the coincidence engine

the coincidence engine

A Novel

sam leith

Crown Publishers
New York

Copyright © 2011 by Sam Leith

All Rights Reserved
Published in the United States by Crown Publishers, an imprint of the Crown Publishing Group, a division of Random House, Inc., New York.
www.crownpublishing.com

Crown and the Crown colophon are registered trademarks of Random House, Inc.
Originally published in paperback in Great Britain by
Bloomsbury Publishing, London, in 2011.

Library of Congress Cataloging-in-Publication Data
Leith, Sam.
The coincidence engine : a novel / Sam Leith. —1st ed.
p. cm.
1. Intelligence service—United States—Fiction.   2. Mathematicians—
Fiction.   3. Mathematical instruments—Fiction.   4. Probabilities—Fiction.
5. Coincidence—Fiction.   I. Title.
PR6112.E46C65 2012
823'.92—dc22

2011021838

ISBN 978-0-307-71642-2
eISBN 978-0-307-71644-6

Printed in the United States of America

Jacket design by Gregg Kulick
Jacket photography by Marcopolo, Feature Pics

1 3 5 7 9 10 8 6 4 2

First American Edition

For Alice, who makes me feel lucky

AUTHOR'S NOTE

It is customary to announce on this page that all resemblances to characters living or dead are entirely coincidental. It seems only courteous to acknowledge, though, that in preparing the character of Nicolas Banacharski I was inspired by the true-life story of the eminent mathematician Alexandre Grothendieck. "What is a meter?" is Grothendieck's line. But *The Coincidence Engine* is a work of fiction: I don't know any maths, and Banacharski is no more Grothendieck than Robinson Crusoe was Alexander Selkirk.

People may also complain that I have taken liberties with both the laws of physics and the geography of the United States of America. I can only respond that reality, in this book, does not exactly get off scot-free.

SL, London, September 2010

"They've found the pilot."

Twelve hundred miles away in New York, Red Queen breathed out.

"What do we know?"

"More or less nothing. Hospital sweep sent up flags. Field agents in Atlanta called it in. He's in Mobile. Name of Arno Fisk. I'm headed over there now to talk to him."

"Condition?"

"Cuts and bruises. Some—well. They're saying some cognitive issues."

In the background, Red Queen could hear wind across the mouthpiece of the phone. Behind that, the sound of heavy traffic moving fast: trucks pounding south on the interstate.

"It's not clear. He was dressed as a pilot, but he's not a pilot. There's nothing on him in the FAA database. He was unconscious for some time. What I hear—"

The wind picked up and the next few words were inaudible.

"—consciousness. I need to go."

"OK, go," said Red Queen.

The phone went down in its cradle.

Red Queen's desk was broad and made of dark wood. The top was covered in red leather. It was out of place. It belonged among other antiques—not in this oblong box with its ozonic air conditioning and its twenty-four-hour fake sunlight. There were no books in the room. An uncomfortable two-seat sofa, against the wall, faced the desk. On the other wall there was a locked cabinet. There were no windows.

A corner of the leather surface of the desk looked like it had been chewed by mice. Red Queen picked at the leather with a fingernail for a moment, staring at nothing.

Then Red Queen turned to the computer, waggled the mouse to bring the screen alive, and brought up the Intercept to read it again.

Bree, on the highway, hung up the phone on the timber wall of the Snacky Shack and walked round to the door. It was late morning and the sun, already hot, bounced off the dusty glass and winked at her. She'd been driving for three hours already. Red Queen could wait half an hour while Bree got waffles.

Bree was the only person in the place—an awkward L-shape that had once been a barn, or an auto-shop or something. Formica tables, pairs and fours. Booths lined the window onto the highway and Bree sat in the furthest one of those, with her back to the corner wall. She sat a while, watched the traffic tick past, waited while the waitress finished scratching in her hair with her pencil.

The waitress leaned down by the chef—a good-looking Latino wearing a greasy checkered dishcloth as a bandana—and produced a laminated menu the size of an occasional table. She dropped it wordlessly in front of Bree, left, returned with a clear plastic beaker of iced water, set that wordlessly down, fished a pad from her pouch and pointed at it, expectantly, with her head-scratcher.

"Morning," said Bree.

"Mornin'," said the waitress.

"Belgian waffles," she said. "Three eggs over medium, Canadian bacon, chicken sausage and sourdough toast; two rounds."

The waitress wrote it down.

"You want a side of fries with that?"

Bree's eyes flicked up from the menu.

"No fries," she said. "And no grits."

The waitress looked at her. Bree looked back.

"Thank you," said Bree, and smiled sweetly.

Thirty minutes later Bree was back heading south in the brown Chrysler with the windows up and the air conditioning on, and by mid-afternoon, she was rolling into Mobile. She left the interstate and took Airport Boulevard.

Providence Hospital was a white building west of the center of town. Bree drove in under a quaint old archway, swung the front of the car round and parked up under a shade tree, just out of the sight line from the main entrance.

She got out and the weather hit her. It was as if the humidity had tugged the leash on her breath. She'd worked up just enough of a sweat for it to chill on her, unpleasantly, when she stepped into the air-conditioned lobby. She ignored the potted palms and crossed to the desk.

"Visiting Fisk, room 325," she said. "Helen Fisk. I called earlier."

She showed the woman her ID. The woman didn't seem interested. Bree wrote "Helen Fisk" in the register, went to the elevator and went up.

It was a nice hospital. Someone cleaned it. Her flats didn't stick. She'd been in hospitals where only people in heels—and Bree hadn't worn heels since she could remember—were really qualified to make it down the corridors.

The room that the man who seemed to be called Fisk was supposed to be occupying was down a long corridor and through some doors. Bree had a pretty good sense of direction. West, it should be facing, over scrubland and away from the parking lot and the main part of the hospital. She listened at the door a little, then when she was satisfied nobody was in Fisk's room, knocked softly.

She didn't wait for an answer, but opened the door, slipped in, closed it behind her.

The room did face west. The blind was half lowered, and afternoon light came through the bottom half of the window and slanted across the foot of Arno Fisk's bed.

Fisk was awake but he looked a little glassy. He had dark hair, spilling from a bandage wrapped round the top of his head, and a purple, very shiny bruise bulbing out the right side of his forehead and casing the orbit of his eye. Underneath his right eye the skin was wasp-striped black and yellow.

There was something dark—looked like dried blood—in his nostrils, and a single butterfly stitch on his lip. He was a mess. Bree couldn't see what was going on under the blanket, but both the arms above it—resting side by side on the tray table over his waist and looking uncomfortable—were in casts to the elbow.

She'd been in the room for a couple of seconds before his eyes rolled toward her, as if in surprise, and focused a foot or two behind her left shoulder. They were shiny, and such a dark brown that the pupils and the irises, at this distance, were hard to tell one from the other. Even smashed up, he was a handsome man, though more tanned than Bree thought was ideal.

"Come in," he said. It came out: "Cerrm urh?" Then he looked surprised again.

Bree walked up to the bed. She didn't bother affecting hesitation. According to the medical notes the agents in Atlanta had skimmed, there had been no permanent brain damage or intracranial bleeding. Just a prize-winning compendium of fractures, breaks, and abrasions—consistent, one of Bree's colleagues had said, with the rough prognosis for an eight-year-old child with rickets spending a half-hour in an industrial tumble dryer.

This spaciness was probably just drugs. If they had him self-administering he'd be no use to Bree, or anyone.

"Mr. Fisk," Bree said.

His eyes said, "Who wants to know?" and his mouth said, "Urr?"

"Mr. Fisk, my name is Dana Hamilton. I'm from the Federal Aviation Authority."

She reached into her top pocket and showed him Dana Hamilton's business card. He frowned at her wrist. Closer up, she could see where his pupils ended and where his irises began. His irises were fingernail-thin, chocolate-colored halos. He looked like a badly mangled bushbaby.

"Federr avuh urrdurr?"

"Yes, Mr. Fisk. And may I say what a pleasure it is to meet you today?" Dana extended her hand. There were four fingers extending from the cast on his right arm. Dana shook two of them.

There was a chair by the bed. She pulled it round and sat on it.

"I've come to talk to you about your accident. I work as an insurance assessor for our pilot outreach branch, unexpected eventuality division."

"Whur durr?" said Arno Fisk.

"There are certain anomalies in our records regarding the events of August 11th. We need to straighten out our files. Mr. Fisk, I'm going to level with you. We have no record, precisely— and this is very probably our fault; the full-spectrum security audit ongoing since 2001 has, to be honest, caused as much confusion as it has cleared up—of your pilot's license. You were admitted to the emergency room without ID, and the FAA— under the WelfAir insurance scheme—covered your bills during the time you were unconscious. We're now reaching a stage where we need to action an alternative funding stream for your medical care."

Something stirred in Fisk's face. Somewhere at the murky bottom of his consciousness, what Bree was saying had snagged. That was the idea. If he wasn't too stoned to know he was in the hospital, maybe he wasn't too stoned to realize that whoever was paying for him to be there could stop paying for him to be there.

"Mr. Fisk, we need to establish your eligibility for continued treatment. We need to find some way of reconnecting you to the FAA's database."

This was not strictly true. Bree didn't give too much of a damn about the FAA's database, though she was curious as to who the hell this guy was. No ID, no known next of kin. They'd found his name through teeth while he was still out—busted crown done eight years previously back home in Illinois.

Arno Fisk, thirty-five years old. Born in St. Charles. Moved away when he graduated high school. Moved back, apparently, for long enough to go to the dentist. Moved away again. He'd ended up in Mobile somehow, though he didn't seem to have driven there. There were three Arno Fisks holding driving licenses in Illinois and two in Alabama, and none of the five of them was this guy.

"I'm nurr a pilurr. I tole the pleezmann." He looked tired. "Anno whurr huppen."

"But you were found near the wreckage of a 737," Bree said. "You were found *in* the wreckage of a 737. Strapped into what was left of the pilot's seat."

"Anno whurr."

"You know what happened?"

"AnnNO."

"You don't know what happened?"

Fisk subsided slightly, and his eyes refocused dead ahead.

"Mr. Fisk, you were dressed as an airline pilot." She reached a little. What the hell. "As I'm sure you know, there are federal penalties attached to the improper impersonation of an officer of the Federal Aviation Authority, or an accredited pilot of that same body." She softened her voice. "We're sure you meant no harm, but it's very important that you tell us everything you remember about the events leading up to your being found."

She looked at him, her eyes moving over his unbruised cheek. The skin was olive-colored. It looked like it would smell nice. He kept staring ahead.

"Look, I'm honest? We just want to know where the plane came from. There were no identifying markings on the fuselage— at least none recognizably attributable to any known airline. No passengers were found. No planes were missing. We checked all the schedules in the continental United States for the two weeks

6

surrounding the time you were found. We checked private flights—and there aren't a large number of 737s in private hands; we checked scheduled flights; we checked extraordinary rendition flights. There weren't any scheduled flights across the South in any case, because of the hurricanes."

This was mostly but not entirely true. They had recovered some identifying markings. One section that seemed to belong to the tailplane, according to the file, was made of tin-plated steel and stamped with a date of no readily decipherable significance in the summer of 2009. It seemed overwhelmingly likely it belonged to a can of beans.

"As far as anyone knows, this 737 airplane appeared out of nowhere. It didn't crash, it didn't fall out of the sky—there was no sort of impact evidence. OK? Planes don't come out of nowhere. They are big things. Then it broke up—without burning or exploding—at or near ground level. And it scattered itty-bitty little bits of metal debris over three square miles of Alabama back-country, and left a guy with half his bones broken, strapped to a chair, hanging in a tree."

Arno Fisk, to whom some of this was getting through, attempted to look as baffled as Bree. It was a very creditable attempt.

"That was you," she added.

Bree tensed as she heard the handle of the door twist. A nurse came in, sideways, turned and looked startled to see a visitor. She was carrying a clear plastic jug of water. She frowned, then smiled politely, and was opening her mouth to speak when Bree interrupted her.

"Oh, thank you. Arno's mouth was getting so dry, wasn't it, hon? Just there, sweetie, thanks. No, a bit to the right. Perfect. I'll take care of his glass." She put a little urgency into her tone, stopped just short of steering the nurse back out of the room by her hip. She could see the nurse making a snap decision; to go with the flow rather than submit to the awkwardness of challenging Bree's ownership of the space. One more firm "thank you" was enough to see her off.

Bree had all sorts of outs, but unnoticed was best—unnoticed was always best. She knew the name on the register was different from the name she'd used to Fisk, and figured there'd be no trouble with it in a routine hospital visit to a badly if bizarrely injured man. She'd leave confusion, rather than suspicion, behind her if she left anything at all. But she'd rather leave it behind her than have it turn up while she was still there. As far as the nurse was concerned, if she checked, this was the cute Fisk guy's fat older sister. And if Fisk wondered why this lady was calling him "hon," well . . .

He made a noise. She turned back to him. Fisk was looking a little more focused, as if he'd made a decision to pull himself, as far as he could, together.

"Uh durr rumberr much. I' was Sadderday. Uh wuzz a li'l drunk."

The words came out slowly, and clearly with effort. "Uh hadd a beer. Bit. Nommuch. Cuz uh wuz goin'a work. Uh member geddin dress. Geddin in car. Id was winndy."

"You were going to work. What time was this?"

"Uh dunnuh. Evennuntime. Late. Iz dark. Winndy."

He pushed his lips together and out, like a chimp puckering up for a kiss, and exhaled through them almost soundlessly: hwhhh-hhhhhhooooo. His eyelids drooped and his cheeks tightened in a secret smile. Some sort of morphine surge. Hwhhhhhhhh . . .

"Winnndy . . ." Hwhhh . . .

"Yes, it would have been windy. There were hurricane warnings. A lot of people had left town. And you were going to work?"

"Sssss."

"Why? Nothing was leaving the ground that night."

"Gudda work. Goo money."

"Where do you work? You work as a pilot?"

"Nuh! Nudd a piludd." He was trying to pull himself together again.

"You were dressed as a pilot. Could someone have done that to you while you were unconscious?"

If someone had done that to him, Bree could have added, they had a sense of humor. According to the admittedly sketchy paperwork she'd been able to obtain through the Atlanta relay, he was dressed in the uniform of a TWA pilot from the mid-1980s. A defunct airline. An emergency-room orderly's sniggering e-mail to his college buddy had added the even more peculiar detail that, underneath his pilot's uniform, he had been wearing satin thong underpants with a tiger-stripe print. These had been soiled.

"Nuh. Uh dress muhself. Took muh uhn cloze inna bag."

"Where do you work?"

He shook his head floppily and frowned. "Anywhur. Uzz jus' anyone books. Wuzz jub up by—ahhh—Gumbuh Lake."

Gumbo Lake was an enormous swamp ten or fifteen miles to the north of where Fisk had been found. Fisk's tree had been a couple of miles west of Axis, off the 13, which went up to Mount Vernon.

"What sort of job were you doing?" As she asked, Bree realized she knew the answer.

"Ubba darnzer."

"A dancer. You're a stripper."

"Ubba *darnzer*," he insisted, but his face, even through the drug haze, looked bashful and a little bit pleased with itself. He attempted what would have been a well-practiced, flirtatious, long-lashed look. The effect was not as he would have intended, but the attempt was enough that Bree could feel herself coloring at the base of her throat. She felt cross.

"Uh wuz onna urrway," he continued, not noticing or minding much. "Saw uh member. Uz drivin'. Larss thing uh member. Driving." The casts bumped on the table as he attempted a shrug, then winced as he remembered what trying to shrug with two broken arms and a fractured collarbone felt like. "Then uhz year."

"You don't remember anything else? You didn't stop, didn't get out of the car, didn't meet anyone?" Like, anyone carrying a commercial passenger plane? Bree thought but did not say.

"Ur gur. *Nuh.*" He struggled a little in the mist. "Yerrr. Uh gud ou'. Uh member. Or nuh. Uh think. Gudda pee."

Oh shit, thought Bree, not knowing if or how she was supposed to help him do that—and it seeming likely it would bring another nurse.

"Pee. Beer. Heh. Uh gudda."

Bree realized, with relief, he was still remembering. He looked confused again. "Uh gud urr. Iss winnndy." He made the whooshing noise again.

And then his face shone and his lids sagged. "Uzz inna plane . . . Inna . . . Hadda mos' amazin' dream . . ."

Bree got up. She didn't know what she knew, and she couldn't think of anything else to ask because she didn't know what she didn't know. That was normal. That was her job.

"Saw rrainbow," said Fisk. "Byooofu'. 'Mazin' dreammm . . ."

"Thank you, Mr. Fisk," she said, but he wasn't really noticing. She left.

As she crossed the parking lot to the Chrysler, she ran over the conversation in her memory. She didn't speculate. There was never any value in speculating. But something nuggeted in her mind.

"I'm not a pilot," he had said. "I told the policeman."

Bree, who had seen the records, thought: What policeman?

An amazing dream.

Fisk, subsiding back into morphine sleep. Going down through the layers. There was a humming of bees. The air all around him was wet and it smelled of tin and electricity. The trees were dark, dark green and the sky was gray in all directions.

He was driving a car. Not his own car. He knew in the dream that it wasn't his own car, but it somehow belonged to him. The car was a vintage Plymouth as big as a whale. Fisk wallowed in a wide front seat upholstered in blood-covered leather. Fat drops of rain were splatting and dragging across the windshield, hauled sideways by the wind.

Rain was wetting his cheek. Fisk had the windows open. He knew he had a passenger, on the front seat with him—he could see them from the corner of his eye—but he couldn't bring himself to look round. He wasn't scared of his passenger—*sharer*, he thought; my passenger is my sharer—but something prevented him from turning his head to look. His eyes were on the road.

He cruised on the speed limit. Fifty-five miles per hour, but the scenery changed only very slowly. He felt unease as he looked ahead, at the road pulling toward him lickety-split, and the scenery making its way sluggishly past like a moving staircase with the handrail out of sync.

A bit away from the highway, before the treeline, he could see the gator fence. There were gators lined up behind it. They were moving their limbs slowly, purposefully. One, then another huffed and lolled and then, with lazy weight, started to haul themselves up the fence vertically, link by link. He noticed the passenger (*sharer*, he thought again) was gone. Nobody was there.

The wind picked up, flapping erratically into the driver-side window. It was sheety and gusty and it tasted like batteries on his tongue. Fisk suddenly realized that the car wasn't moving at all. The road continued to spool toward him, but it was a special effect, like in an old movie. He realized he needed to pee.

He was outside the car, standing by the highway. Fisk was experiencing something halfway between memory and hallucination.

He didn't remember getting out of the car, but he could see it. There was somebody, he couldn't see who, driving it, and somebody on the passenger side. The wheels were turning—whitewalls blurred—but it was keeping level with him.

Here in the wind he felt scared. The wind caught his cuffs and belled his sleeves out with a great sad sound like a foghorn. The navy fabric of his uniform trousers, wet from the rain, clung to his legs like Saran wrap. His captain's cap flipped up and vanished horizontally, end over end, out of his sight before he could turn to see it. He turned his back to the wind. The sky ahead, back down the highway where he had come from, over the delta, was black as stone.

He moved his hand to his zipper, and POOM! He was nowhere.

2

"The coincidence engine is starting to work. I saw it with my own eyes."
The Intercept was from nobody. It had been more or less sieved from static. Shortwave frequencies, an echo of an echo. The original signal was, they thought, perhaps, a fax; it still retained some formatting features. But its origin and its destination were unknown, and the very fact that they found it continued to be a source of bafflement. It was a one in a million shot: the equivalent of getting a crossed line and hearing your best friend's voice from the other side of the world.

It wasn't even a term the Directorate's officers had been specifically searching for. But "coincidence engine" was close enough to send up a flag: they'd been combing for "probability," "paradox" (since that had been the inaccurate but hard-to-shake term that had briefly attached to the project), "singularity," "Heisenberg" (in variant spellings), and a half-dozen other key terms and areas. Red Queen, who made no secret of not being a scientist, explained to the Directorate's staff that they were looking for "weird stuff and people who seem to know about miracles."

But then that was more or less a description of what they'd been doing ever since those wackos around the second Gulf War revived the Directorate of the Extremely Improbable. Red Queen would have preferred to work in the State Department, and Red Queen had made this noisily clear—which was almost certainly why Red Queen had the job. In this department, producer capture was not a good idea.

But the arrival of the Intercept, coming so soon after the hurricanes and the satellite photograph, had seemed too much of a . . . well, there it was.

Someone had flagged it, and now it was here.

The hurricane blew through the junkyard and it made a plane. I saw it. First the gathering wind, and then the sky was filled with metal clashing and screaming and spinning. Rivets swarmed. Currents of air dashed and twirled plates, chairs, tin cans, girders and joists, pinging and banging off rocks. Noise like you never heard. Unholy howl. Rushing and screaming.

Knock, knock, knock and the metal clashing and curving and denting and sticking with great screams. Beyond conception. Beyond seeing. The panel of a trailer. The corrugated sides of a container cracking and flattening. A flash in the middle of it, right in the middle, of a tiny man suspended in air, pedalling his legs like he's treading water and his tiny mouth open and his eyes little dots of terror. Something forming around him.

And finally the wind calmed and the thing was made, the metal miracle. Water running in beads down its flanks under the heavy sky. To the west, the cloud broke and in the distance the sky was bright, like through a tunnel. There was a double rainbow. And on the other side, the sky was a sheet of black. A terrible promise.

The rotors of the engines were idling in the last of the wind. And sitting high in the air, strapped safely in the cockpit, was the pilot—mouth opening and closing, eyes wide, staring into the enormous sky. It works. I saw it.

Its author, Red Queen reflected, sounded about as well adjusted as that guy who eats flies in the Dracula movie. But the thing about the plane had caught their attention.

And there had been a hurricane. This they knew. Hurricane Jody had moved through the Gulf of Mexico for three days in the first week of August, feeding on the warm air rolling off the coast in the unending heatwave. It refused to blow itself out and refused to come ashore.

Occasionally, like a big dog twitching its tail, it brushed against the land. In the early morning of the 24th, a kiss-curl of the fatal weather system—it looked like a wisp of cloud on the satellite image—had flattened four miles of the Florida Keys.

The contents of two recently evacuated trailer parks had been lifted sideways, chewed to splinters in the hurricane's mouth, and sprayed seaward like refuse from an industrial woodchipper. A film crew from Fox News went with them.

The hurricane's retreat had taken a near-perfect hemispherical bite out of the coastline. Thousands of tons of yellow sand were pulled into the sea. Small boats sailed inland through the air and anchored among defoliated palm trees.

The hurricane had retreated, circled at sea, ambled south and west.

It came ashore again sixty-one hours later, on a stretch of coastline where the civic contingency planners had not expected it. The center of the storm had started moving northwest at twenty knots. Its leading edge sucked a renowned Louisiana gambler bodily through the window of a riverboat casino, never to be seen again, and a steel roulette ball punched four inches into the tree stump to which the boat was moored. The storm's left flank had sideswiped a single loop of the coastal highway, gridlocked with late-departing refugees, killing forty-eight motorists and 122 pedestrians.

Then, abruptly, it changed direction again and headed back out to sea, brooded.

And then, on the night of August 10th, it had headed inland again, and it did not stop at the coast. It had made landfall east of Mobile and headed up and over the delta with savage speed.

3

It was still just light in Glisson Road when Mary Hollis arrived home.

The bag in her hand, from the Marks & Spencer at the station, contained a fish pie, a small bag of prepared carrot batons and a half-bottle of red wine with a pink twist-off cap. Summer was on the way out. She felt a faint winter chill through her blouse.

She put the bag down and fished in her handbag for her keys. As she did so, a movement—barely more than a disturbance of the air—registered in her peripheral vision. She glanced briefly up the street toward the road that led to the station. Nothing there.

Silly woman, she said to herself aloud. Silly old bag. Only since she retired last year, though, had she started to notice herself looking over her shoulder when she turned the corner from Hills Road, or feeling nervous if she had to pass a man on the same side of the street. During all the years she worked up at the college, she had regarded the undergraduates as overgrown teenagers—unruly nephews and slatternly nieces, as exasperating and unthreatening as badly trained Labradors.

"All right, Mrs. H?" bellowed in a cockney accent by a public schoolboy. "Where's your gentleman caller, eh?"

"Mind your own business."

Now, already, they had started looking bigger and more strange. If she was out at night and she heard young men walking behind her, she'd dawdle at a bus stop, or pause on the main road under a street light, to let them pass before she turned off.

Sometimes, when they looked drunk, she'd make an excuse to drop into a shop.

She was sixty-five, and she realized that she had started thinking of herself as an old woman. She had started thinking about what she looked like to others. Not the little vanities of make-up or hair—but the way her profile was changing. She felt as if she was growing smaller, taking shorter steps—as if she was gradually feeding herself to her fear.

She found her keys in the bottom of her bag, turned the heavy deadlock and rattled the sticky little brass one into the Yale. The hall was dark and smelled of polish. She picked up her supper, and turned on the light.

She tasted copper in her mouth, and felt her face go cold.

The drawer had been pulled out of the hall table and her letters were spilled over the floor. The rug had been pulled up and was rucked up at the other end by the foot of the stairs. Every one of her framed photographs had been knocked from the walls and there were big jagged pieces of broken glass across the floorboards, a different color where the rug had been.

She felt her skin prickle. She made herself breathe, took a step and reached for the telephone on the hall table. It was an old brown plastic push-button BT model. She'd never owned a mobile phone.

It was when she fumbled the receiver that she realized her hand was shaking. It clattered heavily onto the table. She picked it up and brought it to her ear. There was no dialing tone.

Ahead of her, the darkness leading through to the kitchen seemed to breathe. She wanted to ask whether there was someone still there, but she didn't want to know the answer and her mouth was too dry to speak.

The door behind her was still open, and the street outside felt suddenly more cold and strange. She took a step away, not wanting to turn her back on the other end of the hall, and pushed her spine against the door jamb. She turned her head to look out. In the dusk just across the street there was an elderly man. He was disheveled. Above his gray beard there was a kindly, perplexed face. He was standing still, watching her. Then something seemed to startle him. He turned his head sharply, as if looking over his shoulder.

She stepped back out of the house and called to him, or tried to. As she raised her hand, though, he turned and dipped his head, walking back up toward the main road.

"Sir!" she yelped. "Sir! Excuse me!"

His pace seemed to quicken and then, just as he was coming up to a street light, something she could not account for happened. He seemed, simply, to vanish. There was a shimmer, and where a second ago she had been watching him there was now no more than a heat haze—a smear in the air.

A man's shadow on the pavement shortened as it approached the streetlight, then lengthened on the far side, at the pace you might walk on a brisk spring evening, and then disappeared.

By the time the police arrived, it was full dark and Mary was two doors down with Mrs. Smart at number 62.

Angela Smart had left an open pan of pasta boiling in the kitchen and opened the door to a tremulous knock. She found the old woman standing there. She wore a shapeless greatcoat and hat, and was clutching a plastic bag from Marks & Spencer up against her chest. She seemed agitated.

"Mary?" she had said. She knew Mrs. Hollis from the occasional Neighborhood Watch meeting, and to say hello to in the co-op, sort of thing. She had long had her pegged as a meddlesome ratbag of the first water. "Is everything OK?"

"I'm terribly sorry to trouble you. I think I've—I've been burgled. May I use your telephone to call the police?"

There was a moment where it just hung there, and neither woman knew what to say.

"But come in, of course. Come in. My goodness, were you there? Are you hurt—you poor thing . . ."

She reached a hand to the other woman's arm, and saw her shoulder shrink back and her eyes drop. Her hand tightened round the thin green bag.

"I'm very well, thank you. I'm sorry. I mean, I'm fine. I think they've gone—but my telephone isn't working at the moment."

Mrs. Hollis's tight politeness was as brittle as porcelain. If she touched her, she felt sure that she'd start to tremble and cry. She didn't know quite how to cope with that, so she said: "Of course. Yes. I'll put the kettle on."

She made Mrs. Hollis a cup of tea. Mary Hollis, who had not since she was a young woman and been told it was common taken sugar in her tea, had two lumps. Installed on the sofa, she sipped, and scalded her lips, looking around the living room with a bland show of curiosity.

The police showed up a little later. A man and a woman. She, a trim blonde in her early twenties; he, a thyroidal beanpole of a lad who looked barely out of his teens, and whose Adam's apple bobbed up and down his neck like a fisherman's float after a motorboat has passed.

The WPC called Mrs. Hollis "dear," which would have annoyed her had she been more composed. Her silent companion looked ahead, gulped and bobbed.

They went back into her house a little later. The interior of the house matched the wreckage in the hallway. Her single mattress had been heaved over and there were knife slashes through the fabric of the bed frame.

The little room she used for her study had received the most thorough going-over—books pulled from shelves and scattered open-faced on the floor; slicks of paper spilling from the disembowelled desk. She gasped, little fluttery gasps, as the woman officer asked her, patiently: what's gone?

She didn't know. The feeling wasn't so much loss as violation. And there had not been that much to go, as she would reflect later sitting alone in her ruined room—she declined with a politeness she regretted Mrs. Smart's offer of a bed for the night. No. She couldn't possibly.

Not that much. They'd left her radio, the old television set. They probably wouldn't have recognized as valuable the fine old edition of *Peter Pan* that had been her mother's, the one with the Rackham illustrations. It, too, had been flung to the ground. She replaced it on the shelf.

The jewelry box on her dressing table had been upturned, its contents scattered onto table and floor below. She fished the big turquoise-and-silver brooch from the carpet when the police left, put it carefully back into the box. She started tidying. Gathering these little precious things back together, amid the destruction of the room, felt like combing the hair on a corpse.

The knife slash through the fabric of the bed frame was especially horrible—a casual, instrumental violence. She imagined herself on the bed, on her back, the knife descending. The man with the knife looking not at her, but through her, toward something else.

"You must have surprised them," the policewoman had said before she left, making a note in her pad.

Mary didn't think she'd surprised them, still less scared them. Nobody had rushed past her or clattered in the bowels of the house as she opened the door. Nobody had hoofed it over the garden fence. They'd been here, and they'd not wanted her jewelry or her nice books or her television. They'd not cared what they broke.

She fingered the piece of paper the woman had given her—a form, something to do with being a victim of crime—and looked over again at the slash on the bed. Where the knife had hit the frame, the wood had splintered.

Mary had said nothing to the police about the man she thought she saw vanish. She wondered if she'd been hallucinating. She didn't want them thinking her dotty. Downstairs, she picked up the cushions and replaced them on the sofa. She slept on there that night, still in her clothes.

Mary was right about that much. They had not been interested in her jewelry, the men who had turned over her house, and they would not have been scared of her. They had not, in fact, been interested in her house, her nice books, her jewelry, her television or anything else. They went by the names Davidoff and Sherman, and they had been intending, in fact, to burgle another house altogether.

But the small flat Mike Hollis lived in on the other side of Cambridge from his aunt was a sublet, and the address and phone number appeared in the book under his landlord's name. So when discreet inquiries were made of Google by the accident-prone employees of MIC Industrial Futures, those inquiries yielded an M. Hollis in Glisson Road. And when those inquiries were cross-checked by the same accident-prone employees with the payroll system of Emmanuel College, Cambridge—a comically easy hack, they had thought—they confirmed "M. Hollis" at that address, and in receipt of the sort of miserly monthly check that corresponded to their understanding of what research fellows in mathematics could be expected to earn. They were right about only one thing—research fellows in mathematics do earn about the same as a long-standing college administrator would expect to draw as a pension. But they are paid by the faculty of mathematics, and not by the college.

So, twenty-four hours after ruining Mary Hollis's home and her peace of mind for no good reason, the two men were standing in a room that smelled of dry-cleaning and swivel chairs and paper plates of stale biscuits covered in cling film.

Davidoff stood with insolent blankness, big hands nested behind his back, chin up. His hair was sandy and his cheeks permanently windburned so he always looked as if he had just shaved with a blunt blade. Sherman was smaller—wire-haired, sallow, all muscle and nerve. He was like a longdog constructed from twisted rubber bands. They were making their report.

Their report was that they had nothing to report. In search of their employer's fugitive piece of hardware, they had burgled a blameless old woman. On the evidence of her house she, also, knew no more about the device than you'd expect an elderly secretary to know. Then that old man had turned up. They'd no idea if he'd been a husband, a lodger, or what—he'd looked more like a tramp than anything else—but he had appeared as if from nowhere, and Sherman feared— though he did not tell Ellis this—that the guy had got a look at his face.

What had he been doing there? Everything had been quiet. No burglar alarm, no nothing. They'd watched the old woman leave earlier in the day, and lock the front door behind her.

It had given Sherman the fright of his life. The man had just appeared at the top of the stairs and started walking calmly down toward them. Sherman and Davidoff had bolted as soon as they'd seen him.

They had "struck out—nil for one," as Davidoff, wearing his affected Americanism with an irritatingly complacent air, had put it on the way in. Davidoff seemed almost to relish failure; or perhaps he simply liked watching Ellis cross. What was being handed down to MIC's head of security was, it was reasonable to speculate, about three times as nasty as what he was capable of passing on to those below him.

"Gentlemen," said Ellis, which was his customary overture to a bollocking. He thought it made him sound superior. "Gentlemen, I don't need to remind you that a very great deal of this company's time and money is invested in the recovery of this device. And I don't need to remind you, either, that if it falls into the wrong hands—that is, any hands other than our own—my position is going to look very weak indeed.

"And that means that your position, gentlemen, is going to look even weaker still. This is incredibly *fucking* important, this thing," he said, letting his profanity hang in the air for a bit.

There were people who knew how to swear, Sherman reflected, and people who thought they knew how to swear, and Ellis, with that stupid little vein throbbing self-importantly in his forehead, fell into the latter camp.

Ellis prided himself on his swearing, you could see. It was important for his self-esteem, as an ocean-going civilian sub-craphat, to be able to swear in front of ex-servicemen. Sherman worked really hard to see if he could bring himself to be even the faintest bit intimidated by Ellis. He could not. Davidoff, Sherman could respect. Davidoff was a squarehead, but he was quite a dangerous squarehead. Ellis was . . . His thoughts drifted off.

"This is the future of this company. We own this thing. We paid for it. And our proprietors are not going to sit back and give it away for free to any teenage geeks, Islamist loons, Marxist wackjobs, or any fucking fucking blue-hatted save-the-world fucking ponce-fucker."

Ponce-fucker, eh?

"Fortunately, we have a lead. Our friend in the States has learned of a young man connected to the Banacharski Ring who has just unexpectedly upped and flown across the Atlantic. No warning. Just went. And there's no good reason we can see why he might have decided suddenly to go on holiday by himself."

Ellis knitted his fingers together, and cracked his knuckles.

"His name is Alex Smart. Postgraduate student, close associate of this Hollis. While we were looking at the supervisor, this lad skipped out and there's very good reason to believe that he has the device. He was booked on a flight for San Francisco, but he wasn't flying direct. For no reason we can readily understand, unless he was trying to discourage pursuit, he flew via Atlanta. Two different airlines. Tickets booked at different times—the first through an agent. Only the second was on his own credit card. But the onward flight was grounded by the hurricane. He never got back on a plane, according to our intel."

Intel? thought Sherman. He noticed that Ellis had a monogram on his shirt. He enjoyed hating him for a bit.

"We've lost track of him," Ellis continued. "But so have they. So enough messing about. Do not shoot anyone if you can help it, do not get shot yourself, and if and when you find it helpful to do something illegal, do not get caught doing it. I need scarcely remind you that we have no status either in the UK or in the States. You are private citizens. Whatever favors our proprietors are able to call in when from time to time we find ourselves in a legal gray area, you can be sure they will not call in for you. If you get in trouble, MIC will disavow you so fast your heads will spin."

"Disavow" could mean lots of things. Which was, Sherman thought, probably why the two of them were being better paid than they would be if they'd been working for private hire even in Iraq.

Ellis looked at them both, one after the other, and then enunciated, slowly: "Go to America, find him, and get our toy."

"America's quite big," said Davidoff. "How do you suggest we go about that?"

Sherman was surprised when Ellis replied: "There is one idea. Look—this device affects the way probability works, as we understand it. Like a magnet in iron filings. We think the effect is more powerful when it's closer by. But it's eccentric. For some reason one of the things it seemed to affect strongly, if the literature is to be believed, are these."

Ellis, who had remained sitting throughout this conversation, reached into the drawer of his desk. He pulled out something attached to a tangle of white wires and put the tangle on the desk.

"There's one each," he added.

"The literature," said Sherman.

Davidoff's big hand went down first. He fished up a small square of plastic that brought some of the white wires with it. He looked at it.

"This is an iPod," he said.

"An iPod Shuffle, yes," said Ellis. "It's preloaded."

Sherman picked the other one up and looked at it.

"What are we supposed to do with these?"

"Listen to them," said Ellis. "Listen for patterns. Songs that seem to keep repeating; runs of the same artist; albums that come out in order." He looked a little sheepish. "Even things like . . . songs that begin with the same word, or something."

"This is what we're supposed to use to hunt down this super-weapon, or whatever it is. An iPod. Are you having a laugh?"

"I hate rock music," said Sherman.

Three hours later he and Davidoff were on a plane.

4

"Does the name 'Banacharski' mean anything to you?" Red Queen asked.

The man looked confused and disoriented, as he was entitled to. Four hours previously he had been teaching a class of students in MIT. Three hours and forty-five minutes previously, he had been on his way off campus when a couple of men in suits had started steering him by the elbows as if—he had thought with indignation—he were not a small, bald professor of mathematics but a small, bald bicycle.

Two hours previously he had been, for the first time, in a helicopter. An actual black helicopter, tilting over Boston and heading out into the country. During that short, fast journey, Professor Hands had become quite convinced that his voluntary work leafleting for a human rights organization had made him a target for extraordinary rendition. His whole short body had been flushed, moment by moment, with the chemicals of terror and the lip-trembling self-righteousness of a liberal academic facing a non-fatal kicking from the forces of reaction.

America, he knew, was a totalitarian enemy of free speech— but it didn't actually kill middle-class white men. He expected to endure pain, speak eloquently, and become a cause célèbre. He imagined Chomsky talking about him on CNN; Glenn Beck denouncing him by name on Fox.

Now they were asking him about Banacharski.

"Of course it does," the man said. "He's a very distinguished mathematician. Or was, I suppose—depending on who you want to believe. But this has to do with Banacharski? I can't see why he'd be of any interest to the CIA."

"We're not the CIA, Professor Hands," said Red Queen. "We do a different job than they do. Remember all those bits of paper you signed earlier?"

He nodded.

"They don't mean very much. They say that you're breaking various national security laws if you disclose the existence of this organization, let alone disclose the contents of our conversation, but the nature of what we do means that we could never actually drag you through open court if you break the agreements.

"So we're adult about this. However, I do want to impress on you two things. One of them is that if you tell people about us, these people will think you are mad. Your first point of contact with us was, was it not, with two burly men in dark suits wearing wraparound sunglasses?"

Hands nodded.

"You were brought here in an unmarked black helicopter."

Hands nodded again.

"And here you are, three floors below street level in New York in a secret"—Red Queen chuckled—"a secret underground hide-out. Talking to somebody with a name out of *Alice in Wonderland*." Red Queen's palms turned upward. "It might be enough to earn you a sabbatical, but your accommodation would probably be chosen for you."

Red Queen gave him a friendly smile. "We are a serious organization. What we do is extremely important. And we really do want your help. Contrary to the fantasies of all very highly educated and very poorly educated people, the government is truly not engaged in a conspiracy against the people. We do everything we can, in secret and in the open, to prevent them messing things up.

"So just listen to what we have to say, and to give us the benefit of what you know. Sit around here, talk, have a cup of coffee, come on board. And do us a favor: be an adult—and keep what we talk about to yourself. We need to be able to speak frankly with you."

Hands followed the gesture and looked around the room. It was an odd room. Though it was windowless, on the wall behind Red Queen's desk there was something in the shape of a window that was giving off light, like a lightbox. The floor was pleasantly enough carpeted, and beside him there was a cardboard cup that said "Starbucks" on it. Hands picked it up.

"Plus," Red Queen added, fixing him with a harder stare, "horrible things will happen to you if you speak about this. Really horrible."

This was not true, in fact. Doing anything particularly horrible to a US citizen, particularly a member of a liberal institution of higher education, was almost always far more trouble than it was worth.

It was way, way outside the remit of the DEI—they didn't even have agents licensed to use lethal force—and even the FBI didn't do as much of that as people thought they did. If you want to keep a low profile, the two golden rules are: don't start leaving a trail of bodies, and don't, whatever you do, involve the FBI at any level. As for the CIA . . .

In any case, it was enough to focus the little professor's attention. Even if he suspected all of this, he didn't know it and he wouldn't be likely to want to test the thing out. He had been warned, flattered and warned. He was short, and Red Queen was tall. He was sitting on a low sofa without a table in front of him, and Red Queen was sitting upright behind a desk. He was as ready as he'd ever be.

"OK," Red Queen continued. "Banacharski. The organization I work for has been very interested in Nicolas Banacharski for several years . . ."

Professor Hands, as Red Queen knew, was a number theorist with a very strong interest in Banacharski's work. And Red

Queen knew, too, most of the basic facts of Banacharski's life.

"Well, ehm, Banacharski was a prodigy. Born in Germany. Father was a Russian Jew, died in the camps. He won the Fields in the sixties—you know, the big mathematical medal?"

"I know."

"Amazing work. Very, very high levels of abstraction. He more or less invented—well, completely reshaped—the field I work in. The Fermat solution wouldn't have been possible without his work. But he's barely been heard from since the early nineties. I don't know where he is. Nobody does."

"Presumably he knows where he is," said Red Queen.

"I wouldn't bet on it. He'd be in his eighties now, and he—you know—went *mad*."

Hands scratched the back of his neck. He still looked a little uneasy.

"Banacharski had—well, they started as strong convictions. He was in Paris for '68 and he started to become more and more political. There'd been a chair created for him at the Sorbonne. He'd worked there for a decade or so, perfectly normally. Then he threw it up in 1972 on the grounds that his chair was partly funded by the military. He was a pacifist."

"That's what was said."

"It's the only explanation. He was still working at this stage, but he was getting crankier. Started claiming there was going to come some sort of scientific apocalypse by the end of the century if the physicists weren't kept in check. Then he upped and off."

"Off?"

"Vanished." The mathematician was starting to forget his surroundings and enjoy his story. "He was living in communes, going Buddhist, vegan, some people said—stopped using beds for a bit. There were stories that he went round trying to sell buckets of his own feces to farmers as fertilizer. He turned into a mad monk. He was notionally attached to the University of

Toulouse, but"—he blew air out between his lips and shrugged—"he was doing his own thing. Proofs, papers—he mostly just wrote thousands of pages of what he called 'meditations.' There'd be fragments of proofs in them, amazing proofs—some of them are in libraries. But he was cracked. That's how the story goes.

"One morning in the early nineties his girlfriend returned home to find he'd had a kind of manuscript bonfire in her garden. He was never seen again."

"Literally never seen again?"

"More or less. These letters go out, though—of the long and rambling sort. People in the community, you know—they try to piece together what he's doing. He claims to have given up on math. He's living by himself and working something like twelve hours a day on mad material—some huge manuscript about the physics of free will."

"That's where we come in," said Red Queen. "We know about the letters. We were keeping an eye on them. Does the name Isla Holderness mean anything to you?"

"Yes," said Hands, and there was a moment before something dropped into place behind his eyes. Red Queen looked expressionlessly at him. "Uh, yes. She's a mathematician in my field. She's one of the last people who saw Banacharski. She went to look for him in the Pyrenees."

Red Queen exhaled. "You know the story."

" 'What is a meter?' "

Red Queen nodded in recognition. "What is a meter?" Banacharski's weird riddle: the last communication with Holderness before he disappeared for the final time.

"OK. We're on the same page. We know a bit more than you about some of it. But I'll lay it out. Our organization is called the Directorate of the Extremely Improbable. It's a silly name, but it's always been called that, and the silliness acts as a sort of camouflage. We could just as easily have brought you here in a green helicopter, and had you picked up by men wearing clear eyeglasses and button-down shirts from Gap. As it is, we don't sound like what we are. That is the idea.

"Our job is to assess threats to national security that we don't know exist, using methods that we don't know work. This produces results that we generally can't recognize as results, and when we can recognize them as results, we don't know how to interpret them."

Red Queen continued to look at him levelly.

"It's frustrating work. Here."

Red Queen fished in a desk drawer, pulled something out, and lobbed it across the room to the little mathematician, who caught it. "This is a souvenir from the days when we used to have our own memorabilia."

He turned it over. It was a bronze medallion. Engraved on it was the pyramid-and-eye logo from the dollar bill. Above it, a scrollwork banner carried the initials "DEI." Curving below, a scroll carried the words "Ignota ignoti."

"Unknown unknowns," Red Queen said. "That's what we do. We deal with things we don't know we don't know about. Once we know we don't know about them we hand them over to the CIA, who"—Red Queen sighed—"generally continue not to know about them.

"Predecessors of the DEI have existed as long ago as the Salem witch trials. We had operatives in the Culper Ring during the Revolutionary War. This, at least, is how the story within the organization goes—but there's no real evidence for any of it.

"We were shut down for reasons nobody within the organization understands after the Kennedy assassination, but then, come the run-up to the second Gulf War, certain senior members of the administration became very interested indeed in the sort of paranoid *X-Files* material that was traditionally associated with the Directorate. Donald Rumsfeld, as Secretary of Defense, reinstated our work. Our off-books budget suddenly reappeared. It got big.

"Below where we're sitting this compound goes twelve stories down. There are tea-leaf readers, distance seers, chaos magicians, and tarot tellers. Dicemen. Catatonics. Psychokinetics, psychic healers, lunatics. Haruspices. Illuminati. Idiot savants. Hypnotists. Bearded ladies. Oracles. All drinking the same coffee, and all paid for by the American taxpayer."

Red Queen didn't seem entirely sold on the tea-leaf readers, it occurred to Hands, but it didn't seem his place to point it out.

Instead, he said: "So, ah, what *is* your interest in our mad genius?"

"Banacharski?" Red Queen said. "We don't think Banacharski was mad. We think Banacharski was trying to build a weapon."

5

Alex didn't know what made him stop in Atlanta.

He'd been rebooked onto an onward flight to San Francisco, after the hurricane, but he had never gone to the airport. He had sat on the bed in his motel looking at the clock, his suitcase packed on the bed beside him.

The time when he had planned to leave for the airport had passed. Then the time when he'd need to leave to have a hope of making the flight. Then the time that the gate would have closed. Had he looked out of his window he'd have been able to watch his flight lift into the air. He thought about the empty seat on the plane, carrying a ghost of him to San Francisco, another reality peeling off this one and heading its own way.

He imagined the ghost traveling into town, walking down Market Street, the khaki-colored buildings and tramways and clean sunlight. It would be weary, T-shirted, happy. He imagined walking up over toward Chestnut, and surprising Carey at Muffin Tops while she was pouring coffee for a customer. Then—blank. Nothing. He wasn't imagining Muffin Tops. He was imagining Central Perk from *Friends*. And he wasn't imagining Carey. He was imagining Jennifer Aniston. And his images of the city were a mash-up of Carey's postcards and Google Street View.

He couldn't imagine Muffin Tops. He couldn't imagine Carey. That future was illegible. Instead he was in Atlanta, in a motel room with its brown curtains drawn against the daylight, while his more purposeful ghost flew across America to surprise his girlfriend.

He couldn't stay, and he couldn't go. He didn't feel sad, or scared, or anything at all. He'd flown here on an impulse, and now the impulse had left him and no other impulses had arrived to take its place. He examined the feeling, or lack of it. He felt like if he stabbed a knife into his leg it would make a dull thunk, and then stick out as if he'd driven it into a wooden table leg.

He took out the small cherrywood box and thumbed it open in his lap. The ring was inside, a half-moon of silver metal standing proud of its little velvet cushion. Where there might have been a solitaire diamond, there was instead a double loop in the metal: the lemniscate.

He shut the box with a snap, opened it again, shut it again. What a small thing it had been to decide to change his life. He tried to remember whether he had decided to ask Carey to marry him before he'd seen the ring in the antiques shop, or whether the idea had come fully formed into his head when he'd seen its object expression in the world. He couldn't.

He remembered wanting the ring, and knowing he wanted the ring, and knowing what it was for. The ring had cost about half what he had in the bank. The infinity symbol. He'd thought it was cool. Now he thought it was tacky.

He didn't know if it would fit. He didn't know if Carey would say yes. He didn't know what he'd say if she did. He didn't feel hungry. Eventually, as the afternoon slid into the evening, he turned on the television.

"Isla Holderness," Red Queen continued. Hands was more or less at his ease, now. And he was curious to know how this story would unfold. A weapon? That sounded wrong. Banacharski was a fierce pacifist.

He knew Holderness's story well. It had done the rounds in the mathematical world. She was the woman who had found Banacharski. She'd started as a disciple and they'd exchanged some letters. She wanted to see if she could talk him out, talk him back in. She'd schlepped through tiny villages in the Pyrenees armed with an old photograph of the mathematician. She'd found him, living in a shack in the hills, living like a monk.

Banacharski, to her surprise, had been friendly. The shack was a mess, by all accounts. Banacharski slept on a pallet on the floor, and—in one version Hands heard—lived on grass. Hands wasn't actually sure that was possible.

Somehow, though, he took to Holderness. He had even been flattered to hear that, since his disappearance, one or two of his conjectures had been proved, but he said he'd stopped doing mathematics. Then he'd started ranting about the devil and the physics of free will. He believed that an agency—he called it the devil, though Holderness hadn't been sure whether or not he meant it as a metaphor—was interfering in measurements, making precise knowledge impossible, minutely bending space time.

After she returned to England, they began to correspond. It went well at first. He indicated, so the story went, that he intended to make her the custodian of his legacy—that he'd pass her his findings. Then one day a letter arrived, apparently, demanding the answer to a question: "What is a meter?"

Holderness had no idea how to answer it. A sheaf of further letters arrived before she had even finished composing her reply. The first was incoherently angry, filled with scrawled capitals and obscenities. It accused her of being in league with the Enemy. It arrived on the same day as another that appeared to threaten suicide. The third arrived a day after the other two. It was addressed to "The Supposed Isla Holderness." Every mention of her name in this letter was surrounded by bitterly sarcastic inverted commas. "Since you are not who you say you are, you know that I cannot be who you say I am," it opened. It was signed "Fred Nieman." Holderness had set off to find him. She had found the shack burned to the ground and Banacharski, again, gone.

"He thought Isla Holderness was a spy," said Red Queen.

"Why would he have thought that?" said Hands.

"He was intensely paranoid," said Red Queen. "Also, he was quite right. She *was* a spy. She worked for us. We'd been monitoring all her correspondence with him. His letters dropped hints of what he was working on—I think he thought that was what was keeping her interested; after all these years of isolation, the human contact was welcome, and he was flattered by her interest. But you have to remember this was a deeply, deeply paranoid man. The hints were purposely fragmentary. We had to stay at arm's length, and she was deep cover.

"We thought we had the breakthrough, but 'What is a meter?' completely threw us. It threw her too. But she waited to respond.

"That was when it became clear something was very wrong. Banacharski vanished. Then we thought Holderness had gone rogue. We knew enough about what this man was like to know that the longer she left her response, the more likely it was that he'd flip his wig. We'd sent the clearest possible instructions on receipt of the 'What is a meter?' letter that she should go immediately, in person, to see him and find a way of talking him round. But instead she spent a week trying to work out the answer to his riddle.

"She was responding to none of our signals to come in. She didn't use the dead-letter drops, and the messages she was sending stopped making any sense: newspaper buying, for instance. There was a complex series of codes surrounding what paper she bought, at what time of day, and how much change she used.

"All of a sudden she seemed to be buying newspapers completely at random. It took us a while to cotton on to what had actually happened."

"What *had* happened?"

"It turned out that—actually—Banacharski was wrong. Isla Holderness was just what she professed to be: an academic mathematician who was interested in his work."

"I don't follow you."

"He was right but he was wrong. Isla Holderness was a spy. But that was a different Isla Holderness. We made a huge mistake. This woman with Banacharski wasn't our Isla Holderness, and she wasn't spying on him. It was another woman with the same name. And she'd been buying newspapers completely at random all along."

Red Queen looked a little bitter about this.

It was hard enough keeping track of all the DEI's agents, and the organization's institutional reluctance to commit anything to paper for fear of being counter-surveilled made it more or less impossible.

Many DEI field agents didn't even know they were working for the DEI—and a good few of them actually thought they were spying on it for one of the several fictitious cover agencies that it ran. Red Queen occasionally pretended to be unsure whether the DEI was a real organization or, itself, a red herring.

Hands looked mystified. "So where was your Isla Holderness while the other Isla Holderness was with Banacharski?"

"Thousands of miles away in a cave network in northern Pakistan," said Red Queen, gloomily. "She had spent the previous three years infiltrating with unprecedented success—not that we knew about how she was getting on at the time, since we'd forgotten she was there—bin Laden's inner circle."

"What?" said Hands. "*Osama* bin Laden? The terrorist?"

"No," said Red Queen, brightening up a bit. "As it turned out, not."

The car was a box of smoke. It pulled into the parking lot of the International House of Pancakes where Bree had made the rendezvous and stopped in the rank of parking spaces across from where she was waiting in the shade of a tree.

Through the windshield, Bree could see nothing. It was like a white-out in there. The driver's-side door opened, and the car exhaled—a roll of what looked like dry ice furling out under the door and dissipating above the hard top. A hand, holding a cigarette, gripped the edge of the roof. A foot—a giant foot, like a beached canoe—appeared under the edge of the door, and a very tall man scissored out and stood upright, looking around, as the smoke cleared.

Bree reckoned he was about six foot three. He had a thin face, and short pale gray hair. She walked up with a hand in her pocket, and she could see his attention register her.

He put the cigarette in his hand into his mouth and pulled on it very heavily.

"Hello," he said, without taking his sunglasses off. "I'm Jones."

"Bree."

They didn't shake hands, though an awkward moment passed when they could have. They stood opposite each other in the hot parking lot, and even from this distance Bree could smell the smoke on him. There was a parchmenty grayness, close up, to his skin. It was like wasp paper under his eyes.

He indicated the car with a gesture of his arm. "This is my . . . wheels."

He looked oddly pleased with himself.

Bree had been told a little about Jones. She still didn't understand it, not exactly, but she was comfortable with that. Red Queen had said only that Jones's "condition" was going to be an advantage in the hunt—and that Bree shouldn't be disconcerted if he seemed a little eccentric. Bree had, in her time, spent days staring earnestly into crystal balls alongside people who, in Brooklyn accents, assured her that they were 500-year-old Mittel-European Gypsies. She had a wide tolerance for the eccentric.

She guessed she'd find out about Jones as they went along; provided she didn't asphyxiate first.

"Jolly Rancher?" she said.

She held out her hand, and the thought came to her momentarily that she might have been pulling a dog biscuit from her pocket. Jones looked at it, and paused as if confused.

"Yes—please," he said.

He took one of the little candies from her hand. Bree noticed with satisfaction that it was the peach flavor, which was the only one she hated. Jones unwrapped it fastidiously. He removed the cigarette from his mouth, popped the Jolly Rancher in, and replaced the cigarette.

"Thank you," he said.

Bree took one of the green-apple flavor, and after a moment or two they climbed into Jones's rental car and they slammed the doors and Bree wound down her window and Jones pumped the air conditioning to full and lit another cigarette and then they drove out of the IHOP parking lot and into the world.

Alex's mental fug lasted most of that evening. He had watched pinky faces on CNN until he had got bored, then he'd turned over to the orange faces on Fox News, then—briefly—the BBC, where he didn't know whether it was the familiar rust-colored graphics or the familiar green-yellow face of the correspondent standing by the railings in Downing Street that made him feel homesick.

Then he flipped again, to a show called *I Want a Million Dollars NOW!* Some girls in bright swimsuits were screaming at each other.

He had noticed that the wall of his room, by the door to the bathroom, had a bottle opener fixed to it with screws. So you could lever the crown top off a bottle of beer, presumably, before you took it into the toilet to settle in for a shit.

Alex didn't have a bottle of beer. There was a little plasticky coffee-maker on the table by the television, though. He had plugged the two-pin plug in, filled the glass pot awkwardly from the shallow sink, filled the coffee-maker's reservoir from the pot, replaced the empty pot on the hotplate. Beside it there was a plastic basket designed, apparently, to fool the passer-by into thinking it was made out of bright blue wicker. He had picked up the heat-sealed plastic envelope that said "Coffee," and torn it open. It contained, apparently, a giant tea bag full of coffee, some of which had spilled out of the torn tea bag onto the table.

He had picked up the other plastic envelope, a paler brown, which contained the decaf. He had liberated the giant tea bag intact this time, smoothed it into the round space for it in the top of the coffee-maker, flipped the hinged holder so it sat back over the pot. Then he had replaced the two-pin plug, which had fallen out of its slot. Then he had flipped the switch on the base of the coffee-maker so it glowed orange, and waited for the machine to cough and splutter to a natural death.

Then he had unsheathed one of the two white styrofoam cups from its plastic wrapper, poured the scalding caramel-colored coffee into it, waited for it to go cold, then drunk it.

Now he had run out of things to do.

Alex had never been to America before. Having set out with a sense—now, he saw, entirely bogus—of purpose and adventure, he felt suddenly small and pathetic and alone.

In his imagination, it had been a vector transformation. Going to America would, necessarily, make him equal to the setting. America, far away, looked big: he would become big as he traveled toward it. America, close up, was enormous. And he, traveling toward it, had become even smaller. He imagined himself labeled "Shown actual size."

There was an entire country out there to be seen, and he couldn't bring himself to leave his motel room even to eat. How hard could it be to walk round the corner and get a pizza, or go to a bar? He knew he was exacerbating things by inactivity. He felt low enough to do nothing but not so tired that he could go to sleep. Now the numbness was fading, the pleasurably dismaying shock of simply not doing what he intended and expected to, he found it hard to put the wasted cost of the flight out of his mind.

And while he sat here his mind was moving, never quite settling, on a survey of his situation. He was twenty-four years old. The most important thing in his life, for three years, had been a PhD that his gut told him he wouldn't finish. Now it was a girl whom his gut had told him that he would marry, and in marrying whom, his gut told him, he would change his life. Now his gut had vanished. He was gutless. He looked down, miserably, at his gut, as if he imagined someone was watching whom he ought to impress with his wryness if not his resolution.

Nobody was watching. He zoned back in. A bikini girl on the television shouted, at a buff-bodied and gormless male competitor: "Alix!"

He flicked the channel, and a British sports commentator said with lugubrious sonority: ". . . run . . ."

Flick.

". . . run?"

Cricket, this time. Flick.

". . . run away as far and as fast as you can . . ."

A cowboy film. Flick.

". . . circumstances are conspiring there . . ."

Politics. Flick.

"Out!"

Tennis. Flick.

"To get you . . ."

An advertisement for an ambulance-chasing personal injury lawyer whose swiftly scrolling small print was just beginning to make its way up from the bottom of the screen.

Click. Alex turned the television off. Something nagged at him—a feeling right at the back of his mind, almost below the level of consciousness—that someone somewhere was trying to tell him something. He shrugged it off.

He decided, finally, to make himself go for a walk. He swung his legs off the bed, and himself up onto his feet. He pulled back the chain from the door, shrugged his jacket on, and with not the slightest enthusiasm left the room, crossed the broad balcony and took the single flight of stairs down to the car park.

The light was orange and the night hot and tarmacky and strange-smelling. It was about nine o'clock, he reckoned. The motel consisted of an L-shaped block of rooms two stories high, up to the foot of which parked cars nosed shell by shell. The motel was about a third full. Looking behind him as he crossed the tarmac, he could see a guy with his face in shadow, drinking a can of something on the balcony, two rooms down from his room.

At the registration office, strip light blared from the Perspex window where the teenage night clerk sat watching television. The door adjacent was half lit, with a sign hanging on it saying "Closed" and the brightest light source the Mountain Dew decal on the vending machine.

Alex walked past the office and onto the broad highway: three lanes in either direction. He turned right. There wasn't much traffic. To his left, a pickup and a family car waited for the over-head lights to turn green.

There were no pedestrians. On the opposite side of the road was a long car park on the other side of which was a Pet Superstore, a CVC chemist and a 7-Eleven. On his side of the road was noth-ing at all: a pavement, a broad grass verge, a low hedge. There was some sort of office building set back from the road behind a network of drives and flower beds.

It took him ten minutes to reach the end of what he presumed to be the block, and still there was nothing doing. He kept walk-ing. He assumed that this was not downtown.

It took him another ten minutes to reach the end of the next block. There was a twenty-four-hour photo shop. It was closed. He kept walking. It took him twenty minutes more to reach a drive-through McDonald's on the other side of the road. Alex felt a shade ashamed to have traveled to America and to be eating at McDonald's, but he was now tired and he thought that something comforting and familiar might see off his self-pity if it didn't exacerbate it.

He walked up toward the ordering window. There was one car—an SUV—pulled up by it, a meaty forearm and a measure of beard protruding from the driver's window. It rolled on with a jerk, and Alex walked up to the booth.

"Ah." He tried to see past the kid behind the microphone to a menu somewhere, though he didn't need it. "I'd like . . . two plain hamburgers please. Small fries." This had been the food Alex had ordered while alone, and passing McDonald's, for years. "And a—"

He was interrupted by the blare of a horn, close enough to cause him to jump with fright. Ice-white headlights washed past him, and the horn went again.

"Hell do you think you're doing? I could have killed you! Get in line, you little prick!" a woman with a frightened face shouted at him from the driver's window of her station wagon. He realized that behind the SUV had been a queue of two cars, one of which had not seen him walk past it in the pool of dark beside the cashier's window and had nearly broken his legs.

The cashier looked amused. "Ma'am?" he said.

Alex, hot with shame, retreated and let the car jounce up to the window. The woman's attention left him. He walked down the curved grass verge. The car behind pulled up to the station wagon's bumper as if pointedly. Alex walked down further.

He stood by the offside back wheel of the car behind. Whoever was in it showed no sign of acknowledgment. Another car pulled in behind. The station wagon lurched off from the window. The car behind which Alex was queuing moved off to take its place— and the car behind Alex, as if he were invisible, moved up in turn behind its bumper.

"Hey!" Alex felt himself saying—or would have, had he not felt the ridiculousness of him saying it before it left his lips. "Ahem!" would have been no more dignified or effective. He didn't think he had the courage to go and remonstrate with the driver. He was a pedestrian. He was nobody.

Alex stepped off the verge and stood behind the rear bumper of the car that had jumped the queue. He didn't look to see what if any expression the man in that car was making in his rear-view mirror.

It took about a minute for the car to move off. Another had pulled in behind him. He could see the shadow of his own legs across the bumper and boot of the car in front. Then it was gone, his shadow lengthened across the tarmac, and the car behind him honked its horn.

He held his ground, and moved forward deliberately. Finally, he reached the window.

"Two hamburgers. Medium fries. Regular fries. And a Sprite please."

He ate his supper out of the paper bag on the verge. The burgers were not like they were at home. They were hotter, flimsier. The buns were different. More scrunched-up, somehow.

He felt, again, lonely. He walked back to the motel without meeting another pedestrian.

When he got up the stairs the man on the balcony was there again. He couldn't reach his door from the staircase without walking ten feet toward him, so he bobbed his head and said: "Night."

"Night," said the man, in what sounded like a British accent.

6

Davidoff was lying on the bed nearest the window when Sherman came back in. He had his white earplugs in and was rapping his knuckles in the same annoying way on the wooden bed frame. That was what he had been doing to cause Sherman to go outside in the first place, Sherman remembered.

On the table was the wreckage of a service-station sandwich.

Still standing up, Sherman plugged his own iPod into his ears and pressed play.

There was a high squalling guitar noise and then what sounded like a teenage girl's voice even higher through a gale of feedback. Sherman winced: a teenage girl with serious emphysema, apparently.

"Waaansathoudahsawyou . . ." the girl's voice wailed, ". . . innacrowdiyazybaaaah . . ." A drumbeat started to thump insistently in the background, and another wave of guitarry fuzz came over the top. Sherman pulled out the headphones.

"This is pointless," he said, just loudly enough to break Davidoff's reverie. The younger man picked his big head up a little and looked at him. He stepped over and pulled out one of Davidoff's earbuds, at which he frowned. Music leaked from the dangling earbud: ". . . bompTSSSSS, bompbompTSSSSS, bompTSSSSS, bompbompTSSSSS."

"What?" said Davidoff.

"Are you receiving your directions from the cosmos all right there, mate?"

"No," said Davidoff. "I'm listening to REO Speedwagon."

Sherman dropped Davidoff's earbud so it dangled by the bed, inhaled, and shuffled impatiently. It bugged him to be doing so little. It also bugged him that Davidoff pronounced REO "reeyo," but that was just part of a wider discontent.

They had arrived late the previous night into an airport still clogged with backlogged passengers, and after picking up a car and driving around had finally hit on this unlovely motel. They had spent the day getting the lay of the land.

Davidoff had either bought the daft idea that this next-generation weapons system could be tracked down with the use of a last-but-one-generation MP3 player; or he had embraced the possibilities Ellis's plan offered for bunking off. He had spent most of the day with the earbuds in, nodding away to himself, now and again saying something moronic like: "I've just had 'Love in an Elevator,' 'The Only Way Is Up,' and 'Stairway to Heaven.' Do you think we're closing in on it?"

"Fuck. Do. I. Know, mate," Sherman would respond with unfailing regularity.

His own iPod was clearly broken. Since they'd arrived in the motel it would play nothing but that Neil Young racket over and over again.

The money on this job was good—if Ellis was going to pay them to listen to music, on his own head be it—but the doing nothing was not. Sherman would have been happier back in the desert, slotting ragheads from a long way away. He wondered about slotting Davidoff from less far away.

He took another can of Mountain Dew from the small fridge, cracked it open, and went outside to drink it and wonder what to do next.

"So we got this."

Red Queen showed Hands another photograph. It was the satellite image of the airplane.

"It's an airplane," said Hands.

"Yes," said Red Queen. "This is a satellite image taken from space. When the weather is doing what the weather was doing over most of the Southern states last week, satellites can't see much of anything. There's cloud, rain, electrical interference. This is the only image we've got."

The image, though distinctively the shape of a plane, was blurry and pixelated. It was more than half obscured by a wisp of gray-white that Hands assumed must be cloud.

He adjusted his glasses with his right hand and looked at it again.

"I still see a plane. I only just see a plane. As you say, it's not a very accurate picture. So what's special about it? What does it have to do with me?"

"What's special about it is—" Red Queen hesitated. "There are two things special about it. First, this plane is sitting on the ground, nowhere near anything that looks like an airport. It's in the middle of a field. So how did it get there? And second is that this plane doesn't exist. Didn't exist."

"What do you mean?"

"It's a 737. There aren't that many of them made. They register every one. We have access to those registers. All accounted for. This one not. This plane appeared from nowhere."

A look passed across the professor's face that conveyed, with a pink wrinkling of the forehead from eyebrows to scalp, that he was still wondering, from time to time, whether he was the victim of a practical joke.

"Ri-i-ght."

He decided to show willing.

"So how do you think the plane appeared from nowhere?"

"This image was taken not far from a large scrap-metal disposal facility in Alabama, in the immediate aftermath of Hurricane Jody. We think the hurricane assembled the plane."

"That's completely absurd," said Hands. "Hurricanes don't build planes anywhere outside undergraduate philosophy lectures."

"Who knows," said Red Queen levelly. "Perhaps the hurricane was showing off. But that's the only working explanation we have. And we got this."

Red Queen showed Hands the Intercept. Hands frowned at it. Noting the spots of pink on his cheeks, Red Queen expected him to dismiss the Intercept one sentence in. He got to the end, though—and again, there was something indecipherable in his expression as he read.

"I don't know anything about engineering, or about satellites, or about—whatever *this* is supposed to be. But I'm afraid this is complete garbage," he said. "The whole thing. Impossible."

"Improbable," said Red Queen.

"Garbage. Impossible."

"Improbable enough to be effectively impossible."

"No, just impossible."

"We think that what Banacharski was making was a machine that would make impossible things probable."

Hands looked uneasy at this point. Red Queen watched him very closely.

"That sounds highly—"

"Yes. Improbable. Extremely improbable, in fact."

"So where is this plane, then? Surely your . . . men in black helicopters"—Hands pronounced the last phrase with notable distaste—"will already be halfway to Area 51 with it."

Red Queen looked pained.

"Our men in black helicopters, if you want to be crude about it, didn't get anywhere near it. Professor Hands: do you remember what happened twelve hours after Hurricane Jody?"

Hands looked blank.

"Hurricane Kim." The second storm had been even faster and more violent than the first, curving in from the north. "By the time another human being was in a position to stand where the satellite image shows that plane, there was nothing but fragments of twisted scrap metal spread out over the surrounding area as far as the eye could see."

"So who wrote this?"

"You tell me."

Hands emitted a long sigh, and decided it was time to come clean.

"Me," he said. He took a sip of the coffee from the paper cup. It was stone cold.

Red Queen's eyebrows climbed half an inch. "Really?"

Alex woke up feeling better. He showered, trying not to let the discolored nylon shower curtain touch his body. The curtain sucked onto the whole of his flank in a big wet kiss, held there by static electricity. But the towel was clean enough, and Alex stood on the scrunched, wet mat in front of the sink afterward and in the yellow light shaved for the first time since he had left London.

He dressed in jeans and a clean white T-shirt, then put on his blue denim jacket, then opened the curtain onto the scrubland out behind the motel. The sun was dazzling white and the sky pale. He thought better of the jacket and took it off, rolling it up under two straps of his rucksack.

You are always nearer by not keeping still. That was a line from a poem Carey had quoted to him. It had made him think of centrifugal force—the way the earth falls constantly away from us.

He wondered, fleetingly, about calling Carey. But he didn't know yet what he was going to say to her—and he didn't want to spoil what was supposed to be a surprise. He realized, though, that he'd now been gone long enough that he'd be missed. It was—what?

His watch said 9:50.

He wondered if Saul would be at home. He grabbed his phone from the bedside table, thumbed two buttons to unlock it and prepared to dial. Before he was able to touch a button, though, the screen said "Unknown" as if there were a call in progress.

He held it to his ear. There was silence at the other end, but an open silence, a breathing silence, like the sea in a shell.

Alex listened, then he said: "Hello."

As he did so, another voice said "Hello" simultaneously. It was a girl's voice.

He said "Hello" again, quicker this time, and her voice, once more at the same moment, like an echo so instantaneous as not to be an echo at all, said "Hello." Then he paused and heard the breathing sound.

He had had his own voice in his ear when the girl had been speaking, but he was pretty sure now that the girl's voice belonged to Carey.

He felt a chill. He must have speed-dialed her by accident. He pressed the red button and spiked the call.

He dialed his brother, listening to tiny, insect click-clacks and then the long distant ring of a transatlantic connection. Saul answered on the third ring.

"All right, bumface?"

"All right, Saul."

"I would like you to know," said Saul, in a voice of some seriousness, "that I have now owned every last level in *Peggle*."

"Saul, I have literally no idea what you're talking about. Is this one of your computer games?"

"Not just any computer game, my friend. I'm talking *Ultra Extreme Fever*, Beethoven's 'Ode to Joy,' *Magic Hats* . . . Compared to this, *Plants Versus Zombies* sucks balls."

"*Plants Versus Zombies*? Was that the one with the—"

". . . Plants and the . . . zombies? Yes. And the sucked balls. I knew that hoity-toity Oxbridge education wasn't lost on you. Now I'm insis—"

"Never mind that. Saul: I'm in America . . ."

There was a pause. The forward progress of Saul's onslaught had been impeded, momentarily, by this new piece of information. The phone was on the end of the breakfast bar in Saul's flat, and he imagined Saul's whole-body gesture of surprise and interest catching Tim's peripheral vision. Tim's *Evening Standard* would go down and he would make a silent question mark with his face.

"Alex. He's in America!" Saul would be mouthing to his boyfriend, his eyes wide. The image was so clear to him Alex felt homesickness lurch in his stomach.

Saul started to sing "I wanna be in Ameh-ri-cah" but Alex cut him off with "Saul—," and his voice changed, became more serious. "Skidoop, what are you doing in America? Are you OK?"

"I'm fine, Saul. I just had a thing where—I wanted to get away. It's not a big deal . . ."

A thought occurred to Saul.

"Are you with the girl?"

Alex said nothing for a moment and Saul ran, in triumph, with the silence. "My *God*! Tim! This is so exciting. This is more exciting than anything that's ever happened. Alex has eloped with the American girl! He's going to go live on a farm in Iowa and make sweet love to livestock and breed a*dor*able little one-eyed children in dungarees . . ."

"I haven't eloped," Alex said. "Saul, I'm not with Carey. Look, I haven't got long—I'm calling on my mobile phone. I didn't tell anyone I was going, and I'm fine, but I don't want people to worry about me or call the police or anything."

"Where *are* you? Where in America?"

Alex looked out of the window.

"Atlanta," he said.

"*Atlanta?*"

He ignored the question. "Can you call Mum and tell her—I don't know what you tell her, actually. Don't tell her I'm here, though. Please. Tell her I'm staying with you if you have to. Make something up."

"What happened, little brother? Are you a*lone*?"

"Nobody's here. I'm fine," Alex said. "I'm going to go and see Carey, but I'm not sure what's going to happen."

Saul seemed to digest this.

"You're not going to go all *Thelma and Louise* on us, are you?"

"No," Alex said. "I'm not going to go all *Thelma and Louise*. I promise."

"Well, you have a fabulous holiday, then. And seriously: take care."

"Thanks. See you soon, Saul."

"Laters, bumface," said Saul. And he rang off.

Alex put the phone in his hip bag. He had a plan in mind. On the road, he'd be able to think. He opened the door of the room and stepped onto the balcony. The man who had been there last night was nowhere. He walked down the stairs and across the car park to check out.

The clerk said the nearest Hertz office was back out by the airport. Alex crossed the highway and waited for the bus. The bus shelters here didn't have benches, like in the UK. This one didn't even have a shelter. Alex dropped his rucksack between his feet and leaned back on a concrete post. A tramp with a piled shopping cart was approaching from the direction Alex was watching for the bus. He was the only other person Alex could see, and wore a gray felt hat of shapeless design, filthy brown trousers hanging low on his waist, and some sort of twist of webbing slung round his bare chest. He was barking like a seal. "Raup! Arrp!" he said. "Aaarrp!"

Alex could hear it from some way away. With each exclamation, the shopping trolley, with its cargo of stuffed 7-Eleven bags, would take a jolting bunny-hop forward and its owner would whip his head round to the left. It looked like a nervous tic, or like he was anxious that something unwelcome was on the point of arriving unannounced on his left shoulder. Alex couldn't think of why exactly anything would want to go near the man's left shoulder.

"Aarrp! Raaup!" Alex looked at his feet. There was no sign of a bus.

The tramp made slow progress up the road. The barking sounds he emitted sounded more and more like dry heaves with each moment that passed. And from what Alex could see out of the corner of his eye, what he was expecting to arrive on his shoulder wasn't welcome. His eyes were rolling like those of a terrified horse.

When he got level with Alex, whose existence he had not appeared to notice, he suddenly whipped his head the other way, so his face was pointing straight into Alex's, and shouted: "BOO!"

Alex's stomach flipped and he jumped back in fright. He stumbled over the rucksack at his feet and landed with a painful thump on his coccyx. He scrambled to get his feet under him.

Leaning against his shopping trolley, the tramp was wheezing with laughter.

"Faggin' aaaRRGH! Gotcha. Faggin' liberal!"

Alex's face flushed with blood but, fearing violence, he snatched up his rucksack and took a step back. The tramp scissored into another burst of mirth, then apparently took fright again, and his head jerked back round to look over his shoulder.

"Arrrp!" he exclaimed, then looked piercingly at Alex.

"Spare sssigarette?" he said, sending a hot gale of rotting pilchards in Alex's direction. There was a furze of white stubble on the bulb of his chin and his cheeks were sunken. His lips moved and ticced, flashing teeth the color of toffee. His right hand probed under the webbing round his chest and scratched absently at his left nipple.

"Hnuh? Eh?"

Alex shook his head.

"Asshole," said the tramp genially, and stood, left arm on the trolley, laughter passed, sizing Alex up. Alex coughed officiously and looked distractedly past the tramp down the road. There was still no sign of the bus.

"Sorry," he said. The tramp shrugged, and barked again. Alex looked at his feet. It occurred to him to whistle a thin tune, but his mouth felt dry. And then, as they stood there with Alex looking at his feet, the tramp grabbed Alex by a twist of shirt and walked in until the hot physicality of him, sour stink of skin, dried sweat, rancid mouth smell, enveloped the younger man.

Alex's eyes flicked up. And the everyday madness in the man's face had been replaced by something different. He looked as if he was having a seizure. The muscles on his neck were standing up, and a coil of vein went across one.

"Nobody's here," he hissed. You could hear the wet breath whistling against his wrecked teeth. "Trust nobody. Nobody can help you. Bring them together. Bring them back. Forgive."

The tramp was breathing very hard now, and he had Alex clenched to his chest. But whatever he was doing wasn't directed at Alex, apparently. His eyes were milky, absent, staring into Alex's face as if seeing someone else there, or as if seeing someone through him. He opened and closed his jaw wordlessly. A creamy crust of foam moved where his lips met.

Alex grabbed him by the shoulders—his skin was like dry rubber to the touch—and pushed him off. The tramp's hand released the hank of T-shirt, leaving a smudge of dark grime.

"Isla . . . Kara . . . Ana . . ."

"Are you—are you all right?" Alex tried. The man's voice had changed and his face looked—grief-stricken.

"Nameless," the tramp said then. "Nameless ones. All the nobodies . . ."

Then something passed—whatever neurological event had upset him, whatever mental weather had passed across his brain, blew itself out. The man swayed, blinked as if confused, and then his focus found Alex again. He stepped back as if a little embarrassed, and put a tetchy, proprietorial hand on the bar of his supermarket cart.

Out of the corner of his eye, Alex saw the bus arriving. It swung into the stop where they were standing and the door opposite the driver opened with a slap and hiss. Alex shouldered his pack and hopped quickly on, fumbling a rolled-up dollar bill into the feeder and wriggling down to the end of the bus, sitting on a hard plastic seat.

A couple of seconds later, he heard the tramp's voice. He had climbed onto the bus, and was now arguing with the bus driver. Alex saw him fishing in his horrible trousers and waving something at the driver.

"My money stink? My money stink? Zat it? Faggin' liberal."

The bus driver said something Alex didn't catch.

". . . take a piss right here, lady. Just ask."

He started a second, more purposeful rummaging in the horrible trousers before the driver shot out an arm and snatched the note from his hand. The door slammed shut behind him.

"Heh," he said, and ambled stinkily down the aisle of the bus. Ignoring several vacant pairs of seats, he hoisted himself into the one next door to Alex, sat down and looked straight ahead. He seemed to have stopped barking.

"Spare cigarette?" he asked, then answered his own question with a long sigh. "Nahhh."

Alex wanted to move, but he was sort of wedged in, and he didn't like to seem impolite.

"Ah, sir, your . . . things . . ." Alex pointed at the window.

The tramp shrugged.

"Ah, none of that stuff means . . . it's just stuff, you know?" He looked as if with the slightest curiosity out of the window at his shopping cart, orphaned on the sidewalk as the bus lurched away.

The tramp fished a single bent cigarette out of his trousers and put it in his mouth. He didn't light it.

"Don' need bags of stuff when I got . . . my freedom. I can do anything, go anywhere . . ." He delivered this in a tone of flat unenthusiasm. "Yessir. Whee. Free will. The open road."

He paused, apparently reflecting on all that the glorious exercise of his freedom had brought him.

"Where you from, kid?" he asked.

Alex became conscious of a certain stiffening in the neck of the Korean girl a few seats in front. A raisin-skinned old woman down at the driver end of the bus adjusted her bag on her lap and looked pointedly out of the window. Everyone was pretending not to be listening. Alex felt acutely self-conscious.

"Ah. Cambridge."

"Mass?"

"What? Oh. No. England. Britain, England."

The tramp's head bobbed thoughtfully.

"You—" Alex coughed—"know it?"

"Yarp. Posted there. Inna war."

Another long pause, as the tramp seemed to zone out. Whenever he stopped talking his marine funk seemed to cycle chromatically through a range of species: now tuna, now kipper, now lobster-on-the-turn.

"Fred," the tramp said.

Alex felt himself color.

"Alex." He twisted awkwardly in his seat and shook Fred's hand. Always him, he thought. Always him. How much longer was it going to be before he asked for a—

"Dollar? Y'lemme a dollar, pal?" His voice now a confidential growl.

"I—"

"Gotta get inna shelter. I get inna shelter I can—look . . ."

Fred, surprisingly limber, ducked his head down, grabbed his own foot and levered it up on his knee. His shoe was like a Cornish pasty, split at the seams. The filling looked unappetizing. He pulled it off, revealing a foot that had seen a lot of life. Its crowning glory was the nail on the big toe: a full inch long, with dry blood crusted at the base, it was the shape and color of a tooth rather than a toenail.

"Horrible," he said.

"Um," said Alex.

"They got clippers inna shelter. Lend me thirty bucks."

"Thirty?"

"All I ask."

"I'm really terribly—"

"Forty. Pal. I'm mentally ill."

The unlit cigarette bobbed and wagged as if it were glued to his lower lip. The back of the Korean girl's head looked fascinated by the exchange.

"I get fits. Pal. Alex. I can't work. There's a bullet in my brain. Right here, look." He grabbed Alex's hand and guided it to a place at the top of his forehead near his hairline where there was a scar. He pushed Alex's fingers against it and there was a disconcerting boneless give under the skin.

"Wenn in. Docs could never get it out. I pick up radio signals. Get visions. I know what's going on. You better gimme forty dollars."

"I don't—I'm really sorry. I haven't got that much money. I'd like to help, but—"

"Pal."

"I've—will this . . . ?" Alex pulled a note from his pocket. Shit. It was a twenty. Fred snatched it.

"Humph," said Fred. Then: "Wait up." He produced something from his horrible trousers. It was a very, very crumpled one-dollar bill and a stub of pencil. "I got your change. Hah." He unfurled the bill and held it in front of Alex's face. He twitched his finger and thumb, seigneurially. Alex found it very irritating.

"Thank you," he said a moment later, snatching the bill from the air. Nineteen dollars down. And sitting next to a tramp on the bus. Alex put the bill in his pocket. It felt like their business was transacted, and they sat on in a tense silence, Alex looking out of the window and breathing, shallowly, through his mouth.

They pulled up to a stop, finally, within sight of the wire-fenced expanse of the airport car farm.

"Bye," said Alex.

The tramp said something, but it was a little slurred. It sounded like "I'll see you around."

Alex wriggled past him and walked with relief down toward the front end of the bus to alight. Fred stayed where he was, and as the door shut behind him Alex heard from the inside of the bus what sounded like the bark of a seal.

What Hands told Red Queen about the Intercept was not what Red Queen had been expecting to hear. Not by a long chalk. What Red Queen took for signs of guilt or complicity had been, as it turned out, something entirely other. It had been embarrassment.

His first action when asked what he knew had been to protest, in a squawk whose sheer volume spoke of outraged innocence: "Nothing! Nothing at all!"

Red Queen had known, from early on, that there had been something odd about the professor's response to the Intercept, something shifty. When put on the spot, he had gone crimson.

"I don't know what you mean," he said, "by trying to humiliate me this way. But if I hadn't been transported here in a style quite beyond the means of even my wealthiest students, I'd long since have thought this a sophomore prank.

"Where did you get this from?" he asked, in the too-shrill voice of a man who was now all bluster.

"Professor Hands," said Red Queen, "where we got it from is far less important than your having written an eyewitness account of the event that is at the center of our investigation, and then lied about it. There is a man in the hospital in Mobile with severe injuries as a result of this event—an event that we have no choice but to treat as an act of war. You have professed not to know anything about this event, or its architect, but you are one of a handful of people on earth who works, at a high level, in Banacharski's field. At the moment you are looking very much indeed like a prime suspect. You are on the point of becoming"—Red Queen finished with a hard stare—"a known unknown. And that entitles me to hand you over to some people who will be a lot less nice to you."

Hands had the face of a man in whom panic and bewilderment were wrestling like drunken teenagers at a pajama party.

"But I don't know anything about this—event, as you call it. This document: I should have told you what it was but I was, I don't know, embarrassed. It's—"

"It's an exact description of the formation of an airplane out of a junkyard!"

"It's fiction!"

"Professor Hands, I put it to you that it is not. Look." Red Queen's hand stabbed, again, at the blurry satellite photograph. "That is an airplane. Right there. In Alabama backcountry. An airplane."

"No, I mean this has nothing to do with anything. The passage you read, yes, I wrote it. But years ago." The professor took his glasses off and started to clean them. The pink on his skin had intensified to the point where it was coming out in creamy spots of white at the cheeks and the angles of his forehead. "I wrote that a decade ago or more. It's *fiction*. I was trying to write a science-fiction novel—I, I don't know. Call it a *jeu d'esprit*. It's silly. Pure nonsense. It was about someone who builds a sort of magic probability machine. That was the first page."

"A novel. Like a what—like you'd buy in a bookstore?" said Red Queen, who knew perfectly well what a novel was, and didn't want to bother to pretend not to know what a *jeu d'esprit* was.

"Yes," Hands, now a little piqued. "With pages and writing. Just like you've probably seen on TV." He regrouped, replaced his glasses. "Mine never got as far as the bookstore stage. I considered self-publishing, but after I'd had rejection letters from a number of agents I decided that, probably, I was a mathematician not an artist."

The panic was leaving him. What he said next was tinged with something almost wistful.

"I loved—as a child—loved reading science fiction. I was of that generation of children for who Einstein was a hero—and the lunar landings. I ended up in pure math—and that's a whole other story—but it was science fiction that got me on the path. I had the idea I could do it myself." He pursed his lips a little. "Evidently, I couldn't." After leaving it for a little while, he said: "So, where did you get this from?"

"Nowhere, more or less. It was highly corrupt when it came in. From general surveillance. We think it was originally a fax, but it was impossible to isolate where it was coming from or where it was going."

"Well," said Hands, "I can tell you for sure that it's nothing to do with me that it's come to you. My only remaining copy of the manuscript has been in a cardboard box in my garage in Cambridge for years, and is likely to remain there."

Red Queen put on a mulling-it-over face. It was possible Hands was lying, though it seemed unlikely, and trying to work out what truth he was lying to conceal was the high road to a migraine. If this was an eyewitness account, it would have had to have been from someone standing in the middle of a hurricane. And detail after detail didn't make sense. How could they have heard the noise above the wind?

Red Queen felt irritable; then, not.

"So this thing was written ten years ago?"

"At least. At least."

"Yet it describes exactly what happened in Alabama."

"No. It describes exactly what I invented ten years ago," said Hands prissily. "It's only you who says this thing has happened with the airplane—and only this satellite picture as evidence."

"Let us say it describes what happened."

"It had an unreliable narrator."

"Zip it. It describes what happened. And less than a week after what happened happened, someone transmitted it and it came to us. Doesn't it slightly stretch credibility to imagine that this is a coincidence?"

"Ah," said Hands. "I think I see what you're driving at."

Red Queen let him run. It seemed worth giving him a little satisfaction, a moment of control.

"So you're saying," said Hands, "that a document describing an imaginary coincidence engine, arriving just after something that might be a real coincidence engine takes effect, is proof that the real coincidence engine actually exists?"

"We work with what we've got," said Red Queen.

7

Jones and Bree had spent the morning doing what Bree thought of as old-fashioned detective work, not that she had ever been a detective. The Mobile line of inquiry having gone nowhere, Red Queen had now told her to find this kid from England who they knew "the other side" was looking for. Bree didn't ask who "the other side" was; in the DEI it could mean anything.

Red Queen had shuffled the DEI's ring of skeleton keys and pulled passenger manifests for commercial flights out of Atlanta. He had been supposed to be on a flight. They had staked out the airport. He hadn't showed up. Red Queen had also slipped into the Customs and Immigration database and found the photograph they'd taken at border control in Atlanta when he'd got off his plane from England. It showed a lean, long-jawed young man. Early twenties, tired-looking, perhaps from the flight. Tousled blond hair, a slightly off-center nose. This was an improvement on the photograph on his Facebook profile, which was a picture of a duck.

There had also been a few frames grabbed from the CCTV in the luggage hall. In one of them he walked in—you could only see the back of his head because of the positioning of the camera—and crossed to the luggage carousel, where he stood unhelpfully behind a pillar. He had been carrying a briefcase—apparently his hand luggage from the plane—but what he fished off the carousel had been a backpack. It had seemed odd, to Bree—people who travel with backpacks don't usually have briefcases as their hand luggage. The camera had lost him as he went through customs.

There was one more of him getting into a taxi at the rank outside the airport. He still had the backpack on him, and a fanny pack round his waist. But no briefcase. Bree had pointed it out when the pictures came through.

"I know," Red Queen had said. "We're working on that end of it. You stay on Smart. Don't approach him for the moment. Just find him, and stay on him, and as soon as you do, tell me. If he's got this thing on him, he could be . . . unpredictable."

Alex Smart's "unpredictability" was the reason, according to Red Queen, that Bree had been teamed with Jones. The current thinking about this thing, if it existed at all, which Bree somewhat doubted, was that it was somehow affected by what people around it expected.

"Do you know about the observer's paradox?" Red Queen asked.

"Is that the one with the cat in a box?" Bree said.

"I've got people here who know all about it. Essentially, it says that you affect something by looking at it. Or you can't look at something without affecting it."

"How's that?"

"I'm not the expert. It's something to do with physics."

"If you stare into the abyss, the abyss also stares into you," Bree said.

"You're joking," Red Queen said.

"Yes," Bree said. "I am joking. Tell me about the observer's paradox."

Bree felt annoyance in the quality of the pause. Bree didn't know, quite, why she felt the need to get on Red Queen's nerves, but she knew that her boss seemed to be unusually tolerant of it. It was, perhaps, the nature of the work they did: facetiousness was a way of expressing skepticism. Too much DEI stuff head-on and you started circling the plughole. The material you were dealing with started to seem plausible. You didn't want to end up in one of the deep levels, gibbering about impossible angles, elder gods and colors unknown to man.

Red Queen continued. "We know that this thing does weird things to chance. Right out on the end of the bell-curve things. It's not like it weights the dice a bit. It's like it makes the dice land on one corner and stay there, or makes all the spots fall off spontaneously. Well, this plane."

"If it did assemble this plane—"

"Which we're assuming for the moment it did. This plane is not purely random. It's a thing. It's an idea. It has to do with an expectation—whose, we don't yet know."

"Why should it be?"

"That's what they think. That's what we're working on. In quantum mechanics you can't look at something without affecting it—that's for very, very tiny things, at least. But if they could . . . well, the working theory is that this has somehow turned that round—there's a professor we pulled in—MIT guy, came highly recommended—who says that it might be designed to 'weaponise the observer's paradox.' It will take what you're expecting, and then something else will happen. Or, if you're expecting it to do that, perhaps it will make the original thing that you were expecting happen after all. Before you stopped expecting it."

"How does it know what you're expecting?"

"When you stare into the abyss . . ."

"Now you're being facetious."

"Yes. We don't know. If we did, we'd have built it ourselves."

"So it's affecting random events and making them not random?"

"Not quite. It's more as if it's doing things that are surprising."

"Plane appears in Alabama," conceded Bree. "That's surprising."

"Yes," said Red Queen. "It is."

"So, Jones," Bree said later. It was lunchtime and they were eating burritos. Bree hadn't wanted to broach what she'd been told about Jones with him until she'd had the chance to size him up. But now she'd spent more time with him, she'd got a better sense of the way in which Jones's condition might relate to the job in hand. Besides, she was curious. "You're hard to surprise?"

Jones looked at her levelly. He had taken off his sunglasses and his eyes were a striking ceramic gray. He was, Bree thought, quite attractive. They had, earlier on, reached an accommodation on the smoking issue. Bree's asthma, aggravated by Jones's perpetual smoking—how many packets a day did he get through?—had reduced her to near-speechless wheezing.

She had wound down first her window, then—pointedly—his, then cranked the air con up to full blast. He hadn't so much as interrupted his stream of cigarettes, so much as asked her whether she minded if he smoked. Nothing of the sort.

Finally, she had said: "Jones, I'm dying here." He had looked at her with quizzical sharpness. "Would you mind, please, not smoking while we're in the car together?"

"You want me to stop smoking cigarettes."

"Yes. Please."

"Certainly."

And, with no signs of ill will, he had.

As soon as they'd got out at the Taco Bell, though, Jones had lit a cigarette. They were outside in the children's play area. Bree had ordered first: two beef combo burritos and a big Sprite. Jones had ordered the same thing. Now Bree was eating her second burrito. Jones was still on his first, because he was smoking in between mouthfuls.

"Hard to surprise," he said. "No. Impossible to surprise."

He took a drag from his cigarette, and continued to chew. He showed—as he tended to—no real sign of continuing to speak. Bree pressed him.

"This special condition of yours," she said. "Tell me about it. Why are you not possible to surprise? See everything coming, do you? Got it all figured out?"

"No. I don't see anything coming. I don't expect things," he said without inflection. "I'm apsychotic."

"You're what?"

"Apsychotic. Not 'psychotic.' It means no soul. My doctor told me to explain it this way: I don't have an imagination."

Bree chewed her burrito and looked at him.

Jones waited a bit, then continued to speak. He sounded dutiful, as if what he was saying had been learned by rote. "I say my doctor told me to use that phrase, but I do not know what it means. I cannot imagine an imagination. I do not know what you mean by 'surprise.' I can't talk about 'future.' Things take place. I do not expect them. I do not expect anything else. I have no expectations at all."

"Whoa," said Bree. "Jones, how can it be possible for a person not to have an imagination?"

"There are areas of the brain that associate objects that are not the same together, that associate"—he hesitated, frowning—"imaginary objects with real ones. Those areas in my brain are not the same. Imaginary objects don't exist for me. I can't understand how they exist for everybody else. I cannot use metaphors. I don't know what it would mean to do so. Dr. Albert said it's 'like explaining color to a blind man.'"

Bree continued to chew and continued to look.

"I don't understand that," added Jones, "either."

"There exist more extreme forms of my condition. I can use language. I can read photographs and even some pictures. I know that"—he pointed to her burrito—"this food is called a burrito and that both this food"—he pointed to his—"and that food"—he pointed back to hers—"is the same food, called burrito. Olga Thurmer, twelve, in Oslo, has severe apsychosis. She cannot—Dr Albert says this is a joke—'see the wood for the trees?' She went to a wood. The wood was not 'tree and tree and tree and tree and tree and tree': she gave all the trees proper names. She could not see what they had in common.

"James Hart, seventy-two, in Brisbane, Australia, has severe apsychosis. He has never spoken. Nelson Kogbara, thirty-four, in northern Nigeria, has severe apsychosis. He cannot perceive the borders of objects. When objects move in space he does not recognize them. Ava Howard, twelve, and her identical twin sister Ana, from Bushey in the United Kingdom, have severe apsychosis. They cannot tell themselves apart. Han Fa, ninety-nine, from—"

"OK," said Bree. "OK. Stop. So you can talk."

"It means I can't think about anything that doesn't exist. I can't"—he seemed to reach for a phrase that did not come naturally—"see things coming. I don't desire things in the future."

"You seem to like cigarettes," said Bree, who was already starting to wonder about the wisdom of letting Jones drive the car.

"That's a chemical craving. That's habit. I don't make mental pictures about cigarettes. It's hard to explain. I don't fear things in the future."

"Apparently not," said Bree. "Do you know what those cigarettes are doing to your lungs?"

"Yes," said Jones, and didn't say anything else.

"Ain't hearda your Mr. Smart," the guy in the hat said in the umpteenth motel Sherman and Davidoff tried. Best Western, Motel 6, Holiday Inn, Marriott, Days and Crown Plaza had, as Davidoff had predicted, come up blank. Now they were onto the small places, the ones without computerized directories you could get into; and, probably, the ones that might waive the need to show a passport or a driving license.

These were the sorts of places he'd be staying. The chances, mind, that if he was bothering to stay in this sort of place he'd be doing so under his own name, were slimmer. But they'd nothing else to do, and Sherman had insisted on at least trying so that they could say they had tried. It beat listening to Neil Young over and over again, and as long as he hadn't been through the airport he was not likely to have got far from Atlanta. A picture of him might have been helpful, though.

The old man was running a thumb down a paper register on an old clipboard. "You can leave a message. Maybe he shows up," he said, evidently moved to compassion by Sherman's affecting story. "I'd sure hate for him to miss his momma's funeral."

They had briefly entertained the idea of leaving a message at the first place that had offered them the option. But it seemed more likely to do harm than good. If he was deliberately moving about, he'd be unlikely to return to somewhere he'd been. And if he'd been there, or was there, under a false name, he wouldn't like finding a message under his real name. And if he hadn't been there he'd like finding a message for him even less. Whichever way you looked at it, he seemed unlikely to call an unknown number and arrange to meet even a kindly-sounding stranger in a non-public place in order to be robbed.

But Davidoff—who was lazy and irritable—wasn't giving up. They stepped a little bit away from the clerk's window.

"How about: you've won the lottery, call this number?" the bigger man suggested, pulling the sweaty patch on the front of his T-shirt away from his skin.

"Davidoff, of all the bad ideas you've had in your long career of having bad ideas, that is the most idiotic."

"Seriously," he said. "I'd call the number if I got that message."

Sherman had let that hang in the air as its own reproach.

Davidoff thought for a bit longer. Then he said: "No ticket."

"No ticket," said Sherman. "No ticket. No American citizenship. No reason for the Georgia state lottery ever to have heard of him. Mind you, he does have a machine that wins lotteries."

"No way," said Davidoff.

"Don't pretend not to remember," Sherman said. "You were there when we were briefed. Didn't Ellis say that in the early days, when they'd sent two experienced people after this thing, both of them won the lottery within a week of each other and instantly quit the company? Real problem. They thought it was the machine doing it."

Davidoff turned his palms upward and smiled at the memory. "Yeah. That's why winning the lottery was on my mind," he admitted. Then, looking at his feet: "I spent two hundred pounds on tickets."

Sherman wasn't going to share with his partner that the same idea had occurred to him, at least briefly, before being dismissed. I mean, what if this thing really was that powerful? He'd conceived the suspicion that Ellis somehow wanted them to believe the story about the lottery winners, or at least know it. But if this magic device really did keep evading pursuit by making its pursuers so rich they gave up the chase, he didn't imagine that Ellis would have assigned them to the task of hunting it down with quite such obvious relish.

No. Ellis had probably not been telling them the whole truth. It seemed far more likely, he reflected, that this probability machine had decided to change tack and start putting its pursuers off by, for instance, having them be hit by a meteorite, eat a Snickers bar infested with MRSA, or suffer a plague of agonizing boils. It might bend the very laws of probability around it . . . but that was no reason to think it would necessarily be nice. If you could choose carrot or stick, you'd choose stick, wouldn't you? Every time.

As he went over these speculations in his head, it occurred to Sherman that he'd started thinking oddly. He had used the word "decided" of a piece of inanimate technology. He'd cast himself as its "enemy," come to that. He'd started to think of this machine itself almost as a person: as if it, rather than the guy carrying it, was the one making the decisions. He had started to acquire the paranoid impression that this fugitive piece of property might not *want* to be recovered.

"Two hundred pounds?" he said. "You muppet. Did you win?"

"Three numbers. A tenner."

"Unlucky."

"Yes. No note then?"

"No note, lad. Now. Have we gone through all the motels?"

Davidoff looked at the page they'd torn from the phone directory.

"Yup."

Something nagged at Sherman. "Davidoff?"

"Yup."

"Did we try our own motel?"

Davidoff let his jaw hang open for a moment while he considered the proposition.

"No," he said at length. "We didn't."

"Well, shall we go back and have a look, then?"

It took them thirty-five minutes to drive back to the Hazy Rest Motor Inn through rush-hour traffic.

The adenoidal kid in the faded Skynyrd T-shirt was back manning the office. Sherman noticed that the boy had painted his fingernails black. They offered, by now with more briskness than conviction, their line about why they were trying to find out whether there was an Alex Smart in the motel.

"Aren't you the guys in room 9?"

"Yes," Sherman said.

"Here y'go. Yeah. Yeah. He was here. English dude, yeah? I thought you were like together or something. Two doors down in room 7."

He shuffled the register round so Sherman could read it.

Alex Smart. Checked out late that morning. They'd probably passed each other on the balcony.

They thanked the clerk and went back to the car where Davidoff had parked it across two spaces at an angle. They sat back down and Sherman thought for a while.

"What are the chances of that happening?" Davidoff asked. He put his sunglasses on and looked out of the window. Sherman thought he was probably admiring himself in the reflection. Something occurred to Sherman.

"Car hire companies," he said.

"Can't we check them online?" Davidoff grunted. "And get some lunch while we're at it?"

"No," said Sherman. "Most of them are at the airport. He's only got a few hours on us at the moment, but by the time we finish buggering about on the Internet he'll be long gone and they'll all be shut. Let's go."

Davidoff sighed, turned the key, and wheeled round the car park just over-fast enough, and stopped at the junction with the highway just over-abruptly enough, to signal his exasperation.

They made good time. Twenty minutes later the two men were at the Hertz office in a Portakabin in the airport rental car park. They joined the queue behind a tall kid wearing a rucksack, Davidoff tapping his feet impatiently, Sherman looking about him, sucking his teeth, wondering the best line to spin the clerk . . . Conversational was what was needed, he thought. A bit of finesse. Use the English accent. Something about a stag party that got separated . . . phone not working in America . . . groom in danger of not making it to the church on time. That might— well, that or something like . . .

"Smart," said an English voice, and Sherman's awareness returned to the room. "S-M-A-R-T. Yes. As in clever."

Well, I'll be, Sherman thought. The boy in front of him in the queue pushed a British passport and driving license across the counter. The woman smiled indulgently but professionally. Sherman risked a slight craning of the neck. Yes. Come to think of it, he did look vaguely familiar from the motel.

Davidoff wasn't paying any attention. Sherman gently put finger and thumb around the bones of his elbow and dug the tips in harder than was necessary.

Davidoff hissed something and his head whipped round. He looked at Sherman crossly. The kid in front didn't notice. Sherman made his face tense and looked at the boy's back. Davidoff cottoned on. He blinked and frowned.

"All right, Mr. Smart, you need to sign here"—she circled something quickly with her biro—"and here and here"—a couple of dashed crosses. The boy cocked his head, started scribbling.

"Here are your keys. The car's a silver Pontiac, mid-size. It's in space number 137, row 8. Remember to return it full."

"Thanks." The boy shouldered his rucksack and walked out of the building.

"Next," she said, turning her empty smile on the two men waiting in the line. They looked at each other, then one of them mumbled about having forgotten something and they walked out of the office and round to the right, where young Mr. Clever had gone. She looked at her nails and wondered what Chef Boyardee was going to prepare for her dinner tonight.

Outside, Sherman and Davidoff walked among the rows of cars keeping the kid in sight. They pretended to be looking for a car of their own—though Davidoff's nervousness meant that he had to be prevented from hard-targeting behind the nearest SUV whenever the boy glanced round. As soon as they'd made the boy's car and noted down the number plate, they returned to their own, parked up outside the fence within sight of the exit. Davidoff turned the engine on and let it idle.

He'd be nervous driving a new car. They had no way to know whether or not he'd driven in America before, but it was a safe bet he'd take a bit of time to familiarize himself with the controls. Sure enough, it was getting on for five minutes before the silver Pontiac rolled out of the car park and turned, hesitatingly, onto the road and rolled west.

The two men gave him six car-lengths or so of a start, and then pulled out behind him and began to follow.

He joined the 285 heading north toward the west side of the city. Davidoff was driving. Sherman opened the glove compartment and pulled out the little map of the area that they'd given him at the hire car place. Their own car, too, was a rental and they hadn't thought to buy an atlas. Sherman thought that if the kid headed out of town that was a decision they might regret.

The silver Pontiac pulled out ahead of them and was momentarily obscured by a white eighteen-wheeler. It had "Xpress Global Systems" written on the side in blue block capitals, and underneath, in smaller letters: "A division of MIC Industrial Futures."

"Fancy that," Sherman said whimsically. "On our team."

"What?"

"The truck."

"Uh?"

Davidoff squinted.

"This haulage company or whatever it is. Works for the same people we do. We should flash our lights."

Davidoff grunted again, plainly having not the faintest idea what Sherman was talking about. He pushed the pedal down and came up behind the truck, glanced in his wing mirror and pulled out round it. A corner of the silver car became visible again, back in the slow lane, a few cars ahead. As they got closer, though, Sherman frowned.

As their angle on the front of the truck narrowed, a second silver Pontiac came into view, on the tail of the other. At this range it was hard to make out the number plates. One of them was their boy, but the other one . . .

"Better get a bit closer. There's another silver bloody car up there. We don't want to lose—"

There was a bang.

Davidoff abruptly pumped the brake and Sherman was thrown forward. Something flew up from the road, very fast, and smacked the top half of the windscreen before bouncing up off and behind them. Sherman, startled, looked round and looked behind. Something black disappearing under the wheels of the car following.

"What was—?"

Davidoff, frowning a little but with the car under control. Up ahead Sherman could see the front tire of the eighteen-wheeler flapping in rags. The driver was slowing down, trying to get a slight fishtail under control. Davidoff let the car fall back, then powered forward past it. They'd lost a couple of hundred meters on the Pontiacs.

"Blowout," he said. "Step on it. We're losing them."

Ahead, there was a cloverleaf junction and the traffic was slowing down as a column of cars joined the freeway from the right. The two Pontiacs, further on, went under the shadow of an overpass. A car joining the freeway shot across their bows without signaling. Davidoff muttered something and braked again.

It was a silver Pontiac. It lurched out wide into the left-hand lane, accelerated round an SUV, waggled back into the middle lane and shot off up under the overpass.

"It's—hang on . . ." Sherman could see, through the traffic ahead, the other two silver Pontiacs. The third caught them up. "We've got to catch up with the—"

"I can see," said Davidoff in a voice at once distracted and alive with irritation. "I'm trying but these—SHIT!"

The people in this place were maniacs. They were carved up again, this time someone swinging in from behind, then undertaking and cutting back in front of them, before going wide and, with a honk of horns, screeching round that SUV.

Another—oh, for crying out loud.

As Davidoff concentrated on trying not to be crashed into, Sherman scanned the road ahead. He could now see four identical silver Pontiacs. At least four. One of them—one of them was taking the exit. It was marked Arthur Langford Parkway East. He couldn't make out the license plate.

"Davidoff—he's leaving. He's taking the exit." Davidoff wrenched the wheel. They were in the slip road. Just as they were about to be committed, Sherman had second thoughts.

"No! It's the other one! Don't take the exit! Stay on the road."

Davidoff swore again, wrenched the wheel back and they crossed the stripy lines back onto the main road, narrowly missing the sand-filled oil drums protecting the junction. A dirty white Toyota behind them roared up the exit, missing their rear bumper by a smaller distance than Sherman was comfortable with, its horn emitting a wail of outrage.

He could see three Pontiacs several car-lengths ahead. Davidoff was making valiant efforts to catch up with them, weaving freely in and out of all four lanes of traffic. To their right, Sherman became aware of another line of traffic sloping down a ramp and waiting to join the freeway—the westbound traffic from the road they'd just passed under. Rush hour was approaching and these would be the first people making their way out from the center of town into the western suburbs. The Pontiacs, where he could make them out, glimpsing the tops of their roofs, were just past where the traffic merged.

The traffic had slowed to twenty or thirty miles an hour. The sun winked off an angle of one of the cars waiting to join the freeway and Sherman glanced sideways. Just ahead and to the right of them, spilling into the traffic ahead, were three more silver Pontiacs, tailing a wood-paneled station wagon, which was itself tailgating another silver Pontiac.

Sherman had lost count. Seven, was it? Maybe eight. A rise in the road a little later on allowed him to see them all at once, spread out across four lanes and a couple of hundred meters of the road ahead.

Sherman had by this stage formed a hunch. The boy was leaving town, and he was most likely to head west. West was where the airplane thing had happened. West was where he was supposed to be flying, or had at least bought a ticket to. West was the best bet. Two Pontiacs whose numbers were impossible to see took off along the eastbound exit.

The main pack of Pontiacs carried on. Sherman leaned forward in his seat, his jaw working. The exit for the westbound carriageway of the interstate came off the left, the fast lane. One of the silver cars, its indicator winking for a good forty seconds before it made its way into the faster traffic, pulled out. The indicator stayed on. It was traveling slightly too slowly—as if its driver wasn't confident about what he was doing.

He had slowed enough to give a glimpse of the first two digits of the number plate . . . B4 . . . 84 . . . B4? Was it?

"Got you," said Sherman. "Follow that one."

Davidoff swung out across two lanes of traffic and entered the slip road only three cars behind the target. None of those cars was silver. "Hope you're sure about this," he said.

"I'm sure," said Sherman. The slip road rose in a gentle left-hand curve from ground level up and over the southbound carriageway of the 285 before cresting and then sloping down to join the fat interstate heading west. The silver car disappeared round the curve ahead of them, and as they coasted over the top of the rise and faced down, they were momentarily dazzled by the sun.

The silver car must have already joined the main road. Cars were shuffling between lanes just off the slipway. The I-20 ribboned off toward the horizon, and as far as Sherman and Davidoff could see—three lanes of faded blacktop—the roofs of cars reflected the sun's coppery light like the scales of a snake. It was beautiful, all those cars crawling westward together.

Every car for as far as the eye could make out was silver. Every one—Sherman knew at that moment in his guts—was a Pontiac.

"Let's go back to the motel," he said. "We may have to think again."

Davidoff steered them off at the next exit and they looped back round toward Atlanta, Sherman dialing Ellis's number, letting his thumb hover over the green button to call, and then thinking better of it.

8

There did seem to be an awful lot of silver cars on the road, Alex thought as he drove out of the city. Odd. Perhaps there was a factory nearby.

Then he was back into his thoughts. Those thoughts. They seemed less pernicious, less circular, less—if he was honest about it—*thinky* than the thoughts he had been having beforehand. Always nearer by not keeping still. Now he was moving and his thoughts were calm to the point of being almost contentless.

He was even able to avoid thinking about some of the things he usually found himself thinking about. He had decided not to think about the effect on his credit card of hiring a car for two weeks, and lo and behold, here he was, not thinking about it. He had decided not to think about the likelihood that he'd fail to finish his PhD, lose his funding and have to move back in with his mum, and lo and behold, here he was not thinking about it. He had decided not to—well, he was really not thinking about that. He ran through a whole list of the things he wasn't thinking about—some more quickly than others, and none of them bit him.

"I might take up not thinking for good," he said aloud to himself—something he realized he had started to do over the last couple of days. Not thinking was working splendidly. He knew from the atlas on the passenger seat that he was headed for the west, and that it would take him a few days to get there. All he knew was that the next big town was Birmingham. That was fine.

He weaved past another of those silver cars. They seemed to be thinning out. This was much better, he decided, than driving in the UK. Once you got the hang of driving on the right, obviously. No roundabouts. No changing gear. As a teenager, Alex had driven into the back of a stationary Volvo as a consequence of a misunderstanding that had involved both roundabouts and changing gear.

Now, here, this was very satisfactory. No roundabouts, no gearstick—no corners, practically. The highway was dead straight, and cool air from the air con blew onto his arms.

The car had a docking station for his iPod. Letting his eyes leave the road in brief guilty bursts, he put on the Talking Heads. "Things fall apart," David Byrne announced to the car. "It's scientific!"

Alex sang along with "Road to Nowhere," and then "Psycho Killer," and just as his own jollity started to sound forced to him, "Once in a Lifetime" came on and his mood turned.

It was a song about a man waking up to find himself in and out of time. . . . Then a rushing chorus, something about water rushing over and under and everywhere. Was it a song about drowning? If so, it was a very exultant one. Alex felt uplifted and estranged. Nobody was with him. He realized he didn't know, again, whether he was happy or sad. The music decided for him.

When he'd been a child, sitting in the back of the car, the music on the radio had been the soundtrack to his life. He'd watched fence posts, pylons, stanchions tick past—slowly up ahead, then too fast to see when you looked at them right at the side of the car, then slowlier behind. He had sat, entirely absorbed in himself—or, rather, himself entirely absorbed in what was around him. Watching the English countryside roll by. On the long journeys from Cambridge down to their Cornish holidays in summer: red clay churned in fields to each side. This was where his mother was from. Eurythmics. His father taking him to boarding school. Springsteen. Coming back late at night, sleepy, from the airport when they'd taken their first holiday to Corsica. He must have been ten, then. Tom Waits singing about an "old '55."

Alex started experimenting with the cruise control button. If you pressed it, the car kept to its speed. You could put your feet on the floor—even dare yourself, just momentarily, to take your hands off the wheel until the car, very gently, started to slide toward the lane markers at the edge of the road and you grabbed the wheel again, just between finger and thumb.

He remembered hearing about "cruise control" as a child, and imagining it at first to be something they had in America where the car drives itself. Someone later had told him a story of how someone had put on cruise control on a long desert highway and fallen asleep. A very slight bias on the steering—no more than a fraction of a degree—had caused the car to wander off the road and out into the flat scrub desert. The man had woken up maybe half an hour after the the car had coughed its last of petrol and rolled to a halt. There had been no sign of a road or a river or another human being in any direction: just level low scrub, and dry dirt, and behind his car a long and imperceptibly curved pair of tire tracks in the dust, slowly being erased by the evening wind. Nobody had come to get him. He had died there.

This story had stayed with Alex. What looks like a straight line turns out to be a curve. A tiny fraction of error could scale; a trivial multiplier could propagate into a cascade. A fragment of a degree in the angle of approach was the difference between a stable orbit and slingshotting into deep space; a fraction of a second's lag in a clock could make a GPS system put an airplane into a mountain. The curvature of a miniscus could scatter light, or focus it to a point.

When Alex had been traveling in his gap year, he'd gone to Tibet. He'd left Lhasa on a local bus bound across the Himalayas for Kathmandu, him and his big brother—then on his summer holidays from university. It had taken a couple of days, rattling over the passes where the air was thin and the sky was blue-white. The high points in the passes were marked with cairns of stones, and bleached prayer flags, muddy snow in pockets of the ground.

When they stopped to get out at one place to take photographs, Alex remembered thinking how you could plot lines radiating out from his position there by the bus. At any moment, to move along one of those lines in one of those directions would be to die. He was entirely safe in the bus—but walk thirty feet to the left and you'd tumble down a steep bank of scree. Set off to the right, let the bus leave you behind, you'd be dead of exposure in forty-eight hours, maybe.

You could do that at any time, anywhere. You were almost never more than a strange decision or an accident, or a movement of a few feet, from extinction. Alex had started to imagine himself as the center of a spiderweb of lines, constantly adjusting, on the map. At the end of each one a black X. As you walked beside a busy road, on the road side of you the lines would be compressed to no more than a couple of meters—to the other side they'd extend hundreds of meters, maybe. Stand on the edge of a cliff and the lines would fan out from your feet all along the clifftop—and the same would be true of every other human being. Everyone would carry their own invisible, unmonitored, 360-degree asterisk of harm.

If you credited the alternative universe idea, in every one of those universes there would be a you who had taken a different one of those decisions, suffered a different one of those accidents. There were versions of you who would have jumped or stumbled across every micrometer of that cliff face. And every moment spawned a new position of you in the world, a new 360-degree signpost to catastrophe, a new sheaf of alternative yous in alternative worlds around each of whom radiated another set of fresh positions, divergences, threats.

That idea had struck Alex most vividly when he was eighteen, but it had stayed with him. He became aware of it reentering his thoughts: not threatening, but a source of wonderment. At any moment at all he was one sharp twist of the steering wheel away from the universe not existing. How on earth, with all that risk, had it survived so long?

A game he started to play with himself was to see how long he could keep cruise control on. He fixed it for the speed limit, and everyone was overtaking him. He dabbed the brake to override it, then tried to keep a steady distance behind the car in front and thumbed the button.

Over a few minutes, he found, his car was up toward the back bumper of the car in front. The trick then was to signal and move out without touching either brake or accelerator. You had to be lucky—if a big truck was passing you at the wrong time and you were boxed in, you'd have to brake . . . but you could cut it pretty fine.

It was absorbing. As the sun got lower and redder, and the mile markers told him Atlanta was further and further behind him, he felt settled again.

He'd never done anything like this before. He felt in and out of himself, lost and in charge. Nobody now knew where he was. Not his mum, not anybody. He was starring in a film that nobody was watching. He was unobserved.

It reminded him of his friend Rob's joke when they'd been undergraduates together.

"Erwin Schrödinger's bombing down the M4 in his Porsche." He remembered Rob saying this, and just how he'd said it—Rob in his horrible velvet jacket and his black corduroy trousers, lolling on Alex's green beanbag. Rob's voice cracked and dry from weed.

"You've got it wrong, Rob. It's not Schrödinger."

Rob, pink-eyed, thinking.

"No. Crap. Heisenberg, right. Sorry. Heisenberg is bombing along the road . . ."

Now Alex laughing very hard, helium-pitched giggles. Carey, then, who they were both trying to impress, simply looked perplexed, smiling her oval smile. The joke—Heisenberg is pulled over by the police, and when asked if he knew how fast he had been going retorts: "No, but I can tell you exactly where I am"—had taken Rob hours to tell, and even longer to explain afterward.

"It's—you know about Heisenberg's Uncertainty Principle, right?"

"I heard of it," she said. Carey was doing English and American Studies on a two-year exchange scheme. She was a year older than either of them. Her hair was brown and curly, and she was better at smoking weed and holding it together than either of her suitors. She'd done it all through high school.

As Rob had lumbered through the contrived explanation of the contrived joke, she had smiled at Alex with a studied bashfulness he thought might, just, be coquettish. Then Rob, still on the edge of hysteria, had moved onto a joke whose punchline was "Zorn's Lemon"—he remembered that, and Carey, not understanding the joke at all and finding it even funnier because of that, burst with laughter. She fell back on the scratchy old carpet and lay there with her knees up and her chest shaking with laughter. Her mouth was pink and her teeth were very white, and she snorted a little when she breathed in. Alex could have died with love, then, just looking at her.

Three days later, to Alex's astonishment, she kissed him after the college dance. He was drinking vodka and lemonade out of a plastic cup, and the room was very dark and very, very noisy. The lights were maybe ten minutes away from coming up. In the middle of the low-ceilinged common room drunken undergraduates were staggering and stamping in a big hairy many-legged alcohol-smelling tangle. Alex was looking into the middle of it, a little glassily, when Carey appeared beside him. She had taken the plastic cup out of his hand and put it on the floor, and then she leaned in decisively and kissed him on the mouth.

That had been—nice. And afterward they had staggered out of the room like a three-legged race and into the midnight air smelling of grass from the lawns. Without the darkness and the thumping noise, Alex had felt drunkenness wearing off and self-consciousness intruding. But then, quite briskly, she had taken him to her girl-smelling single bed in her room across the quad and had taken charge of getting the sex out of the way, as if her soft belly and miraculous breasts and unexpected tattoo had been no more to her than the facts of her own body.

Then she'd gone to sleep on her back, snoring very softly, and Alex had lain awake not minding that her neck was cutting off the circulation to his arm. Her breath smelled slightly sweet from Coca-Cola and slightly alcoholic from rum. The duvet was askew, and one of her breasts was exposed, spilling down toward her armpit, where he could see a patch of sore skin and a bit of stubble. She had a mole on the soft skin just where her neck met the hinge of her jaw.

On Sunday morning, when he woke up, Alex had shyly and, as he thought, politely made an excuse about having to be in the library, kissed her awkwardly and said something non-committal and gone.

That was how their relationship had started. When Carey arrived in the college she was sexually confident, easily flirtatious, at home in her skin. Now, having quietly worshipped Carey for months, domesticating the relationship by making a friend of her, he'd actually gone to bed with her.

But the relationship between Carey and Alex had not, as he had expected, fizzled out in embarrassment and apology. At the cost of a certain showy huffiness from Rob, who felt excluded and maybe liked Carey more than he had let on, they had gone from friendship to established coupledom almost without passing through the in-between stage of tugging and scrabbling and kissing in public.

They were at ease, and that seemed to suit them both well enough. Alex found passion, or the expectation of passion, unsettling. Why make something private so public? And the courtship thing—he knew he had to do it but the self-exposure it involved and the risk and the game-playing and the humiliation . . . If you liked someone and you fancied them, why did you have to go through all that?

Carey had taken that out of his hands. They knew each other. Alex knew that she liked peanut butter on the cheapest white bread she could find, that they had the same Veruca Salt album, that she got on well enough with her foster-father, argued with her foster-mother, had no sisters and was liked better by boys than she was by girls. He put this down to jealousy; she was pretty, and neither worked it nor apologized for it. It was a fact about her.

Alex didn't know what attracted her to him, though. Men fancied Carey; women did not fancy Alex. Alex's place, ordinarily, was as the nerdy but unthreatening best friend of girls whom he chastely worshipped but who didn't think of him that way. Carey, on the other hand, had befriended Alex—and yet she also wanted to sleep with him. She did think of him that way. It was almost unprecedented, this state of affairs, and he intended to reward her with his loyalty. But it made him understand her less.

He wondered for a long time whether she was attracted to him by something she imagined he had that he didn't; or whether later, that illusion having vanished, the relationship was sustained by her affection for something else about him, such as his family, with the dull and affectionate stability that hers lacked; or whether there was something lacking in her—a simple failure of nerve or imagination that led her to idle in his shallows when with her looks and confidence she could have been with anyone else she wanted.

He studied his face in the mirror, sometimes, wondering what she saw there, and not liking what he did. Alex, when he looked at himself, saw a weak chin and watery features. He had eyes that flinched away from the camera. In the family photograph, blown up big and behind glass on the half landing of the old house, the two brothers stood in front of their parents: Saul already as tall as their mother, wearing his four-square smile; Alex's head minutely blurred with motion, eyes down and to one side, hooding his lids. The old wallpaper from that same room in the background, gold striping the green.

But it went on, nevertheless. Alex never asked Carey whether he had been a factor in her choosing to do her postgraduate work in Cambridge. And—at her request—they still hadn't moved in together. She said she was "funny about sharing space." But the fact that he loved her, after they had been going out for three years, was something he took for granted. It was another fact about her, like her beauty and the fact that he didn't understand her.

She wasn't delving, introspective, exhausting in that way some girls he'd known had been—even though, as he knew, she'd had it tougher than most of the thoroughgoing neurotics he'd been out with previously. She didn't talk endlessly about her emotions, or expect him to. Good.

Alex, there and here, had made some miles without even thinking about it. He'd noticed the state line going past about an hour back. The afternoon was mellowing, and he was in Alabama. He turned off the air con, wound down the window. Warm air came in, the smell of gasoline. He thought of singing Lynyrd Skynyrd to himself but the urge to sing had left him.

What Alex didn't know, as he was moving west, was that things were happening all around him.

Ahead of him, in Birmingham, a man stopped dead on the steps of the 16th Street Baptist church, in slanting sunlight, startled by the sound of birdsong. He shook his head. In the chattering of half a dozen birds on a telephone wire he could have sworn he had heard the first few bars of "Amazing Grace."

In the time it took Alex to pass through the Talladega National Forest, every shop in the state of Alabama sold out of Chicken & Broccoli Flavor Rice-A-Roni. In one shop in Gadsden, a fight broke out over the last packet on the shelf. A pregnant woman, overcome by her craving, pulled a gun on the teenage boy who had beaten her to it. She did not shoot.

In two small towns, equidistant to north and south of the I-40, the highway down which Alex was traveling, two men fell back in love with their wives for the first time in forty years. The names of both men were "Herb," and both of them had woken up that morning and rubbed their stubble sleepily while looking in the mirror and thought about shaving but decided not to bother. One of them was to live happily ever after. The other one was to fall down a well on his next birthday.

All over the state, brothers and sisters bumped into each other by chance as one was leaving the dry-cleaner's, and the other was running in to try to pick up her laundry.

In Las Vegas, still many miles away, the odds tilted for the first time very slightly against the house in low-stakes blackjack. Red Queen would be told about this in due course—as soon as it became detectable.

Unknown to anyone but you, in the Gulf of Mexico a sailfish of prodigious size, aided by a freakish current off the coast, spent thirty minutes keeping pace exactly with Alex's car. Then a shark took it.

Other things were happening. Things unknown to you, but known to me.

And other things, I suspect, were happening that are unknown even to me.

9

You need to know, though, what happened when Isla Holderness met Banacharski. That's where this begins. It begins with a woman with short, dark blond hair, and a handsome pointed nose, and windburned cheeks, walking up a cart track in the French Pyrenees. This is May 1998, and the hills are very beautiful. Buttercups nod in the cold wind.

Isla is carrying an old-fashioned backpack—it belonged to her father, and has a frame made of hollow aluminum poles. She has on thick hiking socks, made of gray wool, and jeans tucked into them. She is tired. She has been walking and—where possible—hitchhiking around this area for nearly two weeks now. In her pocket is a passport-sized photograph snipped from an academic journal. It has been creased and recreased.

It shows a thin man frowning with an expression of, she judges, concentration or toleration of having concentration broken. His hair is dark, and very close-cropped, nearly a skinhead—a reaction, perhaps, to a hairline already prematurely receded. It suits him. His cheekbones are sharp and he looks handsome. He's looking not at the camera, but downward and slightly to one side. Something like amusement plays around his mouth. The photograph is ten years old.

She is excited, because she thinks she may have found him. She started from Carcassonne, and she has been walking from town to town, going deeper into the countryside. She told her colleagues, most of them at least, that she was going on a walking holiday. Nobody mentioned Banacharski, except Mike—Mike, she thought, liked her—who when he heard she was going to the eastern Pyrenees said: "Off for a tryst with your boyfriend, I shouldn't wonder."

She is on a walking holiday. She's thirty-two years old and she's happy. She has been camping most nights, not more than one night in three treating herself to an inn. It's warm in the days, but most mornings she wakes in her tent with dew on her feet. She hasn't got much money. She eats chunks of *saucisson sec* with a penknife, and tears bits of bread to go with it. She has, in a compartment of her backpack, a jar of cassoulet and a tin of pineapple pieces for an emergency.

But when she passes through each village, she shows the photograph. She enjoys doing what a tourist would do—sitting in the village square, if there is one; eating her lunch quietly. She asks, with her halting French. At first it was hard. Now easy.

"Cet homme—un ami . . . vous savez ou il est?" She'd show the photograph. Cheeks would be rubbed, grunts emitted, more grizzled friends summoned over sometimes.

"Il s'appelle Nicolas. Nicolas Banacharski. Il est un . . . il fait le mathematique . . ." Here, she'd find herself feebly miming something halfway between a scribble on an imaginary table and a scribble on an imaginary blackboard. Her mime for mathematics was no more necessary, nor more plausible, than her mime for telephoning, or typing—the former consisting of an imaginary Bakelite earpiece and the latter of a peculiar ragtime piano solo played at the level of her clavicles with her eyebrows around her hairline.

Still, all this seems to endear her to the gruff old Frenchmen. Most of them seem to have heard some stories of a crazy mathematician. She has been following, generally, whichever wave of an arm her last informant offered. She's tried to pick market towns when there were markets. But she isn't hunting. Her idea is simply to have a holiday—to give it shape by hoping she'd stumble across the great man, but that isn't the point of it, not at all.

Then, yesterday, she was buying her lunch in a *boulangerie* in Nalzen and waiting for the orange-haired old chimp to ring up her sandwich. She was wondering how long that display of Chupa Chups lollipops had been there, when she looked out of the window over a display of baroquely iced cakes and exquisitely lacquered strawberry tarts.

It was him. To the life. He was going past on a bicycle, lolling, with one hand on the handlebars and the bicycle describing lazy, open sweeps back and forth across the empty street.

The woman squawked as Isla barged out of the shop to give chase. She left her backpack in the shop, yanked open the door and hop-skipped after him in her ridiculous socks.

"M'sieu! M'sieu!"

Half of her had imagined that if she ever met him he'd run or yell at her. She wasn't quite prepared for him simply to stop. He braked, and turned round. He looked startled, but not yet annoyed.

"Pardon . . . pardon . . ."

"Quoi?"

"Nicolas?"

"Quoi?"

"Je suis Isla."

His look was shifting from startled and sympathetic, to alarmed.

"Isla Holderness—*nous avons* . . ." She remembered he spoke English. They'd exchanged letters in English. "It's me, Isla. We've—I mean, I've sent you letters. I'm Isla Holderness."

"Mam'selle . . ."

The man on the bicycle was kindly. He stayed put for her stammering explanation, and was gentle in telling her that the words "Isla Holderness" meant nothing to him in any order at all, and that he was certain they had never exchanged letters. He was a handyman, not a scholar—he had used the word "scholar," clumsily, when she'd said "mathematician." He laughed when she showed him the photograph, though. He had to admit, it looked like him. No, no apology necessary. *Au contraire.* His name was Pascal. *Enchanté.*

But a mathematician? Lived alone? Pascal thought he might know him. Yes, bald. Not looking like this, though. He was an eccentric, sure enough—Pascal didn't remember his name but it might have been Nicolas. He looked at the photograph, blotting out the lower half of the face with his thumb and looking at the eyes. Isla could see they were different, now, Pascal and Banacharski, about the eyes.

They were still standing in the street. It was a small town and no cars had come. Pascal rolled his bicycle back and forth with his hips, turned the handlebars lazily with his free hand. He seemed to be smirking.

"Peut-être." It was an old photograph. He couldn't tell. But there was this *type* living in a shack up above Tragine. Pascal had gone to fix his septic tank. Had a lot of paper. He was— Pascal made a waving gesture with his hand . . . Big beard, Pascal said. Like a *blaireau.* People talked about him. Jewish, he thought. Maybe an inventor?

He left her after a few minutes, scribbling his phone number, as an act of gallantry, with a blunt stub of pencil on a bit of cardboard torn from a packet of cigarette papers. She folded this once and tucked it into the coin pocket of her jeans. They had made friends, though as she watched him cycle away she noticed that the bicycle was wagging less than previously and his head was wagging more.

She went back into the *boulangerie* and endured a foul look. The baguette, which she ate sitting on a low wall in the sunshine, was delicious. She spent the night in a field outside Freychenet, more excited than she was prepared to acknowledge to herself.

Now Isla is walking up, leaving the last outbuildings of the farm she passed behind her. The cart track is dry, and the sun has baked worm-curls of mud on it. Her new walking boots bash satisfyingly and painlessly off them. As a contour slopes round she glimpses the roof of a wooden cabin. The quarter-acre of land in front of it has been raked out flat and hoed, and there are lines of bamboo poles with brilliant green-yellow bean shoots curling around them. Chickens scratch in the dirt.

She doesn't think that Banacharski knows she is coming to look for him. She underestimates how small these towns are, and how close together. Banacharski knows she's coming.

He didn't know, at first, whether he wanted to be found. But now he sees her starting up the path toward him, smiling, and he thinks that he has been too lonely for too long.

"So, Jones," said Bree. "This thing. This thing you have."

It had been bugging Bree all afternoon, and she had been bugging Jones with it. It wasn't something Bree could quite make sense of. And—she being a naturally skeptical person—it wasn't something she completely believed, either. It was far from impossible that this was something Red Queen was doing just to mess her about. That Jones was a spy, or an actor, or some other damn thing. Indeed, that this whole thing might be some sort of fieldwork assessment exercise.

Jones didn't say anything.

They were in the car, and Jones was looking out of the wind-shield at the road. They were on the road west out of Atlanta heading for Birmingham. The sun was low in the sky ahead of them. They reckoned the kid was on the move, and that he was heading west.

Bree had asked how they knew that and Red Queen had said something about triangulation. They had tried the idea of using fluctuations in the ambient spread of probabilities to track the device. They conjectured that its effect on the world might leak out from it—little subtle ripples of unlikelihood, little freaks, unexpected variations from the mean could be discerned if you looked at large enough bodies of data. Their conjecture—unless what they were seeing was no more than the effects of chance itself—seemed to have been borne out.

They were monitoring regular big spreads: sports events, the patterns of roulette wheels and hands dealt in the major gambling centers of the North American mainland. Of course—and Bree would never have doubted it—they had access to those data in real time. Over the last several hours there had been spikes, outliers, runs of aces, improbable snake eyes, statistically significant fluctuations.

Red Queen didn't go into detail—just hints. Bree imagined low-level employees sitting in safe houses in all fifty states flipping quarters every ten seconds and noting down the results: "Heads, tails, heads, heads, tails, heads, heads, heads, heads, coin landed on edge, heads, heads, heads . . ." Whatever was measurable was measured.

Wispy though it was, all these variations, plotted together, seemed to signal some sort of gradient, something geographical, arranged around a moving focus. And the data was consistent with that focus heading westward at approximately the speed of an automobile traveling down a highway. Crudely, as Red Queen explained it, the closer to this thing you got, the less likely it was that you'd roll a four one time in six. Dice were behaving themselves on the eastern seaboard, Red Queen said. Dice were becoming more unruly to the west.

That, then, was the weather report: that was the state of chance. Things were getting more unlikely in the southwestern United States of America, with a front of downright implausible moving in from the east. Conditions in Atlanta and points east were calming, with nobody expected to beat the house for the foreseeable future.

★   ★   ★

"This thing," Bree repeated. "Does it make life fun?"

"I don't understand." Jones said that to a lot of inquiries. Bree had learned to persevere. She stopped talking, and looked at the side of his face like he was a Sudoku.

"Knock knock," said Bree.

Jones didn't say anything.

"I said: knock knock. You know about that, Jones. Don't pretend you don't. You grew up in some laboratory somewhere you never got told knock knock jokes?"

"I know knock knock jokes. I just don't know why they make you laugh."

"So you know what you say?"

"I know."

"So say it."

"Who's there," said Jones, but he said it without a question mark.

"Boo," said Bree.

"I've heard that one," said Jones.

"Say it for me, Jones," said Bree with a wheedling intonation. If you'd been watching carefully you could have identified her coaxing manner as flirtatious, almost.

"Boo who."

"Don't cry," said Bree. "It's only a joke."

Jones continued to stare out of the windshield. Bree reached into the glove compartment and took out a Slim Jim and unwrapped it and began to chew. That hadn't been a success.

"Slim Jim, Jones?" she said.

"No thanks," said Jones.

"OK," said Bree, a mile or so later on. "Not big on sense of humor. No GSOH, like they don't say in the lonely hearts listing. Jokes don't make you laugh."

Jones didn't say anything.

"Jeezus, Jones. I'm trying to needle you here. Throw me a bone."

Jones continued to look out of the windshield with bland attention to the road.

"OK. Needle means like . . . Bone means like . . . Means say something."

"What would you like me to say?" said Jones.

"Make conversation."

Jones left it a while. He seemed to be involved in some sort of mental effort. Bree could have sworn the hand with which he ordinarily smoked—the main hand with which he ordinarily smoked, given he seemed to be ambidextrous in this regard—twitched toward his pants pocket.

"Knock knock," said Jones eventually.

"Who's there?" said Bree.

Jones didn't say anything for a bit.

"Who's there?" said Bree. "Jones, you have to—"

"Mister," said Jones.

"Mister who?" said Bree.

"Mister Jones," said Jones. Bree laughed. Jones didn't.

"Hah, Jones," said Bree. "I like it. You were joking . . . Nice work . . ."

She cracked open another Slim Jim—they were minis—by way of celebration. Jones continued to stare benignly at the road, but she saw something around his eyes, in his frown, that looked a little haunted.

She waited a bit.

"You weren't joking," she said. "Were you?"

"No," said Jones. "I was trying."

"You were funny. Sort of . . . inadvertently." After the highway had gone by for a bit more, uneventfully, Bree continued. "Knock knock jokes aren't really funny, anyway," she said. "They're more like corny. So it's funny when they're not funny?"

"I know that," said Jones. "I know other people find things funny. It's one of the concepts I find difficult to understand. Funny is what?"

"Do you not laugh, Jones?"

Jones thought quite hard about this; as did Bree, who was trying to remember if she'd heard him laugh since they'd met.

"No," he said eventually, in a tone of voice that suggested that the question was an odd one.

"Not even if I tickle you?"

"No," said Jones. "I think that reflex is attached to anticipation. I don't have that. But I don't laugh. I know a lot of jokes. I remember every joke anyone tells me. I remember everything anyone tells me. I have an eidetic memory. It's one of the things that allows me to function. Someone tells someone else a lie and they laugh. I know that's how it works. But it doesn't work for me. If I know the joke, I know what's going to happen. If I don't know the joke, I often don't know it's a joke. It's just— nonsense. It confuses me."

Bree remembered, suddenly, the way her own daughter had been when she was five or six. That was when they'd been living in Washington, again, in the long narrow apartment with the air-con unit in the window at the end of the hallway that made all that noise.

Bree remembered Cass saying two things, the two things connecting up. First was when she had overheard Bree talking to Al, when they were still talking, and Al had said something that had made Bree laugh. A joke, not one of his dirty ones. Bree had been a couple beers in, probably laughing harder than whatever Al had said deserved.

"What, Mommy? What?" Bree had repeated the joke, but Cass had just looked confused. Did that really happen? Why not? Why did you say it did?

That phase lasted months—a curiosity about jokes, matched with a total failure to understand them. They seemed to be everywhere. Suddenly her schoolmates were all telling these jokes and Cass would bring them home, wondering, almost to the point of tears.

Cass—prim with indignation, hands behind her back in the blue dress, toe of the red shoe pivoting on the linoleum. "No, Mommy. That's not true. No. That's a lie."

The problem was that Cass didn't understand the difference between a joke and a lie—and Bree, though she knew there was one, had not been able to explain it to her daughter. She had not, come to that, even been able to explain it to her own satisfaction.

Later, when Cass started to lie in earnest, the thing recurred from the other end. "Did you do your homework?" "Did you study for the test?" "How was school?" These routine questions would be answered yes, and yes, and lovely thank you, Mommy. It was only when the teachers called to ask why Cass had failed the test, why she'd come to school without her homework, why she'd bitten another child so hard she'd drawn blood, and Bree confronted her, that she'd protest, "I was joking! It was a joke!"

"Cassie, did you take Mommy's keys, honey?"

"No, Mommy, I promise. Daddy took them."

And Cass would have a blazing row with Al. And then the keys would show up, in Hampton Bear's bear house in the corner of Cass's room.

"I was joking, Mommy! I was joking!" she would shriek as Bree, especially if it was late in the evening, smacked the backs of her legs red. Long time gone.

"What's the matter?" Jones said.

"Nothing," said Bree. "Bit of my Slim Jim went the wrong way." She coughed and thumped her chest and wiped her eyes on her sleeve and went into the glove compartment and came out again.

"OK, Jones," she said. "Irish knock knock joke. You say knock knock."

"Knock knock."

"Who's there?"

"Mister."

"No, it's—" she started. Jeepers he was hopeless. Then she realized he was, earnestly, trying. That made her feel . . .

"OK, Jones," she said. "Don't bother. Just drive." Trying, she thought.

The light was going down ahead of them, spreading out over the sky. It was cloudy in that direction. They drove on through Birmingham without stopping, at Bree's suggestion, and got takeout from a Wendy's on the outskirts, also at Bree's suggestion. Jones ordered what Bree ordered, which was one fewer burger than she would have liked. Bree liked Wendy's. The hot foil wrappings felt classier than Mickey D's, and she liked the way the burgers were square even though the buns were mostly round. She liked that you could nibble the corners off, salty and greasy and chewy and hot.

They ate leaning back against the doors of the car where it was parked in the lot. The restaurant was light and the light spilled into a kids' play area with a slide in the shape of an elephant and a see-saw anchored to the PlayCrete by a spring. It had a smiling plastic Wendy face, with ginger bangs and braids, atop the central boss. Wendy's eyes were dark.

Bree felt tearful. She slurped her big orange soda. Jones, on the other side of the car, smoked gratefully, and the drift of the smoke smelled good.

As they drove, afterward, Bree stopped trying to establish what went on in Jones's head. That was Jones's business, she reckoned. She liked him.

They drove on from the Wendy's and kept going to Tupelo, where when Bree saw the illuminated vertical beacon of a Motel 6 glowing she asked Jones to pull in and they decided to stop for the night. They would contact Red Queen in the morning. Bree wondered what had happened about the disappearing case—the one he'd had at the airport and then hadn't had.

They booked two adjacent rooms, both for cash. Jones helped Bree with her small traveling bag, put it in her room for her then came out to the walkway. It was round ten thirty, maybe eleven.

"Jones," she said. "Sleep well."

"Yes. Thank you. You sleep well also."

There was a moment of neither moving. Jones seemed to be looking for a cue.

She stood opposite him a minute, and thought of hugging him and then laughed aloud, a little nervously, and turned round and went into her room before she had time to register his quizzical expression.

Bree lay on her back on her bed in her clothes and looked at the ceiling. She thought of Cass. It was some time before she went to sleep. She wasn't aware of falling asleep at all. But she woke still in her clothes and with the lights on, where she had been lying earlier, with a disoriented feeling. That meant she had been asleep. The clock on the wall said it was 2 a.m. She could hear a noise.

Cheap thin motel walls, she thought, as her startlement abated and she got a sense of where she was. Barely more than partitions. It would be some couple going at it. But the noise wasn't the grunt and huff of sex, not even the stagy wailing some women seemed to put on when they found themselves in motel rooms with thin walls next to Bree when she was trying to sleep.

It was the high, animal, keening sound of someone in distress. Bree rolled her feet onto the ground and reached into her bag for the small, light handgun she carried and had never had to fire. She knew that this was a serious job. If this thing was as powerful as she understood it to be, she knew the DEI would not be the only people looking for it; they probably weren't even the only government agency looking for it. There were interests at work in it that would use violence. Red Queen had as much as told her so.

She sat with the gun in her two hands, getting her breathing steady, listening. The sound rose and fell, came and went. It wasn't the sound of someone being hurt. It was the sound of crying: the jagged hee-hawing of someone winded by grief. It was coming through the wall separating her room from Jones's. It sounded too high to be a grown man's voice.

Bree got up, rolled on the outsides of her feet to her door, and slowly turned the handle. Outside the air was still muggy. There was a dirty yellow halogen light illuminating the porch, and mosquitoes blatting against it. She eased the door behind her closed—a soft click, and a moment of panic before she remembered her key card was safe in her pocket—and she could no longer hear the bellow of the air conditioner.

She took a couple of steps down to Jones's door. It was closed. The sound was coming through the thin plywood. She kept the gun in her right hand, but let it fall down behind her thigh. She knocked, softly, with the knuckles of her left hand on the door.

The sound stopped, abruptly. She stood breathing there for a minute, then knocked again.

"Who is it?" It was Jones's voice. She had, momentarily, a flash of remembering the knock knock jokes.

"Jones?" she said.

"Bree?"

"Yes."

The door opened. Jones was there, and from behind him there came a gust of old cigarette smoke. He had his trousers on, and no top. He was well muscled. In one hand he had a toothbrush and in the other a lit cigarette, and his eyes were red and sore. He looked at her a moment, winced, and resumed brushing his teeth. Foam appeared around his mouth.

"Jones?"

"What?" he said, removing the toothbrush. He put the cigarette up to his mouth and took a pull. The end was dabbed with shiny foam when he took it out. Then he turned round and went back into the room. His room was exactly like Bree's, except that beside the laminated no-smoking sign on the bedside table was the polystyrene cup from the bathroom, filled with butts.

Jones tapped his ash into this cup, went into the bathroom and spat noisily.

"I was just going to bed," he said.

"What the hell's up? Was that you crying?"

Jones looked at her as if slightly affronted.

"Yes," he said.

"Easy, Jones," Bree said. "What's the matter?"

"My mother is dead," Jones said.

"Oh, Jones. I'm sorry. Shit. You should have said. What happened?" Bree moved in, awkward because of her bulk and because of Jones's semi-nakedness and his being a colleague and being covered in toothpaste and waving a cigarette. She thought she ought to hug him but contented herself with reaching up and squeezing his shoulder. Jones's face crumpled, then recovered. He sat down on the bed.

"Jones, look, we'll—where's home? Do you want to drive there? Did you just hear?"

Jones sat down on the bed, and Bree sat down with him.

"No," said Jones. "My mother has been dead for twenty-four years."

Bree didn't say anything for a bit, then she said: "*Twenty-four years?*"

"My mother has been dead for twenty-four years."

"I heard you, Jones. I mean: what? What's making you cry? Twenty-four years is a long time."

"She's still dead," said Jones.

"Jesus, Jones. Of course. I know, but it's like you just found out—"

"It *is* like I just found out. I always cry before I go to sleep," said Jones. "I have emotions. I don't have an imagination: I can't see things that aren't there. But I have emotions. I had something and it made me happy and I lost it and now I don't have it."

"Tell me about her," said Bree. Bree thought of Cass again, and then stopped the thought. "What do you remember about her?"

"Everything," said Jones.

"You're—"

"I remember everything she ever said to me. Everything she ever wore. Every time she touched me. Every smell and taste of her." Jones sighed. "I have an eidetic memory. That is my condition. Everything that ever happens to me I remember it exactly. If I didn't have that I couldn't function."

"But."

"Why would I not be sad when I am alone?"

"Jones, people get over things. They have to. You can't just—"

In the light from the wall lamp, Jones's face was a sick yellow. He looked miserable. He got up and went to the sink, rinsed his toothbrush and stood it in the other polystyrene cup.

"I can't. I know that this is not like other people. It's not important. It is what happens to me. But I have no way of 'getting over things.' I have no expectations, no desires that live in what you call the future. That is what apsychosis means. Everything I want is in the past. Everything I want to happen has already happened. Everyone I love is already gone, and I can remember everything about them."

Bree didn't know what to say, so she didn't say anything. Jones lit another cigarette from the butt of the last. Bree felt sad and annoyed and a bit awkward.

"Would you like me to leave you alone?" she said.

"I don't . . ."

"OK, I get it. You don't know what it would be like. But you must know—from your experience—if you're happier when you have someone with you or if you're happier when you're alone."

"I'm happier when you are with me," said Jones.

"OK then," said Bree. And she kicked off her shoes and lay down on the bed. When he finished smoking he turned off the light and lay down, apparently without self-consciousness, on the bed next to her. The keening noises he made rose a little, then settled, as Bree put one of her arms over him and held him as he fell to sleep.

10

Isla walks up between two rows of beanpoles toward the cabin. She thinks: nobody is here.

A cane chair, empty, sits outside the cabin. The windows are shuttered. There is an outer door, with a gauze screen in it, that looks like it once had some paint on the wood. It's very slightly ajar, and she pulls it open. She waits a minute, listening to nothing, then knocks on the inside door. She waits, turns on her heels and looks around her. There's no reply, still, from inside, so she walks round the side of the cabin. There's a sloping roof coming off the wall a bit below shoulder height—mossy slates, sheltering a pair of tall red gas canisters and a neat stack of chopped wood.

The back of the cabin is windowless, and faces an escarpment—there'd be room to wriggle past, but not comfortably. As she peers round she sees a cat vanish into the crawl space under the cabin. It smells of sawdust and wet earth. He's in the woods somewhere, presumably. She wonders about leaving a note, decides against.

She puts her face up against one of the windows, cups her hands around her eyes so she can see in. The room looks bare—there's a dark rug of some sort on the floor, some sort of pallet up one end, drifts of yellow paper stacked on and around a table on the blank wall. On the table is an old-fashioned hurricane lamp.

The yellow paper . . . This is it. The letters all came on long sheets of ruled yellow paper from legal pads. The writing disciplined, intense, very small. She is remembering the first letter she had: two years ago, out of the blue, apparently in response to something she had written about him.

"Dear Miss Holderness," it had begun. "The order of things is changing." The letter was written in English, albeit some of it curiously constructed.

It had been addressed in scrawled block capitals with her first name gone over several times in ink, care of "EtUdes/RecOltes," University of Nice. On the back was a poste restante address in Carcassonne.

He had read, he said, the short introductory commentary she had written—there'd been some sort of dodgy French translation—on the value of his work to number theory for this small mathematical journal with its tiresome capitalization.

She hadn't believed it at first. Clearly Mike was winding her up. But would even Mike write forty pages just for the sake of a joke? And Mike didn't know the maths well enough, she realized as she went on, to have written some of the material in the letter. Then she thought that it meant something momentous: if it was Banacharski, and he was still reading journals, it meant he might still be doing maths.

A subsequent page suggested otherwise. He had bought some artichokes at the market, and they had been wrapped in a photocopy of her article. This, Banacharski said, was of tremendous importance.

"I ate these artichokes. There were four of them. And I counted each one the number of their petals, and counted each one the number of the fibers around their hearts. This took me several days. I have started to see what you are talking about. Your article shows a deep grasp of theory. Not in the meanings of your words, which are banal, but in the patterns of your words. You know this. I am now starting to learn. The problem is in disorder."

Isla had been taken aback by this. She'd thought her article sensible enough.

There had followed—taking up most of the letter—a long, long string of numbers—a series with no apparent pattern to it. Then there were operations on these numbers. Some of these, as far as she could make out from the marginal notes, were derived from the number of letters in the successive words of her article; some had to do with the frequency with which given letters had recurred in the article; some had to do, in a complex way, with artichokes.

Banacharski was trying to sieve some sort of order out of the randomness. Nobody could do this. He was constructing equations, finding relationships, whittling the number string down . . . he was—as far as she could tell—trying to wrestle the data into abstract algebra. He was trying to use it to describe a shape in space time, or a manifold of that shape. He digressed, occasionally, into some impenetrable speculation about the symmetries of the artichoke.

His letter closed: "Write to me. There is not enough data. The work I am doing is important." Important was underlined three times.

Isla had tried to follow what was going on. He was mad, that was clear enough. It was a scarily powerful mind, she thought, in deep distress. She had been halfway through writing back when the second letter had arrived. It had been shorter, with moments of lucidity. "I am fighting with devils," it said. "Forgive me."

She had written back, finally, with her home address in Cambridge—he never used it, continuing to write care of the magazine, whose name he sardonically recapitalized, she noticed, in every letter. She said nothing about artichokes. She was chatty, factual, friendly—and did everything she could to flatter him. She told him about work that had been done on his work. Two major conjectures, she said, had been proved. He hadn't been active for seven years.

His letters had gone in and out of lucidity. None was shorter than twenty pages. The longest was eighty-six pages. They appeared at intervals of anything between two and ten days. One or two of the letters contained fragments that made straightforward mathematical sense. In most, the equations seemed to be somehow . . . bent.

Isla discussed them with a few colleagues, including—though she came slightly to regret it—Mike, but was shy of showing them to anyone. She felt somehow protective. She had a sense that Banacharski trusted her.

Frustration started to infect them, though, as time went on. For the last six months, things seemed to be gathering pace. He underlined heavily, used confusing ellipsis, the ascenders and descenders on his letters becoming longer and angrier. Some of his choices of word seemed odd, stilted—and he started to capitalize words at random within the text of his letters. He went on and on about something he called "*the churn*," or the "*in-between space*." It was as if she was supposed to understand something he was trying to communicate and was failing to.

His last letter—all of them, previously, had been signed, simply, "NB"—was signed off "Affectionately, and in despair, Nicolas."

All this has led her here. And she is looking, now, through the window of what must be his shack as a cloud passes over the sun and brings, in this high place, a slight chill.

She takes her face from the window and turns round and there he is. He is standing at the end of the wooden wall of his cabin, smiling at her. The first thing she takes in is the skin of his face. It is blotchy—a pattern of brown freckles alternating with a cross pink color like sunburn. His eyes are deep-set. His lips are fat, old-man lips. His beard is dark gray, with a badger-stripe of white down one side, and spreads wide to his chest, across a striped and grubby shirt, open three buttons down.

Around his waist, higher than his trousers, is a length of what looks like baling twine, snarled in a scraggy version of a bow knot. He salutes her, then casts his eyes down and away, then looks up at her again. He beckons, flapping one hand while look-ing at his feet.

His feet are in flip-flops. His toenails are filthy.

"*Alors, oui, entrez donc*," he says, shuffling round the corner and opening the screen door then the other one.

"I'm Isla," she says.

"Of course," he says, as he opens the door and ushers her in. There's a strange look in his eye, she thinks.

"Honestly?" said Hands. "I think you have a problem."

The interview had gone on late into the evening, though you would not know in the unchanging light of the room that it had done so. Functionaries had been and gone. Hands had spent several hours looking through sheaves of photocopies: selections from Banacharski's letters, classified reports from Directorate sources in MIC, what scraps of intelligence were available.

The coffee in the cup marked Starbucks had been replaced by more coffee in another cup marked Starbucks and Hands had been given a very large cookie containing very large raisins, which he had eaten hungrily. The atmosphere was near enough genial.

"The way you might want to think about it is this," said Hands, cupping his left elbow with his right hand and rubbing it thoughtfully. "If what you've described to me is correct, and I must stress *if*, then this device, or engine if you will, is going to be highly unpredictable in its behavior. Highly unpredictable."

Red Queen let him run.

"There's a point at which mathematics and advanced phys-ics shades over, in a way it's hard for laypersons to understand, into philosophy. It's not the fact that it's hard for the outsider to understand, no. It's more the *way*. Laypeople, you see—laypeople very often get the wrong end of the stick. Headline writers, arts graduates, pompous novelists. They get very attracted to metaphors, you see. You know how it is: they thought Einstein had proved that 'everything was relative'; whereas actually he proved something much more interesting than that. Then there was quantum mechanics and the stick they got hold of the wrong end of was the wrong stick altogether." Hands allowed himself a professorial little chuckle at his own joke. "Then chaos theory. Dear me. What I mean to say is: it's not that all this mathematics is a metaphor. It's the other way round. It's that—sorry, I'm not explaining it very well. What we do doesn't reflect the universe. It describes it. See? There isn't a realm of ideas and then the world . . . it's more like . . . ideas are part of the world. And if this machine does what you seem to think it does, it's possible that what has happened is that something that ordinarily belongs for all intents and purposes to the realm of ideas is, effectively, acting in the world."

"Are you going to tell me what this machine might be doing, Professor?" said Red Queen.

"I'm getting round to it. You'll have to forgive my thinking aloud."

Hands was leaning forward and the elbow-rubbing was slowing and increasing in time with his diction. He paused.

"Mind control?" said Red Queen.

"No. I don't imagine so. Probably rather the absence of it. One of the big mysteries is consciousness. What is creating what I'm thinking, and what—assuming, that is, that we're not all brains in a jar, or the hallucination of some being in another universe altogether—is creating what you're thinking and what does it mean to think? Consciousness, ideas, imagination, selfhood—all the things that make you you and me me. These obviously arise from electrical impulses in the physical brain. And the best accounts of consciousness we have—which is to say, no real accounts at all—speculate that the ghost in the machine, so to speak, may be a function of these impulses interacting at a quantum level."

"OK."

"So the brain—consciousness itself—isn't separate from the system of matter and energy in the rest of the universe. It's part of it. Maybe a very tiny part of it, but that doesn't matter. Chaos theory says that something very, very tiny in the data of a system that feeds back through itself can create very, very dramatic results. So it's not theoretically impossible that something that started life as an idea might have an effect in the world."

"What are the chances?"

"Well—we don't know, obviously. I'd say it would be very, very unlikely. Very unlikely indeed. It hasn't happened before, as far as anyone knows. But then, if Banacharski has found a way of making a machine that affects probability—which would be odd because probability doesn't itself exist, necessarily; at least not in the sense that most people might understand it . . ."

"Then you're supposing," said Red Queen, "he made a machine with his brain. And this machine made it possible for his brain to make the machine. Isn't that a bit circular?"

"I'm speculating," protested Hands. "That's all I'm in a position to do." He looked a little hurt. "I'm a professor of mathematics, anyway: not of yet-to-be-discovered physics."

Red Queen stood up, walked round the desk, returned to the chair, performed a lazy roll of the neck.

"So it won't look like a machine, necessarily?"

"I don't suppose so, no."

"No knobs, buttons, flashing lights, wires?"

"I doubt very much it runs on a battery."

Red Queen's watch said it was a quarter to midnight.

They were interrupted by a rap at the door of the room, followed before either had the chance to respond by a man of medium height, with a splash of gray in his hair, wearing a dark suit. His manner was brisk.

"Porlock," said Red Queen.

The man bowed his head slightly. "Word from Our Friends. They think they've found the suitcase the boy dropped at the airport. They're bringing it in." Our Friends was Directorate slang for what might have been called the executive branch. Friends got things done. Theoretically, they were partner agencies. But Red Queen regarded their involvement in this—in anything—as at best a necessary evil.

"What was it? Where was it?"

"He didn't leave it. He passed it, as you thought, to someone in arrivals."

Hands sat on the sofa mutely watching the exchange.

"Who?"

"Courier."

"For who?"

"An agency. His name was misspelled on the manifest. That's why the initial sweep didn't pick it up. The client was MIC."

Red Queen tensed, looked at Hands, then went out into the corridor with Porlock. Porlock pushed the door to behind him so that Hands could no longer hear their conversation.

"What was it?"

"An encrypted hard drive."

"How did you get it?"

"The courier had an accident. Not the boy, the pickup guy. Non-fatal. Best Our Friends could do. We thought you'd want it."

"I do. Put everyone on this. People with big brains and eyeglasses. Tell me when you've cracked the drive."

"Could this be it?"

Red Queen shrugged. "Seems unlikely if the analysts are saying the thing's on the move. Something's making the weather out there."

"Weather?" said Porlock.

"Figure of speech. I mean something's stirring things up. And whatever it is, this hard drive is the best clue we have to what it is and where it's going."

Porlock turned on his heel and clicked off up the corridor. Red Queen went back into the room, where Hands was shifting in his chair, looking faintly grumpy.

"Professor Hands. I'm sorry again to keep you so late. Now, this is important. You said earlier you thought we had a problem. What did you mean by that?"

Hands sat back in the sofa and rubbed the bridge of his nose hard with his thumb and forefinger.

"Nicolas Banacharski was one of the most brilliant mathematicians of the twentieth century. No question. He had a very powerful mind. But he was—is, if he's still alive—cracked. That is often part of the way things go with mathematicians who work at a very high level. If this thing he's made is a leakage of that mind into the world, and if it's working like a feedback loop . . . it will get more powerful and more unpredictable the more it operates."

"And it won't have an off switch."

"I have no idea. I'm not imagining this thing as something that has an off switch. I'm imagining it as something that will tend to produce effects that have to do with human minds. The very fact that you say it's affecting probability is the troublesome bit."

"I don't follow."

"Probability isn't something you can affect like—I don't know—like a magnet affects iron filings. When you load dice you're not affecting probability—you're affecting physics. You're making one side heavier. Probability isn't a force. It doesn't *do* anything. The earth hasn't got a probability field in the way it has a magnetic field or a gravitational field. Luck—" He blew out through his lips. "Luck is something that exists simply in the brain of the lucky or unlucky person. It's an *idea*, not an actual thing."

"We have Gypsies," said Red Queen. "Down on the fourth level. We have cats on their tenth lives. We have lucky clover.

Rabbits' feet. The Pentagon stockpiled rabbits' feet during the first Gulf War. They *requisitioned* rabbits' feet. They were issued."

Hands shook his head. "No luck. Just things, so to speak, taking place. Your brain is programmed to notice things that seem strange, to invent correlations and to make theories about them. Winning streaks."

"If I won the lottery, I'd be lucky," said Red Queen. "I'd be amazed." Red Queen was not lying about this. Red Queen didn't play the lottery.

"Yes, you'd think so. But are you amazed every week when someone wins the lottery?" Hands answered his own question: "No. Because someone always wins the lottery. The thing is: that's not surprising at all. That's just something happening. One person in a million, or however many players you have, will always win. You're only surprised when it's you. From the point of view of the universe this is not at all unusual. A coincidence isn't something strange that happens; it's something that happens that you think is strange."

Red Queen looked blank, frowned.

"Let me try to explain again," said Hands, his slightly frayed but pleasurably superior sense of himself reasserting itself; his seminar tone sneaking back in. "So if this machine is, as you say, affecting probability, it is affecting something that doesn't exist in the first place. It's affecting an idea in someone's head. An idea about expectation, or even *desire*. And then that idea is affecting things—substantial physical things—in the world. Its operation is as paradoxical, so to speak, as its very existence."

"I don't really have the leisure to think about this philosophically, Professor, interesting though that may be," said Red Queen. "I need to know how to find it, and how to get it under control."

"There," said Hands, "I don't know if I can help you. If it has to do with ideas—and if it is tending to behave in such a way as to be so to speak 'improbable'—what it does will get more and more improbable. It will begin to feed back into itself."

"It will get weirder?"

"In all likelihood, yes. I was talking earlier about cascade effects. You know, like when a truck starts to fishtail on the freeway, and then . . . it just goes and it spins out altogether. Something predictable, after a certain point, becomes very, very unpredictable. At the ends of these series, very close to zero or very close to infinity, the line doesn't just curve slightly—it goes . . ." Hands's right arm wearily described a rocket taking off across some sort of imaginary graph. "What I mean is that something that we know to exist but that is highly, highly improbable—something at the point where the rules really seem to break down altogether—is called a singularity."

"Like a black hole?"

"Yes, a black hole *is* a singularity, in physics. When it comes to the laws of physics, all bets are off, so to speak. But singularity means something slightly different across different disciplines . . . Are you paying attention to me?"

Red Queen was not—was, rather, thinking about the patterns they'd been plotting in gambling odds in the big centers. Porlock's clever idea. They'd let the numbers Doppler off against each other—Atlantic City and Vegas and bootlegged data for Tijuana; all-night poker hands flowing through the big Internet servers; roulette on reservations; anything that might pick up a sort of after-echo of the effect, like background radiation. Porlock had looked as smug as all hell when he'd brought the results, plotted through the day. It had suggested, however approximately, a vector: a field of disturbance heading due west from Atlanta, emitting a steady, Geiger-counter-like crackle of the unpredictable.

In Red Queen's head, a map of America. Porlock thought these gambling centers might be a way of plotting a course. But a line between Atlanta—the place where the boy had stopped and handed this package to his employers—and San Francisco— the place where the boy was apparently heading before he decided to go off-map . . . it went more or less through the Nevada Desert.

"Vegas. What would happen?"

"Sorry?"

"I'm thinking aloud. Let's say, sake of argument, this is a terrorist action . . ." Red Queen got up from the desk again, paced down one side of the room, now ignoring Hands altogether. "You have a coincidence machine. You want to cause maximum damage. Where do you go?"

"I don't follow you."

"You go to Vegas. You go to—what would happen if . . . if . . . everything came up black all at once?"

"Well, I'm no expert on this, but generally casinos lay off odds. On average the people who bet red will cancel out the people who bet black. Rather as I was saying"—Hands was keen to get back to his lecture—"the behavior of a roulette wheel or a deck of cards—a straight one, so to speak—is perfectly predictable over a long period. That's why the casino always wins. The most freakish results all cancel each other out, and—"

"But *say*, Hands"—this was the first time Red Queen had not called him "Professor," and there was a definite edge of impatience in it—"*say* everyone happened to have bet on black. Or nobody bet on black. Then it came black. Or say"—an image suddenly presented itself in Red Queen's mind—rows and rows of women sitting like tortoises in velour leisure suits, in front of the slots in the waxy yellow light—"say every slot machine in Vegas paid out its top jackpot at once. What would happen?"

"Theoretically—"

"Theoretically hell. This would be—would be an act of war. It would wipe out companies, pension plans, stocks. It would cause chaos. This would be like dropping a coincidence bomb on America."

"I suppose, in—"

"Professor, I need to make some phone calls, now. I would appreciate it if you were able to give us a little more of your time."

"Actually, as I was going to say," Hands returned, "I see that gambling or stock markets would present a problem, economically speaking. But I'm—when I said you had a problem I meant something rather more serious than that. A run of numbers in a gambling parlor is one thing, but a singularity is a problem of a quite different order of magnitude."

"I don't see."

"There is something that baffles physicists about the beginning of the universe. We know a little about what gravity was like, in the very first moments of time. And the chances of the initial state of the universe having arisen by accident are one in ten to the power ten." Hands's eyes rolled up and right and his tongue appeared in the corner of his mouth. He remembered: "To the power 123."

"What does that mean?"

"That is fantastically improbable."

"I thought you just said that there was no such thing as probability."

"Not as a force, no. But let's talk as if probability exists as you understand it. For the sake of argument. The state of gravity at the beginning of the universe was so improbable that the odds-to-one against it are so great that if you wrote a 0 on every single atom in the universe, you still wouldn't be able to write it down. I'm saying this machine could do something much more damaging than bankrupting a couple of casinos or crashing the United States's economy."

"There is nothing more damaging than crashing the United States's economy," said Red Queen. "Trust me."

"No. I don't think you understand me. This machine could, if it—strange to put it this way—took a *shine* to the notion, pull our universe inside out through its own asshole." Far from being dismayed by the prospect—in the way Red Queen was dismayed, deeply dismayed, by the prospect of explaining a threat to the economy to the boss—Hands seemed positively to perspire with excitement.

"Is that professor-speak?" said Red Queen.

"Yes."

"Singularity," said Red Queen thoughtfully.

"Yes."

"Universe pulled inside out?"

"Yup."

"Asshole."

"Yes."

"I wasn't asking. Professor Hands, we would appreciate it if you stayed in overnight. I'll have someone bring you a toothbrush. The universe being pulled inside out through its own asshole," Red Queen repeated wonderingly. "Nice. Well. That's a bridge we'll cross when we come to it. Keeping this thing from getting anywhere near Binion's Lucky Horseshoe Casino is the problem I propose to tackle first off."

Red Queen got up and walked out of the room.

As Alex drove west, whistling on his way, little strangenesses proliferated in the world around him.

In one town in Nevada, the cashpoints malfunctioned. Hundreds and hundreds of dollars poured onto the pavements and were blown down the street by the wind. Children chased them. Adults chased the children. Some adults attempted to return the money to the banks. The banks blamed a lightning strike.

In Baton Rouge, a man in a tall hat removed it and a hummingbird flew out. He stopped in astonishment, not noticing the hummingbird, seeing nothing remarkable in the white sunlight on the sidewalk, overwhelmed only by a sense of déjà vu so powerful he forgot for an instant who he was.

Every narcoleptic in Mississippi went out at once. All of them were crossing roads at the time. People thought there was a plague. Cars backed up, honking, at pedestrian crossings as the pedestrians slept. And here, there, and everywhere sleepers shared the same broken dream: of an old man in a shack in the mountains, a rainbow in the dark sky, a terrible wind. None of them remembered the dream.

11

Alex had the idea of going to bed in Memphis, but he realized not long after dark that he wasn't going to make it. So, just around the time his eyes were getting tired and the road was starting to seem strange, he stopped at a motel outside Tupelo. He got a room, and asked the clerk where he could get food at this time of night.

He drove the car down the road to a restaurant called Steak Break. There—eyeing through the near-pitch-darkness of the dining room the portion being eaten by a courting couple at the next-door booth, he ordered just a starter—"chicken tenders," which turned out to be giant, volcanically hot kidney-shaped chicken nuggets—and a baked potato, which came soggy-skinned, waxy-fleshed, wearing a tinfoil leisure suit and a pompadour of whipped buttter.

It tasted comforting. Beer came in a large, fridge-cold glass. He had two sudsy pints as he ate. The waitress said something about his accent, and he wondered briefly, flattered, if she was trying to flirt with him.

The couple left and he was the last customer there. The waitress followed the couple to the door—dark wood, four patterned-glass panels, tiny curtains on a brass rail—and flipped over the wooden "We're Open!" sign on its chain.

It was only quarter past ten. As he sat in the restaurant his phone pinged. He looked at it. Two messages. One must have arrived earlier in the car, while he was driving.

The first one was from Rob. It said: "One for all and all for one? (3, 3, 2, 3, 4)."

For Alex and Rob, the crossword game was a sort of distant intimacy, mixed up with showing off, mixed up with competition. They'd been doing it since a drunken evening in their second year as undergraduates. Months could pass between them, but then one of them would think of one and the other would get it.

The first one after that evening had been a scrap torn from an A4 pad in a college pigeonhole: "Cows hidden from Nazis? (3, 6, 5, 2, 4, 5)." Alex had scribbled "The Secret Dairy of Anne Frank" on the note there and then in the porter's lodge and popped it back into Rob's pigeonhole.

Latterly they'd come through as text messages. Never a proper letter or an e-mail. Never, since the first days of it, in person. The rule—though again, it had never seemed to be actually formulated or discussed—was that until you'd guessed the last one you couldn't send one of your own.

Rob was better at it than Alex. Alex thought about this as he chewed his potato. Something something in something something? Something something of something something? Something something to something something? The something something something something?

That set him off thinking about the sentence Rob had once asked him to make sense of: "Dogs dogs dog dog dogs." When Rob had explained it—*dogs that other dogs pester (dog) in turn pester other dogs*—Alex had tried it on Carey. She'd failed to be as impressed as he'd hoped. She'd said, with a sad sigh: "Yeah. That's about the way it goes."

Rob had been interested in the way the sentence was jointed. Carey, having had it cracked open for her, had simply lit on the meaning—the least important part. Rob had been interested in whether it also worked for fish: fish fish fish fish fish. Carey had said that was stupid because fish didn't fish—and if let's suppose they did, the ones that had been fished would hardly be in a position to do any fishing themselves.

Alex had let it go, pleased simply to be with her on a summer lawn by the river.

The second text message, the one that had just arrived, was from Carey. "Where are you, boy? Weird things are happening. Have a good afternoon. Miss you. Talk tomorrow? Night."

Alex wondered what he'd say. He'd phone her. If he did, would the dial tone, or caller-ID, tell her he was in America, though? A payphone? Would that be different? He didn't want to freak her out. He didn't want to spoil the surprise.

The box with the ring in it—he hadn't felt comfortable leaving it in the room, with its flimsy door—dug into his hip as he leaned forward to flag the waitress for the bill.

"Could I get the check?" he said, enjoying the American words coming out of his English mouth, resisting doing an accent.

The something of something something.

When he got back to the motel he was tired and turned straight in, setting the alarm on his mobile phone for seven thirty. In the middle of the night he half woke up. The room was cool, and through the flimsy curtains he could see the moon over the parking lot. He could hear crying from the next-door room. Then he frowned, turned over, and sank back into sleep.

"There have been disturbances in the mass media," Red Queen said. "Running up to this. That was one of the things that caused us to keep the file open on what seemed to many of us like a lost cause. It seemed perfectly possible the machine was just imaginary: something Banacharski had made up—though, remember, we have some partial material from his communication with Holderness. And, well, some of that material either demonstrated that this machine existed, or it demonstrated the opposite. He was very paranoid. It's possible some of what he told Holderness was disinformation, especially toward the end. But . . ." Red Queen trailed off. "Then the thing with the airplane. The thing with the frogs . . ."

"Frogs?" Porlock said.

"You didn't hear about that?"

Porlock looked slightly irritated.

"Downtown Atlanta? It was on CNN. It led Fox. Frogs fell out the sky. Thousands of them. From very high up. Several citizens were killed."

"I've been working a lot of double shifts. That's been known to happen, though. Don't the frogs get sucked up by tornadoes? We've just had not one but two hurricanes . . ."

"The killed citizens: 60 percent of them were Atlanta-stationed employees of MIC Industrial Futures, Inc.; 40 percent of them were Atlanta-stationed employees of subsidiaries or affiliates of MIC Industrial Futures, Inc.; 10 percent of them was a postman."

"A postman?"

"Yes. We think he was just unlucky. As opposed to the other citizens killed by falling frogs."

"What sort of frogs were they?"

Red Queen admired that sort of attention to detail.

"Mostly the sort of frogs that are hard to identify when you drop them from a mile up. Almost all of them—that is, the epicenter of the frog event, or whatever you call it—fell on MIC's Atlanta offices. They took out the glass roof of the atrium. It was over the cafeteria. A lot of people in hospital with very nasty cuts. The offices are still closed."

"Our Friends are sneaking in and planting more bugs, then . . ."

"Yes. Lots more. MIC, as I don't need reminding you, is the company that was paying Banacharski. From a good way back. They were funding his chair at the Sorbonne. When he resigned in protest at being funded by an arms company it looked like he was resigning in protest at being funded by an arms company, but everything we've since learned suggests that actually he was resigning in order to work directly for the arms company. The letters to Holderness talk about a man, Nieman, an operative for 'the firm,' who's clearly Banacharski's liaison for his research.

He lived for several years with no visible means of support. So MIC are all over this. We think it was their freelancers who went after the guy they found in the plane."

"What about the guy in the plane?"

"Still in hospital. Still a waste of time."

"You know MIC has links to government."

"What arms and baby-milk company doesn't?"

"Very serious links. We are, theoretically, on the same side."

"We are on the same side—but in this, no. This machine is a game-changer. If they get it they'll be their own side. And the frog thing. It can't be chance. As I was saying, though: the mass media."

When Red Queen talked about the mass media, that didn't mean newspapers and television. It meant the hundreds and thousands of the psychically sensitive, wandering mad. To most people, they were a disaggregated army of street-corner crazies, but for the DEI they were an underground railway, an early warning system, a giant biological radio tuned to sketchy transmissions from . . . well, that was the question. Red Queen preferred to remain skeptical, but running the mass media was Sosso's department, down in the underhangar. Red Queen didn't have to worry about it in detail. It was valued. Funding depended on it.

Sosso's theory of it was only ever going to be a theory: whenever anything became empirically testable, it lost its Dubya status and was transferred out of DEI. Dubya was the Directorate nickname for any file coded UU, for "Unknown Unknowns": double-U. But Sosso's theory was this.

Old-style "mediums"—Victorian charlatans in robes and false noses, wired up to jerry-rigged table-knocking devices—purported to have some control over their gifts. But media, to use the correct plural, were actually as passive as air and relatively common. The Chinese were rumored to be "training" them in very large numbers; harvesting Falun Gong and the Tibetan monasteries and "repurposing" the prisoners in permanent detention. That gave even Red Queen the creeps.

What made media media was that only a mind slightly hanging off its hinges could let whatever it was through, and the way it came through was garbled. Low signal, high noise. Any single medium would produce indecipherable gibberish. Yet in aggregation the signals had yielded suggestive results. A hobo in Palo Alto might mumble "Harra fugg . . . a-budda. Zzzzally! Mmmrgfff" at precisely the moment that a heavily medicated paranoid schizophrenic in the Bowditch Hall at McLean's would exclaim, from swampy dreams: "Paternoster! Carthago delenda est! I am Caligula!" And if you combined the sounds of their voices the recording might throw up a fragment of a word in Aramaic.

Sosso, a true believer, liked to use the image of each medium being a single string on a huge harp; you'd hear one note but you needed to hear the chord. Or the assemblage being a pipe organ: the more pipes you could hear the closer to the tune you got.

In a system they'd grimly termed "tag and release," operating over more than two decades through homeless shelters, outpatient mental health units, combat veterans' trauma units, and addiction clinics, thousands of potential media had been identified and fitted with transponders, typically hidden in the fillings of their teeth, or in metal pins fitted somewhere in the skull or jaw where they could benefit from bone conduction.

The second generation of these devices were able to tell when the medium was asleep or unconscious, and flag the signals received accordingly. It was generally believed in the Directorate that sleep—or catatonia, states arising from hypnotic or psychedelic drugs, alcoholic dementia or near coma—was the most likely to yield what Sosso called "accurate" or "high yield" material.

Sosso's team worked on these. They used bleeding-edge voice recognition and translation software to sieve the data, compiling and noting sentence fragments and unusual or foreign words.

They combed different overlays and combinations of voices, experimented with staggering inputs according to the different time zones or lunar phases, squelched the bass or treble, speeded and slowed the recordings, even played fragments backward on the off chance of backward-masked messages. Mostly, they came up mud.

They also tracked the frequencies of particular phonemes—according to time logged and geographical concentration. This was often what yielded the result.

Sosso had a piece of software that allowed her to mouse over a satellite map of the States. On the top-right side of her desktop were two panels—one a ticker tape of sentence fragments that had been tagged as of interest; another a dynamic list of the most common utterances, ranked in order of frequency, available for the last year, last week, last twenty-four hours, last minute.

Marked on the map with mobile red dots were tagged media—mostly, they were concentrated in western California and Florida. Manhattan was red. There was a scarlet dusting over Oklahoma and Montana, too.

If Sosso moused over a dot she could pull up a file: personal history and utterance history broken down statistically. A ticker tape of current utterance could be displayed, over the voice, in real time. The signals from Montana were always lousy, crackly as hell, but in the big cities, they freebooted on the cellphone networks.

Media who said the same thing as each other within a two-minute window would be color-tagged blue for affinity. They'd return to red if a twelve-hour period had passed without a recurrence. If there was a recurrence, or something else significant to suggest a synchronicity, they'd go a brighter blue and slightly increase in size. A very thin blue line would connect them on-screen.

The usual global utterance rankings tended to have mushy collections of sibilants, non-signifying smacky-lip noises, belches and high whinnies of anxiety at the top. Few words made it in.

The less imaginative obscenities sometimes made the top thirty. "Kill" and "help" and "mama" occasionally nudged into the top hundred.

In the days preceding the arrival of the Intercept, the patterns had been altogether stranger. Usually, no more than a couple of blue lines at any one time appeared on Sosso's map: a sketchy dark blue diagonal would connect the Mission District in San Francisco with the French Quarter in New Orleans for, maybe, forty-eight hours. A disconnected line would strike from Fire Island to Key West, flicker, evanesce. Accelerated to the one-second-to-six-hours timescale they used to scan manually for patterns, it looked like a broken 1980s screen saver: a dusting of red dots jittering like midges in the summer air, blue lines appearing at random and then disappearing a second or two later. Rarely, very rarely, one of the blue lines would sprout another line from one end, like an elbow, or two lines would intersect at a non-perpendicular vertex. Then that would go.

In the run-up to the Intercept, lines had appeared and stayed. Sleeping madmen were babbling the same things thousands of miles from each other, at opposite ends of America. These lines on the map formed a double-looping cat's cradle with two huge empty patches. The lines intersected in Atlanta, where an unnamed vagabond—he had signed himself "Nobody" in a smudgy scrawl when he'd been admitted to the Salvation Army shelter where he'd had the seizure and been tagged in '98—was saying, by the look of it, the same thing as his brother lunatics coast to coast.

The utterance charts for the media involved in this event were highly unusual. Underneath the noise, some consistent patterns were emerging: Nobody was producing them most consistently and urgently, but fragments of these utterances were uniting media on a sweeping continuum of tangents up the southeast.

A disyllable or trisyllable that seemed to be "Meat hook," "Me door," "Meet her," "Ammeter," "Umma," or "Ramada" was coming up. "Ankara," "Gon," and "Nameless." "Wadis," or "at ease," or "hotsy," too. Nobody had been able to make any sense of it and, in truth, Sosso would probably have been as freaked out as anybody else if they had. Most of the time Sosso—who was a true believer but inclined to the comforting notion that whatever signals came through from wherever would be deliberately impossible to understand—would affect excitement if they could coax half a line of a Kraftwerk lyric out of the whole of the continental United States.

It was the pattern and consistency of the affinity tags that was striking. It seemed impossible to account for by chance alone. And perhaps, Sosso had speculated, that was all they could hope for.

But in the last twenty-four hours, the blue dot that was the crossing point of the weird figure of eight started moving west—in fits and jerks. Right at that crossing point—still, apparently, ranting like a champ—was Nobody. The transmitter showed he was on the move, and his direction and pace seemed to be shadowing the data from the casino numbers.

12

The point of the journey, for Alex, had become the driving itself. He felt as if he had left his old life—not for a holiday, or for a week, but entirely and irrevocably. He had moved deeper into his solitude. Even while he was moving forward toward Carey, he felt as if he was moving further away from everything else.

Road sadness crept up on him. He used the car stereo less and less. At first, he had driven with the windows down and the air rushing in, but as the hours passed he found the noise not exhilarating but distracting, and he stopped it. He wound the windows up, put the air con on. It made a gentle whoosh. When it got too cold, he turned it off. Then as the car heated he turned it on again. He did this automatively, unthinkingly, until day cooled into evening and he left it off altogether.

The road sadness was half pleasurable: less sharp than his initial homesickness. But it was what was going on, and he gave himself to it. The America he was driving through was familiar to him from films, but it wasn't the America in the foreground of films but in the background: the highway America that was endless and the same everywhere.

He woke up in Tupelo and drove into Memphis. It was late morning and he followed the tourist signs to Graceland but he didn't go in. He drove past without seeing any Elvis impersonators. He stopped mid-afternoon, that day, for food and petrol. And he pressed on.

He got used to the rhythms. His mornings were startled by the brightness of sunlight. He'd wake up in a room in a chain motel, and get up and shower and check out and head onto the road when the sky was still whiter than blue. His mornings were full of optimism. Any time before midday he felt in command. He felt the star of his own film.

He'd stop early, sometimes, for lunch; or he'd have a late breakfast and skip lunch.

The wheels turned and the car hummed and the petrol needle made its half-daily journey across the dial on the dashboard. He would eat fast food, or food from gas stations. He tried monster bags of pork rinds—pretty horrible, actually; giant, chemical-tasting puffs that were to pork scratchings as popcorn is to sweetcorn—and grazed on sour-apple liquid candy. He ate microwave sandwiches and Jack in the Box burgers, nacho cheese and Gatorade. He browsed in chillers, with heavy doors, full of Vitamin Water and cardboard carry-packs of longneck beer.

The vastness of the country impressed itself on him. The road, when he was in between cities, was worn pale gray and yellow: and was only two lanes in either direction. An image came to him of the roads—arteries they call them—as the country's circulatory system. He imagined himself swept along them like a blood cell, a platelet, shouldering past the big trucks, pumped by a huge heart somewhere miles away. That made him think of cells dying, DNA unknitting, fraying, counting down.

He drove for hours and hours in a near trance, adjusting cruise control, watching the road ahead vanish under his car, thinking about Carey and trying to imagine a joint future. Again and again, his imagination failed him.

He could imagine their past well enough. Drunken scamperings in college. Their becoming a fixture of the scene, "Beauty and the Geek"—they'd gone to one fancy-dress party as that. But the future was a blank.

He started to drive into the night. As he crossed over into New Mexico the landscape changed. The neon minarets of the rest stops thinned out, became less frequent in the big desert, in between cities. It was just the ribbon of road and the car and the scrub to either side.

He felt calm but alert, as if he could go on for hours without sleep. Then, as time went on, he felt a little dislocated—as if he had gone on for hours without sleep, but hadn't noticed it. He couldn't tell how fast time was passing, or had passed.

There was a period of about an hour—was it an hour?—when he became hypnotized by the road in his headlights. There were no other cars around. The car seemed to be floating—just ahead of it fifteen feet of tarmac rushing in a blur in the yellow light. No sense of forward motion or acceleration. No sense of time or space passing. He was barely aware of the wheel in his hand.

Far, far ahead in the distance he could see red tail lights, but no road or horizon line to orient them against. They rose slowly, as if levitating into the air. Then they winked out and it was dark as far as he could see.

Alex eased off the pedal a little. The speedo kept steady. He had put cruise control on without noticing it. The red light reappeared—higher than it had been, and still climbing, moving off to the left. Alex started to wonder whether it was a car at all. Had there been mountains?

He looked down in front of him, saw the road coming into existence a car's length or more ahead, churning monotonously toward him, vanishing as it hit the lower sill of the windscreen. Alone, he thought. He raised his eyes.

The whole of his consciousness seemed, now, to be zeroed on that little red light, miles in the distance. Would he, one day, remember this moment? The road fell away underneath him. Nothing was funny. Nothing was sad.

If you moved far enough out, for long enough, you lost your bearings.

The red light vanished again. The car started to climb. Alex imagined around him, unseen, trains creaking and lumbering through the night. Sleeping families. Empty forecourts. Rough sleepers mumbling. In his pocket was the ring that was going to link him to Carey, whoever she was, whoever he was.

A little later, as the Pontiac crested a rise of some sort, Alex saw a glow in the distance—not the sharp point of red that had been the lights of the car in front—rather a diffuse, blue-gray lambency announcing itself on the horizon.

It got closer. It was big—not a building but more a pool of light—huge, by the side of the road, with darkness and the empty land all around it. It was a car dealership, out in the middle of nowhere. There was nobody there. The windows of the building itself were black. It rose up from the car park like the bridge of a container ship. All around it were cars, hundreds of cars, parked hull to hull, with halogen lights burning bone white above them.

It made him think of an elephants' graveyard. Not white bones tanning in the sun, but empty windscreens, roof props, the scratchproof paint shining under the cold arc lights.

Alex rode on, until it vanished behind him, an island of light, unpopulated, in the enormous desert night.

Isla spends the week with Nicolas. At first, he doesn't say much at all, though he behaves as if he was somehow expecting her— an affectation of serene foreknowledge that she doesn't know whether or not to trust.

He ushers her into the shack. She ducks her head under the lintel as she enters. He, behind her, nodding courteously. The shack has a smell of wood and something sweet and dusty, like a church. He follows her in, gestures at a wooden chair that's pushed in against a desk. On either side of the chair are tall stacks of yellow paper. The stacks of paper are everywhere. He sees her looking at them, waves dismissively as if brushing them away, shuffles to the chair and pulls it out, turns it round for her, busily nods and points her at it.

"There, there—please . . . sit."

The old man smiles encouragingly, nodding again faster as she advances.

She sits, nervously. She still has her backpack on so she teeters on the front couple of inches of the seat, smiling back at him, hands on her knees. She keeps suppressing an instinct, like someone meeting a nervous dog, to extend a low palm, gently.

He turns round, fumbles behind one of the piles of paper and fishes out an ancient kettle on the end of a snaking orange extension lead, then fills it from a large earthenware jug. He mumbles to himself in a sing-song voice under his breath as he does so.

As the kettle starts to rattle and cough, he moves over to an arrangement of shallow wire baskets hanging one above the other from chains. She can see a couple of leeks just going dry at the ends, a red net of cashew nuts. The whole assemblage wobbles as he rummages in it, and two handsomely sized eggs, smeared with a dab of dried brown, loll against each other in the bottom basket.

He pulls something out and returns, his tall body hunched over a little as if half out of shyness, half to save himself the effort of standing up only to bend again. On the floor he puts a dark green mug. It is the color of old copper, she can see, on the inside. He produces a cloudy tumbler from somewhere else, puts it down too, and as the kettle passes its crisis of excitement, drops a pinch of some sort of herb into each and tops it with boiling water.

"I don't get many visitors," he says, stirring each with a spoon before handing her the mug, punctiliously, handle first. The infusion smells very strongly of sage. He sits down cross-legged with a great crack of the knees and looks at her, then downward into his beard, whose ends he worries at absently between finger and thumb.

He begins with a cough, and a shrug. "I've been gone a long time," he says. "I know . . . I know . . . I'm very—touched—that you have come to see me. My last letters—I must apologize for . . . well, let's . . ."

He pauses and shakes his head quickly from side to side.

"We'll talk about that later, perhaps. Yes. I'm glad you came."

Isla simply sits there with her face glowing. She tells him how much he is admired, how much she has longed to meet him. After several minutes of this he starts to respond more than monosyllabically.

"Oh, it's a long time since I did mathematics, really. A child's game. A means to an end. My work now is very different." She can see the flattery working on him. "But you know that, don't you?"

He is still reluctant to meet her eyes for more than a moment. But she keeps talking, tries to keep him talking. She picks up on points in their correspondence, passes on faculty gossip—to which he listens with what she suspects is feigned interest, apart from the odd light of recognition, sometimes hostile, when the name of a mathematician of his own generation is mentioned.

At one point during their conversation—this is when Isla thinks she has made a breakthrough—he sees her eyes drifting over to a netting bag of some green vegetables by the pallet where he sleeps.

"Ah, yes," he says, and the twist of his mouth seems almost self-mocking. "Artichokes."

Occasionally she feels something spiky in his mind pushing back at her. He'll ask a question about a point of mathematics, as if testing her, checking she's understood. Sometimes the look when he raises his eye is minutely sharper, more appraising—then the sentences will again trail off and the combing of the fingers through the beard will increase. He continues to sit cross-legged, without apparent discomfort.

As they talk, he hauls over a pottery container filled with pea pods, takes a handful and pushes the container over toward Isla. They shell and eat the peas, which taste woody, but less horrible than the sage tea—and to Isla, who is both hungry and nervous, they are a welcome opportunity to do something with her hands.

That first night, she keeps talking to him till the sun sinks. He lights the hurricane lamp and moths loop in crazy eights around the table. They pass a point where impoliteness has become moot. Only when he notices her start to shiver a little, and tries to give her his blanket, does she make a move. The blanket, she guesses, is the origin of the dusty smell.

"I'm sorry. You are too kind. I must leave you . . ." She dares his first name: "Nicolas. I have to go and pitch my tent." She asks if she can set up her tent down the slope from his house. "Perhaps we can talk some more in the morning; if I'm not intruding?"

"No," he said, wanly. "You are intruding, but you are not an intruder. Perhaps a helper. A sharer."

That night she sets up her tent, laboriously, in the pitch dark. She dreams of goats bleating, and the following morning she is woken by the sound of chickens pecking about at the entrance to her tent. It hasn't rained. Shivering from the dawn, she pokes her head out and sees Banacharski, bent over in his corduroy trousers, scrubbing at something in the dirt up by the front of the shack.

That is how Isla Holderness's week with Banacharski starts. She quietly slots into his life, and he lets her. That first morning, she offers to make him breakfast and he, affecting to be startled by the emergence of this woman from the dew-steaming tent at the foot of his garden, nods. "Come." She uses the eggs she saw—they are fresh enough, and finds a couple more in a dirt bath under the house, one still warm.

The gas canisters she saw outside heat a little tank of hot water Banacharski uses to wash. But he also has a single-ring burner on a bottle of gas and she finds a skillet.

"I don't usually cook," he says.

She makes omelettes, seasoned with chervil she finds growing at a short distance from the house, and they eat them. He, again, insists she take the chair while he sits on the floor.

For most of that morning she helps him potter around the garden, pulling weeds. He does this more than she, but he points, occasionally, and grunts. She doesn't know anything about gardening; she has always lived in big cities. As it goes on, prompted gently, the older man starts to talk a little more—about himself, about the disappearance. He won't say much about it, but when she says something about being overcome by "pressure" he turns to her sharply.

"I am not mad," he says, looking her very directly in the eyes. "I know that that is what they want everyone to think. And it suits me—for my own purposes, for different purposes. But I am not mad. I know exactly what they are doing. EXACTLY."

He turns his head from her and roots at the foot of the hedge, turns back—looking cross, with a dandelion leaf tangled in his beard. "Exactly what they are doing. I am not mad."

That is followed by another long silence and a furious bout of weed pulling.

It is early afternoon when he declares that he has to work. He does so in a sudden snap—a violence of gesture that takes her by surprise. She senses, suddenly, that he's long past when he'd have started ordinarily, as if his gardening has been a distraction he has affected until it has become intolerable. The weeds he has been pulling are some way from his garden. They were there for a reason.

He walks briskly into the shack and shuts the door. Isla goes for a walk. The weather is pleasant enough. She walks a contour of the hill behind the shack, descends into a valley and marches up the other side until there is a pleasant ache in the tops of her legs, thinking all the way. She thinks how to approach him, how to coax him out. She has never done anything like this before.

Will he be finding her attractive? The thought has crossed her mind. He did have girlfriends when he was younger. He probably hasn't had a woman since . . . unless . . . Why should she speculate? He's an old man. She knows Mike would say: is it safe? She feels safe. He's an old man. He's reedy, pot-bellied. If he tried anything she could, with these strong thighs and these arms she goes swimming with . . . she feels safe.

But she wonders, just in the abstract, if he finds her attractive.

And so it goes. She returns later in the afternoon and knocks on the door. He lets her in. He has been in the chair at the table, writing on a yellow pad. He seems in a good mood.

"My new work," he says, tilting the pad toward her. It's in prose, very densely written, studded with what look like algebraic notations. She makes to peer more closely at it, but he snatches the pad away and puts it face down on the desk.

"Tell me, Isla Holderness . . . what do you think happens to us when we think? When we want something?"

Isla raises both her eyebrows, opens her face, looks deferentially blank. Banacharski snorts. They don't talk about his work again that night. But, as last night, she asks whether she can stay in her tent, and perhaps help him tomorrow and he assents with a courteous gesture.

And so they establish a routine. Isla helps him to cook, makes a few efforts to clean up the shack—though she knows better than to touch his mouse-nests of paper, let alone order them or be seen trying to read them. And, gently reasserting her interest, she piece by piece steers him into talking about his work. It is a slow and elliptical process.

"I put it another way," he says one evening, apropos of nothing, and in the middle of what has so far seemed to be a conversation about the virtues of eating raw vegetables (he says he lived happily through one summer eating cow parsley and soaked nettles). "If everything is perfect—if our measurements add up, if we can measure that, and that, and that"—he points with sudden violence to the verticals on the wall of the shack, just in the shadow of the hissing hurricane lamp—"and that angle is so, and that line is so, and that force is so . . . we can build a house. Yes? So when the winds blow, when the hurricane comes, we will be safe. You see?"

Isla learns simply to ignore this sort of thing, not to startle, to go with the sudden shifts in his conversation. His speech is like the patchwork prose of his letters. She had assumed they were written discontinuously, at different times of day and in different moods, as the storms of his madness blew themselves out, as signals swept from nerve to nerve in his brain and clarity came and went. It seems, though, that the shifts are almost instant. It is as if he is participating in half a dozen conversations, and simply tunes in and out of them—sometimes responding to her, sometimes to some cue elsewhere.

"Now in here—" He points to her head. "Now out here—" He waves at the air. "A pretty fantasy. You can measure nearly. Very, very nearly. But you can't measure precisely. True knowledge is impossible. I measure this once, then twice. Which is right? Then a third time. This is—what is the word? An analogy."

Isla asks, is he talking about subatomic particles?

"Not that—yes, that is part of it, but I mean something bigger than that. I mean that everything we are is a mistake in the measurement. Everything. This mistake—this is the devil's gift to us. The devil broke the clockwork. Now . . ." He looks at her, suddenly exultant, and raises his hands, palms outward by the side of his face. ". . . CUCKOO! CUCKOO!"

Late another night, they are talking about time. It is something that Banacharski seems agitated by, a subject he returns to.

"Imagine, see. Time is not a thing, not a thing that flows from one thing to another thing to another. It is a direction—a dimension. Does north flow? Does sideways flow? No. You can't measure time because what do you measure it with?"

At another point he draws a circle on one of the sheets of paper and shows her. "Here and gone do not mean anything," he says. "Look. Make this axis time. This axis space. Here"—he marks a sort of triangle inside the circle, shades it roughly in—"is the map of Alexander the Great in the world. And here. He is not 'gone': look. He is here: on the map between such a place and such a place and so-and-so BC and so-and-so BC."

He draws another blob on another part of the circle. "And here is the map of Nicolas Banacharski in the world. In this world. And here"—he draws another blob, this one overlapping the last—"is the map of Miss Isla Holderness in the world."

That night he becomes a little tearful. "You have to understand, Isla," he says. "When I was a child I was a displaced person. Whenever you have a war, you have displaced persons, shifting from place to place. They are victims of chance. For me, there was the chance of where I was born and when I was born, and the chance that I was born at all. Everything was chance. What my mother saw. Where my father died. It was chance. One lived, one died. Chance that I was born, and not somebody else. I am trying to repair that. Do you understand? Think, like a play on words, perhaps—another chance."

She touches his arm, and she sees wetness on his lips. "I am an old man, Isla Holderness. I am an old man."

Later, he mumbles something she doesn't think about until much, much later.

"Nobody wants me," he says. "Nobody is coming for me. I promised nobody anything . . ." he says at one point. He seems distressed. Isla takes a risk, and puts an arm awkwardly around his shoulder, and a charge seems to go through him. The yellowy whites of his eyes roll sharply toward her. He seems not just self-pitying, but scared.

13

Alex sat up in the bed under the thin motel sheet. He reached over to the little MDF unit screwed to the wall by the side of the bed and found his mobile phone in the half-light. It was the small hours of the morning, though he didn't bother to check the display on the big digital alarm clock. The answer to the crossword game.

"The set of all sets," Alex typed into his mobile phone, and pressed "send."

"In your *face*, Mr. Rob," he said aloud, even though he was alone. He felt immensely comforted. Rob would be on his way to work, he thought. He pictured Rob, on the Noddy Train, as he without fail called the Docklands Light Railway, heading in to the job he boasted about but hated at PricewaterhouseCoopers or DeloitteDeLaZouch or whatever the company was called.

Rob had made such a noise, when they'd been together as students, about not becoming what he called a "spamhat," his blanket term for anyone richer and older than himself whom he suspected of having taken a lucrative job because they had been—deservedly—bullied at school. Rob had been—deservedly—bullied at school.

Alex imagined—no, knew for a certainty—that his text would ping, or zoing, or chirp onto Rob's BlackBerry or iPhone or whatever he now had as he swayed along on the train, and that Rob would be excited by it, and affect to have had his day ruined.

Alex, even though it was late, waited five minutes before sending his next text. It was as well to affect not having been saving it up—but at the same time taking a few minutes to imply a plausible albeit startling facility of mind.

"Inexperienced butler? Sounds like an old film. (3, 5, 3, 2, 5)."

He was woken fifteen minutes later by his phone—on silent—burring against the hard surface of the bedside unit. He reached for it, bleary now, and thumbed the unlock sequence. The little square screen was fish-green. New message.

"Cnut," said Rob's message.

Alex smiled and sighed, replaced the phone on the bedside table and settled back into a happy sleep.

Red Queen's encryption team worked on the hard drive they'd recovered from MIC—the drive the boy had couriered across the Atlantic for them and dropped off in Atlanta. The drive was exceptionally hard to crack, but—the cryptologists reported—not impossible. Progress was being made by brute-force computing. Red Queen regarded that as somewhat suspicious. So did Porlock. Still, they persevered. Resources were diverted. Compartment by compartment, data started to come off the disk.

It bugged Red Queen, though, that the casino metrics suggested the device itself was still on the move. The data coming off the hard drive didn't make much sense, as yet—it certainly didn't resemble, as Red Queen had initially dared to hope, backup blueprints for the machine. So what did it have to do with anything?

Ellis, MIC's head of security, had been working on the hard drive too, or rather working on its absence. MIC couriered several items of varying sensitivity between its offices in London, Washington and Atlanta every day; to say nothing of the material it moved between narco states in South America and AK-infested government buildings in Lagos, Freetown, Mogadishu, and Khartoum. If any of those packages went missing, Ellis was informed.

Commercial competitors—as senior management insisted on calling the private interests, most of them governments rather than companies, and most of them clients rather than competitors, that tended to be interested in ripping MIC off—needed to be discouraged from obtaining sensitive data.

Ellis's anti-theft policy was twofold. The first side of it was straightforward. They used a dozen or more different courier companies in each country, randomising each job and booking them independently and at late notice. All electronic data that they couriered was encrypted and tagged; and all disappearances were investigated.

The second part of the anti-theft policy was slightly more complicated. In the first place, MIC couriered something in the order of five or six times as many packages as it needed to. Only very select personnel knew which contained the important data and which were heavily encrypted dummies. These were what Ellis liked to call "Barium Meal Experiments": they'd tie up a lot of time and expertise, and once broken would yield complex, useless, or deliberately misleading information. Their chief purpose was to cause their interceptors to give themselves away by acting on a red herring—a piece of bogus market-sensitive information that might cause a greedy dictator to tilt at a stock, or a hint that the opposition had bought a surface-to-air missile package for which MIC sold the only effective countermeasure. Sometimes it was more important and more profitable to know who was ripping you off than to prevent them doing so.

They were also, most of them, laden with the sort of high-end Trojan viruses that would install a nice back door, for MIC, in their hosts' computer systems.

They knew, for instance, that the Atlanta package had traveled by air to New York within a few hours of its disappearance from the courier company. But the signal from its tag had abruptly cut out on arrival. It had either been discovered or encased in concrete, or discovered and then encased in concrete.

In New York, the tag had not been discovered, nor had it had been encased in concrete. But it was deep underground, with the DEI's cryptographers. And it was nearly a day before those cryptographers fully cracked it. And a bit over a day when they realized what had happened.

"Like something gift-wrapped in a cartoon," Porlock said without a trace of mirth when he made his report. "Black on face. Hair sticking up."

"Swine," said Red Queen.

The quarantined network they'd been using to open the drive had quietly suffered the computer-virus equivalent of Ebola and would take more time and energy to cure than it had taken to break the encryption in the first place. Among the effects of the virus was that every computer in the network was quietly trying to get in contact with a remote ISP—almost certainly one of MIC's secure nodes—four times per second. They were doing so in vain, since the network wasn't wired to the outside world. But it made Red Queen think of the magic harp in the fairy story, screaming and screaming from under Jack's coat that it had been stolen.

The data on the drive had been mud. One programmer speculated irritably that the extensive personnel file for a company named "Herring Enterprises"—they checked: it had no personnel; it was a Cayman Islands shell—was a private joke.

The DEI's programmer was right. It was a private joke. But it was not a private joke that Ellis was much laughing at. Ellis, too, had missed a trick. When he was first told about the missing package, he had given it little thought. Let his subordinates work it.

He was more preoccupied with trying to find this probability machine, and the routine loss of a BME—as, on checking, he saw it was—was neither here nor there. It was only when it occurred to him that it was Atlanta and that it was about the same time this kid had given those idiotic thugs of his the slip there, that he went back and wondered about a connection.

Could the boy have stolen the package? Could the machine have caused the package to be stolen?

Ellis looked at the loss of the package. It had gone through the airport, routinely, with no problems. The representative of the courier company had picked up the briefcase with the hard drive. But the closure of the Atlanta offices after the incident with the frogs—another thing that had installed the flickering jelly bean of an incipient migraine in the corner of Ellis's field of vision—had meant that he'd returned with the package to his own company's offices with a view to putting it in the safe. Where he'd been mugged and relieved of the suitcase. Two muggers—he didn't get much of a look at them. The loss had been reported to the police, but Ellis didn't hold out much hope of recovering it. Not with someone flying it instantly to New York, which was not what normal muggers did.

Ellis couldn't see a way that the boy, even if he had had an accomplice, could have known about this package arriving at the same time as him; nor where it would be going; nor why he would be interested in it in any case.

Ellis found out which courier company MIC had used, and telephoned their UK office. He was rude to a series of dispatchers until a senior manager looked it up on the computer.

"His name was Alex Smart," said the manager. "Yup. First time we've used him, according to our records. The usual thing—student or something, no criminal record, answered one of our ads online. He got a short-notice flight to Atlanta. We got your parcel sent. Why? Is there a—"

Ellis hung up. Well. That explained how the kid got to Atlanta. MIC bought him a ticket.

If Ellis had been more puckish, he would have said "Swine," but Ellis instead swore unimaginatively, hammered the phone cradle with two fingers and then started to dial again.

"What I have been trying to do," says Banacharski later in the week. His sentences, still, are not always coming out entire. "To build a machine. To undo—these knots."

They have spent a long day together. As usual, Isla has been circumspect. She has tried to make herself useful—has cleaned, even, where the opportunity to do so without looking rude has presented itself. She has retreated when it seems right—particularly when he has insisted that it is time for him to meditate. It hasn't been a problem for her. She has taken herself off on a walk.

She has started to get used to his moods. She doesn't think that she's going to learn from him what she'd hoped—still less, get him to come back to civilization. This was the thing that, though she didn't admit it fully, she'd fantasized about: she, as Perseus, with the gorgon's head to show off. When she was little her dad taught her how to fish. She liked the idea, always, of the skill of bringing something in that was stronger than the line by which it was caught. She has an ego, Isla.

So she doesn't think she's going to bring him in. But she has started to feel for him. She reproaches herself. She always felt for him—even when she'd only read about him she felt she understood him. But now, she feels like she has a responsibility. She sees his mind, like a boat straining at its moorings in a heavy tide, and she feels sorry for him. She wants to soothe it.

"In the war. My father died. My mother lived. My little sister died. I lived. Chance. How do we live with that? How, Isla Holderness? How do we live with it? It is impossible. Nobody can. Nobody can do that." He seems half to be talking to himself.

Then he changes tack again. "There are walls in the air." His hand, in a chopping motion, comes down between her face and his. "Everything is so close to us. These walls: a membrane's distance. We think—our physics, already, almost shows it if you know how to look. Every moment spawns infinities—new universes. A sparrow falls, a sparrow doesn't fall—you know that?"

"The Bible," Isla says.

"Yes. The Bible. Every sparrow, a new universe. Every feather, a new universe. Every wingbeat. What happens—"

"This is the parallel universes idea you're talking about?"

Banacharski waves, impatiently. "Not parallel. No such thing as parallel. That's what the devil, as I told you, made impossible—"

"You're talking metaphorically?"

"Yes! Metaphorically. Yes, I am. Exactly that." He looks, riddlingly, pleased with her—but not as if she has said something he agrees with, she thinks, so much as that he knows she didn't understand. "What he does to the measurements, the devil, that's it. Everything curves. Not parallel. Like soap bubbles, these infinities. Everything touching everything else. You could just step through. If you could only see the walls. If you could hear what all those versions of you are saying, just on the other side. Think of what happens. How do you think of it? You go forward, yes?"

"Ah. Yes?"

"Look." He wiggles his hand like a fish. "Your choice, this or that. Your chance, this or that. You jump out of the trench and the precise angle of the bullet from a machine gun two hundred meters away"—he dashes the tips of his fingers on his temple— "finished. You are hiding in a house, and your baby daughter then—just then, as the guard comes by—she hiccups or she starts to cry—finished."

Isla just looks, keeps looking at him.

"You think this is a chance in a million. This: what kills you. What lets you live. But go back. How you got there. Every tiny chance builds on another tiny chance before it, and before that, to the beginning of the universe. Why are you there then? Why do your parents meet, and why do their parents meet, and how does that one sperm in each one meet that egg? If you look at it like that, look, it is impossible, no? Impossible. My speaking, like this, to you, how did we get here? Start back then. It is like a maze. Take any wrong turning of an infinite number and look: we are not here."

He rocks, now, back and forward a little on his haunches. His right hand turns and turns in his beard. Isla sits on the chair. She catches sight of herself with her hands folded over each other in her lap, primly, like a figure in a medieval painting.

"The only way that what we have here—something as improbable as you, and me, sitting in this room together—can take place is if everything that could have happened, somewhere else, already has. You follow me? So this is what I am working with. How do you solve a maze?"

Isla feels the length of the pause. He is looking at her.

"You follow the left-hand wall?"

Banacharski wheezes with laughter.

"Backward! You start at the end. Then every fork, it is not a problem—it is not a thing that can go two ways. It is just a node that is leading you back home. I mean this—" he waves his hands again—"metaphorically."

He stands up, now, and takes a step or two—agitating his hands.

"I mean that chance is an illusion," he says. "We think one thing happens and not another. But really everything happens. No time passes and nothing is lost and nobody dies. They are living in an infinity of universes, at every moment, for all time . . ."

His eyes look at her, as if from far away. Isla feels creepily, sorrowfully, a sense of how broken his mind is. She knows, then, that she can't stay. She shouldn't have come.

"Just here—" He fishes, again, at his imaginary wall in the air. His lips are moving into a sad smile, and his eyes are wet. "So near. Imagine if you could pass through these walls. Imagine something that would make everything exist at once. Imagine if at every little point you weren't seeing universes splitting off, but universes coming together. You will see the maze entire—it will be not a maze but a pattern, you see? Like on wallpaper. A decoration, not a prison."

Isla's cheeks feel stiff. She smiles at him, arranging her face somewhere between quizzical and accepting.

"Everything that is lost is present," he says. "See? If you can just reach through, with your mind, through the wall, into the

place where something never happens, or doesn't happen yet . . .
Everything that has gone is here. Anything can happen because
everything will happen. Everything true, everything existing,
everything here, now, always . . ."

He looks at her almost imploringly. "Nobody dies. Nobody
goes away. Nothing is ever lost."

The following day, Isla tells him that she has to leave.
Banacharski looks momentarily stricken. Then he shrugs.

It is a bright morning, chillier than the previous one.

"Walk with me," he says. They set off up the hill behind the
house. At first Banacharski says nothing; then, to her surprise, he
links arms with her. The slight tang of him on the air makes her
not revolted, but a little sad.

"I have enemies, Isla," he says. "You know, when you first
came here, you wanted to know why I left the Sorbonne? That
was one of the reasons I had to go. I had the real fear that they
would kill me. No joke. They would kill me before my work
was finished."

"But, Nicolas—why would anyone have wanted to kill
you? Your work was abstract. You were a mathematician, an
academic. You're just being"—she dared it; after a week, she
dared it—"paranoid."

"No!" he snaps. "That is how they try to discredit me. How
they try to make me lower my guard. *Paranoid!* Tchoh! Even
then, I knew my work would have—implications. I let something slip in a lecture, and one of their agents—Oh, believe me,
Isla Holderness. They have agents everywhere. Everything is
connected to everything else, and in this spiderweb there are
good spiders and there are bad spiders."

He has lost his thread.

"You said something in a lecture."

"Yes, yes. Somebody wrote to me. Frederick Nieman, he called
himself. Some kind of joke, I think: *Niemand.* 'Fred Nobody.'
That was how I was to know him. He said he was interested

in my researches into causality. I was not working on causality, then. Not openly. I was still a geometer. But at the time I had started to think about these things: about geometries that were not strictly mathematical: geometries of desire and intention. Nieman had happened on my work by chance, he said. He understood some of the implications. He foresaw a great future for me, he said. And he would pay."

Banacharski huffs, a little, as they reach the top of the hill. She feels him leaning more heavily on her arm.

"They wanted what I was doing, for them and them alone, but they did not understand what I was doing. They thought I could make them a weapon: something that would change outcomes. Make magic bullets. If you sell weapons, you know, everything looks like a weapon.

"I knew, of course—he did not even need to say it—that if I did not do what they wanted they would kill me. I was afraid. I told him that I would share my work with them. This was a company that had done great wrong. It worked, during the war, with the Nazi government. Many, many people were killed with their weapons. But I was scared." He looks ashamed, but at the same time a little defiant. "I told them I could build them a probability bomb. For that, I told them, they needed to pay, and I would need isolation.

"So they paid me, helped me disappear. I disappeared—this was the big joke—after I resigned in protest at the discovery that their money was funding my chair at the Institute. They liked that. Double bluff."

Something in Banacharski's face changes, like when a shift in the angle of the light turns a transparent surface opaque. "I became my own ghost," he says.

"The statement you gave, though," says Isla, "about the systematic corruption of science by the military?"

"Yes," says Banacharski. "They let me attack them because they thought it would help. I was telling the truth. Triple bluff. There is no bomb. There never was. I am engineering reality—not assembling some toy out of nuts and bolts."

They walk on a bit. Isla watches a small brown bird prick and preen in the grass, the beak and head moving sharply.

"But Nieman," he says, as if more to himself than Isla, "I think Nieman is coming back."

"Back? He's been here?" Isla asks.

"No," says Banacharski. "We haven't met. Only letters. He writes to me on yellow paper. Always yellow paper. Like the paper I use. I am afraid about meeting him. But I think he is coming for me anyway."

"What did you do with their money?" Banacharski looks at her sharply. She worries, for an instant, she went too far. She sees something of cunning in his expression—a decision to say something almost taken, then a decision not to.

"You must concentrate, Isla. I stalled them. My work is nearly finished. But they may come for me. They have been losing patience. You know, you need to take care for yourself . . ."

He is now looking down at his wrecked flip-flops.

"There is something I would like you to have of mine, Isla. A gift. You have been someone who has shown me kindness."

Banacharski reaches into the pocket of his filthy trousers and produces something. Isla sees it glint, and then she startles at the pressure as he presses it into her palm. As he does so he looks furtively about him, into the distant trees, the empty ground between.

He withdraws his hand and she looks into her own. It is a ring, right where her lifelines cross—a simple silver thing, with a figure-of-eight design sweeping over the top of it.

"It was my mother's," says Banacharski. "I have nobody. Now I give it to you."

"I can't."

"I have nobody. You take it. That ring will be—how should I say it?—a lucky charm for you."

He gives her a strong, fond look. "Borrow it, then. Think of it as a loan. Come back at the end of the summer. Bring it back to me. God keep you safe."

Isla sets off for home the following day, walking down into the local town, from where she arranges a taxi—it takes her half a day—to get back to Toulouse. That is the last time she sees Banacharski alive.

As Hands described to Red Queen, they continued to exchange letters. But Banacharski's letters had become wilder. Isla, back in Cambridge, felt uneasy—as if there was someone shadowing her. When she went out every morning to get the newspapers, she found herself casting suspicious glances down the aisles at the Co-op. There'd always be someone holding up a pot of yogurt or a tin of sweetcorn, fondling it abstractly, reading the label with studious distraction.

She thought for a time that she might be going mad—that Nicolas's paranoia was rubbing off on her. The magazine continued to forward his letters. Sometimes, the way they were folded in the envelope, a certain looseness about the glue, made her feel like they might have been tampered with. She took to hiding them.

At the same time, other letters started to come—more personal ones, addressed directly to her. The handwriting on the envelopes of these was different—more restrained—though the writing inside was the same.

In the last of these, he wrote: "Don't worry. You have my love. I am nearing the center of the artichoke. Do not trust. Destroy."

Something, she thought, had started to confuse him. The letters were in the same handwriting, but they seemed to be from two different people. The letters that came through the magazine raved about this "machine," which he said was "nearly built." She puzzled over that.

In these letters, he promised her that "when the time was right," he would share his discoveries with her: she was, he said—and here it was triple underlined—"the custodian of his legacy." But he said the time was not yet right. He said he was "storing some parts of the machine" in a place known only to him.

The other letters, the ones that she told nobody about, were love letters, of a sort. That is, they did not profess love directly. But they were personal. They were trying to make a connection. And they talked at length—great length—about his childhood, and what he remembered about the war. Much was about his mother, Ana, the presumed owner of the ring he had entrusted to her. She had lived through the war but cancer got her while Banacharski was in his teens. He talked about his first memory of her, rocking in a chair with him, sitting in her lap wrapped in a woolen blanket. That was at his grandparents' house in Allenstein, what is now Olsztyn in northern Poland. He said he remembered how the blanket had tasted: of dust and pine.

Banacharski enclosed, in these letters, pages from a manuscript he said was "my mother's testament." It seemed to be a memoir of some sort, but it was told in the third person, annotated in pencil by Nicolas, and quoted from in his letters. Between the two narratives—and what of the history of his life remained on the public record—Isla was able to piece together the sequence of events.

One fragment described Ana Banacharski's courtship with Nicolas's father, Sergei Mitrov, in Berlin in the late 1920s. Mitrov was a Russian anarchist who had fetched up there after fleeing the Bolsheviks. She had moved to the city as a student, and they met after she attended a meeting in the radical bookshop where he was staying. She had fallen pregnant, and they moved through Europe together living, unmarried, as a family.

Then came the Spanish Civil War. Mitrov joined the International Brigades, and Ana moved back to her parents' in East

Prussia. Nicolas would then have been seven. Three years later, when Germany annexed Poland, and the persecution of Allenstein's Polish-speaking minority began, Ana fled with Nicolas to France. Ana's story described the old man, her father, waving from the door of the town house—his mustache, his mild smile and the turn-ups on his trousers. It was the last time she saw him.

Mother and son spent the war years in a series of refugee camps. "Her Nicolas, her little Buddha, her watchful child," her narrator wrote. "Ana knew she would have to leave him."

Nicolas's own narrative picked up here. He talked about his memories, the watchful child reporting. At some point they had been reunited with Mitrov. He remembered his mother, terribly distressed, in the camp outside Paris. He had worked out afterward, only from his mother's memoir, that he had had a sister who was stillborn at about that time.

But in 1942 Mitrov was separated from Ana and his son by what Banacharski called "a malign chance." His letters stopped coming. He did not survive the war. Nicolas wrote, curiously, that he had no memories of his father at all.

These communications resembled love letters not in anything explicit, so much as in their intimacy of address, their notes of tenderness, the parallels they drew between past and present. There had been a girl he had known in the refugee community at Chambon-sur-Lignon, he said, called Kara. Isla reminded him of her. She had resembled Isla, he said, though he did not say in what way. He sketched out a chaste friendship between the fourteen-year-old Nicolas and sixteen-year-old Kara, compli-cated by longing. Her father was Danish—a wealthy man in the antiques business. He had not encouraged their friendship. They'd been separated, though he'd had letters from her after the war. She hadn't died. But she had disappeared. In his early twen-ties Nicolas had tried to find her without success.

"Gone," he wrote. "Another gone. Another lost to time."

His letters seemed confiding, tender, anxious that what had

happened to him would be known, and his connection with her maintained.

"Chance—or the illusion of chance—is what divides us one from the other. It is chance that carries us apart. Chance that kills us. But what if chance could make us live? What if chance brought us together again? It is just a matter of seeing it right. Of turning it around."

Isla wrote back, in one letter: "Nicolas, you say it is chance that divides us. But is also chance that makes us live. You lost people by accident. But you also found them by accident. You found me by accident. Every human being on the face of the earth is here—you said it yourself—by chance."

"You misunderstand. Deliberately?" he wrote back. "For everyone who is born hundreds of millions of people—real people—are never born. Who speaks for them? They are nobody. Who will rescue them? What if you could imagine a world in which those people live and are not alone and do not grow old and die? And what if by imagining you could make it so?"

In early autumn, via *EtUdes/RecOltes*, came another letter, sharper in tone than any of the previous. It wondered, with crude sarcasm, whether she was in the employ of "the other side." It asked her to come and visit him. It said he had something to give her. But before, it said, she needed to answer him one simple question: "Nobody has been reading my letters. I have proof positive. I need to know that you are who you are. So answer me this: what is a meter? Reply quickly."

Isla called her colleague Mike about this. She was worried, she said. She sat in the kitchen of her house in Cambridge and showed him the last letter from Banacharski. What could he mean? Mike shook his head. "Buggered if I know," he said. "Your boyfriend is, let's not forget, mad as a badger."

"A meter," she said. "It's a measurement. He's preoccupied by measurements. And he's trying to build a machine. He says he's finished it."

"Clear as flaming mud, love. I'd leave it. Write back and tell him it's something to do with Napoleon. He probably thinks he's something to do with Napoleon." Mike seemed moderately pleased with the witticism. He fetched himself another of Isla's biscuits and moved on to some faculty gossip.

"What is a meter?" he said as he left. "A hundred centimeters, eh?"

Isla did not show Mike the letters she had got privately. And she did not tell him about Ana's ring. She was still turning it over in her mind two days later. She was leaving for her 10 a.m. seminar, running late and with her hair still slightly wet against her neck, when she picked up the post from the tiled hallway. There were two letters, forwarded from Nice. Both were bulging, as if there was more paper in them than their envelopes were strictly designed to bear.

She tucked them under the arm of her duffel coat as she stepped out into the street. She slipped open the first one with a thumbnail, her bag on her lap, as she settled on the top deck of the bus on the way in to the faculty. She felt her cheeks grow cold as she read.

The yellow legal paper was in some places torn with the force of the handwriting. Block capitals alternated with lower case, no one letter joined up with another, and words of German and French mashed into English sentences. The ruled lines on the paper were only ever a loose guide when Banacharski was excitable—but here the lines of his script were flapping off them like an untethered mainsheet in a gale.

It was a wad of incoherent fury, calling her a "thief," a "liar" and a "Judas." It accused her of working with "the enemy, the murderers, the Moloch." The second letter was shorter, and barely in prose at all. On the first page, her name was written in block capitals, dead center, and a series of numbers scribbled underneath—separated by dashes and subject to a whole succession of transformations that brought them out to new numbers.

She leafed through. He was using the letters of her name—it would be Kabbalah, she guessed; he had spoken to her about using Kabbalistic practice for, he said, exploring "the relationship between speech and number."

On the following pages the letters of her name had been anagrammed, and further manipulated into numbers; or, the letters of her name were written out as a matrix, and multiplied by another matrix constructed from the same letters. Her eyes started to swim. He couldn't have slept. Nobody could physically have achieved the rate and ferocity of work in these letters—would not physically have been able to write them down—in the time between them.

They were both dated the same day, though they bore different postmarks and had clearly been held up a few days between Paris and London. Isla, scouring her memory, couldn't swear to it that they hadn't been written on the same day as the original letter posing the riddle. The final page of this second letter ended: "Nothing comes of nothing. Nobody's here. We are divided by nothing. Forgive me." His signature at the bottom was also bristling with numbers, all of them canceled to zero.

She missed her stop. She was twenty-five minutes late for her seminar by the time she got there and she noticed her hands trembling as she wrote on the whiteboard. She felt very afraid. She canceled drinks with Mike and Jude. She spent the afternoon talking to the faculty and the college about a temporary, emergency leave of absence. The first flight she could get to Toulouse was the following lunchtime. It would cost her. She didn't think about that.

The following morning, a third letter arrived. On the envelope it said: "To the Supposed Isla Holderness." She read it on the way to the airport.

"You are not who you say you are. I am not who I was. Nobody is here," it began. Almost every other sentence contained a sarcastic intimacy—"my dearest 'Isla'"; "my trusted 'Miss Holderness'"—as if parodying the man who had written her those private letters about his life over the past couple of months. The brusque kindness she remembered from the shack was gone. She found it unbearable.

It ended with a signature: not "Nicolas" or even "NB" this time, but "Fred Nieman."

And so, fast-forward to Isla, walking round the final curve of the approach to Banacharski's shack, feeling that she knows what she is going to find.

The fire had long gone out, doused in cold rain. But the smell of burning came through, wet burned wood. Droplets stood on melted plastic. The shack was gone—a black stain on the ground, a couple of jutting teeth of carbonised wood. Across the wet grass to either side were wisps and fragments of cinderated paper, the odd rag of sodden yellow in the fingers of the green.

The Calor canister under the wall of the shack had obviously gone. Half of it was there, its skin twisted and blackened. Its shrapnel had half dug turves out of the ground, and the grass was radially scorched on that side. The wooden floor of the shack was gone from the center, where the fire seemed to have started. There were threads of rug toward the outside—where the stump of a piling emerged from poured concrete foundations. A stick of table leg was there.

The wind had blown the fire away up the hill, drying and burning the grass in patches up behind the shack. The beanstalks, the ones nearest the hut, were scorched but those toward Isla were intact, if more overgrown than when she had been here. The leaves were blowsy, the season long gone. Isla walked closer.

Too late, she thought. She had run out of time. He was gone.

She twisted a pod off one of the beanstalks, and thumbed it

open. Inside, a broad bean—the only one full-size—sat in its velvety white cushion like a ring in a jeweler's box.

She walked round the shack, looking for him. She thought of calling for him, but it felt wrong, somehow, to raise her voice. He was gone. She knew that. Not dead—she didn't know why she was so sure of that, but she somehow felt confident of it—but gone. Beyond her help. Nobody could help him.

Her good Gore-Tex boots kept the wet out. She remembered him drawing his diagram: "And here is the map of Nicolas Banacharski in the world. And here is the map of Miss Isla Holderness in the world." She understood now why this was strangely comforting.

In among the bean shoots the chickens picked, pecking morosely at the wet grass, shivering their wings. Had he left them? Their henhouse was intact. She peeked into it. There was straw in there, and the hopper was dry, and full of grain.

Isla walked back down into town, and caused the police to be called. They came up, took a statement—Isla struggling a little with her French—filed a missing persons report, and late that evening told her she was free to go home. She spent the night in an auberge, and set off the following morning, early, resolute, sad: telling herself she had done everything she could and not believing it for a second.

When she arrived back in Cambridge, she came home to find that she had been burgled. Her laptop had gone, as well as her video recorder, the contents of her underwear drawer and medicine cabinet, and the nearly full bottle of vodka she had kept on the dresser. A pane of the front bay window had been smashed. A creditable but, finally, unsuccessful attempt had been made to remove the television.

Also, her jewelry box was gone—and with it, which somehow at that moment felt more important to her than even her own christening presents, Ana's ring. Isla had sat down on her living room floor and, before she called the police, cried for a long time.

Three days later, Isla's house was burgled again. This time, it was Banacharski's letters to her that went. It happened during the day, while she was at the library preparing a lecture. No glass was broken. Nothing of value was taken. Nobody was spotted at the scene.

14

Isla Holderness never saw Ana's ring again. Her laptop, having been sold in a grimy pub on the outskirts of town, was eventually recovered by the police.

Its thief was seventeen-year-old Ben Collings, who was picked up not two weeks later while attempting to pry open the back door of the Co-op at 4 a.m., in the mindset of exuberant criminal incompetence that a gram and a half of his brother's home-made amphetamine sulfate and a liter of white cider could be relied upon to produce. His fingerprints matched the ones he had left on the door of Isla's fridge, and his teeth—as the Cambridgeshire Constabulary's equivalent of the CSI lab was proud to report—precisely matched the profile of the two-thirds of a miniature Melton Mowbray pork pie that he had not stolen from inside it.

Mr. Collings, as the PC who returned Isla's laptop to her explained, was "a worthless little toerag" of precisely the sort who formed the cop shop's most loyal client base.

Collings had offloaded most of Isla's possessions onto his big brother—a toerag of some seniority—who had in turn dispersed them among the pawn shops and market stalls of the town. Ana's ring had ended up in an antique shop the quality of whose merchandise was belied by the tweeness of its name. Herbert Owse's Antiquarian Omnium Gatherum stood on Burleigh Street, and was manned by a rubicund numismatist with a wild beard and a liking for checked shirts and moleskin waistcoats. His socks, though this is of scant relevance here, were held up with suspenders. His name was not Herbert Owse.

It was into this shop, however, that Alex Smart ducked while cutting down Burleigh Street one afternoon on his way from the cinema—where he had been spending the afternoon not working on his PhD and not thinking about the fact that he wasn't working on his PhD—to the pub where he was meeting a friend in order to continue doing same.

Alex, who was not in the habit of browsing in antique shops and would not have been able to afford antiques even if he had, had gone in to escape a sudden shower of rain. The shower of rain proving unusually persistent, he was obliged to make a furious pretense at interest in the shop's contents. Away he browsed, under the jovial eye of the proprietor, occasionally asking questions.

"This piece," he said. "Eighteenth century, is it?"

"Art deco," the proprietor replied.

"Hm," said Alex, opening and closing a cabinet door. "Very good . . . hinges, it's got. Are they original?"

"Yes."

"Very good. I was thinking of something like that for my mum. Likes hinges, she does. How much is it?"

"Eight hundred and seventy-five pounds."

"Oh. Oh my. Really?"

"Yes."

"Well—bit more, you know. Embarrassing, but a bit more than I was actually thinking of, you know. Spending."

The supposed Owse made brisk play of returning his attention to the notes he was making in a ledger with a stubby pencil. Alex walked the shop's narrow aisles, keeping one eye on the rain through the bow window. The shop exuded a considerable aura of brownness: wooden floorboards, patches of curly-cornered carpet, brown cabinets and brown bookshelves and brown leather books.

Alex inspected an umbrella stand in which a number of pawky specimens shuffled their spokes. He read the spines of some of the old books, most of which were the sorts of things you might expect to be bought and sold by the yard rather than for their titles—volumes 4 to 8 of something called *The Cyclopedia of Practical Agronomy*; the second volume of a Victorian translation of *Don Quixote*, with illustrated plates.

Then, peering into a glass display cabinet at a selection of silver-black necklaces and brooches with topaz and coral in dented settings, he saw the ring. As he looked at it he thought—in a way that felt light and easy—that perhaps he would ask Carey to marry him, and that this was the ring that he would present to her.

It was sitting upright in a cheap jewelry box. He liked the design, the antique look, the silvery sheen. The ring set his chain of thought in motion, there, while he waited for the rain to stop. But once he had thought it, it seemed right and natural. It was a thought that had been waiting for a thought-shaped slot in his head to occupy, and there it was. They would get married. He would get a cheap flight to the States, and he would go to San Francisco and surprise her with a ring.

The ring was two hundred pounds. Alex could find that. Just. He'd be eating pasta with butter for a bit, but he could find it. He asked the supposed Owse to put the ring aside for him. Wrote his name and mobile phone number, promised to come back the following day. And by the time he stepped out of the shop into the lane, the bell above the door dinging sweetly, shaking a few drops of rain onto Alex's head, the sun was just breaking through the clouds.

And so to Jones, and to Bree—our two supernatural detectives— hot on the heels of this fugitive device. Jones was driving, and Bree was eating.

Bree had worried about Jones driving. The worry started not long after they had gone over a large and tricky interchange through a just-red light that Bree wouldn't have risked. She had read the cross traffic—three lanes of impatient metal, a terminal moraine of shining chrome, pregnant with the intention of surging over their carriageway at the first click of their light to green. They had seemed to heave. Jones had piloted their car serenely through.

"Jones," she had said, her thigh cramping with the effort of pumping an imaginary brake, "with your condition . . ."

"Uh-huh," Jones had said.

"How good are you at anticipating things?"

"Not very," Jones had said. The speedo had been nudging eighty.

"Things like cars pulling out suddenly, or appearing from dips in the road while you're overtaking . . ."

"Uh-huh," Jones had said. He had appeared to have no idea of the drift that the conversation was taking.

"Are you good at anticipating those?"

"I don't know," Jones had said. "I don't think so. Which cars are you talking about?" He had looked around, scanning the road, meerkatted into the rear-view mirror, peered ahead down the road, as if to see what Bree was referring to.

"Not actual cars *here*," Bree had said. "I mean, any cars. Cars you might anticipate. Cars that might pull out or appear from nowhere."

"Cars that don't exist?"

Bree had realized the problem, and fallen silent. Jones's relationship with time was not, she remembered, the easiest thing to navigate. Nor his relationship with notional cars.

"Jones, your head is a strange thing."

"It is the only head I have," Jones had said. "I have nothing to compare it with."

Bree had thought of a better way of putting it. She had asked: "Have you ever crashed a car?"

"I have fast reactions," Jones had said.

"That's not answering the question," Bree had said.

"Yes," Jones had said.

Bree had shrugged. She had let it go. Someone believed Jones could drive. Someone had given him a license. They hadn't crashed. And Bree hated to drive.

So here they were. Jones driving—slowly, at Bree's insistence—and Bree eating an egg-salad sandwich and a big bag of Doritos. It was a beautiful morning. Everything felt light and good. It was one of those mornings when Bree felt a lightness. The weird thing with the crying had shifted Jones in the way she thought about him. She had thought, at first, that he was handsome. But Bree reckoned she thought everyone was handsome. She hadn't been with anyone for a long time. Then she had thought he was freaky, which he was. But now she felt maternal toward him—and she was surprised to find that feeling warmed her.

"Look at that," she said, holding up a Dorito. "That orange. Nothing in nature is that orange."

Jones looked at her Dorito.

"An orange is that orange," he said.

Bree ignored him. She put her feet on the dashboard. "Damn," she said, munching happily. "What did they do before Doritos?"

Bree and Jones continued west, stopping to use landlines, where they could, to contact Red Queen. Data points came back: here, a probable sighting; there, a CCTV image of the Smart boy in a gas station forecourt. They were going in the right direction, feeling their way half blind after their quarry. They discovered, only twelve hours afterward, that he'd been in the same motel in Tupelo.

Bree did most of the talking. Jones almost never originated conversation, but Bree poked and prodded. Bree had become curious about Jones. She asked him what he did when he wasn't doing what they were doing.

"I'm not usually a field agent," said Jones. "I work in a small department in Washington. I go through data."

Bree raised an eyebrow. "Most of the Directorate's desk work is in New York," she said.

"I work for different agencies," said Jones. "I work in a small department. My condition is useful to agencies looking at data. I can find inconsistencies. I don't suffer confirmation bias."

"What's confirmation bias?" Bree asked. Bree was smart, but Bree couldn't fill out a tax return. When she'd been at school, statistics and math had swum before her on the page. They'd role-played a business class when she'd been a teenager, and when presented with a pretend balance sheet she had gone red and found herself giggling with fright and embarrassment.

"People see patterns that aren't there," said Jones. "They see what they want to see. I don't. I see only what's there."

"Is that rare?"

"They say so. Much of the work I do is with tax. But also climate data. I check the algorithms used to identify terror suspects."

"Sounds interesting," said Bree, thinking otherwise. Sifting data. Jeezus. "You get bored?"

"No," said Jones. "Never." Bree had lost the ability to be surprised by this.

His tone was light and his eyebrows remained in position.

"What do you do to relax?" Bree said.

"I smoke. I do Sudoku. I cook."

"You cook?" Bree said. Her interest was piqued. She couldn't imagine Jones cooking. Bree loved to cook. She cooked a lot. It was one of the things she did to pass the time when otherwise she would have been drinking.

"I was told I needed a hobby," Jones replied. "'Take your mind off things.' I cook every evening and on weekends I cook twice a day. I like food."

"What you can taste of it through all those cigarettes . . ." Bree interjected.

Jones didn't sound in the slightest defensive. "I have a good sense of taste."

"What do you like to cook, then?"

"I've cooked all of Julia Child and *Larousse Gastronomique* and Robert Carrier's *Great Dishes of the World* and Delia Smith's *Summer Collection*. I am on number 467 of Marguerite Patten's *Cookery in Color*."

Bree had an image of Jones, solemn and methodical, dressed in an apron and a chef's hat, in the kitchenette of some anonymous and undecorated apartment in which he would be entirely at home. She imagined him holding a burger flipper. He would look like an illustration.

"Black Cap Pudding," said Jones. "Put a good layer of stoned prunes or blackcurrant jam at the bottom of the basin."

Bree burst out laughing. "What?"

"That is one of 'More Steamed Puddings.' After that I will cook 'Castle Puddings.'" Jones looked almost happy.

"Castle puddings, eh? Whatever floats your boat, I guess. You a good cook, then?"

"No. My food is not always good. The instructions have to be exact. I am not good at guessing. I know a 'lug' and a 'pinch.' But what is a 'good layer?'" Bree resisted cracking wise. "I have been finding Marguerite Patten difficult. Delia Smith is very good. I like Delia Smith."

"My favorite food," said Bree, apropos of nothing, "is . . ."

And then she started to think about what her favorite food was. Once again it had eluded her. Every time she played this game—usually imagining herself on Death Row—it changed, but never that much. She had once looked online at a list of actual last-meal requests, and she realized that she had all the same favorite foods as most prisoners on Death Row. Gray's Papaya hot dogs. White Castle sliders. Fried chicken. Pancakes with bacon. A pint of vanilla ice cream with cookie dough. Cold toast thickly spread with salted butter. Banana cake.

She let her sentence trail off. Time and landscape passed.

"You cook for friends, then, Jones?" Bree said a little later. Picking up a conversation with Jones was easy. It was as if you could put him on pause, like a VHS. "Throw parties?"

"No. I cook for myself. I don't socialize," Jones said matter-of-factly. "People find me unnerving. I have assessments with a specialist, Dr. Albert, and a socialization worker called Herman Coldfield. Herman works for the government. He tells me to think of him as a friend."

"Do you?"

"No."

She almost said: "Got a girlfriend?" but then had second thoughts. Of course he didn't. But did he have sex? Even thinking about Jones's sexual needs, if he had any, creeped her out. She had started to think of him as a child, almost. The idea of him as a sexual being repulsed her. But presumably he did—well . . . something. Everybody did. But sex without imagination; without fantasy; without thinking about what the other person was thinking . . .

Bree pushed that aside, and pictured Jones's life, and felt a little sad. His half-life. That unfurnished apartment—clean, drab, anonymous—in which he would be at home. The bedroom in which he would do his crying, the kitchenette in which he would do his cooking, the shoes by the door each morning waiting for him to step into them and go out into the world without fear or expectation.

That was how it had felt to her, the first months sober. I'll be your friend, Jones, she thought.

And so, across country, the three cars proceeded. There were Bree and Jones, making shift with each other. There was Alex, making lonely time—thinking, driving, enjoying the pleasurable melancholy of the road, listening to the Pixies and Talking Heads over and over again, wondering how he would remember this journey, how he would describe it to his children.

And there were Sherman and Davidoff, making no progress, wondering why their iPods didn't work.

"My name is Bree, and—"

Bree had liked drinking. She had been a good drunk. A happy drunk. When she took the first beer of the afternoon—never before noon; never, at least not till toward the end—and felt its coldness scald her throat, its warmth blossom in her chest, she had been suffused with . . . what? A sense of generosity, of well-being, of peace with the universe.

That was the best bit. Of course, she'd smoked then too, just the odd one. So the cigarette, the first hit. That was good. But the drink was where the action was. A six of Michelob, pearled with frost in the top of the refrigerator. Crack and sigh as the cap came off. The bottle sighed too. Then a big pull from the neck and it was like the lights came up.

Bree had been sociable. She and Al had gone out in the evenings, taken Cass when she was tiny. They couldn't afford a sitter in those days. Nobody was buying Al's paintings, and though he got a bit of work here and there hanging other people's stuff it wasn't enough. Bree had stopped being a cop and was pulling down one quarter of jackshit working part-time at the Pentagon.

That first beer, yes. That had been the kicker. Bree tended to make a point of not thinking about it too much. It had been a long, long time and the craving was weaker. But sometimes it still surprised her, like an old ache. And when she did turn and think about it, the taste of that first mouthful was still fresh in her memory as if it was just gone midday.

Level and confront. My ass. What would you give for just— just once more—the taste? Just once more. No such thing as just once. We know where that leads. But before you die, don't you want to feel that again? The cold filling the mouth, the eyes closing, the eyes opening to an easier world?

It was only later that it got harder. Al got less fun. Bree still maintained this. She knew—she fucking knew, OK, by the end of it—that things had got out from under her, but that didn't mean that she was necessarily wrong about Al getting less fun. She'd started staying out when he'd gone home, and they started to row about Cass.

That always hit a nerve with her. That was when it got vicious.

"You dare say that, you fucking piece of shit. I love that girl. I love her more than anything. I'd kill for her. Kill. I do everything for her."

"Who got her up for school this morning?"

"I was *sick!*"

"Bree, you're drinking too—"

"My drinking has nothing to do with—"

"You were sick because—"

"I got *day flu.*"

"You got—"

"I got her up yesterday, and the day before and the day before, and, 'cause one time—"

"It's not just the one time, love."

"Love" stung her. The softness of it.

"Al, do you even think, ever just think, just once what it's like to be me?" She'd hear herself slur on "ever," losing the second vowel, but she'd plow on. The thought of what it was like to be her made her eyes prickle but she wasn't going to give him the satisfaction, and the emotion was redirected into anger. "I'm holding this damn family together while you try to sell your piece-of-shit paintings." That would wound him, and she'd see him suck it down. Looking back now, it still made her hurt somewhere remembering moments like that when she'd see how hard he was trying. Turning the other cheek. That holier-than-thou stuff enraged her.

"I work, and I cook, and I come home and I look after our damn kid, and if one morning I get sick I'm what, I'm a bad mother? I get a drink—yes, maybe I have a couple drinks because I damn well need to unwind and now you're going to sit in judgment over me?"

"I'm not sitting in judgment." He looked miserable, utterly defeated. Bree had always been strong, always stronger than him. "I love—"

Doors would slam, tears come. "Fuck you, fuck you, fuck you." And Bree would show him what was fucking what by going out and necking a couple.

"I love her more than anything." Bree wondered. You had to say it. You had to feel it. What if it wasn't true?

Bree could look back on all this now and know she was wrong. She didn't like to think too clearly about how wrong—she'd been through that, and you'd go crazy if you spent the whole rest of your life fifth-stepping, Bree reckoned; you'd get addicted to shame.

But what was odd was that as she accessed the memories she didn't feel wrong. She remembered not just what she did and said, but what she felt. And as she inhabited the memory she felt it again. She felt indignant. She wasn't that bad then. Nothing worse than millions of normal people who bring their kids up fine, and whose husbands didn't get their panties in a twist if they had one bourbon over the line most nights. She was dealing with it.

That was what she thought of as her double vision. That indignation was still a part of her. But so was the part that saw something else. And even back then, the part that saw things as they were was there. It simply didn't seem urgent. I'll keep an eye on that, she'd thought.

She knew that her morning routine wasn't great; wasn't how it had always been. She'd make sure she was in the bathroom alone, Al out of the house preferably. Then she'd run the shower and before she got in it she stood over the sink with her hands gripping the sides and she arched over it and retched. She had learned to do this silently, for the most part, feeling her diaphragm spasm. She had to do this for somewhere between thirty seconds and a minute. Most days, a few tablespoons of bitter yellow bile slicked onto the white porcelain. She'd ride it out. That, too, passed, and the nausea left with the bile.

Then she'd breathe in and breathe out. And she'd stand up straight. The shuddering and the retching gone, she would feel a lightness, as if she'd been purged. She'd swill her mouth and the sink with water, and step into the shower, almost bright, ready to face the day.

And even though her work at the Pentagon was paper-shoveling, she kept at it. She arrived on time and she left on time and she worked damn well. Until Al left she was keeping it going. She thought of Al's mousy, too-long hair. The yellow tint to his sunglasses and the brown leather jacket he loved and always wore. The speed and anger of his going.

Bree looked out of the car window. America was passing. It was warm, but the air was thick and the sky was the color of ash. A couple drops of rain fell on the windshield.

Al was still there when she'd started to lose time. They'd had so much time back then, when they were young and new-married, that Bree barely noticed it going missing. When it did, it had been funny—Al shaking his head at how Bree couldn't remember getting home from parties and feigning theatrical outrage when Bree would ask: "Did we . . .?"

"You've *forgotten*?"

Later, though, she lost time more easily, more unexpectedly, more disconcertingly. Time started to vanish in the way that dollars would vanish from her purse—just a tentative five minutes here or there, surreptitiously, calculated so she wouldn't miss it but not calculated well enough. She'd find herself in a different room than she had been, tips of her fingers grazing the door jambs, mouth open to deliver a sentence she had no idea of. She would frown and withdraw. That, at least, early on.

The thefts became more blatant. Money from the purse was not an analogy. Money really had been going missing from her purse. And it was hard to be sure, at first, how much and when. But it was clear Cass was stealing from her. Finally, she confronted her about it and Cass reacted as she always did when cornered: with the sort of indignation only an eleven-year-old can muster. Her whole face shone red as she screamed back. Bree slapped her—not on the face but on the legs.

Al had gone by this time. Had he? Bree couldn't always remember the sequence of events. But that would explain why she was so angry—he'd left them both in the shit, the way he walked out. She was under such pressure then. She couldn't afford child care. And her money was going missing. And Cassie was bed-wetting and Bree was exhausted and her good-for-nothing husband had meanwhile lit out for the territories with an armload of his own paintings. It was the first time she'd hit her daughter.

"Never steal. Never steal from your mommy, never. You hear me?" Blood thumping in her ears, rage misting everything. Cass's yell, as the blows landed—suddenly turning the corner into a shriek, even shriller and even louder.

It was about this time that the sneak-thief started to get bolder. Money started disappearing from the bedside table. And drinks—the emergency half-jack in the wardrobe; the old miniatures of vodka in the ice compartment. And time—great chunks of time would have been pocketed, spirited away. It was very confusing.

Was the same person who was taking the money taking the time? That's all money was, Bree had once heard someone say: frozen time. It became impossible to keep track of things.

The thief was eventually apprehended.

Bree never felt that the Bree who had been doing that stuff was another person, one who had died at those meetings to make way for the shiny new person who was now sitting in the car with Jones. That Bree had continued. In another life, one where Bree had spent a lot less time sitting in smoky, talky rooms on jittering plastic chairs comparing war stories, she was living on, still drinking. She'd be deathbound by now, living through blank, real spaces, passing hours and days into her blackouts like someone patiently feeding a furnace: there, but not there.

And she was here, but not here. She followed this Bree around with the tenacity of a shadow. She was long when the sun was low; almost invisible in the bright of the day. Bree could lose touch with her for just a second, by jumping—but then gravity intervened and Bree wasn't a great one for jumping up and down these days, in any case.

Stupid analogy, Bree thought. Raindrops, an unexpected shower, gathered and ran on the windshield. They felt like another analogy, and she wondered what it was like to be Jones, who had shown no signs of making conversation since lunch, and for whom the slick of water running down the windshield would never be anything other than rain.

Bree thought about not-Bree, drinking Bree. It was as if she had acquired a twin. In that life, this Bree would be shadowing her. Sober Bree, in that world, would be not-Bree: would be just there, hanging around, waiting. The thing that was your deepest, darkest terror: the thing you longed for.

Snap. Cheers, sister.

Except in both these worlds, they had taken Cass away, and Bree wondered momentarily in which of these worlds she was living and why.

15

It was the morning of the third day that they got a sure fix on Alex. It was pure good luck.

Red Queen remembered that the Directorate had a long-gone field agent by the name of Doc, living in the New Mexico desert near the Texas border. Doc was semi-retired on medical grounds after spearheading the Directorate's intensive 2003 investigation into the effectiveness of ayahuasca trances as an intelligence-gathering technique.

The verdict of the investigation—reached not by Doc himself but by those observing his experiments with a clearer head—had been "not very." Doc was loco in the brainpan, no two ways about it.

But Red Queen reached out to Doc anyway, and Doc—who did things, if he did them, for reasons of his own—agreed to drive his tangerine-colored pickup to a bluff overlooking the I-40 and wait for "this cat with the magic ring."

"Magic ring?" Red Queen had said.

"A snake told me about it," Doc had said.

Red Queen had made a mental note. "And his license plate. You have it?"

"Wrote it down. In-scriibed it."

"With a pen?"

"It's cool," Doc had said. "I see auras. He's going to be lit up like a Christmas tree on the Fourth of July. He'll be haloed in rainbows. It'll be like the Northern Lights. I'll see him."

"The license plate . . ."

"It's cool," Doc had repeated before ringing off. But true to his word he had perched above the highway and watched the westbound traffic with lizard eyes. And to Red Queen's voluble astonishment, had not only got a tail on the boy but confirmed that the boy was himself being followed. "Couple of wolf-like cats. None too smart. Violent men. Big one and a small one. Keep losing him. And there's something else. Somebody else. A very old man. He's here and he's not here. Like John Barleycorn or an old shaman I know. I'm moving in," he had added. "Do me good to get within a sniff of civilization. Reckon I've got a fix."

He had left Red Queen listening to the staticky burr of an open line, then Doc had rolled his old wagon down onto the highway, and followed them at a leisurely distance. And it was as that orange car, with its big, bald, white-sided tires was lumbering onto the great artery heading west, that Alex had exclaimed, aloud and to himself: "Don't forget your toothbrush."

Doc said, also to himself, musingly: "Something about a toothbrush . . ."

And two hours later, Doc found a payphone and called Red Queen, who called Bree on her cellphone, and directed her to a superstore in a roadside mall on the east side of Albuquerque in the early afternoon.

"He's there," Doc said. "I'm just not sure when."

Bree and Jones showed up, and did two circuits of the wide parking lot, and weren't able to see the boy, or his car, or anything of that sort.

"Had a feeling, this guy, apparently," said Bree, with a shrug. "Another hit for the Directorate. Still, best we've got. We proceed," she added philosophically, "through hints and accidents."

Jones went to get some tobacco. Bree ambled in to check out the store. She walked the aisles, found nothing. No sign of the kid. Near the door there were a couple of girls with too much make-up, wearing long coats. They were chewing gum. With them was a middle-aged man in a cheap suit, pretending not to be watching her as she came in the door. He had something concealed in his palm. She saw his thumb work at it, and he turned his hand, looked surreptitiously down at it. It glinted. Bree didn't like it.

She turned round and headed outside, intending to take up a position where she could watch the front entrance unobserved. She took a trolley. A trolley would be good. Make it look like she was shopping. Who was that guy? Where was the boy?

Alex ran his tongue around his teeth. His upper incisors were pleasantly slippery. He was worried about the lower set, though. They felt furry, clagged. He had a stark visual memory of his toothbrush, sitting red on the white sink at the last motel. He had left it there, hadn't he?

It was about lunchtime anyway. He'd stop. Two birds with one stone.

"Don't forget your toothbrush," he said aloud to himself, before pulling into the supermarket car park. He slammed the car door, hopped out, and set off for the entrance to the shop.

The store dominated the parking lot: a wide glass frontage that could have done with being cleaned more recently, and big scrolls of paper yellowing in the windows advertising special offers, on beer and cleaning products, mostly. Next door were two smaller shops—a tobacconist and a pizza place.

A dirty great sign, hoisted above the entrance like a hat, announced simply: "SUPERSTORE." The letters were picked out in broken light bulbs. A nondescript cartoon character—it looked like a smiling chocolate button—was giving the world an unwavering thumbs up from next door to the letter E.

MIC's guns for hire had lost Alex's trail again, and Sherman had morosely assented to Davidoff's insistence that they stop driving and get some food. A roadside sign half a mile back had promised pizza. Davidoff used a hand on the roof to haul his big frame from the car and they stood there scanning the scene like children at the gates of Disneyland.

Sherman saw the kid before Davidoff did, and nudged the bigger man. He saw the recognition bloom and take hold in his face like a pilot light. Davidoff's eyes scanned the parking lot, and Sherman knew what he was seeing. There was a hedge down the left-hand side. Maybe a hundred meters of asphalt between the kid and the entrance to the store, twenty meters between the two men and the boy they were chasing.

A fat woman in a T-shirt was pushing a shopping cart out of the store. Nobody seemed to be here other than that. A tall gray-haired guy, a couple of hundred meters away, was leaning up outside the door of the tobacco store next door, smoking. A handful of cars in the lot, empty. Sherman picked up pace. Davidoff broke right, out on a slight trot, as if he was someone jogging to get a parking ticket while his family waited in the car. Sherman closed slower.

Ninety meters, fifteen meters.

The boy was moving on a diagonal. Across the front entrance of the store there was a snake of trolleys—what had once been bright pink plastic faded to brittle white in the weather—shucked into each other. To reach the entrance, the boy would have to walk round the right-hand end of them and up the wheelchair ramp.

If Sherman took the straight line—went left of the trolleys and vaulted up the wrong end of the ramp—he'd get there about the same time as the boy.

Eighty meters, ten meters.

Davidoff way out to the right. Scan left—that angle covered. Was there a back entrance? Probably. Best not let him get into the store in the first place if at all possible. Best not let him bolt.

Seventy meters, ten meters. Easy. Easy.

Ouch! Shit. The fat woman—not at all where he'd expected her to be—had barked her trolley against his shin. Stupid fat—

"Sorry, sorry," she was at once muttering, fussing: "Oh gosh, oh gee. Sir, I'm real sorry—I didn't see where you were . . ." She started, inanely, trying to brush down the lapels of his jacket with her hands . . .

Sherman struggled to keep his temper. He could see the kid reaching the end of the ramp, and here was this woman right in the—

"It's fine, really," he said.

"Oh, you're so kind, I'm sorry, I'm sorry."

"It's *fine*," he repeated, jerking away from her. A bit too snappy an emphasis. She was startled, suddenly looking offended.

"Well, there's no call—"

Oh for fuck's *sake*. "Dammit—"

He pushed her trolley to one side roughly—it clattered to the tarmac, lighter than he had anticipated; he didn't have time to wonder why she was pushing an empty trolley—and hopped past, breaking into an angry trot for a couple of paces, enough to carry him to within nearly grabbing distance of the kid. But as he did so the kid heard something and jerked his head round—saw Sherman looking straight at him, read the tension in his face.

Alex Smart didn't recognize Sherman but something in him knew instantly and viscerally that the man behind him was after him. He gasped, stumbled over on one ankle, recovered, hip-checked the back end of the line of trolleys and sprinted up the ramp for the entrance of the shop.

Shit shit shit. Sherman abandoned all pretense of stalking him and just went flat out. A fraction of a second of indecision—go right and round the line of trolleys, or try to hurdle them—resolved in favor of cutting the corner.

He grunted and put one hand out to grab midway down the caterpillar of trolleys, pushed off the tarmac and swung his legs up to vault—the kid whipping back his head to look with candid fright at the man cutting the corner off between them—feeling as he left the ground the trolleys sliding under his hand, his trailing foot now not clearing but catching the steel railing on the other side—angular momentum bringing him round faster than he could compensate for.

The electric doors of the supermarket whooshed open and Alex ran inside. Sherman crashed down onto the top of the ramp behind him. His left hand broke his fall at the cost of an impact in the heel of his hand so hard the pain detonated in his elbow. He lost a smear of skin—he didn't feel it—then first his left then his right knee crashed onto the hairy black-and-red plastic mat that said "WELCOME" in big letters.

Nothing was broken, but the physical shock—a charge of adrenalin and humiliation—made Sherman very, very angry. The electric doors had half swiped shut behind Alex, but then Sherman's face broke the beam, and they jolted open again. Sherman scrambled to his feet and stumbled through the doors.

He got his head up just long enough to see, confusingly, what seemed to be the bottom half of a girl in a bikini before his forward momentum drove his head into the soft part between her bikini top and her bikini bottoms. There was a shrill squawk, interrupted by the sound of the air being driven out of her lungs by Sherman's head. She went down and so did Sherman, rolling off sideways and sprawling on his back.

It *was* a girl in a bikini—two of them. Both blonde. One of them now on the deck somewhere, the other shying above him on her platform shoes like some sort of horse. As Sherman tried to get his footing and his dignity back, there was the sound of an air horn and his field of vision was obscured by an avalanche of something coming down on him—colors, red, white and blue . . .

He threw his hands up to protect his face, and yelped. Sherman was engulfed in something soft and multicolored and swirling. The air horn gave another great asthmatic hoot and Sherman found himself spitting out something dry in his mouth . . . little bits of paper.

The girl on the floor was crying—or wailing, anyway—and Sherman was sitting in a small snowdrift of red-white-and-blue confetti, half of which seemed to be wrapped in flakes round his tongue. The air horn went off again.

Sherman scrambled to his feet. There was a guy in a white button-down shirt with a tie on, trying to help him up and grinning inanely in his face.

"—tulations! Sir, yes, sir, sorry. Sorry, sir, let us"—the man in the shirt sweeping confetti from Sherman's shoulders, the one girl helping the other girl up—"quite unprepared, quite an entrance, ha ha, but no harm done, no, sir, let me extend the compliments of the store to you, yes, sir—"

"What the *fuck*?"

"Ha ha, sir, no, I'm sorry, sir, there's no need for that kind of language, I think you'll be pleased, sir, to learn—let me help you up with that—sir, this is a very proud moment, a proud moment I say, in the history of this store, to be able to say you are our one MILLIONTH customer!"

And with that the man in the shirt and tie extended the open palm of friendship to the man from MIC and the man from MIC hit him in the face.

Alex heard all this—or some of this—behind him as he ran through the store. He dodged a startled sales assistant, brought down a revolving rack of tennis shirts, gulped air, hurdled a low stool on which until moments before someone had been trying on a pair of trainers, and then seeing half concealed between two racks of off-brand sportswear a beige fire door with a bar across it at waist height rammed his hand into the bar so hard his palm hurt.

The door slammed open and disgorged Alex into a corridor of whitewashed breeze blocks and gray floor tiles. It smelled of stale air and long-ago bleach. Alex let the door shut behind him and ran down the corridor and round the corner, grabbing at a bit of pipework to swing himself round as he went.

He heard his own trainers squeaking on the lino, and his chest hurt at the Y-shaped bit where his lungs met.

There were what looked like storerooms off the corridor to one or other side—gray doors, with wired windows in them. He wondered about hiding in one but the fear of being trapped was too strong. Besides, his body—he didn't know who that guy was, but he knew he needed to get away from him—seemed to be making these decisions for him. He carried on running. At the end of the corridor there was sunlight leaking in round the edges of another door with a bar across it. Alex bet that would be the outside door.

He didn't know how long the guy he'd heard fall over behind him would take to be on him and he didn't want to find out. He barreled into the door. It resisted the first bump, but then he pushed again and the bar yielded and the door opened. He spilled out into the light. He was by an open loading bay of some sort—a thin and inexpertly laid strip of tarmac led round to the far corner of the building and back out.

Ahead there was a shallow bank of scrubby grass, a low wall, a patch of waste ground. Further away, in the distance, the highway. He stopped for a moment and looked around. If he could sneak back down between the outside wall of the store and the hedge he could maybe make it to his car. But he'd have to cross the car park. That guy had moved fast. If he hadn't seen where he'd gone would he have doubled back to try and ambush him? Or would he even now be making his way through the back corridor of the building?

Before he had the chance to speculate further, Alex flinched: in the shadow of the loading bay he thought he saw something move. He turned to face it, but his eyes were still adjusting to the brightness. There was something there, though. Definitely something there. He stepped a bit further back—

At that precise moment the fire door banged open again with some force. Out of the door came Sherman, looking as he was:

furious. The door itself swung out and struck Davidoff—who had been unfortunate in the moment he picked to pounce—hard on the top of his forehead. Davidoff, behind the door, went down like a rail of shirts, but not before the momentum of his charge had sent the door slamming back onto his colleague. Sherman, weighing not more than three-quarters what Davidoff did, himself fell over, again, right at Alex's feet.

Alex, not sure at all what had just happened, looked down at the crazy man—who, he noticed, had a gun in his sock and looked like he was proposing to start pointing it at Alex just as soon as he got round to not being on the ground again—and bolted for the corner. If the bad guy was now behind him, the decision where to run had become a whole lot more straightforward.

Jones had caught up with Bree outside the superstore. Jones was smoking and Bree was wondering what to do when Alex emerged from the gap between the low trees and the left-hand side of the store running at full pelt across the parking lot toward them.

Bree looked at Jones, whose expression was perfectly blank. Let him go, thought Bree. This was too public. They knew what car he was driving. The brief was to follow. Protect.

"Like a bat out of hell," Bree murmured as the boy closed the gap between them. She felt a stirring of anxiety in her gut as to what was following him, then quenched it and put on her best bovine bystander expression.

Like a bat out of hell. She wondered about the origins of the phrase. Why were bats, especially, keen to leave hell? The boy ran right between the two of them, legs pumping almost comically high, breath coming in rags and tatters.

Something occurred to her as she watched him go.

"You have no idea," she said to his departing back, "what's going on, do you?" He took a corner—Scooby-Doo legs—and was fumbling at the door of the silver Pontiac and then was in it, overrevving the engine before he got it in gear, then taking a wide loop round the near-empty parking lot and grounding the undercarriage with a scrape as he bounced down the awkward gradient onto the street. He was gone.

The guy Bree had hit with her trolley earlier came out from the same place more or less as Alex was getting into the car. He had something in his hand that he stowed quickly inside his jacket as he saw Bree. At around the same moment, the front doors of the store slid sideways and out came—to Bree's considerable surprise—some sort of store detective in a brown uniform, along with a pair of cut-price beauty queens and a really distressed-looking guy with a wad of crimson toilet tissue clamped to his nose and nosebleed all down his cheap shirt and what looked like confetti in his hair.

The guy with the gun in his jacket clocked them. Bree could see him making a swift calculation. He broke into the sort of awkward, loping run that someone who has just sustained a crunching blow to the coccyx might adopt. First he seemed to be making for the road on foot, the store detective making a half-hearted attempt to lumber in pursuit and the nosebleed guy waving one arm and shouting something from the safety of the doorway. Then, a way away, Bree could hear something that sounded like a siren and the man thought better of it and swerved toward a car parked near the entrance to the lot. He was gone before the store detective got halfway across the space between them.

The guy's car was a rental. Bree shrugged. Everyone's car seemed to be a rental. She had the plate. Red Queen would run something up.

" 's go," she said. "I made the plate. Did you make the plate?"

Jones nodded. "Every one in the lot."

"Jonesy," said Bree. "There is a use for you after all."

"There was another man," Jones said. Bree looked at him with eyebrows raised. "He came past me when I was buying cigarettes.

I saw them talking." Bree was thinking—what with them both having been standing in the middle of the parking lot for the last ten minutes and the guys in the stripey cars about to show up—that it was time for them to be off.

"Wait," said Jones, and vanished at a run toward the far side of the building.

"Jones!" said Bree.

A police car rolled, siren blipping off, into the parking lot and pulled up outside the line of trolleys in front of the store. The store detective and the nosebleed guy mobbed the window as the cop got out. Arms were waved. Bree couldn't afford to stay still and risk becoming somebody's witness so she moved off, fussing ostentatiously with her trolley, and then stood behind their car pretending to do something in the trunk.

When that got boring, she sat in the passenger seat and started to eat Jolly Ranchers from the stash in the glove compartment, two at a time. She liked to combine the cherry and peach ones. Thinking about recipes kept her calm, she had discovered.

Where the hell had Jones gone? The cop had gone into the store with the nosebleed guy and his entourage. He had his note-pad out and was writing as he went. He looked, from his body language at least, bored. Good. Bree waited some more. She ran out of Jolly Ranchers. She thought about calling Red Queen but then thought she better be safe and wait for Jones and wait for a landline. She wondered if there were some Reese's Pieces at the back of the glove compartment. There were not.

Then the door opened and Jones climbed into the driver's seat. He smelled of stale smoke and something else. He pulled a rag out from the compartment in the door and wiped at his hand. He was looking dead ahead. Under the level of the steering wheel Bree could see—

"Is that *blood*? Jesus. Jones: what the hell? Are you hurt?"

"No," said Jones. "The other man is dead."

Bree was speechless, for a moment.

"You're joking." She felt dizzy.

"Don't joke," said Jones. A fact about himself. He showed her a cellphone. On the screen was a picture of a man's face. He looked startled. There was a penknife sticking out of his neck. His mouth was slightly open. Very little blood. The background was tarmac.

"He was unconscious," said Jones. "I was searching him and he woke up. I didn't know what to do so I killed him. No documents. Only phone. Took his photograph. Might be helpful."

"You killed him?"

"I didn't know what to do."

Jones looked intently ahead, turned on the engine, drove the car out of the lot.

Alex was freaking out. He spent at least as much time looking in his rear-view mirror—for *what*? He barely even got a look at the guy—as out of the windscreen. Within thirty seconds of joining the freeway he'd come so close to rear-ending a truck (he reckoned his front bumper had been about four inches from the sign reading "I Brake For Pussy," which would have been fatal had the driver done as advertised) that he'd given himself an even bigger fright than he'd had round the back of the supermarket. He'd had one nasty near miss as he'd become confused as to what was the inside and what the outside lane when you're driving on the other side of the road. A wailing horn had reminded him.

A panicky attempt to fish his mobile phone out of his left-hand pocket—he was still sketchy as to who he would call but he knew he'd rather have it on the passenger seat than in his pocket—had nearly ended in the sort of disaster they show on the news.

Who the hell was that man? With a gun! An honest to God gun. As he drove, he started to calm down. Just a random lunatic. Another one. America was full of those. But what had happened back there? It looked like the door had bounced off something and hit him. What had the door bounced off?

Alex's appetite for his road trip was dwindling. What was causing him especially strong palpitations was the thought—he didn't know from where—that he recognized that man. Could the man have been stalking him or something? He thought of Rutger Hauer's character in *The Hitcher*: a blond, amused lunatic killing his way through the desert and always, as in a nightmare, seeming to get ahead of the hero. Wherever you showed up, he'd already be there, and would have marked his arrival with some dead bodies or a severed finger in a bowl of chips.

Alex kept going west.

He stopped, two hours later, when his petrol gauge started to wag into the red zone. He found a service station, a busy one. And only when he'd been standing in there for twenty minutes, affecting to browse the Doritos under the reassuring eye of the CCTV camera, watching the arrivals on the forecourt, did he set out on the road again with something like a restored sense of calm.

The guy couldn't possibly be following him. Too much time on his own was affecting his imagination. Even so, he came within an ace of calling Saul, just to hear his brother's voice, sleepy and annoyed, at whatever time it was in England.

16

They'd risked sending the photograph of the dead man in over the dead man's phone.

Red Queen had spent fifteen minutes talking Bree down.

"I did not sign up for this," had been the agent's first words when she'd got a line to the Directorate. "Your guy killed someone in cold blood. We don't do that. We don't do things like that. We have no"—Bree flapped her hand—"no—we have no—we're not—"

"Don't panic," said Red Queen. Red Queen was panicking.

"—we have no jurisdiction. If we were—we're not—"

Bree was hyperventilating, nearly. The DEI wasn't a judicial body. It didn't have any jurisdiction at all. It just had a remit.

"Did you know? Did you know he was going to do that?"

"Don't panic—"

"*Tell* me."

Red Queen left a silence a bit too long. "No, I didn't. He wasn't supposed to . . ."

"You—what—who told him? He's . . . this, this 'thing.' He's like mentally ill, and you've got him—"

"We thought. Our Friends thought—"

"He's what? He's what? Our Friends are involved?"

"Of course they're involved. This is very big. Of course—"

"Jesus, RQ. He could go to jail. I could go to jail. He *murdered* someone. In a Kwik-E-Mart parking lot. With a frigging squad car outside."

Bree breathed in and out, raggedly, gathering breath to continue, goggling at the telephone cable. She felt sweaty.

"Where did he get a knife? What was he doing with a knife?"

"Bree—half the people in this country carry a *gun*—"

"So why didn't he use a gun? What's wrong with him? He's a Friend? Are you saying he's a Friend? I thought he was Directorate—"

"On loan. Their asset."

"Well, how do you know? Was this part of *their* plan?"

Red Queen exhaled.

Bree said: "You don't know, do you?"

The silence lengthened.

Eventually Red Queen said: "None of that matters. You know how important this is. Keep your head. Stay with it. Do your job. We'll look after you. Trust me."

Bree didn't say anything to that, put down the phone, went back to the motel room.

The dead man, as Red Queen had feared, was linked to MIC: off-books payments over five years. Frederick Gordon Noone. Forty-one. A British national, ten-year veteran of the UK's Parachute Regiment, where he was known as "Davidoff" for reasons unclear to Red Queen.

Noone had got his boots sandy in Iraq and Afghanistan. Clean service record. After leaving the regiment he had, along with many like him, touted for private hire and found himself doing a similar job for much more money and with the rules of engagement tilted in his favor. He was on Blackwater's books, briefly—then left. The payments from a slush fund linked to MIC had started shortly after.

The trail pointed to sub-Saharan Africa, some time in South America—training FARC, probably, thought Red Queen. The run-of-the-mill end of MIC's operations involved arming and training terrorists and their opposite numbers in government in most of the major conflicts around the world. Creating customers, was how they thought of it.

No family, apparently. Good. His employers weren't going to be reporting this guy missing any time soon. He'd entered the country on his own passport, a guest visa, but that wouldn't send up flags from USCIS for a while. He'd booked a return ticket, no doubt just for the sake of form, but that was still a fortnight away. Hotel? Car? His partner would probably take care of that.

Good.

That they were fielding someone—one of a team, presumably—with traceable connections to them, traveling under his own name, suggested haste and urgency. They were taking very big risks with this thing. So either they were counting on some powerful protectors or they were starting to flail. More likely the former.

This wasn't Red Queen's usual beat. Not at all. The Directorate seldom if ever staged interventions. It soaked information up, spread spiderwebs, moved as invisibly as possible through the world. If it did something stagy, like bringing in Hands, it called in a favor from Our Friends. But this situation was beyond the usual thing. The executive branch, so to speak, needed the DEI's knowledge. And DEI needed the executive branch.

There was still at least one more guy loose on the ground.

Red Queen spoke to Porlock. Explained the situation, though something about his manner suggested he knew about it already.

"Go to Our Friends. Tell them it's their mess. They need to go, find this dead man before anyone else does, and make him disappear. This needs to be contained, agreed?"

"Agreed."

Sherman waited in the car park of their motel for three hours for Davidoff to return. Better safe than sorry. Then he risked a call to Davidoff's pay-as-you-go.

The phone, on the side table of Jones's room in the motel, trilled and its screen lit up. Jones picked it up and got a pen and wrote down the number but did not answer it.

Jones waited. The phone went again. Same number. Jones carefully wrote it down underneath where he had written the number the first time.

Sherman frowned. He knew the big fella would be pissed off that he'd bolted, but there was no great percentage for Sherman in standing around to make friends with Mr. One Millionth Customer and the meet-and-greet girls, and Davidoff could take care of himself.

He'd last seen Davidoff at the front of the shop before it had all gone tits skyward. He'd slipped off, Sherman assumed, to go round and cover any back exits. Much use he'd turned out to be. How the little sod had managed to hit Sherman with the door, he didn't know, but it had done his shin a mischief and from then on in Sherman hadn't had much of a chance to do anything but follow his nose.

This was a crap job, he thought. A crap, crap job. Everything that could have gone wrong had. And now, when he'd like to have been safely indoors having a chod and a read of the paper, he was sitting in some backwater in the middle of America surveilling his own motel room from a car park—he seemed to spend a lot of time in car parks—or feeding crap tin money into crap tin payphones. Lost idiot wanted. Please call Ed Otis, answers to Sherman.

He didn't know what was keeping Davidoff. He thought about phoning Ellis but then thought about not phoning Ellis and preferred the second thought. He thought about returning to the shop, wondered about whether the car had been seen. He thought not. As far as they were concerned he was just a violent nutter who missed out on a free trolley dash and the chance to have his photograph taken with a couple of village idiot beauty queens.

Finally, he decided he'd rather just go than keep sitting here. He waited till after dark, and then drove. The forecourt and the neon sign were still illuminated but the glass front was shut.

Sherman parked the car a couple of blocks away, and walked back to the shop.

The snake of trolleys, locked and chained in the black light, looked like something's spine. A single car, seemingly abandoned, gleamed gray-white in the middle of the car park. The display windows of the shop faced blankly over the asphalt, eating the dark. Sherman shivered, pushed his hands into the pockets of his jacket and broke into the beginnings of a trot.

There was nothing outside the building. Sherman spent a few minutes in a pool of shade near the exit, watching the windows of the building for the sweep of a flashlight—anything that said "night-watchman." Nothing. He circled toward the back of the building.

A sign directed deliveries to a roughly laid tarmacked strip down the side of the store. He trotted down under the shoulder of the building, into the dark. He could smell diesel and grass. He walked round—down a long wall, one locked door and a shuttered loading bay. All quiet. On the other side of the loading bay was the fire door that had knocked him over that afternoon. There was a dim, hooded light over it. He shuffled down the wall toward it.

He was startled, then, by a rustle in the bushes and froze. A tousled figure—not tall enough to be Davidoff—was standing still out there in a pool of dark, seemingly looking in his direction. As Sherman's eyes adjusted he could see the outline of a rough beard. He'd disturbed a hobo. Dumpster-diving probably. There was another rustle, and the old man stepped back and was gone. He wouldn't have been able to see much of Sherman, not from that distance and with Sherman in the shadow of the building. Probably just heard him.

Sherman waited, then went on. Screened from two sides by the low bank and the hedge, he risked the light, tried the door. There wasn't a handle—just the bar on the inside, and the shop may not have had a nightwatchman but it was bound to be alarmed.

If Davidoff had got trapped in there, he supposed, he could have decided it was better to wait the night out than risk tripping the alarm. He didn't have a car. But that didn't make sense. Davidoff hadn't gone into the shop, not from the front, anyway. And if he was in there he wouldn't know that Sherman had taken the car. And why would he have got locked into the shop in the first place? He had a phone . . . No. Sherman had a bad feeling about his partner.

It was just as he was thinking about this bad feeling he had, about his partner, that Sherman heard the sound of a motor idling outside the front of the shop, then coming closer. It sounded like it was coming down the side of the building, where he'd just walked. It stopped. Then there was the sound of a car door opening, and closing. What made Sherman freeze was that the noise of the car—throatier, a van of some sort—and the noise of the voices sounded like someone trying to be quiet. His route back was cut off.

He moved quickly, scrambling out of the light and over the wall and up the slope into the foot of the hedge. He wriggled down into a long, ditch-like concavity he found in the earth. He could hear low, purposeful voices. The foliage was good above him. He risked raising his head.

Four men—all in dark overalls. They had penlights on them, and they were sweeping methodically, stealthily, down the back of the building and up the slope toward where he was hiding.

Shit. He could bolt onto the waste ground behind and risk running for it. But an image came into his head of being shot efficiently in the back. He stayed, put his head down. If they rolled him, he'd pretend to be a sleeping drunk.

He breathed as shallowly as he could. The dancing penlights, he was relieved to see, were moving up toward the ditch a little further along from where he was. Then one stopped, there was a sharp whisper, and the others converged on it. They'd found something. They were maybe six feet away.

There were now two torch beams. Two of the men had clipped off and stowed theirs to free up their hands. In the play of the light Sherman saw the men haul something up, something heavy. As it came, Sherman knew what it was. He'd seen these things hefted like that often before. They yanked it awkwardly out of the ditch, then each man hooked an arm briskly, professionally, under each armpit—another man picking up the legs. No hesitation, no alarm. One man directing.

The head flopped back as the torso came up. A splash of light flashed over it. Mouth open, eyes open, a slick darkness down one side of the neck. That was where Davidoff was.

The four men bore him away, head jouncing, round the corner of the building at speed. Sherman heard a car door close—quietly, but firmly, then another one. Then the motor started and retreated and he was left alone in the hedge in the dark. He waited there for a very long time, and then he got up, walked a long route back to his car, and drove to a new motel.

It was 4 a.m. He found a payphone and he phoned Ellis.

The first thing Ellis said was: "We know."

17

Bree and Jones hadn't said very much since the incident. Bree, because she was nervous. Any second she expected a siren to hiccup and whoop, and blue-red lights to revolve in the rear-view. She didn't know how far Red Queen's reach went, but there was only so much you could do. Someone would have found the body, she thought. Made their car from a security camera at the store—as usual, she'd ensured Jones parked with the plate toward a low wall and the car well away from the store, but there'd been only one way in and out of the parking lot.

Jones had killed. And Red Queen was leaving him in the field? Leaving Bree with him?

It made Bree feel faintly sick to think about him. That large-knuckled hand settled on the steering wheel had pushed a penknife into a man's neck a few hours previously. And if he was upset by that he wasn't showing it. She'd thought—when she'd found him in distress—that she'd been getting somewhere with him. She'd started to feel something toward him—protectiveness, even.

Bree looked at him as they drove through the city's backstreets in search of somewhere to lie low. His face was expressionless and his eyes seemed to be watching something out of sight. They scanned the road; his right hand passed the wheel round to his left hand as he turned corners. He blinked, occasionally. He didn't talk. It was as if, since the incident, there was nobody there. She felt like she was sharing the car with a ghost.

They had eaten separately and Bree had insisted they check into separate motels, a few blocks apart. She said she'd collect him in the morning and they'd go on. He could cry all he liked.

She dropped him off, took the car back, found her way into another of those rooms. It had low yellow light, like all the other motel rooms in America. There was a bedspread that made you feel sad, and the sort of mirror that turned even a young face into a landscape of pits and pocks and defeated skin. Bree could feel her DNA fraying, her cells ticking down and closing in. She looked at herself in the mirror and wondered what it was like to have fun, not to be scared, not to have to work from the time you got up until the time that, gratefully, you whimpered into sleep. She felt very, very sober.

Not that she'd sleep. The incident at the store, the sight of the dead man's face, was going to see to that. Ever since she had been tiny, Bree had been terrified of dying and death. She hadn't been able to visit her father in the hospital. She'd never seen a dead body. Didn't know how anybody could do so and carry on. The very thought of it was enough to bring up a small tremor in her hands.

Whenever you read about dying in books or films it always seemed to picture it as the world darkening and growing silent and getting further away: an old television dwindling away to a white dot, starting at the edges; an inky inrushing in the vision, and the volume going down. That, Bree thought, would be nice. A nice rest.

Bree's night terrors cast it differently. What Bree was frightened of was that far from the world going away and shutting the door politely behind it, the opposite would happen. She was worried that the drab world was the only thing standing between her and something much, much gaudier—like the flimsy curtains they put round hospital beds. When that ripped, she knew deep in her bones, the murmur of daily sense data would rise to a screaming hurricane and she would be overwhelmed, drowned, vanished, obliterated but somehow still there just to take it all in like someone with their eyelids stapled open in a violent cartoon.

When she'd gone to the Freaky Fields with Jess and Anton and taken acid in school—and boy oh boy, was that ever one of her less bright ideas—she'd had a glimpse of it, what it would be like. It had started with a lemony creeping up her cheeks—something like a grin, and they'd been talking and throwing the red ball around until her teeth started to taste funny and she heard sentences a fraction of a second before she spoke them.

The burr of the light in the yellow grass, the too several voices of her friends, the panoply of facial muscles she was expected to find uses for, the way reduplicative fragments of nonsense words and phrases started muscling into the side of her mind ("unde-funnady," "downshudder," "slidewise") . . . she felt panic rising around her like the puddles of silvery water around her hips.

It felt like she'd been flying the light aircraft of her conscious-ness for years without incident, on automatic pilot. And here she was suddenly and abruptly switched to manual: strapped into the cockpit of a 737 and seeing bank after bank of winking lights and switches and multiple joysticks and tiny dials: far too much information coming in. She hadn't needed to think about how to smile, or to pronounce the word "funny," or to separate out the different information coming in from her ears, her eyes, her skin, and her own thoughts.

Now the filters had been removed and she was overwhelmed. She knew then, as she set in for the long haul of a catatonically bad, never-to-be-repeated trip, that this was what dying would be like—only an infinite progression of powers worse.

She hadn't been able to explain it well to her ex-husband, when he'd found her sweating and shaking beside him in the still hours of the morning. She hadn't been able to explain it to the therapist he'd made her see before he'd given up on her and gone.

She hadn't been able to explain it to her mother when it had first struck her. Everyone's frightened of dying. Everyone. But not everyone thinks about it all the time. It was the first thing she remembered from her childhood. Fear in the bones.

She had been six years old. She knew that, because her younger brother Gill had just been born. He was lying there in his cradle up the corridor, asleep already. Bree had had her bath like always and now, with a too-big, grown-up's towel around her shoulders and her flannel pajama bottoms on, the pale blue ones, she was brushing her teeth in front of the mirror over the sink in her bedroom.

The sink was too high. She could rest her chin on the edge of it only, so she stood on the orange plastic toy crate like her mother had shown her. Now the porcelain was cold on her belly. Her dad had come home and her mother had gone downstairs to fix him a drink.

She reached up to the toothbrush holder fixed to the tiling behind the sink. The holder had a flat plastic cartoon of Snoopy's kennel, with Snoopy and Woodstock sitting on the roof. The body of the kennel, like Snoopy, was white. The roof was red. Woodstock was a splotch of yellow. Bree's toothbrush was red and had a little picture of Snoopy on the handle.

She squeezed a pea-sized burr of toothpaste onto the bristles and started to brush around her front teeth in the conscientious circles she had been taught. She remembered, or perhaps imagined, looking at herself in the small mirror, her short blonde hair dark from the bath and tousled and her mouth foaming.

Milk teeth, little round pearls. Soon grown-up teeth, she knew. Then what? Round she brushed. I am Bree, she had thought, looking in the mirror. Nobody else is Bree, only me. It struck her as strange. It had occurred to her that she was a person, a separate person from everyone else, that she was alone in her head—she hadn't expressed it to herself this way, she thought, not at the time; but she could remember the feeling and it corresponded to that—and that she was moving toward something like abandonment. She felt suddenly overwhelmed, like when she was lost in the supermarket. She knew too that she couldn't, having once had this thought, ever unthink it.

The Snoopy toothbrush holder wasn't friendly. It was inert: just a plastic thing, a small object in a huge universe. Bree's mother had come upstairs to find her crying disconsolately, still moving the toothbrush in automatic circles across her teeth, and powerless, with a mouthful of peppermint foam and no vocabulary for it, to explain the feeling.

She had learned to explain it later, to herself. And she had learned to distract herself from thinking about it; but it was there knocking under the floorboards in her apartment, winking at her from the back of the refrigerator, waiting for her in the closet.

She found herself goggling, occasionally, at the people who walked past her every day, wearing their haircuts on their heads and going about their business, and seeming never to have stumbled on this dreadful thought—or if they had stumbled on it, having forgotten it.

In her twenties, she had developed a recurrent half-dream: something that would creep in between her being awake and the little mischiefs of sleep starting to derail her mind. She had learned to control it with pills and rituals and work, but the dream was essentially a dramatization of what was going on in her conscious mind. In these dreams, she died. And instead of things getting quiet and dark and receding, Bree had the sense of something rushing in on her: something that had always been there, but had been hiding—held at bay by the walls and floor and sky, by the surfaces of things. Now her protections fell away. There was a sudden undoing of reality: something unpicking the angles of the corner of the room, the sky unzipping, the floor's tessellations of atoms untoothing and a downflooding of light.

At the same time, the sound of something approaching from a very long way off that would also somehow be just the other side of the walls: a gathering roar, which would make it physically impossible to think, but would be recognizable as it overwhelmed your ears as the sound of a million million million million individual voices—everyone who ever lived or could have lived— whispering a single word.

Bree used to wake with the sound only of her own blood in her ears, and the sheets wet, and the walls and their vertices in place.

Now the dead man was going to bring that back. Bree wanted a beer, now, very much indeed. More than she had wanted one in the many years she had been going to meetings. She made some strong coffee, took two Dylar, waited for breakfast.

18

Ellis told Sherman: "You finish the job. You finish the job, you get it back to us—you'll get paid Noone's bounty too."

Sherman thought about telling Ellis to have some respect— that a man was dead—but he thought Ellis might actually get off, a little, on acting the tough guy about that, so he didn't. He instead looked with distaste at his mobile phone.

"What am I supposed to do with this kid? He's a British national."

"You do whatever you need to do."

Idiot. Sherman diced up telling him to shove it, but decided on balance that that could backfire badly.

He said: "You're the boss. Where do I start looking?"

Ellis said: "He's going west. He had an onward ticket to San Francisco. You know his car. Assume that's where he's going. There's only one road he's likely to be on. All you have to do is follow it."

So Sherman did. But at the same time, Sherman made other precautions.

And when, the next time he called the number he had for Ellis, he heard only the long "bleeeee" of a disconnected line, he put those precautions into action.

He had not been surprised. Whatever Ellis had said, things got too hot. MIC were gamblers, and like any good gamblers, they had decided to quit while they were ahead.

Sherman remembered what, long before he had thumped him, his father had once said to him when drunk: "Life is hell, most people are bastards, and everything is bullshit."

"Disavowed," he said to himself. "Hell, bastards, bullshit." It remained to be seen whether, to extend the figure of speech, he was one of the losses that MIC would be interested in cutting; or whether they were relying on the lumbering local law to do that for them. He didn't intend to find out.

Don't assume anything, was what he thought. Options open. Keep some outs.

His iPod was working again. It was playing REO Speedwagon. He thought of Davidoff, mispronouncing the name, and felt an unaccustomed anger. Davidoff had been set-dressing for these creeps, safe at their desks in front of their computer screens, totting up the numbers, playing the percentages.

Sherman dropped the car, picked up another one across town, and headed as far and as fast as he could out of this story: making time, making distance, making—as he always had—his own luck.

Alex stopped in a Motel 6, sometime after dark, and called Carey. It was past eleven, but he didn't want to go to sleep without hearing another human voice. The phone rang once, twice, three times, and she answered.

"Care?"

"Hey, baby." Her voice was croaky. "It's late. Where you been?" she said. She said something in the background he couldn't hear.

"What?"

"Nothing. Just talking to someone. Wait up." There was a readjustment. He pictured her wriggling to lodge the phone in the crook of her neck. "'Sbetter. Go on. What's up?"

Alex was leaning against the car. Now he could hear her voice, his earlier panic seemed to calm down. That guy was long gone. Carey's voice was sleepy. He pictured her in the pajamas she wore when she slept alone, with the phone crooked into her neck, half paying attention to the television, or yanking open the fridge, or making gestures at him across the room while she talked.

"I'm in America, Carey."

"You're *what*?" Carey spoke the second word in italics.

"I'm here. I'm in America."

She seemed to take a moment to take it in.

"That's great. I mean—where are you? What? You're in San Francisco?"

"No, not quite. I'm more like—I'm in Albuquerque."

"Albuquerque?"

"Well, I was. Few hours back."

"What are you doing there?"

"I'm coming to see you."

"Oh my God!" She sounded like an actress in a teen movie, he thought, the open vowel on the final word like g*aah*d. Then she said it again, catching herself—that was one of the things he loved about her—sounding like an actress in a teen movie and making herself therefore sound more like one.

"Oh my Gaahd!" she said. She was spontaneous the first time. Her voice sounded now like a smile without the eyes going. It was disconcerting.

"I thought I'd surprise you," he muttered.

Now a peal of laughter, unforced. "You have surprised me, crazy English boy. Oh my Lord, that is so romantic. And so"— her voice got muffled momentarily—"sorry—shut up—not you—so . . ." She had lost her thread.

"Shit," she said. "What. I mean, romantic. But stupid. Seriously. What are you doing in Albuquerque?"

"I don't know," he said truthfully. "I was going to surprise you, but I got this flight to Atlanta—"

"Atlanta?"

"Courier. It was a hub. It was in the right general direction."

"Courier?"

"The flight was really, really cheap. I just needed the onward ticket, and then I missed the connecting flight, so now I'm in a car."

"You drove from Atlanta to Albuquerque?"

"I always wanted to go on a road trip."

"You missed the flight is what. This is such a trip. So you coming to San Francisco?" Her voice sounded suddenly less sure, a little knocked off balance.

"I had this idea—you ever been to Vegas?"

Carey laughed. "You said it like Vegas, without the 'Las.' What a player! Soon you'll be calling San Francisco 'Frisco' and we'll know you're from out of town." Alex felt a little deflated. "I'm sorry, baby. You can pronounce Albuquerque Al-ba-kway-kway and you'll be fine by me. Yeah, I've been to Vegas. My folks drove me up there once when I was like thirteen or something to watch them gamble"—Carey always called her foster-parents her "folks," never her mom and dad—"but I haven't been since. Don't think I did much gambling."

"You want to go? Meet me there?"

"Hell yee-ah. What made you think of that? Going to get us married in the Elvis chapel?" She laughed. Alex didn't. He hadn't actually thought of the Elvis chapel. Well, actually, he nearly had. Like with the ring, he wasn't someone who was very good at feeling his way into whether something was so naff it was cool or just naff. And now there was this awkward dead drop in the conversation. She'd been joking and he hadn't responded with the proper levity and now—oh God—it was like there was this fucking great dead badger sitting between them.

He had to say something. "Of course," he said, failing to prevent his voice from sounding serious.

In their relationship there was something, he realized, that caused them to strike each other at near right angles. They didn't quite get each other; from his point of view, it felt like he was always playing catch-up a little. She was hard to read, but he thought that was what made it work. They missed each other that little bit, and then when they caught up they found the misunderstanding funny. He knew he amused her: otherwise she wouldn't spend all that time giggling at him. And she amused him, he thought—though the more he thought about it the more he realized that probably he loved her more than he found her funny.

There. An unevenness. An unevenness he could live with.

"Yeah," he said. "In the Elvis chapel. Just like Chris Evans and Billie."

"Who?" she said.

"Doesn't matter. Just—can you get the weekend off?"

"Sure. Yeah. I mean. Yeah."

"Well, how long will it take you to get there? I don't—I mean, I think I'm about a day away."

"A day? From New Mexico? That's a long day."

"It's all I've been doing for days. Thinking about stuff."

"Hold up," Carey said. "Just moving into the other room. I'm with someone."

She covered the handset and he couldn't hear anything for a moment or two, then he heard a door close.

"Who are you with?"

"Nobody," she said. "Just a friend from work. So, Vegas. Let's do it. I've got air miles. I think they've got flights for like a hundred bucks. Wow. It's hard to imagine you in the States. You're so . . . British."

She didn't sound overexcited. Alex, for an instant, felt that flatness he had felt at the start of his journey. Not lonely, just numb. Why did anybody do anything?

"So, er . . ." He couldn't think of anything to say.

"OK, sweetie, let's talk tomorrow. I'll see about flights, yeah? Vegas. I like it. Let's do it. Two day's time? Where are you staying?"

"Motels."

"Uh-huh. OK." She sounded distracted again.

He reached into his pocket for the ring, something concrete. He turned it in his hand, and he felt less alone.

★   ★   ★

By lunchtime the following day it was fixed. Alex pushed on to Flagstaff, arriving after night fell. He stopped, checked into a motel. The Grand Canyon was near. He imagined its vast absence as he lay on his bed, trying to get to sleep.

On his heels, had he but known it—had they but known it—were Bree and Jones, still heading west, still trusting—as instructed—to luck.

There was little said in the car as they drove. Bree, slightly giddy from not sleeping, was still thinking about what Jones had done, still seeing the surprise on the face of the dead man, still wondering what it would mean to have done the worst thing in the world and not understand what had happened—if, indeed, that was the situation Jones was in. His sunglasses might as well have been armor-plating. There was nothing in there; nothing Bree could understand.

When he was hungry, he would suggest they stopped, and they would eat in silence, standing by the car, Jones looking in whichever direction he happened to be facing; Bree looking in whichever direction Jones wasn't. After that, again, he just drove, eyes blandly scanning the world.

Bree realized, as the miles rolled past under the blank blue sky, that some part of her hated him not for killing the stranger, but for getting away with it. He had done the worst thing in the world, and nothing had happened to him. He didn't fear the consequence. He couldn't feel the loss of another's life any more than he'd feel the loss of his own.

And was it the worst thing in the world, even? No. The worst thing in the world was what Bree had done. Bree had done that years ago. Bree had lost her baby.

She couldn't remember much of the sequence of events. By that stage the memory thief had become brazen. Just flashes, disconnected points of pain, smeared routines. Cass getting her own breakfast and going to school—her spoon clanking softly on her bowl, audible through the partition wall in Bree's dark box of morning pain. Cass, more than once, helping Bree off the couch and into bed. Cass finding bottles and pouring them out, and later, Cass standing barefaced and shaking, chin up, fronting Bree's rage.

She never hit her. She shook her. Never hit her.

And then Cass's own anger—ever since Al had gone. There was bed-wetting first, nothing said. And then, after she started her bleed, the focusless rage of a teenager. Bree had done everything she could to direct Cass's anger at Al. It gave them something to share. It was Al's fault. Al had gone altogether. How could he do that? How could he abandon his own daughter to . . . to Bree.

Trouble at school. Bree hadn't bothered going in to see the head. Bree remembered screaming at the social worker. Marion—pig-faced Marion, with the flakes of dandruff in the dark greasy bit where her hair was parted. Bree hated her whether or not she was doing her job. But the whole machinery went on. Then there were her appearances and non-appearances in court, her desperation, her fantasies, her sloppy embarrassments of love.

Bree even tried to run with her—skip out and run to another state. She pulled Cass out of bed in the middle of the night. It would be like Thelma and Louise, just us girls, she said. She crashed the car into a hydrant, dead drunk, before they reached the end of the street. The seat belt left a purple bruise on the girl's right collarbone and across her sternum. Bree saw it through the bathroom door, set off by the white of Cass's training bra.

When they asked about her rock bottom in meetings, Bree always said it was waking up in the nuthouse: dawn growing blue in the awful window, and shaking with the need for something to make it go dark again. That was nearly a year later, the year she completely lost. She didn't talk about losing Cass. She couldn't share that.

She said to herself that that had been her real rock bottom—that had been the turning point. But what Bree could not turn to face was that losing her daughter had not been her rock bottom. She had loved her daughter, but she had loved drinking more. She had, in the early days of Cass's absence, almost been relieved. Someone else was looking after her; someone good. She could drink safely now. Nobody was watching her.

She hadn't loved her daughter enough to stop drinking, was what the bottom line was. That was a sentence she uttered to herself only when she was so drunk she knew she would forget it.

Every year, at the approach of Cass's birthday, June 29th, Bree thought: this is the year when I go and find her. She could track her through the care system. She could make the correct applications. This is the year, she would think, when I go and knock on the door of her foster-parents' home—she imagined some white suburb, somewhere warm, with a smell of oranges in the air and a clean SUV parked up in the driveway and all that baloney—and say: "I'd like to see Cassie." That would be the year when she would show the young woman who had once been her daughter a fistful of recovery medallions, and beg for her forgiveness. And then what?

She could see Cass—all the different versions, from the first sight of her. Purple face, whitened with vernix, screaming in the hospital. The double whorl in her hair. The surge of love and exhaustion as she first held her weight—her future coiled into that tiny body. The last words she had heard Cass say had been: "Please. I don't want to leave my mom." She couldn't see Cass now. She was a young woman and her face was nobody's, something indecipherable, unavailable to Bree's imagination.

Most years she went to two meetings that day, and didn't talk about Cass. One year, early on, she came within the crack of a screw cap of a bottle of brandy from relapsing. The thought that she couldn't do it made her desperate to take a drink; the thought that she might one day do it kept her from it.

But she had still never looked for Cass. She could not come face to face, not in that way, with the center of her shame. She thought Cass would forgive her—and she thought that there was no way, no way on earth, that she would be able to bear that.

Are you ashamed, Jones? Can you be forgiven? Bree slept that night in a motel in Flagstaff, forty feet from where Alex Smart slept. She, too, felt the giant absence of the Grand Canyon out in the night, but exhaustion took her this time and she was almost grateful when she had the death-dream instead of any other one.

19

A day and a half later, Alex arrived where he was going. Las Vegas rose out of the desert like a mirage. Even from this distance, it looked like a place that someone had invented, or dreamed about after falling asleep with the central heating on too high and a belly full of Stilton.

Alex arrived in town early in the afternoon, and opened the windows to the dirty heat. He was wondering what the inside of the car smelled like. After the desert, where there was no direction but forward, and no other cars on the road, he found himself again on multi-lane highways, being bullied by SUVs shouldering from lane to lane.

The movement of traffic pulled him down into the center. He found himself traveling slowly, from stoplight to stoplight, down the broad, gaudy Las Vegas Boulevard. The Strip: it was a place at once new to him and familiar—a place that had lived, in jumbled form, in his imagination. He'd seen it overflown endlessly, by helicopter, in the title credits of *CSI*—the Eiffel Tower and the Montgolfier balloon traced in blue neon, the pyramid shooting a beam of light into the sky; the burlesque monumental lions outside the MGM Grand; the anonymous coppery curve of the Wynn. He'd zoomed in on it, too, in Google Earth: monumental schematics from the air; frozen images at street level; granular, gaudy and smeared with light.

Was it as he had imagined it? He didn't know. It seemed to come pre-imagined. But it occurred to him as he drove that he hadn't seen it in daylight before: it wasn't intended to be seen in daylight. The concrete and stone answered the sun with a wan brightness. It looked as worn and bleached out as Christmas tree lights discovered in the attic in summer.

He drove up to the top of town, and pulled into the stacked lot of one of the older-looking, shabbier-looking hotels on Fremont Street. He parked the car and an elevator took him to the lobby. There was an old guy wearing an honest-to-goodness cowboy hat leaning on the desk, staring past the waistcoated clerk at nothing. His face was a pained squint, and red thread veins pooled at the hinge of his jaw. Nobody was attending to him. His jaw tightened and relaxed.

Alex checked in. His room was on the eighth floor—it was shabby and small and brown everywhere and it smelled of old smoke. A double-glazed sliding window in a metal frame looked out onto a stained concrete wall gridded with identical windows, the other wing of the H-shaped hotel. Past that, the view toward the north—simmering low-rise, ribboned with tan overpasses.

He felt, at that moment, exhausted. It was another four hours before he was meeting Carey. He lay down on the coverlet of the bed, and fell asleep there without even taking his shoes off.

He woke up with a feeling close to fright. The air conditioner was roaring. His mouth was gummy, his head sore and sweat had chilled on his skin. The light outside was metallic, now, and when he went to the window the facing wall of the hotel was the color of dirty brass in the old sun.

He should have been looking forward to seeing Carey but he was feeling, again, dislocated, unworthy, indecipherable. It made him panicky.

The problem is that when I'm alone I literally cease to believe that I exist.

He said the words to himself aloud, just to feel the air across his tongue. It was something he'd remembered from somewhere, not his own thought. He looked at his rucksack. It belonged to a stranger. He rubbed the back of his neck. His watch told him it was seven o'clock. He was probably just hungry.

★　　★　　★

They had arranged to meet in the Golden Nugget at eight. Alex had suggested meeting her flight, but Carey said that'd be a drag. She had heard that the casino contained the world's biggest nugget of gold. "Let's meet there! Just you, me and a big gold rock. It'll be cute."

Walking into the casino was like walking into an aquarium. The door—no, the entire wall—was permanently open to the outside. It gaped. The mouth of a whale. Not an aquarium. Not just an aquarium. An aquarium and its contents. A mechanical whale, trawling for human plankton. No need to suck: just leave the mouth open and let them wash in.

Even during the heat of a cloudless day, something seemed to stop the sunshine spilling from Fremont Street into the building: a filter in the air—an invisible baleen plate. Within a couple of steps the crisp hot light bouncing off the pavement outside would be gone. There was only the indecipherable carpet, the high ceiling, and slot machines arrayed in rows and islands under the buttery artificial light. It felt like cigarettes and acid stomach and the headachy buzz you get when you pass through tiredness into the unreal underwater feeling on the other side.

You turned round and the pleasant sunshine outside was a wall of white. Reality was oversaturated. It hurt the eyes. Safer in here. The second time you turned round you couldn't find the opening back to the outside world at all. And now, in the evening, the inside started to colonize the outside. That border was porous, after all. But the unreality inside seeped onto the street like smoke.

A shift in the current and you had turned round, lost your bearings. The direction you struck out in was wrong. The angles were wrong. That wall wasn't that wall. It wasn't even a wall at all. That bar was a different bar.

The slots fanned and pulsed. Through alleys of fluorescent coral, portly men in T-shirts lumbered like groupers. Some grazed on the machines, bland-faced and blissful as fish. Old women perched on stools, human spider crabs, barking their yellowed foreclaws on the panels. Cocktail waitresses moved purposefully, dartingly, alertly. Clownfish.

Alex had somehow imagined the sound in the casino would be a cacophony, but it was soothing. He had expected to hear whirring and clattering—and that was there, if you listened for it—but in aggregate it was a sort of anesthetizing white noise, like the sound of the sea.

Over the top, the bleeps and squelches of electronic noise, snatches of tunes, here and there cataracts of imaginary money pouring into imaginary metal containers, digitally simulated. Behind, the purr of a million coins flipping, a million tumblers coming to rest and then starting in motion again, a million balls settling into sockets, a million cards burring into new configurations.

Alex remembered seeing a documentary, once, about a casino in America where women bought buckets of coins and sat, all day and all night, feeding them into the slot machines. There was something devotional about the act: patiently, unsleepingly, as if in a trance, they fed the coins into slots and pressed the button to spin the reels.

With every press of the button, there came a near-imperceptible tensing in the shoulders: a tiny jolt of hope. Then, as the wheels came to rest, came a readjustment. Every few spins, the machine would cough a handful of coins into its trough, and the women would look rejuvenated, freshened: hope satisfied. The coins would be swept back into the bucket, ready to be fed in.

The machines were playing the people, rather than vice versa, it had occurred to Alex. Nearly half the time, the women would have more coins in the bucket than they had started with—but a tilt of the algorithm, the tiniest pressure of a thumb on the scales, meant that the number of coins in the bucket tended, over the long run, toward zero.

Every small score was not a win, but a rebate: a contribution to the struggle, a prolongation of the period of time in which the player was able to believe that the impossible could happen. As they fed these coins in, whittling their chances down the long curve to zero, the same process was going on in every cell in their bodies.

But here there were no buckets, no coins. The clatter of money was synthesized. Just as the blackjack players, on their fields of baize deeper in the casino, exchanged their cash for plastic chips, the slots players now fed dollar bills into machines. You could see them, out of cash, approaching the machines peevishly, feeding ragged cloth bucks into the machines' mouths, having them whirr and spit back. Rubbing the dollars flat on the top of the machine, straightening out the bent corners, thumbing the face of the dead president, feeding them back in, hoping.

If the casino gods were smiling on them, their money would disappear and stay disappeared, and the machine would politely blurt out a white paper slip. It was this that they would feed into the machine.

Paper money was translated into electrons, which were translated into paper, which was translated into electrons, which were translated into paper, which was translated into electrons, which were translated into paper money.

That made sense. This was a place where money—never something strongly tethered to reality—slipped anchor and became altogether imaginary. And the more imaginary it got, the more like itself it became. This was money in its purest, most contingent form—owned, in the perpetual instant of play, by nobody. It existed in a field of probabilities—between the hope of the impossible and the knowledge of the inevitable.

Alex walked the casino floor. His dizziness subsided and a sort of calm came over him. Seven forty-five. Fifteen minutes to kill. He found the nugget glistering in a glass box. Really quite big—nuggets, as Alex had always thought of them, were no bigger than a Tic Tac. This nugget was supposed to look a bit like a hand, but it looked more like a bit of coral. It looked gaudy. It looked like a fake nugget—as if the gold had been sprayed on from a can.

He had just sat down with a rumpled ten to worship at a nickel slot machine when a hand on his shoulder and a voice hazy with travel said: "Hey."

He turned round and stood up and there was Carey, in the old Dead Kennedys T-shirt she used to sleep in, jeans frayed at the hip, hair down, brown-armed and smiling.

"Hey," said Alex, and felt as happy as he ever had. "You're early."

"So are you," said Carey. Her arms were warm on his neck as he hugged her.

He pulled back and said more or less without drawing breath: "It's so good to see you. Look! Vegas! I'm playing a slot machine. What's up? How was your flight? Enough about you, let's talk about me. My God, I've had this weird road trip, I swear, every lunatic in America has tried to kill me or make friends with me. Where's your stuff?"

Carey lifted her pink vinyl shoulder bag by its strap. "Traveled light. Underwear, change of T-shirt, lipstick in case I need to go hooking to earn back what I lose at poker."

"Want to go back to my hotel and put it in the room?"

"Hell no! This is Las Vegas. Let's hit the town. Waitron! Bring me . . . a daiquiri." There was no waitress anywhere in sight. She waved her arm as if twirling an invisible baton, then shouldered Alex out of the way and slammed the palm of her hand onto the fat SPIN button in the center of the machine's console. It quacked and blurted, shuffled its numbers.

"I win!" said Carey.

"No, you don't," said Alex.

"Oh," said Carey. "No, I don't. Does it make that noise when you lose? Imagine the noise when we win. OK. Cash out. Let's hit the town."

"Hang on," said Alex. He pressed the button again. The reels moved. There was a simulated cascade of falling coins.

"Magic hands," said Alex, waggling his fingers.

"We won," said Carey. "Jackpot!" Three oranges. They were thirty-five cents up.

"We won!" Alex repeated. "Go, us. OK, let's cash out and explore the"—his hand moved toward the CASH/CREDIT button but Carey swiped it away—"town—"

"Are you crazy? We're on a streak."

"There's only ten dollars in there . . ."

"Shhh." She pressed the button again.

An hour and a half later, having never been more than $4.85 up, and having finally gone down to zero, they left to go into town.

Carey and Alex were doing what you do in Las Vegas. They sat at one of the bars in Circus Circus—Carey had demanded that they go in, claiming without a hint of sincerity that she had been frightened of clowns as a child and that it would be good aversion therapy—and played the video poker game embedded in the actual bar. Alex had won $100 on his first go, and Carey had then spent fifteen minutes losing it while they drank their watery screwdrivers.

Then when they got hungry they looked for somewhere to eat and realized that everything was either a cheap chain restaurant or an expensive chain restaurant, so they went to a cheap chain restaurant and had fajitas. The restaurant was dimly lit and noisy with pop-punk music with Mexican lyrics. Teenagers with glow sticks round their necks hip-swayed between tables, taking orders as if they had trains to catch and returning to drop the food off with casual violence.

The meat came on lethally hot metal skillets. The tortillas came in a plastic simulacrum of a wicker basket, accompanied by a plastic simulacrum of a saucer containing a plastic simulacrum of grated cheese.

They bought long, bulbed plastic horns containing pre-mixed margaritas dispensed by a machine, which were only drinkable because they were so tooth-hurtingly cold that you couldn't taste how sweet they were. They took the remains of them out onto the street and walked down the Strip.

When? Not now. Not now. Not now.

They continued to walk until their aimlessness started to become something palpable, an awkwardness between them.

Even ordinarily, Alex would be anxious in this situation. Nothing made him more anxious than the need or expectation of having fun. Vegas was a place devoted to the idea of fun. Everyone, everywhere you looked, was trying to have fun.

Alex had brought Carey here under the pretense of having fun. He worried he wasn't having fun. He worried even more that Carey wasn't having fun, or, at least, that whatever fun they were having—the food was OK, wasn't it? They hadn't lost all their money gambling—was deprived of sunlight and water by the enormous shadow of the fun they should have been having, by comparison with which their own meager portion of fun was a wretched failure.

Oh God. What was he thinking of?

He looked over at Carey to see whether it looked like she was having fun. It was impossible to tell. She wasn't hooting with laughter and throwing her head back. She was just sort of walking down the street looking at stuff. She had a drink in her hand, at least. Good.

Alex had finished his own drink. Ever since he had started worrying about the aimlessness—that is, he had an aim, obviously, but the more he wound up to it the less he was able to communicate with the outside world, and until he had done so his companion would be left with the overwhelming impression of aimlessness—he had been sucking away on his margarita so as to be doing something even if he wasn't saying something.

It was a margarita in a brightly colored plastic cup, a foot long. It said so on the side of the cup. Foot-long margarita. With a foot-long straw. That was fun, surely. That was drinks plus fun. Alex felt utterly adrift.

It was probably ages since he'd said anything. Had she noticed? Was she bored?

He knew he should say something. Say something. That was the thing. But the only thing he could think of to say was "Will you marry me?" and even though that was the exact thing to say the moment was wrong. You couldn't just come out of the blue with it, could you? Just abruptly? She'd think he was a loon. Or, worse, joking.

Here? Not here. Not in the street. Yes. Why not? In the street. This is your life. This is your life, going by, and you're going to look back on this moment as the moment when you didn't take the decision that would have made you happy for the rest of your days on earth. With this American girl you love wholeheartedly.

You know you love her wholeheartedly. You have said so to yourself, and had you a diary you would have written it in your diary. You cannot always, when called on, feel the love as a wave of emotion—not in the way you could when you watched her sleep, before you were a couple, or the way you can when she's somewhere else and you miss her. But you know it's there. It's just—it's something you take for granted. Something you're so quietly sure of you barely examine it.

Action. For goodness' sake. Action. That's all. Just do it.

Alex thought about how he used to trick himself into jumping into swimming pools. You ran up to the edge promising yourself that this was just a practice run and that you were going to stop, and then when you got to the edge you simply kept running and took the view that you would apologize to yourself later for the white lie. Always, a great body-shocking spout of cold water to the chest and crotch, bubbles of air foaming up around the ears and neck, and limbs paddling at once, spastic with surprise.

"Carey," said Alex. He looked past her shoulder. There was nobody there. The Strip was empty as far as the next corner and the sky above was a perspectiveless blue-black. It was warm, and away behind him he could hear the hiss and swish and flop of the fountains outside the Bellagio dancing their exhausted dance.

"Mmm?" Carey was distracted. She took another sip of her margarita and Alex admired with a little wave of desperation the way her cheek pulsed inward as she drew on her orange straw.

Alex felt the ring, in its square box, digging against his hip. He was on the verge of action. He felt a little dizzy. He remembered that once he had tried the swimming-pool trick, a little drunk, in the shallow end of a pool with submerged steps. He had driven the little toe of his right foot into the corner of the lowest step, and gulped a lungful of water. Saul had pulled him out in time for him not to drown. For the next fortnight, his broken toe had been so painful that simply hopping downstairs on the other foot had, with every step, sent an inertial throb of blood into the digit that had caused him to gasp.

He went on, anyway.

"You know what you said about the Elvis chapel?" he said.

"What Elvis chapel?" said Carey, turning her eyes to his. She brought the straw back up to her lips and pursed them around it. She had a look of blank expectation. Alex looked at his feet.

"Well," said Alex. "I wanted to say. Look."

Alex thought of getting onto one knee, here on the pavement, but he knew in this instant—with the certainty that he knew he would never climb Kilimanjaro, or emerge victorious from a fist fight, or play a significant role in the history of the human race, or be unconditionally adored by beautiful teenage girls, and with the faint, humming sadness that accompanied those certainties—that getting down on one knee in public was something he did not have the ability to do.

"Carey, what I'm trying to say is—"

And he could not meet her eye. And then he could. She was still holding her margarita, in its big pink plastic yard-of-ale tube, up in front of her chest. Her arms were slim and golden from the sun, and her big Dead Kennedys T-shirt was not quite formless enough to prevent the curve of her breasts from being visible.

She looked beautiful. Alex felt the moment freeze-framing into a memory. He felt as if he was looking back in time to this moment, from some point in the future. But he still didn't know what happened next. Carey slurped her margarita.

Alex glanced nervously over her shoulder. The street was no longer empty. Three men in white suits, walking abreast, were waiting at the crosswalk ahead. Something familiar about them.

Alex put it aside, turned back to Carey, took a deep breath, closed his fist on the sharp-cornered parcel in his pocket, made himself look directly at her quizzical, almost slightly peevish face. A face saying: yup, what? Get on with it . . .

"Carey. Love. Will you—"

Carey took another big slurp of her margarita. Evidently the last. The straw made a violently diarrhoeic noise in the crushed ice. Alex gave a nervous yip, and then barked with laughter. Carey looked baffled.

"What's funny?"

"Just—the noise your thing made. It's nothing. I don't know. Silly mood, I guess. I'm just happy being here with you. Sorry."

"Don't apologize."

"Sorry."

"Are you OK?" she said. "You've been acting a bit—just since we ate—a bit distant."

"Oh, no, no. Shall we walk? No, I'm fine. I was just thinking about. What do you want to do next?"

The white-suited men were getting closer. As they approached Alex could see what was familiar about them. They were Elvis. All three of them. One fat Elvis and two thin ones. The white suits were jumpsuits. The fat one, disconcertingly, had a star-spangled

V-shape from shoulders to crotch. It was hard to tell how old they were, because they were wearing identical black wigs and identical fuzzy-felt sideburns and sunglasses the size of drinks coasters. But judging by the way they were walking they were epically drunk.

The fat Elvis lurched left, inadvertently shoulder-barging the thin Elvis in the middle, which sent him into the other thin Elvis, who pushed tetchily back.

"—even listening to me?"

"Yes, love, sorry. Look out. Those three drunks."

As the Elvises ambled up level with them, Alex grabbed Carey's elbow and pulled her out of the way. Too late. Fat Elvis barged into the back of her. Carey's drink tumbled from her hand and bounced on the sidewalk.

"Hey!" she exclaimed. The Elvises rolled on, oblivious.

"Hey!" Carey said again. "Why don't you look where you're going? That was my drink, you dick."

Half past them, now, the Elvises turned round. Alex didn't like the expression on Fat Elvis's face.

"You say to me, girlie?"

"I called you a dick," said Carey. She pushed out her lip. When she lost her temper, Carey had a tendency to forget that she was a slightly built woman in her early twenties rather than, say, a light-middleweight boxing champion.

"Don't call him an asshole," said the thin Elvis in the Evel Knievel suit. "'S an accident."

"I've hit a girl before," said Fat Elvis. Alex believed him.

"I didn't call him an asshole," said Carey. "I called him a dick." Her face was flushed. Alex was petrified. "He smashed into me and made me spill my drink. And then he was walking off with-out so much as turning round to say sorry. And he's fat, and he's ugly, and he's dressed like a dick. I call that dickish."

Fat Elvis was taking this in. He paused, swaying a bit. Then he spoke to Alex, dead-eyed.

"You need to keep that mouth of hers under control."

He'd barely reached the end of the sentence when Carey slapped him with a report loud enough to make Alex wince. In films, scenes like this seemed to result in moments of stunned silence, but Fat Elvis moved very fast indeed. Barely had the blow landed than he lurched forward with a roar, grabbing at Carey's wrist. He missed, just, and Carey hopped backward.

Alex, on instinct, bopped Fat Elvis on the head with the only thing he had to hand, which was his empty plastic funnel of drink. What impact it made was cushioned by his nylon quiff, but it knocked him slightly off balance.

As he came back up it was immediately apparent he intended violence. Carey swung her handbag, catching him on one sideburn.

"Hey!" shouted the other thin Elvis.

"Run!" shouted Alex, and run they did, with three drunk Elvises in pursuit.

Alex pounded along the pavement. Carey was a bit ahead of him, lifting up her knees, pistoning her arms, her baseball boots flashing red-white and caramel back at him.

"Pricks! Fucking pricks!" Carey was shouting over her shoulder between breaths.

"SHUT . . . UP!" said Alex, much less fit than Carey. By the end of the block they had pulled away from the Elvises but his breath was already ragged. "You're going—to get—me . . . killed."

They swerved through oncoming pedestrians, dip-diving around stationary gawpers. The cross light was flashing "Walk" and Alex saw Carey make the snap call to go for it. He hop-skipped through the intersection with a blare of horns.

They gained the opposite pavement and Alex bounced off someone's shoulder, earning a shout of indignation, and a splat of what seemed to be ice cream on the cheek, but then Alex looked up and realized they were heading into the thick of a crowd.

Carey, ahead of him, wormed shoulder-forward between two people with cameras and ducked into the crowd.

Behind him, Alex heard the shout of what he guessed was one of the Elvises hitting ice-cream guy head on, buying them a second or two, and then he was into the thickening mass himself.

"Sorry, sorry, sorry, sorry, sorry. . . ."

"Hey—"

"—with my friend . . . sorry, sorry, sorry, sorry . . . ."

There was music to the side, and bright lights. Some sort of show. Alex kept his head down. Behind him, the sound of further collisions.

"—you, Elvis!"

"—the damn way . . ."

He plowed on, keeping his head down. He popped his head up. He could see Carey, lither and pushier, extending her lead.

"Sorry, sorry, sorry . . ."

The crowd was very thick, now. The whole of the pavement had been fenced in with wooden boards and netting, and the crowd was jammed into that space. There were planks underfoot and light—golden, green, and red—was pulsing. Alex's arm barked against a rough rope. A loud fusillade of bangs caused him to whip his head round—above the crowd and back from the pavement he could see what looked like a boat, its rigging scarved with multicolored smoke. Hanging from the rigging were girls in bikinis with eyepatches and pirate hats, waggling their legs.

Alex put his head down and plunged on, wriggling through the thickest part of the crowd. As the crowd thinned he caught up with Carey, grabbed her arm.

He risked a backward glance. He couldn't see the Elvises. He pulled her down and against the wooden barrier between the pavement and the road. They squatted there, between a thicket of legs. As he squatted, his trousers tightened at the hip, and the ring box dug in.

Carey's face was bright with exhilaration. She grabbed the back of his head and kissed him on the lips, then let him go.

"Not funny!" he hissed. "It was me they were going to beat up—" and then he stopped momentarily as he saw what looked like three sets of white legs, trousers tellingly flared, coming through the crowd. He pushed his hand over Carey's mouth and studied the pavement. The legs went past.

"Not funny," he repeated, but now they weren't actually going to be beaten up what had been scary started to seem funny. He was shaky with adrenalin.

"Marry me," he said.

"Sure," she said.

He got up, thighs creaking, from his squat and meerkatted up. There was no sign of the Elvises. A wooden walkway coming off the pavement at right angles led to the entrance to a casino. Alex pointed, steered Carey by the elbow, and jostled through into the lobby.

"Drink," he said.

They walked, Alex still holding Carey's elbow, across the wide hideous carpet in the direction of a large, brassy, over-marbled bar in a thicket of slot machines and palm trees.

Behind the bar was a girl who looked from the waist down like she was playing Dick Whittington in panto at the Yvonne Arnaud theater, Guildford, and from the waist up like she was a bellhop in a pornographic movie.

"Champagne," said Alex. "We'd like, please. Two glasses."

"Sir," she said without smiling.

"Care, you are a psychopath," he said. Carey beamed.

"Not taking shit from Elvis," she said.

The woman set two tall flutes of champagne in front of them. She slipped a silver tray down between them with a paper bill face down on it. Carey picked it up.

"Crap!" said Carey. "That's eighty bucks."

"Don't worry about it," Alex said. "I won in the casino earlier, remember."

"But eighty bucks!"

"Seriously." He made a point of looking into her face as he smiled. "This is a special occasion."

He moved his hand over hers, took the bill, replaced it face down on the silver tray. Then he dropped one leg off the bar stool so he could get into his pocket. He pulled out the box, and he put it in on the fake marble bar top between them. He looked at Carey.

She looked at the box. He could hear the blood rushing in his ears. The moment was right.

"Open it," he said.

Carey looked very unsure. She didn't move at all.

"It's for you," Alex said. "Have a look."

The waitress behind the bar was listening with her back to them, pretending to polish some glasses. Carey fiddled with her hands. He could see that she knew what was in the box, and the expression on her face was one of shock and fear. She pushed the box away from her, no more than half an inch, with the back of her knuckles.

"Open it," he said again.

"What is it?" she said.

"Open it."

She did, sadly, and she looked at the ring, its glitter. And then she looked at him, and she looked away. She looked miserable.

"Carey—" he said. Something cold settled in his chest. This wasn't how it was supposed to go. "Carey. I want us to get married." He heard his voice say that. But now it felt like he was watching the scene from a long, long way away. As if he was sitting on the moon, watching his proposal of marriage stall through a telescope—its details scratchy and distant and oddly painless.

She continued looking at the ring. Her eyes were welling.

"Can we just forget this?" she said in a small voice. Alex was accustomed to Carey having a brisk bossiness, a confidence in her manner—but she seemed floored, lost suddenly. He was sitting at this bar with a stranger.

He took a sip of his champagne.

"Yes," he said coldly. "Of course. So sorry." He reached out and went to retrieve the ring, getting as far as snapping the case shut before Carey yelped and put her hand on his, holding it there. Her knuckles were pale. Her face was contorted. The mole on the corner of her chin—where he'd kissed. It was nothing: a blemish. How suddenly and how absolutely what was familiar had become strange; someone he had imagined part of him was just another human animal.

"Don't, don't, don't," she said. Alex left his hand where it was. He looked at the surface of the bar. He was conscious of the waitress not watching, polishing glasses.

"I've got to go now," he said. His face felt very cold. You can't come back from this. He took his hand away and got down off his stool, not looking at her, and put the ring box back in his pocket and walked toward where they had come in without looking back at her. They hadn't gone deep enough in for casino geography to do its work. He still knew how to get out.

He had just reached where the walkway began when he realized that he hadn't paid for the drinks. He turned and went back, fast, feeling a burst of anger. Carey was where she had been and she was looking at him. Her face was wet, and it opened—the whole face—like she'd seen him giving her a second chance.

He ignored her, pushing up against the bar, snatching at the little silver tray with the bill on it and leaning forward to catch the attention of the waitress. Alex thrust his hand in his right-hand jeans pocket and pulled out some crumpled notes— what were these?—twenty, twenty, ten, a five, ones . . . not enough.

"Alex," she said. She put her hand to his elbow and he jerked it away. He didn't look at her.

He pulled his credit card out of his other pocket. "Waitress," he said with a venom that surprised him. She ignored him. "Waitress!"

The waitress turned round with slow ostentation, took in Carey crying, and looked up at him. If there had been a hint of a smirk, a hint of an arched eyebrow, in her expression Alex would have hit her. Her smile was bright and icy. She hated him.

"I need to pay this bill."

"Certainly, sir."

"Alex, please," said Carey—pulling this time at his forearm. Her face was imploring him. "Please. I'm sorry, please, don't go—don't be so horrible, talk to me, please, I'm sorry . . ."

"You have nothing to be sorry about," he said. "I'm sorry. I made a mistake and"—he pulled away with real violence this time—"get *off* me."

She looked startled.

"Don't touch me, Carey. I'm serious. Do you know what I—"

The waitress came back with the credit-card machine. It ticked and chirred. She passed it to Alex. It was deadweight in his hands. He punched in his pin then waited, looking at the gaudy ceiling of the casino and clenching his jaw.

"Aaaand . . ." the waitress said, pulling the strip from the top of the machine with bright professionalism, hitting a button with the heel of her hand and handing card and slippery receipts to Alex. Her overlong red fingernails fanned in the air as she did it.

Alex turned round and went again, and Carey made no attempt to follow him.

He fought through the crowd that was still hanging round the end of the pirate show and walked in no particular direction up the street, and kept walking.

20

I detest Alex, don't you? I didn't want to mention it, at first, but I can't keep quiet any longer. What sort of a hero does he think he is?

The self-pity! The petulance! And so wet. He didn't want Carey for Carey. He wanted Carey because he couldn't think of anything else to want. But really he didn't know what he wanted. He wanted someone to save him from the awful monotonousness of being Alex.

I was hoping to like him, but I've run out of patience. Poor Carey! It's not her fault she doesn't want to marry her drippy English boyfriend. He could have been kind to her. Now she's feeling wretched and he's off in another of his self-absorbed little tantrums. And Carey did love him, enough, in her way. But she knew that if she said yes he'd think that was the end. She didn't want to be his rescuer, his mother, the person who was to blame for his happiness, a bit part in his small life.

Bree would hate him too, I think, if she knew him. Bree, like Sherman, believes we make our own luck. She may be wrong about that. Not as wrong as Sherman, mind—sorry, I'm getting ahead of myself. But wrong nonetheless. At least she knows what she's doing, though. She works. She keeps her head down. She tries to make amends. She has some discipline—now, at least, she does. She even thought she could help Jones.

Alex has none of Bree's discipline. Carey is suffering, sitting back there in the bar in Treasure Island, crying, while the hard woman who served the champagne and didn't even get a tip, calls her honey and asks her if she wants to talk. She wants to talk.

This is Alex's fault. Alex made all of this happen, by doing nothing. By allowing himself to feel only what he thought he ought to feel, by faking it, by truly knowing he wanted her only when she wasn't part of his story.

Alex made all this happen. And now he's going to have to suffer through it.

The anger faded from Alex as he walked, and the coldness, and in it a peculiar ache took hold. He looked at all the neon and felt a loneliness that carried, somewhere at the heart of it, its own thrill.

That was that. He walked up the Strip, wondering what to do. He couldn't go back. He couldn't go back to his hotel. And the Strip was so long and so full of people, the buildings so massive. Everything was heavy here.

He walked for a long time, waiting at intersections for the sign to say "Walk" and then walking across, and walking to the next huge intersection and waiting for the sign to say "Walk." He kept going, up out past the big hotels. A guy came forward and tried to give him a free glossy magazine. He ignored him.

On the pavement there were cigarette butts, glossy flyers for shows, glossy flyers for girls. Massage and escort. Glossy orange breasts, white smiles, gaudy typefaces, phone numbers, phone numbers, phone numbers. Fake photographs, real phone numbers.

Up ahead he could see a slim concrete tower, bone white, rising from the other side of the Strip. It seemed to go half a mile into the sky. At the top, some sort of observation deck pulsed with light, and as he looked, tiny wheels rotated and swung over the edge and back again. A red light shot up the spire above the observation deck and shuddered back down. Fairground rides, he realized—people allowing themselves a moment or two of the fear of falling, the fear of acceleration, the fear of surrendering control.

Alex kept walking. Further ahead, another blurt of neon: a pair of hearts knitting and unknitting unceasingly, a white cross: a wedding chapel. He needed to be away from here. He took one of the roads off the Strip and walked down it, away from the people and the lights, and when he saw a shabby-looking bar he went into it and sat down.

There was a long bar, a pool table, a jukebox and a funk of smoke. The walls were entirely covered in beer mats and most of what light there was came from old neon on the walls, a green crown-cap bottle the size of a baseball bat and a red horse with a yellow cowboy on it.

"What?" said the barman.

"Whiskey, please," said Alex, and regretted the "please."

"Up?"

"Sorry? Oh. Yeah. Please."

Alex put ten dollars down, and necked the whiskey while the barman brought him his change. It was bourbon, and it gave his throat a sweet scald. He coughed. He put a single dollar bill on the bar for a tip and asked for another.

The barman scratched his neck, poured it, watched Alex drink the second. Alex wasn't used to drinking shots—he didn't normally even like whiskey much, and bourbon less—and a swimmy calm descended on him. He was playing at being someone else. Drinking hard was what you were supposed to do, he thought, in these circumstances.

He had a third, more slowly after a moment of reflux made him gag, and then the fourth was on the house. Alex stared glassily across the bar at the bottles, and behind the mirror in which he could see his own dark reflection, and tried to think about what had happened.

He had been shocked. Now the shock was thawing into shame. Why had he been angry at Carey? It hadn't been her fault. He was mouthing to himself. He'd just sprung it on her. She was shocked. And then he'd reacted instantly, and in the worst way—But the *pity*, that was what got to him. The look of sadness on her face. That was what had humiliated him. She looked *sorry* for him. He couldn't stand to be around her, and that was tough shit on her. What was she thinking of? Coming to Las Vegas with him. She'd come to dump him. That was—Christ, no wonder she'd been embarrassed. What a fucking, fucking idiot. Nice one, Smart. Simpering. The ring. The whole thing. If she'd had any sort of courage she'd have dumped him by text message.

Even in pain, Alex noted, he was still more than capable of feeling the sting of embarrassment.

All that remained to do was to pick up his humiliation and go home. Pay off the car. Pawn the ring—well, he couldn't exactly recycle it, could he? He barked mirthlessly. And then he thought of going to a pawn shop and handing it over for a few dollars. He liked the hurting tawdriness of it. Or just throw it in a bin.

But he *loved* her! Some small abject part of him wailed. He couldn't get round that. And never more so, he thought, than now. Just the thought of her skin made a lump come to his throat. What if he went back? This could be just a row. They could just forget about it. He rehearsed that thought without sincerity.

He ordered another whiskey, and was just leaving the tip on the bar when his phone leaped in his pocket and his stomach fell through the seat of his chair. Carey? He pulled it out. No. Not Carey. A text message.

It was from Rob. The message said: "How Green Was My Valet?" He looked at it blankly. It was like a message from another universe, a time capsule from an age when he had thought stupid jokes were funny. He turned off his phone, settled back at the bar, had another whiskey, went back to feeling sorry for himself. If he drank enough, he reasoned, not only would the truth of his feelings become apparent to him, but the course of action he needed to take would also decide itself for him.

He found himself attending to the background noise of the jukebox. He was reaching just that mood when whatever song comes on will acquire a generalized sense of tragic grandeur. Had "Barbie Girl" or the "Birdie Song" come on, they would have seemed to speak directly to him of the futility of life. As it was, he had mawked his way already through "Simple Twist of Fate," "Born to Follow," and—bizarrely—"Cum On Feel the Noize."

Then, in a ragged tangle of chords, underpinned by a sluggish drumbeat, another song he recognized began, and he rested his elbows on the bar, pushed his cheeks up with the heels of his hands and closed his eyes.

Once I thought I saw you . . . in a crowded hazy bar . . .

His lips moved quietly to the words. She was. She was like a hurricane. She was spontaneous and—were hurricanes spontaneous? Never mind—free and . . . she danced like a hurricane, like hurricanes dance, from one star to another, on the light . . .

Chugging, chiming, sad-defiant. The song made no sense at all, but it seemed in that instant to mean everything to Alex. There were calms in her eyes. And, like a hurricane, Carey had blown the modest bungalow of his happiness flat.

If he hadn't thought the barman would see him, laugh at him and stop serving him, he would have allowed himself a blub.

Alex still had his eyes closed when Sherman emerged from the door of the washroom and started walking down the bar. The toilet, for reasons Sherman didn't want to think about, was entirely painted in textured black gloss paint, and the bulb in there had gone. Sherman had been in this dive long enough— fifteen bottles of Molson long, ever since he'd lost most of his stack at blackjack up on Fremont Street—and the toilet had made his decision for him. Here, in the fanciest town he'd ever been in, he'd found a khazi that would have disgraced a rough pub in Plymouth.

He'd been standing tiptoe on sodden wads of bum roll, the closest he could get to the pan, leaning over forward with one hand steadying himself on the cistern pipe. Occasional glints of light from outside showed a seatless bowl, sprinkled with drops, in the general direction of which he had pissed with ferocious need. He had shaken off, nearly losing his footing as he did so on the slippery floor, and walked out with the full intention of finding somewhere very, very cheap to kip.

And it was then that he clocked the skinny kid at the bar, nodding his head to the music like a nonce. And it occurred to him that something about the kid was familiar.

No, he exhaled quietly. You are shitting me. That's the prick that killed Davidoff.

Sherman's first thought—which was his first thought in pretty much all circumstances in any case—was that something fishy was going on. What were the chances of the little bastard fetching up here? And why? He hadn't seemed keen to speak the last time they'd met.

Could it be Ellis tying up loose ends? One of the reasons Sherman had chosen Vegas was that it was an easy city to get lost in, an easy city to make money safe in. If there was going to be a clean-up operation, Sherman had been determined to make sure he was out of the way of the mop.

He'd been careful—booked a flight to LAX, booked a ticket on a Grayhound bus east with his credit card, not taken it, and paid for another ticket on a bus to Las Vegas with cash. That one, he had got aboard. He'd been here less than twenty-four hours. If they had figured out he was here, they really wanted to find him. And that was very bad news for him.

It *was* the kid, though.

OK, smooth. The smart thing to do was slip out and get lost. But. But. The blackjack—dealer paying 21 twice in a row, Sherman doubled down both times and stuck on 20—the beer, the fact he was going to be staying in some horrible hotel again, the crappy toilet and the general fuck-up Sherman's life had become . . . all of these seemed in some way to be this lad's responsibility. Sherman didn't yet know whether the kid was going to get him killed, but it didn't seem unlikely at this rate.

And then there was Davidoff, also not to be forgotten. Sherman was buggered if he wasn't going to take a run at him one way or another.

But what he wanted to do, which was pick nodding boy up by his scrawny little neck and push his face through the glass shelves behind the bar (it was possible; oh, it was possible, given a bit of a run-up), he was not going to do.

Smooth and easy. The kid hadn't seen him, or if he had he was giving a very good impression of not having done so. Or not caring—which would mean . . . Sherman, pulling back against the wall, scanned the room. There was nobody else in the place. Barman? Unlikely.

The kid really might be there alone. The Gents had been empty. Sherman walked back to where he had been sitting and angled the table so his back was to the room, but he could see the kid in the glass behind the bar. He pretended to keep drinking his final bottle of Molson.

The kid wasn't looking anywhere—he looked drunk, was what he looked. Sherman watched him order another Maker's Mark, pay in cash. Head lolling a bit. Mouthing along to the jukie.

"You, my son," Sherman promised him, "are going to get a very nasty bump on the head indeed before this evening is out. You see if you don't."

The song ended with a squeal, and then a jerk. Then there was a click as the mechanism changed and a tangled chord rolled out, fuzzy with static. A drumbeat thumped and limped behind it. "Like a Hurricane" was starting again. Sherman, remembering the song for some reason, frowned.

21

Alex left the bar, his eyeballs floating. The horizontal hold had gone on the room, and he could feel the fajitas moving in his stomach. He wanted fresh air. The jammed jukebox, playing that one song over and over again, had proved resistant to the barman thumping it, and after letting it play the same song for fifteen minutes the guy had finally gone and pulled the plug, with some violence, out of the wall.

Neil Young had stopped, and the circular riff of Alex's own thoughts had continued: hate and fear, anger and grief, grief and hate, anger and fear, salt, pepper, vinegar, mustard . . .

Alex left the bar and turned away from the Strip and walked. Behind him, a shadow calved off from the shadow of the doorway and crept down the dark lee of the building, skipping occasionally through pools of light and back into darkness.

Alex wasn't hard to follow. Sherman had had an hour to sober up. Alex had had an hour to get drunker. He was staggering like a cow that had been hit with a hammer, away from the bright light, into the darkened residential streets, dragging his tail behind him.

Alex stopped at the edge of a bare lot. They were building something there.

A rough fence of corrugated iron had been raised around it, the gaps covered over with panels of metal netting, through which you could see an uneven expanse of bare dirt, pocked and pitted. Blue-white lights on tall poles scored it with sharp shadows. Orange construction vehicles slept like dinosaurs in the cold lunar daylight.

Sherman stopped behind him. Alex put his hands on his knees, bent forward, rocked back and forth over the ground with his mouth open. It looked like he was going to be sick, but then whatever it was passed. Alex spat, instead, a long spool of saliva descending to the blue ground.

Then he resumed his progress, not once looking back, slipping through a wide gap in the fence and ignoring the signs that enjoined him to wear a hard hat. Sherman followed, stopping at the edge of the site in a pool of darkness cast by one of the tall panels. It was bright as day in that site, but dark outside. If the boy was bait, this would be a perfect killing zone. He didn't want to move in until he was sure he was alone.

He watched Alex move with the aimless deliberateness of the seriously drunk. He seemed to be talking to himself. Then Sherman saw him double back toward him. He ducked his head behind the corrugated-iron sheet and stepped further into the dark. If the boy came out through the gap, Sherman would have the drop on him. He waited.

Then he heard a zip go, and the loud drum roll of someone pissing like a horse against the other side of the fence. A pool of hot urine leaked from under the fence and spread around Sherman's shoes. The smell was pungent. If the boy was setting him up he was no sort of professional.

Step in and shoot? Let the kid die with his dick in his hand?

On second thought, if there was an accomplice, now might be exactly when he would anticipate Sherman making his move. Maybe professional was exactly what he was. So far the boy had done absolutely everything he could, seemingly, to invite Sherman to murder him. He had got drunk. He had shown no sign of even looking around to see if there was anyone following him. He had walked off to a deserted construction site, brightly illuminated, with clear sightlines in. And now he was taking a pee.

The gap in the fence spilled light. There was no way this sort of thing happened by accident. Hold back.

Sherman listened patiently. It ended, and Sherman could hear Alex walking away, further into the site. Sherman waited a long time, and then, finally, followed him.

Alex sat down on a short stack of wooden pallets. He had at last lost his self-consciousness. He sniveled, miserably.

"What am I going to do?" he asked the empty lot. "What am I going to do?" He didn't mind much if he died right there. His mouth was foul with whiskey. He felt sick, but it wouldn't come up. He wanted to go home and sleep forever. He wanted Carey. He wanted to die. He wanted his mum. He didn't know what he wanted.

He took his phone out, and looked at it, and put it away again. He wondered if he might be going mad.

Sherman moved out of the shadow of the fence and into the light. He moved quietly, on the balls of his feet. His gun was in his hand. Alex was half turned away from him, staring into the far corner of the lot, where one of the lights was out and the adjacent two-story building left that side in darkness.

There was a sort of generalized sobbing and wailing going on. Sherman knew at that moment that this was more elaborate than he'd have needed for a set-up. There was no accomplice. This had been nothing to do with MIC at all.

Alex sobbed again. The lad was upset—anyone could see that. And Sherman felt sorry for him, whatever his problem was. But Sherman still intended to shoot him in the face.

He waited until he was close enough to be sure of making a chest shot in a hurry.

"You," Sherman called. "Boy." Alex was still looking away. He made no acknowledgment.

"Alex!" he called. Slightly louder. The boy's head turned in surprise.

Who? Alex saw a man with a gun. He stood up suddenly, feeling very sober. It looked like the man who had chased him at the supermarket. The gun was pointed at him.

"Yeah, pal. You." Alex gave a sudden jolt of fright. Seconds ago, when in no prospect of doing so, he had thought he perhaps wanted to die. Now, presented with a golden opportunity, his body chemistry was telling him the opposite. He discovered that he did not want to die at all. The whiskey vanished from his system. He was sober, and terrified.

"Alex Smart," said Sherman. "You've caused me a lot of trouble, lad. A lot."

Alex struggled to say something. He had never had a gun pointed at him before. He said: "Whu-whu-whu-whu-"

Sherman stepped forward and Alex yelped. "Easy," said Sherman. "Hands where I can see them."

Hands where I can see them? Sherman thought. Does anybody actually say that?

Hands where I can see them? Alex thought. They say that. They actually do say that.

Alex realized he had no idea where his hands were. He discovered that they were straight out in front of him, as if his unconscious had decided it was possible to fend off bullets by the act of protesting politely against them, like someone refusing a canapé at a party. Please don't. I couldn't possibly take a bullet in the gut. I'm watching my weight.

Alex's hands shot up level with his head.

"Sir," he said. "I'm sorry. Whatever it is, I'm sorry. I don't know what you think I've done, but I—I think you've got the wrong person, sincerely, sir." The whiskey hadn't entirely worn off. Alex struggled to pronounce "sincerely, sir."

"You're Alex Smart?"

"Yes. I mean no. Sorry. Yes. Sorry. I didn't mean to lie. I mean. I got confused." Alex was breathing fast and shallow. Terror made everything very clear to him. He could see Sherman's sandy hair and hard little face—or, at least, he was aware of them. All he literally saw was the little black hole in the end of the gun.

He talked to Sherman and looked at the gun.

"I'm Alex Smart, but you must mean a different Alex Smart, I mean. There's been some sort of mix-up. I'm a student."

"Are you?" said Sherman. "That's nice for you."

"I'm at Cambridge. I do maths. I don't do . . ." He trailed off helplessly. He didn't know what it was he didn't do, or—rather—how to articulate the mass of things that people presumably did do that led to people pointing guns at them, but that were so far outside the sphere of all the things Alex did as to occupy a separate category of existence.

"Cambridge, eh? Mummy and Daddy must be very proud of you," said Sherman, in a not altogether friendly way. "But I'm afraid I couldn't give two shits what you do or don't do. Not two shits. You've got this machine. It's not your property. And I want it back."

Alex was even more baffled. What machine?

"I don't know, sir. Please. I don't know what you're talking about—"

I don't know what you're talking about, Alex thought. I actually said that. That's what people always say in films, and they are always lying, and something very horrible always happens to them.

"—I mean, sorry, I know how that sounds, I really don't know, I promise I don't. I don't have any machines. Please. You can search me and everything. Just please don't—" and he couldn't bring himself to utter the words "shoot" and "me" out of the fear that it might put an idea into the man's head which would not otherwise have occurred to him.

Overhead Sherman could hear the sound of a helicopter. It flickered through his head that he should run—that that might be MIC come to disavow him, or the FBI come to take him in—and then he put the thought out of his head and concentrated on killing the young man who he believed had killed his friend.

Sherman hadn't liked Davidoff, not that much. But a point of principle was, as he saw it, at stake. Davidoff had been in his regiment. He had been beside Davidoff when they were digging into a position in the Iraqi desert under fire, and discovering they were on top of a mass grave had given each of the sandbags they filled a name: Abdul, Mustapha, Mohammed. They had spent a night dug into that position. This soggy little prick knew nothing of that. And the only thing that would get Sherman out of the hole he was in with his employers and with the law was in this lad's possession.

"Please," said Alex.

"No," said Sherman. He took a step closer to Alex, who had raised his hands, palms out, like a hostage in a black-and-white film. "Mate, the way I see it is this. You killed my friend. You have this coincidence machine. And this is nothing personal but I'm fed the fuck up asking nicely."

Sherman had at no point asked nicely, it occurred to him fleetingly. But he kept the gun level. This was not personal. No. It *was* personal. He gestured with it for Alex to move—down the fence toward the unlit corner of the site, further into the shadow, further away from the human noise of the street.

"I—I don't know what you're talking about," said Alex. "I've got money. Please. I can help you. Please."

It was as Alex went, stumbling sideways down the fence line, that Sherman realized the boy had suffered a failure of imagination. He didn't realize that Sherman meant to kill him—or if he did realize it he was not allowing himself to believe it. He thought he belonged to a different story. His was a world in which people didn't kill each other, except in foreign countries and on television. At some level, this little twat thought that one day he was going to be telling people about this.

It made Sherman hate him—but also envy him. This wet, spoiled, selfish, privileged little wanker. Sherman was not only going to kill Alex, he realized then, but he wanted to.

If he'd kept his eyes on Alex, Sherman would have seen that realization communicate itself to the young man he was about to kill. He'd have seen a face, streaked with drying tears, turn to fear and bewilderment. Alex in that instant knew, for the first time, what it was to be properly hated; to be hated to death.

Sherman would also have seen Alex's eyes, an instant later, attempt to focus over his shoulder on a pudgy woman in early middle age emerging from the far corner of the yard, followed by a tall man with gray hair. The woman had a gun in her hand.

But Sherman saw none of these things because he was disconcerted by a sudden movement in the corner of his field of vision. Distracted for an instant, he looked down. There was a faint, blurred rectangular shadow on the pavement around him, about the size of a Volvo estate. The shadow was getting crisper and smaller, Sherman thought. And that was the last thing Sherman thought.

Sherman was standing there and then Sherman was gone—vaporised, obliterated.

At first nobody in the yard could process the sound. Offensively abrupt and shatteringly loud, it had a quality of being at once percussive and muffled, like a fat person's thigh bone snapping clean without breaking the skin.

Bree had been aware of something flickering in the upper corner of her field of vision and then, with a tremendous WHUMPH! and a tangible dislocation of the air, what she had been looking at had become without preamble what she now was looking at, and it made no sense.

The man with the gun was gone, and where he had been was an oblong block on the ground at the center of a great asterisk of red. There was black stone and polished wood of some sort dashed to matches, and a spreading stain of bright blood. Down both long sides of the oblong, great fat pillars of wood stuck up skywards. Two, at the end that took the impact, had snapped off and shivered. One of them bounced and rolled away over the uneven ground. Meanwhile, fugitive pieces of what used to be

Sherman were crumbed in the dust of the yard like meat scraps in the sawdust of a butcher's floor.

Alex's mouth opened and closed. His hands remained in the air.

Bree looked at the scene. The impact had sent fine brown dust in every direction, and Bree's next breath caused her to cough. A torn skein of green felt, poking out from under the edge of the table, was soaking black with the blood.

Bree was the first person to talk, and she said: "The *fuck*?"

Jones, standing slightly further away, said: "Snooker table."

Jones was right. What had landed on Sherman was a brand-new, full-sized slate-bed snooker table. It had cost twenty thousand dollars and weighed something approaching a ton and a half. It had been destined for pride of place in a newly built "Sherlock Holmes" suite at the MGM hotel and casino, whither the helicopter that was carrying it had been bound before its cargo had parted company with its bindings.

All this took approximately three-quarters of a second, and that fragment of time was crowned by an instant of tranquil bewilderment. The dust hung in the air, and there was silence.

Alex's hands remained in the air. Bree gaped. Then Bree looked down and saw a bit of Sherman on her boot, and as she was bending over to be sick the stillness was broken by a sound like the crack of a pistol. Something powered into the center of the oblong like a little howitzer and shattered into dust. Then another crack, equally loud. Then another—something, this time, kicking off the oblong and skittering across the uneven surface of the yard, something round and red.

Then another—CRACK!—and another—CRACK!—then the same sound but softened, without the hint of ricochet. Bree could see something blurring out of the sky and punching into the dirt in the floor of the yard. It looked like an apple. She had a fleeting image of the way hailstorms used to begin when she was a kid.

Bree flinched as if she were under fire. Then she felt a sharp agony in her hand and her gun flew out of it and onto the ground. Her arm felt as if she'd been hit on the funny bone with a sledgehammer. A round red apple bounced over the yard. She hunched, thrusting her sore arm into her armpit and bringing the other up to protect her head. Then she felt another whistle down behind her, and another, and two more red apples snapped into existence half buried in the dirt of the yard. Snap, snap.

Then a yellow one. Then a green one. Then a brown one.

Jones was still standing, looking puzzled, when a blue snooker ball struck him on the top-right corner of his forehead, a quarter of an inch below his hairline. The orbit of his right eye collapsed, and blood exploded from his face.

Behind Jones a pink ball punched into the dirt.

Jones flopped forward and landed on his knees. His hands were by his sides. His mouth was open. His cigarette fell out.

A couple of feet further on a black ball hit the concrete in which the fence was set and exploded into dust.

Then Jones's whole long body pitched face first, waist still unbending, into the dirt. He came to rest like that, his head looking down the length of his shoulder across the ground to where Bree was half crouched, expecting at any moment to be struck dead by some kind of English sporting goods traveling at terminal velocity.

The hailstorm stopped. Again, there was silence—though it was the anticipatory and untrusted silence of a pause in shelling.

Jones's legs, still bent at the knee, subsided in a succession of ragged jerks to the horizontal. His mouth opened. Blood was pooling, under the influence of gravity, in the corner of his shattered eye. It flowed over the bridge of his nose and trickled thickly into the corner of his undamaged eye. It looked almost black in the artificial light. His mouth closed.

Bree, picking herself up, her hand still buzzing agonizingly from the impact—one of those balls must have hit the barrel of the gun she was holding—ran-stumbled toward where Jones was lying.

Alex was standing where he had been standing, not more than a body's length or two from the wreckage of the snooker table. His hands were still in the air.

Bree shouted "Stay there!" at him but he didn't show any signs of having heard her. He wasn't going anywhere. He had been chased, and newly shot at, and heartbroken, and rescued from death by a falling snooker table. Now he was out. Not computing. Just staring into space.

Bree reached Jones and knelt beside him. The uneven dirt of the lot was hard through the knees of her slacks. She put her hand on his shoulder. His mouth opened. His unbroken eye shifted focus to look at her face. He looked confused. And he looked, for the first time, afraid.

"Easy, Jones," Bree cooed to him. "It's all right. We're going to get you an ambulance. Ambulance is going to come, and pick you up, and we're going to get that eye—"

Jones blinked, and a smear of blood tinted the white of his eye pink. His mouth closed.

"—get that eye looked at, get it fixed up, an'—we're—don't try to speak—just getting an ambulance right now—"

She felt panic getting a hold on her. She fought it. She realized she needed to call, needed to call a *fucking* ambulance—her hands were shaking. She pulled out the cheap cellphone she had and stabbed at the keys, mistyped twice, hit 911, composed herself as she spoke to the dispatcher.

"Yes, corner of—that's right—it says—" she read the street sign she could see—"down an alley at the yard in back. We've got—yes, badly injured, something fell on him. Hit him on the head. Come quick."

She returned her attention to Jones. Absently, maternally, she realized that she had been stroking his hair. Her hand was sticky with blood. He flapped his mouth again, then half coughed a syllable.

"Not," Jones said.

"Don't try to speak, baby," Bree said. She could see the blood, the shattered skull. Jones was dying, right here, right in front of her. "Don't try to speak. Everything's going to be all right. The ambulance is coming. The table got fucko. We won. The good guys won."

"Not alone," Jones said, and she realized that what was in his eye was not fear but imploring.

"Don't worry, Jones. Not alone, no. I'm right here with you. Not alone."

The blood from the wound in Jones's head passed in a runnel down the corner of his jaw. It dripped from the bridge of his nose. Bree was down low, looking into his good eye, nearly on the ground, trying not to think about the mashed part of his face where the ball had hit. "Not alone," she said. "I'll be with you all the way. In the ambulance. Ambulance is coming. Coming now. Not alone, baby. Not alone."

Jones's eye spooked a little. He looked afraid again, held her gaze as if she was what was holding him to the world. And then the pupil of his eye ballooned until the gray iris was the width of a fingernail paring, and he was looking at nobody.

Bree was still there on her knees beside him, stroking his sticky hair and bawling, when the ambulance showed up twenty minutes later and with nobody to save.

22

Alex went with Bree and Jones's body to the emergency room.

Retrieving the main section of Sherman—as the two para-medics discovered when they tried to lift the snooker table—was going to be a separate project. They called for backup while the lights of the ambulance revolved noiselessly on the main street, red spilling through the gap in the fencing and over the bare pocked earth.

While Jones had been dying Alex had passed out. The last thing he heard was a clattering sound somewhere nearby—the landfall, like giant pick-up-sticks, of a baker's dozen snooker cues and rests of different lengths. His system was lousy with whiskey and adrenalin. Alex's mind had had enough.

"Alive," Bree had said to the paramedics, still with Jones, waving at where Alex was lying. "That one's alive. Bring him."

And they had—hauling the boy's unresisting frame into the back of the ambulance between two of them, letting him lie on the floor at Bree's feet, beside the gurney on which Jones, having given up smoking for good, made his journey to the hospital.

While they were loading the bodies, Bree called Red Queen. She just said: "We've found him. The other side was there. Jones is gone."

"Jones is gone?" Red Queen said. "Where gone?"

"Gone. Dead. We're in an ambulance on the way to the medical center."

"Wait there," said Red Queen. Bree was exhausted. She wondered whether Red Queen would be thinking that Jones dead solved a problem. She didn't know Red Queen well enough to make the call, and didn't have the energy for anger. Alex came round in the ambulance, tried to sit up, lay back down again. Bree took charge of him.

When they got to the emergency room they took Jones away and made Bree sign a form. Jones had no identification on him. She realized she didn't know his first name, so she wrote on the form just "Jones" and circled "Mr." You could also be "Mrs.," "Miss," and "Ms." If you were dead in this hospital, it seemed, they were still interested in whether or not you might be single.

She said that she was his next of kin, and didn't have the presence of mind to give any but her real name. Under "relationship to the deceased," she wrote: "Friend." Her hands were still shaking.

Afterward Bree was asked to wait. She was hustled through the emergency room, and into a public waiting area. The walls were sea green and grainy in the strip light. Alex was already there, and Bree went and sat beside him on a metal seat with fixed armrests. The seats were bolted to the walls. It had the feel of a budget airport departure lounge, except that the room's hard acoustics rang with the wails of the suffering and the mad.

Doctors appeared through double doors, looked anxious, and vanished again. A drunk with some sort of wound in his leg lay across two seats on the facing wall. His dark gray jogging bottoms were streaked down one leg with a wet black stain, and there were smears of blood and dirt on his hands and face. He was muttering something that sounded like "ong, ong, ong" and every few minutes he would shriek out "They're here! They're here! They're here!" and bang his open hand on the metal chair, some ring or bangle he wore making a piercing clangor as he struck.

An old man with matted hair and several days of stubble sat, in the far corner, topless and dirty, with a twist of webbing slung around his bare chest. His head jerked, sporadically, toward his shoulder but his gaze was fixed on Bree. She broke eye contact and looked at Alex.

Alex sat, still wrapped in the foil blanket they had given him in the ambulance, hunched and looking away. His face was a waxen yellow, his deep-set eyes dark with sleeplessness and shock. He focused on nothing.

"The thing, then," said Bree, quietly. "Tell me about it. Where did you hide it?"

Alex took a long time before answering.

"Who are you?" he said, still not looking at her.

"A friend?"

"Really." His voice was dead flat. "I don't know what's happening. You tell me?"

"No," said Bree. "Not really." Alex paused, and zoned out again. Bree's question went ignored. Then, as if remembering something from a dream, he said: "You were at the supermarket, weren't you?"

"The supermarket?" Bree tried to think. She picked at a hang-nail. Adrenalin, washing back out of her system, had numbed her. Everything felt unreal.

"The supermarket. Where the man chased me. The dead man."

"Yes," said Bree. She didn't know what to say after that. The dead man. The other dead man. The other other dead man.

"Why did he chase me?"

"He thinks you have the machine."

"I told him," said Alex. "I don't know what he's talking about."

"No?" Bree looked at him appraisingly. If he was lying he was a good liar. She continued. "Something has gone missing. Something that we think—the agency I work for, that is—and the man who had the gun on you thought—the people he worked for, anyway . . . you have. We've been trying to find you. You and your connection in the city."

"I've got nothing," Alex insisted. "I came here to see my girlfriend."

Bree thought about it for a moment. The calls they'd picked up once they'd got hold of his phone records: the calls to a cell on a San Francisco network; then the phone showing up in Las Vegas. The contact: how could it be otherwise?

"Your girlfriend?" Bree wondered whether she was going to regret the initiative she had taken while Alex had been unconscious in the ambulance. If Jones had died—if Jones had died for this, she had wanted to make sure it had been for something. She wasn't going to let it away.

"Ex-girlfriend, probably. We had—something went wrong that can't be put right."

Bree exhaled. She knew all about things that went wrong that couldn't be put right. She felt a hundred years old.

"This is bigger than that," she said.

"Oh yes?" said Alex. Not sounding convinced.

"Don't be an idiot," said Bree. "People are trying to kill you. That man was trying to kill you. It has to have been the machine that saved you. The coincidence engine."

"What?"

"It affects probability. It might be a weapon. Everybody thinks you have it."

"I haven't got anything. I've never heard of it."

"Well, if you haven't got it, who has?"

"If I've never heard of it it's not very likely I'm going to know that, is it?"

Bree fell silent again. She looked down at her hands. Her right palm was slightly tacky with Jones's blood.

"You need to stay here with us," she said. "My boss needs to speak to you."

"Oh no. No, no," Alex croaked. "I've got rights. I'm not saying anything. I don't know who you are."

"I work for the government."

"A government that puts people in black planes and tortures them? I don't think so."

"Suit yourself," said Bree. "But the other guys will come back. You know that, don't you? You were lucky this time. Lucky.

If you can't decide who to trust, you're going to end up dead, my friend. People are already dying because of this thing. My colleague there."

"A snooker table fell out of the sky," said Alex. "How is that something to do with me?"

"I don't know," said Bree. "I've barely heard of snooker. But it fell on a man who was trying to kill you. And it killed a man who was trying to protect you. He's right in there somewhere"— she pointed down through the double doors into the lit corridor beyond—"being zipped into a bag. That was my colleague. We were coming to try to help you."

"Were you?"

"We didn't want you dead. The other guy did. We were on your side. I am on your side."

"Nobody's on my side," said Alex. "Not even my girlfriend."

Girlfriend? Jeezus. Talk about self-absorbed. She let the pause ride, and picked a bit at her thumbnail.

"Want to tell me what happened?" she said afterward. Bree didn't care about the kid's romantic problems—she had just seen two men die violently at very close quarters, and she wasn't wanting to think very much about the likelihood that whatever killed them would kill her too. People who got close to this thing were dying.

"No," said Alex. "I don't want to talk about it."

Once again, Bree's mind did what it always did when traumatized: it sought refuge in the practical. Bree was thinking. She knew the police would have been called—the immediate assumption being that what had happened to Jones was a gunshot wound—and they were likely to have enough trouble with them as it was, explaining what these four people, some with guns, had been doing there in the first place.

The guard at the entrance to the emergency room was already casting the sort of glances their way that suggested he'd been briefed to prevent them walking out if they wanted to. Or was that paranoia? Red Queen would be able to calm this down. Perhaps.

"It's my girlfriend, see, Carey. She works here. She was a student where I go to university, in Cambridge. I'm studying for a PhD. You know about Cambridge?"

Bree let him ramble. She thought about the way Jones's eye had looked when he was lying there in that vacant lot. Not the damaged eye—the other one. Stone gray in the iris. And that sudden sharp opening of the pupil as he came to grief.

"Anyway, she went home. She's American, from the West Coast. I came out to visit her and I had this idea that I . . . It sounds so stupid now, I know. But I thought she was it. She was . . . it's hard for me to talk about this to a stranger, but . . ."

Came to grief. Why was it people said that?

"I asked her to marry me. She didn't want to, I don't think. She sort of hesitated. No. Got to admit it. She turned me down flat. Just like that. I had a ring and everything. I came all the way here to see her."

As if grief was there already, waiting for you. You don't go away to it. You arrive. The boy burbled on.

"Pretty funny. I was pretty upset at the time, but now—you know, you chalk it up to experience. It was about four hours ago, actually. I mean, I'm still pretty upset about it if truth be told. I wasn't completely—you know, I did what you do. Went out and just left her. You can't—you can't recover from that, you know. But you live and learn, move on. Into every life a little rain must fall. It's not the end of the world. It just feels—" his voice quavered—"like the end of the world . . ."

What was Jones looking at? What was the last thing his eye saw of the world? Had he been looking at her when he died? She couldn't remember.

Bree looked up and across the waiting area. A young black guy, lanky arms shining with sweat, was muttering and yipping. A girl in a hooded top sat with her hands folded in her lap, her lips moving silently. There was blood down one side of her face. A bulky man in a pale blue T-shirt, wedged into one of these chairs, had his right arm wound round and round with toilet roll. He was dozing, coughing out sporadic, apnoeic snores.

There was a noise. Through the door to the outside there came a man dressed in a white jumpsuit and a dark wig with extravagant sideburns holding a wad of bloodied tissue paper to his nose. He still had his sunglasses on.

Bree saw Alex look up, and something that might in another circumstance have been amusement passed across his face.

"It's not, honey. It's not. Not the end of the world," said Bree, because she couldn't think of anything else to say. "Life goes on. You just feel sad for a bit. Maybe a long time. I had a husband. Marriage isn't all it's cracked up to be."

"Are you still with him?"

"Had."

"What happened?"

"He left. I wasn't easy to be married to."

"Did you love him?"

"Yes," said Bree, a flat matter of fact.

"Still?"

"No. Jolly Rancher?"

Alex frowned.

"It's a candy," Bree said. She pulled half of a stick of Jolly Ranchers from her pocket, the paper wrapper in a spiral tatter where she had been attacking them. Alex took one, unwrapped it, put it in his mouth. It clinked against his teeth like sticky glass, then started tasting of sour artificial apple. "My friend liked these."

"I'm sorry about your friend," Alex said. Talking was making him feel—not better, exactly. But it was like not looking down. In the back of his mind there was still this sinkhole, this gap, widening, between what he had thought his future was going to be, and what it was now.

With every passing moment, the gap got wider. It was irredeemable. Bridges crumbling and falling into the sea. Alex replayed Carey saying the one thing, the thing that was impossible: "Can we just forget this?" It was done.

"How does it get better?" Alex said.

"What?" Bree had three Jolly Ranchers in her mouth and was unwrapping a fourth. The Ranchers didn't seem to be imparting the jollity their name promised. It occurred to Alex that there was something about her—a look around her eyes?—that made him think he knew her. As if she were someone he saw often and paid little attention to, and then met in another context: like bumping into your old dinner lady in the supermarket a couple of years after you've left school.

"Better," repeated Alex. "How long does it take?"

"Long time," said Bree. "Wait. Waiting does it. Apparently."

"Look," Alex said. He dug a hand into his pocket, and half stood up, and out of his pocket he pulled a square box. "I even got a ring." He popped the box open.

Bree reached out. Her fingers were chubby, her nails bitten down. She took the ring and turned it round in her hands.

"Pretty," she said. "The number eight. Swirly. Ah . . . I'm sorry, kid." She drew it a little closer to her eyes. "What's that written in it there?" She indicated some scratchy markings.

"Hallmark, I think."

"No. Hallmark looks different. Longer. That's just . . ." Bree angled the ring in the harsh light of the waiting room. " 'AB' it says."

Alex took the ring off her and looked at it more closely. It did—right up by where the band swooped into its figure-eight design. The letters had been worn almost to indecipherability by the warm friction of the finger that had once lived in the ring. Bree remembered something Red Queen had said.

"What do those letters mean?"

"I've no idea," he said truthfully. "I hadn't noticed them. I bought the ring secondhand."

"Used?"

"I bought it from an antique shop."

Banacharski's mother was called Ana. The letters they had intercepted had gone on and on about her. She had died.

"You're lying," said Bree.

The look Alex gave her—weariness mixed with fear—was enough to convince her that he was not. And if this was it—why show her? "Let me see it again," said Bree. She held it up to the light once more. On the leading edge, the metal seemed for an instant to have a diffracted blue light—a blur, as if it had slipped sideways in space.

"When? Where did it come from?"

"Just a shop. A shop in Cambridge. A couple of weeks ago. I happened to stop there—I saw it and I thought it might be nice to . . . you know. To ask her to marry me."

Bree rubbed her eyes. It felt like there was grit in them.

"I think," Alex continued, "I—I don't know. I don't know what made me think she would say yes. I know she's got . . . she's much more experienced than me, is what. And she's got what she calls 'issues around commitment.' She's said that before. She didn't have a normal family, like I did—she was fostered when she was a teenager and never sees her birth parents. Never talks about them."

There was a very long silence between them. Alex drew the space blanket tighter around his shoulders, and Bree tugged at where the fabric of her blouse had wedged into her armpit.

"How did you find me?" Alex asked.

"Dumb luck," said Bree. "We'd lost you. But the man who was chasing you—we had a fix on his cellphone. You can triangulate them. Good as a tracking device. He followed you and we followed him."

"How did he find me?" said Alex. Bree shrugged. A known unknown.

"I don't know what they had on you. My boss thought they were getting information from inside our organization. There's a lot riding on this."

"But why did you think I had this thing of yours in the first place?"

"We were watching the Banacharski Ring . . ."

"The Banacharski Ring? It's a web ring. An academic group. We share papers about maths."

"Ostensibly. Our cryptographers say different."

"Not ostensibly. *Really*. Isla—"

"Isla Holderness?"

"Yes, exactly. Isla set it up after she corresponded with him. It's just a website with a discussion forum attached. My supervisor took it over when she left. He was friendly with Isla when they were at Cambridge together, before her accident."

"Uh-huh? OK. So tell me about your supervisor."

"Mike? Not much to tell. He's a research fellow at my college. We meet for supervisions. I show him my work. Sometimes we have a drink. That's it . . ."

"Mike Hollis?"

Alex looked perplexed. "You know him?"

"No," said Bree. "Colleagues of mine were interested in him."

Alex shook his head. He still had no idea what was going on. He wondered where Carey was now, and then pushed the thought out of his mind.

"Hollis sent an e-mail," said Bree. "He mentioned you. He said he was leaving the ring in your hands. Shortly afterward, you left for America. And here you are with the ring. Are we not expected to find that suspicious?"

"This is a ring I bought for my girlfriend," Alex said, past exasperation, "it has nothing to do with Mike, or Nicolas Banacharski, or anybody else. I bought it. Me, at random, in a shop. Mike was leaving me in charge of the Banacharski Ring's website while he went on sabbatical."

Bree thought: what a mess. None of this made any sense. Another wave of exhaustion hit her. And now, when she thought she'd been bringing a loose end in, she might have been doing the opposite. She decided all she could do was breach it.

"Your girlfriend?" Bree said.

"Carey, yes." He added bitterly: "Ex-girlfriend."

"She the last number you dialed on your cell?"

"I don't remember," said Alex.

"Number ending—" Bree pulled his cellphone out of her pocket and consulted the screen—"137 0359?"

"Give me that!" Alex said, snatching it back from her. She let it go.

"She's on her way here," said Bree. "I called her. Said you were in trouble and to come. She sounded a little drunk. It was hard to make out whether she was taking it in. But I said you were going to be here. Said you needed help."

"What? Why?" Alex, panicking, even through his tiredness. It felt like a humiliation—even after everything, seeing Carey was . . .

"Because you're in trouble, and you need help."

"Trouble?"

"Dead people. Me. You're in lots of trouble." Bree gave it a moment, looked at her well-bitten fingernails. "But you're right. It wasn't for you, not strictly, that I called her. I thought she was your connection here. I thought you were going to pass the machine over to her."

Alex started to say something, but she interrupted. "Yeah, yeah. I know. There's no machine. You're here to see your girlfriend. You don't know what I'm talking about . . ."

"I've got to go," he said. He was standing now. Fidgeting with his hands. His cheeks looked like they had been gouged from limestone. He wasn't acting like someone who had been caught by a government agency trying to smuggle a weapon through a strange country. He was acting like somebody who was unbearably miserable at the prospect of confronting his ex-girlfriend.

Bree made a decision. "Go," she said. "Go. You don't need to be here."

"But I thought . . ."

"Yeah," said Bree. She shrugged, but didn't smile. "So did I. This whole thing started as a mess and now it's a worse one. Go. I know where you are. Go get some sleep." Bree did not add that, having been through Alex's wallet and tagged his mobile phone, she knew how to find him if she needed to. "Enjoy Vegas," she added.

She watched as he walked toward the wide doors. The security guard watched him walk through, then looked back to Bree, then scratched his gut and rearranged his shoulders. That probably figured. Still no police. Perhaps miracles did happen.

Bree leaned back in the seat, comfortable as she could get, and let her eyes close.

23

"Something odd." It was Porlock, standing at Red Queen's desk. Red Queen didn't remember him having had the courtesy to knock on the door. "Look."

He put a sheet of paper on the chewed red leather of the desk. It was a stock chart, showing a company's share price falling off a cliff.

"MIC. Last fifteen minutes. We've been watching them—ever since this started. But this you could get on the evening news. The chief investor just dumped all their stock on the market. All of it. It's bad. A cascade effect. The stock's toxic."

"Is the government invested?" asked Red Queen innocently.

Porlock looked sarcastic.

"Every government that buys or sells arms is invested. The consequences could be—"

"For who? The consequences for who?"

"Everyone," said Porlock, whose usual expression of imperturbability had given way to one that looked almost ironical. Porlock, it occurred to Red Queen, would look ironical aboard the *Titanic.* "This will go through the world economy like a hurricane. Contracts canceled, jobs lost."

"This investor . . ." said Red Queen.

"Nobody knows about him," said Porlock. He swung his hand back and forth in front of his chest like a paddle. "Nobody knew he even existed until recently. There were so many institutional investors in the company that who bothered to check which was what? Until this started happening, and a lot of forensic accounting was done very fast and in breach of all ethics and international agreements. The simultaneous stock dumps. It looked like a concerted attack. Each of them traced back several layers. A name associated with a network of accounts in Switzerland. Sleeping partner. Seemingly bottomless pockets. If there was a share loose, he bought it."

"Nazi gold?" asked Red Queen.

"Nothing that simple, I don't think. Nor that small-time. The Nazis didn't *have* that much gold. MIC was in trouble by '99, sure—not much more than a think tank attached to a logo. There'd been bad press about its wartime history and, like everyone, a lot of investment in new tech that turned out to be imaginary. But it was still an arms company: still big. Still not the kind of thing you take control of with pocket change.

"The last decade saw it turn into what it is now. Everyone assumed that whoever was buying it knew something others didn't, so they bought too. Everyone assumed it was just a successful company, which it was."

"Who is this investor?" Red Queen asked. "We have no file on him? Seriously?"

"No. Not one. But his name comes up in connection with Banacharski. He's called Fred Nieman."

Red Queen thought. "The man who was due to visit Banacharski before he disappeared. Mentioned in the letters."

"And," said Porlock, "the name Banacharski himself used to sign his final letter."

Red Queen raised one eyebrow. In the windowless room there was a sense of something coming to an end. "You think Banacharski's alive?"

"Nobody ever found a body," said Porlock. "And MIC paid him a lot of money over the years. What do you suppose he did with it? Under any number of guises, through third, fourth, fifth, to the Xth-term parties, Nieman's fronts had been buying shares in MIC steadily since the beginning of 1999. He didn't work for MIC. He owned it. Had a controlling interest within a couple of years, if you added it all up. Did nothing with it. No record of any involvement in board meetings, not through any of these fronts, and, you know, agencies like ours—governments, senior pols—it's the sort of thing we'd expect to know. All that happened was the money came in, and made more money, and now it's gone."

Red Queen struggled with the thought. Nieman had been buying stock since around the time of Banacharski's last disappearance. But where would he have gotten this sort of money? The company had gone up in value by powers of ten since then—but that holding, still . . . it would have cost.

"They can't have paid him *that* much money. Not nearly that much money. There aren't more than a handful of individuals on the face of the earth with that much money. And why reinvest it? And why take it out? Why would anybody build it up just to destroy it?"

While he talked, Red Queen moused over the computer. There were jagged red lines on graphs, excitable reporters, flashes of men in dealing rooms with their ties held out sideways from their necks like nooses, shouting. It seemed a wonder planes weren't falling out of the sky.

"Never bright confident morning again," Red Queen said flatly. "Where's the money gone?"

Porlock shrugged. "MIC will be lucky to last until the exchange closes this afternoon," he said. "No government's going to risk trying to bail it out."

"No?"

"They've got game theorists on it. Your department, usually. But, no. Bottom line—nobody wants to jump first. They'd rather just watch the dominoes go down; hope the bomb drops everywhere."

Porlock moved his hand to his tie, straightened it.

"Not good news for you, Porlock," said Red Queen. "Is it?"

"Not good news for anyone," Porlock repeated.

"Especially bad for you." Here, Red Queen sent out a questing thumb to scratch diffidently, almost coquettishly, at the scratched leather of the desktop. Looked down, then up again. "Not sure you'll get paid, after all this, though I imagine you've thought of that yourself."

Porlock frowned. The lightbox on the wall of the room gave his face an unhealthy luster, reflected as twin white rectangles on the balls of his eyes. He looked wary. Red Queen continued.

"Your friend Ellis is going to be out of a job, isn't he?" Porlock's composure started to break. "And I don't think there's much chance of anyone getting a finder's fee now, is there? Money's a little tight over there . . ."

"I still don't follow you," said Porlock, although he did.

". . . and if I'm frank about it, I'm not sure how much use we're going to have for you now there's no MIC for you to pass information to. You've served your purpose, as far as the Directorate is concerned."

"You're accusing—me—of passing information to MIC?"

"Only the information I wanted passed," said Red Queen. "But, yes. Very much so." Red Queen picked up the telephone and spoke without dialing: "Porlock's out. Call in Our Friends to pick him up for that talk. Yes. Thank you." Replaced the receiver.

Porlock bridled. Red Queen looked at him directly, without emotion.

"You'll find your canteen card has been revoked."

Bree jerked awake. She heard her own mouth slap shut, and felt the pig-belch of an interrupted snore detonate in her throat. The green-white sub-aqua light of the waiting area hurt her eyes. She closed them again.

For an instant, she was in and out of sleep. Her thoughts had been sinking down through layers. She was in and out of a sheaf of fragments. Jones's eye, filling with blood, black in the moonlight. Watery recursions: standing at a table, drinking fast and anxiously, someone always about to come in. And then, again, the death-dream: the walls peeling away and the gathering roar of voices.

". . . Nobody knows where he is . . . ?" was a phrase that cut over, in a voice she seemed to know, from nearby. She opened her eyes, and her neck ached, and the ceiling was still there, attached to each wall by a right angle.

"My boyfriend. He's hurt. Someone called me from this hospital. Where the hell is he?"

The voice came, high on the air through the noise of the room—a girl still not long out of her teens, high and hysterical and slightly slurred, somewhere on the other side of the room. Bree didn't know why, but as soon as her dream slipped away, something cold entered her diaphragm and stayed there. Her head moved to find the source of the sound. She felt the room retreating from her.

At the entrance to the corridor deeper into the hospital there was a girl arguing with a woman in a medical orderly's outfit. The girl was turned half away from Bree, and the sleep in Bree's eyes.

". . . you'd just calm down . . ." the orderly was saying.

". . . English, his name is Alex. ALEX SMART. He's got a . . ."

". . . I told you . . ."

". . . Jesus, I can't believe this place, don't you keep any sort of records . . . ?"

". . . I'll ask the duty nurse . . ."

Bree pulled herself out of her chair, started to move toward the scene. Her legs were stiff from the chair. She came up on the girl. Pink vinyl bag hanging from a shoulder strap; faded T-shirt; a rash of goosebumps over the skin of her upper arm. What had he said the girl was called?

"Carey," said Bree.

The girl turned round, wild. Her face was naked and her eyes puffy from drink and crying and sleeplessness, and there was a mole at the hinge of her jaw. Bree wasn't aware of inhaling.

"Cass?" Bree said, with the walls of the world lifting up and light crashing in.

The girl who had once been called Cass and was now called Carey and had lost her mother years ago in that instant forgot her nearly fiancé and her foster-parents and her exhaustion. She stood there in a T-shirt that said "Fresh Fruit For Rotting Vegetables," and opened her mouth in astonishment and said: "Mom?"

"Help you, ma'am?" said the orderly.

It wasn't as Bree had imagined it. It wasn't as Carey had imagined it either. Both of them had run the scenario over and over again. Often, at the same time and in different places—one on one coast, often, one on the other—mother and daughter had fantasized their meeting in any number of ways, their different scenarios echoing in invisible antiphony through the churn.

Carey had imagined herself coldly eloquent—had imagined herself quietly but politely informing her mother that she had shed her name, that she didn't want to see her, that she owed her nothing. Bree had imagined being forgiven.

Carey had imagined meeting her mother. Carey had imagined telling her mother that she had changed her name because she didn't want to hear the name her mother used in the mouth of her foster-parents. Bree had imagined being slapped.

Time didn't stop. The waiting room was the same green. There was no dam-burst of wordless recognition, no automatic hugs, no tears. They just stood, two strangers all the stranger for having known each other, with precisely a meter of impassable space between them.

"Cass—" Bree said again.

Carey looked as if punched. Her mouth worked.

"Cass—"

"I. Mom. I." Everything was rushing in on Carey. She was confused. She said: "You've put on some weight."

Bree nodded, and she felt her eyes filling. Carey shook her head. It was too much to comprehend, too much to deal with. "I need to find my boyfriend," she said, rubbing the back of one hand with her chewed nails. "He's had an accident—"

"Alex," said Bree. "He was here. He's fine."

"I—Mom. I can't cope with this now. I need to—my boyfriend's had an accident. I need to find him, OK? He's upset."

"He's fine," said Bree. "Can we talk?"

Neither of them moved. Bree, after a bit, raised her eyes and folded her arms and said: "I know where he's staying. I'll take you there."

It was in a very quiet voice, and while she was looking at her feet, that Carey said, as they walked out of the waiting area under a dark blue sky lightening with dawn: "I missed you."

They walked out together through the door and the guard by the emergency room didn't challenge them and the police never came.

Carey found the hotel and went up to the eighth-floor room where Bree had said Alex's room would be. There was a double-wide maid in a uniform made from synthetic fibers hip-nudging a cart further up the corridor.

"Alex?" Carey said.

The door to 810 was ajar. She pushed it open and took in the empty bed, the coverlet still the old chaos, the clock winking from the bedside table. Alex was gone. There was no note.

She took out her phone, and called him, but there was no reply. She thumbed to produce a text message, and typed "Sorry," then after a moment's thought deleted it and put her phone back into her pocket and left the room.

Where had the money gone? Red Queen did not know, and never would. It vanished in the night. It was ghost money.

It trickled out like river water making its way to the sea across the fan of rills in a wide estuary, through the investment bodies and front organizations, the blind trusts and offshore black holes, the accounting switchbacks and shell companies. Incalculably diffusive was the vanishing of the mysterious Nieman's holding in MIC, and like a withdrawing tide it left wreckage, glints of tin, the bones of boats, the suck and wheeze of shellfish buried in their holes in the sand.

But it did not disperse. Not exactly. If it was like an estuary, it was an estuary that flowed back toward the river. It found its way into a newly opened numbered account.

And this account had, as if by chance—though nobody knew then—the same number as the account from which, all those years ago, a certain reclusive mathematician was paid a monthly stipend for his research by his contact at MIC. And somewhere far away something began again.

24

What had happened had happened. Things rolled on. There was nothing in the constitution of the universe that said Alex was meant to be with Carey. Nobody would insulate him against failure, and nothing would indemnify him against loss. He had had an idea about the way his future went that had turned out to be wrong. He had had his chance. He was, after all, alone.

Alex had driven out of Las Vegas in the early morning, when the sun was starting to sear the tarmac and gamblers were emerging caffeinated and shuddering and broke into the bleak light of Fremont Street, on their way to bed, those of them that had beds to go to. The last thing he wanted to do was to say goodbye.

Everything had gone its separate way. He wanted to go home. But he wanted to make a gesture, just to himself—wanted to go somewhere where nobody was looking for him.

He drove up and out of the city toward the west. He had the idea to go to Death Valley. He wanted to be somewhere where he would be a small figure in the landscape.

He drove for an hour, maybe two—the same sort of trance descending on him as the city thinned and disappeared behind him as he had felt in the desert on his way in from the east. His sadness was for a short time something objective, something outside himself. It shared with him, but it wasn't the whole of him. Some version of him would go home on a plane, would wonder how to persuade the stewardess to give him an extra bottle of red wine with his meal, would look gritty-eyed at Heathrow from the window of a taxiing plane and see familiar grays and all the mundane apparatus of normality. Las Vegas would be a gaudy dream. He and Carey would avoid each other, would have the odd awkward conversation, would pretend to be friends, then eventually would stop needing to pretend and would actually be friends, or at least would be friendly with each other. And at that point it really would have died and no force on earth would be able to magic it back.

Trucks and cars came and went. Traffic was sparse. A police patrol car sat angled in the wide patchwork of dirt and tarmac between the carriageways, waiting for something to happen. Sunshine made the windscreen opaque, then momentarily the angle was right. The patrolman inside had on a wide-brimmed hat, and his head was held unmoving, like a lizard holds its head.

The ring. No need for theatrics. He kept one hand on the steering wheel, sliding it round to the top, where the plastic was sun-hot under his palm. With the other he thumbed the rocker on the door. The window slid down and dusty heat entered the car. To either side and all around the desert was dry heat, marked with dark green foliage and white sticks, dead scrub. Low hills rose on the horizon line, and above them was white, and above that was blue. High thin clouds stood in the air, wisps of smoke rolled into miserly cigarettes.

A large truck came out of the haze, swelled, and closed the gap between them, then whooshed past, guffing hot smoke and turbulent air through the open window into the car. Its canvas back panels, retreating in Alex's rear-view mirror, said XGS in black-on-white capitals. It thundered away to its destination.

Alex's window was still down. He pulled the ring out of his pocket and with a single movement threw it out of the open window, high and out to the side of the road. It turned in the air, and the wind was going too loud and the car was too far forward for Alex to hear the high "tink" as the ring hit a rock and skittered into the desert where the chances were that nobody would ever find it again.

★   ★   ★

Much later, Bree called Red Queen from the airport.

"There never was a coincidence engine," said Bree. "Was there? You did it yourself, didn't you? The whole lot."

"You think?" said Red Queen, ignoring the second half of what Bree said. "How do you explain this?"

Bree was in the airport. Red Queen was where—New York?

"Explain what?"

"All of this. Everything that happened." ·

"Nothing happened," said Bree. "You did it—at least until it got out of your control."

"Huh?"

"You knew the Directorate was leaking," said Bree. She was testing a theory. She needed to know. "You knew MIC would over-extend themselves looking for it. The satellite image of the plane, that was you: you cooked it up. Easily done: you control the flow of data; we all know that. The guy in the hospital—what was he, an actor? And the Intercept: to make your photo of the plane plausible; or the photo of the plane, to make the Intercept plausible. The boy knew nothing. Nothing. And the rest of it was just chance."

"No," said Red Queen. "I did cook up the plane—the photo-graph of the plane, anyway. That was where it started from. Flying a kite. No more than that. But I don't know anything about the guy in the hospital. And the Intercept was real."

A pause.

"Sort of. Took a long while to unravel what had happened to it. It was part of a crappy story this guy was writing. Professor up at MIT. He wrote it as some sort of therapy, is my theory, if you can get therapy for being a very irritating individual. There was a New York agent he'd sent the manuscript too. A guy called Duck. Duck and Hands. Weird. I guess he was using it as scrap paper, anyhow. He happened to fax something the wrong way up—Professor Hands's golden words. And that was how it came to us. But then it was that same professor I called in to look at the Banacharski material."

Bree felt, as the conversation went on, an ebbing sense of Red Queen's responsibility. Did the hurricane do that? Could that have been possible? But even as Bree was pushing the line she had been determined to push, she felt differently. She wanted to know if Red Queen believed, and going on the attack was the way to do it. But she herself felt different. The machine was real, and it had brushed against her. She couldn't not believe, not now, in the miracle. And the details mattered less and less.

"So the photograph was fake."

"Yes," Red Queen said.

"The plane didn't appear."

"It might have done," said Red Queen. "Actually, it might have done. But we didn't photograph it if it did." Red Queen said nothing for a bit. Then: "We thought the machine didn't exist, but then we started to worry that perhaps it did. It was the Intercept that made me change my mind. The fact that it had nothing to do with the operation I was running, yet described it so perfectly. And the stripper in the pilot's outfit? I had nothing to do with him either, if he had anything to do with this. So then I needed to see Hands—who didn't know anything, as it turned out."

Bree felt deeply, deeply confused. She formed a mental picture of a bucket of Kentucky Fried Chicken.

"But Hands was helpful. Accidentally helpful. He explained that if it could be thought of, it could perhaps exist. Not here—not in this parallel, the chances against that would be inordinately high—but somewhere else. Another parallel where it could have been possible. It could exist. And if it could exist there—it could affect us, it could bleed through. Assuming that here is where we think we are, anyway."

"I don't follow," said Bree.

"There's any number of universes where none of this ever happened. Where none of us even existed. A majority, if I understand it right. There are universes where your favorite food, Bree, is chef salad."

"I doubt it," said Bree.

"Believe," said Red Queen.

"The boy knew nothing," Bree said again. "But that ring—"

"'AB' could be anyone," said Red Queen. Then, after another longish pause and an exhalation of breath: "I think you're right. For what it's worth, and with no evidence at hand, I think you're right. But there. It's gone now."

"It killed people," said Bree, "if I'm right."

"Uh-huh. It did. It killed Jones." The pause hung there on the line between them. "You liked him, didn't you?" Red Queen sounded almost solicitous.

"Not like that," said Bree. "Not at all. I felt sorry for him. His aysiwhotsis—"

"Apsychosis."

"—apsychosis didn't do him a whole heap of good, in the end, did it?" Bree didn't let herself think about the likelihood that after the killing of that man in the parking lot, from Red Queen's point of view Jones's death was in some ways convenient.

Didn't let herself admit, either, that from her point of view, also, at one level, it felt like—like a weight somehow off her mind. She hadn't been able to judge what Jones had done, and she had felt that she needed to judge it. And with Jones dead . . . it was one less knot in the world.

"No," Red Queen was saying. "It didn't. But the boy, knowing nothing—nothing happened to him, did it? It's no use to us, this thing. And there's barely an MIC for it to be any use to, or danger to. Forgetting it exists, or not believing it exists, is probably the safest way to deal with it."

"That's the way the kid dealt with it," said Bree, scratching her leg with her right hand. "Kind of by accident."

"Test subject number one," said Red Queen. "Imagine if he'd

known what he had in his pocket. I've spoken to people. Full discretion. You were right to let him go."

"Jones?"

"Dealt with," said Red Queen.

Bree thought of Alex: gormless, broken-hearted, clearly so far out of his depth that no harm could come to him. In some other life, she thought, he could have ended up her son-in-law.

"Well," said Bree. There was a long enough pause. Bree rubbed the telephone receiver with one pudgy thumb. It was all she knew of her boss. Bree had never met Red Queen face to face. "RQ," she said, "I'd like some time off."

"Huh?" Red Queen sounded surprised. Bree had never asked for time off.

"I get time off, or I quit," said Bree.

"Don't quit," said Red Queen. "Sure. What time off do you need?"

"A sabbatical," said Bree. "I want to spend some time with my daughter."

Red Queen, at the other end of the phone, made a sound like an exclamation mark, and then smiled.

Alex drove on, toward the coast and the big city and the airport. When he could see the city rising in his windscreen, he called Saul.

"Good morning, little brother," Saul said. "Are we married? Have we eloped with a stripper? Are we—"

"Nothing, Saul. Nothing at all. I'm coming home," he said.

There was no coincidence engine. Not in this world. It existed only in Banacharski's imagination and in the imaginations he touched. But there was a world in which it worked, and this world was no further than a meter from our own. Its effect spilled across, like light through a lampshade.

And with that light there spilled, unappeased and peregrine, fragments of any number of versions of an old mathematician who had become his own ghost. Banacharski was neither quite alive nor quite dead, if you want the truth of it. He was a displaced person again, and nowhere was his home.

He had been driven to madness by long life, and time's arrow, and the permanence of loss, and now he was searching ceaselessly for all the versions of everything he loved: here, there, now, then, once and future, everywhere. He was looking for a second chance. Whether he was in heaven or hell was open to question.

Chickens pecking in the wet grass. A smell of dust and pine. A woman's cough. Asphalt. A road going nowhere. The clatter and slap of rain under thunderheads. A figure glimpsed out of the corner of an eye, encountered unexpectedly in an empty room, possessing—momentarily—a stranger's face with something you recognize.

Nobody's here but us.

At ten minutes past ten on a blank gray morning, some weeks after the events of this story took place, Maeve Bannister, at home in Esher, heard the letter box snap shut. She tipped the iron onto its heel, reflexively patted the neat hair on the side of her head, and walked down a carpeted corridor to the front door of the half-timbered house where the man nicknamed Davidoff had grown up.

There were two letters there. One of them was a shiny envelope with slogans printed in color on the outside. She turned it over, and, as she began to walk back down the corridor, paused, turned it over again, and then let it fall unopened into the wicker basket by the coat stand.

The other letter intrigued her. It was a brown envelope, crumpled and water-stained at one edge. "PLEASE FORWARD" was double-underlined at the top-left corner, and she could see where it had originally been hand-addressed in the same black block capitals. All but the edges of them had been obscured by a sticky label pasted on—just the address of the house on it—by a dot-matrix printer. There was an American stamp, canceled, on the shoulder of the envelope and a scrawl of post-office biro beside it.

She walked back to the ironing board and slipped a thumbnail under the flap of the envelope.

Dear Mrs. Noone,

I hope this letter reaches you. It is about your son, Frederick. I am very sorry to inform you that Frederick has passed away. I don't know if you will have been told, but I know that waiting is difficult and I wanted to make sure that somebody informed you.

I am sorry I cannot come to tell you in person, Mrs. Noone, but my situation is very difficult at the moment and I am not at liberty to travel. I hope to visit you with my condolences at my earliest convenience.

I served with Frederick in the Parachute Regiment, perhaps he mentioned me? My name is Edward Otis, but in the regiment I was always called "Sherman" just like he was known as "Davidoff." Perhaps you knew that?

I wanted to say to you that he was a good mate and a brave soldier. Without him I would probably not be here now, and I know he died doing what he loved.

He always talked about you. I wanted you to know, he wasn't alone when he died.

The letter was signed "Sherman." There was no return address.

Mrs. Bannister, who had bought the house after Mrs. Noone's death the previous summer, felt a moment of abstract sorrow, then put the letter to one side and got on with her ironing.

In the desert between Indian Springs and Desert Rock, the heat haze cleared to glass as evening arrived. An old man shuffled along the side of the road. He was bare-chested and smeared with dirt. A shapeless gray felt hat kept the sun from his eyes. His shoulders were tanned to leather by the sun. He was muttering to himself.

You couldn't see where he had come from. He was not here, and then he was here. He scanned the horizon, raised one hand to scratch the side of his face. He had the sense of having been followed, but when he looked around him he could see nothing.

"Waiting for me," he said. "Just the other side in the churn. Damn liberals."

There was something sad about the look of this old man—something in the set of his shoulders that suggested long searching, a habit of disappointment. He shuffled on. His legs were tired, and his worn old toenails chafed through the leather of his shoes.

He walked out from the road into the scrub desert, then bent down, from the waist. His knees bowed out a little and he emitted a grunt. He picked something up off the ground and straightened up. He raised it to his lips, and blew across it.

"Hmm," he said. He polished it with his thumb and held it up to the light. It winked. He put it in one of his pockets and walked on.

The sky was blank as bone. A few fat drops of rain slapped the faded tarmac. The dust began to rise.

ACKNOWLEDGMENTS

With special thanks to all who gave me encouragement—in particular, David Miller and all at Rogers, Coleridge and White, and Michael Fishwick, who saw the point of this before it existed and without whom it probably wouldn't. Thanks to all at Bloomsbury, Kathy Fry, and particular props to Colin Midson, Ruth Logan, Sophia Martelli, and Alex Goodwin. And thanks to Umar Salam, for nurturing my maths-envy.

A NOTE ON THE AUTHOR

Sam Leith is a former Literary Editor of the *Telegraph*. He now writes for many leading publications including the *Guardian* and the *Evening Standard*. His previous books, *Dead Pets* and *Sod's Law*, have been published to critical acclaim. *The Coincidence Engine* is his first novel. Sam Leith lives in London.

A NOTE ON THE TYPE

The text of this book is set in Bembo. This type was first used in 1495 by the Venetian printer Aldus Manutius for Cardinal Bembo's *De Aetna*, and was cut for Manutius by Francesco Griffo. It was one of the types used by Claude Garamond (1480–1561) as a model for his Romain de l'Université, and so it was the forerunner of what became standard European type for the following two centuries. Its modern form follows the original types and was designed for Monotype in 1929.

W9-CKM-757

Handbook of Laser-Induced Breakdown
Spectroscopy

Handbook of Laser-Induced Breakdown Spectroscopy

David A. Cremers
Applied Research Associates, Inc.
Albuquerque, NM

and

Leon J. Radziemski
Research Corporation
Tucson, AZ

John Wiley & Sons, Ltd

Other Wiley Editorial Offices

John Wiley & Sons Inc., 111 River Street, Hoboken, NJ 07030, USA

Jossey-Bass, 989 Market Street, San Francisco, CA 94103-1741, USA

Wiley-VCH Verlag GmbH, Boschstr. 12, D-69469 Weinheim, Germany

John Wiley & Sons Australia Ltd, 42 McDougall Street, Milton, Queensland 4064, Australia

John Wiley & Sons (Asia) Pte Ltd, 2 Clementi Loop #02-01, Jin Xing Distripark, Singapore 129809

John Wiley & Sons Canada Ltd, 22 Worcester Road, Etobicoke, Ontario, Canada M9W 1L1

Wiley also publishes its books in a variety of electronic formats. Some content that appears in print
may not be available in electronic books.

Library of Congress Cataloging in Publication Data

Cremers, David A.
  Handbook of laser-induced breakdown spectroscopy / David A. Cremers and Leon J. Radziemski.
    p.   cm.
  Includes bibliographical references and index.
  ISBN-13: 978-0-470-09299-6 (cloth : alk. paper)
  ISBN-10: 0-470-09299-8 (cloth : alk. paper)
  1. Atomic emission spectroscopy.   2. Laser spectroscopy.   I. Radziemski, Leon J., 1937–
  II. Title.
  QD96.A8C74 2006
  543′.52—dc22   2006006408

British Library Cataloguing in Publication Data

A catalogue record for this book is available from the British Library

ISBN-13 978-0-470-09299-6 (HB)
ISBN-10 0-470-09299-8 (HB)

Typeset in 10/12pt Times by Integra Software Services Pvt. Ltd, Pondicherry, India
Printed and bound in Great Britain by TJ International Ltd, Padstow, Cornwall
This book is printed on acid-free paper responsibly manufactured from sustainable forestry
in which at least two trees are planted for each one used for paper production.

To Tom Loree, scientist and colleague, who started the LIBS project at Los Alamos National Laboratory in the late 1970s

Contents

Foreword

The most significant series of events occurring in the past four decades in the field of analytical atomic spectroscopy have been the invention of the laser and the development of array detectors. These events have led in the past 25 years to the emergence of laser-induced breakdown spectroscopy (LIBS), also called laser-induced plasma spectroscopy (LIPS), laser spark spectroscopy (LSS), and laser optical emission spectroscopy (LOES). This technique has dominated the analytical atomic spectroscopy scene in the last decade much like atomic absorption spectroscopy dominated in the 1960–1970s, ICP atomic emission spectroscopy in the 1970–1980s, and ICP mass spectrometry in the 1980–1990s. Certainly much of the growth of LIBS as an analytical technique is directly attributed to the pioneering research of Cremers and Radziemski. The 1981 papers by Radziemski and Loree certainly began the revolution involving LIBS. The extreme interest in LIBS is apparent when one looks at the rapid increase in publications since 1965, namely fewer than 50/year from 1965 to about 1995 and since then the increase has been nearly exponential with more than 100 in 1997, more than 200 in 1999, more than 300 in 2003, and about 400 in 2004. In addition, the interest in LIBS is obvious when one looks at the number of LIBS sessions at PITTCON and FACSS and the conferences devoted exclusively to LIBS.

Few analytical techniques other than LIBS have ever resulted in such a general interest in the analytical community. Fundamental papers involving the measurement of electron number densities and plasma temperatures; determination of the approach to local thermodynamic equilibrium; the experimental and theoretical aspects of laser breakdown in gases, liquids, solids and aerosols; the modeling of laser-induced breakdown and ablation on solids; the modeling of post-breakdown of solids; and the use of multiple laser pulses in LIBS have all occurred in the physics and chemistry literature. The great attention to theoretical aspects of LIBS has been fueled by numerous and far-reaching applications of LIBS. Applications have involved solids, liquids, gases, and aerosols and specifically metals, environmental particles, including aerosols, water contamination, archaeological studies, artwork dating and cleaning, sampling of biological materials including bacteria and spores, analyses during machining, and homeland security involving analysis of explosives and biological and chemical warfare agents. The analytical interest has resulted primarily because of the multi-element capability, the applicability to virtually all sample types, the low sample requirements (almost non-destructive), the speed of measurements, and the lack of sample preparation. The major difficulty with LIBS involving calibration is a major current research area where calibration-free and absolute analysis are active areas of research activity.

I look forward to the further development of LIBS during the next decade. This book will certainly be useful to all researchers and will be useful to me in a field that has captivated my interest in the past few decades.

Professor J.D. Winefordner
V.T. and Louise Jackson Professor of Chemistry
Graduate Research Professor
Head, Analytical Division
Department of Chemistry
University of Florida, Gainesville, Florida USA

Preface

DC on the left and LR on the right

The invention of the laser has resulted in many technological spin-offs. One that has emerged as a field-deployable, analytical technique is laser-induced breakdown spectroscopy (LIBS), also sometimes called laser-induced plasma spectroscopy (LIPS) or laser spark spectroscopy (LSS). LIBS uses a low-energy pulsed laser (typically tens to hundreds of millijoules per pulse) to generate a plasma which vaporizes a small amount of the sample. Spectra emitted by the excited species, mostly atoms, are used to develop quantitative and qualitative analytical information. Targets have included gases, liquids, and aerosols, with an emphasis on solids. Applications have been many and range from sampling iron and steel, soil for contamination, metals used in nuclear reactors for degradation, artwork for dating, teeth of mummies for evidence of water contamination in the past, and detection of aerosols emitted from smokestacks or during machining operations. In the past five years, new applications have sprung up around sampling of biological materials, planetary exploration, and homeland security. Improved techniques are being developed, and LIBS instrumentation is now available commercially. Experiments have driven improved theoretical and computational models of plasma initiation and expansion.

In the early 1980s there were few groups working on LIBS. In the past decade, however, the field has expanded greatly with many international groups now investigating and developing the method for a variety of applications. The first international conference solely on LIBS was held in Pisa, Italy in 2000. Subsequently, international meetings have been held every 2 years, and meetings focused on work in the European and Mediterranean areas on the odd years.

Several edited books and book chapters published in the last decade and a half provided snapshots of the status of LIBS at the time of their publication. Our goals are somewhat different. In addition to a comprehensive update of the forefront of LIBS development and applications, we review and summarize, for the novice, the principles of plasma spectroscopy and analytical spectrochemistry as it applies to LIBS. Included are new data and archival material to assist experienced as well as new users. Embedded are comments on the many advantages of the method along with its limitations, to provide the reader a balanced overview of LIBS capabilities.

In the first chapter we present a historical review of LIBS development through to the year 2002, based on the peer-reviewed literature. We focus on the earliest time an innovation or application appeared on the scene, rather than tracing every development through to the present day. Of course, continuous improvements in apparatus, techniques, and fundamental understanding drive the reexamination of old applications, and the emergence of new applications spurs improvements in a recurring spiral of progress. Chapter 2 contains a review of the basic principles of plasma atomic emission spectroscopy. A plasma is a local assembly of atoms, ions and free electrons, overall electrically neutral, in which the charged species often act collectively. Natural light emitting plasmas, like the sun, have been known forever. Electrically-induced plasmas have been generated in the laboratory since the 1800s, and laser-induced plasmas have been investigated since the 1960s. In this chapter we deal with the intricacies of LIBS plasma formation, lifetime and decay, in and on a variety of media, focusing on spectral information as the primary diagnostic technique. The use of spectral line properties for determining plasma properties such as temperature and electron density is discussed. Laser ablation and the effect of multiple laser pulses on plasma properties are also reviewed here.

LIBS uses instrumentation similar to that employed by other atomic spectroscopic methods, and each important element of a LIBS apparatus is discussed in turn in Chapter 3. The unique characteristics of LIBS originate from the use of a powerful laser pulse to both 'prepare' the target sample and then 'excite' the constituent atoms to emit light. To generate and capture those signals, a combination of modern laser, detector, timing, and data-gathering instrumentation, with traditional spectroscopic apparatus including spectrometers and their optics is needed. New developments in fiber optics and detector technology are highlighted. The calibration of wavelength and spectral response is treated, along with methods of LIBS deployment from basic set-ups to more advanced configurations.

The next three chapters deal with fundamental concepts in spectroscopic chemical analysis and how they apply to and are modified by the conditions under which LIBS operates. Analytical figures-of-merit are used to benchmark the capabilities of an analysis method and to compare the performance of distinct analytical techniques using a common set of parameters. These include limits of detection, precision, accuracy, sensitivity and selectivity. In Chapter 4 we present a discussion of the more important figures-of-merit and how they are used to characterize LIBS. The basic element of any LIBS measurement is the emission spectrum recorded from a single plasma. Each firing of the laser atomizes a portion of the sample in the focal volume and produces a plasma that excites and re-excites the atoms to emit light. This is then applied either to qualitative analysis as discussed in Chapter 5, or quantitative measurements as presented extensively in Chapter 6. In the former, some basic and practical methods of element and material identification are presented. In the latter, we discuss the ultimate goal, to provide a highly quantitative analysis, hence to determine with high precision and accuracy the concentration of a species in a sample or the absolute mass of a species. We treat how LIBS interacts with different forms of samples, internal standardization and matrix effects. A detailed example of measuring impurities in a lithium solution is presented.

The ability to make remote measurement in field environments is one of the principal advantages of LIBS. This application and three basic techniques for its use are treated in Chapter 7. In the first method, the laser beam is directed over an open path (through air, gas or vacuum) to the target on which a plasma is formed, and then the plasma light is collected at a distance. In the second method, the laser pulses are injected into a fiber optic and transported to the remotely located target sample, while in the third method, a compact probe containing a small laser is positioned next to the remotely located sample and the plasma light is sent back to the detection system over a fiber optic cable. We discuss subjects such as conventional stand-off analysis, the development of very long distance analysis, and details of the physics and engineering of fiber optics.

In Chapter 8 we consider the recent history from 2003 on, emphasizing the latest trends in LIBS research and applications, and focusing on what a new applier of LIBS needs to know to perform state-of-the-art LIBS experiments. Subjects reviewed include fundamentals enhanced by modeling and experiments, double pulse studies and applications to nuclear reactors and detection of biological agents. The chapter ends with a detailed review of the progress towards sending LIBS on a mission to Mars. A book on LIBS would not be complete without some speculations on the most promising directions for the future, methods of expanding LIBS applications, and factors that will speed its commercialization. These are the subjects of Chapter 9.

The appendices contain fundamental information that will be useful to the LIBS community. They include: (A) a discussion of the essentials of basic safety considerations for LIBS operations; (B) a guide for getting a quick start in LIBS development; (C) published detection limits, as well as a unique list of element detection limits using a uniform method of analysis developed for this text, and (D) a list of major LIBS references.

Starting from fundamentals and moving through a thorough discussion of equipment, methods, and applications, we believe that the *Handbook of Laser-Induced Breakdown Spectroscopy* will provide a unique reference source that will be of value for many years for this important new analytical technique.

David Cremers
Leon Radziemski

Acronyms, Constants and Symbols

Item	Definition	Value, units, or comments
$\alpha(\lambda)$	absorption coefficient as a function of wavelength	/cm
AOTF	acousto-optic tunable filter	Chapter 3
APD	avalanche photodiode	a sensitive photodiode type detector
c	speed of light in vacuum	299 792 458 m/s
CCD	charge coupled device	two dimensional array of photodiodes, Chapter 3
COD	continuous optical discharge	
CF-LIBS	calibration-free LIBS	Chapter 8
CW	continuous wave	
CRM	certified reference material	used to calibrate LIBS, Chapter 4
e	electron charge	$1.60217653 \times 10^{-19}$ C
eV	electron volt	$1.60217653 \times 10^{-19}$ J
$\varepsilon(\lambda)$	emissivity as a function of wavelength	
ε_o	electric constant	$8.854187817 \times 10^{-12}$ Farads/m
f#	f-number of an optical system (e.g. lens or spectrograph)	e.g. f# = f/d = (lens focal length)/(lens diameter)
FOC	fiber optic cable	Chapter 3
FOM	figures-of-merit	a set of parameters to benchmark the performance of an analytical method, Chapter 4
FWHM	full-width at half maximum	width of a spectral line at the points of half maximum intensity
Γ	full-width at half maximum intensity of a spectral line	units of wavelength, wavenumber or frequency
HWHM	half-width at half maximum	half width of a spectral line at the points of half maximum intensity
h	Planck constant	$6.6260693 \times 10^{-34}$ J/s
$\hbar$	Planck constant/2π	$1.0545717 \times 10^{-34}$ J/s
ICCD	intensified CCD array	Chapter 3
ICP	inductively coupled plasma	
IPDA	intensified PDA	Chapter 3
IR	infra-red	refers to a spectral region, $\lambda > 700$ nm
k	Boltzmann constant	$1.3806505 \times 10^{-23}$ J/K
LIBS	laser-induced breakdown spectroscopy	
LIDAR	Light detection and ranging	optical methods of remote sensing of materials in the atmosphere
LIPS	laser-induced plasma spectroscopy	alternate name for the LIBS method
LIF	laser-induced fluorescence	

(Continued)

Item	Definition	Value, units, or comments
LOD	limit of detection	Chapter 4
LOQ	limit of quantification	Chapter 4, LOQ = 3.3LOD, usually
LSC	laser-supported combustion	type of plasma wave, Chapter 2
LSD	laser-supported detonation	type of plasma wave, Chapter 2
LSR	laser-supported radiation	type of plasma wave, Chapter 2
LSS	laser spark spectroscopy	alternate name for the LIBS method
LTE	local thermodynamic equilibrium	Chapter 2
LTSD	lens-to-sample distance	
λ	wavelength	nm, angstroms (Å); $1\text{Å} = 0.1\,\text{nm}$
m	electron mass	$9.1093826 \times 10^{-31}\,\text{kg}$
MCP	multichannel plate	intensifier for a CCD and PDA, Chapter 3
NA	numerical aperture	
Nd:YAG	neodymium YAG laser	type of solid state laser typically used for LIBS
NIR	near IR	refers to a spectral region, $700 < \lambda < 3000\,\text{nm}$
OES	optical emission spectroscopy	
PCA	principal component analysis	
PD	photodiode	solid state optical detector, Chapter 3
PDA	photodiode array	one-dimensional array of photodiodes
PMT	photomultiplier tube	optical detector
ppm	parts-per-million	concentration unit, usually stated as w/w
ν	frequency	Hz
n_e	electron density	$/\text{cm}^3$
R-FIBS	remote filament induced breakdown spectroscopy	Chapter 7
RSD	relative standard deviation	Chapter 4
RM	reference material	used to calibrate LIBS, Chapter 4
σ	wavenumber	$/\text{cm}$
s	standard deviation	Chapter 4
T	Absolute temperature	degrees Kelvin (K)
t_b	gate width	time period over which the plasma light is recorded
t_d	delay time	time period between arrival of the laser pulse at the sample to form the plasma and the start of recording of the plasma light signal
Torr	unit of pressure	
UV	ultraviolet	refers to a spectral region, $180 < \lambda < 400\,\text{nm}$
VIS	visible	refers to a spectral region, $400 < \lambda < 700\,\text{nm}$
VUV	vacuum ultraviolet	refers to a spectral region, $\lambda < 180\,\text{nm}$
XRF	x-ray fluorescence	method of element detection

Values from P.J. Mohr and B.N. Taylor (2005). CODATA recommended values of the fundamental constants: 2002. Rev. Mod. Phys. 77: 1–108.

1 History

1.1 ATOMIC OPTICAL EMISSION SPECTROCHEMISTRY (OES)

1.1.1 CONVENTIONAL OES

Since the early 1800s, scientists realized that elements emitted specific colors of light. As atomic theory developed, spectroscopists learned that those colors, wavelengths or frequencies were a unique signature for each atom and ion. Hence spectra became fingerprints of the emitting atomic species. This is the basis for spectrochemical analysis using atoms.

Early sources of spectra were the sun, flames and gas discharges, such as the old Geissler tube. These were plasma sources, with varying degrees of ionization depending on the source conditions. Against the 5000 K photosphere of the sun, we see the Fraunhofer absorption lines due to neutral and once ionized species. In the solar corona highly ionized spectra are observed because of temperatures that reach into the hundreds of thousands of degrees.

Many sources have been developed for spectrochemistry, but two workhorses have been the conventional electrode spark and, more recently, the inductively coupled plasma (ICP). These are illustrated in Figure 1.1 (Plate 1), which also contains a photograph of the laser spark. The electrode spark has excitation temperatures up to 50 000 K, while the argon ICP temperature is more typically about 10 000 K. Typically they are used for laboratory analyses but occasionally are pressed into service for situations requiring more rapid data acquisition. For example, the conventional spark has been used for decades to monitor the steel making process by withdrawing a molten sample which is then solidified and transported to a laboratory located in the plant for rapid analysis. Decisions on additives are made based on these spectroscopic data.

1.1.2 LASER OES

As soon as the laser was developed in the early 1960s, spectrochemists began investigating its potential uses (Radziemski, 2002). An early observation was that a pulsed laser could produce a small plasma in air. The emission from that plasma

Handbook of Laser-Induced Breakdown Spectroscopy D. Cremers and L. Radziemski
© 2006 John Wiley & Sons, Ltd

Figure 1.1 Photographs of a conventional electrode spark, an inductively coupled plasma, and a laser-induced spark. The size scales are different (see Plate 1)

showed the potential for spectrochemical analysis. However, from 1960 to 1980 the analytical capability was so inferior to that of the conventional spark and laser technology was in its infancy, so that the technique was less favored than a related one – laser ablation into a conventional plasma source. Here the laser was used to vaporize a small amount of sample for analysis by, for example, the conventional electrode spark (Moenke and Moenke-Blankenburg, 1973). However, that was not the only way the laser could be used in spectrochemistry.

The development of tunable dye lasers meant that one could illuminate a prepared source of atoms with radiation resonant with a transition in one of the atomic species. Then either the absorption of the laser beam or the laser-induced fluorescence could be used as an analytical signal. These techniques discriminated against background and increased the signal to noise considerably by recycling the same atoms many times. Sometimes the atoms were placed in the laser cavity itself. The intra-cavity absorption technique was a very sensitive spectrochemical method, if difficult to employ generally.

Both absorption and fluorescence are used in many applications. However, because the laser needs to be tuned to a specific transition in a specific species, it is not as broadly useful as a hot plasma in which a variety of species can be excited and monitored simultaneously.

1.2 LASER-INDUCED BREAKDOWN SPECTROSCOPY (LIBS)

Laser-induced breakdown spectroscopy (LIBS), also sometimes called laser-induced plasma spectroscopy (LIPS) or laser spark spectroscopy (LSS) has developed rapidly as an analytical technique over the past two decades. As most commonly used and shown schematically in Figure 1.2, the technique employs a low-energy pulsed laser (typically tens to hundreds of mJ per pulse) and a focusing lens to generate a plasma that vaporizes a small amount of a sample. A portion of the plasma light is collected and a spectrometer disperses the light emitted by excited atomic and ionic species

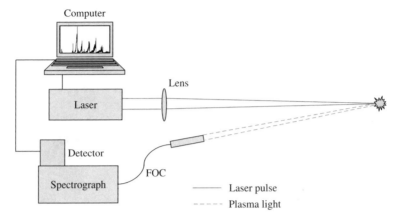

Figure 1.2 A schematic of a simple apparatus for laser-induced breakdown spectroscopy illustrating the principal components

in the plasma, a detector records the emission signals, and electronics take over to digitize and display the results. The **book cover** shows a LIBS spectrum with certain strong spectral features standing out from the continuous background plasma light.

LIBS is an appealing technique compared with many other types of elemental analysis, because setting up an apparatus to perform a LIBS measurement is very simple. One merely focuses a laser pulse in or on a sample, which can be a gas, liquid, aerosol or solid, to form a microplasma, examples of which are shown in Figure 1.3. The spectra emitted are used to determine the sample's elemental constituents. However, the basic physical and chemical processes involved are not so simple. The initiation, formation and decay of the plasma are complex processes. Absorption of the incident laser radiation occurs through the mechanism of inverse bremsstrahlung, involving three-body collisions between photons, electrons, and atoms or molecules. In gases and liquids the plasma creates a shock wave in the surrounding medium transferring energy by means of conduction, radiation and the shock wave. When the experiment deals with a sample surface in a vacuum, the plasma and ejecta expand freely away from the surface at different speeds. Excitation of specific energy levels in different atoms is likewise complex, and depends on factors such as thermodynamic equilibrium and interactions with other atoms and molecules generally lumped under the category of matrix effects. After the laser pulse has terminated (typically within 10 ns), the plasma decays over an interval of one to several microseconds, depending on the laser energy deposited. In vacuum that temporal process is shortened. Most LIBS experiments involve repetitive plasmas with frequencies of 10 Hz or greater.

The spectra observed change as the plasma evolves temporally as shown in Figure 1.4. Soon after initiation, continuum and ionic spectra are seen. The continuum

Figure 1.3 The laser spark (a) in a gas, (b) in a liquid, (c) on the surface of a liquid, and (d) on a beryllium (see Plate 2)

is the 'white light' from the plasma that contains little spectroscopic information and the ions result from electrons ejected by neutral atoms. As the plasma decays, these are followed by spectra from neutral atoms and eventually simple molecules formed from the recombination of atoms. Throughout the temporal history, one observes a diminishing continuum spectral background due to recombination of free electrons with ions. Inspection of the LIBS spectrum reveals immediate qualitative information about sample composition. After calibration, quantitative information can be obtained. These issues will be treated in greater depth in subsequent chapters.

During the past 10 years, the LIBS technique has made significant progress towards becoming a viable commercial technology. Over the years many useful reviews have been published (Adrain and Watson, 1984; Cremers and Radziemski, 1987; Radziemski and Cremers, 1989; Radziemski, 1994; Lee *et al.*, 1997;

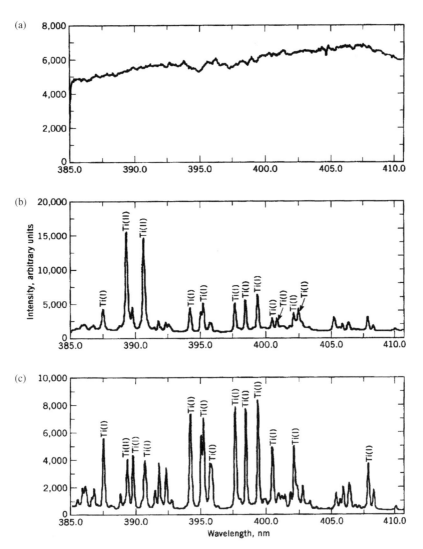

Figure 1.4 Gated titanium spectra of a LIBS plasma illustrating the development of the spectra as a function of the time after plasma initiation. The time intervals are: (a) 0–0.5 μs; (b) 0.5–5 μs; and (c) 10–110 μs

Rusak *et al.*, 1997; Tognoni *et al.*, 2002; Lee *et al.*, 2004). In this chapter we consider the history of the technique and some applications that have spurred its development. We focus on the first time an innovation or application appeared on the scene, rather than tracing every innovation through to the present day. Note however, that contemporary improvements in apparatus, techniques and fundamental understanding are driving reexaminations of old applications. Conversely, the emergence of new applications drives improvements in a recurring spiral of progress.

Table 1.1 Significant milestones in the development of LIBS as an analytical technique applicable to a variety of samples and circumstances

1960	Ted Maiman develops the first pulsed laser
1963	First analytical use of a laser-plasma on surfaces, hence the birth of laser-induced breakdown spectroscopy
1963	First report of a laser plasma in a gas
1963	Laser micro-spectral analysis demonstrated, primarily with cross-excitation
1963	Laser plasmas in liquids were initially investigated
1964	Time-resolved laser plasma spectroscopy introduced
1966	Characteristics of laser-induced air sparks studied
1966	Molten metal directly analyzed with the laser spark
1970	Continuous optical discharge reported
1970	Q-switched laser use reported, results compared with normal laser pulses
1971	Biological materials investigated with LIBS
1972	Steel analysis carried out with a Q-switched laser
1978	Laser spectrochemical analysis of aerosols reported
1980	LIBS used for corrosion diagnostics in nuclear reactors
1982	Initial use of the acoustic properties of the laser-induced spark
1984	Analysis of liquid samples and hazardous aerosols demonstrated
1988	Attempts made to enhance intensities through electric and magnetic fields
1989	Metals detected in soils using laser plasma method
1992	Portable LIBS unit for monitoring surface contaminants developed
1992	Stand-off LIBS for space applications demonstrated
1993	Underwater solid analysis via dual-pulse LIBS demonstrated
1995	Demonstration of fiber optic delivery of laser pulses
1995	Multiple-pulse LIBS reported for use on steel samples
1997	LIBS use in applications in painted works of art and illuminated manuscripts
1998	Subsurface soil analysis by LIBS-based cone penetrometers shown
1998	Reports on the use of echelle spectrometers coupled with CCD detectors
1999	Trace metal accumulation in teeth observed with LIBS
1999	Pulses from different lasers used to enhance LIBS performance
1999	Calibration-free LIBS introduced
2000	Report on commercial instrument for coal analysis
2000	Demonstration of LIBS on a NASA Mars rover
2000	First International conference on LIBS – Pisa, Italy
2002	Second International Conference on LIBS – Orlando, FL
2004	Third International Conference on LIBS – Malaga, Spain
2004	LIBS approved for 2009 Mars mission

Table 1.1 illustrates some significant milestones in LIBS development. These will be addressed individually in the following sections.

1.3 LIBS HISTORY 1960–1980

Shortly after the pulsed ruby laser was invented in 1960 the laser-induced plasma was observed. The first published report mentioning the plasma was a meeting abstract by Brech and Cross in 1962 (Brech and Cross, 1962). Early on, the laser was used primarily as an ablation source with cross-excitation to provide the spectrum. In 1963, Debras-Guédon and Liodec published the first analytical use for spectrochemical analysis of surfaces (Debras-Guédon and Liodec, 1963). Maker *et al.* in 1964 reported the first observation of optically induced breakdown in a gas (Maker *et al.*, 1964). Runge *et al.* in the same year discussed the use of a pulsed Q-switched ruby laser for direct spark excitation on metals (Runge *et al.*, 1964). Linear calibration curves were obtained for nickel and chromium in iron, with precisions of 5.3 % and 3.8 %, respectively. They also analyzed molten metal. In 1966, Evtushenko looked at the effect of sparks from two lasers (Evtushenko *et al.*, 1966). About the same time, Young *et al.* described the characteristics of laser-induced air sparks (Young *et al.*, 1966).

In the period from 1964 to 1967 the first instruments based primarily on laser-ablation with cross-excitation were developed by Zeiss (Germany), Jarrell-Ash (USA) and JEOL Ltd (Japan). Although they could be operated with the laser plasma generating the spectral emissions, most often the laser was used only for ablation followed by cross-excitation with a conventional spark. Because the auxiliary spark could contaminate and complicate the analysis through the introduction of electrode material, auxiliary excitation by electrodeless methods was also developed. The instruments could not typically compete in accuracy and precision with conventional spark spectroscopy, although they could handle nonconducting samples. Some instruments continued in use through the 1990s. An excellent discussion of those devices and the associated techniques is contained in the book entitled *Laser Micro Analysis* (Moenke-Blankenburg, 1989).

Time resolution of the decaying plasma helps to monitor the plasma evolution, to discriminate against the continuum light, and to sort out spectral features. It is especially valuable in reducing interferences between spectral features that appear at the same or adjacent wavelengths but in different temporal windows as illustrated in Figure 1.4. Different detection systems to obtain temporally resolved spectra were used in the 1960s, including a streak camera and rotating mirrors. A method more suited to modern detectors, electronically gating and averaging the signals from many plasmas, was developed by Schroeder *et al.* (Schroeder *et al.*, 1971). As detectors have developed, the preferred methods of time resolution have moved from boxcar averagers, for example, to gated, intensified charge coupled detectors. Fast photodetectors are used to record the temporal profile of plasma emissions from single pulses. An early review of the field was published by Scott and Strasheim in 1970 (Scott and Strasheim, 1970).

During this period, much of the research on the laser plasma and its uses appeared in the Russian literature. For example, Afanas'ev and Krokhin published on the vaporization of matter exposed to laser emission (Afanas'ev and Krokhin, 1967). In 1966, Raizer reported on breakdown and heating of gases under the influence of a laser beam, which was a summary of original work and a review of the state of the art (Raizer, 1966). Biberman and Norman did a thorough analysis of the origins of the continuous spectrum from the laser plasma which underlies the discrete spectral lines (Biberman and Norman, 1967). In 1974, Buravlev *et al.* commented on using a laser in spectral analysis of metals and alloys (Buravlev *et al.*, 1974). Much of the physics covered in the Russian literature was summarized in the classic book by

Raizer, *Laser-induced Discharge Phenomena*, published in English in 1977 (Raizer, 1977). Underlying that is the classic book on the physics of shock waves and high-temperature hydrodynamic phenomena, a text originally published in Russian in 1964, translated into English in 1966, and recently reprinted (Zel'dovich and Raizer, 2002).

Early on it was recognized that physical and chemical matrix effects would have to be dealt with if LIBS was to develop as a quantitative method. Cerrai and Trucco discussed matrix effects in laser-sampled spectrochemical analysis (Cerrai and Trucco, 1968). They focused on the dependence of spectral line intensities on physical conditions such as grain sizes and boundaries. This was followed by a paper by Marich *et al.* concluding that physical effects were more important than chemical ones (Marich *et al.*, 1970). However others, like Scott and Strasheim, found signal suppression due to various effects linked to the components of the matrix (Scott and Strasheim, 1970). It is now accepted that a variety of physical and chemical effects play important roles in signal strength, and repeatability.

Biological media with metallic contamination were investigated by the laser plasma as reported in papers by Marich *et al.* and Treytl *et al.* (Marich *et al.*, 1970; Treytl *et al.*, 1972). The former deals with the effect of the matrix on the spectral emission from a variety of samples, including human serum and liver. The latter provides detection limits for the analysis of metals in biological materials. Metals in the form of reagent grade salts were incorporated into gelatin or albumin matrices. Limits of detection ranged from 2×10^{-15} gm for magnesium and copper to 3×10^{-13} gm for mercury and iron.

A novel variation of the pulsed plasma is the continuous optical discharge (COD). In this case a continuous wave (CW) laser beam is focused to sustain a plasma as long as the laser remains on. The laser is usually of the continuous CO_2 variety. Initiation requires another pulsed laser or a conventional spark. Early papers on this subject were published by Generalov, and Keefer (Generalov *et al.*, 1970; Keefer, 1974). Spectrochemical analysis by the COD was investigated by Cremers *et al.* (Cremers *et al.*, 1985).

Materials processes such as welding were obvious applications of high powered lasers. The plasma literature in that field overlapped with that of spectrochemical applications. In the first of a series of books, Ready (Ready, 1971) provided an overview of the variety of phenomena induced by high power laser pulses. Some of the subjects discussed were: optical damage of materials; the interaction between laser radiation and surfaces resulting in ablation, melting, and crater formation; the effect of laser light on biological systems; and optically induced gas breakdown. The most recent version edited by Ready is a compendium of 30 years of research, the *LIA Handbook of Laser Materials Processing* (Ready, 2001).

Generating a plasma in water was considered first by Buzukov *et al.* (Buzukov *et al.*, 1969). Lauterborn (Lauterborn, 1972) conducted high-speed photography of plasmas in liquids. This was followed by measurements of shock waves and cavities caused by laser-induced breakdown in water, glycerin, and benzene by Teslenko (Teslenko, 1977). These mechanistic studies focusing on the shock wave formation and propagation continued throughout the 1970s.

In the mid to late 1970s aerosols became a subject of research. The effects of dust and particles in the beam as they influenced breakdown were studied by Lencioni (Lencioni, 1973). He found that when long focal-length lenses were used, dust in the beam initiated strings of mini-plasmas. Belyaev *et al.* discussed laser spectrochemical analysis of aerosols in a 1978 publication (Belyaev *et al.*, 1978). In 1979 Edwards and Fleck Jr published on the two-dimensional modeling of aerosol breakdown in air (Edwards and Fleck Jr, 1979). This was followed by a study in 1982 by Ivanov and Kopytin on selective interaction of a train of laser pulses with an aerosol medium (Ivanov and Kopytin, 1982).

A spin-off method of LIBS called TABLASER was described by Measures and Kwong starting in 1979 (Measures and Kwong, 1979). That technique uses an ablation laser pulse followed by a laser pulse through the plume. The second pulse from a dye laser is tuned to a transition in the element of interest and results in laser-induced fluorescence. Interest in this type of arrangement surfaced again in the 1990s.

1.4 LIBS HISTORY 1980–1990

As lasers and other LIBS components became smaller and the *in situ* advantages of the laser plasma became more obvious, additional applications appeared. Interest at Los Alamos National Laboratory was kindled by two 1981 papers on the time-integrated (Loree and Radziemski, 1981) and time-resolved (Radziemski and Loree, 1981) forms of the technique in gases. The term LIBS was originally used in the former 1981 paper, and TRELIBS, identified with the time-resolved version, in the latter. Currently LIBS is the term used for either method.

Los Alamos then funded an internal study of the use of this technique for detection of toxic beryllium dust, resulting in papers on detecting beryllium in air (Radziemski *et al.*, 1983a) and on filters (Cremers and Radziemski, 1985). Figure 1.5 shows a long spark created by using a cylindrical lens, on a rotating stage on which a blackened piece of filter paper has been set for contrast. During that period, Los Alamos scientists studied the detection of hazardous gases (Cremers and Radziemski, 1983), aerosols (Radziemski *et al.*, 1983b), and liquids (Cremers *et al.*, 1984; Wachter and Cremers, 1987). Sensing of steels and other metals in molten or solid forms were also investigated (Cremers, 1987).

Some research focused on diagnostics and enhancements. The plasma generates shock waves that can be heard and recorded as acoustic signals, whose strengths are related to the energy deposited in the medium. The acoustic properties of the spark were first studied by Belyaev *et al.* (Belyaev *et al.*, 1982). Kitamori (Kitamori *et al.*, 1988) started an interesting line of research in particle counting in liquids by using the acoustic effect produced by the plasma. He also made observations of the optical emission. Beginning with the early 1990s, more quantitative uses of acoustic signals were reported, for example by Diaci and Mozina (Diaci and Mozina, 1992), who studied the blast waveforms detected simultaneously by a microphone and a

Figure 1.5   A long spark created by using a cylindrical lens, on a filter set on a rotating stage

laser probe. Starting in 1988, there were several reports of attempts to enhance the plasma by the use of auxiliary magnetic or electric fields. None have reported dramatic success.

Much interest was shown in the initiation of the spark on single microspheres or droplets. Results included a paper by Chylek *et al.* (1986), on the effect of size and material of liquid spherical particles on laser-induced breakdown. This line of research was continued in a paper by Biswas *et al.* (1988) detailing the irradiance and laser wavelength dependence of plasma spectra from single levitated aerosol droplets. Chang *et al.* (1988) discussed laser-induced breakdown in large transparent water droplets.

In the late 1980s interest increased in making LIBS more quantitative by addressing the factors such as differential excitation. These included many works from the Niemax group in Dortmund (Ko *et al.*, 1989; Leis *et al.*, 1989). In the study by Ko *et al.* the stability of internal standardization was investigated. They found that the chromium to iron intensities in binary mixtures were not a function of time after plasma initiation, hence temperature, or completeness of vaporization. This was in contrast to zinc to copper ratios in brass. The conclusion was that internal standardization was not a given in all cases, but the conditions for its use needed to be established for each situation. In the study by Leis *et al.*, the atomization and propagation properties of the plasma plume were investigated.

Studies of toxic and superconducting materials were made. These included analysis of beryllium in beryllium-copper alloys (Millard *et al.*, 1986) and detection of cadmium, lead and zinc (Essien *et al.*, 1988). The superconducting materials community published many papers on laser ablation for deposition of super-conducting thin films, and sometimes addressed the optical emission as a diagnostic technique for process monitoring. A method of monitoring corrosion in the core regions of nuclear reactors was detailed by Adrain (Adrain, 1982) and a working system was described.

At the close of the decade, a book edited by Radziemski and Cremers, *Laser-induced Plasmas and Applications*, summarized the relevant physics, chemistry and applications at that time (Radziemski and Cremers, 1989). It contained detailed chapters updating the physics of breakdown and post-breakdown phenomena, and an updated review of the technique.

1.5 LIBS HISTORY 1990–2000

As the field proceeded into the 1990s, applications and fundamental studies developed rapidly. There were several useful reviews during this decade (Radziemski, 1994; Song *et al.*, 1997; Rusak *et al.*, 1998). Hou and Jones (Hou and Jones, 2000) reviewed several techniques with field capability and presented the advantages and disadvantages of each.

More research groups surfaced in the US and in other countries. In Australia, Grant *et al.* provided detection limits for minor components in iron ore (Grant *et al.*, 1991). This was done with a view to developing a field-based technique. Later Chadwick's group in Australia analyzed lignite and produced a commercial instrument for coal analysis (Wallis *et al.*, 2000). Sabsabi and Cielo (Canada) started publishing their work on aluminum alloy targets with papers in 1992 and 1995 (Sabsabi and Cielo, 1992, 1995). Palleschi's group in Pisa, Italy began addressing applications with respect to pollutant detection such as the paper by Lazzari *et al.* on the detection of mercury in air (Lazzari *et al.*, 1994).

The application of LIBS to remote analysis, begun in the 1980s, developed rapidly in the 1990s. It was an important area of investigation by Cremers' group at Los Alamos. Cremers *et al.* (Cremers *et al.*, 1995) discussed remote elemental analysis by laser-induced breakdown spectroscopy using a fiber optic cable. Angel's group also published on the use of a fiber optic probe to determine lead in paint (Marquardt *et al.*, 1996). LIBS for the analysis of lunar surfaces was first mentioned in papers by Blacic *et al.* and Kane *et al.* (Blacic *et al.*, 1992; Kane *et al.*, 1992). This was followed by a seminal paper by Knight *et al.* (Knight *et al.*, 2000) on characterization of LIBS for planetary exploration, and a report on the use of LIBS on a prototype Martian rover (Wiens *et al.*, 2002). Figure 1.6 shows a K9 rover with the LIBS sensor unit on the mast.

Efforts to make LIBS more quantitative continued. Davies *et al.* (Davies *et al.*, 1996) reported on relevant factors for *in situ* analytical spectroscopy in the nuclear industry. Russo's group at Lawrence Berkeley Laboratory undertook detailed studies of the ablation process as reported by Mao *et al.* (Mao *et al.*, 1995). Winefordner's group at the University of Florida initiated studies of the variables influencing the precision of LIBS measurements. Their first publication in this area was by Castle *et al.* (Castle *et al.*, 1998) where a variety of factors were considered and inter- and

Figure 1.6   The K9 rover in the field with the LIBS sensor mounted on the right side of the mast head instrument suite. (Photo courtesy of NASA Ames Research Center)

intra-shot measurement precisions were calculated. The best precision obtained was 0.03 %. Gornushkin *et al.* reported on a curve of growth methodology applied to laser-induced plasma emission spectroscopy (Gornushkin *et al.*, 1999). A procedure called 'calibration-free LIBS' (CF-LIBS) was developed in Palleschi's group, as explained in a paper by Ciucci *et al.* (Ciucci *et al.*, 1999). In effect, one assumes thermodynamic equilibrium, and uses spectral lines representing the bulk of the vaporized material, to deduce the concentration of the element of interest. Matrix effects continued to be studied. For example, the effects of water content and grain size were reported by Wisbrun *et al.* (Wisbrun *et al.*, 1994). These works and others have sharpened the focus on factors that can enhance or hinder the ability to obtain quantitative results.

Throughout the decade unique applications continued to emerge. Harith *et al.* studied the hydrodynamic evolution of laser driven diverging shock waves (Harith *et al.*, 1990). Quantitative simultaneous elemental determinations in alloys, using LIBS in an ultra-high-vacuum, was reported by Theim *et al.* (Theim *et al.*, 1994). The US Army Aberdeen Proving Ground laboratory under Miziolek began its investigations of LIBS with two publications by Simeonsson and Miziolek (Simeonsson and Miziolek, 1993, 1994). They studied LIBS in carbon monoxide, carbon dioxide, methanol and chloroform, and used a variety of laser wavelengths from 193 to 1064 nm. The group of Aragón, Aguilera and Campos (Aragón *et al.*, 1993) applied LIBS to determining carbon content in molten steel. Poulain and Alexander (Poulain and Alexander, 1995) used LIBS to measure the salt concentration in seawater aerosol droplets. Singh's group published on quantification of metal hydrides (Singh *et al.*, 1996) and LIBS spectra from a coal-fired MHD facility (Zhang *et al.*, 1995).

Art analysis has received much attention, for example as described by Anglos *et al.* (Anglos *et al.*, 1997), who worked on diagnostics of painted artworks using LIBS for pigment identification, and Georgiou *et al.* (Georgiou *et al.*, 1998), who described excimer laser restoration of painted artworks. Vadillo and Laserna published work on depth-resolved analysis of multilayered samples, a technique that is used in forensic archeometry (Vadillo and Laserna, 1997). Applications to biological materials were developed. Samek *et al.* studied trace metal accumulation in teeth (Samek *et al.*, 1999). Pallikaris *et al.* (Pallikaris *et al.*, 1998) reported on the use of LIBS for monitoring corneal hydration, while Sattmann *et al.* started work on polymer identification that resulted in an apparatus to sort plastics (Sattmann *et al.*, 1998).

Determination of the composition of soils and contaminants received considerable attention. Eppler *et al.* (Eppler *et al.*, 1996) reported on matrix effects in the detection of Pb and Ba in soil. Detection limits of 57 and 42 ppm (w/w) for Pb and Ba, respectively, were achieved. A cylindrical focusing lens yielded higher experimental precision than a spherical lens. Miles and Cortes performed subsurface heavy-metal detection with the use of a cone penetrometer system (Miles and Cortes, 1998). A real-time fiber-optic LIBS probe for the *in situ* detection of metals in soils was used by Theriault *et al.* (Theriault *et al.*, 1998).

Much work was directed to improvement in instrumentation and techniques. Undoubtedly the greatest impact was achieved by the introduction of the compact echelle spectrometer mated with the ever-more capable CCD detectors, intensified or not. A good introduction to these subjects can be found in Vadillo *et al.* (Vadillo *et al.*, 1996), who reported on space and time-resolved LIBS using CCD detection. Also Barnard *et al.* (Barnard *et al.*, 1993) commented on the design and evaluation of echelle grating optic systems for ICP-OES, and Harnley and Fields (Harnley and Fields, 1997) wrote on solid-state array detectors for analytical spectrometry. Bauer *et al.* described an echelle spectrometer and intensified CCD combination (Bauer *et al.*, 1998).

Diode lasers may be sources of the future because of their small size and simplicity of operation. An introduction to the subject for laser spectrochemistry was given by Lawrenz and Niemax (Lawrenz and Niemax, 1989). A passively Q-switched Nd:YAG microchip laser was described by Zayhowski (Zayhowski, 2000). The laser was 1 to 2 mm on a side and was diode pumped. Peak powers approaching 0.5 MW were reported.

As lasers with new parameters became available they were put to use on LIBS applications. The result of 60 ps Nd:YAG 532 nm pulses was reported by Davis *et al.* (Davis *et al.*, 1993). Kagawa *et al.* (Kagawa *et al.*, 1994) wrote on XeCl excimer laser-induced shock wave plasmas and applications to emission spectrochemical analysis. Sattman *et al.* (Sattman *et al.*, 1995) discussed analysis of steel samples using multiple Q-switched Nd:YAG laser pulses. Lasers with pulses of different lengths were used and their results compared. Femtosecond, picosecond, and nanosecond laser ablation of solids was discussed by Chikov *et al.* (Chikov *et al.*, 1996). Fedosejevs' femtosecond LIBS group has focused on laser pulses of hundreds of microjoules, dubbed 'microlibs,' as reported by Rieger *et al.* (Rieger *et al.*, 2000). Microline imaging was discussed by Mateo *et al.* in Laserna's group (Mateo *et al.*, 2000). Angel *et al.* reported on using dual pulses and pulses of 1.3 ps and 140 fs (Angel *et al.*, 2001). Both show very low background signals, so time resolution is not necessary; however the low signal levels dictate a higher repetition rate and adequate summing of spectra.

Later in the 1990s the applications turned to very practical problems, such as monitoring environmental contamination, control of materials processing, sorting of materials to put them in proper scrap bins, and slurry monitoring. Barrette and Turmel (Barrette and Turmel, 2000) used LIBS for on-line iron-ore slurry monitoring for real-time process control. Buckley *et al.* (Buckley *et al.*, 2000) implemented LIBS as a continuous emissions monitor for toxic metals. Palanco and Laserna (Palanco and Laserna 2000) studied the full automation of a laser-induced breakdown spectrometer for quality assessment in the steel industry with sample handling, surface preparation, and quantitative analysis capabilities. St-Onge and Sabsabi (St-Onge and Sabsabi, 2000) published on quantitative depth-profile analysis using LIPS on galvannealed coatings on steel. Laser ablation continues as an active area, and is well summarized in a review by Russo *et al.* (Russo *et al.*, 2002).

An emphasis on developing rugged, moveable instrumentation emerged at this time. Optical fibers were built into LIBS systems, primarily for carrying the spark light to the spectrometer, but also for the delivery of the laser pulse as well. More compact echelle spectrographs have been developed. An instrument the size of a small suitcase, used for analysis of contaminants in soils and lead in paint, was made

Figure 1.7   A portable LIBS surface analyzer, circa 1998

in Cremers' Los Alamos laboratory as reported by Yamamoto *et al.* (Yamamoto *et al.*, 1996). A later version of this unit is shown in Figure 1.7. Capability and compactness have improved since that time. The maturity of LIBS was demonstrated by its recent adoption for use in planetary geology on a 2009 mission to Mars.

1.6 ACTIVE AREAS OF INVESTIGATION, 2000–2002

As we entered the new millennium, international meetings in Pisa, Italy (Corsi *et al.*, 2001), Cairo, Egypt (Harith *et al.*, 2002), Orlando, FL, USA (Hahn *et al.*, 2003), Crete (Anglos and Harith, 2004) and Spain (Laserna, 2005) provided excellent summaries of the current status of LIBS applications. New areas of study include increasing exploration of the vacuum ultraviolet region of the spectrum. Biological applications on human teeth, bones and tissue are becoming more common. Pollen, spores and bacteria are being studied to see if unique signatures can be determined. Homeland security applications are proliferating. Surface mapping and imaging modes using line sparks are proving useful to determine surface compositional variations. Sophisticated statistical techniques are being applied to extract signals and reliability factors. New papers are appearing in relevant journals every month. The growth of publications involving LIBS through 2002 is illustrated in Figure 1.8. LIBS instruments are being marketed, especially for materials analysis and toxic materials identification. Because LIBS is the most versatile analytical method yet developed, many applications studied in the earlier LIBS periods have resurfaced because of increased needs or improved instrumental capabilities. Likewise patents

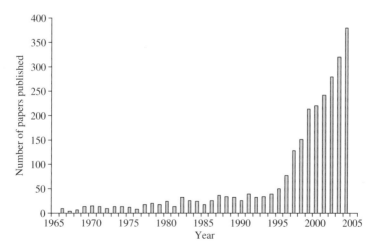

Figure 1.8 LIBS papers per year, 1966–2005. In the last 5 years, about 1140 papers have been published relating to LIBS. (Courtesy of M. Sabsabi)

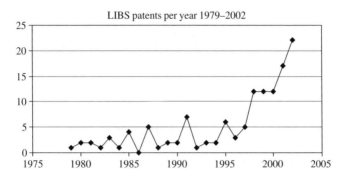

Figure 1.9 LIBS patents per year, 1979–2002. (Courtesy of M. Sabsabi)

involving LIBS are proliferating rapidly, as illustrated in Figure 1.9. All this points
to the fact that interest in LIBS as an analytical technique is increasing, a trend
which we believe will continue in the coming years.

REFERENCES

Adrain, R.S. (1982). Some industrial uses of laser induced plasmas. Ch. 7 in *Industrial
    Applications of Lasers*, ed. H. Koebner, John Wiley & Sons, Inc., New York: 135–176.
Adrain, R.S. and J. Watson (1984). Laser microspectral analysis: a review of principles and
    applications. J. Appl. Phys.17: 1915–1940.
Afanas'ev, V. Yu and O.N. Krokhin (1967). Vaporization of matter exposed to laser emission.
    Soviet Physics JETP 25: 639–645.
Angel, S.M., D.N. Stratis, K.L. Eland, T. Lai, M.A. Berg and D.M. Gold (2001). LIBS using
    dual- and ultra-short laser pulses. Fresenius J. Anal. Chem. 369: 320–327.
Anglos, D., S. Couris and C. Fotakis (1997). Artworks: laser-induced breakdown spectroscopy
    in pigment identification. Appl. Spectrosc. 51: 1025–1030.
Anglos, D. and M.A. Harith (2004). 2nd Euro-Mediterranean symposium on laser induced
    breakdown spectroscopy (EMSLIBS-II). J. Anal. At. Spectrom. 19: 10N–11N.
Aragón, C., J.A. Aguilera and J. Campos (1993). Determination of carbon content in molten
    steel using laser-induced breakdown spectroscopy. Appl. Spectrosc. 47: 606–608.
Barnard, T.W., M.J. Crockett, J.C. Ivaldi and P.L. Lundberg (1993). Design and evaluation
    of an echelle grating optical system for ICP-OES. Anal. Chem. 65: 1225–1230.
Barrette, L. and S. Turmel (2000). On-line iron-ore slurry monitoring for real-time process
    control of pellet making processes using laser-induced breakdown spectroscopy: graphite
    vs total carbon detection. Spectrochim. Acta Part B 56: 715–724.
Bauer, H.E., F. Leis and K. Niemax (1998). Laser induced breakdown spectrometry with an
    echelle spectrometer and intensified charge coupled device detection. Spectrochim. Acta
    Part B 53: 1815–1825.
Belyaev, E.B., A.P. Godlevskii and Y.D. Kopytin (1978). Laser spectrochemical analysis of
    aerosols. Sov. J. Quant. Electro. 8: 1459–1463.
Belyaev, E. B., *et al.* (1982). Nature of the acoustic emission during laser breakdown of
    gaseous disperse systems. Sov. Tech. Phys. Lett. 8: 144–147.
Biberman, L.M. and G.E. Norman (1967). Continuous spectra of atomic gases and plasma.
    Sov. Phys. Uspekhi 10: 52–54.

Biswas, A., H. Latifi, L.J. Radziemski and R.L. Armstrong (1988). Irradiance and laser wavelength dependence of plasma spectra from single levitated aerosol droplets. Appl. Opt. 27: 2386–2391.

Blacic, J.D., D.R. Pettit and D.A. Cremers (1992). Laser-induced breakdown spectroscopy for remote elemental analysis of planetary surfaces. Proceedings of the International Symposium on Spectral Sensing Research, Maui, HI.

Brech, F. and L. Cross (1962). Optical microemission stimulated by a ruby laser. Appl. Spectrosc. 16: 59.

Buckley, S.G., H.A. Johnsen, K.K.R. Hencken and D.W. Hahn (2000). Implementation of laser-induced breakdown spectroscopy as a continuous emissions monitor for toxic metals. Waste Manage. 20: 455–462.

Buravlev, Yu. M., B.P. Nadezhda and L.N. Babanskaya (1974). Use of a laser in spectral analysis of metals and alloys. Zavodskaya Laoratoriya 40: 165–171.

Buzukov, A.A., Y.A. Popov and V.S. Teslenko (1969). Experimental study of explosion caused by focusing monopulse laser radiation in water. Zhurnal Prikladnoi Makhaniki i Tekhnicheskoi Fiziki 10: 17–22.

Castle, B.C., K. Talabardon, B.W. Smith and J.D. Winefordner (1998). Variables influencing the precision of laser-induced breakdown spectroscopy measurements. Appl. Spectrosc. 52: 649–657.

Cerrai, E. and R. Trucco (1968). On the matrix effect in laser sampled spectrochemical analysis. Energia Nucleare 15: 581–585.

Chang, R.K., J.H. Eickmans, W.-F. Hsieh, C.F. Wood, J.-Z. Zhang and J.-B. Zheng (1988). Laser-induced breakdown in large transparent water droplets. Appl. Opt. 27: 2377–2385.

Chikov, B.N., C. Momma, S. Nolte, F. von Alvensleben and A. Tünnerman (1996). Femtosecond, picosecond, and nanosecond laser ablation of solids. Appl. Phys. A 63: 109–115.

Chylek, P., M.A. Jarzembski, N.Y. Chou and R.G. Pinnick (1986). Effect of size and material of liquid spherical particles on laser-induced breakdown. Appl. Phys. Lett. 49: 1475–1477.

Ciucci, A., M. Corsi, V. Palleschi, S. Ratelli, A. Salvetti and E. Tognoni (1999). New procedure for quantitative elemental analysis by laser-induced plasma spectroscopy. Appl. Spectrosc. 53: 960–964.

Corsi, M., V. Palleschi and E. Tognoni (Eds) (2001). Special Issue, 1st International Conference on Laser Induced Plasma Spectroscopy. Spectrochim. Acta Part B 50: 565–1034.

Cremers, D.A. and L.J. Radziemski (1983). Detection of chlorine and fluorine in air by laser-induced breakdown spectrometry. Anal. Chem. 55: 1252–1256.

Cremers, D.A., L.J. Radziemski and T.R. Loree (1984). Spectrochemical analysis of liquids using the laser spark. Appl. Spectrosc. 38: 721–726.

Cremers, D.A. and L.J. Radziemski (1985). Direct detection of beryllium on filters using the laser spark. Appl. Spectrosc. 39: 57–60.

Cremers, D.A., F.L. Archuleta and R.J. Martinez (1985). Evaluation of the continuous optical discharge for spectrochemical analysis. Spectrochim. Acta Part B 40: 665–679.

Cremers, D.A. (1987). The analysis of metals at a distance using laser-induced breakdown spectroscopy. Appl. Spectrosc. 41: 572–578.

Cremers, D.A. and L.J. Radziemski (1987). Laser plasmas for chemical analysis. Ch. 5 in Laser Spectroscopy and its Applications, eds L.J. Radziemski, R.W. Solarz and J.A. Paisner, Marcel Dekker, New York: 351–415.

Cremers, D.A., J.E. Barefield and A.C. Koskelo (1995). Remote elemental analysis by laser-induced breakdown spectroscopy using a fiberoptic cable. Appl. Spectrosc. 49: 857–860.

Davies, C.M., H.H. Telle and A.W. Williams (1996). Remote in situ analytical spectroscopy and its applications in the nuclear industry. Fresenius J. Anal. Chem. 355: 895–899.

Davis, L.M., L.-Q. Li and D.R. Keefer (1993). Picosecond resolved evolution of laser breakdown in gases. J. Phys. D: Appl. Phys. 26: 222–230.

Debras-Guédon, J. and N. Liodec (1963). De l'utilisation du faisceau d'un amplificateur a ondes lumineuses par émission induite de rayonnement (laser á rubis), comme source énergetique pour l'excitation des spectres d'émission des éléments. C.R. Acad. Sci. 257: 3336–3339.

Diaci, J. and J. Mozina (1992). A study of blast waveforms detected simultaneously by a microphone and a laser probe during laser ablation. Appl. Phys. A 55: 352–358.

Edwards, A.L. and J.A. Fleck Jr (1979). Two-dimensional modeling of aerosol-induced breakdown in air. J. Appl. Phys. 50: 4307–4313.

Eppler, A.S., D.A. Cremers, D.D. Hickmott, M.J. Ferris and A.C. Koskelo (1996). Matrix effects in the detection of Pb and Ba in soils using laser-induced breakdown spectroscopy. Appl. Spectrosc. 50: 1175–1181.

Essien, M., L.J. Radziemski and J. Sneddon (1988). Detection of cadmium, lead and zinc in aerosols by laser-induced breakdown spectroscopy. J. Anal. At. Spectrom. 3: 985–988.

Evtushenko, T.P., et al. (1966). Investigation of air sparks by two synchronized lasers. Sov. Phys.-Tech. Phys. 11: 818–822.

Generalov, N.A., V.P. Zimakov, G.I. Kozlov, V.A. Masyukov and Y.P. Raiser (1970). Continuous optical discharge. JETP Lett. 11: 302–306.

Georgiou, S., V. Zafiropulos, D. Anglos, C. Balas, V. Tornari and C. Fotakis (1998). Excimer laser restoration of painted artworks: procedures, mechanisms and effects. Appl. Surf. Sci. 129: 738–745.

Gornushkin, I.B., J.M. Anzano, L.A. King, B.W. Smith, N. Omenetto and J.D. Winefordner (1999). Curve of growth methodology applied to laser-induced plasma emission spectroscopy. Spectrochim. Acta Part B 54: 491–503.

Grant, K.J., G.L. Paul and J.A. O'Neill (1991). Quantitative elemental analysis of iron ore by laser-induced breakdown spectroscopy. Appl. Spectrosc. 45: 701–705.

Hahn, D.W., A.W. Miziolek and V. Palleschi (Eds) (2003). Special Issue, LIBS 2002. Appl. Opt. 42: 5933–6225.

Harith, M.A., V. Palleschi, A. Salvetti, D.P. Singh, G. Tropiano and M. Vaselli (1990). Hydrodynamic evolution of laser driven diverging shock waves. Laser Part. Beams 8: 247–252.

Harith, M.A., V. Palleschi and L.J. Radziemski (Eds) (2002). Special Issue, 1st Euro-Mediterranean Symposium on Laser-induced Breakdown Spectroscopy. Spectrochim. Acta Part B 57: 1107–1249.

Harnley, J.M. and R.E. Fields (1997). Solid-state array detectors for analytical spectrometry. Appl. Spectrosc. 51: 334A–351A.

Hou, X.D. and B.T. Jones (2000). Field instrumentation in atomic spectroscopy. Microchem. J. 66: 115–145.

Ivanov, Y.V. and Y.D. Kopytin (1982). Selective interaction of a train of laser pulses with an aerosol medium. Sov. J. Quant. Electro. 12: 355–357.

Kagawa, K., K. Kawai, M. Tani and T. Kobayashi (1994). XeCl excimer laser-induced shock wave plasma and its application to emission spectrochemical analysis. Appl. Spectrosc. 48: 198–205.

Kane, K.Y., D.A. Cremers, R.C. Elphic and D.S. Mckay (1992). An in situ technique for elemental analysis of lunar surfaces. Joint Workshop on New Technologies for Lunar Resource Assessment (6 April 1992), Santa Fe, NM. NASA-CR-191918.

Keefer, D.R. (1974). Experimental study of a stationary laser-sustained air plasma. J. Appl. Phys. 46: 1080–1083.

Kitamori, T., K. Yokose, K. Suzuki, T. Sawada and Y. Gohshi (1988). Laser breakdown acoustic effect of ultrafine particle in liquids and its application to particle counting. Jpn. J. Appl. Phys. 27: L983–L985.

Knight, A.K., N.L. Scherbarth, D.A. Cremers and M.J. Ferris (2000). Characterization of laser-induced breakdown spectroscopy (LIBS) for application to space exploration. Appl. Spectrosc. 54: 331–340.

Ko, J.B., W. Sdorra and K. Niemax (1989). On the internal standardization in optical spectrometry of microplasmas produced by laser ablation of solid samples. Fresenius Z. Anal. Chem. 335: 648–651.

Laserna, J.J. (2005). Third international conference on laser induced plasma spectroscopy and applications. Spectrochim. Acta Part B 60: 877–878.

Lauterborn, W. (1972). High-speed photography of laser-induced breakdown in liquids. Appl. Phys. Lett. 21: 27–29.

Lawrenz, J. and K. Niemax (1989). A semiconductor diode laser spectrometer for laser spectrochemistry. Spectrochim. Acta Part B 44: 155–164.

Lazzari, C., M. de Rosa, S. Rastelli, A. Ciucci, V. Palleschi and A. Savetti (1994). Detection of mercury in air by time resolved laser-induced breakdown spectroscopy technique. Laser Part. Beams 12: 525–530.

Lee, W.B., J. Wu, Y.-I. Lee and J. Sneddon (2004). Recent applications of laser-induced breakdown spectrometry: a review of material approaches. Appl. Spectrosc. Rev. 39: 27–97.

Lee, Y.-I., K. Song and J. Sneddon (1997). Laser induced plasmas for analytical atomic spectroscopy. Ch. 5 in *Lasers in Analytical Atomic Spectroscopy*, eds J. Sneddon, T.L. Thiem and Y.-I. Lee, VCH, New York: 197–235.

Leis, F., W. Sdorra, J.B. Ko and K. Niemax (1989). Basic investigations for laser microanalysis: I. Optical emission spectrometry of laser-produced sample plumes. Mikrochim. Acta (Wein) 11: 185–199.

Lencioni, D.E. (1973). The effect of dust on 10.6-μm laser-induced air breakdown. Appl. Phys. Lett. 23: 12–14.

Loree, T.R. and L.J. Radziemski (1981). Laser-induced breakdown spectroscopy: time-integrated applications. Plasma Chem. Plasma Proc. 1: 271–280.

Maker, P.D., R.W. Terhune and C.M. Savage (1964). Optical third harmonic generation. Proceedings of the 3rd International Conference on Quantum Electronics, Paris, Columbia University Press, New York, Vol. 2: 1559.

Mao, X.L., M.A. Shannon, A.J. Fernandez and R.E. Russo (1995). Temperature and emission spatial profiles of laser-induced plasmas during ablation using time-integrated emission spectroscopy. Appl. Spectrosc. 49: 1054–1062.

Marich, K.W., P.W. Carr, W.J. Treytl and D. Glick (1970). Effect of matrix material on laser-induced elemental spectral emission. Anal. Chem. 42: 1775–1779.

Marquardt, B.J., S.R. Goode and S.M. Angel (1996). In situ determination of lead in paint by laser-induced breakdown spectroscopy using a fiber-optic probe. Anal. Chem. 68: 977–981.

Mateo, M.P., S. Palanco, J.M. Vadillo and J.J. Laserna (2000). Fast atomic mapping of heterogeneous surfaces using microline-imaging laser-induced breakdown spectrometry. Appl. Spectrosc. 54: 1429–1434.

Measures, R.M. and H.S. Kwong (1979). TABLASER:trace (element) analyzer based on laser ablation and selectively excited radiation. Appl. Opt. 18: 281–286.

Miles, B. and J. Cortes (1998). Subsurface heavy-metal detection with the use of a laser-induced breakdown spectroscopy (LIBS) penetrometer system. Field Anal. Chem. Technol. 2: 75–87.

Millard, J.A., R.D. Dalling and L.J. Radziemski (1986). Time resolved laser-induced breakdown spectrometry for the rapid determination of beryllium in beryllium-copper alloys. Appl. Spectrosc. 40: 491–494.

Moenke, H. and L. Moenke-Blankenburg (1973). *Laser Microspectrochemical Analysis*, A. Hilger, London and Crane, Russak and Co., Inc., New York.

Moenke-Blankenburg, L. (1989). *Laser Micro Analysis*, John Wiley & Sons, Inc., New York.

Palanco, S. and J.J. Laserna (2000). Full automation of a laser-induced breakdown spectrometer for quality assessment in the steel industry with sample handling, surface preparation and quantitative analysis capabilities. J. Anal. At. Spectrom. 15: 1321–1327.

Pallikaris, I.G., H.S. Ginis, G.A. Kounis, D. Anglos, T.G. Papazoglou and L.P. Naoumidis (1998). Corneal hydration monitored by laser-induced breakdown spectroscopy. J. Refr. Surgery 14: 655–660.

Poulain, D.E. and D.R. Alexander (1995). Influences on concentration measurements of liquid aerosols by laser-induced breakdown spectroscopy. Appl. Spectrosc. 49: 569–579.

Radziemski, L.J. and T.R. Loree (1981). Laser-induced breakdown spectroscopy: time-resolved spectrochemical applications. Plasma Chem. Plasma Proc. 1: 281–293.

Radziemski, L.J., D.A. Cremers and T.R. Loree (1983a). Detection of beryllium by laser-induced breakdown spectroscopy. Spectrochim. Acta Part B 38: 349–353.

Radziemski, L.J., T.R. Loree, D.A. Cremers and N.M. Hoffman (1983b). Time-resolved laser-induced breakdown spectrometry of aerosols. Anal. Chem. 55: 1246–1251.

Radziemski, L.J. and D.A. Cremers (1989). Spectrochemical analysis using laser plasma excitation. Ch. 7 in *Laser-induced Plasmas and Applications*, eds L.J. Radziemski and D.A. Cremers, Marcel Dekker, New York: 303–325.

Radziemski, L.J. and D.A. Cremers (Eds) (1989). *Laser-induced Plasmas and Applications*, Marcel Dekker, New York.

Radziemski, L.J. (1994). Review of selected analytical applications of laser plasmas and laser ablation, 1987–1994. Microchem. J. 50: 218–234.

Radziemski, L.J. (2002). From LASER to LIBS, the path of technology development. Spectrochim. Acta Part B 57: 1109–1114.

Raizer, Y.P. (1966). Breakdown and heating of gases under the influence of a laser beam. Sov. Phys. Uspekhi 8: 650–673.

Raizer, Y.P. (1977). *Laser-induced Discharge Phenomena*, Consultants Bureau, New York, NY.

Ready, J.F. (1971). *Effects of High-power Laser Radiation*, Academic Press, New York, NY.

Ready, J.F. (2001). *LIA Handbook of Laser Materials Processing*, Laser Institute of America, Orlando, FL.

Rieger, G.W., M. Taschuk, Y.Y. Tsui and R. Fedosejevs (2000). Laser-induced breakdown spectroscopy with low-energy laser pulses. Proc. SPIE 4087: 1127–1136.

Runge, E.F., R.W. Minck and F.R. Bryan (1964). Spectrochemical analysis using a pulsed laser source. Spectrochim. Acta 20: 733–735.

Rusak, D.A., B.C. Castle, B.W. Smith and J.D. Winefordner (1997). Fundamentals and applications of laser-induced breakdown spectroscopy. Crit. Rev. Anal. Chem. 27: 257–290.

Rusak, D.A., B.C. Castle, B.W. Smith and J.D. Winefordner (1998). Recent trends and the future of laser-induced breakdown spectroscopy. Trends Anal. Chem. 17: 453–461.

Russo, R.E., X. Mao and S.S. Mao (2002). Physics of laser ablation in microchemical analysis. Anal. Chem. 74: 70A–77A.

Sabsabi, M. and P. Cielo (1992). Laser-induced breakdown spectroscopy on aluminum alloy targets. SPIE 2069: 191–201.

Sabsabi, M. and P. Cielo (1995). Quantitative analysis of aluminum alloys by laser-induced breakdown spectroscopy and plasma characterization. Appl. Spectrosc. 49: 499–507.

Samek, O., D.C.S. Beddows, H.H. Telle, G.W. Morris, M. Liska and J. Kaiser (1999). Quantitative analysis of trace metal accumulation in teeth using laser-induced breakdown spectroscopy. Appl. Phys. A 69: 179–182.

Sattman, R., V. Sturm and R. Noll (1995). Laser-induced breakdown spectroscopy of steel samples using multiple Q-switch Nd:YAG laser pulses. J. Phys. D: Appl. Phys. 28: 2181–2187.

Sattman, R., I. Moench, H. Krause, R. Noll, S. Couris, A. Hatziapostolou, A. Mavromanolakis, C. Fotakis, E. Larrauri and R. Miguel (1998). Laser-induced breakdown spectroscopy for polymer identification. Appl. Spectrosc. 52: 456–461.

Schroeder, W.W., J.J. van Niekirk, L. Dicks, A. Strasheim and H.V.D. Piepen (1971). A new electronic time resolution system for direct reading spectrometers and some applications in the diagnosis of spark and laser radiations. Spectrochim. Acta Part B 26: 331–340.

Scott, R.H. and A. Strasheim (1970). Laser induced plasmas for analytical spectroscopy. Spectrochim. Acta Part B 25: 311–332.

Simeonsson, J.B. and A.W. Miziolek (1993). Time-resolved emission studies of ArF laser produced microplasmas. Appl. Opt. 32: 939–947.

Simeonsson, J.B. and A.W. Miziolek (1994). Spectroscopic studies of laser-produced plasmas formed in CO and CO_2 using 193, 266, 355, 532, and 1064 nm laser radiation. Appl. Phys. B 59: 1–9.

Singh, J.P., H. Zhang, F.-Y. Yueh and K.P. Carney (1996). Investigation of the effects of atmospheric conditions on the quantification of metal hydrides using laser-induced breakdown spectroscopy. Appl. Spectrosc. 50: 764–773.

Song, K., Y.-I. Lee and J. Sneddon (1997). Applications of laser-induced breakdown spectrometry (LIBS). Appl. Spectrosc. Rev. 32: 183–235.

St-Onge, L. and M. Sabsabi (2000). Towards quantitative depth-profile analysis using laser-induced plasma spectroscopy: investigation of galvannealed coatings on steel. Spectrochim. Acta Part B 55: 299–308.

Teslenko, V.S. (1977). Investigation of photoacoustic and photohydrodynamic parameters of laser breakdown in liquids. Sov. J. Quant. Electro. 7: 981–984.

Theriault, G.A., S. Bodensteiner and S.H. Lieberman (1998). A real-time fiber-optic LIBS probe for the in situ delineation of metals in soils. Field Anal. Chem. Technol. 2: 117–125.

Thiem, T.L., R.H. Salter, J.A. Gardner, Y.I. Lee and J. Sneddon (1994). Quantitative simultaneous elemental determinations in alloys using LIBS in an ultra-high-vacuum. Appl. Spectrosc. 48: 58–64.

Tognoni, E., V. Palleschi, M. Corsi and G. Christoforetti (2002). Quantitative micro-analysis by laser-induced breakdown spectroscopy: a review of the experimental approaches. Spectrochim. Acta Part B 57: 1115–1130.

Treytl, W.J., J.B. Orenberg, K.W. Marich, A.J. Saffir and D. Glick (1972). Detection limits in analysis of metals in biological materials by laser microprobe optical emission spectrometry. Anal. Chem. 44: 1903–1904.

Vadillo, J.M., M. Milan and J.J. Laserna (1996). Space and time-resolved laser-induced breakdown spectroscopy using charge-coupled device detection. Fresenius J. Anal. Chem. 355: 10–15.

Vadillo, J.M. and J.J. Laserna (1997). Depth-resolved analysis of multilayered samples by laser-induced breakdown spectrometry. J. Anal. At. Spectrom. 12: 859–862.

Wachter, J.R. and D.A. Cremers (1987). Determination of uranium in solution using laser-induced breakdown spectroscopy. Appl. Spectrosc. 41: 1042–1048.

Wallis, F.J., B.L. Chadwick and R.J.S. Morrison (2000). Analysis of lignite using laser-induced breakdown spectroscopy. Appl. Spectrosc. 54: 1231–1235.

Wiens, R.C., R.E. Arvidson, D.A. Cremers, M.J. Ferris, J.D. Blacic, F.P. Seelos IV and K.S. Deal (2002). Combined remote mineralogical and elemental identification from rovers: field and laboratory tests using reflectance and laser-induced breakdown spectroscopy. J. Geophys. Res. 107: 10.1029/2000JE001439.

Wisbrun, R., I. Schechter, R. Niessner, H. Schroeder and K.L. Kompa (1994). Detector for trace elemental analysis of solid environmental samples by laser plasma spectroscopy. Anal. Chem. 66: 2964–2975.

Yamamoto, K.Y., D.A. Cremers, M.J. Ferris and L.E. Foster (1996). Detection of metals in the environment using a portable laser-induced breakdown spectroscopy instrument. Appl. Spectrosc. 50: 222–233.

Young, M., M. Hercher and C.-Y. Yu (1966). Some characteristics of laser-induced air sparks. J. Appl. Phys. 37: 4938–4940.

Zayhowski, J.J. (2000). Passively Q-switched Nd:YAG microchip lasers and applications. J. Alloys Compd. 303: 393–400.

Zel'dovich, Ya.B. and Yu.P. Raizer (2002). *Physics of Shock Waves and High-temperature Hydrodynamic Phenomena*, eds W.D. Hayes and R.F. Probstein, Dover, Mineola NY.

Zhang, H., J.P. Singh, F.-Y. Yueh and R.L. Cook (1995). Laser-induced breakdown spectra in a coal-fired MHD facility. Appl. Spectrosc. 49: 1617–1623.

2 Basics of the LIBS Plasma

2.1 LIBS PLASMA FUNDAMENTALS

Light emitting plasmas have been studied in earnest since the 1920s, and laser-induced plasmas since the 1960s. In this chapter we will deal with the intricacies of LIBS plasma formation, lifetime, and decay in and on a variety of media. Good references to plasmas and relevant spectroscopic diagnostics are books by Griem (Griem, 1964, 1974, 1997), Lochte-Holtgreven (Lochte-Holtgreven, 1968) and Bekefi (Bekefi, 1976), and chapters by Weyl (Weyl, 1989), Root (Root, 1989), Radziemski and Cremers (Radziemski and Cremers, 1989b), and Kim (Kim, 1989) in *Laser-induced Plasmas and Applications* (Radziemski and Cremers, 1989a).

A plasma is a local assembly of atoms, ions and free electrons, overall electrically neutral, in which the charged species often act collectively. Plasmas are characterized by a variety of parameters, the most basic being the degree of ionization. A weakly ionized plasma is one in which the ratio of electrons to other species is less than 10%. At the other extreme, highly ionized plasmas may have atoms stripped of many of their electrons, resulting in very high electron to atom/ion ratios. LIBS plasmas typically fall in the category of weakly ionized plasmas. A schematic overview of the temporal history of a LIBS plasma initiated by a single laser pulse is shown in Figure 2.1. At early times, ionization is high. As electron-ion recombination proceeds, neutral atoms, and then molecules form. Throughout there is a background continuum that decays with time more quickly than the spectral lines. The continuum is primarily due to bremsstrahlung (free–free) and recombination (free–bound) events. In the bremsstrahlung process photons are emitted by electrons accelerated or decelerated in collisions. A recombination occurs when a free electron is captured into an ionic or atomic energy level and gives up its excess kinetic energy in the form of a photon. Time resolution of the plasma light in LIBS allows for discrimination in favor of the region where the signals of interest predominate. The symbol t_d represents the delay from the initiation of the laser to the opening of the window during which signal will be accepted; t_b represents the length of that window. LIBS has also been performed in a double-pulse mode, where two laser pulses from the same or different lasers are incident on the target. The first application of this variation was to liquids by Cremers *et al.* (Cremers *et al.*, 1984). We will discuss its more recent use in ablation of solids at the end of this chapter.

Handbook of Laser-Induced Breakdown Spectroscopy D. Cremers and L. Radziemski
© 2006 John Wiley & Sons, Ltd

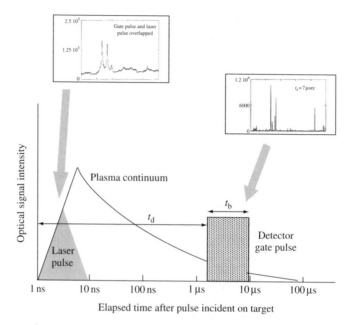

Figure 2.1 A schematic overview of the temporal history of a LIBS plasma. The delay and window are shown. Inserts illustrate the kind of spectra one might observe at the different times

The timescales shown in Figure 2.1 are appropriate for a plasma initiated in air at 1 atm by a 5 to 10 ns 1064-nm laser pulse from a Nd:YAG laser. For much longer (e.g. CO_2 laser) or much shorter pulses (e.g. pico- or femtosecond lasers) the timescale will expand or contract accordingly. As ambient pressure decreases, the plasma lifetime decreases because there is less trapping and recycling of the absorbed energy in the plasma volume. Plasmas formed by the modest laser energies used for LIBS are typically less than 10% ionized at the earliest observable time.

Typical plasma radiation processes are shown in Figure 2.2. When E is given in joules, the frequency, wave number and wavelength of a transition are given by:

$$\nu = \Delta E/h \quad \sigma = \nu/c \quad \lambda = 1/\sigma, \tag{2.1}$$

where ΔE is an energy level difference. [Note: The table of Acronyms, Constants and Symbols contains the definition of characters often used in equations, like h (Planck's constant) or c (speed of light). Symbols used only once are defined under the equation where they are introduced. Occasionally the same symbol is used differently in different equations. In that case it is defined for the particular occasion.] Energy levels are conventionally listed with the ground state as zero, and in pseudo energy units of wavenumber, E/hc, commonly /cm. In that case, the wavenumber of the transition can be read directly from the difference of two energy level values.

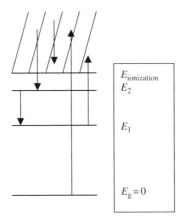

Figure 2.2 Typical transitions in an atom or ion. From left to right: bound–bound; free–bound; free–free; ionization from the ground state; ionization from an excited state

The goal of the LIBS technique is to create an optically thin plasma which is in thermodynamic equilibrium and whose elemental composition is the same as that of the sample. When those conditions are fulfilled, relationships discussed below connect observed spectral line intensities with relative concentrations of elements. Typically these conditions are only met approximately. We will consider each of them in more detail. Given these and other complexities it is somewhat amazing that analytical results can be obtained. But with care they can, so usually these problems are no more than annoyances.

2.1.1 SPECTRAL LINES AND LINE PROFILES

The main diagnostic technique for plasmas involves the relationship between plasma properties and spectral line characteristics. Line widths are related to plasma temperature and electron density. Line shapes and shifts can be a diagnostic for the principal broadening mechanism. There are other diagnostic techniques. Langmuir probes and Thompson scattering can be used to measure electron densities, Schlieren or other interferometric techniques can reveal refractive index changes, and Abel inversion can assist in unfolding properties in the plasma by layer. Even the plasma acoustic emission can be employed for diagnosis. Optical techniques other than the passive observations of emission lines, such as laser-induced fluorescence, can cast light on critical plasma parameters. For an overview of diagnostic techniques see Lochte-Holtgreven (Lochte-Holtgreven, 1968) or Hauer and Baldis (Hauer and Baldis, 1989), and for some recent uses see Section 8.2.

Spectral line profiles are determined by the dominant broadening mechanisms. Pure Doppler broadening results in a Gaussian line profile, shown here in wavenumber units, but which can be converted easily to frequency or wavelength units:

$$I(\sigma) = (4\ln 2/\pi\Gamma^2)^{1/2} \exp[-4\ln 2(\sigma - \sigma_0)^2/\Gamma^2] \qquad (2.2)$$

where Γ is the full-width at half-maximum (FWHM),

$$\Gamma = (8kT \ln 2/Mc^2)^{1/2}\sigma_0 \qquad (2.3)$$

where M is the species mass and σ_0 the central wave number of the transition. Other common effects such as natural line broadening and collision broadening due to collisions with neutrals lead to a symmetric Lorentz profile:

$$I(\sigma) = (\Gamma/2\pi)/[(\sigma - \sigma_0)^2 + (\Gamma/2)^2]. \qquad (2.4)$$

Often the two are of comparable magnitudes, and the resulting profile obtained by convolution of the two is called the Voigt profile. Figure 2.3 compares the characteristics of Gauss and Lorentz profiles of equal full-width at half-maximum (FWHM), and the resulting Voigt profile. The Gaussian will dominate close to the line center, the Lorentz in the line wings. Voigt profiles will depend on the relative strength of the two effects. For detailed analysis of Voigt profiles see Hummer and Rybicki (Hummer and Rybicki, 1971) or Whiting (Whiting, 1968).

The term collision broadening is often used to describe the effect of collisions of neutral atoms or molecules. It exists even in the absence of a plasma, and is seen, for example, in absorption lines that start on low lying energy levels. Collisions with ions and electrons result in Stark broadening. An energy level in an electric field is split into sublevels according to the absolute value of the quantum number m_J representing the z component of the total angular momentum J. Hence, in the

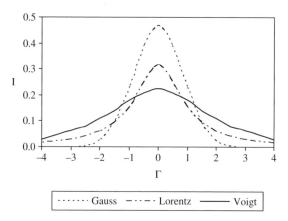

Figure 2.3 Gauss and Lorentz profiles of equal half widths. The Voigt profile is the result of the convolution of the other two

Stark effect in most atoms, the fine structure transitions between levels of different m_J are not symmetric about the unperturbed level position, and an asymmetric, shifted line can be the result. If the splitting of the levels is not too large, the resulting broadening may appear to be symmetric. This is different than for atoms in a magnetic field (the Zeeman effect), where at low fields, isolated sublevels split symmetrically around the parent level.

2.1.2 DETERMINING ELECTRON DENSITIES FROM SPECTRAL LINE WIDTHS

Under normal LIBS conditions, the most important contributions to the line width are the Doppler width and the Stark effect. It is easy to see why the natural line width can be neglected. Natural line widths are related to energy level widths by $\sim \Delta E \Delta t > \hbar$, where ΔE is the width of the level, and Δt its lifetime. For a transition between two energy levels with natural lifetimes of 10 ns, the natural spectral line width is about $\sqrt{2}$ times the level width or 7×10^{-4}/cm. At 500 nm the line width in the example above amounts to 0.002 nm. These are unobservable at the spectrometer resolutions used in LIBS experiments.

The Doppler width depends only on the absolute temperature and the atomic mass of the emitting species. Starting from Equation (2.3) and converting to wavelength units for FWHM, we obtain:

$$\Delta \lambda_D = 7.2 \times 10^{-7} (T/M)^{1/2} \lambda_o \qquad (2.5)$$

where M is the atomic mass of the element and λ_o the central wavelength of the spectral line. Calculated Doppler and Stark widths (discussed below) for some lines commonly observed in LIBS experiments are shown in Table 2.1. Some observations and comparisons will be made after the discussion of Stark width that follows.

As mentioned above, in Stark effect degenerate sublevels identified by the quantum number m_J are partially or completely split, leading either to (1) an unresolved, broadened, and often shifted level center-of-gravity, or (2) a resolved series of sublevels. Selection rules on the transitions between the sublevels allow one to predict the intensity of the resulting line (Cowan, 1981, pp. 498–504). The electric field that causes Stark effect in LIBS plasmas results primarily from collisions with electrons, with small contributions due to collisions with ions. The calculation of the effect of nearby perturbers upon emitting species has historically taken two directions. The quasi-static Holtzmark theory assumes that the relative motion between perturber and emitter is small, so that the perturbation is constant over times on the order of a level lifetime. At the opposite extreme, the impact theory assumes that the emitter is unperturbed except for isolated instantaneous interactions. Griem's books mentioned above contain good detail on the theory behind these calculations and how they lead to expressions for Stark widths.

Table 2.1 Doppler and Stark widths for lines of some elements of interest in LIBS experiments. Widths are calculated full-width at half maximum intensity (FWHM), for a plasma temperature of $10\,000$ K and an electron density of $10^{17}/cm^3$, except where noted

Element	λ (nm)	Atomic mass	Temperature (K)	Doppler FWHM (nm)	Stark width coefficient[a] (HWHM in Å at $10^{16}/cm^3$)	Stark width (FWHM in nm at $10^{17}/cm^3$)
Hydrogen	656.3	1	11 000	0.047		0.4440[b]
Hydrogen	656.3	1	20 000	0.067		
Hydrogen	656.3	1	50 000	0.106		
Hydrogen	486.1	1		0.035		0.8300[c]
Deuterium	656.0	2	10 000	0.033		
He	587.5	4	10 000	0.021	0.1700	0.3400
Li	670.7	6.9	10 000	0.018	0.0138	0.0276
Li	610.3	6.9	10 000	0.017	0.2140	0.4280
Li	460.2	6.9	10 000	0.013	1.2700	2.5400
Li	413.2	6.9	10 000	0.011	3.4100	6.8200
Be	234.9	9	10 000	0.006	0.0009	0.0018
Be (II)	313.1	9	10 000	0.008	0.0537	0.1074
C	193.1	12	10 000	0.004	0.0022	0.0044
C	247.9	12	10 000	0.005	0.0036	0.0072
O	777.3	16	10 000	0.014	0.0315	0.0630
Na	589.2	23	10 000	0.009	0.0157	0.0314
Mg	285.2	24	10 000	0.004	0.0041	0.0082
Al	309.2	27	10 000	0.004	0.0260	0.0520
Si	288.1	28	10 000	0.004	0.0064	0.0128
Si	390.5	28	10 000	0.005	0.0117	0.0234
S	181.4	32.1	10 000	0.002	0.0022	0.0044
K	766.5	39.1	10 000	0.009	0.0415	0.0830
Ca	422.6	40	10 000	0.005	0.0063	0.0126

[a] Coefficients from Appendix 4 (neutrals) or 5 (ions) of Griem (Griem, 1974).
[b] Experimental, at $T \sim 11\,000$ K and $n_e = 2 \times 10^{16}/cm^3$ (Parigger et al., 2003). If this scales linearly with electron density, the approximate value at $n_e = 10^{17}/cm^3$ would be 2.2 nm.
[c] Experimental, at $T \sim 11\,000$ K and $n_e = 9.2 \times 10^{15}/cm^3$ (Parigger et al., 2003). If this scales linearly with electron density, the approximate value at $n_e = 10^{17}/cm^3$ would be 10 nm.

Stark broadened line widths can be used to calculate the electron density in plasmas. For example, the following expressions relate the line width and shift to electron and ion densities (Equations 226 and 227 in Griem, 1974):

$$w_{\text{total}} \sim [1 + 1.75\,A(1 - 0.75r)](n_e/10^{16})w \qquad (2.6)$$

$$d_{\text{total}} \sim [1 \pm 2.00\,A(1 - 0.75r)](n_e/10^{16})d \qquad (2.7)$$

where w_{total} is the measured half-width at half maximum (HWHM), A in this case is a parameter giving the ion contribution [A scales as $(n_e)^{1/4}$], r is the ratio of the mean distance between ions to the Debye radius, and w is the HWHM Stark width caused by the electron density (scaling as n_e as indicated). If A is 0 (no ionic contribution) and the electron density is $10^{16}/cm^3$, the Stark widths can be read from Appendices 4 and 5 of Griem (Griem, 1974). Limitations on these expressions and scaling to other densities are discussed in his 1964 and 1974 books. Expressions (2.6) and (2.7) can be used to determine electron density. There have been other effects added to Stark theories by Oks (Oks, 1999). Detailed recent studies of H_α and H_β broadening, including a more accurate treatment of ion dynamics, have been described by Parigger *et al.* (Parigger *et al.*, 2003) and Gigosos *et al.* (Gigosos *et al.*, 2003).

Table 2.1 contains the predictions of Stark widths and compares them with Doppler widths. The second, third and fourth columns are the parameters needed to apply Equation (2.5), and the resulting Doppler widths are in the fifth column. Stark broadening coefficients, from Appendices 4 (neutral) or 5 (ions) of Griem (Griem, 1974), are given in the sixth column. Stark broadening widths calculated from Equation (2.6) are found in the seventh column. The ionic contribution was neglected, so A was set equal to zero in Equation (2.6). The Stark widths are calculated for an electron density of $10^{17}/cm^3$.

Let us now consider some of the results in Table 2.1. Regarding hydrogen, the Stark widths have recently been re-determined by Oks and Parigger as mentioned above. Published values from the latter work are given in column seven, but these were made at different electron densities. Footnotes *b* and *c* contain the values adjusted to $n_e = 10^{17}/cm^3$. For hydrogen, the Stark widths are considerably larger than the Doppler widths for the temperatures given in the table. Moving on to lithium, values are given for several lines to illustrate the variation of Stark width as the upper energy level gets closer to the ionization potential. Lithium has an ionization potential of 5.4 eV. The upper levels for the four lines listed are: 1.8 eV for the 2p-2s resonance lines at 670.7 nm, 3.9 eV for 3d-2p at 610.3 nm, 4.5 eV for 4d-2p at 460.2 nm and 4.8 eV for 5d-2p at 413.2 nm. While the Doppler FWHM values for these lines vary from 0.01 to 0.02 nm, the Stark widths increase from 0.03 to almost 7 nm. In general, Stark widths and shifts will be largest for the upper levels closer to the ionization limit, and for upper levels that originate in electron configurations that have optical electrons with high angular momentum. Hence f levels are affected more than d levels and so on.

As one goes higher in atomic mass, the Doppler widths get smaller. Hence, even for many strong lines that originate from upper levels that are still far from the ionization limit, the Stark broadening can dominate. Regarding shifts in wavelengths, except for high f levels, these are typically less than 0.1 nm. Whether the Stark widths and shifts of lines from LIBS plasmas are observable depends on the optical and spectral resolving powers of the spectrometer–detector system.

When using LIBS at atmospheric pressure, ambient background species densities of molecular oxygen and nitrogen are on the order of $2 \times 10^{19}/cm^3$. Electron densities measured by Stark broadening are often $10^{18}/cm^3$ at less than a microsecond into the plasma, and $10^{16}/cm^3$ at 5 to 10 μs after the laser pulse. Figure 2.4 contains examples of LIBS electron densities obtained from specific experiments. Of course, if LIBS is performed in different atmospheres, such as 7 Torr of CO_2 on Mars or 90 atm on Venus, these densities will be orders of magnitude different.

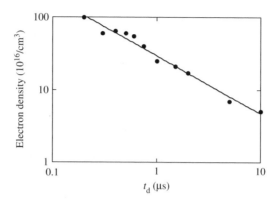

Figure 2.4 Electron densities measured in some LIBS experiments. Data abstracted from Stark widths of F, Ar, N and Cl lines

2.1.3 PLASMA OPACITY

Having introduced the concepts of line profile and line width, we can now discuss the opacity of a plasma. Fundamentally, a plasma is optically thin when the emitted radiation traverses and escapes from the plasma without significant absorption or scattering. The intensity of radiation emitted from a plasma is given by:

$$I(\lambda) = [\varepsilon(\lambda)/\alpha(\lambda)]\{1 - \exp[-\alpha(\lambda)L]\} \qquad (2.8)$$

where $\varepsilon(\lambda)$ is the emissivity, $\alpha(\lambda)$ is the absorption coefficient (/cm), and L is the plasma length along the line of sight to the observer. Note that when α is small:

$$I(\lambda) = [\varepsilon(\lambda)/\alpha(\lambda)][\alpha(\lambda)L] \sim \varepsilon(\lambda)L \qquad (2.9)$$

which is the condition for the plasma to be optically thin.

There are two relatively easy ways of checking for the optical thickness of a plasma. Strong spectral lines of elements have well known relative intensities, sometimes determined from atomic physics coupling theory (LJ, jj, etc.), sometimes determined experimentally. When re-absorption becomes noticeable, the observed intensities will depart from the expected values, the stronger lines effectively saturating. Starting with the most intense lines, they approach a flat-topped profile, evidence of self-absorption (see Figure 8.3 for calculated profiles). In more extreme cases, a single line will appear to have a dip at the central frequency. In such a case the line is said to be self-reversed. The subtle onset of self-absorption poses a problem for converting line intensities to concentrations, as discussed in Chapter 4. Self-absorption is also a major problem for calibration-free LIBS (CF-LIBS) as discussed in Chapter 8.

There are other experimental methods to detect self-absorption. One is to use a spherical mirror behind the plasma and compare the intensity of a given line with and without the mirror in place. When using this method care must be taken to illuminate the spectrograph properly, as discussed in Bekefi (Bekefi, 1976).

2.1.4   TEMPERATURE AND THERMODYNAMIC EQUILIBRIUM

Plasma descriptions start by trying to characterize properties of the assembly of atoms, molecules, electrons and ions rather than the individual species. If thermodynamic equilibrium exists, then plasma properties, such as the relative populations of energy levels, and the distribution of the speed of the particles, can be described through the concept of temperature. In fact, thermodynamic equilibrium is rarely complete, so physicists have settled for a useful approximation, local thermodynamic equilibrium (LTE). All one demands is that equilibration occurs in small regions of space, although it may be somewhat different from region to region. A useful approximation usually exists after a sufficient number of collisions have occurred to thermalize the plasma, which means to spread the energy in the plasma across volume and species. Even then, not all species may be in thermodynamic equilibrium. It is common for heavy species (atoms and ions) and light species (electrons) to equilibrate separately more quickly, and later in time with each other. The fundamental physical reason is that energy between collision partners is shared more equally the closer the masses of the colliding particles. Note that there may be more than one 'temperature.' An example of the direct observation of the equilibration of electron and atom temperatures in a LIBS plasma was given in a paper describing a study of an oxygen plasma induced by CO_2 laser radiation (Radziemski *et al.*, 1985). Figure 2.5 illustrates the convergence of electron temperature, measured by a Langmuir probe, with excitation temperatures measured by the Boltzmann method, where the plasma was initiated by a 10.6 μm CO_2 laser pulse. The probe measurements are represented by the black circles (500 mJ/pulse)

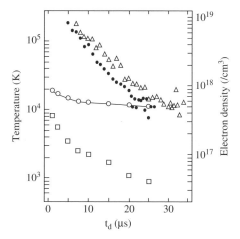

Figure 2.5 Illustration of the convergence of electron temperature measured by a Langmuir probe (black circles, 500 mJ pulse; open triangles, 800 mJ pulse), with excitation temperature measured by the Boltzmann method (open circles). (Reproduced from Radziemski *et al.*, 1985, with permission from Elsevier)

and open triangles (800 mJ/pulse), and the Boltzmann temperatures by the open circles (500 mJ/pulse). The open squares are the electron densities measured using Stark effect line widths. Convergence of temperatures over a period of 25 μs is clearly seen.

A variety of tests have been developed to ascertain whether thermodynamic equilibrium exists. Probably the simplest is that the relative intensities of atomic spectral lines from closely upper spaced levels in the same multiplet agree with predictions from basic theory (White, 1934; Kuhn, 1963). Of course, self absorption and interferences from nearby lines can limit the usefulness of this approach. Another test has to do with the electron density being high enough for collisions to dominate the population of levels. Griem (Griem, 1997, p. 219) discusses various criteria for the hydrogen atom, which depend on the energy difference between the levels involved. The larger that difference, the more difficult it is to establish equilibrium. The worst case in neutral atoms (except for the ground to first excited states of monatomic gases) is the 10.2 eV difference between the ground and first excited state of hydrogen. Griem's analysis suggests that for a temperature of 1 eV ($\sim$11 000 K) and atmospheric pressure, an electron density of 10^{17}/cm^3 would ensure LTE. The approximations imply that LIBS plasmas generated by an irradiance of $>10^8$ W/cm^2, at atmospheric pressure, would be sufficiently thermalized several hundred nanoseconds after initiation. The situation could be different for plasmas formed with femtosecond pulses, or at low pressure. Recent studies referred to in Chapter 8 point to the possibility of multicomponent plasmas.

If experiment determines that LTE exists, the distribution of several quantities, including electron speeds and populations of energy levels or ion stages are dependent on a single quantity, temperature. The Maxwellian velocity distribution function f_M is:

$$f_M = (m/2\pi kT)^{3/2} \exp(-mv^2/2kT) \qquad (2.10)$$

where m is the electron mass and v the electron speed. Relative populations of energy levels, whether atomic or molecular in origin, are given by the Boltzmann distribution:

$$N_j/N_o = (g_j/Z)\exp(-E_j/kT) \text{ with respect to the ground state or} \qquad (2.11)$$

$$N_j/N_i = (g_j/g_i)\exp[-(E_j - E_i)/kT] \text{ for relative population,} \qquad (2.12)$$

where i and j refer to two levels, N_o is the total species population, $N_{i,j}$ are the populations of levels $E_{i,j}$, $g_{i,j}$ are the statistical weights of the levels $(2J_{i,j}+1)$, J is the total angular momentum quantum number of the term, and Z is the partition function usually taken as the statistical weight of the ground state. The spectral line radiant intensity is given by:

$$I = h\nu\, gA\, N/4\pi = (hcN_o gA/4\pi\, \lambda Z)\exp(-E/kT). \qquad (2.13)$$

I is in units of W/sr, ν is the line frequency, and A is the transition probability (Einstein A coefficient). N may be the absolute number or the number density. If the latter is the case, then Equation (2.13) gives the radiant intensity per unit volume of source. The ratio of the intensities of two lines is:

$$I'/I = (\lambda' g' A'/\lambda' g A) \exp[-(E' - E)/kT]. \tag{2.14}$$

Choosing lines for which the g, A and E values and the wavelengths are known, and measuring the relative intensities, enables one to calculate T by the two-line method. If the lines have significantly different line widths, then integrated intensities are the measurement of choice. Figure 2.6 illustrates the parameters useful for determining temperature from the two-line method.

Relative intensities are not easy to measure precisely. A way to improve temperature values is to use many lines simultaneously and perform a graphical analysis. We rearrange Equation (2.13) into the form:

$$\ln(4\pi Z/hcN_o) + \ln(I\lambda/gA) = -E/kT \quad \text{or}$$

$$\ln(I\lambda/gA) = -E/kT - \ln(4\pi Z/hcN_o). \tag{2.15}$$

This is the equation of a straight line with slope of $-1/kT$. Hence if one plots the quantity on the left against E (of the upper state for emission), and if there is a Boltzmann distribution, a straight line is obtained. Some of the crucial factors in obtaining a good Boltzmann plot are accurate line intensities, accurate transition probabilities, and well spaced upper levels. The further apart the extremes of the upper level values, the easier it will be to define the slope of the line. To illustrate, Figure 2.7 shows a LIBS spectrum of basalt, with iron lines used for a multi-line Boltzmann plot indicated by stars. The fundamental data for these lines are contained in Table 2.2 and the resulting plot is shown in Figure 2.8.

From the slope of the line in Figure 2.8, the temperature is determined to be 7500 K.

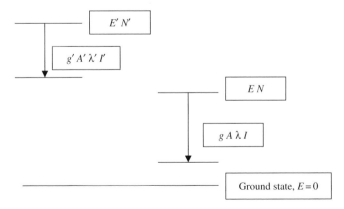

Figure 2.6 Illustration of parameters and energy levels for the two-line method of determining plasma temperature

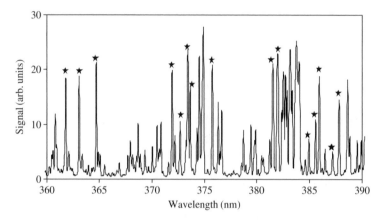

Figure 2.7   LIBS spectrum of basalt and iron lines used in the Boltzmann plot of Figure 2.8

Table 2.2   Neutral Fe [Fe(I)] parameters for a Boltzmann temperature determination (see Figure 2.8)[a]

Wavelength (nm)	E_u (eV)	gA^b	Wavelength (nm)	E_u (eV)	gA^b
361.877	4.42	5.1	382.043	4.10	6.01
363.146	4.37	4.65	384.044	4.22	1.41
364.784	4.31	3.21	384.997	4.23	0.61
371.994	3.33	1.78	385.637	3.27	0.23
372.762	4.28	1.12	385.991	3.21	0.87
373.487	4.18	9.92	387.250	4.19	0.53
373.713	3.37	1.28	387.857	3.28	0.2
381.584	4.73	9.1			

[a] Data from: http://physics.nist.gov/PhysRefData/ASD/index.html
[b] In units of 10^8/s.

The relative populations among ion stages in LTE are given by the Saha (or Saha–Eggert) equation. To use this expression to obtain temperature, called the temperature of the ionization equilibrium, relative intensities of lines from different ion stages of the same atom (occasionally different atoms) are measured. The electron density must be known from other experiments. Figure 2.9 illustrates the quantities involved in Equation (2.16):

$$N(Z,0)n_e/N(Z-1,0) = 2g(Z,0)/g(Z-1,0)(mkT/2\pi\hbar^2)^{3/2}\exp(-\Delta E/kT) \quad (2.16)$$

where $N(Z,0)$ is the population of the ground state of ion stage Z, $N(Z-1,0)$ is the population of the ground state of ion stage $Z-1$, m is the electron mass, n_e is the electron density, and ΔE is the ionization energy of stage Z relative to stage $Z-1$. In terms of relative intensities:

$$I'/I = \lambda g'A'N(Z)/\lambda'gA\,N(Z-1). \quad (2.17)$$

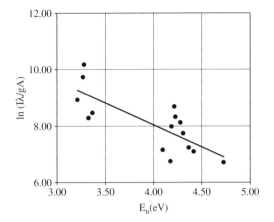

Figure 2.8 Multiline Boltzmann plot based on the data of Table 2.2

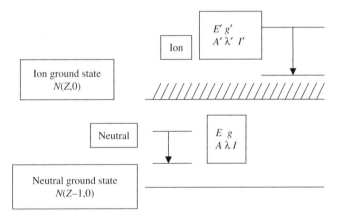

Figure 2.9 Illustration of parameters and energy levels for the Saha method of determining plasma temperature

For a specific application of the methods see Aguilera and Aragón (Aguilera and Aragón, 2004).

In addition to temperatures from atom, ions and the ionization equilibrium, it is possible to measure vibrational and rotational temperatures. Sometimes more than one of these temperatures can be measured simultaneously. If the results do not agree, doubt is cast upon the completeness of LTE.

Temperatures achieved in LIBS plasmas are of course dependent on the energy deposition, hence the fluence and irradiance. For irradiance values of $\sim 10^{10}$ W/cm^2, the temperature is typically 8000–12 000 K at 1–2 μs into the plasma lifetime (t_d). Figure 2.10 contains an example of LIBS temperatures obtained from Boltzmann and Saha analyses.

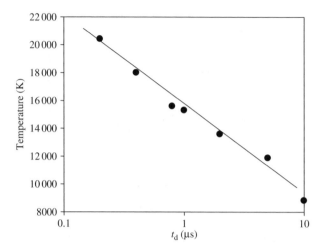

Figure 2.10 Air plasma temperature as a function of time after plasma formation using Saha and Boltzmann data from C and Be lines

2.2 LASER-INDUCED BREAKDOWN

2.2.1 BREAKDOWN IN GASES

There are two key steps that lead to breakdown in a gas. First, there must be some free electrons in the focal volume of the laser beam. Sometimes these are transient electrons liberated by cosmic rays or the natural radioactivity of the earth. At other times they are generated by the first few photons of the pulse itself, being liberated from dust, negative ions such as O_2^-, organic vapors, or through multiphoton ionization of atoms or molecules in the atmosphere. Multiphoton effects are necessary for direct ionization of species like N_2 and O_2 because their ionization energies are much greater than energies of photons normally used. For example, the ionization potential of O_2 is 12.2 eV and of N_2 is 15.6 eV, while Nd:YAG 1064, 532 and 266 nm photons have energies of 1.25, 2.33 and 4.7 eV, respectively. Despite the very small cross-sections for the multiphoton process, irradiances of 10^{10} W/cm^2 are sufficient for weak multiphoton ionization to occur.

The second step in the process of breakdown is generating sufficient electron and ion densities. For the irradiance values typically used in LIBS (10^8–10^{10} W/cm^2), this occurs through avalanche or cascade ionization. At higher irradiance values, significant multiphoton production of electrons can occur through:

$$M + mh\nu \longrightarrow M^+ + e^-, \qquad (2.18)$$

where m is the number of photons. In the classical picture, free electrons are accelerated by the electric field in the optical pulse during the time period between collisions with neutral species. The collisions thermalize the electrons quickly.

A small number of electrons in the tail of the Maxwellian distribution will have enough energy to ionize an atom or molecule through the reaction

$$e^- + M \longrightarrow 2e^- + M^+. \tag{2.19}$$

This starts to produce other free electrons that gain energy from the field and produce more ionization. The process of electron multiplication continues during the laser pulse and results in the ionization of the gas and breakdown. Alternately, electrons can acquire energy from photons in three-body collisions with atoms or molecules (inverse Brehmsstrahlung). As the number of ions increases the electron–photon–ion collisions increase yielding a higher probability of further electron multiplication.

The change in electron density can be represented by the following equation which contains growth and loss terms:

$$dn_e/dt = n_e(\nu_i - \nu_a - \nu_r) + W_m I^m n - \blacktriangledown(D \blacktriangledown n_e) \tag{2.20}$$

where ν_i, ν_a and ν_r are the impact ionization, attachment and recombination rates, respectively, W_m is the multiphoton ionization rate coefficient, I^m is the irradiance (W/cm^2) necessary for an m-photon process to occur, n is the number density of the species being irradiated, $\blacktriangledown$ is the gradient operator and D is the diffusion coefficient for electrons. Values for these coefficients are discussed in depth by Weyl (Weyl, 1989).

The breakdown threshold is difficult to pin down with accuracy because of the many variables involved. These include the characteristics of the medium (dust, ionization thresholds), the laser pulse characteristics (temporal pulse length, wavelength), and the irradiance (related to the focal properties of the optics). The latter also affects the balance between cascade and multiphoton ionization. In general, a pressure independent value for breakdown threshold indicates a dominance of multiphoton ionization.

A thorough investigation of the breakdown thresholds in molecular oxygen and nitrogen using 10 ns, 1064 nm Nd:YAG photons was done by Stricker and Parker (Stricker and Parker, 1982), over pressure ranges from 1 to 50 atm. In this range of pressures, the process was avalanche, not multiphoton ionization. Their value of the breakdown threshold in laboratory air was 8.2×10^{10} W/cm^2. The slope of the curve implied that an order of magnitude increase in the pressure resulted in an order of magnitude increase in the breakdown threshold. For a 7–8 ns Nd:YAG pulse in air, at the frequency fundamental, doubled, tripled and quadrupled wavelengths of 1064, 532, 355 and 266 nm, respectively, breakdown thresholds were measured, and values from others' experiments summarized (Simeonsson and Miziolek, 1994). These and other representative results for breakdown thresholds in atmospheric pressure gases for several lasers and wavelengths are listed in Table 2.3.

Measurements have been made using pulses in the pico- and femtosecond regimes. In 1983, Williams *et al.* published the results of a study of the breakdown threshold in laboratory air using the Nd:YAG frequency doubled to 532 nm, with pulse lengths in the 30–140 ps regime (Williams *et al.*, 1983). Their

Table 2.3 Measured breakdown thresholds for several lasers and gases

Laser, wavelength, pulse length, other	Gas and pressure	Breakdown threshold irradiance (W/cm^2)	Reference
Nd:YAG, 1064 nm, 10 ns	Laboratory air, 1 atm	8.2×10^{10}	Stricker and Parker, 1982
Nd:YAG, 1064 nm, 8 ns	Laboratory air, 1 atm	2.0×10^{10}	Simeonsson and Miziolek, 1994
Nd:YAG, 1064 nm, 8 ns, spot diameter 5×10^{-3} cm	Laboratory air, 1 atm	5.0×10^{11}	Tambay and Thareja, 1991
Nd:YAG, 1064 nm, 7 ps	Nitrogen, 760 Torr	8×10^{14}	Dewhurst, 1978
Nd:YAG, 532 nm, 7 ns	Laboratory air, 1 atm	1.5×10^{10}	Simeonsson and Miziolek, 1994
Nd:YAG, 532 nm, 6 ns, spot diameter 5×10^{-3} cm	Laboratory air, 1 atm	1.0×10^{11}	Tambay and Thareja, 1991
Nd:YAG, 532 nm, 8 ns	Laboratory air, 1 atm	2.5×10^{12}	Bindhu *et al.*, 2004
Nd:YAG, 532 nm, 80 ps	Laboratory air, 1 atm	1.8×10^{13}	Williams *et al.*, 1983
Nd:YAG, 532 nm, 25 ps	Nitrogen, 760 Torr	4×10^{13}	Dewhurst, 1978
Nd:YAG, 355 nm, 7 ns	Laboratory air, 1 atm	2.7×10^{10}	Simeonsson and Miziolek, 1994
Nd:YAG, 355 nm, 4 ns, spot diameter 5×10^{-3} cm	Laboratory air, 1 atm	1.05×10^{11}	Tambay and Thareja, 1991
Nd:YAG, 266 nm, 7 ns	Laboratory air, 1 atm	1.7×10^{10}	Simeonsson and Miziolek, 1994
Nd:YAG, 266 nm, 4 ns, spot diameter 5×10^{-3} cm	Laboratory air, 1 atm	1.06×10^{11}	Tambay and Thareja, 1991
ArF, 193 nm, 10 ns	Laboratory air, 1 atm	9.7×10^{9}	Simeonsson and Miziolek, 1994

threshold values ranged from 1 to 4×10^{13} W/cm^2. Other results from Dewhurst (Dewhurst, 1978) are included in Table 2.3. More information on breakdown will be found in Weyl (Weyl, 1989). Given variations in experimental conditions and changes in laser technology, values indicated here should be used only as a guide to likely results. If the breakdown threshold is a critical parameter, the researcher should do the measurements on the actual system.

Often breakdown thresholds are reported in terms of the corresponding classical electric field. The expression for converting between irradiance and electric field is (Hecht, 1987, p. 44):

$$I = c\varepsilon_{o} \langle E^2 \rangle = 2.6 \times 10^{-3} E^2 \tag{2.21}$$

where I is the irradiance in W/cm^2, $\langle E^2 \rangle$ the time averaged value of the square of the electric field amplitude, with E in V/cm. Hence an irradiance of 10^{10} W/cm^2 corresponds to an electric field of 2 MV/cm.

2.2.2 POST-BREAKDOWN PHENOMENA IN GASES

After breakdown in a gas, absent a surface, the luminous plasma expands outward in all directions from the point at which breakdown initiated. Depending on the irradiance, some of the laser energy may be transmitted through the plasma volume, some scattered, and the rest absorbed. The plasma advances up the beam towards the laser during the laser pulse, because the absorption of the photons is asymmetric in that direction. Hence the plasma has a slight conical shape with the blunt end towards the lens. In the case of gases more transparent to the incident wavelength, more of the energy would be absorbed at the site of the plasma being formed, resulting in spherical expansion.

With the development of continuous, high power CO_2 lasers in the 1960s, continuous laser-induced plasmas in gases became possible. These also are called continuous optical discharges (CODs). The first observation was published by Generalov et al. (Generalov et al., 1970). CODs have been achieved in a variety of gases at pressures ranging from 1 to over 200 atm with 10.6 µm CO_2 lasers employing powers of at least 25 W. The Russian literature often refers to this device operated in a flowing atmosphere as an optical plasmatron. Plasma temperatures are typically below 15 000 K. Keefer (Keefer, 1974) also reported early experimentation on laser-sustained plasmas, and later provided a good review of the field (Keefer, 1989). The use of the COD for spectrochemical analysis was studied by Cremers et al. (Cremers et al., 1985), where a 45 W CO_2 laser was used to generate a plasma in xenon.

2.2.3 BREAKDOWN IN AND ON SOLIDS, AEROSOLS AND LIQUIDS

The majority of problems to which LIBS is applied involve solids in air, to a lesser extent liquids and aerosols. In addition, there can be unwanted breakdown on the surfaces of optical components that will shorten their life and scatter the incoming laser radiation. As a result, breakdown and post breakdown phenomena on or in transparent and opaque dielectrics, metals and liquids is of interest. Optical damage studies are one area of interest. To a great extent the subject is empirical. Thresholds are quite sensitive to the purity of the material, the surface preparation, smoothness and particles that have adhered to the surface. If the laser beam is multimode it may have hot spots that initiate plasma formation below the average threshold values. Typical reported values for LIBS type plasmas on solids are in the range of 10^8–10^{10} W/cm^2.

The availability of pico- and femtosecond lasers has illuminated some of the processes of ablation. Through observations of the onset of ablation, one can obtain an estimate of breakdown thresholds. Papers by Hashida et al. and Semerok et al. discuss both thresholds and ablation rates for 532 nm, 6 ns Nd:YAG and 800 nm Ti:sapphire at 70 fs and 5 ps on copper substrates (Hashida et al., 2002; Semerok et al., 2002). Their results and others are contained in Table 2.4 and follow expected

Table 2.4   Recent measured breakdown thresholds for some laser pulses on solids

Laser, wavelength, pulse length	Surface, gas and pressure	Breakdown threshold irradiance (W/cm^2)	Reference
Nd:YAG, 532 nm, 6 ns	Cu, atm air	1.67×10^9	Semerok et al., 2002
Ti:sapphire, 800 nm, 5 ps	Cu, atm air	9×10^{10}	Hashida et al., 2002
Ti:sapphire, 800 nm, 70 fs	Cu, atm air	2.5×10^{11}	Hashida et al., 2002
Colliding-pulse laser, 620 nm, 90 fs	$BaTiO_3$, vacuum	5×10^{11}	Millon et al., 2003
Colliding-pulse laser, 620 nm, 120 fs	Fused silica, atm air	1×10^{13}	von der Linde and Schüler, 1996 (also investigated were glass, sapphire and magnesium fluoride)
Nd:YAG, 1064 nm, 6.4 ns	Fused silica, argon	5.5×10^{10}	Galt et al., 2003

progressions. If breakdown threshold is an important factor, it should be measured with the samples and laser being used in the experiment.

For transparent materials such as those from which lenses and windows are made, breakdown can occur at the surface or within the material. Thresholds have been measured for four transparent dielectrics (glass, magnesium fluoride, sapphire and fused silica) by von der Linde and Schüler (von der Linde and Schüler, 1996). The results for fused silica are typical and contained in Table 2.4. In general one expects the surface thresholds to be lower because of surface defects such as scratches, pits or dust particles. The most common type of damage in LIBS experiments arises when a laser beam has passed through the focusing lens and is incident on a window as it is proceeding to a focus. If one is not careful, a plasma can be initiated on the window, or on the exit side of the focusing lens by retro reflection.

Aerosol induced breakdown is a complex subject because of the many parameters involved. These include the composition of composite particles, shapes, density, materials, atmosphere and water content. Suffice it to say, that these factors, in general, lower the breakdown threshold. Particles ejected a sufficient distance from surfaces under irradiation may cause single or multiple plasma formation detached from the surface, thereby screening the surface, partially or totally, from absorbing incoming laser radiation. Laser beam blooming, focusing and distortion can also occur.

Breakdown thresholds in water and other liquids have been measured as well. There is great interest in this area in the community performing laser surgery in the eye. Culminating an extensive study, Kennedy et al. published the results of experiments and calculations of breakdown thresholds in a variety of aqueous media (Kennedy et al., 1995). Their goal was to gain an understanding of the role of laser-induced breakdown as a possible ocular damage mechanism. Samples included ocular media, saline, tap and distilled water. Some of their results are listed in Table 2.5. The variations for different types of samples are also presented in the

Table 2.5   Recent measured breakdown thresholds for some laser pulses in liquids

Laser, wavelength, pulse length	Medium	Breakdown threshold irradiance (W/cm^2)	Reference
Nd:YAG, 1064 nm, 7 ns	Tap water	5.6×10^9	Kennedy *et al.*, 1995
	Ultra pure water	1.82×10^{10}	
	Vitreous	1.27×10^{10}	
	Saline	8.31×10^9	
Nd:YAG, 532 nm, 3 ns	Tap water	9.35×10^9	Kennedy *et al.*, 1995
Nd:YAG, 1064 nm, 80 ps	Tap water	1.91×10^{11}	Kennedy *et al.*, 1995
Dye laser, 580 nm, 100 fs	Tap water	5.6×10^{12}	Kennedy *et al.*, 1995
Nd:YAG, 1064 nm, 6 ns	Distilled water	7.6×10^{10}	Vogel *et al.*, 1996
Nd:YAG, 1064 nm, 30 ps	Distilled water	4.5×10^{11}	Vogel *et al.*, 1996

table for the 1064 nm, 7 ns experiments. The results of Vogel *et al.* are included for comparison (Vogel *et al.*, 1996).

2.2.4   POST-BREAKDOWN PHENOMENA ON SOLID SURFACES

When the laser irradiance is high enough to cause a plasma plume, the leading edge of the pulse rapidly heats, melts and vaporizes material into a layer just above the surface. Some of the laser energy then heats the evaporated material. While the plasma is weakly ionized, part of the laser energy continues through to the surface and part is absorbed in the plasma or material behind it. At high enough energy, the plasma can become opaque to the laser beam and the surface is shielded, while the plasma front grows towards the laser as described above. This occurs when the plasma frequency becomes greater than the laser frequency, or in terms of the critical electron density n_c, at:

$$n_c \sim (10^{21}/\lambda^2)/cm^3 \tag{2.22}$$

where λ is the laser wavelength in microns. The cutoff near $10\,\mu m$ occurs at an electron density of $10^{19}/cm^3$. At 1000 nm that value is $10^{21}/cm^3$, and at 250 nm it is $1.6 \times 10^{22}/cm^3$. The latter large values can be reached in the first few picoseconds of plasma formation, leading to absorption of the rising edge of a nanosecond pulse. Later in a nanosecond pulse, absorption by the plasma and heated gas can affect the trailing edge.

Consider the formation of a plasma on a plane surface and expanding up the laser beam, as illustrated in Figure 2.11.

There are three important zones, the plasma front, the shock front and the absorption front. At the lowest intensities the shock front precedes the absorption front which is coupled to the plasma front. In this model, both the energy of the shock deposited in the atmosphere behind it, plus the radiation from the plasma,

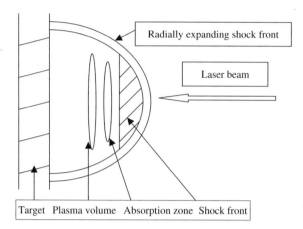

Figure 2.11   Schematic diagram of the development of a laser plasma initiated on a solid surface

are required to move the absorption front towards the laser beam. This is called a laser-supported combustion (LSC) wave. At higher laser intensities, the shock front is strong enough to heat the gas, leading to absorption of the laser beam. Hence the absorption zone comes up just behind the shock front, and both are ahead of the plasma front. This is called the laser-supported detonation (LSD) wave by analogy to what happens in chemical detonations. At the highest intensities, the radiation from the plasma itself is sufficient to heat the atmosphere in front of it to the point at which it becomes absorbing. Hence the absorption zone is coupled to the plasma front. This is called a laser-supported radiation (LSR) wave.

When the incident irradiance is not much larger than the breakdown threshold, the LIBS plasma is typically in the LSD regime when expanding into atmospheric pressure air. Figure 2.12 illustrates schematically the relative positions of the expanding plasma, absorption zone and shock front. At higher irradiances it is better described by an LSR wave, where those three zones have effectively merged. Root (Root, 1989) provided qualitative indications of the variation of velocity, pressure, temperature and density for the three types of plasmas, LSC, LSD and LSR in a one-dimensional approximation. A recent work that models this regime, and then goes on to ablation mechanisms and rates as well as analytical considerations, is given in the significant modeling effort reported by Bogaerts *et al.* (Bogaerts *et al.*, 2003). Their results will be discussed in Chapter 8. After the termination of the laser pulse, the plasma loses energy and decays. Mechanisms include recombination, radiation and conduction.

The effect of a cover gas in certain regimes of pressure is to slow down and confine the plume. Also, the plasma size goes through various regimes as pressure is reduced. At very low pressures the luminous part of the plasma can be very small. Figure 2.13 illustrates the difference in size of plasmas at two pressures, 0.00012 and 7 Torr of CO_2.

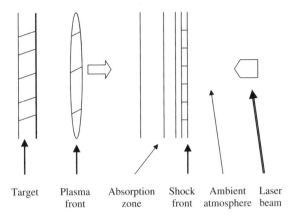

| Target | Plasma front | Absorption zone | Shock front | Ambient atmosphere | Laser beam |

Figure 2.12 Schematic elements of a laser detonation wave (LDW) expanding into an ambient atmospheric pressure gas

2.3 LASER ABLATION

Ablation scenarios are dependent on a multidimensional matrix of parameters including material properties and laser properties. Laser fluences of microjoules to millijoules per square centimeter can cause desorption of atoms and ions with no obvious physical change to the surface. At higher fluences, different mechanisms come into play because, for subsequent pulses, the laser energy is incident upon melted and recondensed matter. The surface reflectivity changes and an ablation crater, with or without elevated walls, forms. The elements of the original sample may have been selectively evaporated so that the redeposited material no longer exhibits the original composition. Important issues in ablation are: the minimum power density to initiate vaporization; the effects of longer or shorter laser pulse lengths; the rate at which ablation proceeds; and the goal of retaining the composition of the sample after ablation into the plasma. We discuss each of these in turn.

An estimate of the minimum power density within a laser pulse required to produce vaporization was given in Moenke-Blankenburg (Moenke-Blankenburg, 1989):

$$I_{\min} = \rho L_v \kappa^{1/2} / \Delta t^{1/2} \, (\mathrm{W/cm^2}) \tag{2.23}$$

where ρ is the density of the target material, L_v is the latent heat of vaporization, κ is the thermal diffusivity of the target, and Δt is the laser pulse length. For pure aluminum, $I_{\min}$ is about $1.75 \times 10^8 \, \mathrm{W/cm^2}$ (Cremers and Knight, 2000).

The effect of laser wavelength is partly through the plasma frequency is described partly through the critical electron density given by Equation (2.22). However this must be coupled with the temporal length of the laser pulse to provide a full picture

Figure 2.13 Size variation of a LIBS plasma at 7 Torr and 0.00012 Torr of CO_2. (Reproduced from Radziemski *et al.*, 2005, with permission from Elsevier)

of effects. Figure 2.14 illustrates the types of surface interactions that can dominate with lasers of different pulse lengths. The potential advantage of picosecond and femtosecond pulses is that absorption and interaction with the surface could be finished before a plasma or plume could form to absorb the laser energy. At terawatt powers the surface material could be rapidly ionized and ejected from the surface by Coulomb repulsion, rather than through thermal effects, as discussed by Russo *et al.* (Russo *et al.*, 2002a).

The maximum mass of material M that can be evaporated by a laser pulse of energy E is estimated to be:

$$M = E(1-R)/[C_p(T_b - T_0) + L_v] \qquad (2.24)$$

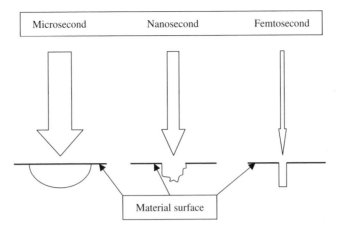

Figure 2.14 Schematics of the interactions of lasers with different pulse lengths on solid surfaces. The microsecond and nanosecond interactions proceed through heating, melting and vaporization. Pulses shorter than the plasma initiation time lead to direct vaporization and the ability, for example, to drill holes with precision

where R is the surface reflectivity, C_p is the specific heat, T_b the boiling point (K), T_0 room temperature (K) and L_v the latent heat of vaporization. This expression can be converted to ablated depth per pulse by using fluence F instead of E, and dividing by the density of the material.

In a study published in 1999, Vadillo *et al.* investigated the effect of plasma shielding on the ablation rate of pure metals as a function of many parameters: cover gas, pressure, fluence, and sample composition (Vadillo *et al.*, 1999). The metals were Zn, Al, Cu, Ni, Fe, Mo, W and Ti. A table of relevant physical constants was provided. Because the samples were drilled through completely, the parameter of μm per pulse was used as the figure of merit for ablation. The laser was an excimer pumped dye laser operating at 581 nm. Ablation rates in air ranged from 0.04 μm/pulse for tungsten at 1.3 J/cm² to 5 μm/pulse for aluminum at 16.7 J/cm². Table 2.6 reproduces some of the results contained in Table 2 of Vadillo *et al.* (Vadillo *et al.*, 1999). Note the leveling off of depth per pulse with increasing fluence, which is caused by increasing plasma shielding with higher fluence. They also observed a significant increase in average ablation rate with decrease in air pressure from 1000 to 250 mbar, but a leveling off below that value.

Finally, they calculated theoretical ablation rates from Equation (2.24) modified to provide ablation depth as described above. They found that, for several metals, the theoretical and observed rates matched within 20% for a fluence of 5.3 J/cm², but deviated for lower and higher fluences. In a different experiment, Semerok *et al.* (Semerok *et al.*, 2002) used Ti:sapphire laser pulses on copper at pulse durations between 70 fs and 10 ps. At 20 J/cm² per pulse, they found ablation rates from 0.24 to 0.15 μm per pulse. Multari *et al.* performed a thorough study of some of the geometric factors related to ablation, such as lens-to-surface distance (LTSD)

Table 2.6 Averaged ablation rate values in μm/pulse for some pure metals, at atmospheric pressure in air, as a function of fluence

Fluence (J/cm²)	1.3	5.3	7.7	16.7
		Depth/pulse (μm)		
Aluminum	1.3	2.5	4.2	5.0
Copper	0.11	0.50	0.38	0.50
Tungsten	0.04	0.20	0.23	0.15

Data from Vadillo *et al.* (1999), with permission from John Wiley & Sons, Ltd

and angle of incidence on the surface (Multari *et al.*, 1996). They observed, for a Nd:YAG 10 ns pulse at 1.06 μm and 185 mJ per pulse, that solid aluminum was ablated at between 10 and 100 ng per pulse, depending on the lens used and the LTSD.

Material ablated into the plasma can have the form of particles (either fresh, or melted and cooled) as well as atoms and/or molecules. Because of the different volatilities of elements and their compounds, the vaporization of elements into the plasma does not necessarily mirror the sample's composition. The result is shown in Figure 2.15 (Yamamoto *et al.*, 2005). Spectroscopic data plotted in the figure illustrate the large departure from stoichiometry possible, in this case for particles ablated from a steel sample. The black circles represent calibrated measurements, the other symbols a variety of LIBS measurements.

It is apparent that minimizing selective vaporization in order to retain stoichiometry is critical. Two phenomena appear to make this minimization more likely. When the energy deposited into the sample is much larger than the latent heat of vaporization for all of the constituents, it is likely that all constituents can be completely vaporized and removed. This is because target thermal properties and constants no longer play a major role. The same effect can be induced by desorbing atoms through nonthermal processes, such as bond breaking and photochemistry on a rapid time scale, faster than energy relaxation can occur at the surface. Ready (Ready, 1971) and Chan and Russo (Chan and Russo, 1991) have commented on the general nature of several regimes. For longer microsecond laser pulses and lower irradiances $<10^6$ W/cm², the thermal nature of the process allows differential vaporization. At $>10^9$ W/cm² and nanosecond pulses, the pressure over the surface inhibits further vaporization until the substrate reaches a critical temperature. Because of the more uniform heating and a more explosive release, the melt ejected should be closer to the sample composition.

The literature is replete with models of the ablation process for a variety of laser and sample parameters. The recent review article by Bogaerts *et al.* (Bogaerts *et al.*, 2003) provides a good summary and list of references for these models, as well as references to the experimental literature. Most of the models start with pulses of a least a few nanoseconds in length, and assume that the interaction with the surface is through heating of the solid, followed by melting and vaporization. Especially

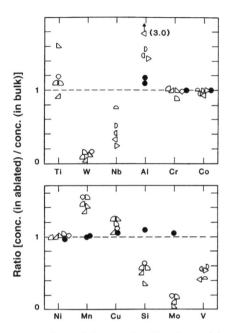

Figure 2.15 Relative concentrations of elements in ablated material and bulk material. This illustrates the large departure from stoichiometry that is possible for ejected material. The case shown is for particles ablated from a steel sample by an acousto-optically Q-switched laser (Yamamoto *et al.*, 2005, with permission from Society for Applied Spectroscopy). The solid black circles represent calibrated concentrations to verify the method

for metals, where the relaxation of photon-excited electrons to the lattice is very rapid, this is a good starting point. For shorter laser pulses, the energy deposition by photons competes with the relaxation time, and a more sophisticated model of the coupling of electron temperature to lattice temperature is needed.

Laser ablation is of interest for many applications other than LIBS, for example for laser-ablation-ICP or ICP-MS. See for example a review by Russo *et al.* (Russo *et al.*, 2002b). Also, extensive use is made of laser ablation and desorption for material deposition in developing thin films and new superconducting materials, as discussed in Miller and Haglund (Miller and Haglund, 1998).

2.4 DOUBLE OR MULTIPLE PULSE LIBS

As mentioned earlier, researchers have used double or multiple pulses for LIBS, in various configurations, because it can result in very large enhancements in signal intensities. Figure 2.16 illustrates the timing between two pulses, where Δt represents the temporal difference between the arrival of the two pulses at the target. Here t_d stands for the delay from the initiation of the *second* laser pulse to the opening

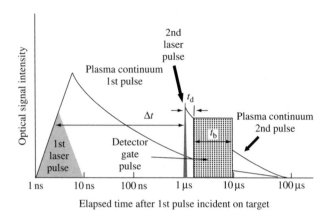

Figure 2.16 The temporal history of a LIBS plasma when two laser pulses are used. The delay between the pulses is Δt, the delay to the opening of the window t_d, and window length is t_b

of the window during which signal will be accepted. Several methods of generating the pulses and arranging them geometrically have been tried. These include:

(1)   multiple pulses within the same flashlamp pulse;
(2)   collinear beams from two lasers focused on the same spot on the target;
(3)   orthogonal beams, typically with one beam perpendicular and one parallel to the surface:

   (a)   where the pulse for the beam parallel to the surface is first in time forming an air spark (pre-ablative);
   (b)   where the pulse for the beam parallel to the surface is second, and reheats the material ablated by the first pulse (reheating).

Figure 2.17 illustrates these configurations schematically.

Proceeding historically, Uebbing *et al.* (Uebbing *et al.*, 1991) used the orthogonal reheating scheme and found enhanced intensities, less dependence on the matrix in which the element was found, but higher (poorer) detection limits. Sattman *et al.* (Sattman *et al.*, 1995), with method (1) above, used bursts of one to six laser pulses within a single flashlamp pulse. The multiple Q-switched pulses were generated by a Nd:YAG laser with one oscillator and two amplifiers. Pulse intervals ranged from 2 to 100 μs. With a goal of improving the performance of LIBS in steel analysis, they found increased material ablation for multiple pulses, compared with a single pulse of energy equal to the sum of that of the individual pulses. For example a 2 × 40 mJ double pulse removed about 1.4 μg while two single noninteracting 40 mJ pulses only removed 1.0 μg. Similarly, line intensities were greater and analytical performance improved. The improvement was ascribed to higher plasma temperatures and electron densities. They continued this work by investigating multiple-pulse steel analysis in the vacuum ultraviolet, finding detection limits of less than 10 μg/g for phosphorus, sulfur and carbon (Sturm *et al.*, 2000).

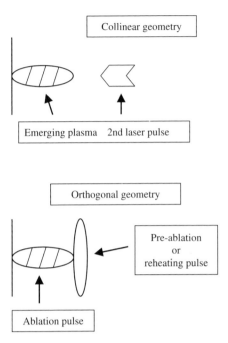

Figure 2.17 Alternative geometries for double-pulse experiments: collinear and orthogonal. In the collinear case, the second laser pulse is incident both on the surface and the plasma formed by the first pulse. In the orthogonal case, the pulse parallel to the surface can come before (air plasma) or after (reheat) the pulse perpendicular to the surface

St-Onge *et al.* reported using two different wavelengths in double-pulse LIBS, 266 nm and 1064 from a Nd:YAG laser (St-Onge *et al.*, 2002). They found enhancements of 5 to 10 times using the two pulses over either of the single pulses, almost independent of which pulse came first.

Several papers from Angel's group dealt with the utility of method (3a), enhancing signals from metals and glasses from 10 to 30 times, as summarized in Stratis *et al.* (Stratis *et al.*, 2001). The mechanism by which the pre-ablation pulse caused enhanced ablation was not clear. Possibilities included sample heating, lowering the pressure above the sample surface, increasing electron density above the surface, and the interaction of the expanding shock on the surface.

2.5 SUMMARY

We have just touched the surface of a rich sub-field of physics and physical chemistry regarding laser plasmas. New data are emerging to clarify complex issues, and some of these will be discussed in Chapter 8. The principles discussed in this chapter will be useful in subsequent discussions that will focus on their application to spectrochemical analysis.

REFERENCES

Aguilera, J.A. and C. Aragón (2004). Characterization of a laser-induced plasma by spatially resolved spectroscopy of neutral atom and ion emissions. Comparison of local and spatially integrated measurements. Spectrochim. Acta Part B 59: 1861–1876.

Bekefi, G. (Ed.) (1976). *Principles of Laser Plasmas*, John Wiley & Sons, Inc., New York.

Bindhu, C.V., S.S. Harilal, M.S. Tillack, F. Najmabadi and A.C. Gaeris (2004). Energy absorption and propagation in laser-created sparks. Appl. Spectrosc. 58: 719–726.

Bogaerts, A., Z. Chen, R. Gijbels and A. Vertes (2003). Laser ablation for analytical sampling: what can we learn from modeling? Spectrochim. Acta Part B 58: 1867–1893.

Chan, W.T. and R.E. Russo (1991). Study of laser–material interactions using inductively coupled plasma-atomic emission spectrometry. Spectrochim. Acta Part B 46: 1471–1486.

Cowan, R.D. (1981). *The Theory of Atomic Structure and Spectra*, University of California Press, Berkeley.

Cremers, D.A., L.J. Radziemski and T.R. Loree (1984). Spectrochemical analysis of liquids using the laser spark. Appl. Spectrosc. 38: 721–726.

Cremers, D.A., F.L. Archuleta and R.J. Martinez (1985). Evaluation of the continuous optical discharge for spectrochemical analysis. Spectrochim. Acta Part B 40: 665–679.

Cremers, D.A. and A.K. Knight (2000). Laser-induced breakdown spectroscopy. In *Encyclopedia of Analytical Chemistry*, ed. R.A. Meyers, John Wiley & Sons, Ltd, Chichester: 9595–9613.

Dewhurst, R. (1978). Comparative data on molecular gas breakdown thresholds in high-laser radiation fields. J. Phys. D. Appl. Phys. 11: 191–195.

Galt, S., M. Sjoberg, M. Lopez Quiroga-Teixeiro and S. Hard (2003). Optical breakdown in fused silica and argon gas: application to Nd:YAG laser limiter. Appl. Opt. 42: 579–584.

Generalov, N.A., V.P. Zimakov, G.I. Kozlov, V.A. Masyukov and Yu.P. Raiser (1970). Continuous optical discharge. JETP Lett. 11: 302–304.

Gigosos, M.A., M.A. González and V. Cardenoso (2003). Computer simulated Balmer-alpha, -beta, and -gamma Stark line profiles for non-equilibrium plasmas diagnostics. Spectrochim. Acta Part B 58: 1489–1504.

Griem,H.R. (1964). *Plasma Spectroscopy*, McGraw-Hill, New York.

Griem, H.R. (1974). *Spectral Line Broadening by Plasmas*, Academic Press, New York.

Griem, H.R. (1997). *Principles of Plasma Spectroscopy*, Cambridge University Press, New York.

Hashida, M., A.F. Semerok, O. Godbert, G. Petite, Y. Izawa and J.-F. Wagner (2002). Ablation threshold dependence on pulse duration for copper. Appl. Surf. Sci. 197–198: 862–867.

Hauer, A.A. and H.A. Baldis (1989). Introduction to laser plasma diagnostics. Ch. 3 in *Laser-induced Plasmas and Applications*, eds L.J. Radziemski and D.A. Cremers, Marcel Dekker, New York.

Hecht, E. (1987). *Optics*, 2nd edn, Addison-Wesley, Reading, MA.

Hummer, D.G. and G. Rybicki (1971). The formation of spectral lines. Ann. Rev. Astron. Astrophys. 9: 237–270.

Keefer, D.R. (1974). Experimental study of a stationary laser-sustained air plasma. J. Appl. Phys. 46: 1080–1083.

Keefer, D.R. (1989). Laser-sustained plasmas. Ch. 4 in *Laser-induced Plasmas and Applications*, eds L.J. Radziemski and D.A. Cremers, Marcel Dekker, New York.

Kennedy, P.K., S.A. Boppart, D.X. Hammer, B.A. Rockwell, G.D. Noojin and W.P. Roach (1995). A first-order model for computation of laser-induced breakdown thresholds in ocular and aqueous media: Part II – comparison to experiment. IEEE J. Quant. Elec. 31: 2250–2257.

Kim, Y.W. (1989). Fundamentals of analysis of solids by laser-produced plasmas. Ch. 8 in *Laser-induced Plasmas and Applications*, eds L.J. Radziemski and D.A. Cremers, Marcel Dekker, New York.

Kuhn, H.G. (1963). *Atomic Spectra*, 2nd edn, Academic Press, New York.

Lochte-Holtgreven, W. (1968). *Plasma Diagnostics*, John Wiley & Sons, Inc., New York.

Miller, J.C. and R.F. Haglund (Eds) (1998). *Laser Ablation and Desorption*, Academic Press, New York.

Millon, E., J. Perrière, R.M. Défourneau, D. Défourneau, O. Albert and J. Etchepare (2003). Femtosecond pulsed-laser deposition of $BaTiO_3$. Appl. Phys. A 77: 73–80.

Moenke-Blankenburg, L. (1989). *Laser Micro Analysis*, John Wiley & Sons, Inc., New York, p. 25.

Multari, R.A., L.E. Foster, D.A. Cremers and M.J. Ferris (1996). The effects of sampling geometry on elemental emissions in laser-induced breakdown spectroscopy. Appl. Spectrosc. 50: 1483–1499.

Oks, E. (1999). Advance in diagnostics for high-temperature plasmas based on the analytical result for the ion dynamical broadening of hydrogen lines. Phys. Rev. E 60: R2480–R2483.

Parigger, C.G., D.H. Plemmons and E. Oks (2003). Balmer series Hβ measurements in a laser-induced hydrogen plasma. Appl. Opt. 42: 5992–6000.

Radziemski, L.J., D.A. Cremers and T.M. Niemczyk (1985). Measurement of the properties of a CO_2 laser-induced air-plasma by double floating probe and spectroscopic techniques. Spectrochim. Acta Part B 40: 517–525.

Radziemski, L.J. and D.A. Cremers (Eds) (1989a). *Laser-induced Plasmas and Applications*, Marcel Dekker, New York.

Radziemski, L.J. and D.A. Cremers (1989b). Spectrochemical analysis using laser plasma excitation. Ch. 7 in *Laser-induced Plasmas and Applications*, eds L.J. Radziemski and D.A. Cremers, Marcel Dekker, New York.

Radziemski, L.J., D.A. Cremers, K. Benelli, C. Khoo and R.D. Harris (2005). Use of the vacuum ultraviolet spectral region for laser-induced breakdown spectroscopy-based Martian geology and exploration. Spectrochim. Acta Part B 60: 237–248.

Ready, J.F. (1971). *Effects of High-power Laser Radiation*, Academic Press, New York.

Root, R.G. (1989). Modeling of post-breakdown phenomena. Ch. 2 in *Laser-induced Plasmas and Applications*, eds L.J. Radziemski and D.A. Cremers, Marcel Dekker, New York.

Russo, R.E., X. Mao and S.S. Mao (2002a). The physics of laser ablation in microchemical analysis. Anal. Chem. 74: 70A–77A.

Russo, R.E., X.L. Mao, H.C. Liu, J. Gonzalez and S.S. Mao (2002b). Laser ablation in analytical chemistry – a review. Talanta 57: 425–451.

Sattman, R., V. Sturm and R. Noll (1995). Laser-induced breakdown spectroscopy of steel samples using multiple Q-switch Nd:YAG laser pulses. J. Phys. D: Appl. Phys. 28: 2181–2187.

Semerok, A., B. Sallé, J.-F. Wagner and G. Petite (2002). Femtosecond, picosecond, and nanosecond laser microablation: laser plasma and crater investigation. Laser Part. Beams 20: 67–72.

Simeonsson, J.B. and A.W. Miziolek (1994). Spectroscopic studies of laser-produced plasmas formed in CO and CO_2 using 193, 266, 355, 532, and 1064 nm laser radiation. Appl. Phys. B 59: 1–9.

St-Onge, L., V. Detalle and M. Sabsabi (2002). Enhanced laser-induced breakdown spectroscopy using the combination of fourth-harmonic and fundamental Nd:YAG laser pulses. Spectrochim. Acta Part B 57: 121–135.

Stricker, J. and J.G. Parker (1982). Experimental investigation of electrical breakdown in nitrogen and oxygen induced by focused laser radiation at $1.064\,\mu m$. J. Appl. Phys. 53: 851–855.

Stratis, D.N., K.L. Eland and S.M. Angel (2001). Effect of pulse delay time on a pre-ablation dual-pulse LIBS plasma. Appl. Spectrosc. 55: 1297–1303.

Sturm, V., L. Peter and R. Noll (2000). Steel analysis with laser-induced breakdown spectrometry in the vacuum ultraviolet. Appl Spectrosc. 54: 1275–1278.

Tambay, R. and R.K. Thareja (1991). Laser-induced breakdown studies of laboratory air at 0.266, 0.355, 0.532, and $1.06\,\mu m$. J. Appl. Phys. 70: 2890–2892.

Uebbing, J., J. Brust, W. Sdorra, F. Leis and K. Niemax (1991). Reheating of a laser-produced plasma by a second laser pulse. Appl. Spectrosc. 45: 1419–1423.

Vadillo, J.M., J.M. Fernandez-Romero, C. Rodriguez and J.J. Laserna (1999). Effect of plasma shielding on laser ablation rate of pure metals at reduced pressure. Surf. Interface Anal. 27: 1009–1015.

Vogel, A., K. Nahen, D. Theisen and J. Noack (1996). Plasma formation in water by picosecond and nanosecond Nd:YAG laser pulses. I. Optical breakdown at threshold and superthreshold irradiance. IEEE J. Sel. Topics Quant. Electr. 2: 847–860.

von der Linde, D. and H. Schüler (1996). Breakdown threshold and plasma formation in femtosecond laser–solid interaction. J. Opt. Soc. Am. B 13: 216–222.

Weyl, G.M. (1989). Physics of laser-induced breakdown. Ch. 1 in *Laser-induced Plasmas and Applications*, eds L.J. Radziemski and D.A. Cremers, Marcel Dekker, New York.

White, H.E. (1934). *Introduction to Atomic Spectra*, McGraw-Hill, New York.

Whiting, E.E. (1968). An empirical approximation to the Voigt profile. J. Quant. Spectrosc. Radiat. Transfer 8: 1379–1384.

Williams, W.E., M.J. Soileau and E.W. Van Stryland (1983). Picosecond air breakdown studies at 0.53 μm. Appl. Phys. Lett. 43: 352–354.

Yamamoto, K.Y., D.A. Cremers, L.E. Foster, M.P. Davies and R.D. Harris (2005). Laser-induced breakdown spectroscopy analysis of solids using a long pulse (150 ns) Q-switched Nd:YAG laser. Appl. Spectrosc. 59: 1082–1097.

3 Apparatus Fundamentals

3.1 BASIC LIBS APPARATUS

LIBS is a plasma-based method of atomic emission spectroscopy (AES) that uses instrumentation similar to that used by other AES methods. The unique characteristics of LIBS originate from the use of a powerful laser pulse to both 'prepare' the target sample and then 'excite' the constituent atoms to emit light. Sample preparation results from the action of the focused laser pulse on the target that removes a small mass of the target in the form of atoms and small particles (Chapter 2). Coincident with ablation is the formation of a microplasma in the focal volume of the laser pulse that excites the ablated atoms. The plasma continues this excitation after the laser pulse. In addition, small ablated particles are vaporized in the hot plasma and the resulting atoms excited.

A typical LIBS apparatus is shown diagrammatically in Figure 3.1 (Plate 3) along with a photo of a simple LIBS apparatus. The main components are:

(1) the pulsed laser that generates the powerful optical pulses used to form the microplasma;
(2) the focusing system of mirror and lens that directs and focuses the laser pulse on the target sample;
(3) target holder or container (if needed);
(4) the light collection system (lens, mirrors or fiber optic) that collects the spark light and transports the light to the detection system;
(5) detection system consisting of a method to spectrally filter or disperse the light such as a spectrograph and a detector to record the light;
(6) computer and electronics to gate the detector, fire the laser, and store the spectrum.

The basic components of any LIBS system are similar but the component specifications are tailored to the particular application. These specifications include physical parameters such as size, weight, packaging, power and utilities required for operation as well as technical specifications pertaining to operational performance. These will be discussed in detail below, but examples include the energy of the laser pulse and the spectral resolution of the spectrograph.

Handbook of Laser-Induced Breakdown Spectroscopy   D. Cremers and L. Radziemski
© 2006 John Wiley & Sons, Ltd

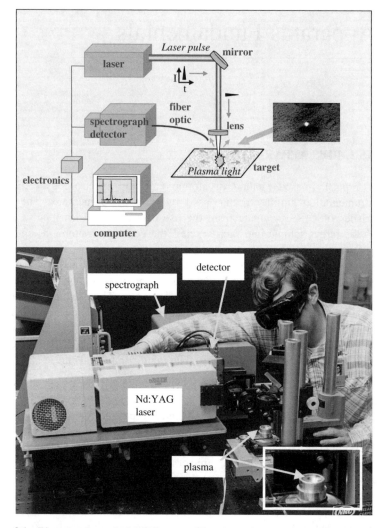

Figure 3.1 Diagram of a typical LIBS set-up. The photo shows a simple LIBS set-up used to analyze material on a filter (see Plate 3)

3.2 LASERS

3.2.1 LASER FUNDAMENTALS

Principles of laser operation in general and the operation of specific lasers are described in detail in numerous books (Svelto, 2004). The discussion here will be limited to the fundamentals of the operation of the flashlamp-pumped Nd:YAG laser which is used for the majority of LIBS measurements. A basic Nd:YAG laser is

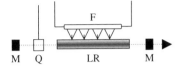

Figure 3.2 Nd:YAG laser configuration. F, flashlamp; LR, laser rod; M, mirror; Q, Q-switch

shown diagrammatically in Figure 3.2. In brief, a flashlamp is fired to produce broadband light (pumping light) extending over the near UV, visible, and near IR spectral regions. A small percentage of this pumping light is absorbed by ions doped into the lasing material (Nd ions in a YAG crystal matrix; YAG, yttrium aluminum garnet). Due to the electronic energy levels of the Nd ions in the laser rod, if the flashlamp pumping is sufficiently strong, a population inversion is established in which the upper level of the lasing atomic transition is more populated that the lower terminating level of the transition. In this case, a photon passing through the laser rod at the same frequency as the lasing transition will experience gain or amplification by inducing decay of some of the ions from the upper to the lower state (stimulated emission). If the rod is surrounded by a resonant cavity composed of two mirrors in which some of this amplified light is directed back into the rod, significant amplification of light at the wavelength of the lasing transition can be achieved.

For LIBS, powerful laser pulses on the order of 5 MW are needed to form the microplasma when focused to a small spot. These high powers are easily achieved using a pulsed and Q-switched laser having moderate pulse energies. In this case, an electro-optic Q-switch shutter is positioned in the cavity to prevent photons at the laser wavelength from making a complete path through the cavity and inducing stimulated emission. In this way, the population inversion between the upper and lower levels of the lasing transition can become very large. When the Q-switch is activated by a suitably timed gate pulse, the Q-switch becomes transparent, allowing photons to make many traverses of the laser cavity resulting in a high power pulse of short duration. A fraction of this pulse leaves the cavity through a partially transmitting mirror (output coupler). For the Nd:YAG laser, the Q-switched pulse length is on the order of 5–10 ns. The pulse is of short duration because once lasing begins, the population inversion is rapidly depleted and lasing terminates. The Q-switch is intentionally closed shortly after the laser pulse to prevent the generation of additional pulses. The Q-switch can be pulsed more than once during the period of flashlamp pumping, however, to produce two powerful pulses for dual-pulse LIBS (Sections 3.2.5 and 8.6).

3.2.2 TYPES OF LASERS

Specifications of the pulsed and Q-switched Nd:YAG laser typically used for LIBS are listed in Table 3.1 along with specifications of some other lasers used for LIBS measurements. These other lasers include the excimer laser (UV wavelengths) and

Table 3.1 Specifications of lasers used for LIBS

Type	Wavelength (nm)	Pulse width (ns)	Rep. rate (Hz)	Comments related to LIBS applications
Nd:YAG (s)	Fundamental: 1064	6–15	ss to 20	(1) Fundamental wavelength easily shifted to provide harmonic wavelengths
				(2) Available in very compact form for small instrumentation
	Harmonics: 532, 355, 266	4–8		(3) Good beam quality possible
				(4) Dual-pulse capabilities in single unit
				(5) Flashlamp or diode-pumped available
Excimer (g)	XeCl: 308	20 ns	ss to 200	(1) Requires periodic change of gases
	KrF: 248			(2) Beam quality less than Nd:YAG laser
	ArF: 194			(3) Provides UV wavelengths only
CO_2 (g)	10 600	200 (with 1000 ns trailing edge)	ss to 200	(1) Requires periodic change of gases or gas flow
				(2) Does not couple well into many metals
				(3) Beam quality less than Nd:YAG laser
Microchip	1064	<1 ns	1–10 k	(1) Good mode and beam quality
				(2) High shot-to-shot pulse stability
				(3) High rep. rates ∼ 10 kHz

s, solid state laser; g, gas laser; ss, single shot.

the CO_2 laser (far IR wavelength) that use gas as the lasing medium. In this case an electrical discharge is produced in the gas that pumps the lasing species. The optimum type of laser used for LIBS depends on the application (Lorenzen *et al.*, 1992) and the desired laser wavelength.

Nd:YAG lasers (flashlamp pumped) are preferred for most LIBS applications because they provide a reliable, compact, and easy to use source of laser pulses of high focused power density. In addition, the fundamental wavelength can be easily shifted to generate pulses with fixed wavelengths ranging from the near IR to the near UV spectral regions. Typical laboratory and compact Nd:YAG lasers are shown in Figure 3.3. The latter type has been incorporated into compact, person portable instrumentation (Yamamoto *et al.*, 1996) and a cone penetromter system (Miles and Cortes, 1998). Some important specifications of these two lasers are compared in Table 3.2. In a few cases, arc lamp pumped, acousto-optically Q-switched lasers have been used for LIBS (Ernst *et al.*, 1996; Yamamoto *et al.*, 2005). These lasers

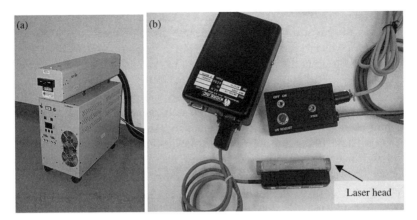

Laser head

Figure 3.3 (a) Typical laboratory Nd:YAG laser (Surelite laser; photo courtesy of Continuum, Inc.); (b) compact Nd:YAG laser (MK-367; photo courtesy of Kigre Laser, Inc.)

Table 3.2 Specifications of the laboratory and compact Nd:YAG lasers of Figure 3.3

Parameter	Laboratory	Compact
Pulse energy (mJ) max.	450	25
Pulse width (ns)	5–8	4
Repetition rate (Hz)	10	1
Energy stability ($\pm\%$)	2	<10
Beam diameter (mm)	<10	3
Beam divergence (mrad)	0.5	1.1
Flashlamp lifetime (10^6 shots)	10	0.3
Mass (kg)	71	1.2
Cooling	water	air
Power requirements	220 V AC; 12 A	12 V DC; 1.2 A

AC, alternating current; DC, direct current.

have repetition rates of several kilohertz but produce pulses with maximum energies up to 20 mJ. These have been used to sample solid surfaces such as metals and soils.

To increase the analytical performance of LIBS measurements, injection seeded Nd:YAG lasers have been investigated. Injection seeding is a method of producing laser output that operates on an ultra-narrow single longitudinal mode by injecting a 'seed' beam into the cavity from a single mode continuous wave diode pumped laser. The seed beam is typically injected into the Nd:YAG laser cavity through a fiber optic. The resulting laser pulse is near transform limited in linewidth and displays a smooth temporal profile in contrast to the intensity fluctuations normally observed from the unseeded laser operating multimode. The shot to shot stability of the laser pulse is enhanced using a seeded pulse. A recent study, however, has shown that in the analysis of gases, injection seeding did not improve analytical precision (Hohreiter *et al.*, 2004). Other factors, such as the elimination of aerosol particles from the gas were found to significantly increase precision.

Pulse widths typically used for LIBS are in the range of 5–20 ns depending on the laser. In recent years there has been interest in evaluating the use of picosecond (10^{-12} s) (Eland *et al.*, 2001a) and femtosecond (10^{-15} s) pulses for LIBS. The majority of work appears be devoted to femtosecond pulses (Eland *et al.*, 2001b; Scaffidi *et al.*, 2003). These pulses are usually generated by a mode-locked Ti-sapphire oscillator pumped by a continuous wave laser such as the solid-state Nd : YVO_4. These lasers are not near the stage of development of the Nd:YAG laser for instrument applications and are more of a laboratory instrument. Use of these lasers, however, has revealed some interesting results in LIBS experiments and their use is expected to continue.

A new type of laser, the microchip laser (Zayhowski, 1999, 2000), has been demonstrated for LIBS analysis (Gornushkin *et al.*, 2004a). These lasers are made by dielectrically coating a thin piece of sold-state gain material to form a simple cavity which is then longitudinally pumped by a semiconductor laser. A saturable absorber is added to one end of the cavity to generate Q-switched pulses. A diagram of the components of the microchip laser is presented in Figure 3.4. Typically, these lasers produce pulses with durations of less than 1 ns and pulse energies in the low microjoule range. Because of the low energy, tight focusing of the laser pulse is needed to produce a plasma.

3.2.3 PROPERTIES OF LASER LIGHT IMPORTANT FOR LIBS

Properties of lasers important for LIBS include wavelength, pulse energy and focused pulse power density (irradiance). These determine whether an analytically useful laser plasma can be generated. For example, some laser wavelengths couple

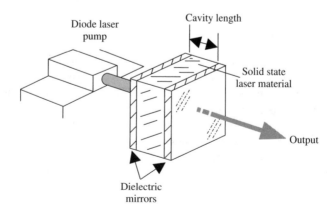

Figure 3.4 Diagram of a micro-chip laser assembly. (After Zayhowski, 1999, with permission from Elsevier)

more readily into a specific material compared with other wavelengths. The CO_2 wavelength (10 600 nm) is highly reflected by a copper target as well as some other metals but this wavelength couples well into glasses and aqueous solutions which have high absorption in the IR. In addition, although a laser pulse may have focused power densities on the order of GW/cm^2, if the pulse energy is too low, sufficient material may not be ablated and vaporized to provide a usefully strong emission signal.

Other important properties include the spatial quality of the laser pulse which determines the minimum spot size to which it can be focused. It may not be possible to focus a beam with poor quality to a sufficiently small spot to achieve power densities required to form a laser plasma. Some laser pulse properties are shown in Figure 3.5 and discussed below.

3.2.3.1   Irradiance

Lasers are unique sources of high irradiance (also termed intensity) light required to generate the laser plasma. The unit of irradiance is W/cm^2 or photons/cm^2. The pulse energies used for LIBS typically range from 10 mJ up to 500 mJ. Given that the energy in a visible photon is $\sim 10^{-19}$ J, the number of photons in a laser pulse used for LIBS ranges from 10^{17} to 5×10^{18} photons. Note that these photons will be in a pulse having a duration of ~ 10 ns for the usual LIBS experiment. For comparison, a thermal light source (blackbody) at a temperature of 1000 K will produce about 10^{12} photons/s from a 1 cm^2 surface area within a bandwidth of 100 nm (a solid state laser will have a bandwidth <0.001 nm), or for comparison, only 10^4 photons in 10 ns.

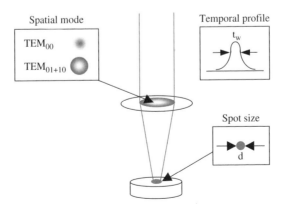

Figure 3.5   Demonstration of some laser properties important for LIBS

3.2.3.2 Directionality

The ability of the laser pulse to propagate over long distances as a collimated beam is important for stand-off and remote LIBS measurements (Section 3.8 and Chapter 7). Here stand-off represents the projection of the laser pulse through the atmosphere or free space over a distance of many meters. Remote indicates transport of the laser pulse through a fiber optic cable. Both methods require a laser pulse with good directional beam qualities. A high quality laser which operates in a single lowest order mode (Gaussian mode) produces a laser beam that replicates closely a uniform plane wave having a constant phase distribution across the wavefront. Such a beam, emerging from the output coupler of the laser of diameter d will propagate as a highly directional, parallel beam for a distance given by $\pi d^2/\lambda$, often termed the Rayleigh range (Section 7.2.2). After this distance, the beam will begin to expand with an angular spread of $\Delta\theta$ where $\Delta\theta = d/\lambda$ is specified as the beam divergence.

3.2.3.3 Monochromaticity

Conventional light sources are broadband, generating light over a wide range of wavelengths. A laser on the other hand, has the ability to generate the majority of its output energy within a very narrow spectral range due to the laser light originating from a well-defined transition in the lasing medium. As noted above, for a solid state laser the bandwidth will typically be <0.001 nm. In terms of excitation properties of the laser plasma, monochromaticity is not typically important. Analytically useful laser plasmas can be generated with IR, visible and UV wavelengths. Certain wavelengths couple more strongly into specific materials making wavelength important for ablation but a highly monochromatic beam is not important because the absorption spectra of bulk materials are usually slowing varying functions of wavelength. Monochromaticity may be important, however, in LIBS instrument design. That is, in some configurations, it may be desirable to use optical components that reflect the narrow band laser wavelength and then pass the broad spectrum of the laser plasma which is collected for analysis (open path LIBS, Section 7.2.3).

3.2.4 GENERATION OF ADDITIONAL WAVELENGTHS

For some target samples, the fundamental frequency of the laser (1064 nm for Nd:YAG) may not be optimum for LIBS analysis. Because of the typically good beam quality from Nd:YAG lasers and their high peak powers, a simple form of frequency conversion (or wavelength shifting) is possible to generate alternate wavelengths. This is accomplished using so-called harmonic generation simply by passing the laser pulse through a suitable birefringent material. Crystals of KDP (potassium dihydrogen phosphate) and KD*P (potassium dideuterium phosphate), which are relatively easy to produce in large sizes and which are transparent

Table 3.3 Energy of fundamental and harmonic wavelengths of Nd:YAG

Wavelength (nm)	Energy (mJ)
1064	450
532	200
355	100
255	55

at the fundamental and shifted Nd:YAG wavelengths, are commonly used. Energy conversions are typically about 50%. In the simplest case, the 1064 nm fundamental is converted to 532 nm (2nd harmonic) which may be further doubled to 266 nm (4th harmonic). By combining the residual 1064 nm wavelength with converted 532 nm, the 3rd harmonic of 355 nm is generated. Table 3.3 lists typical energies available at the harmonic wavelengths for a laboratory Nd:YAG laser with specifications of Table 3.2.

These wavelengths can be used to generate other wavelengths not at harmonic frequencies using Raman shifting methods or by using them to pump dye lasers or OPOs (optical parametric oscillators). This adds complexity to the instrumentation, however.

3.2.5 DOUBLE PULSE OPERATION

Experiments have shown that in many cases the emission signals and signal-to-noise ratio in LIBS measurements can be enhanced through the use of dual laser pulses incident on the target in either a collinear or orthogonal configuration as shown in Figure 2.17 (Scaffidi *et al.*, 2006). For ultimate versatility, two independently operating lasers, separately triggered, provide the maximum versatility. That is, the pulses can be adjusted to overlap temporally or to be separated by any selected time interval and the pulse energies can be adjusted independently. The orthogonal pulse configuration will be easier to align compared with the collinear set-up when using two lasers but for implementation in the field, the collinear set-up is more feasible and will be useable for stand-off analysis. Also, the wavelengths of the lasers may be different to enhance certain effects. The use of a dual-pulse arrangement in which the pulses have different pulse widths has also been investigated (Scaffidi *et al.*, 2003).

In some experiments, where a pulse separation on the order of 40–160 μs is useful and the same wavelength is acceptable, a single laser can provide both pulses. An example is the detection of solids underwater (Pichahchy *et al.*, 1997). Specifically, Nd:YAG lasers that are electro-optically Q-switched can provide dual-pulse operation by using two Marx bank pulse generators to sequentially trigger the Q-switch. The triggering is set-up so the first Marx bank is triggered at the front of the pumping profile of the flashlamp and the second Marx bank is triggered at least 40 μs later but at a delay at which the flashlamp pumping rate is still sufficient to

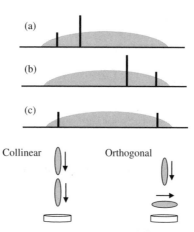

Figure 3.6 Dual-pulse laser operation. Relative intensities of first and second pulses (E_1, E_2) depending on positions relative to the flashlamp profile (shaded). (a) $E_1 < E_2$; (b) $E_1 > E_2$; (c) $E_1 \sim E_2$. Collinear and orthogonal dual-pulse configurations are shown

produce lasing. By adjusting the flashlamp pump energy, the timing between the two pulses and their positions within the envelope of the flashlamp profile, the relative pulse energies can be adjusted (Figure 3.6). Dual-pulse generation by the same laser is especially attractive for the collinear pulse configuration because the same optical system focuses the two pulses.

3.3 OPTICAL SYSTEMS

3.3.1 FOCUSING AND LIGHT COLLECTION

In LIBS, laser pulses can be focused on the sample using lenses or mirrors as shown in Figure 3.7. Typically, a single lens is used to focus the laser pulses to a sufficiently small spot to achieve an analytically useful plasma (a). For systems requiring an adjustable focus, such as industrial process monitoring in which the lens-to-sample distance may be changing, a multi-lens system may be required with the relative positions of the lenses adjusted to locate the focal point on the target (b). Similarly, the laser pulses can be focused using a mirror (c).

Depending on the apparatus, a lens or mirror system may be used to collect the plasma light which is then directed into the detection system (e.g. spectrograph and detector). A single lens is the simplest optical arrangement to collect the plasma light although multiple lens systems may be used in certain cases. Unless constructed specifically to eliminate the effect, lens systems will exhibit chromatic aberration (Hecht, 2001), such that the focal position of the lens system is wavelength dependent (Figure 3.7d). This is due to the dependence of the refractive index of optical materials on wavelength. For example, for quartz, the refractive index

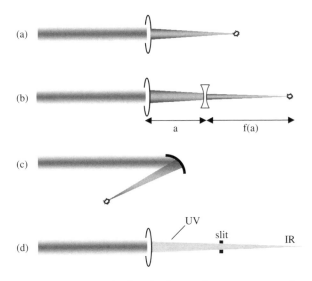

Figure 3.7   Different arrangements for focusing laser pulses to generate a plasma

decreases with increased wavelength so that the focal length will increase with increased wavelength. An advantage of a mirror system is that all wavelengths will be focused at the same position. On the other hand, the use of a spherical mirror in an off-axis configuration will result in astigmatism and coma (Hecht, 2001) distorting the resulting image.

Typically, spherical optics are used to focus the laser beam, which is usually radially symmetric for an Nd:YAG laser. These result in a circular spot focused on the sample resulting in the plasma shown in Figure 3.1 which is radially symmetric with respect to the optical axis of the incident laser beam. By using cylindrical optics, however, a line or long spark can be formed on the target (Cremers and Radziemski, 1985; Arnold and Cremers, 1995; Mateo *et al.*, 2000; Rodolfa and Cremers, 2004). The area sampled by the long spark can be much larger than that sampled by the spark formed by a spherical lens allowing large areas to be more rapidly sampled. An example of such a focusing arrangement is shown in Figure 3.8 with the resulting spark shown in Figure 3.9. By using the donut mode from a laser with an unstable resonator, a long spark with a more uniform intensity distribution can be formed. When the long spark is formed by a Gaussian-like spatial mode, the 'hot spot' would be located in the center of the long spark.

3.3.2   LENSES

In the majority of LIBS systems, the laser pulses are focused into or on the sample using a simple lens. In addition, simple lenses are used to collect the plasma light and

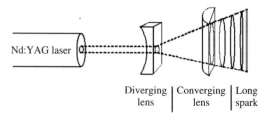

Figure 3.8 Lens system used to form a long spark on a sample

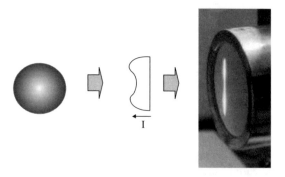

Figure 3.9 Donut mode laser pulse produces a long spark with high intensity lobes at top and bottom. Shown on the right is the long spark formed on filter paper

either focus it into a spectrograph or onto a fiber optic cable. Important parameters of the lens are the focal length, diameter and material. Typical focal lengths for *in situ* measurements range from 50 to 150 mm with lens diameters of either 25 or 50 mm. The diameter of the laser beam from the majority of solid state lasers (or their harmonics) are on the order of 6–8 mm, suitable for the smaller lenses. More sophisticated, multilens focusing systems are needed, for example, for situations requiring variable focus, to focus the laser pulse over many meters, and to achieve the minimum spot size (highest power density on target).

Important properties of lenses are:

(1) Material (e.g. bk-7, quartz, zinc selenide, germanium, NaCl). The lens should have maximum transmission at the laser wavelength and if used to collect plasma light, it must transmit efficiently at the wavelengths being monitored.

(2) Anti-reflection coatings to minimize back reflections (to less than 0.5%, typical) and therefore maximize energy on target. This coating also minimizes reflections from the optic which may be directed back toward the laser or around the room. An uncoated optic will typically reflect about 4% of the light incident normal at each surface so a laser pulse traversing a lens will lose about 8% of the incident energy. For an optical system with many surfaces, the energy loss when using uncoated optics can be large.

(3) Lens type (plano-convex, double convex, etc.). For critical applications, best form lenses that provide the minimum spherical aberration from a spherical lens may be preferred.

(4) Scratch and dig is a measure of the visibility of surface defects, scratches and digs (pits). For most LIBS applications this is not a critical parameter.

3.3.3 FIBER OPTIC CABLES

Fiber optic cables (FOCs) are being used extensively with LIBS because they simplify collection of the plasma light (Figure 3.10). FOCs are particularly useful in applications in which the detection system cannot be positioned close to the target. An example is a subsurface cone penetrometer system in which the plasma may be generated many meters underground but the detection system is located at the surface (Theriault *et al.*, 1998). Prior to the use of FOC, the plasma light was either focused onto the spectrograph slit or the plasma was generated sufficiently close to the slit that a sufficient amount of light would pass through it. If focused on the slit, typically only a thin vertical slice through the plasma enters the spectrograph (Section 7.4.1). Small changes in the position of the plasma will greatly affect the intensity of observed light because the intensity and relative intensities of emissions are strongly dependent on position in the plasma.

A typical fused silica FOC design is shown in Figure 3.11. The fiber transmits the light using total internal reflection and those light rays entering the fiber within the acceptance cone angle (numerical aperture) will be reflected down the fiber with high efficiency (Figure 3.12). The acceptance angle of a fused silica fiber optic is ∼26° so that light will be collected from all parts of the plasma if positioned a few centimeters distant. Although the plasma emits UV light, in most applications 'solarization,' a UV light induced phenomenon that degrades the transmission efficiency of the fiber, does not appear to be a problem.

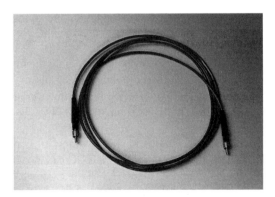

Figure 3.10 Fiber optic cable used to collect plasma light. The SMA connector on this cable will interface to some types of spectrograph entrance slits

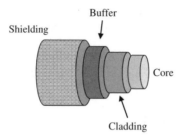

Figure 3.11   Design of a fiber optic

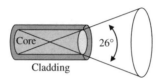

Figure 3.12   Light rays entering the fiber within the acceptance cone will be transmitted

Fiber core diameters typically range from 50 μm to 1 mm for fused silica. The fused silica can be high or low OH content with high OH fiber used in the UV/VIS and low OH fibers employed for the nearIR because of their low water content (<2 ppm) and correspondingly lower absorption. A cladding material of lower refractive index (n_c) than the core fiber (n_f) is used to enhance the light guiding effect. Typical cladding is fluorine-doped silica producing a numerical aperture (NA) of 0.22, where NA = $(n_f{}^2 - n_c{}^2)^{1/2}$. Surrounding the cladding is a buffer to protect the cladding from scratches and other damage that may cause the fiber to break. The composition of the buffer determines the operating environment of the fiber. The typical polyamide buffer offers a wide temperature range (−100 to 400 °C) and solvent resistance. For extremes of temperature (−90 to 750 °C), a gold buffer is used.

Using a FOC, the plasma light can either be focused onto the fiber end to increase light collection or the fiber can simply be pointed at the plasma. Focusing on the fiber increases the sensitivity of light collection to alignment of the optical system. In contrast, pointing the fiber at the plasma reduces this alignment sensitivity (Section 7.4.1).

FOCs can be made in custom lengths having a variety of connector types (e.g. FCSMA905, ST, FC/PC). The composition of the FOC can also be custom tailored for the spectroscopic region of interest (Figure 3.13). For example, fiber materials are specially selected for the VIS/nearIR (350–2000 nm), UV/VIS (200–800 nm), and deep UV (solarization resistant fibers below 230 nm). Outer shielding is typically PVC, Kevlar reinforced PVC or metal shielding.

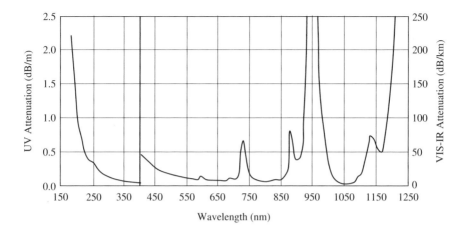

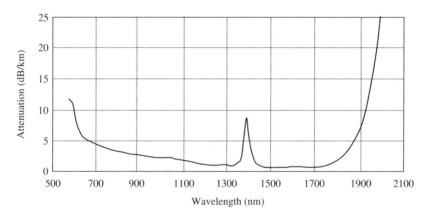

Figure 3.13 Spectral transmission of UV (a) and IR (b) fiber optic materials. (Reproduced from *The Book on the Technologies of Polymicro*, 2005, with permission from Polymicro Technologies, LLC)

The discussion above relates to solid step index fused silica fibers. Other fiber types have been investigated for use with LIBS including graded index solid fibers, hollow-waveguide and photonic-crystal waveguide fibers, and hollow core fibers. Recently hollow-core photonic-crystal fibers have been used to deliver picosecond pulses which were then focused on a solid surface to form a laser spark (Konorov *et al.*, 2003). These fibers can transmit laser pulses having significantly higher fluences than is possible using fused silica fibers. Using the photonic-crystal fiber, however, it was not possible to form an air spark. Recently, it was demonstrated that by using a hollow-core fiber (cyclic olefin polymer-coated silver hollow fibers) an air plasma with high reproducibility can be formed for a straight or slightly curved fiber (Yalin *et al.*, 2005). The ability to form an air plasma was degraded significantly as the fiber was bent further $(1/R > 0.73/m)$. Work remains to reduce bending losses to maximize energy transmission, but this demonstration opens up new possibilities for LIBS applications.

By using a bundle of individual fibers, custom FOCs can be constructed. Two examples are shown in Figure 3.14. One configuration involves a circular bundle at the light collection end of the fiber which is arranged as a linear array at the distal end. The linear array is positioned along the slit of a spectrograph to increase the amount of light directed into the instrument. In another arrangement (trifurcated cable), a circular fiber bundle of fibers is divided into separate bundled cables at the distal ends which can then be directed into different instruments. A common use is to route the collected light to different spectrographs each spanning different spectral regions. For commercial fiber optics, the specifications indicate that for a trifurcated bundle, 27% of the incident light is channeled into each leg while this increases to 43% for a bifurcated bundle. Losses are due to 4% reflection at each end and the packing fraction for fibers in the bundles, which is about 0.9. The positions of fibers in each bundle are randomized so that each of the divided ends will receive equal distributions of the light from the input end.

In addition to collecting plasma light, the FOC can also be used to deliver laser pulses to a remotely located sample (Cremers *et al.*, 1995; Davies *et al.*, 1995). The pulse energy leaving the fiber can be focused with a simple lens system to form the laser plasmas or the bare end of the fiber core may be ground smooth with a radius to serve as a short focal length lens. An example of a FOC probe delivering laser pulses is shown in Figure 3.15. The FOC shown here is delivering about 60 mJ of pulse energy.

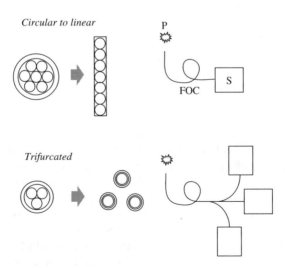

Figure 3.14 Custom FOC configurations

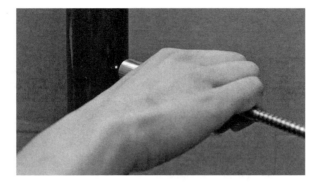

Figure 3.15 FOC probe for LIBS analysis. Using this probe, the plasma light was collected by the same fiber delivering the laser pulse. The plasma light was split off the distal end and directed into the detection system

3.4 METHODS OF SPECTRAL RESOLUTION

3.4.1 INTRODUCTION

As described previously, the light from the laser plasma contains information about the elements composing the material via the set of emission lines characteristic of each element. The laser plasma can be considered as a sum of the white light continuum from the plasma and the discrete emissions from each atomic species and in some cases simple molecules. The complete emission spectrum of each element is unique, no two are identical. Figure 3.16 (Plate 4) demonstrates LIBS analysis using a low resolution spectral system and a higher resolution system. The light from the laser plasma on the right, when viewed through a simple transmission diffraction grating, shows a broad spectrum of low resolution. Strong emissions only from nitrogen in air are observed because air contains 80% nitrogen. When the same spectrum is viewed using a higher resolution spectral system, spectral features due to minor and trace elements in the soil are observed.

Figure 3.16 shows the importance of a high resolution detection system. When monitoring a single line as is often done in many types of atomic emission analyses, the possibility exists of spectral interferences, that is, that two or more elements may have the same emission wavelength or have emission lines sufficiently close in wavelength as to overlap. This overlap may prevent unambiguous monitoring of the element line of choice. If an atom is excited in a low density medium (e.g. a low pressure discharge tube or hollow cathode lamp), the emission lines can be very narrow, with a value of 0.01 nm typical. In a laser plasma, where the density of atomic species will be high, processes are active that will act to increase the width of the line. These include pressure broadening (due to collisions between species) and Stark broadening (due to the high electron density in the laser plasma). Because the plasma decays temporally after formation and the distribution of material in the plasma is very inhomogeneous, these widths can be reduced in some cases

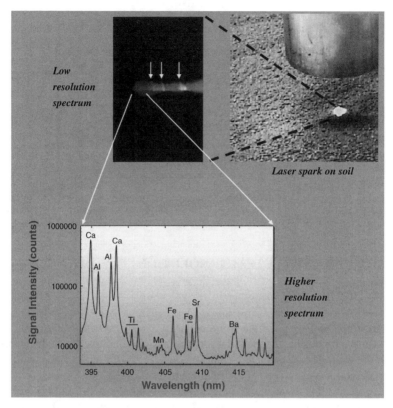

Figure 3.16 LIBS spectrum produced by a simple transmission diffraction grating from the plasma formed at the right on soil. Here only strong lines of nitrogen from air are observed. Higher resolution of the spectrum shows emissions from major, minor and trace elements in the soil (see Plate 4)

by delaying observation to later times after the plasma has decayed, or viewing emissions from different areas of the plasma. Spectral overlap produced by broadening of lines by these processes is fundamental and determined by the physics of the atomic systems, as discussed in Chapter 2. Some practical aspects of measuring emission lines from LIBS spectra that partially overlap are discussed in Section 4.2.

There are several parameters important for describing the performance of a spectral resolution system. These will be discussed below in relation to a grating spectrograph.

3.4.2 SPECTRAL RESOLUTION DEVICES

The method of spectral resolution depends on the application and can be as simple as a spectral line filter to monitor a single wavelength or a sophisticated echelle

Table 3.4 Comparison of methods of spectral resolution

Method	Characteristics
Spectral filter	Single fixed wavelength, small, inexpensive, useful for imaging
AOTF*	Single wavelength, tunable wavelength, useful for imaging
Grating monochromator	Single wavelength, high resolution, tunable, f#~4
Echelle spectrograph	High resolution, broadband spectral coverage, alignment more critical, typical f#>9, requires two-dimensional detector array
Grating spectrograph	Wide spectral coverage, high resolution, tunable, different gratings offers ability to tailor spectral resolution, f#~4

*Acousto-optic tunable filter

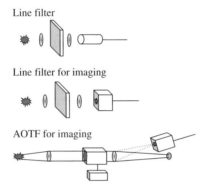

Figure 3.17 Single emission line detection and imaging using a line filter and AOTF

spectrograph that can monitor simultaneously the majority of the useful LIBS spectral region (200–800 nm) for analysis in air. Table 3.4 lists methods of spectral resolution used for LIBS and some methods of single emission line detection are illustrated in Figure 3.17.

3.4.2.1 Spectral filters

Various types of filters are useful for LIBS (Figure 3.18). Long wave pass edge filters, for example, are useful to eliminate second order in spectrographs (e.g. 300 nm will appear at 600 nm unless it is removed by such a filter). Color filters can be used to transmit only the spectral region of interest to reduce light intensity at other wavelengths that may be particularly strong and may lead to high levels of scattered light in a spectrograph. A notch filter transmits over a broad spectral region but exhibits high attenuation within a small band. This filter will be useful for LIBS to filter out scattered 532 nm light when this wavelength is used to generate the laser plasma. This will be especially important if monitoring emission lines near 532 nm. Bandpass filters pass only a selected spectral region with high attenuation outside this region. The wavelength region passed by this filter is determined during

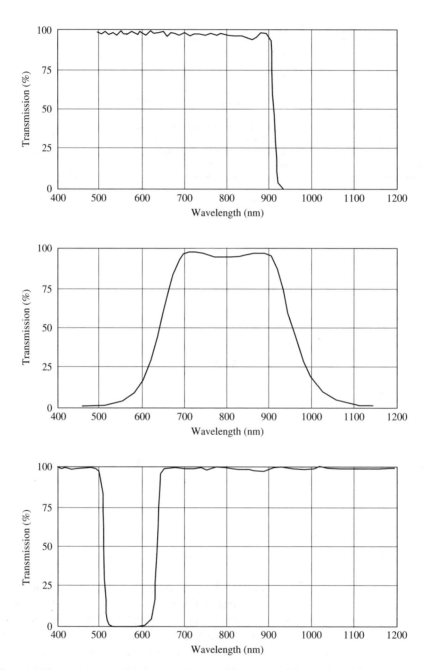

Figure 3.18 Partial transmission curves for edge (a), bandpass (b) and notch (c) filters

fabrication and can be wide or narrow. Line filters or narrow bandpass filters are useful to transmit a certain emission line of interest. These filters would be useful for a simple LIBS instrument designed to monitor only a single or a few fixed emission lines. Such filters can be designed to transmit at a particular wavelength with a bandwidth down to 0.1 nm. They are manufactured using a series of dielectric coatings deposited on a suitable transmissive substrate (e.g. quartz for the UV). Tunable filters are angle sensitive and require a collimated beam of light to achieve maximum performance. Blocking of wavelengths outside the bandpass is typically 10^{-4} and usable clear apertures are in the range 9 to 45 mm. Bandpass transmission at the center wavelength varies with filter specifications but is on the order of 40–70%.

3.4.2.2 Acousto-optic tunable filter (AOTF)

The AOTF is a solid-state electronically tunable spectral bandpass filter. It can be used for imaging in the light of a specific wavelength as well as serving as a simple spectral line selection device (Multari et al., 1996). An AOTF consists of a crystal of tellurium dioxide or quartz with a piezoelectric transducer bonded to one side as shown in Figure 3.19. The piezo transducer is driven at radio frequencies (RF) to generate acoustical compression waves in the crystal that alter the refractive index of the crystal in a periodic pattern. This leads to the generation of a diffraction grating in the material so that a beam of collimated light incident at the Bragg angle is diffracted into the first-order beam. Changes in the frequency of the acoustic wave determine the spacing pattern in the crystal and hence the wavelength of the diffracted light. The power of the applied RF wave (5 W typical) determines the amplitude of the acoustic wave and hence the amplitude of the diffracted beam. The diffraction efficiency can reach ~80% and the switching speed for both wavelength and power is on the order of megahertz. The AOTF requires collimated light (half-cone angle of ~5°) to achieve maximum performance. The use of a quartz crystal requires that the light be linearly polarized.

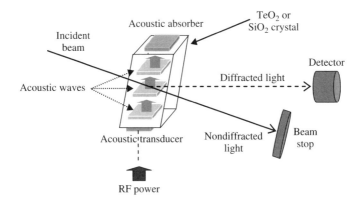

Figure 3.19 Diagram of the operation of an AOTF device

An AOTF set-up is shown in Figure 3.17. AOTF systems can provide spectral selection from 230 out to 4500 nm although a particular system is designed to operate efficiently over a narrower spectral range, typically 300 nm wide, with high efficiency selection of the desired wavelength (~80%). For a particular device, the spectral resolution changes with wavelength over the operational range. For example, for one AOTF operating in the range 400–650 nm, the spectral resolution changes from 1 to 5 nm as the wavelength is scanned from the low to high wavelengths. Optical apertures range from 2×2 to 10×10 mm, useful for imaging. An example of an AOTF-filtered image of a LIBS plasma formed on a metal is shown in Figure 3.20 (Plate 5) (Multari and Cremers, 1996). Here the plasma was viewed in the light of the Cr(I) line at 425.4 nm. The evolution of the Cr emission from a tilted surface as a function of the time delay between plasma formation and observation of the light is shown here.

3.4.2.3 Spectrograph

A basic spectrograph is shown diagrammatically in Figure 3.21(a) (Plate 6). There are different designs (or mountings for the grating) such as the Littrow, Ebert-Fastie, Czerny-Turner, Paschen-Runge, and crossed-Czerny-Turner (James and Sternberg, 1969). The design differences relate to whether one or two mirrors are used for collimating and focusing the light and the position of the slits relative to the grating. The Czerny-Turner is shown in Figure 3.21 and is the most common variant in use. Here, light from the plasma is imaged onto the entrance slit. The light passing through the slit reaches the first mirror which collimates the light, directing it onto the grating. Ideally the grating will be filled with the light reflected by the mirror to achieve maximum resolving power. Light is reflected off the grating at different angles according to wavelength. This light then strikes a second mirror that focuses the light, now in the form of a spectrum, onto the focal plane. An array detector records the light preserving the horizontal distribution of light along the focal plane. In a spectrometer, a slit allows light over a selected narrow wavelength range to pass through to a detector.

Examples of spectra recorded with a spectrograph are shown in Figure 3.21(b). These demonstrate the operation of the spectrograph and the image presented at the focal plane. Here the spectrograph slits were set to a width of several millimeters compared with a usual setting of 100 μm. In this case, an image of the laser plasma in the horizontal and vertical directions is formed at the focal plane at each wavelength of an emitting element. The elements observed here are N, Ca, Al and Si using Al metal as the target. The N emission originates from air. The spectra were obtained at different times after plasma formation and they show how the spectrum evolves with time. At the earliest time, the plasma spectrum is dominated by a spectrally broad background light that shows no strong emission features attributable to an element. At a later time, emissions from N(II) are observed and, as the plasma decays further with time, emissions from N(II) subside and are replaced by emissions from elements in the Al metal. These images show in effect the spatial dependence of the emission from the plasma in the light of each element observed.

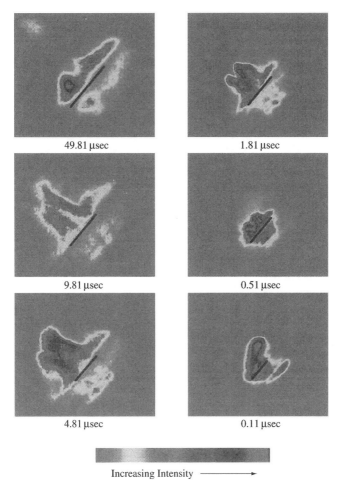

Figure 3.20 Cr emission observed using the AOTF with an ICCD. (Reproduced from Multari and Cremers, Copyright 1996 IEEE) (see Plate 5)

Alternatively, individual slits can be located at the positions of emission lines along the focal plane. A light detector is then placed behind each slit to record the emission signal. An example is shown in Figure 3.22 together with a photograph of detectors positioned behind the focal plane of a 1 m focal length vacuum Paschen-Runge polychromator.

The f#($=1/2 \times$ NA) of the spectrograph is determined by the diameter of the mirrors (d) and the distance from the entrance slit to the first mirror (f) according to f# $= f/d$. The lower the f#, the more light gathering capability of the instrument. For a 0.5 m spectrograph, a typical f# is 4. The longer the focal length, the greater

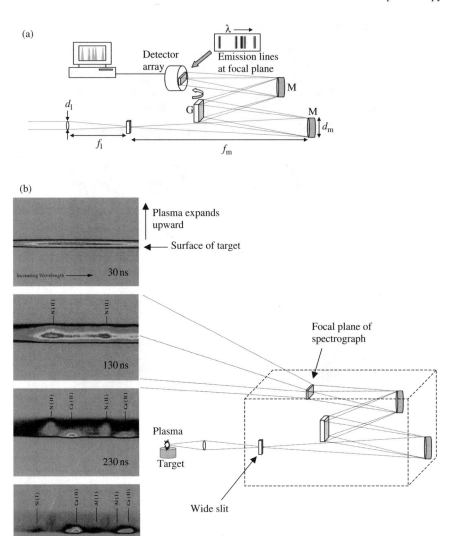

Figure 3.21 (a) Detection of LIBS spectrum using a Czerny-Turner spectrograph and array detector. (b) Examples of LIBS spectra recorded at the focal plane of a spectrograph. (Multari *et al.*, 1996, with permission from Society for Applied Spectroscopy) (see Plate 6)

dispersion of the instrument. Typical specifications for a 0.5 m spectrograph are listed in Table 3.5.

To achieve maximum light throughput, it is important that the f# of the spectrograph matches the f# of the optical system directing the light onto the entrance slit. This is accomplished by proper selection of the lens (diameter and

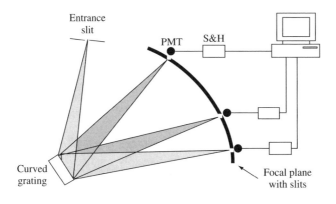

Figure 3.22 Polychromator system with PMTs positioned behind slits in the focal plane. The PMT signal is processed, for example, using a sample-and-hold circuit (S & H). PMT = photomultiplier tube detector

Table 3.5 Specifications for a 0.5 meter spectrograph

Optical design	Imaging Czerny-Turner
Focal length	500 mm
Grating	1200 lines/mm, 68 × 68 mm
Aperture ratio (f#)	4–6.5
Resolution (10 micron slit, 4 mm high)	0.05 nm
Reciprocal linear dispersion	1.7 nm/mm
Focal plane	27 mm wide × 14 mm high

focal length) used to focus the light onto the slit. Using an f# for the filling optics smaller than the f# of the spectrograph will overfill the mirror and grating resulting in scattered light.

An important parameter is the spectrograph resolving power expressed as:

$$R = \lambda/\Delta\lambda = nN \tag{3.1}$$

where n is the order of the spectrum and N is the number of lines on the grating illuminated by the light to be dispersed. Note that the resolving power is wavelength dependent and increases with the spectral order but it is independent of the size and spacing of the ruling in the grating. For a value of $R = 2500$, for example, at a wavelength of 250 nm, emission lines separated by 0.1 nm could be resolved. Spectrographs can have very high resolving powers, on the order of a million or higher.

The dispersion of a grating spectrograph is a measure of the spread of wavelengths. The angular dispersion, defined as $d\theta/d\lambda$ is the angular separation of two wavelengths whose difference is $d\lambda$. It is readily obtained by differentiating the fundamental grating equation which results in:

$$d\theta/d\lambda = n/a\cos\theta \qquad (3.2)$$

where θ is the angle between the normal to the grating and the diffracted beam and a is the ruling spacing, the reciprocal of the number of lines per unit length. For example for a grating of 2400 grooves/mm, the ruling spacing is 0.42 μm. As a gets smaller or the order number gets larger, the dispersion increases. However, the practicing spectrochemist is more interested in the spread of wavelengths across the width W of a focal plane, hence $\Delta\lambda/W$, called the reciprocal linear dispersion. To obtain that expression we start by defining the linear dispersion as:

$$dy/d\lambda = f d\theta/d\lambda \qquad (3.3)$$

where y is a linear dimension in the focal plane parallel to the dispersion, and f is the focal length of the focusing optic, such as the second mirror in the Czerny-Turner arrangement. Then the reciprocal linear dispersion is:

$$d\lambda/dy = a\cos\theta/nf. \qquad (3.4)$$

As a numerical example we will consider a fast (i.e. low f# value) vacuum spectrograph that we used for a vacuum ultraviolet (VUV) study (Radziemski et al., 2005). It had 2400 lines/mm, 5 cm wide grating, a 30 cm focal length mirror, and was used in first order. For wavelengths between 150 and 200 nm the diffraction angle was close to 45°. So:

$$d\lambda/dy = 420\,\text{nm} \times (0.71)/300\,\text{mm} = 1.0\,\text{nm/mm}. \qquad (3.5)$$

The CCD detector had 1024×1024 pixels, each 13 μm square. Hence the width W of usable focal plane was about 14 mm. Using the reciprocal linear dispersion, one could record about 14 nm of spectrum at one spectrometer setting.

Although spectrographs are more than a century old, new designs are being developed for LIBS. A high-resolution dual-grating Czerny-Turner spectrograph was demonstrated for spectral imaging with LIBS (Gornushkin *et al.*, 2004b). In addition, high performance, very compact spectrographs incorporating array detectors are marketed by several manufacturers. An example is shown in Figure 3.23 along with some specifications.

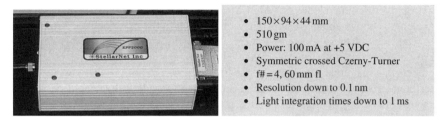

- 150 × 94 × 44 mm
- 510 gm
- Power: 100 mA at +5 VDC
- Symmetric crossed Czerny-Turner
- f# = 4, 60 mm fl
- Resolution down to 0.1 nm
- Light integration times down to 1 ms

Figure 3.23   Compact, fiber-optic-coupled spectrograph. (Source: Stellar-Net www.StellarNet.us)

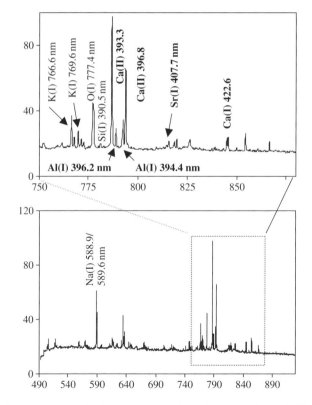

Figure 3.24   Spectrum obtained using a spectrograph similar to that shown in Figure 3.23

An example of a spectrum obtained with a similar instrument is shown in Figure 3.24. This is a spectrum of a certified soil sample obtained at a distance of 5.3 m with the sample maintained in 7 Torr of CO_2 to simulate the Mars atmosphere. The spectrum spans 490 to 930 nm and the detector was a CCD array. This spectrum demonstrates several issues discussed above. First, a limited, although wide spectral range is spanned by the spectrograph but many important lines of elements in soil below 490 nm are not observed in first order. Second, spectra of strongly emitting elements (Al, Ca, Sr, Si) are observed in second order at wavelengths above about 780 nm. These are shown in the expanded spectrum at the top. The lines of these elements appear at twice the wavelength. In this spectrum there is no strong interference of the elements appearing in second order with elements having emission lines in the range 750–775 nm. If there were strong interference between first- and second-order lines, an edge filter could be used to remove either element emissions above 750 nm (so second order would be observed unobstructed) or an edge filter could be used to eliminate emission below 450 nm so second order would not appear. Third, the wavelength spacing between elements in second order is double that for the first-order spectrum. Monitoring elements in second order is a method of achieving greater resolution and dispersion. Fourth, second order may be used to monitor elements at lower wavelength simultaneous with elements at greater wavelengths without requiring a second spectrograph tuned to lower wavelengths.

3.4.2.4   Echelle spectrograph

The 'workhorse' of LIBS analysis has been the spectrograph combined with either a photodiode array (PDA) or CCD array (Section 3.5). In recent years, however, the echelle spectrograph has been used more extensively and several compact versions have become available (Bauer et al., 1998).

As shown in Figure 3.21, the conventional spectrograph uses a diffraction grating to produce the spectrum. This spectrum is recorded at the focal plane using a PDA or CCD. The spectral range recorded is limited by the width of the focal plane and the size of the array detector. Except in special cases, in which the vertical intensity distribution of the plasma light along the slit is used, the CCD is used in vertical binning mode with the intensities along the slit added to produce an intensity at each wavelength monitored along the focal plane.

Using an echelle spectrograph, the two-dimensional capabilities of the CCD can be utilized to increase the spectral range significantly. A diagram of an echelle spectrograph is shown in Figure 3.25. The echelle grating is a diffraction grating in which the number of lines/mm is much less than typically used in a conventional spectrograph (600 versus 2400). Because it is used at a high angle, the echelle produces spectra of very high dispersion but only over a short wavelength range in each grating order. The different orders of the grating will overlap and these are

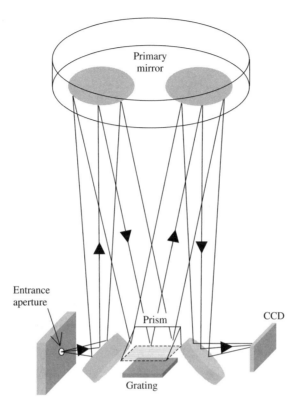

Figure 3.25 Diagram of an echelle spectrograph. (Designed and Manufactured by Optomechanics Research Inc.)

spatially separated using a cross-dispersing element such as a prism. In this way, the various orders are stacked vertically in the echelle spectrograph focal plane. The two-dimensional detection capabilities of the CCD are then used to record the different orders resulting in the image of the orders or the echelleogram shown in Figure 3.26.

The different orders are easily seen in the echelleogram with longer wavelengths located at the bottom portion. The light 'spots' along the different orders correspond to emission from a specific element line. The echelleogram is useful to calibrate the echelle wavelength and adjust the optical alignment of the instrument. For spectral analysis, however, software is used to transform the echelle image to a spectrum. An example of a spectrum is shown in Figure 3.26. Note that the spectrum spans the main spectral region useful for LIBS analysis that extends from 200 to 800 nm. As with conventional spectrographs, different gratings can be used to increase instrument performance in certain spectral regions. Table 3.6 presents a comparison of two commercially available echelle instruments.

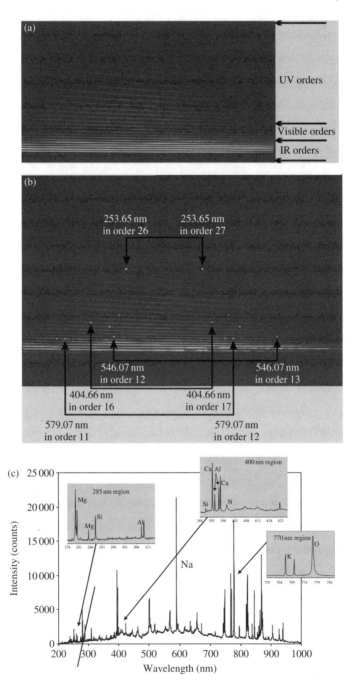

Figure 3.26 (a) Arrangement of orders in the focal plane of an echelle spectrograph. (b) Emission lines from Hg lamp in the focal plane used to calibrate the wavelength. (c) LIBS spectrum of soil recorded using the echelle spectrograph and ICCD. (Photos courtesy of Catalina Scientific, Inc.)

Table 3.6 Comparison of two echelle spectrographs (standard models, ICCD detector)

Parameter	Model 1	Model 2
Spectral range (nm)	190–1100	200–780
Spectral resolution ($\lambda/\Delta\lambda$)	1700	20 000
Focal length (cm)	20	25
Mass (kg)	4	4
Size (cm)	$12.7 \times 15.2 \times 32$	$14 \times 16 \times 32$

3.5 DETECTORS

The type of detector used with LIBS depends on many factors including the number of elements to be monitored and the type of spectral method used. A comparison of detectors typically used for LIBS is presented in Table 3.7. Using a line filter to monitor a single emission line as shown in Figure 3.17 requires only a sensitive light detector. Common examples are photomultiplier tubes (PMTs) or photodiodes, especially, sensitive avalanche photodiodes (APDs) (Squillante *et al.*, 2003). A variant of the APD, the Geiger photodiode has also been demonstrated for detection at low light levels (Myers *et al.*, 2003). The output of these devices is

Table 3.7 Comparison of some detectors used for LIBS

Detector	Characteristics
Photomultiplier tube (PMT)	Measure instantaneous light intensity; temporal responses <1 ns; useful to map out decay response of plasma light; spectral response tailored to spectral region; inexpensive; compact; used with line filter or monochromator to provide single wavelength detection
Avalanche photodiode (APD)	Solid-state detector; high gain; fast response; rugged; compact; high signal-to-noise ratio; high quantum efficiency; fabrication as an array
Photodiode array (PDA)	Provides one-dimensional spatial information about light intensity along array; light intensity integrated with temporal response determined by readout time; used with spectrograph to provide simultaneous detection over a certain spectral range
Intensified PDA (IPDA)	PDA characteristics plus time-resolved detection down to few ns; more expensive than PDA
Charge coupled device (CCD)	Provides two-dimensional spatial information about light intensity on array; light intensity integrated with temporal response determined by readout time; used with spectrograph to provide simultaneous detection over a certain spectral range through vertical binning of pixel signals; intensity distribution along vertical dimension can be used in certain applications (e.g. long spark) or multiple FOC input at entrance slit to monitor spectra from different regions simultaneously
Intensified CCD (ICCD)	CCD characteristics plus time-resolved detection down to few ns; more expensive than CCD

a current in proportion to the intensity of incident light. These are not integrating devices as they provide a signal simultaneous in time with the incident light intensity. Therefore these can be used to monitor a selected spectral feature as a function of time. The current is typically integrated on a capacitor for a certain time period and the resulting voltage is the signal. Alternatively, the voltage can be digitized to produce a signal in the form of counts.

The 'workhorse' of photodetectors is perhaps the PMT which is compact, rugged, highly sensitive, and relatively inexpensive. PMTs come in a variety of sizes and the photocathode material is selectable to maximize sensitivity in certain spectral regions. A diagram of the operation of a PMT is shown in Figure 3.27(a). A light pulse striking the photocathode material results in the ejection of electrons that, through electrostatic focusing, travel through a set of dynodes coated with a secondary emissive material. An electron striking this material will eject additional electrons resulting in electron multiplication as the electron pulse produced by the light pulse, travels down the dynode chain. The large number of electrons is collected at the anode and results in a current signal with amplifications of 10^6 possible. In addition, PMTs that are 'solar blind,' that is, that do not detect IR or visible wavelengths are available. A diagram of a PMT and integrating circuit is shown in Figure 3.27(b).

Using a PDA, spectral information over a wide range can be recorded on each laser pulse. A diagram of a PDA is shown in Figure 3.28. The device is a linear array of closely spaced diodes with a typical diode size being 25 μm wide ×2.5 mm long.

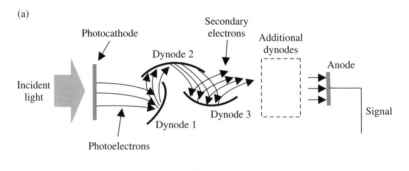

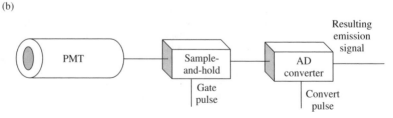

Figure 3.27 (a) Diagram of the operation of a typical side-on PMT. (b) PMT with integrating and digitizing signal processing

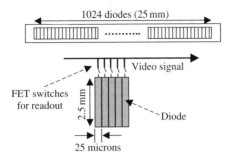

Figure 3.28 Design of a linear PDA

The number of diodes ranges from 256 to 2048 although other configurations are possible. Light striking the diode removes charge and the amount of this charge is the signal. Following the exposure time period, the diodes are read out by measuring the amount of charge that must be added to each diode to achieve neutral charge. The diodes are read out sequentially.

Using a CCD, spectra over a wide range can also be recorded. The CCD, however, is a two-dimensional device so the x–y spatial distribution of light incident on the device can be recorded. Typical pixel sizes range from $13 \times 13\,\mu m$ up to $26 \times 26\,\mu m$. The design of a CCD is shown in Figure 3.29. The arrangement shown here is 512×1024 elements although many other array sizes are available. Like the PDA, the CCD integrates the incident light. Read-out of the array destroys the stored data and readies the array for the next record cycle. The CCD is readout by shifting all the rows vertically downward into the shift register which is then readout sequentially. After the pixel information (1024 separate pixels) in the shift register is read out, all rows are shifted down again and the new data in the

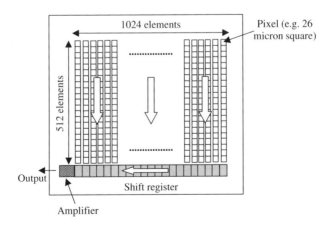

Figure 3.29 Design of a CCD

shift register is read out. For a 512 pixel vertical array, 256 such shifts are required to completely read the array. Both the PDA and the CCD can be used to record a spectrum presented at the focal plane of the spectrograph. With the CCD, the intensity in the 512 pixels in each column are added or vertically binned to produce a single intensity at a particular wavelength in the focal plane. Using the CCD, however, information about the vertical distribution of light along the slit can be recorded also (Figure 3.21). This information can be useful, for example, if imaging a long spark along the entrance slit of a spectrograph. The vertical information will yield the distribution of a particular emission feature along the slit. That is, for each plasma, a map of the distribution of elements along the spark axis of those elements being monitored along the horizontal dimension of the CCD array (wavelength coverage) will be obtained. By scanning the long spark over a surface, a two-dimensional map of the intensity distribution can be constructed. An example is shown in Figure 3.30 (Plate 7).

A comparison of a typical PDA and CCD is presented in Table 3.8. An obvious advantage of the CCD is its two-dimensional capability, important for some applications such as imaging. For LIBS measurements in which the spectrum presented at the focal plane of the spectrograph is to be recorded, the two systems can be used somewhat interchangeably. There are certain applications, however, in which each has an advantage. For example, for low light levels, the CCD is preferred because of its lower dark current. The low dark current makes the CCD the detector

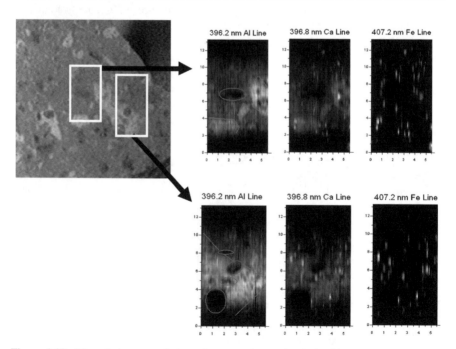

Figure 3.30 Map of element emissions along a rock sample obtained by scanning a series of long sparks along the surface (see Plate 7)

Table 3.8 Comparison of PDA and CCD array detectors (no MCP intensifiers)

Characteristic	PDA	CCD
Pixel size (example) (μm)	25×2500	13×13; 26×26
Saturation level (no. e)	125×10^6	650 000
Dark current (e/pixel/s)	600 000	100
Signal to noise (max.)	10 000:1	800:1
Electrons/count	1900	10
Spectral response (nm)	180–1100	180–1100

of choice for long integration times (>10 s) such as might be used with an echelle system where readout of the array after each shot is not feasible. On the other hand, the PDA is best for single shot measurements in which the signal levels are high or near the saturation level of the detector.

In LIBS, the decay of spectral features occurs on the microsecond time scale for a plasma generated using nanosecond laser pulses. On the other hand, typical readout times of 1024×1024 arrays are on the order of a millisecond. Therefore, to obtain time resolved detection of an image, a shutter of some sort must be used to capture the image at a specific time after plasma formation. Clearly, for events on the microsecond time scale, mechanical shutters are too slow. An electronic shutter of some sort is required. Typical shutters used with array detectors are microchannel plates (MCPs) (Wiza, 1979). These are two-dimensional devices, like array detectors, that can be gated on and off very rapidly, on the order of a few microseconds for example, to permit or prohibit the passage of light. A diagram of an MCP is shown in Figure 3.31. MCPs consist of a thin sheet of glass tubes (~10–100 μm diameter) with length to diameter ratios of 40–100. The size of the MCP determines the number of tubes and arrays ranging from 10^4 to 10^7 individual

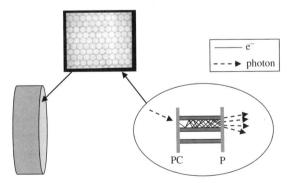

Typical size ~ 15–42 mm diameter
Gain ~ 10^3
No. channels ~ 10^4–10^7

Figure 3.31 Diagram of an MCP

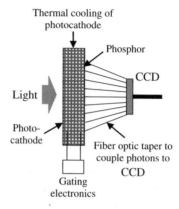

Figure 3.32 Diagram of a typical ICCD

tubes. Gating is provided by applying a high voltage (~1.5 kV) between the front and back sides of the device. With the voltage applied, when a photon strikes the photocathode (PC), an electron is liberated that travels via multiple reflections down a narrow channel in the MCP. The insides of the tubes are manufactured to produce the desired secondary electron yield. In effect, each tube is a continuous dynode structure resembling a PMT. Because the electron is accelerated by the applied voltage, it acquires kinetic energy, and frees other electrons as it travels down the narrow channel. A single electron can give rise to as many as 10^3 electrons at the back end of the MCP. Electrons striking the luminescent phosphor screen (P) at the back of the MCP produce photons, many more photons than the single photon that initiated the electron cascade process. By adjusting the voltage, the gain of the MCP can be controlled. Note that MCPs are light gates only and do not record or store the incident light.

The detector of choice for many LIBS applications is the intensified CCD (ICCD) detector. These units are a CCD coupled to an MCP to provide time-gated detection of the laser plasma. A diagram of one configuration of an ICCD is shown in Figure 3.32. ICCDs can be used for time-resolved imaging, for example, with the AOTF or a line filter, or can be used with a spectrograph (Figure 3.21). Intensified PDAs (PDA + MCP) are also used for LIBS for time-resolved detection.

3.6 DETECTION SYSTEM CALIBRATIONS

3.6.1 WAVELENGTH CALIBRATION

In order to associate an emission line with a particular element, the recorded wavelength must be known within a certain precision. Following this, compilations of emission lines can be consulted to narrow down the choices and select the most appropriate element. Important factors to consider when selecting the appropriate element of origin are discussed in Chapter 5. Single line filters are made for a particular wavelength (±tolerance) and these do not need to be calibrated although the bandpass wavelength can depend on extremes in temperature and the angle of incidence of the incident light on the filter surface. But polychromators and spectrographs must be wavelength calibrated using a calibration source having lines that can be unambiguously identified and associated with a specific wavelength. A common method of calibration uses a spectral lamp such as a 'pencil style' mercury or Hg lamp or hollow cathode lamp. The 'pencil' lamps are often preferred because they are a compact and stable source of narrow and discrete emissions lines. The Hg lamp in particular is widely used and the pattern of emissions lines readily identified for easy calibration. Lines for the Hg lamp are listed in Table 3.9 and in general these provide good spectral coverage for many important regions of the LIBS spectrum. For high resolution detection systems were wavelength coverage is reduced, another spectral source with a higher density of emission lines will be needed requiring the use of other calibration lamps, such as an iron hollow cathode. In addition to Hg, other readily available 'pencil style' lamps include Xe, Ar, Ne and Kr with lines in different spectral regions. The spectrum from these sources is recorded using the same experimental set-up used to record the LIBS spectrum. For calibration, at least two lines of known wavelength, ideally at each end of the recorded spectrum, are needed to calibrate the wavelength. When using only two lines, the assumption is that the dispersion remains linear across the spectral range

Table 3.9   Hg calibration spectrum (Data sourced from Sansonetti *et al.*, 1996, with permission from Optical Society of America)

Wavelength (nm)	Intensity[a]
253.6521	300 000
289.3601	160
296.7283	2600
302.1504	280
312.5674	2800
313.1655	1900
313.1844	2800
334.1484	160
365.0168	5300
365.4842	970
366.2887	110
366.8284	650
404.6565	4400
407.7837	270
434.7506	34
435.8385	10 000
546.0750	10 000
576.9610	1100
579.0670	1200

[a] Relative units with the measured value of the 436 nm line arbitrarily set to 10 000.

so that a simple linear interpolation fit can be performed of wavelength versus position in the focal plane or versus wavelength setting on a monochromator. This approximation is fine for the width of array detectors, however, over a longer wavelength interval a better solution is to have identified lines at several positions across the focal plane so that a polynomial can be fit to the data to correct for nonlinear dispersion.

An example of wavelength calibration is shown in Figure 3.33. Figure 3.33(a) shows a LIBS spectrum obtained by analyzing a barium solution deposited on a filter. The detection system was an echelle spectrograph and ICCD detector. From the general area of the spectrum observed, a number of strong barium lines have been identified from compiled wavelength tables and these are labeled on the spectrum. The pixel number associated with each line is also indicated. Using the data of barium wavelength and corresponding pixel number (four points), we can fit the data as shown in Figure 3.33(b). The linear fit is excellent indicating constant linear dispersion across the focal plane. From the fit we can convert each pixel number to a corresponding wavelength and the resulting spectrum is shown in Figure 3.33(c). Using the calibrated spectrum, additional lines in the spectrum not used for calibration can be identified and these are listed on the calibrated spectrum. The H(I) line arises from the high concentration of hydrogen atoms from the filter material and sodium is ubiquitous in nature, found in many materials analyzed using LIBS.

3.6.2 SPECTRAL RESPONSE CALIBRATION

Each component of a LIBS detection system has a certain spectral response curve associated with it $r(\lambda)$. That is, the response depends on wavelength such that not all wavelengths are transmitted through or reflected off optical components with the same transfer efficiency. In addition, the detector used to record the light has a response function that is wavelength dependent. The end result is that the complete detection system (fiber optic, spectrograph, detector, lenses, etc.) will show a sensitivity that is wavelength dependent. In some cases it may be important to know how the response of the detection system varies with wavelength. As an example, the relative intensities of emission lines in different regions of the spectrum may be compared independent of the detection system response. In principle, the total response of a detection system may be computed from the separate response curves of the different components. Consider Figure 3.34 which shows response curves for the spectrograph, detector, and fiber optic cable. The responses have been normalized to 100 as most often it is the relative response of the system that must be computed with absolute response seldom used. By multiplying the different response curves, the total response $r_{TOT}(\lambda)$ can be determined:

$$r_{TOT}(\lambda) = r_{FOC}(\lambda) \times r_{SPEC}(\lambda) \times r_{DET}(\lambda). \qquad (3.6)$$

For the curves of Figure 3.34, $r_{TOT}(\lambda)$ is plotted after normalization to 100. To correct a LIBS spectrum then for the spectral response of the detection system,

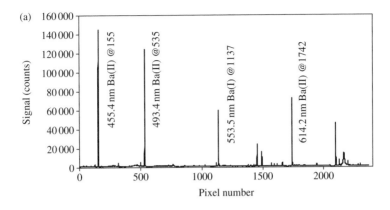

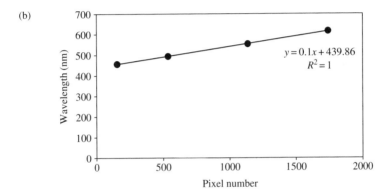

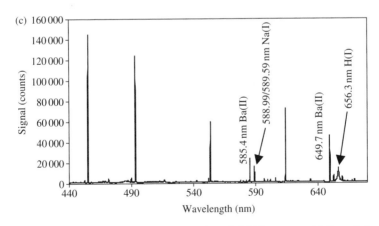

Figure 3.33 Demonstration of wavelength calibration of a LIBS spectrum. (a) Recorded spectrum of signal versus pixel number. Four barium lines are identified and wavelengths indicated. (b) Barium wavelength versus pixel number for the four lines producing an equation relating wavelength (y) to pixel number (x). (c) Resulting calibrated spectrum with additional lines identified using wavelengths assigned by calibration

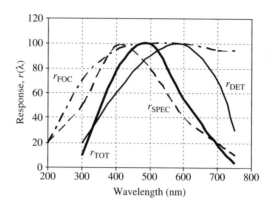

Figure 3.34 Response curves for different components of a LIBS detection system along with the total response curve

the signal at each wavelength of interest $s_{MEAS}(\lambda)$ is multiplied by the quantity $r_{TOT}(\lambda')/r_{TOT}(\lambda)$ or

$$s_{CORR}(\lambda) = s_{MEAS}(\lambda) \times r_{TOT}(\lambda')/r_{TOT}(\lambda) \tag{3.7}$$

where λ' is some fixed wavelength to which the responses at the other wavelengths are compared. Typically, λ' may be selected as the wavelength for which $r_{TOT}(\lambda) = 100$.

In practice, the response of each detection system component will probably not be known accurately and there are differences between each individual component and the manufacturer's specification sheet. In addition, changes in components over time, due to factors such as degradation of spectrograph mirrors through oxidation of the coating and accumulation of surface contaminants such as pump oil, will change the response curve. The best method of correcting for spectral response is to use a calibrated light source. A tungsten lamp is used for wavelengths from about 250 to 2400 nm and deuterium lamps are used for UV wavelengths in the region 200–400 nm.

These lamps, typically traceable to a recognized calibration laboratory such as NIST (National Institute of Standards and Technology), are supplied with a calibration curve $I_{CAL}(\lambda)$ or table of data from which such a curve can be prepared. The lamp will be operated at a specified current from a well-regulated power supply and in a certain geometrical set-up to direct light from a specific portion of the lamp into the detection system. The lamp will be positioned at the same location as the LIBS plasma would be formed and the lamp spectrum $s_{LAMP}(\lambda)$ is recorded. Then $r_{TOT}(\lambda)$ would be computed as:

$$r_{TOT}(\lambda) = s_{LAMP}(\lambda) \times I_{CAL}(\lambda')/I_{CAL}(\lambda). \tag{3.8}$$

The $r_{TOT}(\lambda)$ values determined in this way would be used as described above to compute $s_{CORR}(\lambda)$. Here λ' is a selected fixed wavelength to which the other intensities are compared.

3.7 TIMING CONSIDERATIONS

In the case of time-resolved detection for either imaging or spectral detection, careful timing between the laser pulse and the gate pulse to the detector is essential. A timing diagram describing the timing events in a LIBS measurement is presented in Figure 3.35.

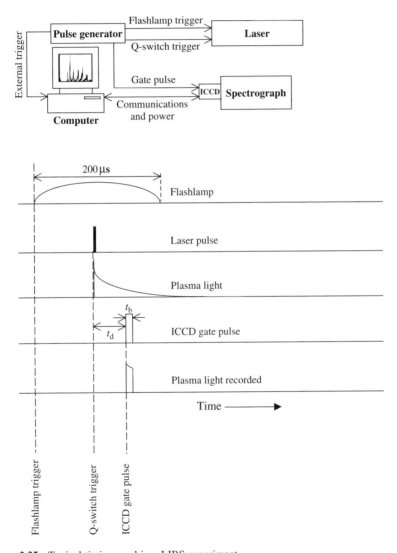

Figure 3.35 Typical timing used in a LIBS experiment

In the case shown, the laser flashlamp and Q-switch are triggered by a pulse generator synchronized to the data acquisition system controller by a computer. The pulse generator produces an external trigger that clocks the detector readout with the laser pulse. A four-channel pulse generator is used so that each of the three pulses (flashlamp, Q-switch, gate, trigger) can be independently varied with respect to each other. This permits, among other things, the gate pulse to be positioned at zero delay with respect to the laser pulse or even positioned prior to the laser pulse (negative delay), useful for certain experiments.

In high repetition rate measurements, special care must be given to timing considerations. For example, a 1024 pixel PDA can be read out at a relatively fast rate so that the spectrum produced by each laser pulse can be independently recorded and stored. A typical rate will be 40 Hz. Readout times for a CCD detector can also be fast if the pixels are vertically binned, that is, if the CCD is not used in the image mode. When used in the image mode, however, as required by an echelle detector or for imaging studies, readout times will be much slower as each pixel must be read and stored separately. To prevent the finite readout time from limiting the repetition rate of the laser and hence the speed at which a measurement can be made, on chip averaging of the plasma light can be used. In this case, the CCD is not read out after each pulse but instead, the light from many plasmas are collected or averaged on the chip. The stored intensities are then read out after a certain number of pulses (e.g. 100 pulses, or 10 s for a 10 Hz) laser. Time resolved detection is still possible with an ICCD in this integrating mode as the intensifier can be gated rapidly on and off at the laser repetition rate. The integrated light in this case will represent time resolved detection.

3.8   METHODS OF LIBS DEPLOYMENT

Because the LIBS plasma is formed from laser light with its unique properties, LIBS is adaptable to a variety of different deployment methods. The typical LIBS set-up is shown in Figure 3.1. Additional arrangements are shown in Figure 3.36. Some of these are described later as examples of actual LIBS instruments. In Figure 3.36(a), the laser pulse is injected into a fiber optic cable for transport to the target. The emerging laser pulse is focused by a lens system to generate the laser plasma. The plasma light is then collected by either the same fiber optic or a second fiber and then transported back to the detection system. Obvious advantages of this system are that the laser and detection system can be positioned away from the target which may be located in a hazardous (e.g. high radiation) area. In addition, the probe at the end of the fiber can be very compact.

In a second configuration shown in Figure 3.36(b), a compact laser (e.g. Figure 3.3) can be housed in a small probe which is located adjacent to the target sample. The plasma light is collected by a fiber optic and transported back to the remotely positioned detection system.

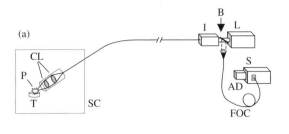

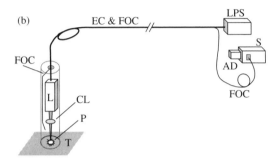

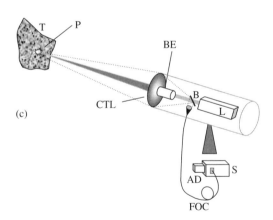

Figure 3.36 Three possible configurations (a–c) for LIBS analysis in addition to direct analysis (Figure 3.1). L, laser; B, beamsplitter; FOC, fiber optic cable; I, pulse injector for FOC; CL, lens; T, target; P, plasma; S, spectrograph; AD, array detector; CTL, collection lens; EC, electrical cables; LPS, laser power supply; BE, beam expander

In the third configuration, the laser pulses are focused at a distance onto the remotely located target (Figure 3.36c). Typically, a beam expander will be used to expand the beam which is then focused onto the target using a multiple lens system. The plasma light can be collected by the same optical system as shown in Figure 3.36(c), or a separate co-located light collection arrangement. This stand-off detection system can analyze samples at many meters distance. The achievable range depends on the spatial quality of the laser pulse as well as pulse energy and power density.

REFERENCES

Arnold, S.D. and D.A. Cremers (1995). Rapid determination of metal particles on air sampling filters using laser-induced breakdown spectroscopy. Am. Ind. Hyg. Assoc J. 56: 1180–1186.

Bauer, H.E., F. Leis and K. Niemax (1998). Laser induced breakdown spectrometry with an echelle spectrometer and intensified charge coupled device detection. Spectrochim. Acta Part B 53: 1815–1825.

Cremers, D.A. and L.J. Radziemski (1985). Direct detection of beryllium on filters using the laser spark. Appl. Spectrosc. 39: 57–63.

Cremers, D.A., J.E. Barefield and A.C. Koskelo (1995). Remote elemental analysis by laser-induced breakdown spectroscopy using a fiber optic cable. Appl. Spectrosc. 49: 857–860.

Davies, C.M., H.H. Telle, D.J. Montgomery and R.E. Corbett (1995). Quantitative analysis using remote laser-induced breakdown spectroscopy (LIBS). Spectrochim. Acta Part B 50: 1059–1075.

Eland, K.L., D.N. Stratis, T. Lai, M.A. Berg, S.R. Goode and S.M. Angel (2001a). Some comparisons of LIBS measurements using nanosecond and picosecond laser pulses. Appl. Spectrosc. 55: 279–285.

Eland, K.L., D.N. Stratis, D.M. Gold, S.R. Goode and S.M. Angel (2001b). Energy dependence of emission intensity and temperature in a LIBS plasma using femtosecond excitation. Appl. Spectrosc. 55: 286–291.

Ernst, W.E., D.F. Farson and D.J. Sames (1996). Determination of copper in A533b steel for the assessment of radiation embrittlement using laser-induced breakdown spectroscopy. Appl. Spectrosc. 50: 306–309.

Gornushkin, I.B., K. Amponsah-Manager, B.W. Smith, N. Omenetto and J.D. Winefordner (2004a). Microchip laser-induced breakdown spectroscopy: preliminary feasibility study. Appl. Spectrosc. 58: 762–769.

Gornushkin, I.B., N. Omenetto, B.W. Smith and J.D. Winefordner (2004b). High-resolution two-grating spectrometer for dual wavelength spectral imaging. Appl. Spectrosc. 58: 1341–1346.

Hecht, E. (2001). Optics, 4th edn, Addison-Wesley, Reading, MA.

Hohreiter, V., A.J. Ball and D.W. Hahn (2004). Effects of aerosols and laser cavity seeding on spectral and temporal stability of laser-induced plasmas: applications to LIBS. J. Anal. At. Spectrom. 19: 1289–1294.

James, J.F. and R.S. Sternberg (1969). The Design of Optical Spectrometers, Chapman and Hall, London.

Konorov, S.O., A.B. Fedotov, O.A. Kolevatova, V.I. Beloglazov, N.B. Skibina, A.V. Shcherbakov, E. Wintner and A.M. Zheltikov (2003). Laser breakdown with millijoule trains of picosecond pulses transmitted through a hollow-core photonic-crystal fibre. J. Phys. D: Appl. Phys. 36: 1375–1381.

Lorenzen, C.J., C. Carlhoff, U. Hahn and M. Jogwich (1992). Applications of laser-induced emission spectral analysis for industrial process and quality control. J. Anal. At. Spectrom. 7: 1029–1035.

Mateo, M.P., S. Palanco, J.M. Vadillo and J.J. Laserna (2000). Fast atomic mapping of heterogeneous surfaces using microline-imaging laser-induced breakdown spectrometry. Appl. Spectrosc. 54: 1429–1434.

Miles, B. and J. Cortes (1998). Subsurface heavy-metal detection with the use of a laser-induced breakdown spectroscopy (LIBS) penetrometer system. Field Anal. Chem. Technol. 2: 75–87.

Multari, R.A. and D.A. Cremers (1996). A time-resolved imaging study of Cr(I) emissions from a laser plasma formed on a sample at nonnormal incidence. IEEE Trans. Plasma Sci. 24: 39–40.

Multari, R.A., L.E. Foster, D.A. Cremers and M.J. Ferris (1996). Effect of sampling geometry on elemental emissions in laser-induced breakdown spectroscopy. Appl. Spectrosc. 50: 1483–1499.

Myers, R.A., A.M. Karger and D.W. Hahn (2003). Geiger photodiode array for compact, lightweight laser-induced breakdown spectroscopy instrumentation. Appl. Opt. 42: 6072–6077.

Pichahchy, A.E, D.A. Cremers and M.J. Ferris (1997). Detection of metals underwater using laser-induced breakdown spectroscopy. Spectrochim. Acta Part B 52: 25–39.

Radziemski, L.J., D.A. Cremers, K. Benelli, C. Khoo and R.D. Harris (2005). Use of the vacuum ultraviolet spectral region for LIBS-based Martian geology and exploration. Spectrochim. Acta Part B 60: 237–248.

Rodolfa, K.T. and D.A. Cremers (2004). Capabilities of surface composition analysis using a long laser-induced breakdown spectroscopy spark. Appl. Spectrosc. 58: 367–375.

Sansonetti, C.J., M.L. Salit and J. Reader (1996). Wavelengths of spectral lines in mercury pencil lamps. Appl. Opt. 35: 74–77.

Scaffidi, J., J. Pender, W. Pearman, S.R. Goode, B.W. Colston Jr, J.C. Carter and S.M. Angel (2003). Dual-pulse laser-induced breakdown spectroscopy with combinations of femtosecond and nanosecond laser pulses. Appl. Opt. 42: 6099–6106.

Scaffidi, J., S.M. Angel and D.A. Cremers (2006). Recent and future trends in dual-pulse laser-induced breakdown spectroscopy. Anal. Chem. Rev. 78:A24–A32.

Squillante, M.R., J. Christian, G. Entine, R. Farrell, A. Karger, M. McClish, R. Myers, K. Shah, D. Taylor, K. Vanderpuye, P. Waer and M. Woodring (2003). Recent advances in very large area avalanche photodiodes. Proc. SPIE 5071: 405–410.

Svelto, O. (2004). *Principles of Lasers*, 4th edn, Springer, Berlin.

Theriault, G.A., S. Bodensteiner and S.H. Lieberman (1998). A real-time fiber-optic LIBS probe for the in situ delineation of metals in soils. Field Anal. Chem. Technol. 2: 117–125.

Wiza, J.L. (1979). Microchannel plate detectors. Nucl. Instrum. Methods 162: 587–601.

Yalin, A.P., M. DeFoort, B. Wilson, Y. Matsuura and M. Miyagi (2005). Use of hollow-core fibers to deliver nanosecond Nd:YAG laser pulses to form sparks in gases. Opt. Lett. 16: 2083–2085.

Yamamoto, K.Y., D.A. Cremers, L.E. Foster and M.J. Ferris (1996). Detection of metals in the environment using a portable laser-induced breakdown spectroscopy (LIBS) instrument. Appl. Spectrosc. 50: 222–233.

Yamamoto, K.Y., D.A. Cremers, L.E. Foster, M.P. Davies and R.D. Harris (2005). LIBS analysis of solids using a long-pulse (150 ns) Q-switched Nd:YAG laser. Appl. Spectrosc. 50: 1082–1097.

Zayhowski, J.J. (1999). Microchip lasers. Opt. Mater. 11: 255–267.

Zayhowski, J.J. (2000). Passively Q-switched Nd:YAG microchip lasers and applications. J. Alloys Compd. 303–304: 393–400.

4 Determining LIBS Analytical Figures-of-Merit

4.1 INTRODUCTION

Analytical figures-of-merit (FOM) are used to benchmark the capabilities of an analysis method and to compare the performance of distinct analytical techniques using a common set of parameters. The main FOM often used to characterize an analytical method are: (1) limits of detection, (2) precision and (3) accuracy, although other parameters such as (4) sensitivity and (5) selectivity are sometimes included. Definitions of FOM and standardized methods of determining them can be found in publications by the International Union of Pure and Applied Chemistry (IUPAC, 1997) and the International Organization for Standardization (ISO, 1993, 1997, 2000). Here we present a discussion of the more important FOM and how they are used to characterize LIBS.

4.2 BASICS OF LIBS MEASUREMENTS

Whether qualitative or quantitative analysis, the basic component of any LIBS measurement is the emission spectrum recorded from a single plasma. Each firing of the laser atomizes a portion of the sample in the pulse focal volume and produces a plasma that excites and re-excites the atoms to emit light. The plasma light is collected and recorded resulting in a measurement. The recorded quantities may be a spectral region (e.g. obtained using an ICCD detector) or the emission wavelength of a single line or set of lines (e.g. PMT detection using a polychromator) as described in Chapter 3. From the spectrum, the intensities of the analyte(s) emission line(s) is (are) determined. Here we discuss details related to analysis of the emission spectrum.

Examples of LIBS analyses that produce complex (Cr) and relatively simple (Be) spectra are shown in Figure 4.1. These spectra were obtained by scanning a series of laser sparks along filter paper on which atomic absorption standard (AAS) solutions were deposited. These solutions are relatively free of contaminants so the observed

Handbook of Laser-Induced Breakdown Spectroscopy   D. Cremers and L. Radziemski
© 2006 John Wiley & Sons, Ltd

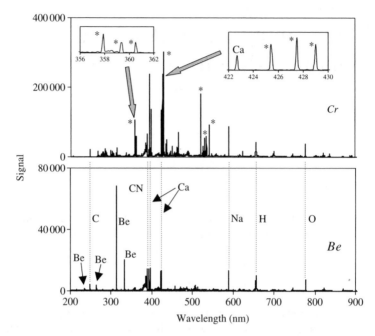

Figure 4.1 Comparison of LIBS spectra of Cr and Be solutions deposited on a filter showing differences in complexity (line density). Emissions from C, H and O are due to the filter material. Cr lines indicated by an asterisk (∗)

lines, with the exception of C, H and O from the filter material, are due to the deposited element. The elements Ca and Na are ubiquitous in nature and are also observed. The elements in the filter have a few strong lines to interfere with lines due to Cr and Be. The insets on the Cr spectrum show, at higher spectral resolution, the strong Cr lines in the UV and blue spectral regions. Strong emission from the molecule CN is also observed as described below.

The LIBS spectrum resulting from interrogating a basalt rock sample is shown in Figure 4.2. This spectrum spans the most important spectral region for LIBS, 200 to 800 nm, over which most elements exhibit at least a few strong emission lines. This spectrum shows a very high density of emission lines resulting from the complex composition of the basalt rock and the sensitivity of the LIBS method.

There are several factors to consider in identifying an emission line with a particular element and these are discussed in Chapter 5. In all cases, however, the wavelength of the emission line is the prime identification parameter. Element wavelengths are listed in a number of compendiums (Striganov and Sventitskii, 1968; Reader *et al.*, 1980; Phelps, 1982; Winge *et al.*, 1985; Sobel'man, 1996; Reader and Corliss, 1997; Payling and Larkins, 2000). Typical entries by element in such compilations include the wavelength, ionization stage, relative intensity

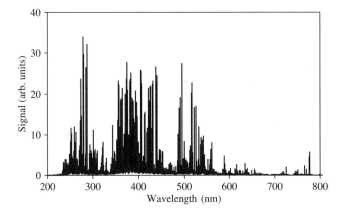

Figure 4.2 LIBS spectrum of basalt recorded using an echelle spectrograph

and energy level designations with energies. Here we use the nomenclature that (I) signifies the neutral atom, (II) represents the once-ionized atom, etc., so that O(I), O(II) and O(III) represent the neutral, once-ionized and doubly ionized oxygen atom, respectively.

In addition to emissions from atoms, emissions from simple molecules are observed from some samples. In general, high concentrations of the elements composing the molecules must be present for molecular emissions to be observed. Typical examples include AlO (Chapter 5) from Al metal interrogated in air, YO from the superconductor ($YBa_2Cu_3O_7$), and C_2 and CN from graphite sampled in air. These simple molecules are formed as the atoms recombine in the cooling plasma. Typically, the ambient air supplies the O atom of the molecule. An example of a LIBS spectrum from graphite analyzed in air is shown in Figure 4.3. A compilation

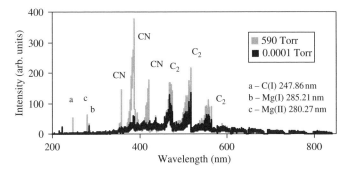

Figure 4.3 LIBS spectrum of graphite in air showing emissions from a few elements and simple molecules formed as the plasma temperature decays

of emission wavelengths for simple molecules likely to be found in a LIBS plasma is presented in Pearse and Gaydon (1963).

Examination of the LIBS spectrum will reveal those elements in the sample that are present at concentrations above the minimum detectable by the method. Compiling a list of elements in a sample is useful for qualitative analysis (Chapter 5). In most cases, however, the interest lies in the intensity of an emission line or set of lines which is used for quantitative analysis (Chapter 6). The discussion of methods to determine the intensity of an emission line begins with a closer look at a very small spectral region of the complex spectrum of Figure 4.2. This is shown in Figure 4.4 with lines due to the elements Ti, Al and Ca labeled. The strongest line shown is that of Ca(II) at 396.2 nm. The Ti line lies in a spectral region where it is free of a spectral interference (i.e. overlap) with another line. The Ti line shape is well defined. The Al line is largely interference free but there is a small interference on the right side of the line due to another element, probably Ti. The Ca line, on the other hand, shows interference from lines on the long and short wavelength sides of this line. The cross-hatched region in each case is the sum of the emission line intensity and the background or white light from the plasma. Depending on the detector, background due to dark noise in the detector can be subtracted out of the recorded spectrum, often automatically, which we will assume is the case here. It should be noted that a detection system such as a polychromator with PMTs mounted behind a slit will record the sum of the emission signal and white light background. Because the recorded light intensity is ascribed to a single wavelength corresponding to an analyte wavelength, the sum of the signals will be processed. There is no way to determine what fraction is due to the emission line and what part is due to the background light when recording a single wavelength. In contrast, in the case of an array detector (PDA , CCD or ICCD, etc.) the intensity as a function of wavelength is recorded and processing of the line and line shape and background subtraction can be carried out.

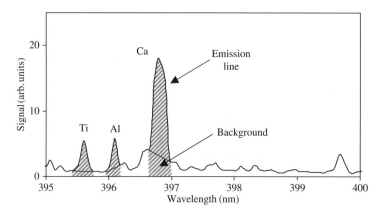

Figure 4.4   Expanded region of Figure 4.2 showing individual lines

In determining a line intensity, the simplest case to consider is that of Ti in Figure 4.4. The net emission signal is determined by establishing the baseline on either side of this 'clean or isolated' line, drawing an imaginary line between these two points and computing the area or height above this line. A simple algorithm can be written to readily process this type of data. The software for some array detector systems has this capability built in. Determining the analyte signal in the case of Al is more complex as there is an adjacent line that represents a small interference with the Al line. The simplest method of determining the net emission signal is the same as described above – draw an imaginary line between the low and high wavelength side of the Al line which, in our example, is still well defined even in the presence of the interference. As in the case for Ti, the net emission signal is computed as the area above the imaginary line. The most complex case is that of Ca with interferences on either side but here again a good approximation to the net Ca emission signal can be determined by computing the area of the imaginary line between the low and high wavelength side of the Ca line. This procedure, although containing some error, has been shown to give adequate results.

Another method of determining the area of a line is shown in Figure 4.5 for the 422.6 nm Ca(I) line from the spectrum of Figure 4.2. There is an interference on the left side of this line but the right side is free of interference. A baseline level can be established using the flat region around 423 nm and this is indicated by the dashed line. Finding the peak of the line and computing the area in the shaded region yields one half of the line area with background. One-half the baseline is easily subtracted and the resulting value is doubled to give the net analyte signal.

The calculations of line areas described above can easily be carried out by writing simple computer programs to process the spectral information from an array

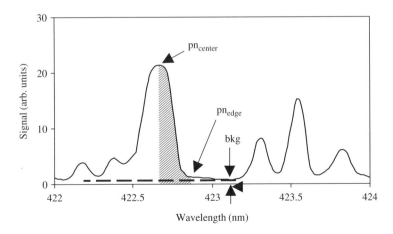

Figure 4.5 Determining the area of the Ca(I) 422.6 nm line by splitting the line

detector. These data will be in the form of signal at a particular pixel number (pn) which corresponds to a certain wavelength: signal(pn). In the case of Figure 4.5, the line area will be computed as:

$$\text{Area} = 2 \times [\Sigma \text{signal}(pn_i) - bkg] \tag{4.1}$$

where the sum extends from $pn = pn_{center}$ to pn_{edge} and bkg is the background intensity adjacent to the line. The background (bkg) is that corresponding to one-half the line width.

In the most rigorous evaluation of line intensities, each emission peak could be fitted with an assumed line shape. Then the intensity of the analyte of interest is de-convoluted from the other interfering lines (Kauppinen *et al.*, 1981; Barth, 2000). This is illustrated in Figure 4.6. From the line shape, the net analyte signal can be extracted. Whether this procedure leads to improved data is a function of the degree of overlap and the relative intensities of the analyte and the interferent(s). Clearly, as the analyte intensity decreases in intensity relative to the interferent(s) intensity(ies), such a procedure will improve the data. On the other hand, it is often possible to use another emission line of the element of interest if the line of choice exhibits strong interferences.

In the majority of cases, essentially the same results will be obtained using the peak height and peak area of a line. This is shown on Figure 4.7 where the height and area of the 769.9 nm K(I) line are plotted on the same calibration curve graph versus concentration. The height values were normalized to the area value at the maximum concentration to accentuate the similarities in the results. On the other hand, if comparing the intensities of two lines, one of which may be strongly affected by Stark broadening, for example the H(I) (alpha) line at 656.29 nm, the integrated intensities should be used.

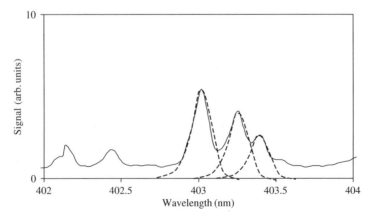

Figure 4.6 Mn line spectrum extracted from Figure 4.2 showing the overlap of the adjacent lines at 403.08, 403.31 and 403.45 nm

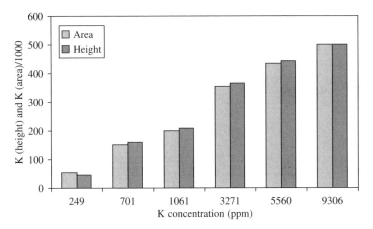

Figure 4.7 Comparison of peak heights and areas obtained for the K line at 769.9 nm for powdered basalt samples spiked with different concentrations of KCl

4.3 PRECISION

Emission of light from the LIBS plasma is a short-lived event (Figure 2.1) that involves collecting light over a time period of only ~20 μs, for example. For comparison, a measurement using a continuous excitation source such as the inductively coupled plasma (ICP) may involve collection of light from the excited analyte over a period of 5 s which corresponds to collecting the light from 250 000 laser plasmas or running a 10 Hz laser for 6.9 h! Clearly, the total signal recorded in a practical LIBS measurement is much less than that recorded using a continuous source, assuming equal excitation. In addition, the laser plasma is a pulsed excitation source that both prepares (atomizes) and excites the sample on each shot. Inherent shot-to-shot instabilities related to the achievable stability of the repetitive laser pulses and perturbations of the plasma by characteristics of the sample and the sampling procedure, all serve to limit measurement 'repeatability.' Here repeatability is the closeness of one measurement with other measurements carried out under the same experimental conditions.

Measurement repeatability is described by the term precision – a measure of the agreement of a set of results (x_i) among themselves. Precision is usually expressed in terms of the deviation of a set of measurements (number $= n$) from the arithmetic mean (M) of the set of repeated measurements. This deviation is calculated as the standard deviation (s) given by

$$s = [\Sigma(x_i - M)^2/n - 1]^{1/2}. \qquad (4.2)$$

Using s, the percent relative standard deviation (%RSD) can be computed as:

$$\%RSD = 100\% \times (s/M). \qquad (4.3)$$

It should be noted that in some cases, a measurement will involve a single LIBS spectrum. An example is the determination of the composition of a single small particle such as in an aerosol laden air stream. In other cases, a series of individual measurements will be collected and the shot-to-shot evolution of the LIBS spectrum is analyzed. An example is repetitive ablation of a geological sample to monitor the change in composition as the outer (weathered) layers are ablated away and the composition of the underlying bulk sample is analyzed. The result is a histogram of composition as a function of depth. Another example is the real-time monitoring of material flow for process control or effluent analysis. Note that for these single shot measurements, precision cannot be determined ($n = 1$) and would not have any significance as the sample would be changing shot-by-shot. On the other hand, computing s for such a set of data could be used as a designator for the extent of change observed in a sample or process, rather than a measure of the repeatability of the process itself (e.g. the standard deviation in the sample composition among individual particles exhibited a value of 30%).

Aside from these 'special cases,' to increase LIBS analytical performance, typically, many individual measurements (i.e. individual spectra) are recorded and the results are combined to produce an average measurement. The average measurement may be repeated several or many times using the same experimental parameters. Each of these similar measurements is called a 'replicate.' In a measurement, the sample is assumed to be a constant or that a sufficiently large number of individual spectra are averaged to account for variations in sample properties. Spectra are also averaged to account for shot-to-shot differences that may result from somewhat different plasma excitation on each shot. The number of measurements averaged together to produce a single LIBS measurement is determined by many factors including:

(1) sample homogeneity (depth and lateral homogeneity, more uniform samples will require fewer measurements to obtain a representative determination of composition);
(2) desire to maximize precision and accuracy within the performance of the method;
(3) required analysis duty cycle (number of measurements/time);
(4) sampling method. (Is the lens-to-sample distance constant? Are ablated particles intercepting subsequent laser pulses and perturbing plasma formation?)

When making replicate measurements, the experimental conditions are maintained constant. The results of these replicate measurements (e.g. six is typical) are used to determine measurement precision and increase the accuracy of a determination. A demonstration of the change in precision with number of individual spectra averaged to produce a single measurement is shown in Figure 4.8. The sample was a homogeneous uranium solution with the laser pulses focused on the surface of the liquid to form the plasmas. In this example, averaging a large number of spectra to produce a single measurement was found to increase precision which, in these

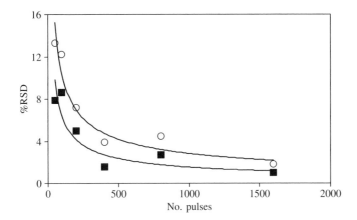

Figure 4.8 Measurement precision (%RSD) versus number of pulses used for a measurement. Sample was uranium metal in nitric acid (Wachter and Cremers, 1987). Net uranium signal (open circles) and uranium signal ratioed to an adjacent region of background continuum light (black squares)

measurements, was limited by movements of the liquid surface due to the shock wave produced by the laser pulse. These data show a significant gain in precision as the number of averaged pulses increased from 50 to 500 and that a precision of 1% was obtained for the ratioed analyte signal using 1600 laser pulses (10 Hz laser, 2.7 min analysis time).

It should be emphasized that precision is a measure of the repeatability of a measurement. High precision does not imply an accurate measurement.

4.4 CALIBRATION

4.4.1 CALIBRATION CURVES

For quantitative analysis, a calibration curve of instrument response (e.g. element signal) versus absolute mass (gram, nanogram, etc.) or concentration (%, parts-per-million or ppm) of the element to be detected is usually prepared. A general calibration curve is shown in Figure 4.9 and some aspects of this curve are sometimes seen in LIBS literature for calibration over a wide range. Ideally, there will be a linear relationship between the element response and the mass or concentration over the entire range investigated and a linear fit to the data would pass through the origin (0,0). Also, in the best case, the signal will double in magnitude if the concentration doubles. Actual calibration curves deviate from these ideal qualities. The range of concentration of mass (or concentration) over which the calibration curve is linear is termed the *linear dynamic range*. Nonlinear behavior is sometimes observed at the lower and higher concentrations. The slope of the calibration curve

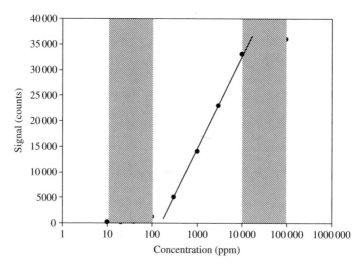

Figure 4.9 Generalized calibration curve with three regions of different sensitivity clearly evident

at a certain concentration is termed the sensitivity and it is the change in signal for a given incremental change in the concentration (or mass). Clearly, as the slope increases, a fixed change in the observed signal relates to a smaller change in the concentration. Often the calibration curve will be plotted as mass (or concentration) versus signal.

The curve of Figure 4.9 shows a loss of sensitivity at high and low concentrations, on either side of the central linear region. The loss of sensitivity, or flattening of the curve, at low concentrations can be due to:

(1) a spectral interference with the analytical line with the concentration of the interfering species remaining constant as the analyte concentration decreases;
(2) a constant background concentration of the analyte being determined that is not included in the stated concentration of the analyte;
(3) incorrect determination of the analyte signal so that a portion of the background signal is included in what is assumed to be only the analyte signal.

An example of an unexpected source of error related to (2) occurred in our laboratory during a measurement of Hg in soil. Using the 546 nm Hg(I) line as the analyte LIBS signal, a strong signal at 546 nm was recorded even for 'pure' or 'clean' soil. The line was observed when analyzing other materials and the signal was finally traced to a light leak in the plasma light collection system. The Hg emission from fluorescent lights in the laboratory contributed a constant signal to the analyte signal excited by the laser plasma.

Considering (1), whether a species interferes with or overlaps the analyte emission signature in a LIBS measurement is related to the resolution of the detection system and the timing parameters used to record the spectrum. A review of wavelength tables will show that few analyte lines have true spectral interferences in the sense of two adjacent lines having the identical wavelengths. There will be some difference in the wavelength but perhaps a very small difference, on the order of 0.01 or 0.001 nm or even less. In practice however, the line width and the spectral resolution method will determine if the lines interfere. The lower the resolution of the method, the greater will be the chance of spectral interference.

At early times (e.g. $t_d < 1\,\mu s$), the spectral lines may be broadened to the extent that they overlap whereas for a longer delay ($t_d \sim 2\,\mu s$) the broadening may decrease so the lines are sufficiently resolved to be individually monitored without interference. This time dependent broadening is due to effects such as Stark broadening and Doppler broadening (see Chapter 2) that vary with the decaying plasma. In the presence of such broadening, interfering lines cannot be resolved using even a high resolution spectrograph, as the broadening occurs in the analyte itself. Some of these line broadening processes become less important as the plasma decays after formation. A good demonstration of such line broadening is provided by the hydrogen line at 656 nm. At early times in the LIBS plasma, $t_d \sim 0.1\,\mu s$, this line can be on the order of 10 nm wide whereas at later delays, $t_d \sim 1–2\,\mu s$, this will be reduced to a few tenths of nanometers. The sensitivity of this hydrogen line to the electron density (Stark effect) is sometimes used as a measure of the plasma electron density (Section 2.1.2).

The loss of sensitivity at high concentrations is most often due to 'self-absorption.' Self-absorption typically is observed for emission lines in which the lower level of the transition is the ground state or close to the ground state. Because transitions are element specific and quantized or of a specific wavelength, a given species has the highest proability of reabsorbing a photon emitted by a member of the same species. Because of the high density of atoms in the microplasma and its characteristically high temperature and electron density gradients, the outer layer of the plasma will be populated by 'cool' atoms, residing mostly in the ground state. The central core of the plasma will contain a higher density of excited atoms. As these atoms decay to the ground state, the emitted photons corresponding to resonance transitions will have a high probability of being absorbed by the 'cooler' atoms in the outer layers, thereby reducing the observed intensity of the emission line. As the concentration of the atoms in the target sample increases, the number of 'cooler' atoms in the outer layer increases and self-absorption becomes evident (Figure 4.10). A good example of self-absorption observed in a LIBS experiment is shown in Figure 4.11. Here the shapes of the emission lines depend on ambient pressure with the peaks recorded for 580 Torr reduced in intensity at the center (self-reversed). The lines appear broad in relation to their height because of the high concentration of K(I) in the sample. These K(I) emissions end in the ground state and the upper levels are at 1.6.1 and 1.62 eV making them particularly susceptible to self-absorption. The effect of self-absorption on the ability to obtain quantitative results using LIBS has been considered in detail (Lazic et al., 2001).

A loss of sensitivity in the calibration curve can also be due to saturation of the detector response, that is, the intensity of light upon the detector is so great that there no longer is a linear response of the detector signal to the change in light

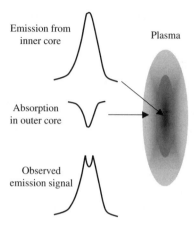

Figure 4.10 Diagram illustrating the origin of self-absorption

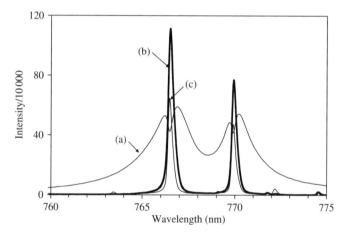

Figure 4.11 Example of strong self-absorption observed from a laser plasma formed on pressed KCl powder. The two large peaks correspond to strong K emissions. (a) 580 (b) 7 and (c) 0.0001 Torr pressure (Harris *et al.*, 2004)

intensity. In the linear operating regime of the detector, a change in the incident light intensity by $x\%$ should change the signal by $x\%$. This is most often evaluated using a neutral density filter to reduce the light intensity a known amount and monitoring the resulting signal.

If the nonlinear behavior of a calibration curve is due to some change in excitation provided by the plasma as the sample changes, the curve can often be 'straightened out' by plotting the analyte signal ratioed to another element known to be in the sample at a constant concentration. An example is shown in Figure 4.12. The left plot displays a calibration curve that is clearly not linear with the absolute Cu signal

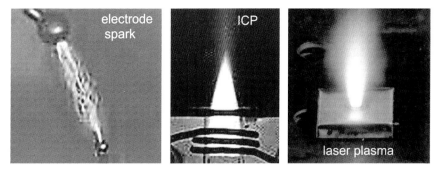

Plate 1 Photographs of a conventional electrode spark, an inductively coupled plasma, and a laser-induced spark. The size scales are different (see Figure 1.1)

Plate 2 The laser spark (a) in a gas, (b) in a liquid, (c) on the surface of a liquid, and (d) on a beryllium (see Figure 1.3)

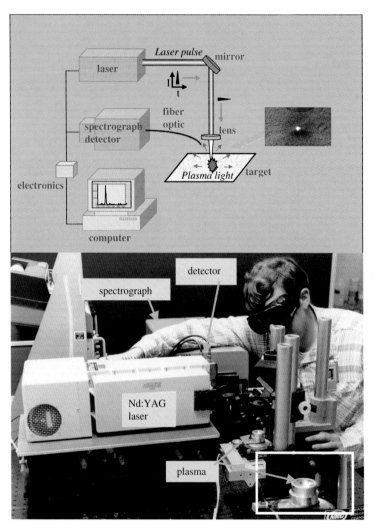

Plate 3 Diagram of a typical LIBS set-up. The photo shows a simple LIBS set-up used to analyze material on a filter (see Figure 3.1)

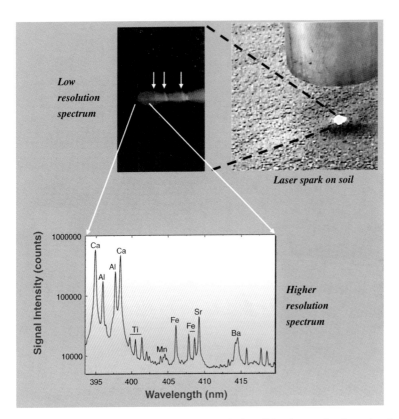

Plate 4 LIBS spectrum produced by a simple transmission diffraction grating from the plasma formed at the right on soil. Here only strong lines of nitrogen from air are observed. Higher resolution of the spectrum shows emissions from major, minor and trace elements in the soil (see Figure 3.16)

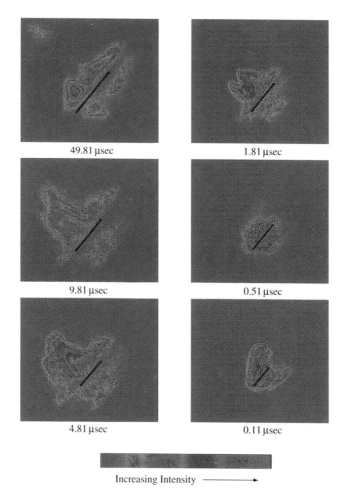

49.81 µsec   1.81 µsec

9.81 µsec   0.51 µsec

4.81 µsec   0.11 µsec

Increasing Intensity ⟶

Plate 5 Cr emission observed using the AOTF with an ICCD. (Reproduced from Multari and Cremers, Copyright 1996 IEEE) (see Figure 3.20)

(a)

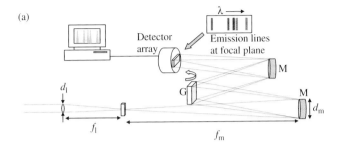

(b)

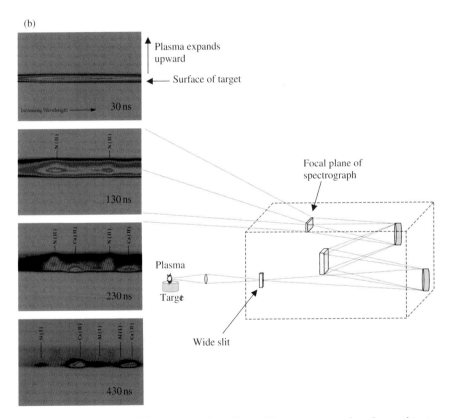

Plate 6 (a) Detection of LIBS spectrum using a Czerny-Turner spectrograph and array detector. (b) Examples of LIBS spectra recorded at the focal plane of a spectrograph. (Multari *et al.*, 1996, with permission from Society for Applied Spectroscopy) (see Figure 3.21)

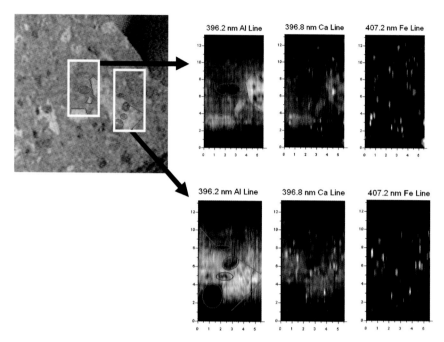

Plate 7 Map of element emissions along a rock sample obtained by scanning a series of long sparks along the surface (see Figure 3.30)

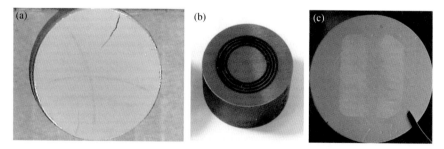

Plate 8 Examples of some calibration samples. (a) Pressed basalt certified reference material showing the tracks produced by translating the sample under repetitive laser sparks. (b) Steel certified reference material showing concentric tracks produced by a high repetition rate laser. (Yamamoto *et al.*, 2005, with permission from Society for Applied Spectroscopy.) (c) Calibration filter containing an analyte at a certain surface concentration (e.g. ng/cm²). The tracks produced on the sample by scanning the filter under a series of long sparks formed on the surface are visible (see Figure 4.16)

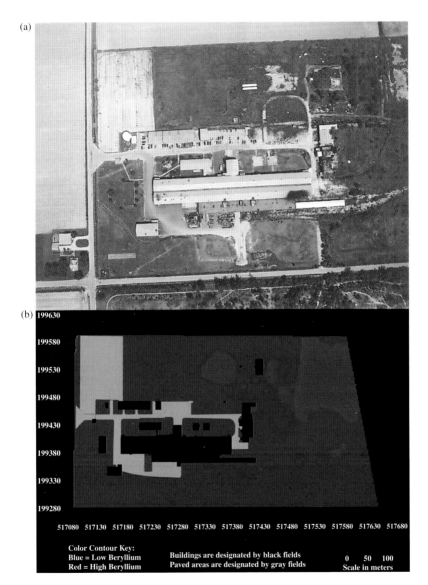

Plate 9 (a) Aerial photo of a former beryllium facility at Luckey, Ohio, USA. (b) Map of main features and locations of high and low beryllium concentrations. (Photo and figure courtesy of Science and Engineering Associates, Inc.) (see Figure 5.23)

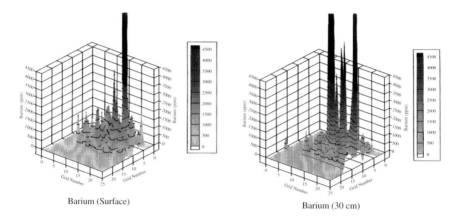

Barium (Surface)   Barium (30 cm)

Plate 10 Barium concentrations in soil determined using the field portable LIBS instrument of Figure 5.21(b). The grid refers to spatial position along the area of contamination with the determined concentrations plotted on the vertical axis. Each measurement required about 2 min, including sample exchange in the instrument (see Figure 5.24)

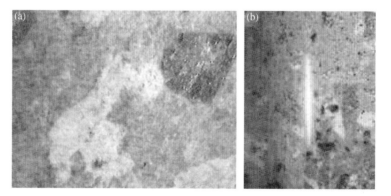

Plate 11 (a) Close-up photo of a ground surface of a rhyolite rock sample. Distinct features are 1–2 mm in size. (b) Analysis of the same rock using a long spark (1 cm) to average over inhomogeneities (see Figure 6.7)

Plate 12 Demonstration of stand-off LIBS using a laboratory instrument to interrogate a cliff bank. The spark is shown in the inset. The distance was 24 m between the spark and the optical system (focusing and light collection) (see Figure 7.2)

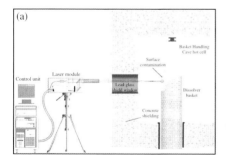

Plate 13 (a) Schematic showing the deployment of the remote LIBS instrument to monitor surface contamaintion. (b) Laser beam of the instrument being directed through the lead glass shield window (Applied Photonics, 2004a. Courtesy of Applied Photonics, Ltd) (see Figure 7.7)

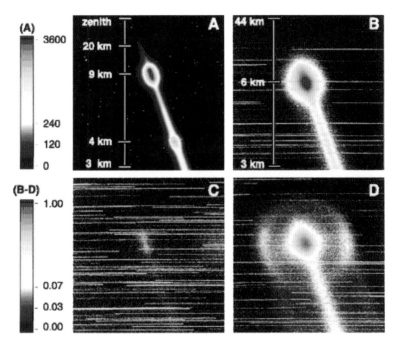

Plate 14 CCD camera images of filaments produced by a femtosecond laser beam propagating vertically through the atmosphere. The femtosecond pulses were produced by the Teramobile. (A) Fundamental wavelength, exhibiting signals from more than 20 km and multiple-scattering halos on haze layers at 4- and 9-km altitudes. (B–D) White light (385 to 485 nm) emitted by the femtosecond laser beam. These images have the same altitude range, and their common color scale is normalized to allow direct comparison with that of (A). (Reprinted with permission from Kasparian *et al.*, 2003) (see Figure 7.10)

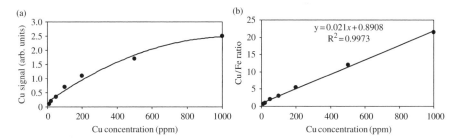

Figure 4.12 LIBS calibration curves for Cu in a synthetic silicate sample using 10 mJ pulses

plotted versus Cu concentration from a set of synthetic silicate samples. There is a significant loss of sensitivity at the higher concentrations. Plotted in Figure 4.12(b) is the ratio Cu/Fe. The resulting calibration curve is linear. Plotting the analyte signal ratioed to an 'internal standard' element is a well known method of correcting for some nonlinear behavior. The caveat is that the concentration of the internal standard element must be constant.

The slope or sensitivity of the linear portion of the calibration curve in Figure 4.9 is dependent on experimental factors. Shown in Figure 4.13 is the relationship between

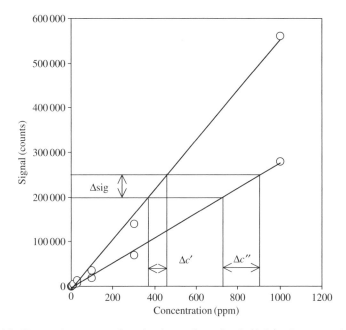

Figure 4.13 For a given uncertainty in the analyte signal (Δsig), the uncertainty in the concentration determination decreases with increased sensitivity ($\Delta c' < \Delta c''$)

a change in the signal and a corresponding change in the analyte concentration. Clearly, as the slope increases, for a given uncertainty in the signal (Δsig), the uncertainty in the concentration to be determined decreases. Therefore, it is desirable to have maximum sensitivity in the technique.

For LIBS, increases in the laser pulse energy and the gain of the detection system, both instrumental parameters, will increase the slope. The slope will also be affected by sampling conditions such as the atmosphere above the sample. An example of the change in calibration curve slope with laser pulse energy is shown in Figure 4.14. The increase in slope with energy can be traced to (1) increased mass ablation of the sample leading to a higher number of excited species and (2) an increase in the size of the plasma producing greater excitation of ablated species.

The dependence of slope on pressure shown in Figure 4.15 requires some explanation. The increase in slope observed for 7 Torr pressure is the net result of the competing processes of increased ablation and reduced excitation. The number of collisions decreases as the pressure is reduced but the number of atoms in the plasma increases with ablation. The latter is the predominate mechanism down to a pressure of a few torr. Ablation increases with reduced pressure because of reduced plasma shielding that permits more of the incident laser pulse energy to reach the sample surface. For pressures below about 1 Torr, plasma shielding becomes negligible and the mass ablated remains uniform for further pressure decreases. In this low pressure regime, reduced excitation due to reduced pressure (reduced collisions) controls species excitation and the element signals decrease with pressure. For pressures below about 0.001 Torr, ablated species are no longer confined near the surface as these are ejected out into the surrounding free space immediately upon irradiation by the laser pulse. In this case the time between collisions becomes so great that further pressure decreases do not affect species excitation.

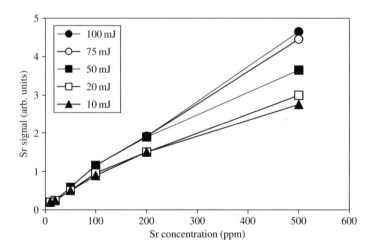

Figure 4.14 Sr calibration curve as a function of laser energy

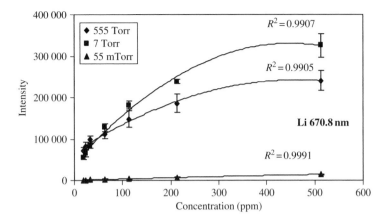

Figure 4.15 Calibration curves for Li at various pressures. The distance between the target and the LIBS system was 4 m (stand-off measurement, Chapter 7)

4.4.2 CALIBRATION STANDARDS

The LIBS method, as any other analytical technique, requires calibration to obtain optimum results in a quantitative analysis. As discussed in Chapter 8, methods are being developed for calibration free-LIBS but this technique has not been widely deployed as the method is still being refined and the quality of the results has been sample dependent. For this reason, active calibration is typically employed with the calibration curve developed using a set of standards or calibration samples having a composition as close as possible to the unknown sample. This provides for the best results as factors such as matrix effects are minimized because the standards and the unknown samples have the same bulk composition. Of course, in some cases the sample to be analyzed may be a true unknown with little or no knowledge about the matrix.

Calibration standards for soil analysis can be prepared, for example by obtaining clean soil and then adding known amounts of the analyte of interest (e.g. potassium), as a compound for example (potassium chloride), to the soil to produce a set of samples having analyte concentrations spanning the range of interest. By weighting out the samples fairly precisely, acceptable calibration samples can be prepared. It may be, however, that the chemical form of the analyte compound added to the calibration samples may be different from the form of the analyte in the unknown specimen thereby possibly affecting the observed emission signals through matrix effects.

Because LIBS interrogates a sample with little or no preparation, the method requires that the form of the calibration standard match that of the interrogation method. That is, solid samples will be used to calibrate a LIBS system developed to analyze metal samples, airborne samples will be used to calibrate the response of a LIBS air sampling system in which the laser plasma is formed directly in air, and surface depositions of a material will be developed to calibrate a method of analyzing swipes upon which contaminated material has been deposited. Some different calibration samples are shown in Figure 4.16 (Plate 8).

Calibration standards for many types of samples can also be obtained commercially from a large number of governmental and industrial laboratories. These include reference materials, certified reference materials, primary standards, etc. Table 4.1 lists the definitions of these different sample types as they relate to LIBS and which may be encountered in selecting and developing calibration samples.

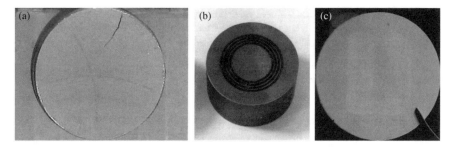

Figure 4.16   Examples of some calibration samples. (a) Pressed basalt certified reference material showing the tracks produced by translating the sample under repetitive laser sparks. (b) Steel certified reference material showing concentric tracks produced by a high repetition rate laser. (Yamamoto *et al.*, 2005, with permission from Society for Applied Spectroscopy.) (c) Calibration filter containing an analyte at a certain surface concentration (e.g. ng/cm^2). The tracks produced on the sample by scanning the filter under a series of long sparks formed on the surface are visible (see Plate 8)

Table 4.1   Some definitions related to LIBS calibration

Calibration curve	A graphical representation of the relationship between a signal and the amount of an analyte in a sample. Additional variables or analytes may be used in calibration in which case a calibration surface or hypersurface is formed (multicomponent analysis)
Standard or calibration sample	A material having one or more composition values of interest that can be presented to the analytical instrument for calibration purposes
Reference material (RM)	A material having one or more composition values of interest that are sufficiently homogeneous and well established within certain limits to be used for the calibration of an analytical instrument, the assessment of an analytical method, or for assigning values to other materials
Certified reference material (CRM)	A reference material, accompanied by a certificate, having one or more composition values of interest certified by a procedure or a series of procedures which establishes traceability assuring an accurate realization of the composition value. The certified value is usually accompanied by an uncertainty at a stated level of confidence

4.5 DETECTION LIMIT

The limit of detection (LOD) as defined by the IUPAC is (IUPAC, 1997):

> The limit of detection, expressed as the concentration, c_L, or the quantity, q_L, is derived from the smallest measure, x_L, that can be detected with reasonable certainty for a given analytical procedure. The value of x_L is given by the equation $x_L = x_{bi} + k s_{bi}$ where x_{bi} is the mean of the blank measures, s_{bi} is the standard deviation of the blank measures, and k is a numerical factor chosen according to the confidence level desired.

Because the relationship between the measure (or signal) and the concentration (or mass) is given by the slope of the calibration curve $m = \Delta c_L / \Delta x_L$, we have $c_L = c_{bi} + k s_{bi} m$ but c_{bi} is typically zero (no analyte concentration in the blank sample) so that $c_L = k s_{bi} m$. This is the formula that is often used to compute the LOD with $k = 3$. Ideally, a $k = 3$ value would correspond to a confidence level of 95% but because s_{bi} is determined from a small number of measurements, a 90% confidence level is more reasonable. The detection limit should be considered the minimum amount of the analyte that can be present and be determined to be present, rather than the minimum amount of the sample that can be actually measured. For quantification purposes, $k = 10$ and the limit of quantification is given by LOQ = $10 s_{bi} m = 3.3$LOD. Debate over FOMs, especially the detection limit, is ongoing and a bibliography relating to the detection limit is presented at the end of this chapter.

It should be realized that the LOD can be affected by many measurement parameters such as laser pulse energy and the values of t_d and t_b used for detection as well as sample characteristics. The condition of the surface polish of a metal sample and laser pulse irradiance, for example, have been shown to affect the LOD for Mo in stainless steel (Cabalín et al., 1999).

4.6 ACCURACY

Accuracy is a measure of how close a measurement result is to the 'true' value of the property measured. Of course, the true value would have to be determined by a perfect measurement technique which in reality does not exist. Even if an 'unknown' sample were made from pure components, there would always be some uncertainty in measuring out the compounds that would be combined to make the 'unknown' sample. We therefore resort to what is termed the 'conventional true value' or 'accepted true value.' An example would be the concentration of an analyte specified for a certified reference material (Table 4.1). The 'certified concentration' would be determined by averaging analytical determinations of that analyte from a number of different analytical methods.

The error in accuracy may be defined as the difference between the measured value (x_m) and the 'accepted true value' (x_{atv}):

$$\text{Error} = x_m - x_{atv} \qquad (4.4)$$

Errors in accurately measuring a quantity can be due to many factors and these can be classed as systematic (or determinate) errors and random errors. Systematic errors are due to a fault in a procedure or instrument. For example, in a LIBS measurement, if the laser pulse energy was not maintained constant (instrument drift) or it had a different value than the laser energy used for measurements used to construct the calibration curve, errors in determining an analyte concentration will occur. Such an error can be minimized by assuring the constancy of laser pulse energy and other experimental parameters.

Random errors cannot be avoided and are due to fundamental limitations on the experimental procedure. For example, the laser pulse energy can never precisely be set to the same value used to construct the calibration curve and there will always be some drift in the laser energy at a level below which the energy cannot be controlled any more precisely. From this definition, it is clear that random errors can be minimized to some extent by making replicate measurements. It is just as likely that a random error will produce a positive error as a negative error and to a certain extent these will cancel out.

The accuracy is often expressed as percent accuracy error which is computed as:

$$\%\text{accuracy error} = \text{absolute value of } [(x_m - x_{atv})/x_{atv}] \times 100\%. \quad (4.5)$$

Accuracies of LIBS measurements determined using geological samples and in direct air sampling evaluations are presented in Section 6.8.

REFERENCES

Barth, A. (2000). Fine-structure enhancement – assessment of a simple method to resolve overlapping bands in spectra. Spectrochim. Acta Part A 56: 1223–1232.

Cabalín, L.M., D. Romero, J.M. Baena and J.J. Laserna (1999). Effect of surface topography in the characterization of stainless steel using laser-induced breakdown spectrometry. Surf. Interface Anal. 27: 805–810.

Harris, R.D., D.A. Cremers, C. Khoo and K. Benelli (2004). Unpublished data.

IUPAC (1997). Compendium of Chemical Terminology, 2nd edn, IUPAC, Research Triangle Park, NC.

ISO 3534-1 (1993). Statistics–Vocabulary and Symbols – Part 1: Probability and General Statistical Terms, ISO, Geneva.

ISO 11843-1 (1997). Capability of Detection – Part 1: Terms and Definitions, ISO, Geneva.

ISO 11843-2 (2000). Capability of Detection – Part 2: Methodology in the Linear Calibration Case, ISO, Geneva.

Kauppinen, J.K., D.J. Moffatt, H.H. Mantsch and D.G. Cameron (1981). Fourier transforms in the computation of self-deconvoluted and first-order derivative spectra of overlapped band contours. Anal. Chem. 53: 1454–1457.

Lazic, V., R. Barbini, F. Colao, R. Fantoni and A. Palucci (2001). Self-absorption model in quantitative laser induced breakdown spectroscopy measurements on soil and sediments. Spectrochim. Acta Part B 56: 807–820.

Payling, R. and P. Larkins (2000). Optical Emission Lines of the Elements, John Wiley & Sons, Ltd, Chichester.

Pearse, R.W.B. and A.G. Gaydon (1963). The Identification of Molecular Spectra, Chapman and Hall, London.

Phelps III, F.M. (Ed.) (1982). *MIT Wavelength Tables, Volume 2: Wavelengths by Element*, MIT Press, Cambridge, MA.

Reader, J., C.H. Corliss, W.L. Wiese and G.A. Martin (1980). *Wavelengths and Transition Probabilites for Atoms and Atomic Ions*, Natl. Stand. Ref. Data Ser., Natl. Bur. Stand. (US) 68: Part I.

Reader, J. and C.H. Corliss (1997). Line spectra of the elements. In *CRC Handbook of Chemistry and Physics*, 77th edn, ed. D.R. Lide, CRC Press, Boca Raton, FL.

Sobel'man, I.I. (1996). *Atomic Spectra and Radiative Transitions*, 2nd edn, Springer-Verlag, Berlin.

Striganov, A.R. and N.S. Sventitskii (1968). *Tables of Spectral Lines of Neutral and Ionized Atoms*, IFI/Plenum, New York.

Wachter, J.R. and D.A. Cremers (1987). Determination of uranium in solution using laser-induced breakdown spectroscopy. Appl. Spectrosc. 41: 1042–1048.

Winge, R.K., V.A. Fassel, V.J. Peterson and M.A. Floyd (1985). *Inductively Coupled Plasma-Atomic Emission Spectroscopy, Physical Sciences Data Volume 20*, Elsevier, Amsterdam.

Yamamoto, K.Y., D.A. Cremers, L.E. Foster, M.P. Davies and R.D. Harris (2005). Laser-induced breakdown spectroscopy analysis of solids using a long-pulse (150 ns) Q-switched Nd: YAG laser. Appl. Spectrosc. 59: 1082–1097.

BIBLIOGRAPHY FOR DETECTION LIMITS

Analytical Methods Committee (1987). Recommendations for the definition, estimation and use of the detection limit. Analyst 112: 199–204.

Analytical Methods Committee (2001). Measurement of near zero concentration: recording and reporting results that fall close to or below the detection limit. Analyst 126: 256–259.

Boumans, P.W.J.M. (1994). Detection limits and spectral interferences in atomic emission spectrometry. Anal. Chem. 66: 459A–467A.

Currie, L.A. (Ed.) (1988). *Detection in Analytical Chemistry: Importance, Theory and Practice*, ACS Symposium Series 361, American Chemical Society, New York: Ch. 1.

Currie, L.A. (1997). Detection: international update, and some emerging dilemmas involving calibration, the blank, and multiple detection decisions. Chemom. Intell. Lab. Syst. 37: 151–181.

Currie, L.A. (1999). Detection and quantification limits: origins and historical overview. Anal. Chim. Acta 391: 127–134.

Garner, F.C. and G.L. Robertson (1988). Evaluation of detection limit estimators. Chemom. Intell. Lab. Syst. 3: 53–59.

Long, G.L. and J.D. Winefordner (1983). Limit of detection: a closer look at the IUPAC definition. Anal. Chem. 55: 712A–724A.

5 Qualitative LIBS Analysis

5.1 INTRODUCTION

As discussed in Chapter 4, the basis of any LIBS measurement is the plasma spectrum which contains information about the elements in the target sample. This information is in the form of emission lines located at specific wavelengths, the intensity of the lines and the relative intensities of the lines. This information is important for analyzing the sample. The analysis can either be qualitative or quantitative. *Qualitative analysis* seeks to establish the presence of a given element in a sample. *Quantitative analysis* seeks to establish the amount of a given element in a sample. As a subset of qualitative analysis we can add material identification. This type of analysis can arise if the identification of the samples lies within a certain limited set of materials. An example is the identification of metal alloys of which there are a limited number (Jurado-Lopez and Luque de Castro, 2003). Some examples of the different types of qualitative analysis that have been used with LIBS are listed in Table 5.1. In this chapter we discuss qualitative analysis and material identification.

5.2 IDENTIFYING ELEMENTS

The basalt spectrum of Figure 4.2 contains a high density of lines. Due to the high resolution of the echelle spectrograph used to record this spectrum, many closely spaced lines can be resolved and elements identified. Analysis of this spectrum indicates emission lines attributed to the elements (e.g. Al, Ba, Ca, Fe, K, Li, Mg, Mn, Na, Sr, Ti). In all cases, each element in the basalt has many lines of different intensities in the spectrum. The assignment of a line is a blend of science, art, and experience. Topics to consider when identifying lines are presented below.

(1) *Knowledge of the sample.* For example, basalt is known to have high concentrations of Si, Al, Ca, Fe, K, Mg, Mn, Na, P and Ti, etc., but recordable concentrations of other elements such as Eu, Sm, U, elements that may have lines closely adjacent in wavelength to the strong lines of these elements (spectral interference) are unlikely to be found, unless the sample is contaminated by these elements.

Handbook of Laser-Induced Breakdown Spectroscopy   D. Cremers and L. Radziemski
© 2006 John Wiley & Sons, Ltd

Table 5.1   Examples of qualitative analysis using LIBS

Purpose	Procedure
Identification of complex molecules by element intensities (Dudragne et al., 1998)	Ratios of slopes of calibration curves were compared with stoichiometric atom ratios to identify starting molecules
Sorting of wood products treated with CCA (copper chromated arsenate) (Moskal and Hahn, 2002)	Form laser plasmas on wood surface and monitor for Cr emission
Identification of organic compounds in air (Portnov et al., 2003)	Intensity ratios of C, H, O, N, C_2 and CN
Identification of alloys used in jewelry manufacture (Jurado-Lopez and Luque de Castro, 2003)	Rank correlation method used to compare spectra of 'unknown' samples with those in a spectral library
Identification of precipitates on surfaces of Al alloys (Cravetchi et al., 2003)	Spectra in the region 320–410 nm were compared to distinguish the precipitate from the Al alloy
Identification of the composition of dirt on steel plates during manufacture (Orzi and Bilmes, 2004)	The presence of Fe particles in the surface dirt layers of manufactured steel plates

(2)   *Relative intensities of lines from wavelength tables.* From wavelength tables (references in Chapter 4), the relative intensities of lines can be determined and these can be used as a guide to assist in identifying lines. It should be realized, however, that relative line intensities are source dependent and that current wavelength tables were not compiled using the laser spark.

(3)   *The ionization stage of the element.* Assume that two elements are equally likely to be found in a sample. If the two elements have lines that spectrally interfere and one line belongs to a neutral species and the other belongs to a doubly or triply ionized species, it is most likely that the line belongs to the neutral species. Although once-ionized species are often observed in a LIBS plasma, the observation of higher ionization stages is unlikely in air. The lines of species with ionization potentials of 6 eV or less are more likely to be observed whereas species corresponding to >10 eV are unlikely to be present in sufficient numbers to be observed.

(4)   *The experimental conditions.* Certain experimental conditions can determine the species observed. For example, in air, emissions due to Fe(I) and Fe(II) are observed with the ionization potential of Fe(I) being 7.87 eV. In a vacuum, however, Fe(III) can be observed even though the second ionization potential is 16.18 eV. In another example, focused power densities on the order of 1 MW/cm², corresponding to a welding laser pulse, incident on an aluminum sample creates a plume that results in the excitation of neutral species but no ionized species are observed. The temperature of the plume measured using a Boltzmann plot (Chapter 2) indicates 3000 K.

(5) *Observation of multiple strong lines.* Many elements have several strong emission lines and if one line is observed the other strong lines of the element should be present. For example, if the strong Al(I) lines at 394.4 and 396.1 nm appear, the strong Al(I) lines at 308.2 and 309.3 nm should also be observed.

An example using the basalt spectrum of Figure 4.2 and the tentative identification of the strong line at 288.1 nm as due to Si(I) will demonstrate the procedure of line identification. Within 0.05 nm of the 288.1 nm line are lines due to Sm, Gd, Cd, Cs, Pr, Ca and Tm with the Gd line being somewhat strong as listed in the wavelength tables. However, from knowledge of typical soil composition, it is very unlikely that Sm, Gd, Pr and Tm will be in soil unless it happens to be contaminated. In addition, these are not usual contaminants found in soils unlike Pb, As, Zn, etc., which can occur due to mining and industrial processes. On the other hand, Ca is ubiquitous in nature being found almost everywhere naturally and it is present in soil at a high concentration. A look at wavelength tables, however, will show that the Ca line in question is due to doubly-ionized Ca, with Ca(III) having an ionization potential of 11.871 eV which is very high. For this reason, we would not expect to see strong Ca(III) lines appearing in a LIBS spectrum. The element Cs is also observed in many materials so it could be a candidate for the line we are tentatively attributing to Si(I). The Cs line is due to once-ionized Cs with the first ionization potential being 3.894 eV, sufficiently low that the Cs(II) line would be observed in a LIBS plasma. To further evaluate the presence of Cs we look for the two strong blue lines of Cs at 455.528 and 459.317 nm. In our spectrum there is a line close to 455.528 nm which could be due to Cs if the wavelength calibration of the spectrograph is off a small amount. There does not appear a feature at or near 459.317 nm, however, that we can attribute to the other strong Cs line. Therefore, it seems like Si(I) is the best identification of the 288.1 nm line. This is further supported by the appearance of a relatively strong line at 390.55 nm that is listed in the wavelength table as being about one-third the intensity of the 288.1 nm Si(I) line.

One factor that affects all LIBS measurements, even the simple identification of elements in a sample, is the condition of the surface. LIBS is essentially a surface analysis technique although repetitive sampling at the same location can be used to ablate through the surface to underlying layers. Surface detection is a useful capability in some applications, however, for example, to detect stains on a surface in the presence of a large mass due to the underlying substrate. Other analytical methods which can penetrate through the surface layer (e.g. x-ray fluorescence) to sample a large volume of the substrate composition would be attempting to monitor a small signal from a thin layer of surface material on top of a large signal from the bulk target. On the other hand, repetitive ablation at the same spot can be used to ablate through a thin weathered layer on a rock (~100 μm thick) to record changes in composition as the underlying bulk rock is approached. An example of this is shown in Figure 5.1. Figure 6.8, discussed below, shows the spectrum from a Tl stain on an aluminum plate.

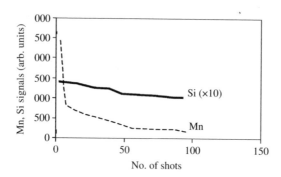

Figure 5.1 Change in element signals as the weathered surface of a granite rock is repetitively ablated. The Si(I) signal was multiplied by a factor of ten for plotting here

5.3 MATERIAL IDENTIFICATION

Patterns in the spectrum formed from element line intensities can be used to identify a material from a given set of materials. Consider asbestos, a highly fibrous silicate mineral composed of the elements Mg, Ca, Si, Al, O, H and C which are ubiquitous in nature. It is not the elements in asbestos that are dangerous but the structure of this material that determines toxicity. Fibers longer than $5 \mu m$, less than $5 \mu m$ wide with a length/width ratio >3 are most toxic. Sensitive detection is needed to monitor for residues of asbestos as according to one study the 'evaluation of all human data provides no evidence for a threshold or a safe level of asbestos exposure.' Fortunately, LIBS has good detection capabilities for the elements in asbestos. Asbestos is typically found around construction areas as it was added to building materials to give them strength, fire retardant abilities, color, and in some cases, simply as filler because it was an inexpensive material. For this reason, because LIBS is an element detector, to identify asbestos using LIBS its spectrum must be distinguishable from common building materials. A comparison of the asbestos LIBS spectrum in the wavelength range 382–406 nm is shown in Figure 5.2 along with LIBS spectra of cement and a ceiling tile. Upon inspection of the spectra they are clearly distinguishable based on the appearance/absence of some lines and the relative intensities of lines due to different elements. The results of a comparison of the asbestos spectrum with four different ceiling tile compositions, cement, wallboard and pipe insulation is presented in Table 5.2. The results show that based on mostly qualitative evaluation of the different spectra, using three different classes of signal levels (low, medium and high), asbestos can be identified from the other materials.

As another example, consider the identification of rock type based on recorded emission lines in the UV spectral region. Figure 5.3 displays spectra from bulk rock samples of basalt and dolomite and certified rock powder standards of these same rock types. The bulk rock and powders originated from different geological locations. A cursory examination of the different spectra and evaluations based on

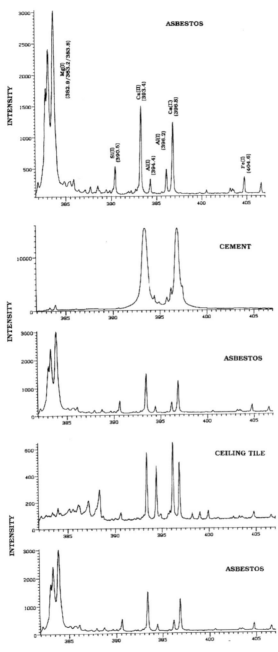

Figure 5.2 Qualitative analysis using LIBS. Comparison of LIBS spectra of asbestos, cement and ceiling tile in the region 382–407 nm. Although composed of ubiquitous elements (Al, Mg, Ca, Fe), these different materials, likely to be found together, are easily distinguished by inspection of the spectra

Table 5.2 Comparison of asbestos and building materials spectra

Material	Element detected					
	Mg	Si	Ca	Al	Ti	Fe
Asbestos	XXX	X	XX	X		
Tile 1	X	X	XX	X		
Tile 2			XXX	XX	XX	
Tile 3	X		XX	XX	X	X
Tile 4	X	X	XX	X		
Pipe insulation		XX	X	XXX	X	
Wallboard	X		XXX			
Cement		X	XXX	XX		

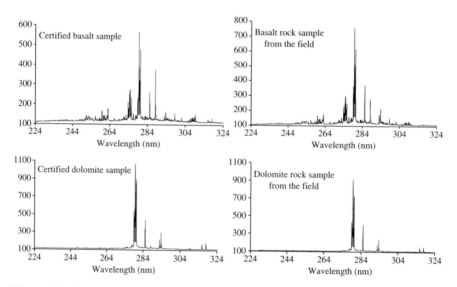

Figure 5.3 Comparison of spectra from bulk rock and powdered samples of basalt and dolomite

the positions of lines and relative line intensities show that the bulk rock and powder standards for the common rock types agree and are significantly different from the other type. Including other rock types such as granite would show the ability of LIBS to distinguish this variety from basalt and dolomite.

Another type of material identification can be practiced by 'atom counting.' Although LIBS cannot give structural information directly about the starting target material, it can reveal in certain circumstances, the number of a certain atomic species in a sample. An example is shown in Figure 5.4. Here two CFCs (chlorofluorocarbons) and the gas SF_6 as pure materials were mixed with Ar gas and were analyzed using the same apparatus under identical analysis conditions. The F/Ar ratio was determined over a certain concentration range. The slope of the

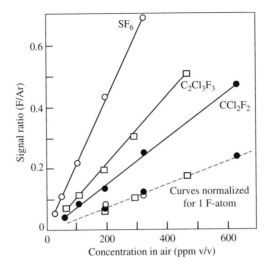

Figure 5.4 Calibration curves for different F-containing atoms. The dashed curve results from dividing the data for each species by the number of F atoms in that species (i.e. 6, 3, 2) (After Cremers and Radziemski, 1983)

calibration in each case is related to the number of F atoms on the pure gas species. Dividing each signal of the corresponding species by the number of F atoms results in the overlapping dashed line curve shown in the figure. This indicates that in the case of pure materials and a calibrated system, a material can be identified from a certain set of possible species. By including other atoms in the calibration procedure, the identification can be made more selective. In the case of CFCs, the Cl atom could be included in a LIBS analysis and these atoms counted.

5.4 PROCESS MONITORING

Besides acting as an excitation source to form a plasma that can be analyzed to determine composition, the laser pulse can also process a material to do work. An example is surface cleaning. Surface cleaning using a high repetition rate (kHz) acousto-optically Q-switched laser is shown in Figure 5.5. Some advantages of using a laser for cleaning are (1) fine control of the cleaning operation as the laser pulse spatial size and location can be precisely controlled, (2) remote cleaning because only optical access to the sample is required (e.g. through a window) and (3) the ability to monitor in real-time and remotely the cleaning process spectroscopically. As a demonstration of laser cleaning and process monitoring, a brief study of removing and monitoring AlO layers from aluminum is described. This work (1) demonstrates surface cleaning, specifically that oxide layers can be removed from an Al surface easily, rapidly and remotely using a laser and that (2) the oxide removal process can be monitored optically in-process and *in situ*.

Figure 5.5 Laser cleaning of a surface using a high repetition rate laser. The laser beam (kHz repetition rate) is rastered across the surface as the Al sample is translated below the beam generating the cleaned area (Yamamoto *et al.*, 2005, with permission of Society for Applied Spectroscopy)

5.4.1 EXPERIMENTAL

The experimental arrangement is shown in Figure 5.6. Pulses from a Q-switched Nd:YAG laser were focused on the surface of aluminum samples using a cylindrical lens (150 mm focal length). The samples were contained in a large chamber purged with Ar gas to minimize re-oxidation of the surface following oxide removal by the laser pulses. High-purity Ar (less than 20 ppm impurities) was used as the purge gas. The laser pulse energies were between 100 and 400 mJ, the pulse width was 10 ns, and the laser repetition rate was 1–25 Hz. The aluminum samples were 0.64 cm thick disks mounted axially to permit rotation during the experiments so fresh aluminum surfaces could be continually exposed to the laser pulses. A small motor was used to rotate the samples. Because of the high peak power densities of the focused laser pulses, 'line sparks' about 5–7 mm long could be formed on the samples. Examples of line sparks are shown in Figures 1.5 and 3.9. These sparks ablated the surface material from the samples and at the same time atomized and excited the removed material for a LIBS analysis. In these experiments, the spark light was imaged onto

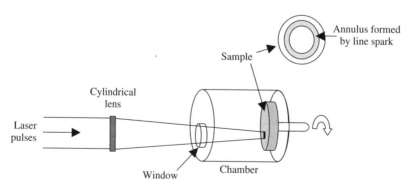

Figure 5.6 Apparatus used to monitor plasma emissions during surface cleaning of Al metal in an Ar gas atmosphere

the entrance slit of a small spectrograph and the light detected by an intensified array detector. Two types of samples were used: Al disks as machined and Al disks that had been black anodized to increase the thickness of the oxide surface layer.

The removal of oxide from the sample surface was monitored spectrally during the cleaning operation by recording emissions from (1) a trio of neutral oxygen lines [O(I)] near 777.4 nm and (2) a series of aluminum oxide bands (AlO) in the blue spectral region. The O(I) lines were not spectrally resolved in these experiments. The AlO spectrum monitored here is shown in Figure 5.7. Because the atmosphere surrounding the sample was purged with pure Ar gas, the spectral features due to O(I) and AlO recorded here were due mainly to the evolution of O from the surface of the sample by the action of the laser pulses.

5.4.2   RESULTS

5.4.2.1   Monitoring Oxide Removal Using O(I) Emissions

Figure 5.8 shows spectra obtained by repetitively sparking the same area of an unanodized aluminum surface. The strong line on the left of each spectrum is due

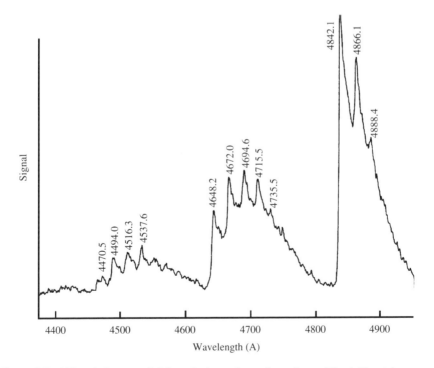

Figure 5.7   AlO emission recorded from the laser plasma formed on oxidized Al metal

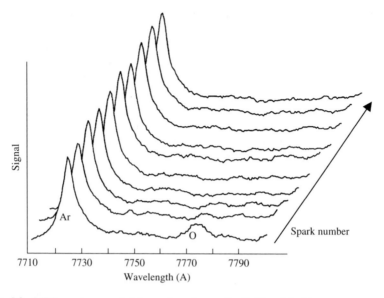

Figure 5.8 LIBS spectra recorded from a bare (unanodized) Al metal plate

to argon emission. The oxygen line is small but clearly shown on the first spectrum on the right at 777.4 nm. The strength of the oxygen line decreased rapidly as the number of sparks increased and it is absent from the last spectrum shown here. The intensity of the O(I) line is plotted in Figure 5.9 versus shot number for three different independent experiments. Essentially the same temporal histories were obtained in each experiment.

Figure 5.10 shows the results of an identical experiment carried out using an anodized aluminum sample. The oxygen line is much stronger on these spectra because of the greater thickness of the oxide layer. In fact, the oxygen emission increased during the first few sparks, then decreased somewhat and eventually leveled off to a nearly constant value. The increased O(I) signal [and Ar(I) signal] observed on the first few shots can be attributed to increased coupling of the laser energy due to repetitive sparking at the same area. Data for two similar experiments carried out under these conditions are plotted in Figure 5.11.

The residual oxygen signal observed even after 49 shots had been formed at the same location on the anodized aluminum sample (Figure 5.11) can be attributed to the residual oxide layer at the perimeter of the ablation region. This oxide layer was evidently still being sampled by the 49th pulse. The validity of this explanation was verified by ablating a small continuous region of the surface by slowly rotating the sample while repetitively sparking the surface at 25 Hz. The sample was then exposed to air to produce oxidation and then the center portion of the previously ablated region was resparked and the O(I) emission recorded. These results are presented in Figures 5.12 and 5.13 and they show that when the heavily oxidized

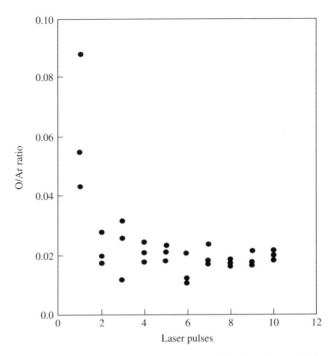

Figure 5.9 Intensity of O(I) emission versus shot number for a bare Al metal plate. Results for three experiments are shown

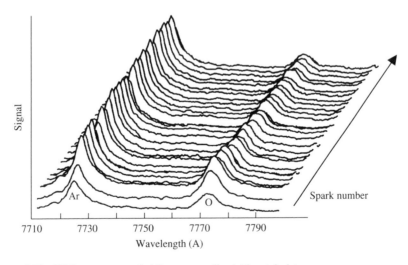

Figure 5.10 LIBS spectra recorded from an anodized Al metal plate

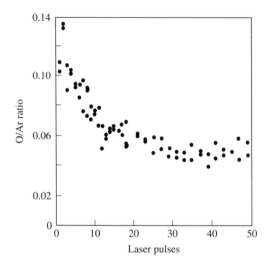

Figure 5.11 Intensity of O(I) emission versus shot number for an anodized Al metal plate. Results for two experiments are shown

region around the ablated area was removed, the O(I) emission signals were reduced to a very low level after several shots.

5.4.2.2   Monitoring Oxide Removal Using AlO Emissions

A series of experiments similar to those described above was carried out by monitoring the AlO emission in the blue spectral region. Signals from the unanodized aluminum were weak and not useful to monitor the change in oxide thickness. Figure 5.14 shows the AlO signals recorded by repetitively sparking an anodized surface. As observed for O(I) emissions (Figure 5.11), even after many shots the AlO signal remained strong. These data are plotted in Figure 5.15. Data obtained by repetitively sparking a previously cleaned region of an originally anodized sample is shown in Figure 5.16. Here, as shown above in the case of O(I) emissions, the AlO signals recorded after many shots were smaller than those observed by sparking a fresh anodized surface.

5.4.2.3   Rate of Oxide Removal

The rate of removal of oxide from the anodized samples was observed visually: the gray metallic color of aluminum metal was clearly distinguishable from the black color of the anodized coating. By rotating the sample under the laser pulses and changing the laser repetition rate it was possible to determine an approximate rate of removal of the heavy anodized layer. This rate was about $0.3\,cm^2/s$ for the laser operating at 10 pulses/s. The time required to clean an area of $1300\,cm^2$ is about 72 min under these conditions: lasers of the type used here, however, can be

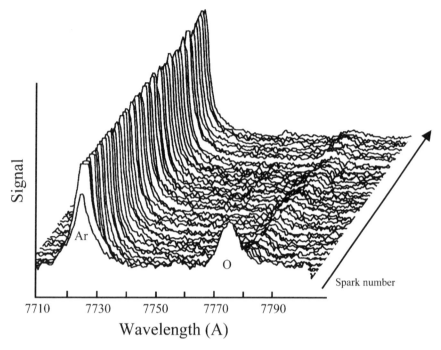

Figure 5.12 Intensity of O(I) emission after removal of anodized area surrounding the ablation region showing much reduced residual O(I) signal compared with Figure 5.10

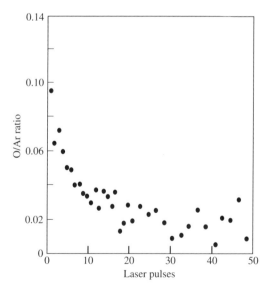

Figure 5.13 Intensity of O(I) emission versus shot number for an anodized Al metal plate after removal of anodized region surrounding the ablation region. Compare with data of Figure 5.11

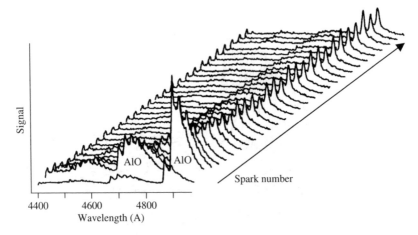

Figure 5.14   AlO emission recorded from repetitively ablating an anodized Al metal plate

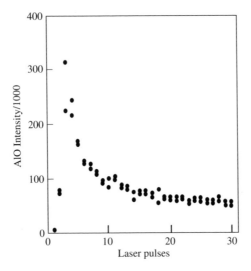

Figure 5.15   Intensity of AlO emission versus shot number for ablation of an anodized Al metal plate

operated at 30 Hz and the laser beam expanded in one dimension to generate a 'long spark' about 12 mm long on the sample. This effectively increases the cleaning rate by a factor of $(30/10\,\text{Hz}) \times (12/6\,\text{mm}) = 6$ so the area of $1300\,\text{cm}^2$ could be cleaned in about 12 min. It should also be pointed out that excimer lasers with pulse repetition rates of 100–200 Hz having beam dimensions larger than those used here could be used to increase the cleaning rate significantly compared with that calculated here.

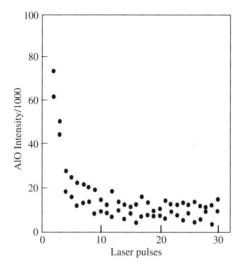

Figure 5.16 Intensity of AlO emission versus shot number for an anodized Al metal plate after removal of anodized area surrounding the ablation region. Compare with data of Figure 5.13

5.4.2.4 Surface Condition after Cleaning

The condition of the aluminum surface after cleaning depends to some extent on the parameters of the laser pulse and how it is focused on the sample. In the experiments described here, there was some reduction in the macroscopic smoothness of the surface as observed visually under a microscope. Much of this roughness occurred at the perimeter of the long sparks and was due to the strong focusing of the laser pulses.

5.4.3 CONCLUSIONS

The work described here has shown that (1) a previously oxidized surface can be efficiently cleaned by scanning the surface with a repetitively pulsed laser beam, (2) the metal surface can be roughened to some extent by the action of the laser pulses, and that (3) the removal of the oxide can be determined spectroscopically by monitoring the O(I) emission in the case of a light or heavily oxidized surface or by monitoring the AlO emission in the case of heavy oxidation. It may also be possible to monitor oxide removal via an increase in emission from the metal lines as the oxide layer is ablated.

5.5 MATERIAL SORTING/DISTINGUISHING

The ability to perform a LIBS measurement using only a single pulse has a number of applications. One application is the sorting of a group of materials according to composition. The speed with which such sorting can be carried out depends on several factors including (1) surface condition of samples in the group, (2) the type of analysis (only major elements or minor elements, trace elements) and (3) the closeness of compositions of samples in the group.

5.5.1   SURFACE CONDITION

Clearly, because LIBS is a surface analysis method, it is important that the surface composition be indicative of the bulk composition. Repeated ablation by a series of laser sparks can be used to ablate away unrepresentative surface layers but this will preclude a rapid analysis. Depending on the surface condition only a few laser ablations may be needed to obtain a representative sample or 10 s or 100 s of ablative shots may be needed. The repetition rate of the laser will of course enter into the analysis as a higher repetition rate laser will allow a more rapid analysis if many ablative pulses are needed to interrogate the bulk sample.

In cases where the bulk composition is of interest, the surface contamination thick and repetitive sampling is not feasible, LIBS can yield ambiguous results. Examples are shown in Figure 5.17. Here we present spectra abstracted from spectral signatures of an aluminum metal substrate. Aluminum samples were retrieved from a recycling operation feedstock and interrogated without cleaning using a single LIBS spark (50 mJ energy pulse) directed at each sample. The clean sample shows only strong emissions from Al lines at 394.4 and 396.1nm. Weathered surface #1 shows some traces of dirt (no loose dirt) on the surface but the underlying aluminum was visible. In this spectrum the strong Al lines are apparent along with weak lines due to strong emissions from Ca, a common contaminant. Sample weathered #2 (clearly dirty, but the underlying surface still visible) shows strong emission from lines attributed to Al (the substrate), Ca (stronger than recorded from weathered #1 relative to Al), Pb and Fe. The Al samples were collected along with other metals and would have come into contact with these metals during handling. The heaviest surface contamination was observed for sample weathered #3 which visually showed heavy accumulation of dirt that completely obscured the surface. The corresponding spectrum shows strong emissions from Ca (stronger than Al, the substrate), Fe and again Pb. The Al emissions are actually weaker in intensity than many of the lines due to other elements. Because the surface was completely obscured for this sample, the origin of the Al emission was from the contaminant(s) rather than the bulk metal.

5.5.2   TYPE OF ANALYSIS

The criteria for sorting materials can be designated at different levels. For example, if the starting group contains a number of materials differing only by a few elements and those elements are minor or trace levels, then the surface condition of the samples will require more averaging to increase data quality to more accurately

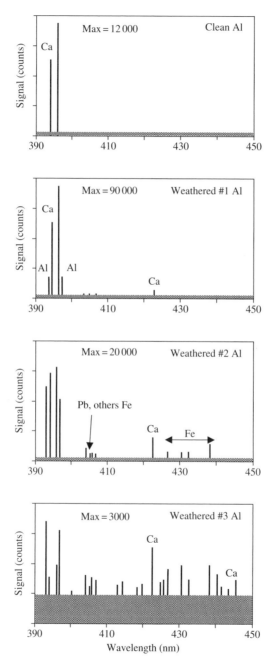

Figure 5.17 LIBS spectra from aluminum metals with different degrees of surface contamination. The grey area indicates the average height of the background intensity

determine the sample composition and to observe differences in concentrations between these elements in the samples which, depending on the sample, may differ by only a few percent. On the other hand, if sorting is to only be carried out at a level corresponding to sorting by only the main element with differences between minor and trace elements unimportant (e.g. ferrous alloys from aluminum alloy and copper alloys) then only a few shots may be needed. This is demonstrated in Figure 5.18 in which a series of nine different metals (Al, Ti, In, Fe, Cu, etc.) were presented to a series of repetitive laser sparks and a single spectrum from a single spark recorded from each sample. As the results show, and detailed analysis of the data verifies, using only a single spectrum, the different metals can be sorted with 100% accuracy. Note that only a small spectral region (317.9 to 418.0 nm) was used for this type of sorting. Other spectral regions could be included to increase the accuracy of sorting and to include other metals not having distinct spectral features in the region displayed in Figure 5.18.

5.5.3   SORTING MATERIALS OF CLOSE COMPOSITION

The more difficult type of analysis is that involving a set of samples having small compositional differences. Examples include steel alloys and aluminum alloys, which can differ by only a few percent in a few elements. Another example occurs with the identification of different rock samples within a type. As shown above, it is relatively easy to discern the differences between different rock types such as

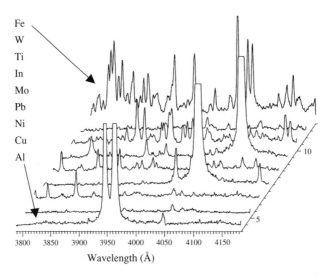

Figure 5.18 Sequential LIBS spectra recorded from nine different metals each 'analyzed' by a single laser plasma at a rate of 19 samples/s. The list of elements corresponds to the order of the spectra shown

Table 5.3 Composition differences between six basalt samples

	Columbia	688 Rock	Olivine	GUW BM	NCS GBW	Hawaiian
Sr (ppm)	346	169.2	468	220	1100	389
Si (%)	79.4	48.4	46.85	49.51	44.64	73.2
Ba (ppm)	683	200	172	250	527	130
Ti (%)	3.61	1.17	1.62	1.14	1.42	4.36
Mn (%)	1.52	0.167	0.15	0.14	1.31	1.29
Ca (%)	12.21	12.17	9.6	6.47	8.81	19.57
Al (%)	20.64	17.36	17.06	16.25	13.83	20.66
Fe (%)	23.46	17.99	10.09	9.67	21	20.93

basalt, dolomite, granite, etc. Sorting materials within a rock type, looking for small compositional differences is more demanding. A simple experiment will demonstrate, however, the use of LIBS for this application. Consider six basalt samples having the compositions listed in Table 5.3. Spectra of these six basalts are presented in Figure 5.19 for the spectral region from 380 to 470 nm. The spectra are overlapped and appear to be very similar. By constructing calibration curves for the six basalts for the elements listed in Table 5.3, linear calibration curves are obtained and the element concentrations for the corresponding basalt sample lie in the correct position on each curve. Representative curves for barium and silicon are shown in Figure 5.20. Using these results, it is possible to unambiguously identify each of the six basalts using the calibration curves.

5.6 SITE SCREENING USING LIBS

LIBS instruments can be readily deployed to evaluate areas for high and low levels of contaminant materials. This includes monitoring the workplace to determine the presence and locations of contaminant dusts (in air and on surfaces) and the screening of soils for toxic materials such as result from mining operations (e.g. Berkely Pit, Montana). LIBS instruments can be readily configured for this application and examples are shown in Figure 5.21. These include instruments that can be transported to a field site to provide on-site analysis in a mobile laboratory or instruments that can be deployed in the field for *in-situ* measurements. The basic design of these instruments follows the general LIBS configuration shown in Figure 3.1. The actual application will determine the type of components used (e.g. laser energy, repetition rate) and the sampling configuration. The instruments shown in Figure 5.21 include a backpack LIBS system that is battery-operated, with the laser mounted in the hand-held probe to directly sample surface or soil contamination. The second device is a transportable LIBS system into which collected samples are introduced and analyzed in less than 1 min by a series of laser plasmas directed at the surface. The third instrument, shown in Figure 5.22, is intermediate to these two instruments. It can be deployed in the laboratory or field and accepts collected samples of about 4 g soil.

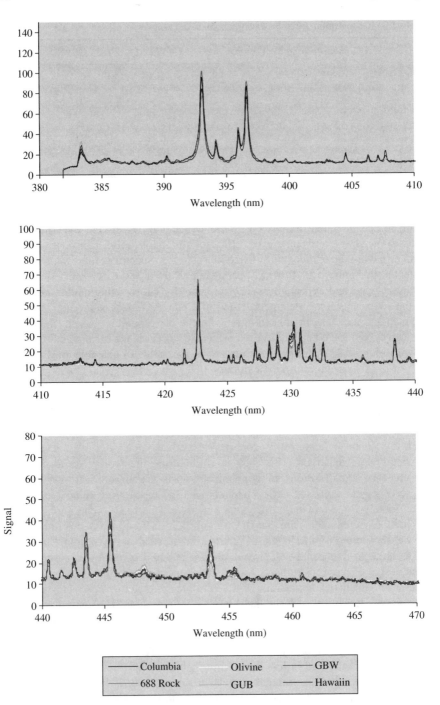

Figure 5.19 Overlapped spectra of six basalts samples (Table 5.3) showing similarity of the spectra

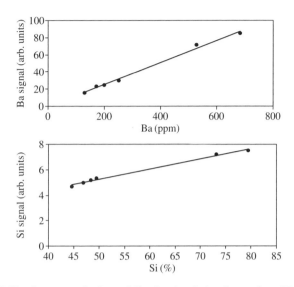

Figure 5.20 Calibration curves for Ba and Si using the six basalt samples of Table 5.3

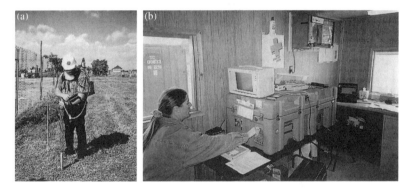

Figure 5.21 (a) Backpack LIBS instrument shown here for direct soil analysis. (b) Transportable LIBS instrument for the analysis of collected samples. Both units were deployed at Luckey, Ohio to characterize a former beryllium processing site. (Photos courtesy of Science and Engineering Associates, Inc.)

Figure 5.22 Portable soil analyzer (ca. 1994). (a) Packaged instrument. (b) Instrument in use. (c) Analysis of loose soil sample. Soil samples are placed in small cup, rotated and analyzed using a compact Nd:YAG laser, a 0.125 m spectrograph, and a CCD

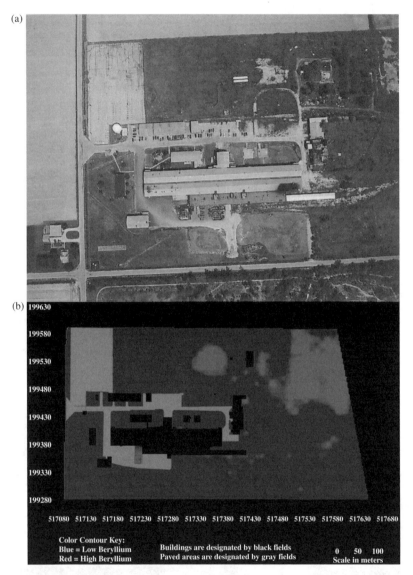

Figure 5.23 (a) Aerial photo of a former beryllium facility at Luckey, Ohio, USA. (b) Map of main features and locations of high and low beryllium concentrations. (Photo and figure courtesy of Science and Engineering Associates, Inc.) (see Plate 9)

Actual screening results are shown in Figure 5.23 (Plate 9). An aerial view of a former beryllium processing plant at Luckey, Ohio is shown together with a map of beryllium contamination throughout the property. This map was produced from data obtained using the instrumentation shown in Figure 5.21. High

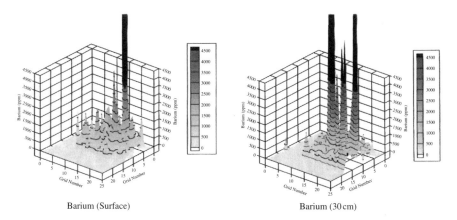

Barium (Surface)   Barium (30 cm)

Figure 5.24 Barium concentrations in soil determined using the field portable LIBS instrument of Figure 5.21(b). The grid refers to spatial position along the area of contamination with the determined concentrations plotted on the vertical axis. Each measurement required about 2 min, including sample exchange in the instrument (see Plate 10)

beryllium concentrations are indicated by red and the blue areas reveal lower level contamination.

Another example of soil screening is shown in Figure 5.24 (Plate 10). An open field area was contaminated by barium nitrate. The area had been exposed to the weather for many years and some of the water soluble compound had leached into the ground. Using the transportable instrument shown in Figure 5.21(b), collected samples were analyzed and maps of barium concentrations at depths down to 30 cm were developed. Two such maps are shown in Figure 5.24.

REFERENCES

Cravetchi, I.V., M. Taschuk, G.W. Rieger, Y.Y. Tsui and R. Fedosejevs (2003). Spectrochemical microanalysis of aluminum alloys by laser-induced breakdown spectroscopy: identification of precipitates. Appl. Opt. 42: 6138–6147.

Cremers, D.A. and L.J. Radziemski (1983). Detection of chlorine and fluorine in air by laser-induced breakdown spectrometry. Anal. Chem. 55: 1252–1256.

Dudragne, L., Ph. Adam and J. Amouroux (1998). Time-resolved laser-induced breakdown spectroscopy: application for qualitative and quantitative detection of fluorine, chlorine, sulfur, and carbon in air. Appl. Spectrosc. 52: 1321–1327.

Jurado-Lopez, A. and M.D. Luque de Castro (2003). Rank correlation of laser-induced breakdown spectroscopic data for the identification of alloys used in jewelry manufacture. Spectrochim. Acta Part B 58: 1291–1299.

Moskal, T.M. and D.W. Hahn (2002). On-line sorting of wood treated with chromated copper arsenate using laser-induced breakdown spectroscopy. Appl. Spectrosc. 56: 1337–1344.

Orzi, D.J.O. and G.M. Bilmes (2004). Identification and measurement of dirt composition of manufactured steel plates using laser-induced breakdown spectroscopy. Appl. Spectrosc. 12: 1475–1480.

Portnov, A., S. Rosenwaks and I. Bar (2003). Identification of organic compounds in ambient air via characteristic emission following laser ablation. J. Lumin. 102–103: 408–413.

Yamamoto, K.Y., D.A. Cremers, L.E. Foster, M.P. Davies and R.D. Harris (2005). LIBS analysis of solids using a long-pulse (150 ns) A-switched Nd: YAG laser. Appl. Spectrosc. 50: 1082–1097.

6 Quantitative LIBS Analysis

6.1 INTRODUCTION

The ultimate goal of any analysis technique is to provide a highly quantitative analysis, that is, to determine with high precision and accuracy the concentration of a species in a sample (e.g. parts-per-million), the absolute mass of a species (for example, ng in a particle), or determine a surface concentration (e.g. ng/cm^2). A quantitative analysis begins with determining the response of a system for a given concentration or mass of the analyte of interest. This usually takes the form of a calibration curve as discussed in Chapter 4. As noted there, the calibration is usually strongly dependent on the analysis conditions. So for quantitative analysis, the conditions used to prepare the calibration curve must be the same when the 'unknown' sample is analyzed. In a LIBS analysis there are many parameters that affect the precision and accuracy of a measurement. Some of these can be controlled, such as the stability of the laser pulse energy, and others are dependent on the sample and sampling procedure over which there may not be a high degree of control. The advantage of LIBS, that materials can be sampled directly with little or no sample preparation, is also a challenge to the method, because the physical and chemical properties of the sample can have a strong effect on the ability to obtain quantitative data. A list of important parameters that affect a LIBS analysis is presented in Table 6.1 and some of these are shown in Figure 6.1.

6.2 EFFECTS OF SAMPLING GEOMETRY

It has been well documented in LIBS measurements that changes in the geometrical aspects of the measurement system can strongly affect analysis results. This includes the methods of focusing the laser pulses on the target and of collecting the plasma light. For example, the power density incident on the sample is a strong function of the lens-to-sample distance (LTSD) and the power density determines, in part, emission line intensities, the relative intensities of lines, and the mass of sample ablated. The dependence of mass ablated from aluminum metal on the LTSD, for laser pulses focused by spherical and cylindrical lenses of 75 mm focal length, is shown in Figure 6.2 (Multari *et al.*, 1996). The mass ablated is clearly a strong

Handbook of Laser-Induced Breakdown Spectroscopy D. Cremers and L. Radziemski
© 2006 John Wiley & Sons, Ltd

Table 6.1 Factors affecting quantitative analysis using LIBS

Source	Factor	Comments
Laser	Laser pulse energy, laser pulse power, repetition rate	Typically stable to within a few percent for constant temperature operation
Detector	Detector gain	Keep constant or calibrate response if gain is changed
	Linearity of response	Operate in region of linear response or change gain to maintain linearity
Sampling parameters	Lens-to-sample distance	May be maintained through an automated focusing system; less a problem for longer focal lengths; use of a collimated beam to form the plasma can minimize effects
	Changes in optical path transmission to/from sample	Absorption/scattering of laser pulse over optical path to sample by gases and aerosols
	Change of atmosphere above sample	Gas pressure and composition affect ablation and plasma properties
Sample	Uniformity of composition	Sufficient averaging to obtain representative sample
	Uniformity of surface	Sufficient averaging to obtain representative sample
	Chemical matrix effects	Under certain experimental conditions, effect may be reduced
	Physical matrix effects	Under certain experimental conditions, effect may be reduced

function of LTSD with the cylindrical lens showing a stronger variation with changes in the sampling geometry. The total mass ablated from the metal was measured in these experiments. It should be noted, however, that the distribution of total ablated sample between atoms and sample mass removed as particles may change with LTSD. Clearly, changes in the distribution of ablated material between atomized sample and particles will affect the observed emission signals.

The plasma temperature is also a function of LTSD as shown in Figure 6.3, again for the two types of lenses and an aluminum metal sample used for Figure 6.2 (Multari et al., 1996). These data were recorded using a fiber optic cable pointed at the plasma formed on the samples to collect light from all parts of the plasma. In addition, the position of the focusing lens was changed rather than the sample position so the geometry between the fiber optic and sample would remain constant for the different LTSD settings. Both lenses show a strong dependence of temperature on LTSD with a temperature variation of about 30% for the spherical lens for the range over which a useful analytical plasma could be formed. As with ablation, the cylindrical lens shows a more restricted range over which a plasma was initiated.

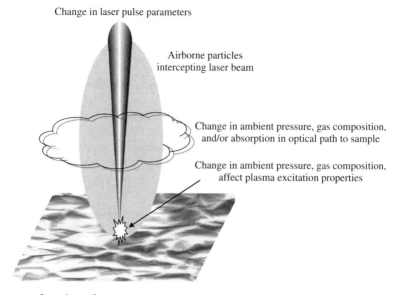

Change in laser pulse parameters

Airborne particles
intercepting laser beam

Change in ambient pressure, gas composition,
and/or absorption in optical path to sample

Change in ambient pressure, gas composition,
affect plasma excitation properties

- Irregular surface
- Changes in surface absorptivity at laser wavelength
- Changes in surface composition with depth and horizontal position
- Composition different from calibration samples

Figure 6.1   Some factors affecting quantitative analysis in LIBS

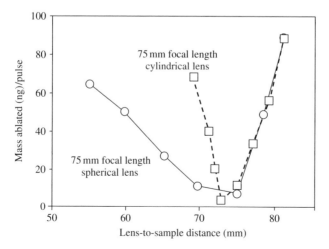

Figure 6.2   Mass ablated from aluminum metal as a function of LTSD for spherical and cylindrical lenses (75 mm focal length). (After Multari *et al.*, 1996, with permission from Society for Applied Spectroscopy)

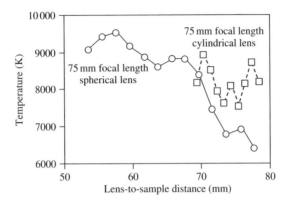

Figure 6.3 Dependence of plasma temperature on LTSD for plasmas formed by spherical and cylindrical lenses (75 mm focal length). (After Multari *et al.*, 1996, with permission from Society for Applied Spectroscopy)

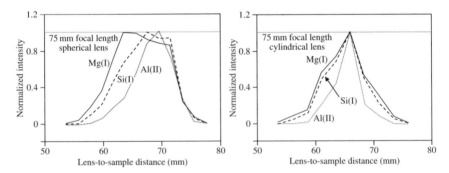

Figure 6.4 Normalized intensities of three emission lines as a function of LTSD. Plasmas were formed by spherical and cylindrical lenses. (After Multari *et al.*, 1996, with permission from Society for Applied Spectroscopy)

The results of a different experiment are shown in Figure 6.4, which contains the normalized dependence of emissions from Al(II), Mg(I) and Si(I) as a function LTSD on soil samples, for the same two lenses (Multari *et al.*, 1996). The emission lines used were 281.62, 285.21 and 288.16 nm, respectively. Samples were soil pressed into a pellet to provide a smooth and uniform surface for analysis. These were translated under the repetitive laser sparks and the spectra were averaged. As the data show in both cases, the emission signals are a strong function of the LTSD for the two lenses, the most intense emissions occurring at a LTSD less than the lens focal length. For the spherical lens, the emission intensities remain above the normalized value of 0.5 over a range of about 14 mm (60 mm < LTSD < 73 mm), while for the cylindrical lens the range is somewhat smaller, about 10 mm (60 mm < LTSD < 69 mm).

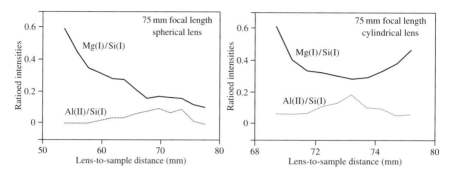

Figure 6.5 Ratioed intensities of two emission lines as a function of LTSD. Plasmas were formed by spherical and cylindrical lenses. (After Multari *et al.*, 1996, with permission from Society for Applied Spectroscopy)

Figure 6.5 shows the intensity ratios of Mg(I)/Si(I) and Al(II)/Si(I) as a function of LTSD for the two lenses. Ideally, the ratio should be independent of LTSD assuming that excitation parameters (e.g. temperature, Figure 6.3) within the plasma change the same for the two species involved in the ratio. The somewhat large variation in the ratio with LTSD shown by these data suggests that the different species are experiencing different excitation with LTSD values.

6.3 OTHER SAMPLING CONSIDERATIONS

The calibration curve is one good diagnostic to probe different matrix effects in LIBS analysis. The dependence of calibration curves on pressure has already been briefly discussed in Chapter 4. Specifically of interest is Figure 4.15, which shows that as the ambient air pressure is reduced, the slope of the calibration changes significantly. With reduced pressure, the slope increases and maximizes for pressures in the region around 10–100 Torr. Then the slope decreases significantly as the pressure is further reduced. The two main competing processes at work here are changes in mass ablated and changes in excitation parameters with pressure (e.g. electron density and temperature; Knight *et al.*, 2000). As the pressure is decreased, the mass of material ablated increases significantly but it levels off for pressures below about 10 Torr. On the other hand, as the pressure is reduced, the excitation of species in the plasma decreases because the collision rate, responsible for excitation in the cooling, decaying plasma, decreases linearly with pressure. The net result of the two competing processes is a peak in element excitation at pressures of a few tens of torr. It must be realized, however, that other factors are at work which also affect the observed element emission intensity. As the pressure is reduced, the atomic species are no longer confined to the initial plasma volume at the surface and they can escape more readily into the region above the surface. At very low pressures, on the order of microns, atoms are ejected from the surface and are quickly transported out of the region of the laser pulse/material interaction zone at the surface. Because of its low mass, hydrogen would escape more quickly than any other element. Under these conditions, after the laser pulse is turned off ($\sim$10 ns for Q-switched Nd:YAG lasers), the excited species may no longer be in the field of view of the light collection system giving an apparent decrease in excitation, which may also be different for different atoms. All of these factors are active and must be considered.

Another interesting effect of pressure is demonstrated by Figure 6.6 (Sallé *et al.*, 2005). Here we show calibration curves for Ca(II) at 393.3 nm for certified

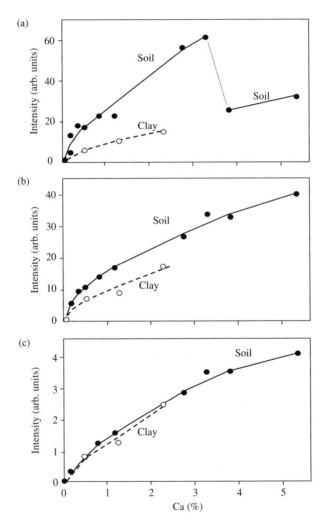

Figure 6.6 Comparison of calibration curves for Mn in soil and clay samples at three pressures. (a) 585 Torr; (b) 7 Torr; (c) 50 mTorr. (After Sallé *et al.*, 2005, with permission from Elsevier)

soil and clay samples at three different pressures. The compositions of these matrices are significantly different with clay samples being characterized by high aluminum content. These data show two interesting effects. First, at 585 Torr (Figure 6.6a), the calibration curves for the two matrices are significantly different with a greater slope observed for the soil sample. As the pressure is reduced, the slopes of both curves decrease but the slope of the curve corresponding to soil decreases to a greater extent compared with the curve for clay. At the lowest pressure, 50 mTorr, the curves appear to overlap. That is, reduced pressure has reduced significantly a matrix effect yielding highly collinear calibration curves.

Secondly, we note that the soil data for the curve at 585 Torr do not show a steady correlation of Ca signal with Ca concentration. The data appear 'noisy' and at the two highest concentrations the correlation breaks down completely. As noted above, however, as the pressure is reduced the soil data become more smoothly correlated and this is especially evident for the two highest Ca concentrations as these values now lie along a smooth calibration curve. At the lowest pressures, the correlation among the soil data becomes even stronger. Clearly, the sampling parameter of ambient pressure significantly affects the analytical results and it does so by reducing some chemical matrix effect.

Because LIBS is a surface analysis method, surface deposits such as weathered layers (Figure 5.1) or dirt (Figure 5.17) can interfere with the determination of the underlying bulk composition. In some cases, repetitive ablation can remove these layers sufficiently to permit sampling of the bulk materials. In addition to such surface effects, the inherent inhomogeneity of the sample can complicate a determination of sample composition. In fact, the question may arise as to what is the true composition of an inhomogeneous sample. Differences in composition can be spatially large so that if 1 mm^3 of a sample was extracted and analyzed the results may be quite different from those obtained by extracting and analyzing a 1 cm^3 volume of the sample. This is demonstrated by the photo of a rhyolite rock surface shown in Figure 6.7 (Plate 11). The close up photo shows visual inhomogeneities in the rock surface that are on the order of 1–3 mm. Because of the typically small size of the focused spot used to form the laser plasma (100–200 μm), the element signals will be strongly dependent on the position of the focal spot on the sample. A long spark, also shown in Figure 6.7, can be used to average over some of these inhomogeneities.

Another example of sampling characteristics is presented in Figure 6.8 which shows the results of scans with a long spark over an aluminum surface contaminated with a Tl containing solution. The features show how the Tl is distributed on the surface. As the sparks are scanned along the surface, emissions from Al and Fe from the metal are clearly evident in the spectral region around 358 nm. As the sparks begin to interrogate the Tl deposited as a solution (then dried) on the plate, strong Tl emissions are observed in combination with a suppression of emissions from the Al and Fe in the substrate. Effectively, the dried deposited solution is inhibiting sampling of the underlying metal: the dried layer is shielding the metal

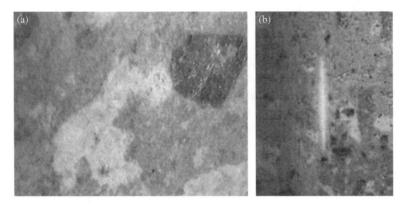

Figure 6.7   (a) Close-up photo of a ground surface of a rhyolite rock sample. Distinct features are 1–2 mm in size. (b) Analysis of the same rock using a long spark (1 cm) to average over inhomogeneities (see Plate 11)

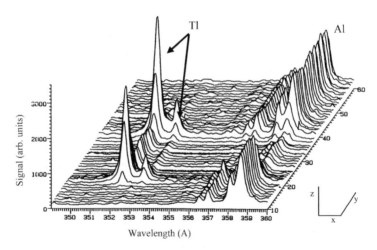

Figure 6.8   Sequential spectra recorded by scanning a series of long laser sparks along an Al metal plate contaminated by a Tl solution. The three lines to the left of the Al line are due to Fe. The location of the Tl is coincident with a suppression of emissions from Al and Fe in the metal. Wavelength (x); shot number (y); signal (z)

surface from the incident laser energy. It is interesting to observe how the Tl signals increase at the start and finish of the scan across the Tl contaminated region. This correlates with a visible inspection of the dried Tl containing solution on the metal, which shows deposition as a ring-shaped pattern on the surface.

6.4   PARTICLE SIZE AND INCOMPLETE VAPORIZATION

Physical factors can affect LIBS analysis. When analyzing a powdered sample or an aerosol, one such factor is particle size. This was demonstrated by one set of experiments. BeCu particles of four different size groups were deposited on filters and interrogated using LIBS. The particles were sized in a cyclone separator, collected and then suspended in water. By placing a known volume of the well-stirred suspension on filter paper (6.4 mm diameter), a known mass was deposited. The actual Be mass in an aliquot of each suspension size was determined by depositing an aliquot of each solution on replicate filters which were then analyzed using ICP analysis.

Six replicate LIBS analyses were performed using a freshly prepared filter for each analysis. The laser pulse energy was 20 mJ. The Be signal data for each particle size group were plotted and are shown in Figure 6.9. There is a strong dependence of the calibration curve slope on particle size (in μm), with the slope increasing as particle size decreases. The results indicate that a greater mass of Be is being accessed as the particle size decreases suggesting a physical matrix effect. If the larger particles are incompletely vaporized, the resulting Be signal will be lower than that obtained from smaller particles that are completely vaporized. The data of Figure 6.9 indicate that the boundary between complete and incomplete vaporization resides around a particle size of about 2 μm. These results agree with a separate determination of complete particle vaporization which indicated that, for 320 mJ, the maximum size particle that could be vaporized is on the order of 2.1 μm (Carranza and Hahn, 2002). Assuming that all laser pulse energy is directed toward ablation, a simple calculation predicts that a copper particle (the major component of BeCu used here) of diameter ~150 μm should be completely ablated by 20 mJ. Therefore, it appears that only a fraction of the laser energy is going into vaporization.

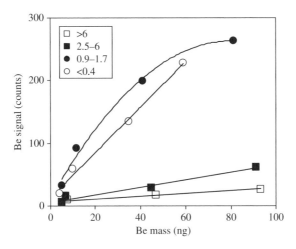

Figure 6.9   Calibration curves for Be(II) at 313.1 nm for different sizes of BeCu metal particles (in μm)

6.5   USE OF INTERNAL STANDARDIZATION

As discussed in Chapter 4, use of an internal standard can often minimize shot-to-shot variations in the LIBS emission signal, increasing measurement precision and correcting nonlinear behavior in calibration curves. The LIBS signal in this case is the analyte signal ratioed to the emission from the internal standard element. This correction was demonstrated in Figure 4.12. Another example of the use of an internal standard is shown in Figure 6.10. To obtain these data, a series

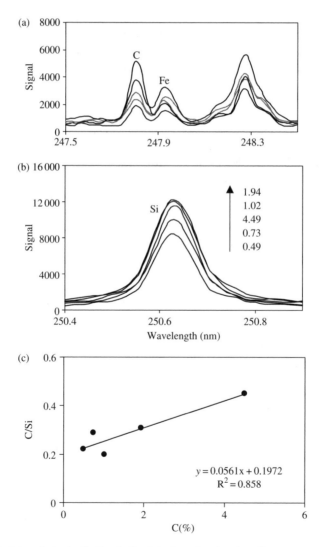

Figure 6.10   Internal standardization in the detection of carbon in soil

of soil samples from approximately the same geographical location were collected, homogenized, and then analyzed by a conventional combustion analysis method to determine total carbon content. The values found for the different samples were 0.49, 0.73, 1.02, 1.94 and 4.49 wt%. These samples were then analyzed using the laser plasma from pressed samples of each member of the collected soil series. The C(I) line at 247.86 nm was recorded simultaneously with the Si(I) line at 250.6 nm using an echelle spectrograph. These emissions are shown in Figure 6.10 for each of the five samples. Silicon was assumed to be at a constant concentration in the soils as the samples were obtained from approximately the same location. The carbon content will vary more widely than silicon with changes in location due to processes such as plant growth and decay which produce large changes in carbon content over a small area.

Figure 6.10(a) shows the carbon and iron signals for the five samples. The spectra as grey lines are out of order with respect to the carbon concentration in the samples. The carbon peak should increase in intensity with carbon concentration in the soil. Figure 6.10(b) shows the silicon signal for the different samples. The curves are labeled as indicated by the arrow according to the corresponding carbon content of the soil sample. Ideally, the silicon signals would overlap to a high degree showing concentration uniformity in the samples but here we see that there is a strong variation in the silicon signal with the sample. This is true even though the experimental conditions were kept constant for all measurements and the variation was attributed to differences in ablation and plasma excitation occurring during the different analyses. Figure 6.10(c) shows the resulting carbon calibration curve using silicon as an internal standard. The results indicate that even though the carbon signals do not monotonically increase with carbon content and the silicon signal, the internal standard, varies strongly from sample to sample, a usable, though not perfect, calibration curve can be prepared using internal standardization.

6.6   CHEMICAL MATRIX EFFECTS

The effect of different species on the analyte in the LIBS plasma is a manifestation of a chemical matrix effect. Other plasma sources exhibit matrix effects but the LIBS plasma can be highly sensitive to these because of the high density of material in the plasma. It is well known that in some plasma sources the introduction of an easily ionizable element, such as cesium, can move the neutral – ion equilibrium concentration of an analyte toward the neutral species (e.g. Le Chatelier's principle). The increase in electron concentration introduced by the easily ionizable element will increase electron–ion recombination and hence result in a greater number of neutral species (Eppler *et al.*, 1996).

A good example of a matrix effect is shown in Figure 6.11. Here we show LIBS data for Mn(I) (set of lines around 403 nm) obtained using certified stream sediment samples and synthetic silicate samples. The concentrations of the major elements in the sediment samples vary from sample to sample but the concentrations of these

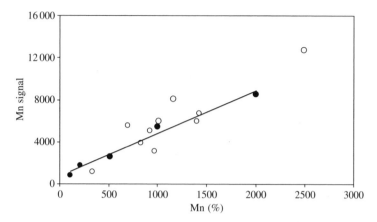

Figure 6.11 Calibration curve for Mn in (open circles) sediments and (closed circles) synthetic silicate samples. The linear fit is to the (closed circles) data

same elements in the synthetic silicate samples remain constant. Major element concentrations for both sample matrices are listed in Table 6.2 with the ranges of major species for the sediment samples listed as they are sample dependent. The data of Figure 6.11 show that greater correlation between Mn signal and Mn concentration was obtained using the constant matrix composition of the synthetic silicates compared with the sediment samples. These data suggest that the variations in the major element concentrations of the sediment samples perturb the Mn emission intensities precluding a high correlation between signal and concentration.

LIBS measures the total abundance of an element in a sample because the plasma breaks down the original target sample into its component parts (e.g. F-atom counting, Section 5.3). In principle, all information about the starting material structure and bonding is lost. It has been shown, however, that the signals obtained from an element depend on the compound form of the starting material (Eppler *et al.*, 1996). A simple example of this is shown in Figure 6.12. Here we show signals from Pb(I) (405.7 nm) and Ba(II) (233.5 nm) compounds ratioed to C(I) (247.8 nm) and Cr (425.4 nm). Masses of the compounds were added to the soil so the concentration

Table 6.2 Major elements in synthetic silicate and stream sediment samples

Sample	Major species (wt%)									
	SiO_2	Al_2O_3	Fe_2O_3	$CaMg(CO_3)_2$	Na_2SO_4	K_2SO_4	Na_2O	K_2O	CaO	MgO
Synthetic silicates (all)	72	15	4	4	2.5	2.5	—	—	—	—
Sediments (range)	32–75	10–29	2–13	—	—	—	0.1–3.3	0.2–3.4	0.2–8.3	0.3–2.4

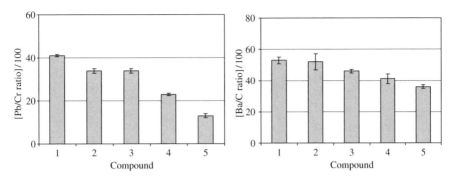

Figure 6.12 Dependence of Pb(I) and Ba(II) signals on compound form in a solid matrix. For Pb(I): 1, -O; 2, -CO_3; 3, -Cl_2; 4, -SO_4; 5, $(NO_3)_2$. For Ba(I): 1, - CO_3; 2, -O; 3, -SO_4; 4, -Cl_2; 5, $(NO_3)_2$. (Data from Eppler *et al.*, 1996)

of the analyte was constant. The precision bars indicate one standard deviation from a set of six replicate measurements. As the data show, the Ba(II) and Pb(I) signals depend on the compound when ideally they should be comparable. The source of these differences could be due to a chemical matrix effect in which the element constituents of the counter ions (e.g. CO_3, Cl_2SO_4, etc.) in the compounds change the excitation and emission characteristics of Ba(II) and Pb(I). Alternatively, the differences could be due to difference in the mass of each compound ablated because of the different heat capacities, vaporization temperatures, and/or absorption at the laser wavelength, characteristic of the different compounds.

6.7 EXAMPLE OF LIBS MEASUREMENT: IMPURITIES IN LITHIUM SOLUTIONS

The report presented below demonstrates the procedures, analyses and results used to evaluate LIBS for the detection of impurities in LiCl solutions. The report was prepared for an industrial sponsor and was aimed at benchmarking LIBS capabilities. Of particular importance was the ability to perform such measurements on samples contained in a sealed environment, such as a processing stream with no direct physical access. The results demonstrate many aspects and characteristics of a quantitative LIBS study. Certain aspects of LIBS measurements discussed in other chapters of this book (e.g. Chapter 4), such as self-absorption, spectral interferences, and the calculation of precision and detection limits are demonstrated.

6.7.1 OBJECTIVE

The objective of this study was to assess the analytical capabilities of LIBS for the detection of impurities contained in aqueous solutions of 10 M LiCl.

The impurities are Ca, Mg, Si, CI, K, Na, Fe, Cr, Ni and C. This report describes: (1) the experimental instrumentation and test methods used for LIBS measurements; (2) calibration curves for each impurity over the range 50–2000 ppm; and (3) detection limits and measurement precision for each impurity over the concentration range of interest.

6.7.2 EXPERIMENTAL

6.7.2.1 Apparatus

The experimental set-up used for the LIBS measurements is shown in Figure 6.13. The pulses from a Q-switched laser were focused on the surface of the solutions contained in sealed quartz vials through the side of the vial as shown. Surface excitation was used instead of forming the laser spark in the bulk liquid because of previous indications of improved detection limits. The light from the spark was collected by a lens and imaged onto the entrance slit of a spectrograph. The spectrally resolved light was detected by a time-gated intensified photodiode array. A pulse generator was used to trigger the laser and to send a gate pulse to the detector head. The gate pulse determined the time interval over which the detector collected light from the spark. This interval was in most cases 2–200 μs after spark formation. In this way, the strong background continuum radiation from the plasma, which occurs within the first few microseconds after spark initiation, was eliminated from the measurements. The experimental equipment and conditions are listed in Table 6.3.

6.7.2.2 Preparation of Solutions

The solutions were prepared in the following manner. First, a large volume of a 10 M solution of LiCl/water was prepared from analytical grade powders of the salts and deionized water. Then, smaller volumes of each of these solutions were measured out and known masses of analytical grade powdered salts containing each of the impurities were weighed out and dissolved in the LiCl volumes to produce a

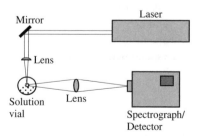

Figure 6.13 LIBS apparatus to evaluate the detection of impurities in Li-containing solutions

Table 6.3 Experimental conditions for LIBS experiments

Laser	Quanta-Ray DCR-1A, Nd:YAG
Wavelength	1064 nm
Pulse length	10 ns
Pulse energy	200 mJ
Repetition rate	10 Hz
Optics	
Focusing lens	2.54 cm diameter, 5 cm focal length
Imaging lens	quartz, 2 in. diameter, 10 cm focal length
Detection system	
Spectrograph	0.5 m focal length, SPEX Industries
Gratings	1200, 2400 and 3600 lines/mm
Detector	Tracor Northern TN-6500 controller with TN-6132 photodiode array
Vials	Analabs, type 35 quartz spectrometer cell (50 mm diameter × 50 mm long)

2000 ppm solution. Portions of these solutions were then diluted with the portions of the master LiCl solutions to give impurity solutions having concentrations of 50, 100, 200, 400 and 800 ppm. Only one impurity was present in each solution (i.e. the impurities were not mixed). For the LIBS measurements, a fixed volume of each solution was put into a clean vial and sealed. Keeping the volume constant maintained the distance between the liquid surface and focusing lens constant.

6.7.2.3 Experimental Procedure

Calibration Curves

Calibration curves were prepared by measuring the emission signal averaged from 600 laser sparks formed on the surface of each solution containing a specific impurity over the 50–2000 ppm concentration range. The photodiode array controller automatically averaged the spectra as they were accumulated and calculated the area under the emission peak. The area of the peak obtained by analyzing each of the six different solutions for a specific impurity was plotted against impurity concentration to produce a calibration curve. A curve was prepared for each impurity in this way.

A list of the analytical lines used for each impurity is presented in Table 6.4. These lines are, in general, those that give the maximum detection sensitivity in emission spectrochemical analysis. Compared with other elements, lithium has few emission lines and the strongest unresolved emissions of Li(I) at 670.78 and 670.79 nm did not interfere with detection of the impurity atoms examined here.

Measurement Precision

The precision of the LIBS measurements was determined by performing ten replicate measurements of the impurity signals at high and low concentrations and calculating

Table 6.4   Analytical lines of impurity elements

Element	Line (nm)	Element	Line (nm)
Ca	393.37 (II)	Na	589.59 (I)
Mg	279.55 (II)	Fe	248.33 (I)
Si	288.16 (I)	Cr	267.716 (I)
Cl	837.59 (I)	Ni	231.60 (II)
K	766.49 (I)	C	247.86 (I)

(I), neutral atom; (II), once-ionized atom.

the standard deviation. Elemental signals were averaged from 200, 600 and 1800 laser sparks corresponding to measurement times of 0.33, 1 and 3 min, respectively.

Detection Limits

The limit of detection (LOD) was determined by computing the slope (m) of the calibration curve ($\Delta c / \Delta x$, where x is the signal) at low concentrations and using the formula LOD $= 2sm$, where s is the standard deviation of 10 measurements made for a specific impurity at the lowest concentration of 50 ppm (Chapter 4).

6.7.3   RESULTS

6.7.3.1   General Considerations

Typical spectra obtained for this report are shown in Figure 6.14. Here the strong emissions from once-ionized Mg are clearly evident in Figure 6.14(a) obtained by averaging the light from 100 sparks. The detector gate was set so the spark light from 1 to 201 μs after spark formation was integrated. Emissions from Li(I) and Mg(I) are also evident in the spectrum. The spectrum shown in Figure 6.14(b) was obtained by integrating the light from 10 to 210 μs. The intensities of the Mg(II) lines shown here relative to the Li(I) and Mg(I) lines are much less than that shown in the spectrum in Figure 6.14(a). This demonstrates the general rule that lines from ions decay more rapidly than neutral lines as the plasma cools. Figure 6.15 shows the spectrum obtained from a 250 ppm Ni in 10 M LiCl solution (Figure 6.15a) and the spectrum recorded from a 'pure' 10 M LiCl solution (Figure 6.15b) over the same spectral region. The Ni emission lines are clearly evident and no 'background' spectral features are present from the solution containing only LiCl. Figure 6.16 shows the spectrum obtained from a 250 ppm Cr in 10 M LiCl solution (Figure 6.16a) and the spectrum obtained from a 10 M LiCl solution (Figure 6.16b) over the same spectral region. Two Cr lines are completely free of spectral interferences but a strong Li line interferes with a strong Cr line in this spectral region.

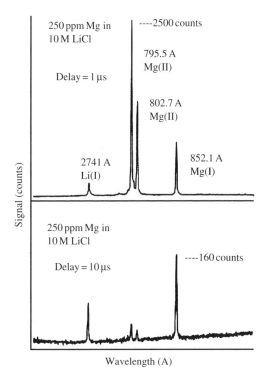

Figure 6.14 LIBS spectrum of Mg lines at two delay times. Sample was Mg in a LiCl solution

Analysis of carbon with LIBS presented a problem at the carbon concentrations of interest here. Carbon signals were obtained from a 'pure' solution of 10 M LiCl and even from deionized water. The latter was attributed to excitation of carbon dioxide in the air above the solution. This carbon signal was reduced significantly by purging the vial with argon gas before sealing it prior to analysis. A strong residual carbon signal was obtained from the 10 M LiCl solution even when it was purged with argon gas. Initially, this emission signal was attributed to a somewhat strong Li(I) line located at 247.5 nm but the dispersion of the detection system was such that features 0.3 nm apart [the C(I) line lies at 247.8 nm] were easily identifiable as distinct lines. Therefore, the carbon signal in the LiCl solution was attributed to carbon impurities in the powder used to prepare the solution.

6.7.3.2 Calibration Curves

Calibration curves for the LIBS measurements are presented in Figures 6.17, 6.18 and 6.19. The elemental signals have been normalized to the signal measured at the

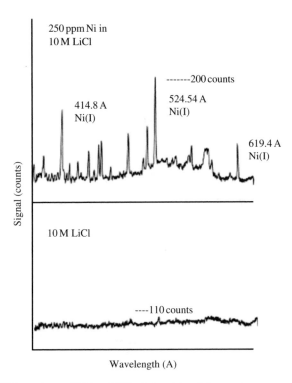

Figure 6.15 LIBS spectrum of Ni in a LiCl solution (a) and the spectrum recorded from the neat LiCl solution (b)

highest concentration of 2000 ppm studied here. In most cases, the calibration curves are linear over the range shown. The two exceptions are calcium and carbon. At high calcium concentrations, the calibration curve shows a loss of sensitivity (slope) which is probably due to self-absorption. The calibration curve for carbon shows a loss of sensitivity at low concentrations. This is probably due to a background carbon signal from carbon in the atmosphere above the solution in the vial which could not be eliminated completely and carbon impurity believed to be in the LiCl powder as discussed above. Chlorine could not be detected in these solutions even at concentrations as high as 2000 ppm. This is probably due to the high energy (10.4 eV) of the strong IR neutral chlorine transition normally used for analytical work and the weaker excitation obtained by forming the spark on a liquid.

6.7.3.3 Precision

The precision of the LIBS measurements is presented in Table 6.5. The values listed in this table are a compilation of results obtained for the different impurities. In general, the same range of measurement precision was obtained for the different

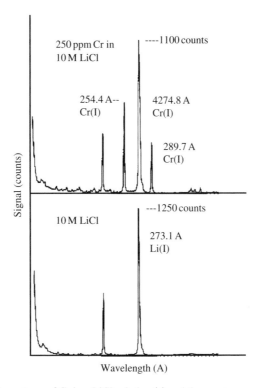

Figure 6.16 LIBS spectrum of Cr in a LiCl solution (a) and the spectrum recorded from the neat 10 M LiCl solution (b). Two Cr lines are completely free of spectral interferences but a strong Li line interferes with a Cr line in this spectral region

Table 6.5 Measurement precision

Integration period (sparks)	Precision (%)
200	5–8
600	4–6
1800	1–3

impurities and no distinct trends were observed (i.e. in repeated measurements, no impurity appeared to yield better measurement precision than another impurity) indicating the measurement precision obtained was characteristic of LIBS itself. As expected, there was an increase in precision as the integration period (number of sparks or elapsed time) increased.

6.7.3.4 Detection Limits

The detection limits for the different impurities are listed in Table 6.6.

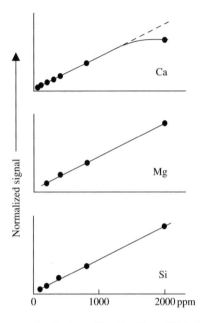

Figure 6.17 Calibration curves for the impurities Ca, Mg and Si in LiCl solutions

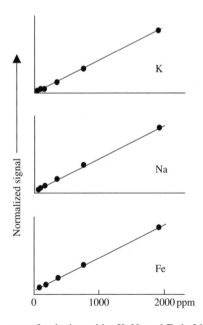

Figure 6.18 Calibration curves for the impurities K, Na and Fe in LiCl solutions

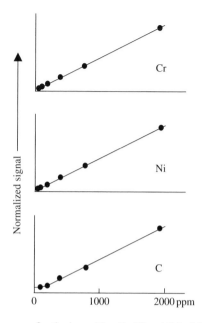

Figure 6.19 Calibration curves for the impurities Cr, Ni and C in LiCl solutions

Table 6.6 Detection limits (in ppm) for impurities in LiCl solutions

Impurity	LOD	Impurity	LOD
Ca	1	Na	0.02
Mg	200	Fe	20
Si	60	Cr	20
Cl	–	Ni	20
K	1	C	50

LOD, limit of detection.

6.7.4 DISCUSSION OF RESULTS

The LIBS detection limits determined for many impurities are sufficiently low to meet requirements of certain applications. The detection of carbon, however, one important impurity, will be compromised for analyses conducted in air. In addition, the analyses are sufficiently rapid to provide for real-time continuous monitoring. Because the surface of the solution is significantly agitated by the shock waves set-up by the spark, the mass of sample analyzed varies from spark to spark. This can be averaged out of the measurements to some degree by averaging a large number of sparks for each measurement.

The advantages of the LIBS method are its noninvasive and remote detection capabilities. Samples can be analyzed in place, all that is required is optical access to the material to form the spark and collect the emitted light. For maximum measurement accuracy, the LIBS method must be periodically calibrated using standards similar to the unknown solutions to be determined. A method must be developed to introduce the calibration samples into the sealed environment containing the unknown samples. There are many variables that depend on experimental conditions that can affect the excitation properties of the plasma. For example, it has been shown that the LTSD is critical in LIBS analysis so the calibration samples must be introduced in such a way as to duplicate this parameter.

6.8   REPORTED FIGURES-OF-MERIT FOR LIBS MEASUREMENTS

LIBS analytical figures-of-merit (FOM) have been reported in the literature for a variety of samples under different measurement conditions. The majority of these measurements have been conducted in the laboratory but there have been some reports of tests done in the field with LIBS results compared with analyses obtained using conventional methods. An extensive list of detection limits derived from the LIBS literature is presented in Appendix C. When reviewing this list it should be noted that detection limits were determined in different ways, some based on the procedures of Chapter 4, and with others estimated based on the signal to noise ratio at one concentration. In addition, specific experimental parameters (e.g. laser pulse energy, delay times, etc.) varied between different studies. The literature reference should be consulted for specific information regarding the detection limit computation.

In determining LIBS accuracy, the LIBS result must be compared against the true or assumed concentration of an element in the sample. Care must be exercised in comparing such results, with special consideration given to evaluating the method or methods used to determine the 'accepted true' concentration in a sample (Section 4.6). For example, some accepted methods of determining elements in soils do not necessarily access all forms of the element. These may only determine the concentration of the element that is in a certain oxidation state with the other oxidation states representing compounds that are not accessed by the analytical technique. LIBS, however, accesses all forms of an element. In such cases, the LIBS value can be expected to be higher that the value determined by the other method.

The accuracy of LIBS has been determined less often than measurement precision and detection limits but there are several reports that show the capability of LIBS using different data reduction methods. For example, Figure 6.20 presents data obtained from the analysis of standard reference materials (SRMs; Colao *et al.*, 2004) using calibration-free LIBS (CF-LIBS), a method discussed in Section 8.3.

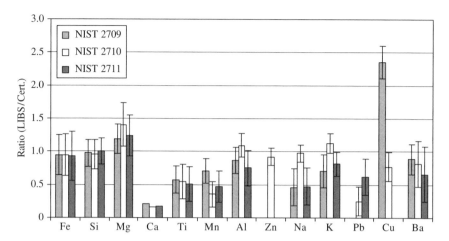

Figure 6.20 Display of LIBS accuracy using certified standard reference materials. (Data from Colao *et al.*, 2004)

The SRMs were powdered samples having a high uniformity of composition with the accepted true values of element concentrations determined by several methods and then averaged. Using such samples represents a good test of LIBS analysis capabilities. Plotted in Figure 6.20 is the predicted element concentration divided by the certified concentration. Ideally, the ratios will be unity but we note there is element dependent deviation from this value. The precision bar on each result denotes the ± uncertainty in the predicted values indicated by the authors. The underestimations of the concentrations of Ca, Na and K were attributed to saturation of the observed emission lines although an effort was made to exclude lines known to exhibit strong saturation effects from the analysis. The data show that the best correlations were obtained for the major elements Fe, Si and Mg.

The same authors, using CF-LIBS and mineral samples, compared LIBS results with those obtained by SEM-EDX (scanning electron microscope equipped with an energy dispersive x-ray spectrometry micro-analytical tool). These results are shown in Figure 6.21 plotted in the same way as described for Figure 6.20.

In data from another study, LIBS results for Antarctic sediments were compared with certified values (Lazic *et al.*, 2001). These results are presented in Table 6.7. The accuracy error was computed according to Equation (4.5) except the absolute value was not included to show over- and underestimations of the concentrations. The predicted concentrations were based on an algorithm that takes into account self-absorption and contributions from regions in the plasmas with different densities resulting in a model that corrects for nonlinearity between emission intensities

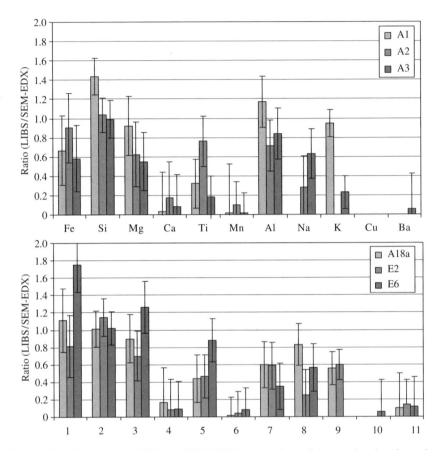

Figure 6.21 Comparison of LIBS and SEM-EDX determinations of elements in mineral samples. (Data from Colao *et al.*, 2004). The labels A1, A2, etc. refer to different samples

and element concentrations. The achieved accuracy was related to the element type and its concentration in the samples as well as the number of samples used to develop the initial calibration data. Elements at high concentrations (Na and Al) were underpredicted and this was related to incomplete correction for self-absorption in the outer plasma layers. The high value obtained for zinc was attributed to some overlap of the Zn line with adjacent strong intensity emission lines.

In another test of LIBS analysis accuracy, or at least, correspondence with accepted analysis methods, on-line continuous monitoring was demonstrated for emissions from incinerators (Buckley *et al.*, 2000). The LIBS plasma was generated in the exhaust stream of the incinerators and metals were injected into the exhaust stream for analysis. Along with *in situ* LIBS sampling, exhaust samples were

Table 6.7 Accuracy of LIBS measurements for Antarctic reference sediments (Lazic *et al.*, 2001)

Element	Certified concentration (ppm)	Accuracy error (%)	Element	Certified concentration (%)	Accuracy error (%)
Zn	53.3	+40	Na	1.97	−32
Ni	9.56	10	Mg	1.52	−14
Mn	446	−5	Fe	2.44	−17
Cr	42.1	2	Ca	1.58	6
Ba	464	1	Al	6.71	−35

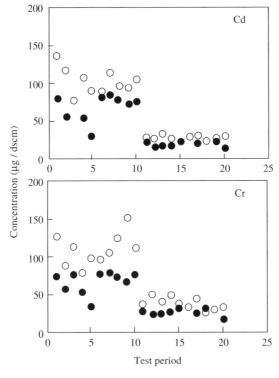

Figure 6.22 LIBS analysis results compared with Method 29 for *in situ* monitoring of elements in an incinerator. LIBS (open circles) and Method 29 (closed circles) data. (Data from Buckley *et al.*, 2000). dscm, dry standard cubic meters

removed and element concentrations were determined using EPA Method 29 (EPA Multi-Metals Sampling Train). The results for cadmium and chromium are shown in Figure 6.22. Each test period corresponded to 1 h of system operation. Each measurement involved averaging spectra from 600 laser plasmas.

Depending on the test period, the results show moderate or high discrepancy between the LIBS measurements and those made using Method 29. On the other hand, in general, the trends in the airborne concentrations of these two elements and other elements monitored tracked reasonably well with the changes determined using Method 29. The overall results for all elements monitored indicate an average difference or accuracy error between the two methods of 63% with beryllium showing the greatest deviation. If the beryllium results were excluded, the overall difference was reduced to 37%.

6.9   CONCLUSIONS

LIBS can be used to provide quantitative analysis of a variety of samples in many settings, both in the laboratory and in the field. As shown here by example, however, each application has some unique characteristics which must be dealt with in order to optimize performance. As the practice of LIBS develops, procedures for obtaining quantitative results reproducibly will be developed, probably for the easiest cases first. These would likely be analysis of metals under reproducible conditions, in a quasi-laboratory environment. Quantitative measurements in the field will likely be the most difficult situation. Nevertheless the method has prospects for providing some information rapidly in field conditions, which cannot be said of most other analytical techniques.

REFERENCES

Buckley, S.G., H.A. Johnsen, K.R. Hencken and D.W. Hahn (2000). Implementation of laser-induced breakdown spectroscopy as a continuous emissions monitor for toxic metals. Waste Manage. 20: 455–462.

Carranza, J.E. and D.W. Hahn (2002). Assessment of the upper particle size limit for quantitative analysis of aerosols using laser-induced breakdown spectroscopy. Anal. Chem. 74: 5450–5454.

Colao, F, R. Fantoni, V. Lazic, A. Paolini, F. Fabbri, G.G. Ori, L. Marinangeli and A. Baliva (2004). Investigation of LIBS feasibility for in situ planetary exploration: an analysis on Martian rock analogues. Planet. Space Sci. 52: 117–123.

Eppler, A.S., D.A. Cremers, D.D. Hickmott, M.J. Ferris and A.C. Koskelo (1996). Matrix effects in the detection of Pb and Ba in soils using laser-induced breakdown spectroscopy. Appl. Spectrosc. 50: 1175–1181.

Knight, A.K., N.L. Scherbarth, D.A. Cremers and M.J. Ferris (2000). Characterization of laser-induced breakdown spectroscopy (LIBS) for application to space exploration. Appl. Spectrosc. 54: 331–340.

Lazic, V., R. Barbini, F. Colao, R. Fantoni and A. Palucci (2001). Self-absorption model in quantitative laser induced breakdown spectroscopy measurements on soil and sediments. Spectrochim. Acta Part B 56: 807–820.

Multari, R.A., L.E. Foster, D.A. Cremers and M.J. Ferris (1996). The effects of sampling geometry on elemental emissions in laser-induced breakdown spectroscopy. Appl. Spectrosc. 50: 1483–1499.

Sallé, B., D.A. Cremers, S. Maurice and R.C. Wiens (2005). Laser-induced breakdown spectroscopy for space exploration applications: influence of the ambient pressure on the calibration curves prepared from soil and clay samples. Spectrochim. Acta Part B 60: 479–490.

7 Remote LIBS Measurements

7.1 INTRODUCTION

Remote measurements using LIBS are carried out in three ways. In the first method, the laser beam is directed over an open path (through air, gas or vacuum) to the target on which a plasma is formed and then the plasma light is collected at a distance. The distances achievable depend on the method of forming the plasma (conventional focusing using a lens or mirror system or femtosecond-induced 'filamentation') and on the method of collecting the plasma light. Even though a robust plasma may be formed, sufficient light must be collected to record a useful spectrum. This method puts severe requirements on laser, optics and detection system performance. In the second method, the laser pulses are injected into a fiber optic and transported to the remotely located target sample. The pulses exiting the fiber are focused to form a plasma on the adjacent sample and the plasma light is collected using the same fiber optic or a second fiber. The advantages of these two methods are that the LIBS instrumentation (laser, spectrograph and detector) can be located at a distance from the target. This opens up a range of new applications for the technique and for this reason remote LIBS analysis has been an area of intense activity in recent years. In the third method, less often used than the other methods, a compact probe containing a small laser is positioned next to the remotely located sample and the plasma light is sent back to the detection system over a fiber optic cable.

Advantages common to all remote LIBS methods are:

- Ability to analyze targets located in certain environments where access by personnel and/or nondisposable equipment is limited (e.g. areas of contamination by toxic, radioactive materials or a confined area).
- Application to process control where analysis must be done rapidly and from a distance (e.g. molten metals and glasses).

Open path LIBS has the added advantages of:

- analysis of physically inaccessible targets (e.g. geological features on cliff faces);
- interrogation of targets located in hazardous environments where any physical access is prohibited but optical access is possible (e.g. through a window on a glove box);

Handbook of Laser-Induced Breakdown Spectroscopy   D. Cremers and L. Radziemski
© 2006 John Wiley & Sons, Ltd

- rapid analysis of distinct, widely separated targets from a single vantage point;
- screening of large surfaces by scanning laser pulses along a surface;
- no possibility of damage to or contamination of equipment by locally harsh environments.

Fiber optic LIBS has the advantages of:

- reduced requirements on instrument performance in comparison with the laser (e.g. greater pulse energies) and optical system (high light collection efficiency) required for open path LIBS;
- direct line of sight to the target is not required;
- shielding of personnel from the open path laser beam;
- greater stand-off distances possible than with open path LIBS.

Compact probe fiber optic LIBS has the advantages of:

- high beam quality delivered to the adjacent target by laser pulses directed to the sample without the use of a fiber optic;
- higher pulse powers can be directed onto the target compared with fiber delivery;
- no damage to fiber optic by high power laser pulses;
- lower pulse energies can be used as the laser pulse is focused directly onto the adjacent target;
- shielding of personnel from open path laser beam;
- greater stand-off distances possible than with open path LIBS.

Open path, remote laser-based spectroscopic measurements have been carried out for many years under the umbrella name of LIDAR (light detection and ranging). These measurements include elastic scattering, absorption, fluorescence and Raman spectroscopy, which offer particle and molecular detection at distances exceeding a kilometer. LIBS has not been included in LIDAR because until recently, these measurements have been restricted to a maximum distance of only a few tens of meters. Recent developments, however, aim to extend the range to a kilometer or more in the near future. Because LIBS is an element detection method, it will provide a new capability to LIDAR methods, complementing the chemical molecular information available from current LIDAR methods.

Of all the remote LIBS techniques, open path LIBS is of particular interest because measurements can be carried out in a truly 'stand-off' mode without any intrusion into the sample region. The only requirement is line-of-sight optical access. In contrast, remote LIBS with a fiber optic and conventional methods of elemental analysis require that some physical device, be it a source and/or detector, be positioned adjacent to the sample or that the sample be retrieved and then transported to the analyzer. Such conventional analysis methods include electrode spark and arc spectroscopy which use metal electrodes, the inductively coupled plasma which sustains the continuous plasma using RF power directed into a coil, and x-ray fluorescence which requires that the source and detector be close to the target. These requirements limit the use of these methods for some important applications and often increase analysis times. In contrast, the unique capability of open path LIBS, combined with the other LIBS advantages, opens up exciting new applications of the technology that cannot be addressed by any other elemental analysis methods.

Two different methods of open path LIBS measurements have been demonstrated which generate the analytical plasmas based on different physical processes. The first method demonstrated we call 'conventional remote LIBS' in which the laser pulse is focused onto the target by a lens or mirror-based optical system to produce power densities sufficiently high to induce ablation and form the microplasma. This method typically has used nanosecond laser pulses with the required energy dependent on the target distance and the characteristics of the optical system. Conventional open path LIBS has been demonstrated at a range of 80 m using nanosecond lasers typically used for *in-situ* LIBS. The second method employs nonlinear processes induced by the high power densities achievable using femtosecond laser pulses. The properties of these pulses can be tailored to form self-guided 'filaments' in a transparent medium (e.g. air) that will propagate over long distances and produce LIBS excitation of a sample. Currently, this method requires the use of large sophisticated laser systems but it has the potential to extend LIBS analysis capabilities to very long distances with kilometer ranges predicted.

Because LIBS uses powerful lasers to generate the laser plasma, extreme care must be taken in deploying LIBS systems for remote analysis. The laser pulse can represent an ocular and skin hazard to the public and the operator and can serve as an ignition source for explosive/flammable materials. Safety concerns are especially paramount for open path LIBS where it may be difficult to control access to the laser beam. The hazards will generally increase as the path length increases and procedures should be developed to ensure the safe use of all remote LIBS systems. These concerns may preclude the use of remote LIBS in some cases. Other safety issues associated with LIBS are discussed in Appendix A.

7.2   CONVENTIONAL OPEN PATH LIBS

7.2.1   APPARATUS

The vast majority of open path LIBS measurements have been conducted using the 'conventional' method of forming the plasma at a distance. A generalized apparatus is shown in Figure 7.1.

Two important requirements of remote conventional LIBS are (1) generating a robust plasma at distance and (2) collecting sufficient light for analysis. These requirements put constraints on the specifications of the laser, optical system, spectrograph and detector. As the distance increases, system requirements become more critical.

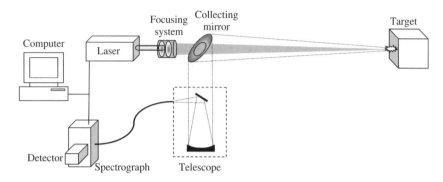

Figure 7.1 Schematic of a LIBS system for conventional open path, remote LIBS

Figure 7.2 Demonstration of stand-off LIBS using a laboratory instrument to interrogate a cliff bank. The spark is shown in the inset. The distance was 24 m between the spark and the optical system (focusing and light collection) (see Plate 12)

The visual appearance of the laser plasma formed on a cliff face is shown in Figure 7.2 (Plate 12). This plasma was formed at a distance of 24 m using a laboratory Nd:YAG laser (10 Hz, 300 mJ/pulse). At this distance, useful spectra were recorded using a 100 mm diameter collection lens with the light focused on a fiber optic connected to a 0.3 m spectrograph equipped with an ICCD (Blacic et al., 1992).

7.2.2 FOCUSING THE LASER PULSE

Depending on the analysis distance, the laser pulses may be focused using a simple lens, a pair of lenses (to vary the position of the focal point), or a more elaborate optical system may be employed to first expand the diameter of the laser pulse and then focus the pulse at a distance onto the target. The use of high quality anti-reflection coated optics is important to maximize the power density on the target. In situations where instrument mass is important (e.g. spacecraft), a mirror system, such as a Cassegrainian telescope, may be desirable as mirrors can generally be fabricated having less mass than an equivalent lens. Mirrors have the added advantage of being free of chromatic aberration. Typically, the focusing system would be adjustable so targets at various ranges can be interrogated from a fixed position.

To form a robust laser plasma, a minimum power density on the target is required. For a given laser pulse power, the power density generated on a remote sample will depend mainly on the minimum achievable spot size which is a function of distance. For a high quality (e.g. Gaussian) laser beam, the spot size is governed by spherical aberrations in the optical system and by the diffraction limit. The laser pulse power directed toward the sample can be reduced through absorption and scattering by the atmosphere and by aerosol particles and this possibility must be considered for each application.

To demonstrate some concerns that must be considered for a remote LIBS system, we first evaluate factors affecting the minimum spot size for a simple single lens system. As noted above, the main factors are spherical aberration and diffraction. For spherical aberration, the smallest spot size (d_{aber}) at the focus is given by:

$$d_{aber} = f(d/f)^3[n^2 - (2n+1)k + (n+2)k^2/n]/32(n-1)^2 \qquad (7.1)$$

where d is the input beam diameter, n is the refractive index of the lens material at the laser wavelength, f is the lens focal length and

$$k = R_2/(R_2 - R_1) \qquad (7.2)$$

where R_1 and R_2 are the radii of curvature of the lens. Using the usual sign convention for lenses, for a plano-convex lens with light incident on the plane side $k = 0$ and for light incident on the convex side $k = 1$.

On the other hand, the spot size determined by diffraction for a beam of wavelength λ is given by:

$$d_{diff} = 2.44\lambda f/d. \qquad (7.3)$$

Insight as to which effect predominates for given f and d values can be obtained by setting $d_{aber} = d_{diff}$ and solving for f as a function of d. An example is shown in Figure 7.3 for 1064 nm light.

For practical LIBS systems, the diameter of the laser beam, even after expansion by a simple Galilean telescope will typically be less than 4 cm whereas focal lengths of interest will be several meters or more. In this case, according to Figure 7.3, the minimum spot size attainable at the focus will be determined by the diffraction limit rather than spherical aberration which becomes important for shorter focal length lenses and smaller beam diameters. For $d = 4$ cm, spherical aberration determines the minimum achievable spot size for $f < \sim$40 cm whereas

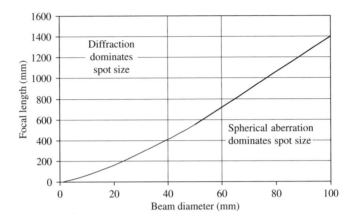

Figure 7.3 Relationship between f and d for $d_{aber} = d_{diff}$

diffraction is the determining factor at longer focal lengths. Therefore, if working in the diffraction limited focusing regime, expanding the beam diameter prior to focusing will produce smaller spot sizes and higher power densities on the distant sample.

Another important parameter is the Rayleigh range (z_R) of the beam at focus which is given by (assuming a diffraction limited spot size, $d_0 = d_{diff}$):

$$z_R = \pi d_0^2/\lambda = \pi 5.95\lambda(f/d)^2 \tag{7.4}$$

and is shown in Figure 7.4. The Rayleigh range is important because it is one computable measure of how accurately the focus must be adjusted to produce the greatest power density on the remote target. Note that z_R is defined as the distance from the beam waist (d_0), or point of minimum beam diameter after focus, to the position at which the area of the beam has doubled. Symmetry of the Rayleigh range before and after the beam waist is assumed. According to Equation (7.4), the Rayleigh range varies as the square of the focal length and as the reciprocal of the square of the input beam diameter. As a sample calculation, for $d = 4$ cm, $f = 10$ m and a 1064 nm Nd:YAG beam, $z_R = 124$ cm.

For conventional remote LIBS, the spot size on the sample must be minimized to generate the strongest plasma. Operationally this condition may be achieved by

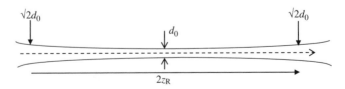

Figure 7.4 Rayleigh range for a focused Gaussian beam in relation to the minimum spot size d_0

repetitively firing the laser and adjusting the focal position until the 'best' plasma is formed on the sample. The 'best' plasma can be indicated by the intensity of white light from the plasma, or by the sound produced by the laser pulse induced shock wave, or by monitoring the intensity of element emissions. At best focus, these should all be maximized. In an automated system, target distance can be determined using a rangefinder based on a number of methods including time-of-flight, phase shift, triangulation and interferometry. The first two listed are appropriate for LIBS instruments and some characteristics are summarized in Table 7.1.

The precision to which the focus must be determined to form a useful plasma depends on distance. The greater the distance, the longer the Rayleigh range and hence precise focusing becomes less crucial.

The Rayleigh range is a parameter useful to estimate an operating range for an optical system in which the diffraction limited spot size must remain below a certain value assuming a certain laser beam quality. The useful operating range for a LIBS system can be determined operationally and provides actual performance capabilities. An example of data recorded during such an evaluation is shown in Figure 7.5. To obtain these data, a $\times 20$ beam expander was used to expand and then focus at a distance Nd:YAG pulses of about 3 mm starting diameter. The pulse energy was 100 mJ. For each selected distance, the LIBS signal from Al metal was maximized by adjusting the beam expander focus to produce the maximum LIBS signal from Al(I) at 394.4 nm. Then the metal sample was moved both toward and away from the beam expander and the position in each direction at which the signal decreased to 10% of its maximum value was noted. For the particular system used here, the value of 10% was selected because the Al(I) signal at this intensity was still regarded as sufficiently strong to be useful for quantitative measurements. The total distance between the two end 10% end points is plotted in Figure 7.5 as a function of target distance. For comparison, the Rayleigh range for $d = 20 \times 3\,\text{mm} = 60\,\text{mm}$, $f = 10\,\text{m}$, and the Nd:YAG fundamental wavelength is 55 cm for this system. This compares well ($z_R = 2 \times 55\,\text{cm} = 110\,\text{cm}$) with the usable range of about 1 m displayed in Figure 7.5.

Table 7.1 Methods of measuring target distances for LIBS

Method	Operation	Range	Accuracy	Laser
Time-of-flight	Round trip travel time of a short duration laser pulse directed at the target is measured	10 m–tens of km	<1 mm	Pulsed laser diode
Phase shift	Shift in phase between a reference pulse and the pulse reflected off the distant target is measured	0.2–200 m	<1.5 mm	Pulsed laser diode (beam divergence = 0.16 × 0.6 mrad; 15 ns pulse; 0.95 mW)

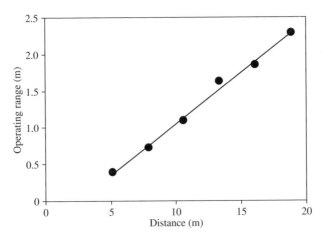

Figure 7.5 Useful operating range of a LIBS system over a range of stand-off analysis distances

7.2.3   COLLECTING THE PLASMA LIGHT

Remote LIBS systems have been developed in which the plasma light is collected collinear with or off-axis to the path of the laser pulses directed to the target. Collection along the same axis as the laser pulses eliminates parallax as the distance to the target (r) changes. In the collinear arrangement, the plasma light is diverted from the path of the laser pulses using, for example, a beam splitter or mirror with a central clear aperture. In one configuration the beam splitter will have a coating that passes the laser wavelength but reflects the plasma light over a wide spectral range. Such coatings are not ideal for wide spectral band detection as there will be some spectral regions that are not efficiently reflected from the beam splitter due to the coating. Using a mirror with a central open aperture as shown in Figure 7.1 avoids this problem but some fraction of the returning plasma light is lost. Of course, here again it is a trade off. For long distances, the outgoing laser beam will be expanded requiring a large central aperture resulting in greater loss of returning light. In either case, the diverted and collected light is then directed into the detection system.

The plasma light can also be collected using the arrangement shown in Figure 7.6. A lens is shown here as focusing the laser pulses onto a fiber optic and the laser pulses are directed onto the target by a 100% reflecting mirror, the converse arrangement of Figure 7.1. A mirror could be used to collect and focus the returning plasma light onto the fiber optic in place of the lens. If using a lens, an important consideration is chromatic aberration. This effect is a result of the refractive index of the lens material being wavelength dependent so that different wavelengths will be focused at different points along the optical axis (Figure 3.7d). Unless achromatic lenses, lenses in which the effect has been corrected, are used, lens focusing will require that the fiber optic be moved relative to the collecting lens to optimize the recorded intensity for different spectral regions. Chromatic aberration becomes an

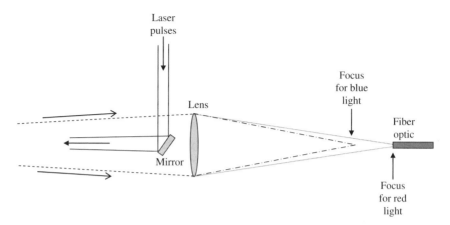

Figure 7.6 One method of collecting plasma light using a single lens. Unless the lens is achromatic, the optimum focal position on the fiber will be wavelength dependent

important consideration, especially when using an echelle spectrograph (Section 3.4) where the spectrum collected on a single shot can encompass a large spectral range (e.g. 200–800 nm). The apparatus shown in Figure 7.1 and the arrangement of Figure 7.6 with the lens replaced by a mirror will be free of this effect.

Of course, with either mirror or lens focusing, some adjustment of the light collection system, just as in the case of focusing the laser pulse, will be required to inject maximum collected light into a fiber as the distance from the target to the optical system (r) changes. Note that in all the light collection configurations discussed here, the collected light will vary as $1/r^2$.

7.2.4 RESULTS USING CONVENTIONAL LIBS

Remote LIBS based on conventional focusing has been used mainly for the analysis of solid targets with ranges up to 80 m reported. Liquid samples have been interrogated at distances of a few meters. Because of the high power densities required to induce air breakdown, the analysis of gases at long distances has not been reported using conventional focusing methods and practical size lasers.

One of the first reports of remote LIBS analysis was described in 1985 by Zuev *et al.* (Zuev *et al.*, 1985). A 'spectrochemical LIDAR' instrument was developed based on a Cassegrainian telescope, spectrograph, and photographic or photomultiplier detection of the collected light. A CO_2 laser (300 μs pulse width and 500 J) was used to generate the laser plasma. Although the focused power densities at distance were not sufficient to produce an air plasma, plasmas were formed on aerosol particles within the telescope focal region at ranges of 50 to 150 m. The elements Ca, Al and Na from the particles were detected along with oxygen and nitrogen emissions from air.

Another early report of stand-off analysis of solids was published in 1987 (Cremers, 1987). One goal of this work was to demonstrate the rapid sorting of metals according to the main metal constituent rather than long range measurements so distances were less than 3 m. Laser pulses were focused on metal samples using a single lens and the light was collected by a bare fiber optic bundle pointed at the plasma. No attempts were made to optimize the experimental set-up to extend the range, but using this simple arrangement, useful signals were obtained as far as 2.4 m using a single focusing lens and no spatial expansion of the laser pulse. This work showed 100% success at the rapid identification of metals according to their main element component (Cu, Zn, Al, Ni, Sn, Mo, Ti or Fe). The use of repetitive ablation to clean a surface was described and the method was evaluated for the analysis of steel at 0.55 m.

In 1991, LIBS was demonstrated for the remote analysis of geological samples outdoors in air at a distance of 24 m using a laboratory laser and detection system (Blacic et al., 1992). The equipment was positioned on a cart and moved outside the laboratory to interrogate a cliff bank (Figure 7.2). A simple three-lens system was used to focus the pulses so the focal distance could be adjusted to achieve different stand-off distances. Spectra were readily collected in bright sunlight allowing an evaluation of the target material composition. The goal of this preliminary work was to promote LIBS as an instrument for future planetary missions. Subsequent investigations on the development of LIBS for space exploration are discussed in Chapter 8.

Although stand-off analysis is usually performed using solid samples, one study has described the analysis of liquids at distances of 3–5 m using both off-axis and on-axis methods of plasma light collection (Samek et al., 2000). Plasma light was collected on-axis using a novel method of separating the laser beam from the plasma light based on frustrated total internal reflection. Different methods of sampling liquid samples were investigated with the majority of measurements employing a laminar flow water jet. In one experiment, however, a radioactive solution of Tc in a Petri dish was analyzed at a distance of 3 m. A low pulse repetition rate of 1 Hz was used to minimize splashing of the solution. Based on the concentration of Tc in the sample and the signal strength it was estimated that Tc levels down to 25 mg/l should be observable.

A custom, mobile LIBS system was developed for stand-off analysis (1 m) of major elements in a mineral melt (1600°C) in an industrial environment (Panne et al., 2002). The plasma light was collected at an angle to the path of the laser pulses instead of collinearly. A variation in the LIBS signal of Si was observed due to changes in position of the mobile instrument in relation to the melt. This was believed to be due to collection of the light at an angle which resulted in monitoring different regions of the expanding plasma. Variations in signals could probably be minimized through a collinear geometry (Figure 7.1). Operational parameters such as pulse irradiance and gate delay and width of ICCD detection were optimized in terms of the signal to noise ratio. This permitted all major elements in the melt (Ti, Fe, Mn, Mg, Ca, Si, Na, Al) to be identified within the brief interrogation time of 1 s corresponding to ten laser pulses. To evaluate process monitoring, LIBS measurements were made from a melt at analysis intervals separated by 60 s along with manual retrieval of a sample from the melt for subsequent analysis by x-ray fluorescence. Runs extending over 80 and 130 min were carried out and compared. Good correlation was observed between the LIBS and x-ray fluorescence data (elements Si, Fe, Al, Ca, Mn, Mg) with a slight shift in the pattern (element signal versus time) attributed to a small mismatch between the sampling times.

Analysis of stainless steel at a distance of 40 m was demonstrated using an open-path LIBS system (Palanco et al., 2002). Light was collected off-axis to the path of the laser pulses. The long Rayleigh length of the beam at 40 m was found useful to minimize the effect of surface irregularities on the analysis with an RSD of 14% determined for the absolute signal precision as the sample position varied ±1 m from the position of optimum laser focus. The ratio Cr/Fe was found to be highly uniform over the range ±5 m from the laser focus. In addition, spectra from six stainless steels samples were collected and emissions from Ni, Mo and Ti compared. Using these data in a three-dimensional pattern recognition algorithm showed that the six steels could be accurately classified using only three elements.

Based on a collinear optical design in which the plasma light was collected along the same path as the laser pulses, Palanco and Laserna (Palanco and Laserna, 2004) developed and described an open-path LIBS analysis system. Performance of the system was evaluated and the feasibility of extending the analysis range of such a LIBS system based on conventional focusing was discussed.

Using a Nd:YAG laser, spectrograph, and ICCD, samples including plant material, soil, rock and cement collected from an industrial environment were analyzed at 12 m distance in the laboratory (Lopez-Moreno et al., 2004). The experimental arrangement was similar to that of Figure 7.1. Depth resolved measurements and the effect of surface condition on the analysis were evaluated. Factors affecting analysis results such as moisture content, surface uniformity and sample orientation were evaluated. Detection limits for Cr and Fe were determined to be about 0.2 wt% from calibration curves prepared using a set of slag standards. These curves were then used to determine the Cr levels in some of the collected environmental samples. The change in Cr signals (concentration) with shot number on the different samples was used to draw conclusions regarding aspects of environmental pollution. Using the large depth of focus of the optical system at 12 m, three-dimensional maps of Cr, Fe, Ca and Mg distributions in a rock sample were made over the volume 20 mm × 18 mm × 0.54 mm depth.

Using the same apparatus, except that the collected plasma light was directed into a fiber optic and a HeNe laser, collinear with the Nd:YAG pulses, was used to aim the system, the same group monitored the corrosion of stainless steels in a high temperature environment (Garcia et al., 2004). The experiments were conducted in the laboratory at a distance of 10 m with the steel samples maintained in an oven. The oxidation of the surface was monitored and qualitative differences observed between the intensity of element emissions from the corroded, scaled steel surface and a clean steel surface. Specifically, after only 10 min exposure at 1200 °C, the scaled layer was found to be Fe-rich with reduced levels of Cr, Ni and Mo compared

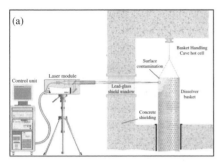

Figure 7.7 (a) Schematic showing the deployment of the remote LIBS instrument to monitor surface contamination. (b) Laser beam of the instrument being directed through the lead glass shield window (Applied Photonics, 2004a. Courtesy of Applied Photonics, Ltd) (see Plate 13)

with the starting material. Depth profiling of the corroded layer showed depletion of Cr at the surface with the Cr signals increasing as a result of repetitive ablation that interrogated the underlying bulk material.

An open-path transportable LIBS apparatus was used to analyze molten steel on a factory floor (Palanco *et al.*, 2004). The sample was heated in a crucible in a small scale induction furnace of 1 kg capacity. The distance between the instrument and the crucible was about 7.5 m with two mirrors in between to direct and focus the laser pulses vertically downward onto the molten sample surface. Measurements showed the ability to monitor in real-time changes in the composition of the melt (e.g. Ni added). Calibration curves for Ni and Cr were prepared by adding these elements to stainless steel. From the curves, detection limits of 1190 and 540 ppm were determined for Ni and Cr, respectively.

Stand-off LIBS was used at a distance of about 5 m to determine the composition of contaminants deposited on dissolver baskets at a spent nuclear fuel reprocessing plant (Applied Photonics, 2004a). Radiometric analysis of the contaminants had identified the radionuclide components but another method was needed to identify the nonradioactive materials. An analyzer system was deployed including the laser and optics to form the laser plasma remotely on the basket through a thick lead-glass window and collect the plasma light [Figure 7.7 (Plate 13)]. The material was analyzed *in situ* and determined to be zirconium molybdate which was an insoluble material formed during the reprocessing procedure.

7.3   STAND-OFF LIBS USING FEMTOSECOND PULSES

7.3.1   CONVENTIONAL REMOTE LIBS USING FEMTOSECOND LASER PULSES

LIBS measurements are typically carried out using nanosecond laser pulses. These pulses are 5–10 ns in duration, contain energies ranging from a few millijoules up to 500 mJ, with the fundamental wavelength of 1064 nm preferred for most applications. The pulse powers are in the range of 0.3 to 50 MW with corresponding focused power densities of 3.8 to 6.4 GW/cm^2 (for a 0.1 mm diameter spot size). Nanosecond lasers are preferred for LIBS because they are technologically well-developed, rugged and reliable, and very compact systems are available for incorporation into instruments. Picosecond and femtosecond lasers, however, generating pulses of durations on the order 10^{-12} and 10^{-14} s, respectively, have been investigated for LIBS applications and some advantages have been found. Unfocused powers from these lasers range from hundreds of megawatts to tens of terawatts.

Because of the broad spectral content of femtosecond pulses, an important concept in discussions of femtosecond lasers is chirp. A chirped pulse is one in which the different wavelengths or colors are not distributed uniformly over the envelope of the pulse. Chirp may be viewed as an increase or decrease in the frequency of a light pulse with time as monitored from a stationary position as the pulse passes by the observer. Chirp can be used to tailor certain pulse properties to maximize excitation characteristics when used for LIBS.

A pulse can be positively or negatively chirped. Positive chirp occurs when the leading edge of the pulse is red-shifted in relation to the central wavelength and the trailing edge is blue-shifted. Negative chirp is the opposite situation. Because the refractive index of a material depends on wavelength, different wavelengths pass through a medium at different velocities. In this way, by passing a chirped pulse through a sequence of prisms, the chirp can be adjusted to be either positive or negative. The refractive index of glass and most materials (e.g. air) increases as the wavelength decreases so that longer wavelengths travel with greater velocities. Therefore, a positively chirped pulse will become more positively chirped and show an increase in pulse width as it passes through air. For instance, a 70 fs pulse of 16 nm spectral content will be chirped into a 1 ps pulse after traversing 1 km of air and the peak pulse power is reduced by a factor of 10 (Wille *et al.*, 2002). On the other hand, a negatively chirped pulse transmitted through the atmosphere will exhibit reduced chirp and a shorter pulse width (Figure 7.8). By controlling the chirp in an output pulse, the pulse width, the pulse power, and hence the position of plasma formation from the laser can be controlled.

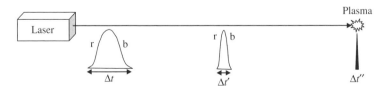

Figure 7.8 A negatively chirped pulse [blue (b) proceeds red (r)] is temporally compressed by traveling through an atmosphere ($\Delta t > \Delta t' > \Delta t''$). When the pulse has been sufficiently compressed, producing a high power density, a plasma is formed at a certain distance

Remote LIBS analysis of targets has been carried out using femtosecond pulses focused onto a target as in conventional LIBS (Figure 7.1). Femtosecond pulses (795 nm, 10 Hz, up to 350 mJ, 75 fs) were directed from the laboratory onto the solid target at 25 m using a simple mirror telescope to expand ($\times$3) and then focus the pulses (Rohwetter *et al.*, 2004). The femtosecond laser could also be adapted to produce picosecond and nanosecond pulses for comparison of results. A second telescope (10 cm primary mirror diameter) was used to collect the plasma light at a position adjacent to but not collinear with the path of the incident laser pulses. Some main results of this study were: (1) femtosecond and picosecond pulses can be used for remote analysis with a detection limit of 100 ng computed for Cu at 25 m using femtosecond pulses; (2) femtosecond pulses produced a cleaner LIBS spectrum than either the picosecond or nanosecond pulses, with the femtosecond spectrum free of emissions from elements in the ambient gas; (3) emissions from the femtosecond- and picosecond-produced plasmas decayed at about the same rate as those from a ns-pulse produced plasma (microsecond timescale); (4) adjusting the femtosecond-pulse chirp to produce the minimum duration laser pulse at the target (i.e. maximum power density) does not produce the strongest emission signal. The optimum signals were obtained by adjusting the chirp for each type of target material.

7.3.2 REMOTE ANALYSIS BY FEMTOSECOND PULSE PRODUCED FILAMENTATION

As noted above, using nanosecond pulses of reasonable energy (i.e. <500 mJ), ranges of tens of meters are possible with LIBS. For this reason, LIBS has not been included in the arsenal of spectroscopic methods employed for long range LIDAR measurements ($\sim$km). Because of the high optical powers generated by femtosecond pulse lasers, on the other hand, a variant of LIBS is possible based on atmospheric filamentation produced by these pulses (Kasparian *et al.*, 2003). Filamentation occurs when a sufficiently powerful femtosecond pulse propagates through air or other medium transparent at the laser wavelength. The process is based on the Kerr effect in which the refractive index of a medium is changed by an applied electric field. The induced change (Δn) is given by:

$$\Delta n = n_2 I \tag{7.5}$$

where n_2 is the nonlinear index of refraction particular to the medium and I is the optical intensity. When a Gaussian-shaped light pulse passes through the transparent medium the change in refractive index will be greater at the spatial center of the pulse and less at the edges, following the intensity distribution across the pulse profile. For air $n_2 = 3 \times 10^{-19} \, cm^2/W$ and the induced changes will form a positive lens acting to focus the light pulse. This focusing results in ionization of the transparent medium and formation of a plasma that acts to defocus the beam. When the pulse power exceeds a certain critical power, a dynamic equilibrium exists

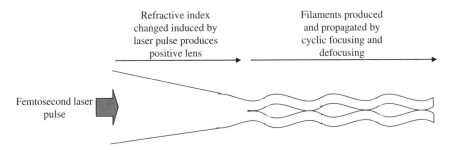

Refractive index
changed induced by
laser pulse produces
positive lens

Filaments produced
and propagated by
cyclic focusing and
defocusing

Femtosecond laser
pulse

Figure 7.9   Filaments over long path lengths are generated by the dynamic equilibrium between focusing (Kerr effect) and defocusing (plasma formation) which occurs along the path of the laser pulses

between the two processes resulting in self-trapping of the propagating laser beam near the optical axis of the beam. For air, the critical power is several gigawatts. This trapping is shown in Figure 7.9. The self-trapping generates filaments of 'white light' or a spectral continuum over distances much longer than is achievable using a conventionally focused beam. Images of filaments produced in air are shown in Figure 7.10 (Plate 14). About 10–20% of the laser pulse energy is directed into the filaments.

Filament lengths of 200 m are typical with filaments up to 2 km long being observed. Filament diameters have been measured to be about 0.1 mm. The intensity inside the filaments is on the order of 4×10^{13} W/cm^2 (Kasparian *et al.*, 2000). At powers 10–100 times above the critical value, multiple filaments are formed that propagate along the beam direction. Frequencies other than the laser frequency are generated as a result of self-phase modulation within the filament producing a 'white light.' A significant portion of this continuum is radiated in the forward and backward direction of pulse propagation aiding remote detection of the spectroscopic signal from the filaments.

7.3.3   TERAMOBILE

Currently compact and field-deployable nanosecond laser systems are available for stand-off LIBS using conventional focusing. On the other hand, femtosecond laser systems generating powers on the order of 10^{14} W that are needed for filamentation studies are currently laboratory instruments because of their complexity, size and requirement for a controlled operating environment. These laboratory devices will become more readily adapted for field use as the technology improves. These efforts will be driven by the unique capabilities that femtosecond lasers promise in several areas related to LIBS and other applications. For the past several years, field applications of femtosecond pulse technology have been demonstrated and evaluated by the Teramobile, a joint collaboration between French and German organizations (Wille *et al.*, 2002). The Teramobile is a laboratory contained inside

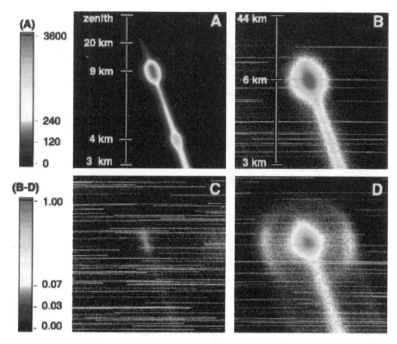

Figure 7.10 CCD camera images of filaments produced by a femtosecond laser beam propagating vertically through the atmosphere. The femtosecond pulses were produced by the Teramobile. (A) Fundamental wavelength, exhibiting signals from more than 20 km and multiple-scattering halos on haze layers at 4- and 9-km altitudes. (B–D) White light (385 to 485 nm) emitted by the femtosecond laser beam. These images have the same altitude range, and their common color scale is normalized to allow direct comparison with that of (A). (Reprinted with permission from Kasparian *et al.*, Copyright 2003 AAAS) (see Plate 14)

a standard freight container that can be transported to different field sites. The laboratory includes a transportable femtosecond laser system producing terawatt laser pulses and associated detection and analysis instrumentation for evaluating the operation of the system for different applications.

7.3.4   REMOTE LIBS USING FEMTOSECOND PULSES

Using self-guided filaments produced by femtosecond laser pulses, remote filament-induced breakdown spectroscopy (R-LIBS) has recently been demonstrated (Stelmaszczyk *et al.*, 2004). The output pulses (80 fs, 250 mJ, 10 Hz) of the Teramobile were collimated to 3 cm diameter and directed at metal targets (Cu and steel) located 20–90 m distant. The pulses leaving the laser system were negatively chirped (corresponding pulse width of 800 fs) to begin filament production in front of the target at 7–8 m. In this way, filaments were produced on the target surface and one pattern is shown in Figure 7.11. The backward emitted light

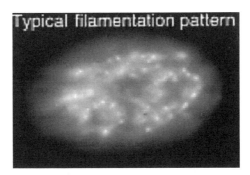

Figure 7.11 Filaments produced on a metal target at >20 m. (Reprinted with permission from Stelmaszczyk *et al.*, 2004. Copyright 2004, American Institute of Physics)

from the filaments was collected by a telescope (20 cm) and recorded by a spectrograph and ICCD. The LIBS spectrum was examined in the 500–550 nm region and emissions from Cu(I) and Fe(I) were recorded at 90 m. Over the 20–90 m range investigated, the LIBS signal from the target surface was independent of distance, indicating that target excitation by the filaments did not change with distance. Considerations of signal-to-noise changes with distance showed that with this nonoptimized system, a distance of 150 m could be realized for LIBS detection (signal to noise ratio ∼ 1). Expected improvements in the detection system efficiency on the order of 100 should permit measurements at ∼1 km range, comparable with the distance observed for filament propagation (Rodriguez *et al.*, 2004).

In a subsequent study by the same group, the range of R-FIBS was extended to an Al target located 180 m from the laser (Rohwetter *et al.*, 2005). Comparisons were made between the R-FIBS spectra and the spectra from conventional LIBS produced by picosecond and nanosecond lasers. The main result was that the R-FIBS spectra were free of emission lines due to oxygen and nitrogen similar to the spectra obtained using femtosecond pulses for conventional LIBS (Rohwetter *et al.*, 2004). Based on the results of this work, the feasibility of kilometer range R-FIBS was considered and experimental requirements estimated.

7.4 FIBER OPTIC LIBS

7.4.1 FIBER OPTICS FOR LIGHT COLLECTION

The use of fiber optics has greatly benefited applications of LIBS in two ways: by providing new methods of collecting the plasma light and by delivering the laser energy to the target. In this section we discuss benefits related to collection of the plasma light. Using a fiber, the plasma light does not need to be directly focused onto the entrance slit of a spectrograph or passed directly through a filter, etc., using a relay optical system. This lends great versatility to instrument design and permits the detection system to be remotely located away from the target as shown in Figure 3.36. Fiber lengths of many tens of meters have been reported in the literature. In addition, with lens focusing onto a slit, typically only a portion of the plasma volume is monitored (Figure 7.12). Because of the highly inhomogeneous distribution of material in the plasma and the strong spatial gradients in excitation parameters in the small plasma, minute changes in the position of the plasma on the slit can significantly change the appearance of the recorded spectrum in terms of emission line intensities as well as relative intensities. For *in-situ* measurements, this sensitivity to alignment is reduced by collecting the plasma light with a bare fiber optic pointed at the sample. Because of the wide acceptance angle of the fiber optic (26 and 58°, respectively, for a fused silica and glass fiber) small changes in the plasma position will not significantly affect the collected plasma light (Figure 7.12). In addition, using a fiber in this way provides collection of light from all parts of the plasma, that is, the plasma light is spatially averaged. Data showing the dependence of the Fe signal on plasma position are shown in Figure 7.13 for each arrangement. In the first case, the plasma light is imaged on a spectrometer slit ($100\,\mu$m wide) by a 50 mm focal length lens (1:1 magnification). Movements of the lens by 0.5 mm reduce the signal to half the maximum value. Movements become more sensitive as the lens focal length increases. Using a fiber optic to collect the plasma light decreases the sensitivity to plasma position. As shown in Figure 7.13, a change in the plasma position on the target in the vertical direction of 3.5 cm produces a 25% change in the observed signal. The fiber to plasma distance was 55 cm.

The amount of light collected by a fiber decreases with distance (r) as $1/r^2$, the same as for lens imaging. Because the end of the fiber is typically small, say 0.6–1 mm diameter, the collection angle from a point source like the laser plasma is also very small with the equivalent f# of the system being about 116 (for 55 cm distance). The amount of light into the fiber can be increased using a lens to focus the plasma light onto the end of the fiber. The cone of light focused onto the fiber

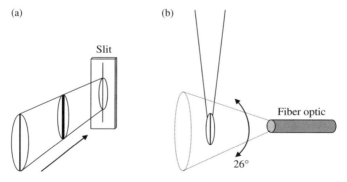

Figure 7.12 (a) Focusing the plasma light onto a spectrograph slit. Because of the narrow slit (e.g. $100\,\mu$m), the signal is sensitive to image position. (b) Collecting light with a fiber optic reduces sensitivity because of the 26° acceptance angle for light

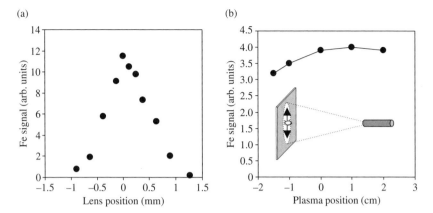

Figure 7.13 Variation of recorded signal as a function of (a) lens imaging plasma on a slit and (b) position of the plasma on the target in the vertical direction with plasma light collected by a fiber optic. The distance between the fiber and sample was 55 cm for (b)

by the lens should be within the acceptance angle of the fiber so that the majority of light incident on the fiber will be transmitted (matching the numerical apertures, Section 3.3.3). Light outside the acceptance cone will not be transmitted. Of course in using lens light collection with a fiber, the sensitivity to plasma position increases as for direct imaging on a slit with a lens. The advantages of remote detection capability as regards light collection are still preserved, however.

7.4.2 FIBERS FOR LASER PULSE DELIVERY

A second benefit of fiber optics is the ability to transmit sufficiently high pulse irradiance through a fiber so an analytically useful plasma can be formed at the distal end of the fiber. In this way, the laser system as well as the detection system can be located remotely from the target as shown in Figure 3.36. It is even possible to collect the plasma light using the same fiber optic that transmits the laser pulse. A probe incorporating these capabilities is shown in Figures 3.15 and 7.14. Typically, low OH fused silica step indexed fiber optics are used to transmit the laser pulse. The fibers used to transport the laser pulse have diameters in the range of 0.4–1 mm. Smaller diameters cannot handle the pulse energies required to form the laser plasma and larger diameters, although available, are not flexible enough for some applications. The laser pulse can be injected into the fiber using the arrangement shown in Figure 7.15. The fiber is positioned behind the focus of a long focal length lens (>200 mm) with the distance between the lens and fiber input face adjusted so that the diverging beam fills about 75% of the fiber end. A lens with a short focal length will generate an air spark at the focus and will introduce rays into the fiber at an angle that exceeds the acceptance angle, resulting in high transmission losses.

Figure 7.14 Generation of a laser plasma on soil using a small probe with a single fiber that delivers the laser pulse and collects the plasma light

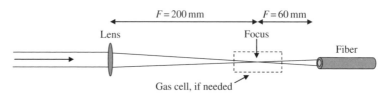

Figure 7.15 Method of injecting laser pulses into a fiber to remotely form the laser plasma

The air spark can be eliminated by placing an evacuated or gas-filled cell at the focus (Davies *et al.*, 1995). The divergence of the laser beam into the fiber can also be controlled using a simple Galilean telescope which eliminates the sharp focus that may produce a laser spark in air. This arrangement is shown in Figure 7.16. In this case, the evacuated cell is not needed.

Generally, the fiber can accommodate the pulse powers used for LIBS, but coupling the energy into the fiber without damaging the fiber input face is the major problem. To achieve maximum power transmission, the end face of the fiber must be optically smooth and perpendicular to the beam. Proper focusing of the beam is critical to prevent intense laser light leaking into the cladding that may damage the polymer cladding or buffer coating. The epoxy used for bonding the fiber to the connector can be affected as well. For this reason, a silica/silica fiber

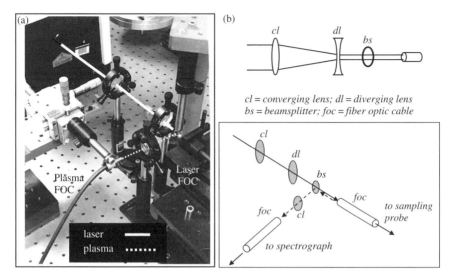

Figure 7.16 (a) Photo and (b) diagram showing one method of using the same fiber to transport the laser pulse and collect the plasma light. A Galilean telescope is used to inject the pulses into the fiber optic

is often used in a specially designed mounting or connector to better tolerate the high power densities and rapid heating levels. It is also recommended that the beam not completely fill the core diameter. Some factors affecting fiber damage by laser pulses are listed in Table 7.2.

The coupling efficiency of the laser energy into a fiber may be increased through the use of a fiber optic with an integral taper at the end. With the larger area of the taper input end, the pulse power incident on the fiber can be reduced to minimize damage and for beams that are multimode and not easily focused, more energy can be injected into the larger taper end. It should be realized that in using a tapered fiber, the numerical apperture (NA) of the light into the taper must satisfy certain conditions to achieve maximum coupling down the fiber. The important relationship is:

$$\mathrm{NA_{in} = NA_{out}}(d_{\mathrm{out}}/d_{\mathrm{in}}). \tag{7.6}$$

Here $\mathrm{NA_{in}}$ and $\mathrm{NA_{out}}$ refer, respectively, to the numerical aperture of the taper input and of the base (nontapered) main fiber over which the laser pulse will be transmitted. The input and output diameters of the taper are d_{in} and d_{out}, respectively. For a fused silica base fiber, $\mathrm{NA_{out}} = 0.22$ and for a taper of $d_{\mathrm{in}}/d_{\mathrm{out}} = 3/1$, the result is $\mathrm{NA_{in}} = 0.073$. A value greater than this will result in losses of the input beam energy through the core/cladding interface due to a reflection angle inside the core exceeding the angle for total internal reflection. Tapers as large as 5/1 can be accommodated in fiber manufacture with the taper occurring over 10–15 mm of the fiber end.

A system of using the same fiber for transporting the laser beam and collecting the plasma light is shown in Figure 7.16. Here a Galilean telescope (single converging

Table 7.2 Factors influencing fiber damage for laser pulse transport

Fiber input face condition	• quality of end polishing • cleanliness • cleaving
Fiber material	• purity/quality of silica • optical attenuation of laser wavelength
Laser parameters	• wavelength • pulse power, pulse width, pulse energy
Launch conditions	• power density on fiber input face • spot size on face • spatial distribution of light at input face • alignment on input face • numerical aperture of input optics

and diverging lenses) was used to generate a slightly diverging beam going into the fiber optic. The return light from the plasma was collected using a beamsplitter consisting of a small quartz plate ($\sim$8% reflection collection efficiency).

7.4.3 APPLICATIONS OF FIBER OPTICS

An early investigation of the use of fiber optics to deliver a laser pulse of sufficient power density to perform a LIBS measurement was reported for underwater analysis (Nyga and Neu, 1993). Separate XeCl lasers (308 nm) were employed, each laser being fiber optic (600 μm core diameter) coupled to deliver pulses to the surface of a calcite sample located under water. The first pulse formed a bubble on the sample and the second laser pulse interrogated the calcite surface inside the bubble simulating in this way interrogation of the calcite in air. The plasma light was collected by the fiber delivering the second laser pulse. A portion of this light was split off and the LIBS spectrum recorded using a spectrograph and ICCD.

The first extensive investigation of the use of optical fibers to deliver the laser pulse to the sample over a long distance was described by Davies *et al.* (1995). A separate fiber was used to collect the plasma light. As the application was intended for eventual use in a nuclear reactor with doses of gamma radiation, attenuation of wavelengths ranging from 296 to 1064 nm was investigated for certain radiation exposure times. A core diameter of 550 μm was chosen for use with laser pulses of 50 mJ energy to accommodate the high power densities without damaging the fiber. Concentrations of some elements of interest were observed as low as 200 ppm and calibration curves were prepared for several elements using certified ferrous metal standards. Use of the system for distances up to 100 m was demonstrated.

In the same year Cremers *et al.* described the use of the same fiber optic to deliver laser pulses to a sample for LIBS and to collect the plasma light (Cremers *et al.*, 1995). Detection limits for Ba and Cr in soil were presented along with calibration curves. Detection limits obtained using the fiber were comparable with those determined for the same elements using direct focusing (nonfiber optic coupled) LIBS.

There have been several other published works dealing with fiber optic coupled LIBS. A representative list is presented in Table 7.3. Some of these involved fiber optic delivery of the laser pulse energy and fiber collection of the plasma light at the source. Others have used a small laser in a probe positioned adjacent to the target with the plasma light collected by a fiber and transported back to the remotely located detection system.

Table 7.3 Literature relating to fiber optic coupled LIBS

Application	Comments (ref.)
Cone penetrometer system	Describes the construction and use of a truck mounted system for subsurface analysis of contaminated sites (Saggese and Greenwell, 1996)
Fiber optic system for detecting lead in paint	Some analytical results are presented for the detection of Pb in paint using the fiber optic system (Marquardt *et al.*, 1996)
Transportable LIBS analyzer for soil contamination	Soil sample analyzer either by insertion into device or through fiber optic coupling of laser pulses to soil. Instrument shown in Figure 7.17 (Cremers *et al.*, 1996)
Cone penetrometer system	Subsurface sampling head designed in which plasma is formed at the interface between a quartz window and soil. Single fiber used for laser and plasma light (Theriault *et al.*, 1998)
Fiber optic probe that combines LIBS, Raman and imaging	LIBS measurements demonstrated using granite rock. Raman spectra obtained of single TiO_2 and $Sr(NO_3)_2$ particles and Raman images of the same particles were recorded (Marquardt *et al.*, 1998)
Aspects of injecting high power laser pulses into a fiber	Useful technical information for those interested in getting started with fiber delivery of pulses for LIBS (Neuhauser *et al.*, 2000)
Fiber optic probe described and used to analyze Al alloy samples	Detection limits for elements in Al alloys obtained with the fiber optic probe were compared with those obtained by direct focusing of the laser pulses (Rai *et al.*, 2001)
Fiber optic probe developed for the *in situ* determination of the elemental composition of a molten alloy	Experimental parameters of the system (e.g. laser pulse energy, gate delay, etc.) were evaluated for different solid alloys. Following this, the system performance was tested using molten alloys in a laboratory size furnace (Rai *et al.*, 2002)
Determine the Cu content of stainless steel steam generator tubes in the reactor of a nuclear power station	A fiber optic coupled LIBS system (75 m umbilical length), shown in Figure 7.18, was used with separate fibers for laser pulse delivery and plasma light collection (Whitehouse *et al.*, 2001; Applied Photonics, 2004b)
Nuclear reactor control rods were screened to determine those containing low Si concentrations subject to corrosion and failure	Control rods were interrogated using a fiber optic coupled probe positioned in a hot-cell through a 10 m umbilical cable. The control rod target was first cleaned using several hundred shots. This was followed by the LIBS analysis using 100 shots (Applied Photonics, 2004c). The LIBS system was similar to that of Figure 7.18

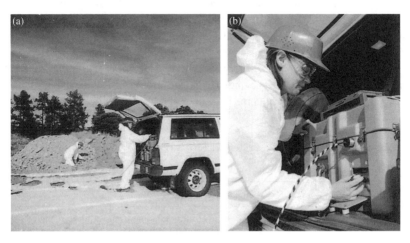

Figure 7.17 Transportable LIBS system soil analysis. (a) Fiber optic delivery of pulses to soil mound. (b) Insertion of soil samples into instrument for analysis (see Table 7.3)

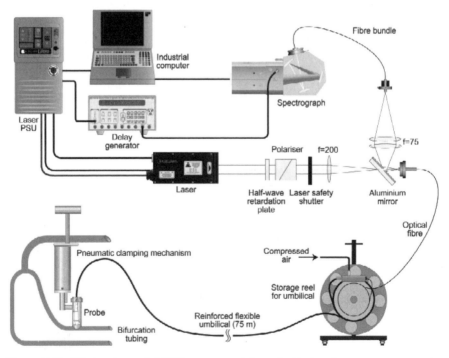

Figure 7.18 Fiber optic coupled LIBS system used for analysis of nuclear reactor components. (Courtesy of Applied Photonics, Ltd, see Table 7.3)

REFERENCES

Applied Photonics (2004a). Remote characterization of high-level radioactive waste at the THORP nuclear reprocessing plant: laser-induced breakdown spectroscopy (LIBS): application note 002. Applied Photonics Limited, North Yorkshire, UK (www.appliedphotonics.co.uk)

Applied Photonics (2004b). In-situ compositional analysis of economizer tubes within the sub-boiler annulus of an AGR pressure vessel: application note 005. Applied Photonics Limited, North Yorkshire, UK (www.appliedphotonics.co.uk)

Applied Photonics (2004c). In-situ batch identification of Magnox reactor control rods: application note 006. Applied Photonics Limited, North Yorkshire, UK (www.appliedphotonics.co.uk)

Blacic, J.D., D.R. Pettit and D.A. Cremers (1992). Laser-induced breakdown spectroscopy for remote elemental analysis of planetary surfaces. Proceedings of the International Symposium on Spectral Sensing Research, Maui, HI.

Cremers, D.A. (1987). The analysis of metals at a distance using laser-induced breakdown spectroscopy. Appl. Spectrosc. 41: 572–579.

Cremers, D.A., J.E. Barefield and A.C. Koskelo (1995). Remote elemental analysis by laser-induced breakdown spectroscopy using a fiber optic cable. Appl. Spectrosc. 49: 857–860.

Cremers, D.A., M.J. Ferris and M. Davies (1996). Transportable laser-induced breakdown spectroscopy (LIBS) instrument for field-based soil analysis. SPIE 2835: 190–200.

Davies, C.M., H.H. Telle, D.J. Montgomery and R.E. Corbett (1995). Quantitative analysis using remote laser-induced breakdown spectroscopy (LIBS). Spectrochim. Acta Part B 50: 1059–1075.

Garcia, P.L., J.M. Vadillo and J.J. Laserna (2004). Real-time monitoring of high temperature corrosion in stainless steels by open-path laser-induced plasma spectrometry. Appl. Spectrosc. 58: 1347–1352.

Kasparian, K., R. Sauerbrey and S.L. Chin (2000). The critical laser intensity of self-guided light filaments in air. Appl. Phys. B 71: 877–879.

Kasparian, J., M. Rodriguez, G. Méjean, J. Yu, E. Salmon, H. Wille, R. Bourayou, S. Frey, Y.-B. André, A. Mysyrowicz, R. Sauerbrey, J.-P. Wolf and L. Wöste (2003). White light filaments for atmospheric analysis. Science 301: 61–64.

Lopez-Moreno, C., S. Palanco and J.J. Laserna (2004). Remote laser-induced plasma spectrometry for elemental analysis of samples of environmental interest. J. Anal. At. Spectrom. 19: 1479–1484.

Marquardt, B.J., S.R. Goode and S.M. Angel (1996). In situ determination of lead in paint by laser-induced breakdown spectroscopy using a fiber-optic probe. Anal. Chem. 68: 977–981.

Marquardt, B.J., D.N. Stratis, D.A. Cremers and S.M. Angel (1998). Novel probe for laser-induced breakdown spectroscopy and Raman measurements using an imaging optical fiber. Appl. Spectrosc. 52: 1148–1153.

Neuhauser, R.E., U. Panne and R. Niessner (2000). Utilization of fiber optics for remote sensing by laser-induced plasma spectroscopy (LIPS). Appl. Spectrosc. 54: 923–927.

Nyga, R. and W. Neu (1993). Double-pulse technique for optical emission spectroscopy of ablation plasmas of samples in liquids. Opt. Lett. 18: 747–749.

Palanco, S., J.M. Baena and J.J. Laserna (2002). Open-path laser-induced plasma spectrometry. for remote analytical measurements on solid surfaces. Spectrochim. Acta Part B 57: 591–599.

Palanco, S. and J. Laserna (2004). Remote sensing instrument for solid samples based on open-path atomic emission spectrometry. Rev. Sci. Instrum. 75: 2068–2074.

Palanco, S., S. Conesa and J.J. Laserna (2004). Analytical control of liquid steel in an induction melting furnace using a remote laser induced plasma spectrometer. J. Anal. At. Spectrom. 19: 462–467.

Panne, U., R.E. Neuhauser, C. Haisch, H. Fink and R. Niessner (2002). Remote analysis of a mineral melt by laser-induced plasma spectroscopy. Appl. Spectrosc. 56: 375–380.

Rai, A.K., H. Zhang, F.Y. Yueh, J.P. Singh and A. Weisburg (2001). Parametric study of a fiber–optic laser-induced breakdown spectroscopy probe for analysis of aluminum alloys. Spectrochim. Acta Part B 56: 2371–2383.

Rai, A.K., F.Y. Fang and J.P. Singh (2002). High temperature fiber optic laser-induced breakdown spectroscopy sensor for analysis of molten alloy constituents. Rev. Sci. Instrum. 73: 3589–3599.

Rodriguez, M., R. Bourayou, G. Méjean, J. Kasparian, J. Yu, E. Salmon, A. Scholz, B. Stecklum, J. Eisloffel, U. Laux, A.P. Hatzes, R. Sauerbrey, L. Wöste and J.-P. Wolf (2004). Kilometer-range non-linear propagation of fs laser pulses. Phys. Rev. E 69: 036607-1–036607-7.

Rohwetter, Ph., J. Yu, G. Méjean, K. Stelmaszczyk, E. Salmon, J. Kasparian, J.-P. Wolf and L. Wöste (2004). Remote LIBS with ultrashort pulses: characteristics in the picosecond and femtosecond regime. J. Anal. At. Spectrom. 19: 437–444.

Rohwetter, Ph., K. Stelmaszczyk, L. Wöste, R. Ackermann, G. Méjean, E. Salmon, J. Kasparian, J. Yu and J.-P. Wolf (2005). Filament-induced remote surface ablation for long range laser-induced breakdown spectroscopy operation. Spectrochim. Acta Part B 60: 1025–1033.

Saggese, S. and R. Greenwell (1996). LIBS fiber optic sensor for subsurface heavy metals detection. Proc. SPIE 2836: 195–205.

Samek, O., D.C.S. Beddows, J. Kaiser, S.V. Kukhlevsky, M. Liska, H.H. Telle and J. Young (2000). Application of laser-induced breakdown spectroscopy to in situ analysis of liquid samples. Opt. Eng. 39: 2248–2262.

Stelmaszczyk, K., Ph. Rohwetter, G. Méjean, J. Yu, E. Salmon, J. Kasparian, R. Ackermann, J.-P. Wolf and L. Wöste (2004). Long-distance remote laser-induced breakdown spectroscopy using filamentation in air. Appl. Phys. Lett. 85: 3977–3979.

Theriault, G.A., S. Bodensteiner and S.H. Lieberman (1998). A real-time fiber-optic LIBS probe for the in situ delineation of metals in soils. Field Anal. Chem. Technol. 2: 117–125.

Whitehouse, A.I., J. Young, I.M. Botheroyd, S. Lawson, C.P. Evans and J. Wright (2001). Remote material analysis of nuclear power station steam generator tubes by laser-induced breakdown spectroscopy. Spectrochim. Acta Part B 56: 821–830.

Wille, H., M. Rodriguez, J. Kasparian, D. Mondelain, J. Yu, A. Mysyrowicz, R. Sauerbrey, J.P. Wolf and L. Wöste (2002). Teramobile: a mobile femtosecond–terawatt laser and detection system. Eur. Phys. J. AP 20: 183–190.

Zuev, V.E., A.A. Zemlyanov, Y.D. Kopytin and A.V. Kuzikovskii (1985). *High Power Laser Radiation in Atmospheric Aerosols*, D. Reidel, Boston.

8 Examples of Recent LIBS Fundamental Research, Instruments and Novel Applications

8.1 INTRODUCTION

We began this book by a thorough review of experiments and results on LIBS from the years 1960 through 2002. After that we reviewed the fundamentals of the physics of the plasma, the apparatus, and the analytical considerations. Throughout the book, some examples of complete LIBS systems have been discussed. In this chapter we look at the recent history from 2003 onward with a view towards emphasizing the latest trends in LIBS research and applications, in general focusing on what a new practitioner needs to know to perform state-of-the-art LIBS experiments.

Although the thrust of much recent LIBS work has been on applications, a review of recent activity shows that much is also being done on the fundamental physics of plasma formation and expansion, as well as modeling of the ablation process. Because the understanding of the plasma and ablation influences the choice of apparatus and its settings, we deemed this an important area to review.

8.2 FUNDAMENTALS

Energy absorption in and propagation through a plasma is an older area of investigation that has been revisited. Bindhu *et al.* (2004) described the energy absorption and propagation of laser created sparks in air and in argon using as a diagnostic a high-speed 2 ns resolution camera to photograph the plasmas. All plasmas were generated with the 532 nm second harmonic of Nd:YAG, with an 8 ns pulse width. One of the results was a new measurement of the breakdown threshold in atmospheric air yielding 2.5×10^{12} W/cm^2. The temperatures and electron densities were determined through standard techniques, the latter using the widths of N(II) and Ar(II) lines. The authors estimated the free-electron bremsstrahlung

absorption depth (in/cm) using an expression given originally by Zel'dovich and
Raizer (Zel'dovich and Raizer, 2002):

$$\alpha_b = 1.37 \times 10^{-35} \lambda^3 n_e^2 T_e^{-1/2} \qquad (8.1)$$

with the wavelength in micrometers and electron density per cm^3. Using this
expression, they calculated the absorption depth in argon and in air at a variety
of energies and axial spark distances. The absorption depths ranged from 0.02
(air, 200 mJ) to 0.14/cm (Ar, 200 mJ). Their conclusions supported many previous
observations, for example that the plasma appears to shift towards the laser.
Figure 8.1 shows the estimated speed of plasma propagation towards the laser beam
for air and argon sparks, as a function of laser energy. The speeds vary from about
1 to 3×10^7 cm/s. They also plotted the amount of laser energy lost in the forward
direction of the beam, due to absorption and scattering, as a function of laser energy.
Above 50 mJ per pulse, more than 80% of the laser energy is lost to the forward
direction.

The LIBS plasma has inhomogeneities that can lead to spatial differentiation. This
fact could be important in choosing the temporal window in which to accumulate
spectroscopic data. The following papers highlight different aspects related to
inhomogeneities.

Corsi *et al.* (Corsi *et al.*, 2003) monitored the spatial and temporal evolution of
a plasma from a steel target using time of flight and shadowgraph techniques.

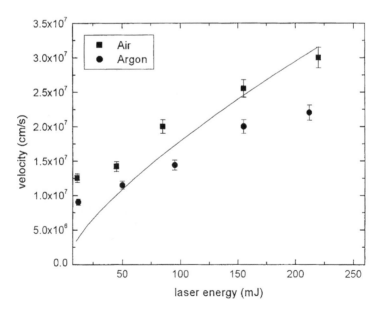

Figure 8.1 The estimated propagation velocity of the spark towards the laser beam as a function
of laser energy, for sparks in argon and in air. (Reproduced from Bindhu *et al.*, 2004, with
permission from Society for Applied Spectroscopy)

The laser was a Nd:YAG with a maximum energy of 600 mJ at 1064 nm, and a 7 ns pulse width. They found two regions in the plume, one characterized by air and continuum emissions produced by shock wave ionization, and the other by emissions from ablated material. At 250 μm from the target they calculated speeds of expansion of 1.2×10^6 cm/s and 1.2×10^5 cm/s for the continuum and neutral chromium fronts. More separation is seen at lower laser irradiances as shown in Figure 8.2. At 2×10^9 W/cm^2 the nitrogen emission intensity peaks considerably earlier than the iron or chromium lines monitored. At 2×10^{11} W/cm^2, all species lie on the same rise–time curve although their decays differ. They concluded that one needed a sufficiently high laser fluence and acquisition delay time to assure the homogeneity needed for analytical applications.

The homogeneity of laser plasmas was investigated using the curve of growth method, using five Fe(I) lines (Aguilera et al., 2003). The laser was a Nd:YAG at 1064 nm with a 4.5 ns pulse length. Two time windows were observed, 4–5 and 15–18 μs. The curve of growth technique was used to determine plasma parameters. In that formalism, the line shapes as a function of temperature and concentration were modeled, and their widths compared with observed line widths. During the early temporal interval, large gradients between inner and outer plasma areas in temperature and iron atom densities were observed. By the later window, with the plasma expanded and somewhat cooled, a single region model explains the uniform temperature and ion atom density. In the 4–5 μs window, the inner region was 1 mm long, had an iron atom density of 4×10^{16}/cm^3 and a temperature of 9400 K. The longer outer region was 4 mm in length, and exhibited an iron atom density of 2×10^{14}/cm^3 and a temperature of 7800 K. At 15–18 μs, a single and more uniform regime was observed, with a length of 4 mm, density of 6×10^{14}/cm^3, and a temperature of 6700 K. The agreement between modeled and experimental line shapes implied that the Stark effect was the dominant broadening mechanism in the plasma.

Aguilera and Aragón focused on temperatures obtained from neutral and ion spectral lines, and on the errors that can result from the inhomogeneous nature of the plasma (Aguilera and Aragón, 2004). They studied the different temperatures that can be obtained from Boltzmann and Saha plots. Experimentally they generated a LIBs plasma using a Nd:YAG laser with 100 mJ per pulse, and investigated the results in a temporal window of 3–3.5 μs. Abel inversions coupled with curves of growth were used to obtain a three-dimensional picture of the plasma. When spatially integrated, the Saha and Boltzmann approaches gave different temperatures, 9100 K versus 13 700 K. However, when spatially resolved, data from the same volume gave the same temperature, 13 160 K. The difference was explained by the spatial variation of the plasma temperature and densities leading to a difference in spatial locus for populations in the upper levels of transitions for neutrals and ions.

Plasma models are becoming more comprehensive and detailed. The paper by Gornushkin et al. reported on experiments performed to validate a radiative model of a LIBS plasma expanding into a vacuum (Gornushkin et al., 2005). They specifically addressed the inverse problem, which means finding initial conditions by comparing

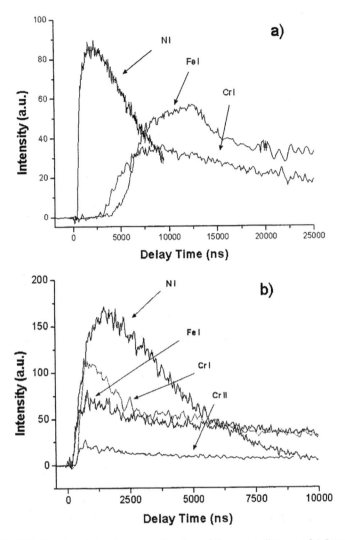

Figure 8.2 Intensity of emission lines as a function of time, at a distance of 1.5 mm from the target. The irradiance values were (a) ∼1.5 × 10⁹ W/cm² and (b) ∼2 × 10¹¹ W/cm². At the higher irradiance the rise times for all lines are very similar. (Reproduced from Corsi *et al.*, 2003, with permission from Society for Applied Spectroscopy)

calculated synthetic spectra with experimentally measured ones. Effectively they deduced the composition of the material from the calculated spectra. The plasma was considered to be characterized by a single temperature and electron density. Two separate problems were considered, first reproduction of the spectra from a single element like aluminum, and then multicomponent samples. From two to six elements and up to 500 spectral lines were involved in these calculations.

The experimental part used a Nd:YAG laser at 1064 nm producing a 0.2 mm spot at 16 GW/cm^2. They calculated the Boltzmann temperature with Fe(II) lines, as a function of position and time, centered around 60 ns into the plasma. The calculated value, averaged over all space and time points around that window, was 17 200 K, compared with the measured value of 16 500 K. The next step in their work will be to include expansion into an atmosphere through shock waves and introducing a second temperature and other factors that could be responsible for deviation from equilibrium.

Bogaerts *et al.* (2003) combined a review with original modeling work on laser evaporated plasma plume expansion into a vacuum, and ablation as it leads to vaporization and particle formation. They modeled the interaction of a nanosecond pulse with a copper target in vacuum. Some of the parameters studied were melting and evaporation of the target, the plume expansion and plasma formation, the ionization degree and density profiles of neutral, once-ionized and doubly ionized copper and electrons, and the resultant plasma shielding. Calculations were performed for a 266 nm wavelength with a 10 ns Gaussian pulse width. The peak irradiance chosen was 10^9 W/cm^2 which, when integrated over the pulse, corresponded to a fluence of 10.6 J/cm^2.

We highlight a few of the many interesting results of this work. The first is the surface temperature as a function of time at the conditions specified above. In the model, the temperature rises to 6000 K during the laser pulse and then decays over the next 100 ns to about 2000 K. The surface recession rate peaks at the peak of the laser pulse, then decreases and slows considerably when the surface temperature drops below the boiling temperature. They also calculated the variation of these quantities as a function of irradiance between 1×10^7 and 1×10^{10} W/cm^2. Plasma formation takes place at 5×10^8 W/cm^2. The surface temperature is about 2000 K at 1×10^8 W/cm^2, and begins to level off at about 7000 K shortly after plasma formation. The surface recession rate has a similar dependence on irradiance, although the melt depth continues to increase through 1×10^{10} W/cm^2 where it is 200 nm. At higher irradiance values, the leveling off of surface temperature and recession is due to the onset of plasma shielding and the direction of energy into increasing the plasma ionization. The authors make many comparisons with experimental work that confirm their general direction. The next step in this evolving work is to model the expansion into one atmosphere of a cover gas, such as air or argon.

8.3 CALIBRATION-FREE LIBS (CF-LIBS)

The technique of calibration-free LIBS (CF-LIBS) (Ciucci *et al.*, 1999) is gaining acceptance in certain experimental situations. Starting from the relative intensities of spectral lines, one constructs a family of Boltzmann plots corresponding to all constituents in the plasma. The concentration of the constituents can then be calculated from the intercepts of the lines on the *y*-axis. One then forces the concentrations of the observed constituents to add up to 100% of the material in the plasma. In CF-LIBS, the plasma is assumed to be in local thermodynamic equilibrium (LTE) and optically thin. It is often not optically thin for strong lines, however. Then spectral-line self-absorption becomes a major issue for the technique. Many lines ending on the ground states of elements, often suspect for self-absorption or self-reversal, have been excluded from the analyses to avoid prejudicing the results. Research recently focused on correction for self-absorption.

The basis of the correction scheme proposed in Bulajic et al. (Bulajic et al., 2002) is to construct curves of growth for spectral lines of interest. Figure 8.3 shows calculated profiles for Cu(I) 324.7 nm as a function of species density. In this simulation, the line starts to become flat-topped at an electron density of $5 \times 10^{15}/cm^3$. Further increases in electron density over $10^{17}/cm^3$ would have shown self reversal at the line center.

The recursive algorithm developed proceeds to calculate species densities from input parameters, estimates self-absorption, recalculates species densities, and so on. The intricacies of Gaussian, Doppler and Voigt profiles are considered. According to the authors, convergence takes place in 10–15 cycles. They compared LIBS results with and without corrections applied to values from standard NIST steel and precious alloy samples. For the NIST 1172 sample, the improvement they achieved is shown in their experimental values reproduced in Table 8.1. The span of concentrations over which this method works is impressive.

An additional difficulty in CF-LIBS arises in accounting for the contributions of all species. Many of the elements detected by LIBS will have neutral and

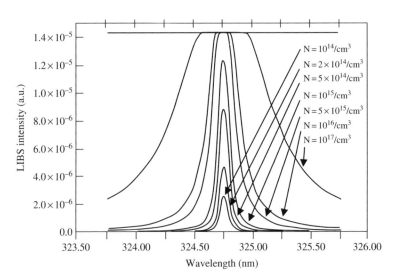

Figure 8.3 Modeled intensity profile of the Cu(I) line at 324.7 nm as a function of species density. (Reproduced from Bulajic et al., 2002, with permission from Elsevier)

Table 8.1 Improvement in analytical performance when a self-absorption correction is added to CF-LIBS. Concentrations are in w%. The standard is a NIST 1172 certified value

Element	CF-LIBS	Corrected for self-absorption	Certified value
Mn	2.0 ± 0.5	1.7 ± 0.2	1.76
Cr	22 ± 6	19.9 ± 1	17.4
Fe	60 ± 8	68.5 ± 2	67.72

Data from Bulajic *et al.* (2002), with permission from Elsevier

once-ionized states. If spectral lines from both states have not been observed, it is necessary to use the Saha equation to calculate the missing species concentration. The neutral and once-ionized contributions must be added together in order to get the total concentration of that particular element. One assumes that the temperatures of all the elements are the same, which would be the case in LTE. That is likely to be the case for neutral elements, but there is evidence of deviation in temperatures between neutral and once-ionized species. Also, as demonstrated above, plasmas can have different temperatures in different spatial regions.

Calibration-free LIBS has been tested for applications of LIBS on Mars. Colao *et al.*, in a thorough, practical study, applied the technique to terrestrial samples of soils and volcanic rock, similar to what can be expected on Mars (Colao *et al.*, 2004a). The laser was a tripled Nd:YAG operating at 355 nm, and the atmosphere simulated was that of Mars. Validation was performed with standard reference materials and scanning electron microscopy coupled with energy-dispersive x-ray analysis (SEM-EDX) on the same samples of siliceous soils and rocks. In summary, LIBS provided an accuracy better than 20% on all major elements except calcium, and better than 60% on minor elements. The conclusion was that, as a remote system operating in real-time without internal standards, it would be very useful for preliminary analyses. A prior knowledge of the sample composition, through combination with data from a different technique such as x-ray fluorescence, would enhance the LIBS results. Sallé *et al.* (Sallé *et al.*, 2005a) reported continued development of this method at the 36th Lunar and Planetary Science Conference.

8.4 LASER AND SPECTROMETER ADVANCES

Gornushkin *et al.* (Gornushkin *et al.*, 2004a) reviewed the rapidly developing microchip-laser as it might apply to LIBS. The ones used for LIBS are passively Q-switched Nd:YAG sources of sub-nanosecond, multikilowatt pulses at high repetition rate. Pumping is done by continuous wave diode lasers to produce 1064-nm pulses a few hundred picoseconds long. Advantages include single mode output which contributes to stability, low pulse to pulse amplitude variation, almost Gaussian intensity profiles, 10 kHz repetition rates, a single linear polarization state, and small ~ 2 mrad divergence. The short pulse length combined with the $\sim 10 \mu J$

output are disadvantages, however, in plasma formation. Tight focusing is necessary to achieve breakdown, which leads to a short working distance. In their feasibility study, they demonstrated that quantitative analysis was possible using nongated detectors. Their microchip laser was a diode-pumped passively Q-switched Nd:YAG laser, operated at 1064 nm, 550 ps pulse widths, 7 μJ pulse energy, with a repetition rate of 5.45 kHz. The laser pulse was focused to a spot of 8 μm diameter. It was necessary to keep the target rotating to sustain the plasma because at the high repetition rate the melt does not have time to solidify between laser pulses, and the threshold for breakdown on the melt is significantly higher than on the solid. They observed that 0.5 to 20 ng per pulse could be removed from metal foils and silicon wafers and with that they obtained detectable spectra. The zinc resonance line was self-reversed. Comparison of cadmium spectra with a spectral library allowed qualitative identification. Limits of detection were poor, however. They concluded that more powerful microchip lasers with energies of more than 50 μJ per pulse would be needed to make this technology useful. These devices are beginning to appear commercially.

A flashlamp-pumped acousto-optically Q-switched Nd:YAG laser (AO-laser) was used to study the effect of high frequency 150 ns pulses for LIBS analysis (Yamamoto et al., 2005). Pulse energies of 10 mJ and frequencies up to 6 kHz were investigated. The typical laser power was 0.07 MW, with a spot size of about 0.25 mm, hence an irradiance of 140 MW/cm². The high repetition rate led to increased spatial and depth sampling. Targets included steels, soils, surface stains and dusts on aluminum. Detection limits for Cr, Cu, Mn, Ni and Si in steel were obtained from calibration curves, and ranged from 0.11 to 0.24%. The minimum detectable mass of 1.2 pg/shot was achieved for strontium. Plasma characteristics were compared with those generated by the more common electro-optically Q-switched Nd:YAG laser. Temperatures varied from 7000 to 4000 K over the first 2 μs of the plasma. The authors commented that the maximum sampling rate for time-resolved detection of light from individual plasmas will be limited by the readout time of the detection system.

Recently a clever design for a dual-grating high-resolution spectrometer was described by Gornushkin et al. (Gornushkin et al., 2004b). At its core it is a Czerny-Turner spectrometer but with a second grating placed close to and almost at right angles to the first grating. A spectrum from the first grating continues through the spectrometer as usual. The zero-order light reflected from the first grating falls on the second grating, is dispersed, and turned by a mirror so that it too proceeds to the focal plane. A two-dimensional CCD detector in the focal plane of the spectrometer allows simultaneous recording of two spectral intervals which are offset vertically to be distinguished, one from the other. The two gratings can be driven independently; hence two intervals between 200 and 800 nm can be observed and imaged. These are 2–3 nm wide for a 2400 grooves/mm grating and 4–5 nm for a 1200 grooves/mm grating. This instrument will be useful in applications where two simultaneously displayed spectral windows are needed. This includes cases where two or more lines need to be observed in different spectral regions for temperature measurements.

8.5 SURFACE ANALYSIS

Vadillo and Laserna reviewed the use of LIBS for surface analysis (Vadillo and Laserna, 2004). They considered many issues: the thermodynamic factors governing plasma formation, energy threshold effects, the ablation threshold fluence, coupling efficiency, the effect of laser pulse width, the sensitivity to the surface, and the effect of the lateral resolution. Material begins to be removed at the ablation threshold fluence, when the energy deposited exceeds the local heat of vaporization. They then considered surface applications, the lateral distribution of elements, depth profiling, and the imaging of different atomic species. Some of the factors that interact include spatial resolution (one wants smaller spot size), data acquisition speed (one wants high speed) and sampling flexibility. Their ample discussion of depth resolution merits comment. Depth resolution was defined as the depth range over which the signal observed changes a specified amount, when profiling a sharp interface between two media. The depth resolution Δz, by convention, is the depth range over which the signal changes from 84 to 16% of its full value. In mathematical form Δz is given by:

$$\Delta z = \Delta p \; \text{AAR} \quad \text{with AAR} = d(p_{0.5})^{-1} \tag{8.2}$$

where Δp is the number of laser shots needed to reach 84 and 16% of the signal, AAR is the averaged ablation rate, d is the thickness of the layer being investigated, and $p_{0.5}$ is the number of laser shots required to reach the interface. Although Equation (8.2) predicts the best resolution (lowest Δz) when the ablation rate is lowest, the authors comment that experiment has shown this occurs at moderate irradiance levels (Mateo *et al.*, 2001). Their overall conclusion is that surface analysis is a field which is growing quickly and will move forward with new applications year after year.

Scanning across a surface with an elongated spark to map inclusions or other deviations from the substrate has become an area of interest. Rodolfa and Cremers investigated the rapid determination of the spatial distribution of elements on surfaces like aluminum and rhyolite rock (Rodolfa and Cremers, 2004). Cylindrical optics were used to create a linear spark ~ 1 cm in length, as shown in Figure 8.4. Light emitted by atoms excited along the spark was collected and provided a spatial profile of elemental composition in the sample when analyzed with a spectrometer and gated ICCD detector. Two configurations were used. With a slit in the focal plane, the resulting data represented the emission intensity along the exit slit at a single wavelength. Replacing the slit with a two-dimensional ICCD detector allowed multiple elements to be monitored at the same time resulting in a two-dimensional intensity graph of the elemental distributions. Moving the spark across the sample surface as spectral data were recorded at regularly spaced intervals allowed them to determine spatial distributions across an area, as illustrated in Figure 8.5. There an image made by printer toner on paper was detected through the iron spectral signature. In another experiment, rescanning the same barium spot six times showed a lower than exponential decay of the signal, and by implication the material was lost to the next scan.

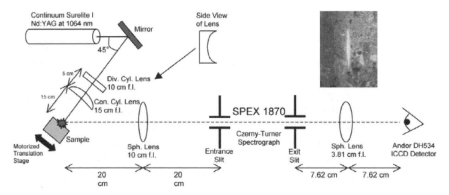

Figure 8.4 Experimental apparatus for surface scanning techniques using LIBS. A Nd:YAG pulse goes through a diverging cylindrical lens of focal length 10 cm with its axis arranged horizontally. The beam then goes through a converging cylindrical lens of focal length 15 cm with a vertical axis to produce the long spark on the sample. Light from the plasma is imaged on the spectrometer slit using a spherical lens of 10 cm focal length, and light from the exit slit is focused on the camera with a spherical lens of focal length 3.81 cm. The schematic illustrates the production of the long spark. The inset is a photo of a long spark on rhyolite. (Reproduced from Rodolfa and Cremers, 2004, with permission from Society for Applied Spectroscopy)

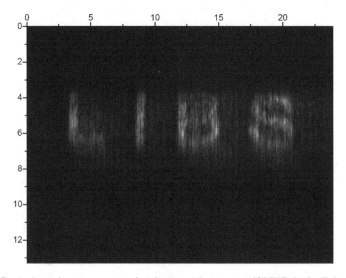

Figure 8.5 An intensity map across printed text, a 14-pt sans-serif LIBS, in the light of Fe(I) at 404.6 nm. Dimensions on the axes are millimeters. (Reproduced from Rodolfa and Cremers, 2004, with permission from Society for Applied Spectroscopy)

Mateo *et al.* reported an automated line-focused laser ablation method for mapping of inclusions in stainless steel (Mateo *et al.*, 2003). The Nd:YAG laser beam at 532 nm was focused to a micro-line on the sample surface. That reduced the number of laser pulses necessary to generate chemical maps and hence improved the speed of data collection. It resulted in a flat topped beam profile which led to very

reproducible craters in terms of depth per pulse. Resolution was about 5 μm along
the line and 50 μm between lines. Light from the sample was projected through a
Czerny-Turner imaging spectrograph onto a CCD detector, resulting in two- and
three-dimensional maps of inclusions in the steel sample. The constituents included
Mn, Mg, Ca, Al and Ti. There was an approximately 50-fold reduction in the number
of pulses and the time to complete an analysis using the micro-line method over
the point to point method. Topographic studies were conducted to demonstrate the
utility of the method. In one of these, they generated a three-dimensional map of
aluminum inclusions in stainless steel. The dimensions of the volume sampled were
875 μm in length, 600 μm in width and 56 μm in depth. The depth profiling of the
aluminum inclusions stood out in this three-dimensional representation. The laser
energy was 33 mJ/pulse. It required 2.5 min to scan this volume, much improved
over the point to point method. Nevertheless the total volume interrogated was less
than 0.03 cm^3, so the method will still be limited to extended spot sampling on a
steel surface.

Bette *et al.* demonstrated high speed scanning LIBS at up to 1000 Hz for the
detection of inclusions in and on steel (Bette *et al.*, 2005). Simple grinding of the
sample surface was sufficient for preparation. A Paschen-Runge spectrometer with
an individual photomultiplier for each line was used and covered the wavelength
range from 130 to 777 nm (oxygen emission lines at each end). Up to 24 elements
could be monitored simultaneously. The system could analyze areas with dimensions
up to 110 by 45 mm. For the first time, light elements such as C, N, O, P and
S could be quantified simultaneously. A diode-pumped Nd:YAG laser at 1064 nm
was used to scan the sample. Only one laser pulse was applied per position.
The spherical lens focusing arrangement resulted in crater diameters of 16–20 μm.
Figure 8.6 shows a 40 × 40 mm area of a steel sample scanned with a step of 100 μm.

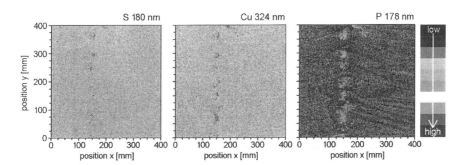

Figure 8.6 Segregation and dendrites in steel. A 40 × 40 mm area of a steel sample was scanned
with a step of 100 μm, with 400 × 400 measurement points performed in 15 min. All mappings
were captured during the same scanning measurement. The sulfur, copper and phosphorus channels
show a segregation zone oriented in the *y* direction. (Reproduced from Bette *et al.*, 2005, with
permission from Journal of Laser Applications. Laser Institute of America*, Orlando, Florida.
www.laserinstitute.org. All rights reserved)
Note: * The Laser Institute of America disclaims any responsibility or liability resulting from the placement and
use in the described manner.

A total of 400×400 measurements were made in 15 min. The sulfur, copper and phosphorus channels showed a segregation zone, a linear zone of enhanced elemental concentrations, oriented in the y direction.

8.6   DOUBLE PULSE STUDIES AND APPLICATIONS

Advances in double pulse techniques through 2002 were reviewed in Chapter 2. Figure 2.17 shows different geometrical arrangements in use and these are summarized below:

(1)   collinear multiple pulses within the same flashlamp pulse;
(2)   collinear beams from two lasers focused on the same spot on the target;
(3)   orthogonal beams, typically with one beam perpendicular and one parallel to the surface:

   (a)   where the pulse for the beam parallel to the surface is first in time forming an air spark (pre-ablative);
   (b)   where the pulse for the beam parallel to the surface is second in time, and reheats the material ablated by the first pulse (reheating).

Several experiments and papers have recently tried to address the causes of the 10- to 100-fold increase in intensities with double-pulse LIBS.

The Saclay group investigated quantifying the intensity changes for double pulse LIBS in orthogonal geometry (Gautier *et al.*, 2005). This paper starts with a good summary of the major variations of this technique and appropriate references. They carried out their double pulse experiments on aluminum samples in atmospheric pressure air. Two lasers were used, one at 532 nm and a second at 1064 nm. Experiments were done in the 3a and 3b arrangements using pre-ablation and reheating schemes. In the reheating experiments, only emissions from lines with high excitation energy levels were enhanced. The results are summarized in Figure 8.7 which shows, for the Mg(II) line at 280.27 nm, the increase in intensity for double pulses compared with simple pulses of increasing laser energy. At the same ablation laser energy, the reheated signals always were greater than the simple-pulse signals by factors of 3 to 5. Results were related to the capacity of the plasma to absorb the energy of the reheating pulse leading to increases of plasma temperature. However the same enhancements were not found in reheating for the Mg(I) 285.2 nm line, because the principal effect of the reheating pulse was to increase the temperature of the plasma. This in turn led to higher ionization, which depleted the neutral fraction, counteracting the thermal increase in the neutral Boltzmann population. In the pre-ablation spark dual pulse scheme (3a), the increases might be linked to the change of atmospheric pressure created by the spark before the ablation step. For their orthogonal beam experimental set up, the reheating scheme (3b) was found to be better than the pre-ablation method for improving LIBS sensitivity.

In this study by the Pisa group (Cristoforetti *et al.*, 2004), single pulse and double pulses were introduced in the parallel configuration (2) using two Nd:YAG lasers

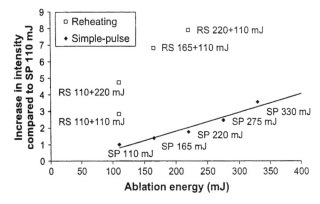

Figure 8.7 Results obtained with different laser energies in the reheating scheme (RS, open squares) and simple pulse (SP, black diamonds) for the Mg(II) 280.27 nm line. The delay between the two pulses in the RS scheme was 200 ns. (Reproduced from Gautier *et al.*, 2005, with permission from Elsevier)

at 1064 nm. The target was a brass sample and air pressures were varied from 0.1 Torr to atmospheric pressure. Neutral and ionized lines were used as diagnostics. Several pressure dependent phenomena were recorded. In one case, the double pulse enhancement of 4 for the Cu(I) 521.5 nm line at atmospheric pressure disappeared below 100 Torr. In another, the pressure effect on the enhancement due to double pulse delay was recorded. The group interpreted these effects as being consistent with changes, as a function of pressure, in the shock wave expansion and gas density in the cavity caused by the laser plasma. The authors concluded that a more detailed model accounting for residual plasma atom effects and electron densities found by the second laser pulse would be useful for more complete modeling of the double pulse process.

Laser microablation and plasma reheating with collinear laser pulses in the 50 fs to 10 ps regime were studied by Semerok and Dutouquet (Semerok and Dutouquet, 2004). A laser at 800 nm with a maximum of 20 μJ per pulse was incident upon a Michelson interferometer to provide the two beams. The results were divided into three delay regions. For delays less than 1 ps, the double pulse effect was similar to that of one pulse of the same energy. The 1–10 ps regime was one of partial plasma shielding. The 100–200 ps delay was found optimum for plasma re-heating by the second pulse, favoring plasma reproducibility and maximizing radiation intensity.

Despite the many experiments, the explanations of the enhancement effects observed are only slowly emerging. They will certainly depend strongly on interpulse delay. At delays below 1 ps, as indicated above, the effects diminish, showing no improvement over single pulse excitation. Once the plasma is formed coupling enhancement may dominate and then plasma shielding. At longer delays, sample heating and atmospheric number density may affect enhancement mechanisms. At even longer delays, the first plasma may have sufficiently cooled and recombined as to present ambient conditions to the next pulse. Much interesting work remains to be done.

8.7 STEEL APPLICATIONS

Steel analysis has always been a popular application for LIBS. It has been applied to multi-elemental analysis of slag samples from a steel plant, as reported by Kraushaar *et al.* (Kraushaar *et al.*, 2003). Avoiding sample preparations, liquid slag was captured in special probes, cooled, and then analyzed with LIBS. In order to obtain useful results, a preliminary chemical analysis of the slag is an essential input parameter because elemental concentrations can range up to 30%. In this work the authors compared four methods of standardizing the LIBS spectra: using (1) no internal standard; (2) one internal standard; (3) a sum of internal standards; and (4) a multi-variate calibration. In the latter case, all the integrated signals are chosen as input parameters, and they span a vector space. The calibration model determines the direction in the vector space that correlates most closely with the reference concentrations of the calibration samples. This direction is used for a linear calibration function. To test which of the calibrations matched most closely the x-ray fluorescence (XRF) determination of concentrations, the mean r^2 coefficient was determined. It varied in the order given above as: 0.65, 0.85, 0.90 and 0.96. Calibration curves show a much better fit of the calibration line for the multi-variate analysis. Much of the work was done on homogeneous samples of representative concentrations, to avoid confusing sample inhomogeneities with fundamental capability. The next major step in improving the results is to optimize the slag sampling method to favor more homogenous samples from the converter and the ladle. The technique's repeatability for the main elements and their oxides, CaO, SiO_2 and Fe_{total} were 0.6, 1.5 and 0.7%, respectively.

The use of LIBS across an open path of 10 m to analyze stainless steel samples in high temperature conditions had been reported by Garcia *et al.* (Garcia *et al.*, 2004). Despite the good properties of stainless steel, at high temperature it can lose its protecting oxide layer and accumulate superficial oxidation called scaling. LIBS represents a simple non-contact method to generate information about the sample in the area affected by the laser. In this work, a Nd:YAG laser beam was expanded to about 70 mm in diameter and then focused with a lens system. Light from the plasma was collected from up to 10 m distance with a Galilean telescope and focused on the entrance slit of a small Czerny-Turner spectrometer with an ICCD detector. Stainless steel samples were placed in the geometrical center of an oven whose door was opened for a short time for rapid measurements. The ratios of elements such as chromium to chromium plus iron, observed in a matter of minutes, presented quantitative information about the dynamic growth of the scale layer. Depth of the scale layer was determined by the number of laser pulses required to reach the underlying matrix material. Modeling using kinetics for oxidation of 316L stainless steel indicates a $t^{1/2}$ dependence of the growth of the scale layer with time. Figure 8.8 shows experimental verification of this trend. The authors concluded that a reasonable start has been made on making this a usable technique. An improvement would allow analyzing the scale composition which could not be done here because it flaked off the sample irregularly.

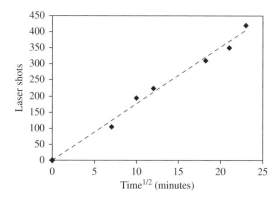

Figure 8.8   Linear dependence of the number of laser pulses needed to reach the matrix, on the square root of the exposure time at 900°C. The sample was AISI 316L stainless steel. (Adapted from Garcia *et al.*, 2004, with permission from Society for Applied Spectroscopy)

8.8   LIBS FOR BIOLOGICAL MATERIALS

Because of terrorist activities, LIBS is being considered for detection and classification of biological aerosols. Hybl *et al.* (Hybl *et al.*, 2003) approached the problem with two objectives: (1) the discrimination potential for aerosol sensing in dense particulates; and (2) identifying biological agents in single particles. For the first they used a broadband, less-tightly focused LIBS system which could not distinguish individual particles for laboratory measurements on an anthrax stimulant *Bacillus subtitles var. niger* (Bg). The laser was a Nd:YAG at 1064 nm, 50 mJ per pulse and 7 ns pulse width. Spectral resolution was provided by two grating spectrometers covering the regions from 200 to 650 nm and 613 to 825 nm. The results were compared with those for common, naturally occurring biological aerosols like pollen and fungal spores, to determine LIBS potential for discriminating biological agents from natural background aerosols. A principal component analysis (PCA) was used to set up a robust set of standards for discriminating between biological material and matrix such as dirt. A three-dimensional color visualization of their results illustrated the capability of PCA in discriminating among several different types of samples: Bg, fungal spores, media and pollen. Many caveats were discussed. The single particle experiments were done with a narrowband, more tightly focused optical system that could spatially resolve individual particles. Their conclusion was that there was sufficient sensitivity to detect Ca, Mg and Na in Bg, but again there were a variety of caveats. Incomplete vaporization or fragmentation of larger particles, particles that only are partially in the plasma, and particles of different sizes are complicating issues. Some of these have been addressed by using cascade impactors to segregate particles of different sizes. They concluded that the technique can result in useful elemental ratios in common biological materials, to discriminate between interferences and biological warfare agents. Its capabilities remain to be tested in a real field environment, however.

Three contributions to the LIBS 2002 Conference (Orlando, FL, USA) addressed different aspects of the analysis of pollens, bacteria, spores, molds and protein (Boyain-Goita *et al.*, 2003; Morel *et al.*, 2003; Samuels *et al.*, 2003). The first of these considered dual analysis by LIBS and Raman. Where LIBS was useful in providing atomic analysis, Raman provided discrimination between biological and mineral samples. The second group analyzed six bacteria and two pollens in pellet form. They concluded that a cumulative intensity ratio was a possibility for a discrimination technique because of its linearity and reproducibility. In the final work, biosamples were loaded onto a porous silver substrate. PCA was used to reduce the data from individual LIBS shots. Their conclusion was that there was adequate information to discriminate between different biomaterials. As always in the realm of analytical techniques, discrimination between similar spectral signatures in a multicomponent environment will be required for the success of any of these approaches. It is likely that simultaneous information from more than one technique would enhance the reliability of the results.

Dixon and Hahn (Dixon and Hahn, 2005) investigated the detection of spores of *Bacillus* as aerosols. A flow system was developed to ensure that only a single particle was in the LIBS spark volume. Detection was based upon observing signals from the Ca(II) lines at 393.4 and 396.9 nm. Also a scheme based on the ratio of calcium to magnesium or sodium was attempted. Their conclusion was that, with their current apparatus and analyses techniques, real time detection of *Bacillus* spores in ambient conditions is not feasible. They noted that the differences between the target and similar particles are rooted in their molecular structure, not in an easily discernible ratio of atomic species. Statistical strategies for improving the LIBS capability for discriminating between benign and toxic agent simulants were also treated by Munson *et al.* (Munson *et al.*, 2005).

8.9   NUCLEAR REACTOR APPLICATIONS

An extreme application of LIBS in a hostile environment is the analysis of materials in a nuclear reactor. Three examples from Applied Photonics Ltd will illustrate LIBS capabilities for remote *in-situ* measurements in a location inaccessible to other analytical techniques.

Monitoring materials in a nuclear power plant is one of LIBS most challenging assignments. Whitehouse *et al.* reported on remote material analysis of nuclear power station steam generating tubes by LIBS (Whitehouse *et al.*, 2001). The objective was to determine the copper content in 316H austenitic stainless steel superheater tubing within the pressure vessel of a nuclear power reactor. It was known that high copper concentrations (Cu > 0.4%) were correlated with low ductility and an increased risk of cracking. Hence the analytical goal was to distinguish three levels of copper content in the joints, low (Cu < 0.06%), intermediate (0.06% < Cu < 0.2%), and high (>0.4%). For safety reasons, a long umbilical fiber optic was required to separate the analytical instrument from the target. The apparatus is shown in Figure 7.18. Figure 8.9 illustrates the convoluted path of the 75 m fiber optic from the sampling region to the laser equipment. Power density transmitted through the fiber had to be kept low to prevent damage to the fiber, so 5.5 mJ per shot, resulting in ∼1 GW/cm² on target was chosen. It was found that a burn-in time of 400 laser pulses was required, after which the next 800 pulses provided reliable data on the samples. Ratios of selected lines of copper and iron were used for the calibration and analysis. Important parameters determined were an estimate of the detection limit (0.036%), precision (3.7%) and accuracy (±25%). A sample of one faulty joint was removed after LIBS analysis, and laboratory analysis confirmed the LIBS result.

In the same vein, other applications followed that original report, as found on the Applied Photonics Ltd web site (www.appliedphotonics.co.uk). For example, baskets used to catch reprocessed nuclear material were accumulating an unknown waste material. It was determined that the baskets should be changed, but their fate awaited the analysis of the waste product. A laser beam was allowed access to the baskets through a lead glass window in the concrete shielding (Figure 7.7; Plate 13). The LIBS analysis showed that the contaminant material was rich in zirconium and molybdenum, which determined that a low level storage facility would suffice for the baskets.

As underwater spent fuel cooling ponds were being decommissioned, it was necessary to characterize and identify components and material stored in the pond prior to their removal. Doing this under water while the material is submerged offers advantages in safety, speed and overall cost reductions. The unique part of this analysis apparatus was a gas nozzle that cleared the way for a LIBS spark to be formed on submerged solid material, as shown in Figure 8.10. Hence the LIBS analysis could proceed in a gas rather than a liquid medium. The probe was usable

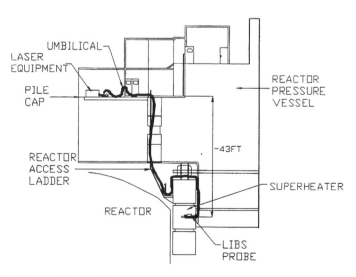

Figure 8.9 Sectional view of the Advanced Gas Cooled Reactor vessel showing the umbilical fiber optic. (Reproduced from Whitehouse *et al.*, 2001, with permission from Elsevier)

Figure 8.10 A 75 mm diameter aluminum disk submerged in water being analyzed by a LIBS instrument. Gas emerging from the nozzle clears the path for a LIBS spark to be formed on the surface. (Source: Applied Photonics website, Applications Note 004, 2005, with permission from Applied Photonics Ltd)

at depths up to 10 m and a gap of 2 mm at the end of the probe was generated by the gas pressure. A variety of materials could be identified quickly because of their unique spectral signatures.

8.10 LIBS FOR SPACE APPLICATIONS

One of the more exotic and exciting recent applications of LIBS is for instrumentation on space missions to planet surfaces. Although widespread interest in the use of LIBS for space applications is recent, consideration of the use of a laser for space missions dates back to the 1980s. In 1986 the Max Planck Institute commissioned a German firm to conduct a study of instrumentation for a flyby asteroid mission (Vertes *et al.*, 1993). A multi-instrument analysis package concept (FRAS or 'Facility for Remote Analysis of Small Bodies') was developed. A laser would be used to remotely interrogate the target surface. Instruments were to include: time-of-flight laser ionization mass spectrometry, secondary ion mass spectrometry, laser-induced fluorescence, and UV spectrometry along with remote Raman spectrometry and surface profile measurements. Although laser plasma spectroscopy was a well-established method in the scientific literature and commercial laboratory instruments developed, it was not included as an instrument. LIBS may have been considered but not implemented for some reason.

Two Mars-bound Soviet space craft, Phobos 1 and 2, launched in 1989 carried laser-based instruments for chemical analysis. The instruments, named LIMA-D, involved firing laser pulses at the Martian moon Phobos from a 30 m distance during a flyby (Sagdeev *et al.*, 1985). The laser was to evaporate an area of 1–2 mm in diameter to a depth of 0.002 mm and the chemical composition of the resulting gas cloud traveling away from Phobos was to be analyzed by a mass spectrometer. Element masses between hydrogen and lead would be determined. Unfortunately, a combination of equipment failures and ground control problems precluded successful use of the LIMA-D instruments on both spacecraft.

Current technological developments in lasers, spectrographs and detectors have made the use of LIBS for space exploration feasible. These developments, in addition to its many advantages compared with past and current methods of elemental analysis deployed on space craft, have brought LIBS to the forefront. These prior methods are XRF on the Viking (Clark *et al.*, 1977) and Venera (Hunten *et al.*, 1983) missions and alpha-proton x-ray spectrometry (APXS) on the Pathfinder (Economou, 2001) and Mars exploration rovers (MER) (Rieder *et al.*, 2003). LIBS promises to greatly increase the scientific return from new missions by providing extensive data relating to planetary geology, one main goal of space exploration. Planetary geology is important because it can answer questions dealing with (1) the physical and chemical evolution of the solar system, (2) what the early solar system was like, and (3) compare processes that occurred on other bodies with geologic processes on Earth. Also, a geologic analysis can tell us something of a planet's history such as whether earlier conditions were favorable for life (e.g. indications of past water).

Advantages of LIBS that make the method particularly attractive for space applications include:

- rapid elemental analysis (one measurement per pulse);
- stand-off or remote analysis at tens of meters;
- small analysis area of ≤1 mm, even at distance (Figures 8.11 and 8.12);
- detect elements in natural matrix without sample preparation;
- ability to detect all elements (high and low atomic number);
- low detection limits for many elements (element specific, 2–1000 ppm);
- compact, lightweight, and able to operate in severe environments;
- eliminate ambiguous results from current instruments (e.g. IR);
- remove dusts and weathering layers with pre-analysis ablation pulses;
- easily combined with other spectroscopic methods (e.g. Raman and LIF).

Figure 8.11 Ablation crater formed on basalt at 3 m distance. Depths ablated per pulse ranged between 0.5 and 1 μm

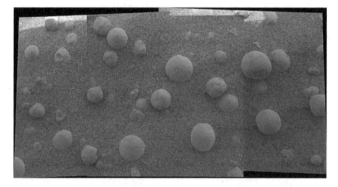

Figure 8.12 Extreme close-up of round, blueberry-shaped formations in the Martian soil near an outcrop at Meridiani Planum. The image is one of the highest resolution images ever taken by the microscopic imager deployed on the Opportunity rover. Image is 3 cm across (with permission from NASA)

Perhaps the most important advantage of LIBS is stand-off analysis and point detection. These allow the interrogation of interesting geological features that may not be accessible to either an *in-situ* detector (APXS) or sample retrieval arm (XRF). Examples of interesting geological features discovered by the MER Opportunity rover that would benefit from a LIBS analysis are shown in Figure 8.13(a) and (b). The layers shown (about 1 cm thick) could be directly accessed by the laser plasma formed at a distance. A laser plasma formed on a cliff bank on Earth is shown in Figure 8.13(c). The point sampling capability of LIBS demonstrated in Figure 8.11 could be used to interrogate small samples such as the 'berries' captured by the Opportunity microscopic imager (Figure 8.12).

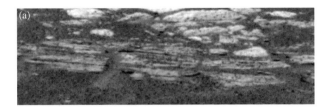

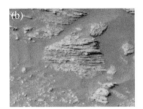

Figure 8.13 (a), (b) Images (courtesy of NASA/JPL/Cornell) taken by the Opportunity rover at the landing site (Meridiani Planum). (c) Laser plasma formed on a cliff face at 24 m distance in air on Earth. The horizontal strip in (c) is the result of moving the laser beam to interrogate different locations.

Stand-off and rapid analysis capabilities of LIBS will greatly increase the number of samples that can be analyzed during the limited mission lifetime. For comparison, a very small number of samples were analyzed on the Surveyor missions 5, 6 and 7 (2, 1 and 3 samples, respectively) (NASA, 1969). Over an operational period of 322 days, the Soviet Lunokhod rover conducted 25 soil analyses and traveled 10 540 m. In 1 month of operation, the Sojourner rover of the Pathfinder mission returned 10 chemical analyses of Martian soils and rocks (Golombek *et al.*, 1997) from a 100 m^2 area. For LIBS, it is anticipated that a measurement of 75 laser shots can be carried out every 2 min with the time between different targets projected to be 5 min, determined by the time to optically acquire and focus the targeting system. Based on these projections, a LIBS stand-off method of analysis will greatly increase the scientific return from future missions.

Several studies have addressed the feasibility of LIBS for space exploration. The results of some of these are summarized in Table 8.2. Currently, preliminary tests have demonstrated some capabilities of LIBS for analysis at close-up and stand-off distances and for atmospheric pressures and compositions simulating Mars, Venus

Table 8.2 Studies of LIBS for space exploration applications

Demonstration of LIBS analysis of a cliff bank in air at 24 m using lab equipment outdoors. Discussion of requirements for a flyable LIBS system (Blacic *et al.*, 1992)

Remote analysis of an Apollo 11 rock simulant at 10.5 m using lab components. Demonstration that stand-off LIBS has sufficient sensitivity to monitor the elements Si, Ti, Al, Fe, Mg, Mn, Ca, Na, K, P, Cr at concentrations in the rock simulant (Cremers *et al.*, 1995)

Detailed study of stand-off LIBS (up to 19 m) using moderate pulse energy (80 mJ) with samples in 7 Torr CO_2. Preliminary evaluation of analytical capabilities. Demonstration of stand-off LIBS at 19 m using a micro-laser (Knight *et al.*, 2000)

Preliminary field evaluation of a compact LIBS system (2–3 m) operated on a NASA rover, qualitative analysis capabilities such as rock identification, and comparison with IR spectroscopy (Wiens *et al.*, 2002)

Study and optimization of experimental factors affecting plasma emission under Mars atmospheric pressure and composition conditions at 1 m distance (Brennetot *et al.*, 2003)

Study of plasma emission characteristics and determination of optimal experimental parameters for samples interrogated in air and in a simulated Mars atmosphere (0.225 m) (Colao *et al.*, (2004a)

Under Mars atmospheric conditions, a comparison was made between analysis results obtained by CF-LIBS and SEM-EDX for close distances (0.15 m) (Colao *et al.*, 2004b)

Evaluation of stand-off LIBS for analysis of water ice and ice/soil mixtures at 4 and 6.5 m under Mars atmospheric conditions (Arp *et al.*, 2004a)

Study of the S and Cl detection at stand-off distances (3–12 m) in a Mars atmosphere (Sallé *et al.*, 2004)

Demonstration (~1 m) of LIBS at 90 atm pressure for application to a Venus mission. Strong effect of pressure on some element emissions observed (Arp *et al.*, 2004b)

Study of the use of the vacuum ultraviolet (VUV) for *in-situ* monitoring of elements in geological samples in a Mars atmosphere. The residual 7 Torr CO_2 gas will prohibit detection of VUV lines at stand-off distances (Radziemski *et al.*, 2005)

Study of the effect of atmospheric pressure on the *in-situ* analysis of soil and clay samples and the effect of pressure on some matrix effects (Sallé *et al.*, 2005b)

Comparison of LIBS capabilities at atmospheric, Mars and low pressures (simulating the Moon, asteroids) for *in-situ* and stand-off analysis (5.3 m). Emission intensities at low pressure are strongly reduced (Harris *et al.*, 2004)

---

and the Moon. Corresponding pressures are Mars (7 Torr CO_2), Venus (90 atm CO_2) and the Moon (~10^{-9} Torr). Figure 8.14 shows how the emissions from four elements depend on pressure for targets of Mars, the Moon and other airless bodies. The behavior shown here can be understood as the result of the pressure dependence of competing processes on collisional excitation of species in the plasma and ablation of the target (Knight *et al.*, 2000). The data indicate that signals are actually enhanced under Mars conditions (7 Torr) compared with the other pressures. For pressures below about 0.001 Torr no changes in element signals were observed with further pressure decreases down to 0.00002 Torr (lowest pressure monitored in Figure 8.14). Therefore, it is believed that measurements made at pressures below 0.001 Torr should simulate an airless body such as the Moon very well in terms of LIBS excitation. LIBS signals are significantly reduced at the lower pressures limiting the range of stand-off measurements (Harris *et al.*, 2004).

Another target of interest is Venus characterized by pressures on the order of 90 atm and temperatures of 725 °C. Photographs of the Venus surface taken by Venera

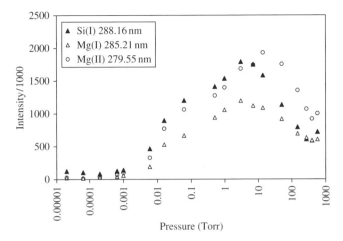

Figure 8.14   Element signals as a function of pressure determined at the *in-situ* analysis distance of 7 cm (Harris *et al.*, 2004)

14 (Figure 8.15) show a transparent, though thick, atmosphere through which a laser beam may be propagated. The use of LIBS at high temperatures has not been shown to be a problem with molten glass and metals being analyzed. There are some data relating to LIBS analysis at high pressures on the order of 30 atm (Noda *et al.*, 2002). More recent work has shown that measurements providing useful LIBS spectra can be carried out at higher pressures (Arp *et al.*, 2004b). Figure 8.16 shows basalt spectra obtained at 90 and at 0.77 atm for comparison for a sample distance of 1 m. At room temperature, CO_2 liquefies at pressures above about 58 atm and so nitrogen gas was used instead. Lines of some major elements in the sample exhibit strong self-absorption whereas other lines do not appear affected by the pressure. This indicates that analytical lines will have to be carefully selected but that at

Figure 8.15   The Venusian surface as recorded by Venera 14. (Courtesy of NASA and NSSDC)

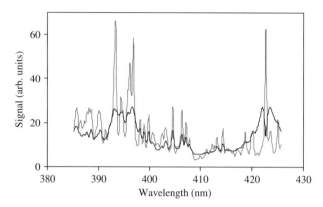

Figure 8.16 Spectra of basalt rock at 0.77 atm (grey line) and 90 atm (black line). The recorded signals were strong and were reduced by 10 000 for plotting here. (Modified from Arp *et al.*, 2004b, with permission from Elsevier)

least qualitative analysis should be possible. The hostile environment on Venus will require that the LIBS system be shielded from the high surface temperatures and pressures. This will necessitate that the instrument be confined to the interior of the insulated lander with remote analysis provided through a window. Although the spectra of Figure 8.16 were obtained at only 1 m distance, the strength of the signals show that stand-off analysis of many meters should be feasible.

Some representative LIBS limits of detection for stand-off analysis of soil samples maintained in a 7 Torr CO_2 atmosphere are presented in Table 8.3. In general, LIBS has sufficient sensitivity to monitor the majority of elements of interest to geologists at useful concentrations. On the other hand, some elements such as Cl and Br may be present at levels below current LIBS detection limits (e.g. Cl ∼ 1.2% and Br ∼ 20–1000 ppm at certain locations on Mars established by the MER). Observation of lines below 200 nm may improve that situation.

Another advantage of LIBS is that it is readily combined with other laser and nonlaser-based spectroscopic methods that use essentially the same instrumentation and have remote analysis capability. The combination of LIBS/Raman is currently

Table 8.3 Stand-off LIBS detection limits for elements in soils and soil simulants (100 mJ/pulse; 19 m; 7 Torr CO_2) (Knight *et al.*, 2000)

Element	LOD (ppm)	Element	LOD (ppm)
Ba	21	Ni	224
Cr	39	Pb	95
Cu	43	Sn	84
Hg	647	Sr	1.9
Li	20		

LOD, limit of detection.

being investigated. A LIBS system can readily be converted into a Raman system by the addition of two minor components. This is shown in Figure 8.17. By inserting a doubling crystal in the laser beam path to generate 532 nm second harmonic light and a narrowband filter to block the scattered second harmonic light from the sample, Raman measurements can be provided using the same detection system. The use of Raman at stand-off distances has been demonstrated (Sharma *et al.*, 2003). Using a compact LIBS sampling head and inserting a small KD*P crystal in the beam path, Raman spectra have been recorded at several meters.

While laboratory work has shown the general capabilities of LIBS for future space missions, work has begun on demonstrating that compact LIBS instrumentation can provide useful analytical results. A micro-laser has been used to record useful LIBS spectra at 19 m with the soil sample maintained in a 7 Torr CO_2 atmosphere. In addition compact spectrographs are being evaluated for use on such missions. Mass, size and power requirements are stringent requirements for space applications necessitating the development of high performance systems.

Preliminary field tests of a LIBS instrument have been carried out using commercial off the shelf components (Wiens *et al.*, 2002). The compact system consisted of a sampling head (~0.5 kg) housing the laser and adjustable focusing and light collection optics (Figure 8.18a). The detection system employed a small

(a)

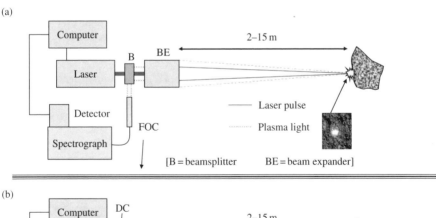

(b)

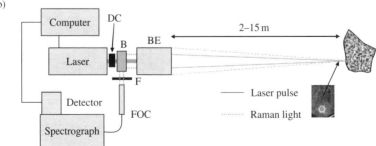

Figure 8.17 A LIBS system (a) is readily converted to a Raman system (b) by the addition of a doubling crystal (DC) and filter (F) to block scattered laser light.

a

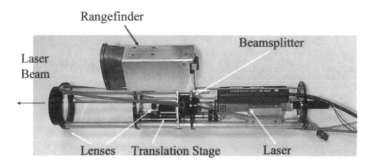

b

Figure 8.18 (a) LIBS sampling head mounted on mast of test rover. (b) LIBS system integrated on test rover. Spectrograph and detector were positioned in the body of the rover

Figure 8.19 LIBS instrument shown on board the MSL rover for the planned 2009 mission. (Rover artwork courtesy of NASA/JPL)

grating spectrograph and ICCD detector. The sampling head and LIBS system were mounted on a rover during a field test in 2000 (Figure 8.18b).

As a result of work by an international team which included studies of LIBS capabilities for Mars analysis (Table 8.2) and engineering work on development of a flyable laser, optical system, and spectrograph, a design for a LIBS instrument has been selected as an instrument on the 2009 Mars Science Laboratory (MSL) rover. The LIBS analyzer and micro-imager combination (named ChemCam) is projected to provide elemental analysis data at a range from 2 to 12 m from the rover. As in the field test instrument (Figure 8.18b), the laser and optical system will be mounted on the mast, ~1 m above ground. Electrical and fiber optic cables will provide information and control links between the spectrographs laser power supply. An artist's conception of LIBS operating on the MSL rover is shown in Figure 8.19. Current specifications indicate this rover will be the largest ever landed on Mars (900 kg mass). The rover is planned to traverse a 6 km path on the Martian surface over the projected >1 year mission lifetime.

REFERENCES

Aguilera, J.A., J. Bengoechea and C. Aragón (2003). Curves of growth of spectral lines emitted by a laser-induced plasma: influence of the temporal evolution and spatial inhomogeniety of the plasma. Spectrochim. Acta Part B 58: 221–237.

Aguilera, J.A. and C. Aragón (2004). Characterization of a laser-induced plasma by spatially resolved spectroscopy of neutral atom and ion emissions. Comparison of local and spatially integrated measurements. Spectrochim. Acta Part B 59: 1861–1876.

Arp, Z.A., D.A. Cremers, R.C. Wiens, D.M. Wayne, B. Sallé and S. Maurice (2004a). Analysis of water ice and water/ice soil mixtures using laser-induced breakdown spectroscopy: application to Mars polar exploration. Appl. Spectrosc. 58: 897–909.

Arp, Z.A., D.A. Cremers, R.D. Harris, D.M. Oschwald, G.R. Parker and D.M. Wayne (2004b). Feasibility of generating a useful laser-induced breakdown spectroscopy plasma on rocks at high pressure: preliminary study for a Venus mission. Spectrochim. Acta Part B 59: 987–999.

Bette, H., R. Noll, G. Müller, H.-W. Jansen, C. Nazikkol and H. Mittelstädt (2005). High-speed scanning LIBS at 1000 Hz with single pulse evaluation for the detection of inclusions in steel. J. Laser Appl. 17: 183–190.

Bindhu, C.V., S.S. Harilal, M.S. Tillack, F. Najmabadi and A.C. Gaeris (2004). Energy absorption and propagation in laser created sparks. Appl. Spectrosc. 58: 719–726.

Blacic, J.D., D.R. Pettit and D.A. Cremers (1992). Laser-induced breakdown spectroscopy for remote elemental analysis of planetary surfaces. Proceedings of the International Symposium on Spectral Sensing Research, Maui, HI.

Bogaerts, A., Z. Chen, R. Gijbels and A. Vertes (2003). Laser ablation for analytical sampling: what can we learn from modeling? Spectrochim. Acta Part B 58: 1867–1893.

Boyain-Goita, A.R., D.C.S. Beddows, B.C. Griffiths and H.H. Telle (2003). Single-pollen analysis by laser-induced breakdown spectroscopy and Raman microscopy. Appl. Opt. 42: 6119–6132.

Brennetot, R., J.L. Lacour, E. Vors, A. Rivoallan, D. Vailhen and S. Maurice (2003). Mars analysis by laser-induced breakdown spectroscopy (MALIS): influence of Mars atmosphere on plasma emission and study of factors influencing plasma emission with the use of Doehlert designs. Appl. Spectrosc. 57: 744–752.

Bulajic, D., M. Corsi, G. Cristoforetti, S. Legnaioli, V. Palleschi, A. Salvetti and E. Tognoni (2002). A procedure for correcting self-absorption in calibration free-laser induced breakdown spectroscopy. Spectrochim. Acta Part B 57: 339–353.

Ciucci, A., M. Corsi, V. Palleschi, S. Rastelli, A. Salvetti and E. Tognoni (1999). New procedure for quantitative elemental analysis by laser-induced plasma spectroscopy. Appl. Spectrosc. 53: 960–964.

Clark III, B.C. A.K. Baird, H.J. Rose Jr, P. Toulmin III, R.P. Christian, W.C. Kelliher, A.J., Castro, C.D. Rowe, K. Keil and G.R. Huss (1977). The Viking X ray fluorescence experiment: analytical methods and early results. J. Geophys. Res. 82: 4577–4594.

Colao, F., R. Fantoni, V. Lazic and A. Paolini (2004a). LIBS application for analyses of Martian crust analogues: search for the optimal experimental parameters in air and CO_2 atmosphere. Appl. Phys. A79: 143–152.

Colao, F., R. Fantoni, V. Lazic, A. Paolini, G.G. Ori, L. Marinangeli and A. Baliva (2004b). Investigation of LIBS feasibility for in situ planetary exploration: an analysis on Martian rock analogues. Planet. Space Sci. 52: 117–123.

Corsi, M., G. Cristoforetti, M. Hildalgo, D. Iriarte, S. Legnaioli, V. Palleschi, A. Salvetti and E. Tognoni (2003). Temporal and spatial evolution of a laser-induced plasma from a steel target. Appl. Spectrosc. 57: 715–721.

Cremers, D.A., M.J. Ferris, C.Y. Han, J.D. Blacic and D.R. Pettit (1995). Remote elemental analysis using laser-induced breakdown spectroscopy. Proc. SPIE 2385: 28.

Cristoforetti, G., S. Legnaioli, V. Palleschi, A. Salvetti and E. Tognoni (2004). Influence of ambient gas pressure on laser-induced breakdown spectroscopy technique in the parallel double-pulse configuration. Spectrochim. Acta Part B 59: 1907–1917.

Dixon, P.D. and D.W. Hahn (2005). Feasibility of detection and identification of individual bioaerosols using laser-induced breakdown spectroscopy. Anal. Chem. 77: 631–638.

Economou, T. (2001). Chemical analyses of Martian soil and rocks obtained by the Pathfinder alpha proton x-ray spectrometer. Radiat. Phys. Chem. 61: 191–197.

Garcia, P.L., J.M. Vadillo and J.J. Laserna (2004). Real-time monitoring of high-temperature corrosion in stainless steels by open-path laser-induced plasma spectrometry. Appl. Spectrosc. 58: 1347–1352.

Gautier, C., P. Fichet, D. Menut, J.-L. Lacour, D. L'Hermite and J. Dubessy (2005). Quantification of the intensity enhancements for the double-pulse laser-induced breakdown spectroscopy in the orthogonal beam geometry. Spectrochim. Acta Part B 60: 265–276.

Golombek, M.P., R.A. Cook, T. Economou, W.M. Folkner, A.F.C. Haldemann, P.H. Kallemeyn, J.M. Knudsen, R.M. Manning, H.J. Moore, T.J. Parker, R. Rieder, J.T. Schofield, P.H. Smith and R.M. Vaughan (1997). Overview of the Mars Pathfinder Mission and assessment of landing site predictions. Science 278: 1743–1748.

Gornushkin, I.B., K. Amponsah-Manager, B.W. Smith, N. Omenetto and J.D. Winefordner (2004a). Microchip laser-induced breakdown spectroscopy: a preliminary feasibility investigation. Appl. Spectrosc. 58: 762–769.

Gornushkin, I.B., N. Omenetto, B.W. Smith and J.D. Winefordner (2004b). High-resolution two-grating spectrometer for dual wavelength spectral imaging. Appl. Spectrosc. 58: 1341–1346.

Gornushkin, I.B., A.Ya. Kazakov, N. Omenetto, B.W. Smith and J.D. Winefordner (2005). Experimental variation of a radiative model of laser-induced plasma expanding into a vacuum. Spectrochim. Acta Part B 60: 215–230.

Harris, R.D., D.A. Cremers, K. Benelli and C. Khoo (2004). Unpublished data.

Hunten, D.M., L. Colin, T.M. Donahue and V.I. Moroz (Eds) (1983) Venus, The University of Arizona Press, Tucson: 45–68.

Hybl, J.D., G.A. Lithgow and S.G. Buckley (2003). Laser-induced breakdown spectroscopy detection and classification of biological aerosols. Appl. Spectrosc. 57: 1207–1215.

Knight, A.K., N.L. Scherbarth, D.A. Cremers and M.J. Ferris (2000). Characterization of laser-induced breakdown spectroscopy (LIBS) for application to space exploration. Appl. Spectrosc. 54: 331–340.

Kraushaar, M., R. Noll and H.-U. Schmitz (2003). Slag analysis with laser-induced breakdown spectrometry. Appl. Spectrosc. 57: 1282–1287.

Mateo, M.P., J.M. Vadillo and J.J. Laserna (2001). Irradiance-dependent depth profiling of layered materials using laser-induced plasma spectrometry. J. Anal. At. Spectrom. 16: 1317–1321.

Mateo, M.P., L.M. Cabalín and J.J. Laserna (2003). Automated line-focused laser ablation for mapping of inclusions in stainless steel. Appl. Spectrosc. 57: 1461–1467.

Morel, S., N. Leone, P. Adam and J. Amouroux (2003). Detection of bacteria by time-resolved laser-induced breakdown spectroscopy. Appl. Opt. 42: 6185–6191.

Munson, C.A., F.C. De Lucia Jr, T. Piehler, K.L. McNesby and A.W. Miziolek (2005). Investigation of statistics strategies for improving the discriminating power of laser-induced breakdown spectroscopy for chemical and biological warfare agent simulants. Spectrochim. Acta Part B 60: 1217–1224.

NASA (1969). Surveyor program results, NASA SP-184, Scientific and Technical Division, Office of Technology Utilization, NASA, Washington, DC.

Noda, M., Y. Deguchi, S. Iwasaki and N. Yoshikawa (2002). Detection of carbon content in a high-temperature and high-pressure environment using laser-induced breakdown spectroscopy. Spectrochim. Acta Part B 57: 701–709.

Radziemski, L.J., D.A. Cremers, K. Benelli, C. Khoo and R.D. Harris (2005). Use of the vacuum ultraviolet spectral region for laser-induced breakdown spectroscopy-based Martian geology and exploration. Spectrochim. Acta Part B 60: 237–248.

Rieder, R., R. Gellert, J. Bruckner, G. Klingelhofer, G. Dreibus, A. Yen and S.W. Squyers (2003). The new Athena alpha particle X-ray spectrometer for the Mars Exploration Rovers. J. Geophys. Res. B108 (E12): 8066.

Rodolfa, K.T. and D.A. Cremers (2004). Capabilities of surface composition analysis using a long LIBS spark. Appl. Spectrosc. 58: 367–375.

Sagdeev, R.Z., G.G. Managadze, I.Yu. Shutyaev, K. Szego and P.P. Timofeev (1985). Methods of remote surface chemical analysis for asteroid missions. Adv. Space Res. 5: 111–120.

Sallé, B., J.-L. Lacour, E. Vors, P. Fichet, S. Maurice, D.A. Cremers and R.C. Wiens (2004). Laser-induced breakdown spectroscopy for Mars surface analysis: capabilities at stand-off distances and detection of chlorine and sulfur elements. Spectrochim. Acta Part B 59: 1413–1422.

Sallé, B., P. Mauchien, L.-J. Lacour, A. Maurice and R.C. Wiens (2005a). Laser-induced breakdown spectroscopy: a new method for stand-off quantitative analysis of samples on Mars. Lunar and Planetary Science XXXVI, abstract 1693.

Sallé, B., D.A. Cremers, S. Maurice and R.C. Wiens (2005b). Laser-induced breakdown spectroscopy for space exploration applications: influence of the ambient pressure on the calibration curves prepared from soil and clay samples. Spectrochim. Acta Part B 60: 479–490.

Samuels, A.C., F.C. DeLucia Jr, K.L. McNesby and A.W. Miziolek (2003). Laser-induced breakdown spectroscopy of bacterial spores, molds, pollens and protein: initial studies of discrimination potential. Appl. Opt. 42: 6205–6209.

Semerok, A. and C. Dutouquet (2004). Ultrashort double pulse laser ablation of metals. Thin Solid Films 453–454: 501–505.

Sharma, S.K., P.G. Lucey, M. Ghosh, H.W. Hubble and K.A. Horton (2003). Stand-off Raman spectroscopic detection of minerals on planetary surfaces. Spectrochim. Acta Part A 59: 2391–2407.

Vadillo, J.M. and J.J. Laserna (2004). Laser-induced plasma spectrometry: truly a surface analytical tool. Spectrochim. Acta Part B 59: 147–161.

Vertes, A., R. Gijbels and F. Adams (Eds) (1993). *Laser Ionization Mass Analysis*, John Wiley & Sons, Ltd, New York: 529–532.

Whitehouse, A.I., J. Young, I.M. Botheroyd, S. Lawson, C.P. Evans and J. Wright (2001). Remote material analysis of nuclear power station steam generator tubes by laser-induced breakdown spectroscopy. Spectrochim. Acta Part B 56: 821–830.

Wiens, R.C., R.E. Arvidson, D.A. Cremers, M.J. Ferris, J.D. Blacic and F.P. Seelos IV (2002). Combined remote mineralogical and elemental identification from rovers: field and laboratory tests using reflectance and laser-induced breakdown spectroscopy. J. Geophys. Res. (Planets) 107 (E11): FIDO 3-1–3-14.

Yamamoto, K.Y., D.A. Cremers, L.E. Foster, M.P. Davies and R.D. Harris (2005). Laser-induced breakdown spectroscopy analysis of solids using a long-pulse (150 ns) Q-switched Nd:YAG laser. Appl. Spectrosc. 59: 1082–1097.

Zel'dovich, Ya.B. and Yu.P. Raizer (2002). *Physics of Shock waves and High-temperature Hydrodynamic Phenomena*, eds W.D. Hayes and R.F. Probstein, Dover, Mineola, NY.

9 The Future of LIBS

9.1 INTRODUCTION

The laser spark as a curious phenomenon, a 'graduate student parlor trick,' and subject of off and on research, has been around since shortly after the invention of the laser in 1960. The name LIBS appeared first in 1981 in connection with serious interest at Los Alamos in the development of laser spark spectroscopy for a variety of applications. Thus LIBS as a true analytical technique, is about 25 years old. Complex technologies, like the laser, can take 30–40 years to mature into techniques that support a variety of applications (Radziemski, 2002). The increase in attention being given to LIBS is manifest in the increasing numbers of papers, patents and international groups working on it. Some have termed it a future 'super star' analytical technique (Winefordner *et al.*, 2004). What is needed to advance the technique? What is possible? Where is LIBS going as a technology?

9.2 EXPANDING THE UNDERSTANDING AND CAPABILITY OF THE LIBS PROCESS

Understanding the processes by which LIBS plasmas are created and develop leads to control, reproducibility, increased analytical capability and acceptance. Some of the improvements made over recent years are:

Optics related:

- Lens-to-surface distance control, especially useful for an eroding surface, and irregular surfaces encountered in the field, such as metal and plastic scrap sorting.
- Collimation of the laser beam so that is has a substantial Rayleigh range, reducing the effect of surface roughness.
- Fiber optics to carry the laser beam close to a target and retrieve the emitted light.
- Development of very compact, low f-number echelle spectrographs to provide complete spectral coverage in a small package.

In the future we may see aspheric optics for shaped focusing, fibers with higher damage thresholds, and newer hollow fibers.

Laser and technique related:

- Separation of the ablating process from the excitation process, that is double-pulse LIBS.
- Use of different laser pulse widths, primarily from femtosecond to hundreds of nanoseconds.
- Using UV wavelengths in bond-breaking.
- Use of high frequency, low energy per pulse lasers for an increased rate of spatial or depth sampling.

Several laser advances could affect LIBS. Microchip lasers with higher power could be used individually, or in arrays depending on the applications. Arrays of microlasers could lead to new surface scanning techniques, or generating plasmas only at their overlap. Field deployable, robust, inexpensive femtosecond lasers would facilitate LIBS use in cases where the avoidance of plasma shielding was an important factor. The use of femtosecond lasers for long range propagation without focusing optics is just now being investigated (Rohwetter *et al.*, 2005) and holds promise for applications at distances out to a kilometer. Also it has been observed that raising the temperature of a surface can increase the subsequent ablation rate. It would be interesting to use a laser pre-heating pulse plus the ablation pulse to see how far this can be pushed. For surfaces that absorb at $10\,\mu m$, a combination of CO_2 and Nd:YAG lasers may provide interesting results.

Modeling the plasma process:

- Modeling the expansion of the plasma into a vacuum has led to the observation that the plasma is not homogeneous in temperatures and densities at different points in its lifetime.

Most LIBS applications occur in air or in a controlled atmosphere. Sophisticated models that are designed to include plasma expansion into a variety of atmospheres at a range of pressures will be very helpful in advancing the understanding of the interaction of the plasma with the ambient environment. These will have to consider chemistry as well as shock physics, and may shed light on the origin of some observed matrix effects.

Other:

- Better understanding of the effect of the ambient atmosphere, its nature and pressure. For example, work in Mars type atmosphere shows that the plasma has a maximum in brightness in the 5–15 Torr range.
- Development of calibration-free techniques based on plasma properties.

9.3   WIDENING THE UNIVERSE OF LIBS APPLICATIONS

For many years the laser was a solution searching for a problem, because the laser was a discontinuous rather than a continuous innovation. It had to generate its own applications. This was the situation with LIBS in the 1970s and 1980s. Now there is no lack of ingenuity from both LIBS researchers and technologists in devising new applications for LIBS. From the planets, to carbon in terrestrial soils, to the depths of the oceans, there are thoughts about how its analytical capabilities might enhance and cast light on a variety of theories, from global climate change to planetary evolution. Here are some evolving capabilities that are opening the door to further innovations.

Surface scanning by LIBS is finding more and more applications. There are two ways to scan surfaces: point by point with a small spark formed by spherical optics or line by line with a spark formed by cylindrical optics. The use of the latter technique is growing, for surface scanning of steel, or examining surfaces for contamination. Going over the same area repeatedly adds a third dimension to the technique, and can result in profiling the depths of inclusions that reside on or very near to the surface. Because only micrometers of depth are ablated per shot at most, the technique at this point is still limited to the top fraction of a millimeter of a surface.

Combining LIBS with other techniques to interrogate molecules can bring different types of analytical information to bear synergistically and make this application practical. LIBS is inherently a way of linking spectral signatures from atoms to species concentrations. Although some progress has been made in correlating LIBS signals with molecules, the direct connection will always be tenuous. On the other hand, combining it with techniques that have molecular identification capability could provide added benefits. The most likely emerging combination, discussed in Chapter 8, is LIBS plus Raman (Sharma *et al.*, 2003; Thompson *et al.*, 2005). With a simple change of a component or two, a LIBS interrogation can turn into a Raman measurement. The combination of data will be powerful. Likewise LIBS and fluorescence has possibilities because of the prevalence of molecular fluorescence. Advanced data reduction and display techniques may be employed to provide more reliable signatures of potentially dangerous biological aerosols.

Remote environmental sensing with LIBS may get an assist from NASA's Mars exploration. Much effort is going into the development of remote LIBS and imaging for the ChemCam project to be mounted on the Mars Science Laboratory (2009) rover. A possible spin off is a miniature terrestrial rover, smaller than the Teramobile (Wille *et al.*, 2002), for detection of hazardous materials in spills, evaluation of potentially contaminated ground (such as New Orleans after Katrina), detection assignments connected with security of military personnel, the detection of improvised explosive devices, and homeland security applications.

A US Department of Energy report (US Department of Energy, 2004) cites the installation of LIBS at a full-scale commercial aluminum operation. The LIBS probe provides *in-situ*, real-time measurement of melt constituents and temperature with a system costing between US$65 000 and US$250 000 depending on the application. The probe enables manufacturers to eliminate furnace idle time due to off-line measurements and reduces product rejections due to variations in melt composition.

New spectral regions can lead to useful signatures. Regions in which LIBS spectra have not yet been investigated in detail include the IR beyond 900 nm and the VUV below 100 nm, down to the x-ray region.

9.4 FACTORS THAT WILL SPEED THE COMMERCIALIZATION OF LIBS

The potential manufacturers of LIBS instruments are faced with the problem of many applications, with a few units needed for each. To keep costs down, easily assembled modules are called for. These may include separate modules for the laser and propagation optics, spectrometer/detector, light-capturing optics, electronics and sampling head. Some Micro-Electrical-Mechanical-Systems (MEMS) integration may be possible. Training a technical staff is an important issue. Laser safety is a must both during technique and apparatus development and in everyday use for applications. (See Appendix A for details.)

9.4.1 LIBS STANDARDIZATION AND QUANTIFICATION

For several years now, a group of six laboratories has been preparing a round-robin test of LIBS results on identical samples, using data taken separately at each location. The effort is led by M. Sabsabi, and the goal is to present evidence to the analytical community of the reproducibility and accuracy of LIBS results. This validation of the quantification that LIBS can provide is an important step in placing this technique on an equal footing with other, more developed methods. An early meeting of this group agreed that the following issues were important:

- ionic to atomic line intensity ratio measurements as sensitive measures of reproducibility;
- sampling approach and optimization;
- practical resolution measurements;
- scale of limit of detection;
- drift diagnostics.

9.4.2 ROUTINE LIBS USE IN INDUSTRIAL APPLICATIONS

Accepted use will stimulate the positive reputation of LIBS in the industrial community. Much recent research has resulted in concepts, designs, or prototypes for instruments that could be developed. Some of these have been discussed in previous chapters of this book, such as the open-path LIBS analysis system developed by Palanco and Laserna (Palanco and Laserna, 2004) and described in Chapter 7, and the deployed nuclear reactor materials interrogation system of Whitehouse *et al.* (Whitehouse *et al.*, 2001), treated in Chapter 8.

A recent article by Noll *et al.* (Noll *et al.*, 2005) discusses the operating performance of inspection machines used in industrial settings. The particular application is called Laser Identification of Fittings and Tubes (LIFT). More than 1.5 million products have been inspected in the past 5 years to verify the materials used and prevent materials errors from occurring.

In 2001 the Industrial Materials Institute (IMI) of the National Research Council of Canada (NRC) installed a LIBS system at an industrial plant for continuously monitoring the composition of a liquid process stream. This sensor has flawlessly operated 24 h per day, 7 days per week, for over 2 years, at a rate of one measurement per minute, and has completely replaced previous analytical practice.

Based on promising early work on pharmaceutical analysis (St-Onge *et al.*, 2002), some in collaboration with Merck Frosst Canada & Co., Pharma Laser Inc. was founded in 1997 and is now offering a commercial LIBS instrument, which has been sold to pharmaceutical companies in Canada and the United States. This fully automated instrument has been designed to support pharmaceutical research and development and, more importantly, to be used on the production floor for the unattended at-line analysis of up to 26 tablet samples/analysis, a full sample set taking only on the order of 15 min to analyze. Currently the instrument is principally used in a research and development environment for formulation development and process optimization.

9.4.3   AVAILABILITY OF COMPONENTS AND SYSTEMS

Potential LIBS users need to be aware of some commercial venues for obtaining LIBS apparatus or systems, and ways of obtaining assistance in deploying LIBS. Below we list some companies, addresses where given, web sites active in late 2005, and a short description of products, without endorsing any company's products. These are companies that are connected with LIBS more specifically. There are many others that supply lasers, timing electronics, and other components that one can find on the web or through buyers guides. A useful method for new users to find up to date information is to use web search engines with key words like 'LIBS apparatus' or 'LIBS applications.' Also a search of the web sites of LIBS conferences can reveal relevant company information, such as for the LIBS 2005 meeting (www.ilt.fraunhofer.de/emslibs2005/):

Acton Research Corporation, 15 Discovery Way, Acton, MA 01720, USA; acton-research.com (spectroscopic equipment).
Andor Corp. USA; andor.com (CCD and ICCD detectors and Spectrographs).

Applied Photonics Limited, Unit 8, Carleton Business Park, Carleton New Road, Skipton, North Yorkshire BD23 2DE, UK; appliedphotonics.co.uk (LIBS applications and instrumentation).

Catalina Scientific Corp., 1870 West Prince Road, Suite 21, Tucson, AZ 85705, USA; catalinasci.com (echelle spectrometers and software).

Energy Research Corporation, 2571-A Arthur Kill Rd, Staten Island, NY 10309, USA; er-co.com (LIBS applications for environmental analysis).

Fraunhofer Institute for Laser Technology (ILT), Steinbachstr. 15, 52074 Aachen, Germany; ilt.fraunhofer.de (industrial applications of LIBS).

Industrial Materials Institute (IMI) of the National Research Council of Canada (NRC), Boucherville, Québec, CA; imi.cnrc-nrc.gc.ca (LIBS applications).

Foster & Freeman USA Inc., 46030 Manekin Plaza, Suite 170, Sterling, VA 20166, USA; fosterfreeman.co.uk/products/evidence/ecco/ecco.html (forensic LIBS instrument).

Kigre Inc., 100 Marshland Road, Hilton Head, SC 29926, USA; kigre.com (portable LIBS instrument).

LLA Instruments GmbH, Germany; lla.de (LIBS instruments).

PharmaLaser, 75 boul. De Mortagne, Boucherville, Québec, J4B 6Y4 CA; pharmalaser.com (pharmaceutical application).

Ocean Optics Inc., 830 Douglas Ave., Dunedin, FL 34698, USA; oceanoptics.com (LIBS system, spectroscopy components).

Rhea Corporation, 4001 Kennett Pike, Suite 134-452, Wilmington, DE 19807, USA; rheacorp.com (LIBS hardware and software).

Roper Scientific, USA; roperscientific.com (detectors such as CCD and ICCD).

Sollid Optics Inc., 365 Valle del Sol Road, Los Alamos, NM 87544-3563, USA; sollidoptics.com (LIBS support).

StellarNet Inc., 14390 Carlson Circle, Tampa, FL 33626, USA; stellarnet-inc.com (LIBS software).

9.5 CONCLUSION

So where is LIBS in the nonlinear progression from science to mature technology? A good idea has been recognized and this evolving technique is being advanced in more and more laboratories throughout the world. Real-world applications expose difficult technical problems such as those associated with analytical issues (sample inhomogeneity, calibration, precision, accuracy, interferences), instrumental ruggedness, sample access, and ease of data capture and analysis. Components are readily available, and some complete instruments are being sold commercially. There the issues of cost/benefit ratios, capability against competing technologies, and reliability come to the fore. To parallel the development of the laser, one can imagine smaller, lighter instruments, each dedicated to a limited set of problems. Newer optical components could simplify that part of the system. Compact, inexpensive diode lasers may reduce the cost and increase the flexibility of approaches. Figure 9.1 shows what some LIBS instruments might look like in the future.

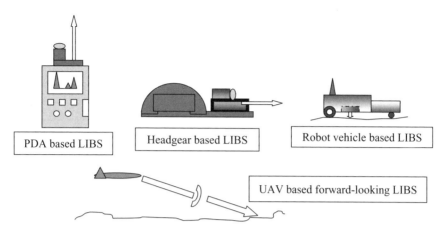

Figure 9.1 Different future embodiments of LIBS technology. How many more can we imagine?

REFERENCES

Noll, R., I. Mönch, O. Klein and A. Lamott (2005). Concept and operating performance of inspection machines for industrial use based on laser-induced breakdown spectroscopy measurements. Spectrochim. Acta Part B 60: 1070–1075.

Palanco, S. and J. Laserna (2004). Remote sensing instrument for solid samples based on open-path atomic emission spectrometry. Rev. Sci. Instrum. 75: 2068–2074.

Radziemski, L.J. (2002). From LASER to LIBS, the path of technology development. Spectrochim. Acta Part B 57: 1109–1114.

Rohwetter, Ph., K. Stelmaszczyk, L. Wöste, R. Ackermann, G. Méjean, E. Salmon, J. Kasparian, J. Yu and J.-P. Wolf (2005). Filament-induced remote surface ablation for long range laser-induced breakdown spectroscopy operation. Spectrochim. Acta Part B 60: 1025–1033.

Sharma, S.K., P.G. Lucey, M. Ghosh, H.W. Hubble and K.A. Horton (2003). Stand-off Raman spectroscopic detection of minerals on planetary surfaces. Spectrochim. Acta Part A 59: 2391–2407.

St-Onge, L., E. Kwong, M. Sabsabi and E.B. Vadas (2002). Quantitative analysis of pharmaceutical products by laser-induced breakdown spectroscopy. Spectrochim. Acta Part B 57: 1131–1140.

Thompson, J., R. Wiens, S. Sharma, P. Lucey and A. Misra (2005). Combined remote LIBS and Raman spectroscopy measurements. Lunar and Planetary Science Conference XXXVI, submission 1517.

US Department of Energy (2004). In-situ, real-time measurement of melt constituents. CPS#980, Office of Energy Efficiency and Renewable Energy.

Whitehouse, A.I., J. Young, I.M. Botheroyd, S. Lawson, C.P. Evans and J. Wright (2001). Remote material analysis of nuclear power station steam generator tubes by laser-induced breakdown spectroscopy. Spectrochim. Acta Part B 56: 821–830.

Wille, H., M. Rodriguez, J. Kasparian, D. Mondelain, J. Yu, A. Mysyrowicz, R. Sauerbrey, J.P. Wolf and L. Wöste (2002). Teramobile: a mobile femtosecond-terawatt laser and detection system. Eur. Phys. J. AP 20: 183–190.

Winefordner, J.D., I.B. Gornushkin, T. Correll, E. Gibb, B.W. Smith and N. Omenetto (2004). Comparing several atomic spectrometric methods to the super stars: special emphasis on laser induced breakdown spectrometry, LIBS, a future super star. J. Anal. At. Spectrom. 19: 1061–1083.

APPENDICES

A   Safety Considerations in LIBS

A.1   SAFETY PLANS

The components used in a LIBS measurement system are typically commercially designed and are generally safe if used properly. The laboratory represents a controlled environment in which experimental conditions can be controlled and safety measures more easily implemented than in the field. Because LIBS is being deployed in the field, under conditions and in locations and with materials that cannot be anticipated here, each situation must be evaluated by those involved in the experiment or application. During the many years we have worked with LIBS the working environments have ranged from a coal gasification system, the Mojave Desert in summer with ~43°C temperatures in the shade, Yucca Mountain in tunneling operations, procedures, and steel making operation. Each location and LIBS measurement had unique safety requirements. To adequately take into account these operating hazards, it is recommended that a safety plan, standard operating procedure, or hazard control plan be prepared that is reviewed by personnel trained in each of the hazards associated with the operation. Examples include, for example, the laser safety officer, occupational health professional, and industrial safety officer. Often it will be advisable that any operations involving chemicals be reviewed by a chemist who may point out hazards not foreseen by the other professionals. Here we present a brief overview of some more common safety related issues that must be considered and in many cases addressed (Table A.1).

A.2   LASER SAFETY

Commercial laser systems are well developed, reliable and safe instruments that must meet certain government regulations. The voltages and currents used in many lasers are hazardous and potentially lethal. Personnel are protected from high voltages and electric shock by interlocks and grounded metal shielding. Interlocks are sometimes defeated so that maintenance and alignment operations can be carried out and extreme care must be taken during these times to assure safe operations. Lasers used for LIBS measurements are generally Class IV with the laser light posing an ocular and skin hazard. Because LIBS is increasingly being used in the field and

Handbook of Laser-Induced Breakdown Spectroscopy   D. Cremers and L. Radziemski
© 2006 John Wiley & Sons, Ltd

Table A.1 Some possible hazards associated with LIBS experiments

Source	Hazard	Information sources
Laser light	Ocular and/or skin damage	ANSI Z136.1 (2000); institution laser safety officer; Laser Institute of America; laser operator's manual (ANSI, 2000)
High voltages (e.g. laser power supplies)	Potentially lethal voltages	Laser operator's manual; institution electrical safety officer; consult with laser manufacturer prior to work on electrical system; arrange work by manufacturer technician skilled in the system (NFPA, 2005)
Handling and storage of materials used with LIBS	Toxic, corrosive, may interact with other materials	MSDS (material safety data sheets, available from the web)
Laser produced aerosols	Inhalation hazard (Be, As, Cr compounds, Tl, silica dusts, etc.)	MSDS; institution industrial hygienist; maximum permissible exposure limits listed by OSHA and ACGIH (ACGIH, 2005a,b)
Laser produced ignition	Explosive mixtures (e.g. H_2 and O_2; aerosolized solvents, liquid solvents)	MSDS; institution safety officer; chemical experts; (Davletshina and Cheremisinoff, 1998)

for remote open path analysis over distances of several meters, special care must be taken in designing and conducting LIBS measurements. Common sense and safety regulations such as ANSI Z136.1 (ANSI, 2000) provide accepted rules and regulations for safe laser use and these should be consulted in all cases. In addition, it should be noted that eye protection will depend on the laser wavelength. For example, eye protection suitable for 1064 nm will not be adequate at the harmonic wavelengths such as 532 nm. The Laser Institute of America in Orlando, Florida, has information regarding laser safety, safety training, and materials and devices to minimize exposure to laser radiation.

A.3 GENERATION OF AEROSOLS

The laser pulse directed at a solid or liquid can generate particulate matter, which although representing a small mass per laser pulse, may accumulate after many shots to toxic levels. For example, the action of a single 100 mJ laser pulse on beryllium metals can liberate 10 ng of material. After 1 min of sparking a sample (10 Hz), very possible during a LIBS measurement or even setting up a LIBS experiment, the amount of beryllium aerosolized can be on the order of 6 μg. If it is recognized that the maximum permissible exposure to airborne beryllium particles is $2 \mu g/m^3$ (8 h work day), it is clear that a situation exits in which regulated safe levels of beryllium may be readily exceeded. The maximum permissible level for beryllium over a 30 min exposure period is $25\,\mu g/m^3$. Beryllium, although recognized as highly toxic under these conditions, is more or less toxic than other materials that may be used in LIBS measurements. Therefore, it is clear that extreme caution must be used when designing and performing LIBS measurements.

A.4 LASER PULSE INDUCED IGNITION

The laser pulses used for LIBS generate a hot plasma that typically contains a small amount of energy that does not represent a strong ignition source for most flammable materials. The amount of heating will be minimal except for high repetition rate lasers (e.g. acousto-optically Q-switched laser at several kHz producing several tens of watts). Most materials when irradiated by these laser pulses will be visually damaged but the damage will generally be minimal. It is obvious in certain operations that the LIBS should not be deployed under usual working conditions. An example is the stand-off analysis of an exposed surface in an underground mine in which flammable gases (e.g. methane) may be present. Another example is the dust laden atmosphere within a grain elevator. These applications must be reviewed critically as the occurrence of an explosion could lead to catastrophic results. It may not always be easy to identify such potentially hazardous situations. For example, cellulose acetate filters when irradiated by a laser beam as shown in Figures 1.5 and 3.9 are not significantly damaged by the action of the laser pulse. Only a small portion of the filter surface is ablated by the laser pulse. The same filter, however, if struck by the laser pulse on edge can be made instantly flammable, with the results resembling flash paper.

REFERENCES

ANSI (2000). ANSI Z136.1 (2000) Standard: Safe Use of Lasers, American National Standards Institute, Washington, DC.
ACGIH (2005a). Guide to Occupational Exposure Values, 2005, ACGIH, Cincinnati, OH.
ACGIH (2005b). 2005 TLVs and BEIs, ACGIH, Cincinnati, OH.
Davletshina, T.A. and N.P. Cheremisinoff (1998). *Fire and Explosion Hazards Handbook of Industrial Chemicals*, William Andrew Publishing/Noyes, New York, NY.
NFPA (2005). National Electrical Code 2005, Edition (NFPA 70), National Fire Protection Association, Quincy, MA.

B Recommended Methods for Commencing LIBS Research on a Variety of Samples

Table B.1 Recommended methods for commencing LIBS research on a variety of samples

LIBS applications	Rec. laser and λ	Laser energy (mJ)	Pulse length (ns)	Rep. rate (Hz)	Focusing; focal lengths (cm)	Line focus	Time gating	Stabilize LTSD	Spectrometer	Detector system
Solid sampling										
Surface analysis of metals (Bette *et al.*, 2005)	Nd:YAG 1064 or 532 nm	50–700	5–10	10	5–50	useful for surface distribution of elements	usually	no	echelle or grating VUV through IR	ICCD, IPDA, PMT
Art history (Burgio *et al.*, 2001)	Nd:YAG 355 nm	2	3–10	single shot	5	no	yes	no	grating UV through IR	ICCD, IPDA, PMT
Nuclear reactor materials (Whitehouse *et al.*, 2001)	Nd:YAG 1064 nm	50 mJ reduced to 5 mJ at fiber	6	20	long fiber optic with telescope	no	yes	yes	grating UV through IR	linear array
Soils and rocks (Harris *et al.*, 2004)	Nd:YAG 1064 or 532 nm	20–150	5–10	10	10–25	useful for surface distribution of elements	usually	could be useful to counter erosion	echelle or grating VUV through IR	ICCD
Liquid sampling (Cremers *et al.*, 1984; Pichahchy *et al.*, 1997)	Nd:YAG 1064 or 532 nm	20–150	5–10	10	20–50 closer risks splashing	no	usually	no	echelle or grating VUV through IR	intensified CCD, linear array or photomultipliers
Gas sampling, aerosols and bioaerosols (Sturm and Noll, 2003; Dixon and Hahn, 2005; Hohreiter and Hahn, 2005)	Nd:YAG 1064 or 532 nm	50–200	5–10	10	5–50 mm	no	usually	no	echelle or grating VUV through IR	ICCD

Table B.1 (Continued)

LIBS applications	Analysis software	System cost (US$k)	Weight (kg)	Assembly time after parts in hand (months)	Single or double pulse	Calibration procedure	Qual. or quant. analysis	Atmosphere and pressure or vacuum	Cell or open to air
Solid sampling									
Surface analysis of metals (Bette *et al.*, 2005)	usually comes with CCD detector	50–100	68	2	single	calibration curves	quant.	ambient air or other gas	either
Art history (Burgio *et al.*, 2001)	usually comes with CCD detector	50–100	68	2	single		qual.	ambient air or other gas	open
Nuclear reactor materials (Whitehouse *et al.*, 2001)	usually comes with detector	400	91	12	single	calibration curves	qual.	ambient air	open
Soils and rocks (Harris *et al.*, 2004)	usually comes with CCD detector	50–100	68	2	single	calibration curves	quant.	ambient air or other gas	both
Liquid sampling (Cremers *et al.*, 1984; Pichahchy *et al.*, 1997)	usually comes with CCD detector	50–100	68	2	double	calibration curves	quant.	ambient air or other gas	open to air, but liquid confined to flow tube
Gas sampling, aerosols and bioaerosols (Sturm and Noll, 2003; Dixon and Hahn, 2005; Hohreiter and Hahn, 2005)	usually comes with CCD detector	50–100	68	2	single	calibration curves	quant.	ambient air or other gas	

qual., qualitative; quant., quantitative.

REFERENCES

Bette, H., R. Noll, G. Müller, H.-W. Jansen, C. Nazikkol and H. Mittelstädt (2005). High-speed scanning LIBS at 1000 Hz with single pulse evaluation for the detection of inclusions in steel. J. Laser Appl. 17: 183–190.

Burgio, L., K. Melessanaki, M. Doulgeridis, R.J.H. Clark and D. Anglos (2001). Pigment identification in paintings employing laser induced breakdown spectroscopy and Raman microscopy. Spectrochim. Acta Part B 56: 905–913.

Cremers, D.A., L.J. Radziemski and T.R. Loree (1984). Spectrochemical analysis of liquids using the laser spark. Appl. Spectrosc. 38: 721–726.

Dixon, P.B. and D.W. Hahn (2005). Feasibility of detection and identification of individual bioaerosols using laser-induced breakdown spectroscopy. Anal. Chem. 77: 631–638.

Harris, R.D., D.A. Cremers, M.H. Ebinger and B.K. Bluhm (2004). Determination of nitrogen in sand using laser-induced breakdown spectroscopy. Appl. Spectrosc. 58: 770–775.

Hohreiter, H. and D.W. Hahn (2005). Calibration effects for laser-induced breakdown spectroscopy of gaseous sample streams: analyte response of gas-phase species versus solid-phase species. Anal. Chem. 77: 1118–1124.

Pichahchy, A.E., D.A. Cremers and M.J. Ferris (1997). Detection of metals underwater using laser-induced breakdown spectroscopy. Spectrochim. Acta Part B 52: 25–39.

Sturm, V. and R. Noll (2003). Laser-induced breakdown spectroscopy of gas mixtures of air, CO_2, N_2, and C_3H_8 for simultaneous measurement of C, H, O, and N. Appl. Opt. 42: 6221–6225.

Whitehouse, A.I., J. Young, I.M. Botheroyd, S. Lawson, C.P. Evans and J. Wright (2001). Remote material analysis of nuclear power station steam generator tubes by laser-induced breakdown spectroscopy. Spectrochim. Acta Part B 56: 821–830.

C Representative LIBS Detection Limits

C.1 DETECTION LIMITS FROM THE LITERATURE

The LOD values listed in Tables C.1–C.3 are from the literature. These values refer to a specific matrix and some additional information that may be of interest is also listed. The literature reference is given along with the wavelength(s) used for detection with the wavelength values taken directly from the source. The original literature source should be consulted to determine the particular experimental parameters under which each LOD was determined and for additional information. The detection limits for an element in a certain matrix determined by different laboratories may be significantly different due to the use of different measurement parameters.

Handbook of Laser-Induced Breakdown Spectroscopy   D. Cremers and L. Radziemski
© 2006 John Wiley & Sons, Ltd

Table C.1 Representative detection limits for elements in selected matrices: gases and liquids

Element	Gas/aerosol in gas (ppm unless other unit specified) LOD (matrix) [ref.] λ in nm	Liquid (ppm unless other unit specified) LOD (matrix) [ref.] λ in nm
Ag		0.43 (water) [Schmidt and Goode, 2002] 328.1
Al		20 (water) [Cremers et al., 1984] 396.15 5.2 (droplet) [Archontaki and Crouch, 1988] 396.15 0.01 (liq. evp. graphite[c]) [Van der Wal et al., 1999] 394.4, 396.15 18 (water) [Samek et al., 2000] 396.15 1 (water ice, CO_2 laser) [Caceres et al., 2001] not found 43 (21 pg) (water) [Huang et al., 2002] 396
As	0.5 (aerosol) [Radziemski et al., 1983] 228.8 600 μg/acm[a] (gas effluent) [Zhang et al., 1999] 278.02 400 μg/dscm[b] (gas effluent) [Buckley et al., 2000] 286.0 400 μg/m^3 (aerosol) [Fisher et al., 2001] 228.81	5 (liq. evp. graphite[c]) [Van der Wal et al., 1999] 274.5, 278.02, 286.04
B		1200 (water) [Cremers et al., 1984] 249.68/249.77 80 (water using RSP) [Cremers et al., 1984] 249.68/249.77 0.054 (electrodep., CO_2 laser[d]) [Pardede et al., 2001] 249.7
Ba		6.8 (water) [Knopp et al., 1996] 455.4 4.9 (Ba^{2+}, water) [Bundschuh et al., 2001] 455.4 0.007 (water) [Lo and Cheung, 2002] 455.4 0.13 (water) [Schmidt and Goode, 2002] 493.4 12 and 66 (ice/10% soil) [Arp et al., 2004] 455.5
Be	0.0006 (aerosol) [Radziemski et al., 1983] 313.1 <0.1 μg/acm (gas effluent) [Zhang et al., 1999] 313.04 1 μg/acm (gas effluent) [Zhang et al., 1999] 234.8 2 μg/dscm (gas effluent) [Buckley et al., 2000] 313.0 40 μg/m^3 (aerosol) [Fisher et al., 2001] 234.86 10 μg/m^3 (aerosol) [Fisher et al., 2001] 313.1	10 (water) [Cremers et al., 1984] 313.04/313.11
Ca	2.9 ng (particle in COD[e]) [Cremers et al., 1985] 393.37 ~3 fg (N_2 gas) [Hahn and Lunden, 2000] 393.66, 396.85	0.8 (water) [Cremers et al., 1984] 393.37 0.4 (droplet) [Archontaki and Crouch, 1988] 393.37

Element		
	0.5 fg (particle in air) [Carranza et al., 2001] 393.37, 396.85 30 fg (aerosol) [Hybl et al. 2003] 422.67	0.13 (water) [Knopp et al., 1996] 422.7 0.01 (liq. evp. graphite^c) [Van der Wal et al., 1999] 393.37, 396.85 0.6 (water) [Samek et al., 2000] 422.67 0.09 (Ca^{2+}, water) [Bundschuh et al., 2001] 422.6 0.003 (water) [Lo and Cheung, 2002] 422.7 0.4–0.1 nmol/l ($CaCl_2$ in water, femtosecond and nanosecond lasers) [Assion et al., 2003] 393.4, 396.8 nm 10 (estimated) ($CaCO_3$ in water) [De Giacomo et al., 2004] 422.7 1 (water) [Yaroshchyk et al., 2004] 393.4 0.020 (droplet) [Janzen et al., 2005] 393.37
C	36 (air) [Dudragne et al., 1998] 833.515	
Cd	0.019 (aerosol in air) [Essien et al., 1988] 228.8 39 µg/acm (gas effluent) [Zhang et al., 1999] 228.8 120 µg/acm (gas effluent) [Zhang et al., 1999] 326.11 5 µg/dscm (gas effluent) [Buckley et al., 2000] 228.8 60 µg/m³ (aerosol) [Fisher et al., 2001] 226.50 120 µg/m³ (aerosol) [Fisher et al., 2001] 228.80	500 (water) [Knopp et al., 1996] 361.2 0.1 (liq. evp. graphite^c) [Van der Wal et al., 1999] 226.5, 228.5 1 (liq. evp. graphite^c) [Van der Wal et al., 1999] 214.44 0.21 (water) [Schmidt and Goode, 2002] 361.1
Cl	8 (freon in air) [Cremers and Radziemski, 1983] 837.6 0.16 (air) [Haisch et al., 1996] 435.8 90 (air) [Dudragne et al., 1998] 837.594	
Co		>0.1 (liq. evp. graphite^c) [Van der Wal et al., 1999] 238–242, 340–348, 349–353
Cr	3.5 ng (particle in COD^e) [Cremers et al., 1985] 425.44 6 µg/acm (gas effluent) [Zhang et al., 1999] 425.44 400 ng/dscm air [Martin and Cheng, 2000] 425.5 5 µg/dscm (gas effluent) [Buckley et al., 2000] 283.6 30 µg/m³ (aerosol) [Fisher et al., 2001] 425.44 40 µg/m³ (aerosol) [Fisher et al., 2001] 428.97	0.1 (water) [Arca et al., 1997] 283.563 0.1 (liq. evp. graphite^c) [Van der Wal et al., 1999] 266–268, 274–279, 283–288 200 (water) [Samek et al., 2000] 520.45 310 (under water, purge gas) [Beddows et al., 2002] 427.28 0.13 (water) [Schmidt and Goode, 2002] 520.9 0.4 (water) [Yueh et al., 2002] 425.4
Cs	1 (water) [Cremers et al., 1984] 852.11	

Table C.1 (Continued)

Element	Gas/aerosol in gas (ppm unless other unit specified) LOD (matrix) [ref.] λ in nm	Liquid (ppm unless other unit specified) LOD (matrix) [ref.] λ in nm
Cu	0.87 ng (particle in COD[e]) [Cremers et al., 1985] 324.75	0.01 (liq. evp. graphite[c]) [Van der Wal et al., 1999] 324.75, 327.4 5 (water) [Samek et al., 2000] 324.75 0.017 (electrodep., CO_2 laser[d]) [Pardede et al., 2001] 327.4 0.0042 (water) [Schmidt and Goode, 2002] 510.6 0.0095 (water) [Schmidt and Goode, 2002] 324.7
Eu		5.0 (Eu^{3+}, water) [Bundschuh et al., 2001] 459.4, 462.7, 466.1 0.03 (Eu_2O_3, water) [Bundschuh et al., 2001] 459.4, 462.7, 466.1 3.3×10^{-5} mol/l (Eu^{+3}, water) [Yun et al., 2001] 459.4, 462.7, 466.1 2.0×10^{-7} mol/l (Eu_2O_3, water) [Yun et al., 2001] 459.4, 462.7, 466.1
F	38 (freon in air) [Cremers and Radziemski, 1983] 685.6 20 (air) [Dudragne et al., 1998] 685.604 40 (C_2F_5H in air) [Williamson et al., 1998] 685.6	
Fe		0.01 (liq. evp. graphite[c]) [Van der Wal et al., 1999] 238–241, 260–263, 273–276 0.05 (electrodep., CO_2 laser[d]) [Pardede et al., 2001] 358.1
Hg	0.5 (aerosol) [Radziemski et al., 1983] 253.6 0.005 (vapor) [Lazzari et al., 1994] 253.65 680 μg/acm (gas effluent) [Zhang et al., 1999] 253.65 80 μg/dscm (gas effluent) [Buckley et al., 2000] 253.7 230 μg/m³ (aerosol) [Fisher et al., 2001] 253.65	10 (liq. evp. graphite[c]) [Van der Wal et al., 1999] 253.65 2.0 (water) [Schmidt and Goode, 2002] 435.8
K		1.2 (water) [Cremers et al., 1984] 766.49 4 (water) [Samek et al., 2000] 766.49 1.2 (0.5 pg) (water) [Huang et al., 2002] 766
Li	1.5 ng (particle in COD[e]) [Cremers et al., 1985] 670.78/670.79	0.006 (water) [Cremers et al., 1984] 670.78 0.3 (droplet) [Archontaki and Crouch, 1988] 670.78 0.013 (water) [Knopp et al., 1996] 670.8

	~3 fg (N$_2$ gas) [Hahn and Lunder, 2000] 279.55, 280.2, 285.21	0.009 (water) [Samek et al., 2000] 670.774
		0.05 (electrodep., CO$_2$ laser[d]) [Pardede et al., 2001] 670.7
		6 and 3 (ice/10% soil) [Arp et al., 2004] 670.8
Mg	1.2 fg (particle in air) [Carranza et al., 2001] 279.55, 280.27, 285.21	100 (water) [Cremers et al., 1984] 279.55
		1.9 (droplet) [Archontaki and Crouch, 1988] 279.55
		0.01 (liq. evp. graphite[c]) [Van der Wal et al., 1999] 279.55, 280.27
	20 fg (aerosol) [Hybl et al., 2003] 285.2	3 (water) [Samek et al., 2000] 285.21
		1 (water) [Charfi and Harith, 2002] 279.55
		1.2 (water, mixed) [Charfi and Harith, 2002] 279.55
		0.1 (water) [Yueh et al., 2002] 279.55
Mn		7.2 (droplet) [Archontaki and Crouch, 1988] 257.61
		10 (water) [Samek et al., 2000] 403.08
		325 (water) [Beddows et al., 2002] 403.08
		0.7 (under water, purge gas) [Yueh et al., 2002] 403.076
		15 and 101 (ice/10% soil) [Arp et al., 2004] 403.0/403.3/403.4
	0.006 (aerosol) [Radziemski et al., 1983] 588.9	0.014 (water) [Cremers et al., 1984] 589.00
	5.2 ng (particle in COD[e]) [Cremers et al., 1985] 589.00	2.2 (droplet) [Archontaki and Crouch, 1988] 589.00
	3.3 fg (particle in air) [Carranza et al., 2001] 589.00, 589.59	0.0075 (water) [Knopp et al., 1996] 589.3
		0.08 (water) [Samek et al., 2000] 588.99
Na		2 (water ice, CO$_2$ laser) [Caceres et al., 2001] 588.99
	100 fg (aerosol) [Hybl et al., 2003] 589.0	0.63 (0.3 pg) (water) [Huang et al., 2002] 589
		2 (water) [Charfi and Harith, 2002] 588.99
		2.5 (water, mixed) [Charfi and Harith, 2002] 588.99
		0.0004 (water) [Lo and Cheung, 2002] 589.0
		1 (water) [Huang and Harith, 2004] 589
		36.4 (water, 1064 nm) [Berman and Wolf, 1998] 341.48, 352.45, 361.94
Ni		18 (water, 355 nm) [Berman and Wolf, 1998] 341.48, 352.45, 361.94
		0.01 (liq. evp. graphite[c]) [Van der Wal et al., 1999] 221–223, 229–231
		0.31 (water) [Schmidt and Goode, 2002] 353.0
P	1.2 (aerosol) [Radziemski et al., 1983] 253.3	

Table C.1 (Continued)

Element	Gas/aerosol in gas (ppm unless other unit specified) LOD (matrix) [ref.] λ in nm	Liquid (ppm unless other unit specified) LOD (matrix) [ref.] λ in nm
Pb	0.21 (aerosol in air) [Essien et al., 1988] 405.8 155 μg/m³ (aerosol in air) [Neuhauser et al., 1997] 405.8 68 μg/acm (gas effluent) [Zhang et al., 1999] 405.78 20 μg/dscm (gas effluent) [Buckley et al., 2000] 220.4 190 μg/m³ (aerosol) [Fisher et al., 2001] 405.78	12.5 (water) [Knopp et al., 1996] 405.8 2 (liq. evp. graphite[c]) [Van der Wal et al., 1999] 261.37, 261.42, 280.2, 283.31 10 (liq. evp. graphite[c]) [Van der Wal et al., 1999] 405.78, 406.21 40 (water) [Samek et al., 2000] 405.78 13.1 (Pb²⁺, water) [Bundschuh 2001] 405.7 0.025 (electrodep., CO₂ laser[d]) [Pardede et al., 2001] 405.7 0.3 (water) [Lo and Cheung, 2002] 405.8 1.1 (water) [Schmidt and Goode, 2002] 405.8
Re		8 (water) [Yueh et al., 2002] 346.046
Rb		0.2 (water) [Cremers et al., 1984] 780.03
S	1500 (air) [Dudragne et al., 1998] 921.29	
Sb	120 μg/acm [Zhang et al., 1999] 259.81	
Si		0.01 (liq. evp. graphite[c]) [Van der Wal et al., 1999] 288.16, 251–253 455 (under water, purge gas) [Beddows et al., 2002] 288.16
Sr		1 and 2 (ice/10% soil) [Arp et al., 2004] 460.7
Tc		25 (water) [Samek et al., 2000] 429.71
Ti		0.1 (liq. evp. graphite[c]) [Van der Wal et al., 1999] 323.4, 334–339 111 and 520 (ice/10% soil) [Arp et al., 2004] 398.2
U		100 (4 M nitric acid/aqueous) [Wachter and Cremers, 1987] 409.02 450 (water) [Samek et al., 2000] 409.02
Zn	0.24 (aerosol in air) [Essien et al., 1988] 481.1	11 (liq. evp. graphite[c]) [Van der Wal et al., 1999] 330.26, 330.29, 334.5, 334.56 0.85 (water) [Schmidt and Goode, 2002] 472.2

RSP, repetitive spark pair.

[a] acm, actual cubic meters.

[b] dscm, dry standard cubic meters.

[c] Liquid evaporated on graphite, dried, and then analyzed using LIBS.

[d] Element electro-deposited and then analyzed on electrode using LIBS and a CO₂ laser.

[e] Particles ablated from element-containing compound into COD (continuous optical discharge).

Table C.2 Representative detection limits for elements in selected matrices: surfaces and solids

Element	Surface (ng/cm² unless other unit specified) LOD (matrix) [ref.] λ in nm	Solid (ppm unless other unit specified) LOD (matrix) [ref.] λ in nm
Ag	(liq. on filter) [Appendix C.2]	200 (UO_2 pellet) [Fichet et al., 1999] 328.0683 60 (PuO_2 pellet) [Fichet et al., 1999] 328.0683
Al	(liq. on filter) [Appendix C.2]	130 (Al_2O_3 in Fe ore) [Grant et al., 1991] 396.2 54, 30 (glass, air 1 and 5 Torr) [Kurniawan et al., 1995] 396.1 16 (zinc alloy) [St-Onge et al., 1997] 308.22 9 (zinc alloy) [St-Onge et al., 1997] 309.27 1–10 (aluminum, echelle) [Bauer et al., 1998] not found 1 (plant material) [Sun et al., 1999] 308.2 200 (UO_2 pellet) [Fichet et al., 1999] 396.1527 60 (lignite) [Wallis et al., 2000] 309.27/309.29 2 (starch-based flour) [Cho et al., 2001] 396.153 18, 3 (wood) [Uhl et al., 2001] 394.403 90 (low-ash lignite) [Chadwick and Body, 2002] not found 7 (steel in Ar) [Sturm et al., 2004] 396.2 1.8–5.7% (soil, 7 Torr CO_2) [Sallé et al., 2005] 396.14
As	440 (aerosol on filter) [Neuhauser et al., 1999] 235.0 910 (quartz filter) [Panne et al., 2001] 235.0	15, 2.7 (wood) [Uhl et al., 2001] 234.984 3.3 (soil) [Lazic et al., 2001] 235.0 0.044 (soil, 7 Torr CO_2) [Radziemski et al., 2004] 189.0
Au	(liq. on filter) [Appendix C.2]	
B	(liq. on filter) [Appendix C.2]	30, 40 (glass, air 1 and 5 Torr) [Kurniawan et al., 1995] 345.1 65 (UO_2 pellet) [Fichet et al., 1999] 249.7733 1.5, 0.3 (wood) [Uhl et al., 2001] 249.773
Ba	18 (solution on Al) [Rodolfa and Cremers, 2004] 413.1 18 (liq. on Al[b]) [Yamamoto et al., 2005] 455.40 13 pg (liq. on Al[b]) [Yamamoto et al., 2005] 455.40 4.4–8 (particles on Al[b]) [Yamamoto et al., 2005] 455.40 3.1–5.6 pg (particles on Al[b]) [Yamamoto et al., 2005] 455.40 (liq. on filter) [Appendix C.2]	180, 99 (glass, air 1 and 5 Torr) [Kurniawan et al., 1995] 553.5 42 (soil) [Eppler et al., 1996] 455.4 265 (soil) [Yamamoto et al., 1996] 455.4 76 (sand) [Eppler et al., 1996] 455.4 600 (UO_2 pellet) [Fichet et al., 1999] 455.4042 100 (PuO_2 pellet) [Fichet et al., 1999] 455.4042 3, 21 (synthetic silicate in 5 Torr CO_2) [Knight et al., 2000] 455.40 30–170 (soil, 7 Torr CO_2) [Sallé et al., 2005] 455.39

Table C.2 (Continued)

Element	Surface (ng/cm² unless other unit specified) LOD (matrix) [ref.] λ in nm	Solid (ppm unless other unit specified) LOD (matrix) [ref.] λ in nm
Be	0.45 (0.5–5 μm particles on filter) [Cremers and Radziemski, 1985] 313.042/313.107 (liq. on filter) [Appendix C.2]	9.3 (soil) [Yamamoto et al., 1996] 313.0/313.1 0.4–1.2 (soil) [Multari et al., 1996] 313.0/313.1
Bi	(liq. on filter) [Appendix C.2]	
Br		350 (UO₂ pellet) [Fichet et al., 1999] 306.7716
		0.0028 mole fraction (org. solid in air) [Tran et al., 2001] 827.2
		0.00029 mole fraction (org. solid in He) [Tran et al., 2001] 827.2
		15 000 and 11 000 (ABS polymer) [Stepputat and Noll, 2003] 827.24
		0.05% (thermoplast) [Radivojevic et al., 2004b] 131.0
		3.75% (thermoplast) [Radivojevic et al., 2004b] 826.5
		1.1% (thermoplast) [Radivojevic et al., 2004b] 833.5
		5.9% (soil, 0.25 Torr CO₂) [Radziemski et al., 2004] 154.1
		5.6% (soil, 0.25 Torr CO₂) [Radziemski et al., 2004] 163.3
Ca		30 (CaO in Fe ore) [Grant et al., 1991] 431.86
		85, 85 (glass, air 1 and 5 Torr) [Kurinawan et al., 1995] 422.6
		1–10 (aluminum, echelle) [Bauer et al., 1998] not found
		1 (plant material) [Sun et al., 1999] 428.3
		60 (lignite) [Wallis et al., 2000] 396.85
		60 (low-ash lignite) [Chadwick and Body, 2002] not given
		850–2200 (soil, 7 Torr CO₂) [Sallé et al., 2005] 393.36
C		65 (steel) [Aguilera et al., 1992] 193.09
		80 (steel) [Aragón et al., 1999] 193.09
		7 (steel) [Sturm et al., 2000] 193.09
		87 (steel) [Khater et al., 2000] 97.7
		300 (soil) [Cremers et al., 2001] 247.8
		3 (steel in air) [Noll et al., 2001] 193.1
		5 (steel) [Hemmerlin et al., 2001] 133.571
		1.2 (steel) [Khater et al., 2002] 97.7
		0.24% (soil, 7 Torr CO₂) [Radziemski et al., 2004] 247.8
		0.32% (soil, 7 Torr CO₂) [Radziemski et al., 2004] 193.1

Cd

400 (aerosol on filter) [Neuhauser et al., 1999] 228.8
400 (quartz filter) [Panne et al., 2001] 228.8
(liq. on filter) [Appendix C.2]

0.51% (soil, 7 Torr CO_2) [Radziemski et al., 2004] 165.7
7 (steel in Ar) [Sturm et al., 2004] 193.1
7 (steel) [Radivojevic et al., 2004a] 193.091
30 (soil) [Wisbrun et al., 1994] PCR using multiple lines
19–306 (soil cone penetrometer) [Theriault et al., 1998] 508.58
8 (starch-based flour) [Cho et al., 2001] 226.502
1.6, 0.5 (wood) [Uhl et al., 2001] 226.502/228.802
6 (soil) [Lazic et al., 2001] 228.8
19, 11 (ABS polymer) [Stepputat and Noll, 2003] 228.80
96 (ABS polymer, on-line analyzer) [Stepputat and Noll, 2003] 228.80

Cl

0.011 mole fraction (org. solid in air) [Tran et al., 2001] 837.6
0.00088 mole fraction (org. solid in He) [Tran et al., 2001] 837.6
7.5% (soil, 0.25 Torr CO_2) [Radziemski et al., 2004] 133.6
1880 (NaCl in pressed sample in He) [Asimellis et al., 2005] 837.59

Co

100 (aerosol on filter) [Neuhauser et al., 1999] 238.4
100 (quartz filter) [Panne et al., 2001] 238.4
(liq. on filter) [Appendix C.2]

Cr

40 (aerosol on filter) [Neuhauser et al., 1999] 267.7
40 (quartz filter) [Panne et al., 2001] 267.7
4.3 (liq. on Al[b]) [Yamamoto et al., 2005] 425.44
3 pg (liq. on Al[b]) [Yamamoto et al., 2005] 425.44
4.4–8.1 (particles on Al[b]) [Yamamoto et al., 2005] 425.44
3.1–5.7 pg (particles on Al[b]) [Yamamoto et al., 2005] 425.44
(liq. on filter) [Appendix C.2]

10 (soil) [Wisbrun et al., 1994] PCR using multiple lines
40 (iron) [Paksy et al., 1996] 425.4
8–69 (soil) [Multari et al., 1996] 425.44
5.8–52 (soil) [Multari et al., 1996] 427.48
367 (steel under water; RSP) [Pichahchy et al., 1997] 425.44
5.2–31.3 (soil cone pentrometer) [Theriault et al., 1998] 425.43
1–10 (aluminum, echelle) [Bauer et al., 1998] not found
6 (steel) [Aragón et al., 1999] 267.72
70 (UO_2 pellet) [Fichet et al., 1999] 520.8436
35 (PuO_2 pellet) [Fichet et al., 1999] 520.8436
7 (steel) [Sturm et al., 2000] 267.72
88, 39 (synthetic silicate in 5 Torr CO_2) [Knight et al., 2000] 267.71
1 (starch-based flour) [Cho et al., 2001] 425.435
<1 (wood) [Uhl et al., 2001] 283.563
2.5 (soil) [Lazic et al., 2001] 425.4

Table C.2 (Continued)

Element	Surface (ng/cm² unless other unit specified) LOD (matrix) [ref.] λ in nm	Solid (ppm unless other unit specified) LOD (matrix) [ref.] λ in nm
		3 (Al alloy, FO LIBS) [Rai et al., 2001] 359.349
		3 (Al alloy) [Rai et al., 2001] 359.349
		30 (soil) [Capitelli et al., 2002] 520.6, 520.8
		204, 256 (Al[a]) [Rieger et al., 2002] 425.4
		2, 4 (ABS polymer) [Stepputat and Noll, 2003] 425.43
		73 (ABS polymer, on-line analyzer) [Stepputat and Noll, 2003] 425.43
		7 (steel in Ar) [Sturm et al., 2004] 267.7
		2100 (slag) [López-Moreno et al., 2004] 520.45, 520.60, 520.84
		11 (Al alloy) [Sallé et al., 2004] 357.869
		1190 (molten steel) [Palanco et al., 2004] not stated, 370–400 nm region
		100, 30 (steel, microchip laser) [López-Moreno et al., 2005] 425
		44–64 (steel[b]) [Yamamoto et al., 2005] 425.44
Cu	19 (aerosol on filter) [Neuhauser et al., 1999] 324.8	20 (soil) [Wisbrun et al., 1994] PCR using multiple lines
	10 (quartz filter) [Panne et al., 2001] 324.8	10 (Al alloy) [Sabsabi and Cielo, 1995] 327.4
	(liq. on filter) [Appendix C.2]	4.8–15 (soil) [Multari et al., 1996] 324.75
		4.5–11 (soil) [Multari et al., 1996] 327.40
		544 (zinc alloy) [St-Onge et al., 1997] 282.44
		520 (steel under water; RSP) [Pichahchy et al., 1997] 324.75
		1–10 (aluminum, echelle) [Bauer et al., 1998] not found
		1 (plant material) [Sun et al., 1999] 324.8
		150 (UO₂ pellet) [Fichet et al., 1999] 324.7540
		90 (PuO₂ pellet) [Fichet et al., 1999] 324.7540
		38, 43 (synthetic silicate in 5 Torr CO₂) [Knight et al., 2000] 327.39
		1 (starch-based flour) [Cho et al., 2001] 324.754
		1.8, 0.3 (wood) [Uhl et al., 2001] 324.754
		3.3 (soil) [Lazic et al., 2001] 324.8
		56 (Al alloy, FO LIBS) [Rai et al., 2001] 324.7
		160 (Al alloy) [Rai et al., 2001] 324.7
		360 (stainless steel) [Whitehouse et al., 2001] 324.75, 327.40
		30 (soil) [Capitelli et al., 2002] 327.4

42, 61 (Al[a]) [Rieger et al., 2002] 324.8
12 (Al[a]) [Rieger et al., 2002] 324.8
22 (Al[a]) [Rieger et al., 2002] 324.8
7 (steel in Ar) [Sturm et al., 2004] 324.8
2 (Al, RSS) [Gautier et al., 2004] 327.4
3 (Al, RSP) [Gautier et al., 2004] 327.4
23.8 (Al) [Ismail et al., 2004] 324
6.3 (steel) [Ismail et al., 2004] 324
100 ng (femtosecond laser, 25 m) [Rohwetter et al., 2004] 521.82
163–353 (steel[b]) [Yamamoto et al., 2005] 324.75
0.40, 0.36 (aluminum alloy, microchip laser) [Freedman et al., 2005] 324.7537

Dy   10 (NaCl) [Ishizuka, 1973] 353.17

Er   30 (NaCl) [Ishizuka, 1973] 349.91

Eu   5 (NaCl) [Ishizuka, 1973] 381.97

F   0.016 mole fraction (org. solid in air) [Tran et al., 2001] 685.6
0.0010 mole fraction (org. solid in He) [Tran et al., 2001] 712.8
300 (NF in pressed sample in He) [Asimellis et al., 2005] 685.60

Fe (liq. on filter) [Appendix C.2]
22 (zinc alloy) [St-Onge et al., 1997] 302.06
1–10 (aluminum, echelle) [Bauer et al., 1998] not found
1 (plant material) [Sun et al., 1999] 404.6
400 (UO_2 pellet) [Fichet et al., 1999] 248.3271
90 (lignite) [Wallis et al., 2000] 238.20
30 (Al alloy, FO LIBS) [Rai et al., 2001] 344.0606
15 (Al alloy) [Rai et al., 2001] 344.0606
500 (soil) [Capitelli et al., 2002] 404.6, 406.4, 407.2
100 (low-ash lignite) [Chadwick and Body, 2002] not found
447,628 (Al[a]) [Rieger et al., 2002] 438.4
1900 (slag) [López-Moreno et al., 2004] 489.2
6 (Al, RSS) [Gautier et al., 2004] 259.9
3 (Al, RSP) [Gautier et al., 2004] 259.9
3–7.5% (soil, 7 Torr CO_2) [Sallé et al., 2005] 404.58
0.32, 0.14 (aluminum alloy, microchip laser) [Freedman et al., 2005] 373.3317, 373.4864, 373.7131

Table C.2 (Continued)

Element	Surface (ng/cm² unless other unit specified) LOD (matrix) [ref.] λ in nm	Solid (ppm unless other unit specified) LOD (matrix) [ref.] λ in nm
Ga	(liq. on filter) [Appendix C.2]	240 (UO_2 pellet) [Fichet et al., 1999] 417.2056 80 (PuO_2 pellet) [Fichet et al., 1999] 417.2056
Gd		200 (NaCl) [Ishizuka, 1973] 367.12
H		10 (zircaloy in He at 15 Torr) [Idris et al., 2004] 656.2
Hg		300, 647 (synthetic silicate in 5 Torr CO_2) [Knight et al., 2000] 435.83 19, 4.6 (wood) [Uhl et al., 2001] 253.652/435.835 84 (soil) [Lazic et al., 2001] 253.7 16, 24 (ABS polymer) [Stepputat and Noll, 2003] 253.65 60 (ABS polymer, on-line analyzer) [Stepputat and Noll, 2003] 253.65
Ho		10 (NaCl) [Ishizuka, 1973] 345.60
In	(liq. on filter) [Appendix C.2]	160 (UO_2 pellet) [Fichet et al., 1999] 451.1323 150 (PuO_2 pellet) [Fichet et al., 1999] 451.1323
K		190, 240 (glass, air 1 and 5 Torr) [Kurniawan et al., 1995] 766.5 3 (starch-based flour) [Cho et al., 2001] 766.490 3.5, 0.7 (wood) [Uhl et al., 2001] 766.491 2000–38 000 (soil, 7 Torr CO_2) [Sallé et al., 2005] 766.49
La	(liq. on filter) [Appendix C.2]	10 (NaCl) [Ishizuka, 1973] 394.91
Li	(liq. on filter) [Appendix C.2]	10, 14 (glass, air 1 and 5 Torr) [Kurniawan et al., 1995] 670.7 35 (UO_2 pellet) [Fichet et al., 1999] 610.3642 40 (PuO_2 pellet) [Fichet et al., 1999] 610.3642 2.5 and 20 (synthetic silicate in 5 Torr CO_2) [Knight et al., 2000] 670.77/670.79 10–20 (soil, 7 Torr CO_2) [Sallé et al., 2005] 670.78
Lu		20 (NaCl) [Ishizuka, 1973] 291.14
Mg	(liq. on filter) [Appendix C.2]	230 (MgO in Fe ore) [Grant et al., 1991] 518.4 0.5 (Al alloy) [Sabsabi and Cielo, 1995] 285.2 130, 28 (glass, air 1 and 5 Torr) [Kurniawan et al., 1995] 383.8

1–10 (aluminum, echelle) [Bauer et al., 1998] not found
1 (plant material) [Sun et al., 1999] 278.0
70 (UO_2 pellet) [Fichet et al., 1999] 285.2129
200 (lignite) [Wallis et al., 2000] 285.21
0.4 (starch-based flour) [Cho et al., 2001] 279.553
<1 (wood) [Uhl et al., 2001] 279.553
7 (Al alloy, FO LIBS) [Rai et al., 2001] 383.829
6 (Al alloy) [Rai et al., 2001] 383.829
90 (low-ash lignite) [Chadwick and Body, 2002] not given
1.8–64 (Al[a]) [Rieger et al., 2002] 285.2
20–32 (Al[a]) [Rieger et al., 2002] 279.6
0.5 (Al, RSS) [Gautier et al., 2004] 280.3
0.2 (Al, RSP) [Gautier et al., 2004] 280.3
28.2 (Al) [Ismail et al., 2004] 285
76.8 (steel) [Ismail et al., 2004] 285
7 (Al alloy) [Sallé et al., 2004] 285.213
160–450 (soil, 7 Torr CO_2) [Sallé et al., 2005] 280.27
0.26, 0.11 (aluminum alloy, microchip laser) [Freedman et al., 2005] 382.9355, 383.2299, 383.2304, 383.8292, 383.8295

Mn

2 (Al alloy) [Sabsabi and Cielo, 1995] 403.1, 403.3
470 (iron) [Paksy et al., 1996] 403.1, 293.3
70 (Al) [Paksy et al., 1996] 404.1
6.7–213 (soil) [Multari et al., 1996] 403.45
1200 (steel under water; RSP) [Pichahchy et al., 1997] 403.08/403.31/403.45/403.57
1–10 (aluminum, echelle) [Bauer et al., 1998] not found
1 (plant material) [Sun et al., 1999] 403.1
60 (UO_2 pellet) [Fichet et al., 1999] 279.4820
110 (PuO_2 pellet) [Fichet et al., 1999] 279.4820
9 (steel) [Sturm et al., 2000] 293.3
0.7 (starch-based flour) [Cho et al., 2001] 257.610
90 (Al alloy, FO LIBS) [Rai et al., 2001] 404.136
10 (Al alloy) [Rai et al., 2001] 404.136
113 (steel alloy, 1064-nm laser) [Bassiotis et al., 2001] 482.352
235 (steel alloy, 355 nm laser) [Bassiotis et al., 2001] 482.352

30 (aerosol on filter) [Neuhauser et al., 1999] 259.4
30 (quartz filter) [Panne et al., 2001] 259.4
22 (liq. on Al[b]) [Yamamoto et al., 2005] 403.08/403.31/403.45
16 pg (liq. on Al[b]) [Yamamoto et al., 2005] 403.08/403.31/403.45
23–51 (particles on Al[b]) [Yamamoto et al., 2005] 403.08/403.31/403.45
16–58 pg (particles on Al[b]) [Yamamoto et al., 2005] 403.08/403.31/403.45
(liq. on filter) [Appendix C.2]

Table C.2 (Continued)

Element	Surface (ng/cm² unless other unit specified) LOD (matrix) [ref.] λ in nm	Solid (ppm unless other unit specified) LOD (matrix) [ref.] λ in nm
		100 (soil) [Capitelli et al., 2002] 475.4, 472.7, 478.3, 482.3
		35, 36 (Al[a]) [Rieger et al., 2002] 279.5
		67, 78 (Al[a]) [Rieger et al., 2002] 403.1
		51, 72 (Al[a]) [Rieger et al., 2002] 294.9
		7 (steel in Ar) [Sturm et al., 2004] 293.3
		8 (Al, RSP) [Gautier et al., 2004] 294.9
		3 (Al, RSP) [Gautier et al., 2004] 294.9
		15.3 (Al) [Ismail et al., 2004] 403
		5.0 (steel) [Ismail et al., 2004] 403
		30, 40 (steel, microchip laser) [López-Moreno et al., 2005] 403.1
		211–454 (steel[b]) [Yamamoto et al., 2005] 403.08/403.31/403.45
		300–450 (soil, 7 Torr CO₂) [Sallé et al., 2005] 403.08
		0.11, 0.05 (aluminum alloy, microchip laser) [Freedman et al., 2005] 403.0753, 403.3062, 403.4483
Mo	11 (solution on Al) [Rodolfa and Cremers, 2004] 407.0	426–1730 (stainless steel, diff. surface finishes) [Cabalín et al., 1999] 550.6
		7 (steel in Ar) [Sturm et al., 2004] 281.6
		80, 90 (steel, microchip laser) [López-Moreno et al., 2005] 384.4
Na		14, 18 (glass, air 1 and 5 Torr) [Kurniawan et al., 1995] 589.0
		70 (lignite) [Wallis et al., 2000] 589.00/589.59
		<1 (wood) [Uhl et al., 2001] 588.995/330.232
		30 (low-ash lignite) [Chadwick and Body, 2002] not found
		70–600 (soil, 7 Torr CO₂) [Sallé et al., 2005] 588.97
N		15–25 (steel) [Hemmerlin et al., 2001] 149.262
Nd		500 (NaCl) [Ishizuka, 1973] 430.36
Ni	270 (aerosol on filter) [Neuhauser et al., 1999] 230.3	20 (soil) [Wisbrun et al., 1994] PCR using multiple lines
	270 (quartz filter) [Panne et al., 2001] 230.3	64 (steel) [Aguilera et al., 1998] 377.6
	(liq. on filter) [Appendix C.2]	1–10 (aluminum, echelle) [Bauer et al., 1998] not found
		50 (steel) [Aragón et al., 1999] 231.60
		6 (steel) [Sturm et al., 2000] 231.60
		12, 224 (synthetic silicate in 5 Torr CO₂) [Knight et al., 2000] 352.45

8.5 (steel in air) [Noll et al., 2001] 231.6
6.8 (soil) [Lazic et al., 2001] 231.6
30 (soil) [Capitelli et al., 2002] 300.3
7 (steel in Ar) [Sturm et al., 2004] 225.4
540 (molten steel) [Palanco et al., 2004] not stated, 370–400 nm region
90 (steel, microchip laser) [López-Moreno et al., 2005] 341.42
0.51, 0.10 (aluminum alloy, microchip laser) [Freedman et al., 2005] 352.4535

P

35 000 (on copper and sulfur) [Franzke et al., 1992] 401.99, 405.78, 406.21, 416.81
<10ppm (on copper) [Franzke et al., 1992] 401.99, 405.78, 406.21, 416.81
460 (aerosol on filter) [Neuhauser et al., 1999] 405.8
60 (quartz filter) [Panne et al., 2001] 405.8
(liq. on filter) [Appendix C.2]

25 (plant material) [Sun et al., 1999] 213.6
9 (steel) [Sturm et al., 2000] 178.3
21 (steel in air) [Noll et al., 2001] 178.3
6 (steel) [Hemmerlin et al., 2001] 178.287
28 (soil, 7 Torr CO_2) [Radziemski et al., 2004] 178.3
7 (steel in Ar) [Sturm et al., 2004] 178.3
36 (steel) [Radivojevic et al., 2004a] 177.495

Pb

10 (soil) [Wisbrun et al., 1994] 405.8
57 (soil) [Eppler et al., 1996] 405.7
298 (soil) [Yamamoto et al., 1996] 405.78
17 (sand) [Eppler et al., 1996] 405.7
10 (concrete) [Pakhomov et al., 1996] 405.78
8000 (lead paint) [Yamamoto et al., 1996] 220.4
5.2–40 (soil) [Multari et al., 1996] 405.78
54 (zinc alloy) [St-Onge et al., 1997] 283.31
405 (zinc alloy) [St-Onge et al., 1997] 287.33
0.7–53.1 (soil cone pene.) [Theriault et al., 1998] 405.78
400 (UO_2 pellet) [Fichet et al., 1999] 405.7820
17, 95 (synthetic silicate in 5 Torr CO_2) [Knight et al., 2000] 405.78
18 (starch-based flour) [Cho et al., 2001] 405.782
17 (soil) [Lazic et al., 2001] 405.8
8.4, 0.6 (wood) [Uhl et al., 2001] 405.782
50 (soil) [Capitelli et al., 2002] 405.7
16, 24 (ABS polymer) [Stepputat and Noll, 2003] 405.78
140 (ABS polymer, on-line analyzer) [Stepputat and Noll, 2003] 405.78

Pr

40 (NaCl) [Ishizuka, 1973] 417.94

Rb

1 (starch-based flour) [Cho et al., 2001] 780.023
(liq. on filter) [Appendix C.2]

Table C.2 (Continued)

Element	Surface (ng/cm² unless other unit specified) LOD (matrix) [ref.] λ in nm	Solid (ppm unless other unit specified) LOD (matrix) [ref.] λ in nm
S		70 (steel) [Gonzalez et al., 1995] 180.7/182.0 8 (steel) [Sturm et al., 2000] 180.73 11 (steel in air) [Noll et al., 2001] 180.7 4.5 (steel) [Hemmerlin et al., 2001] 180.731 1.03% (soil, 7 Torr CO_2) [Radziemski et al., 2004] 180.7 1.77% (soil, 7 Torr CO_2) [Radziemski et al., 2004] 182.6 0.11% (soil, 7 Torr CO_2) [Radziemski et al., 2004] 545.4 7 (steel in Ar) [Sturm et al., 2004] 180.7 73 (steel) [Radivojevic et al., 2004a] 182.034
Sb	280 (aerosol on filter) [Neuhauser et al., 1999] 259.8 550 (quartz filter) [Panne et al., 2001] 259.8	50, 17 (ABS polymer) [Stepputat and Noll, 2003] 259.80 80 (ABS polymer, on-line analyzer) [Stepputat and Noll, 2003] 259.80
Sc	(liq. on filter) [Appendix C.2]	2 (NaCl) [Ishizuka, 1973] 361.38
Si	(liq. on filter) [Appendix C.2]	1500 (SiO in Fe ore) [Grant et al., 1991] 390.55 14 (Al alloy) [Sabsabi and Cielo, 1995] 251.6 600 (iron) [Paksy et al., 1996] 288.158 600 (Al) [Paksy et al., 1996] 288.158 1190 (steel under water; RSP) [Pichahchy et al., 1997] 288.16 1–10 (aluminum, echelle) [Bauer et al., 1998] not found 80 (steel) [Aragón et al., 1999] 288.16 11 (steel) [Sturm et al., 2000] 288.16 200 (lignite) [Wallis et al., 2000] 288.16 5.3, 1.0 (wood) [Uhl et al., 2001] 288.158 400 (low-ash lignite) [Chadwick and Body, 2002] not found 141, 155 (Al[a]) [Rieger et al., 2002] 288.2 283.9 (Al) [Ismail et al., 2004] 288 6.6 (steel) [Ismail et al., 2004] 288 74 (Al alloy) [Sallé et al., 2004] 288.158 200 (steel, microchip laser) [López-Moreno et al., 2005] 288.16 235–319 (steel[b]) [Yamamoto et al., 2005] 288.16 9–45% (soil, 7 Torr CO_2) [Sallé et al., 2005] 288.18 1.87, 0.14 (aluminum alloy, microchip laser) [Freedman et al., 2005] 288.1578

Sm	40 (NaCl) [Ishizuka, 1973] 356.83	
Sn	33 (zinc alloy) [St-Onge et al., 1997] 284.00 54 (zinc alloy) [St-Onge et al., 1997] 286.33 34 (zinc alloy) [St-Onge et al., 1997] 303.41 26, 84 (synthetic silicate in 5 Torr CO_2) [Knight et al., 2000] 303.41 8.2, 2.2 (wood) [Uhl et al., 2001] 286.333	50 (aerosol on filter) [Neuhauser et al., 1999] 284.0 50 (quartz filter) [Panne et al., 2001] 284.0
Sr	42 (soil) [Yamamoto et al., 1996] 407.77 3.1–75 (soil) [Multari et al., 1996] 407.77 5.2–40 (soil) [Multari et al., 1996] 405.78 1–10 (aluminum, echelle) [Bauer et al., 1998] not found 130 (UO_2 pellet) [Fichet et al., 1999] 407.7714 90 (PuO_2 pellet) [Fichet et al., 1999] 407.7714 1.2, 1.9 (synthetic silicate in 5 Torr CO_2) [Knight et al., 2000] 407.77 0.3 (starch-based flour) [Cho et al., 2001] 421.552 30–40 (soil, 7 Torr CO_2) [Sallé et al., 2005] 407.78	8.8 (solution on Al) [Rodolfa and Cremers, 2004] 407.8 3.5 (liq. on Al[b]) [Yamamoto et al., 2005] 403.08/403.31/403.45 2.5 pg (liq. on Al[b]) [Yamamoto et al., 2005] 403.08/403.31/403.45 1.7–3.1 (particles on Al[b]) [Yamamoto et al., 2005] 403.08/403.31/403.45 1.2–3.6 pg (particles on Al[b]) [Yamamoto et al., 2005] 403.08/403.31/403.45 (liq. on filter) [Appendix C.2]
Tb	60 (NaCl) [Ishizuka, 1973] 384.88	(liq. on filter) [Appendix C.2]
Th		(liq. on filter) [Appendix C.2]
Ti	230 (TiO_2 in Fe ore) [Grant et al., 1991] 498.17 410, 350 (glass, air at 1 and 5 Torr) [Kurniawan et al., 1995] 365.3 1–10 (aluminum, echelle) [Bauer et al., 1998] not found 48 (soil) [Lazic et al., 2001] 351.9 4 (Al, RSS) [Gautier et al., 2004] 323.5 3 (Al, RSP) [Gautier et al., 2004] 323.5 1000–2400 (soil, 7 Torr CO_2) [Sallé et al., 2005] 398.92	111 (solution on Al) [Rodolfa and Cremers, 2004] 398.2 (liq. on filter) [Appendix C.2]
Tl	100 (UO_2 pellet) [Fichet et al., 1999] 535.0460	40 (filter) [Arnold and Cremers, 1995] 535.05 100 (aerosol on filter) [Neuhauser et al., 1999] 276.8 130 (quartz filter) [Panne et al., 2001] 276.8
Tm	30 (NaCl) [Ishizuka, 1973] 388.31	
U	1000 (soil) [Cremers and Ferris, 1996] 409.02	
V	38 ($2TiO_2$–SiO_2) [Lucena et al., 1998] 411.18 35 (PuO_2 pellet) [Fichet et al., 1999] 407.7714	90 (aerosol on filter) [Neuhauser et al., 1999] 292.5 60 (quartz filter) [Panne et al., 2001] 292.5 (liq. on filter) [Appendix C.2]

Table C.2 (Continued)

Element	Surface (ng/cm² unless other unit specified) LOD (matrix) [ref.] λ in nm	Solid (ppm unless other unit specified) LOD (matrix) [ref.] λ in nm
Y	(liq. on filter) [Appendix C.2]	2 (NaCl) [Ishizuka, 1973] 371.03
Yb		2 (NaCl) [Ishizuka, 1973] 369.42
Zn	(liq. on filter) [Appendix C.2]	160, 130 (glass, air 1 and 5 Torr) [Kurniawan et al., 1995] 481.0
		1–10 (aluminum, echelle) [Bauer et al., 1998] not found
		1 (plant material) [Sun et al., 1999] 213.930 (soil)
		98 (soil) [Lazic et al., 2001] 334.5
		38 (Al alloy, FO LIBS) [Rai et al., 2001] 330.259
		0.29 (Al alloy) [Rai et al., 2001] 330.259
		30 (soil) [Capitelli et al., 2002] 472.2
		281, 380 (Al[a]) [Rieger et al., 2002] 334.5
		1.36, 0.10 (aluminum alloy, microchip laser) [Freedman et al., 2005] 334.5015
Zr	(liq. on filter) [Appendix C.2]	290, 190 (glass, air 1 and 5 Torr) [Kurniawan et al., 1995] 360.1

PCR, principal component analysis.

FO LIBS, fiber optic LIBS.

[a] LOD depended on concentration of element in the sample and the laser energy.

[b] Using acousto-optic Q-switched laser (150 ns pulse width).

C.2 UNIFORM DETECTION LIMITS

These detection limits were determined using 100 mJ laser pulses from a Q-switched Nd:YAG laser incident on 37 mm diameter filter paper (Whatman 42). Elements were provided by atomic absorption standard (AAS) solutions deposited on the filter over an area of approximately 1 cm^2. The lens focal length was 100 mm. Each measurement consisted of averaging the spectra from 100 laser plasmas. During each measurement, the filter was translated under the laser pulses. Each measurement was repeated six times and the results averaged to provide an element signal at a specific concentration on the filter. Detection limits were determined using LOD $= 3sm$ as described in Section 4.5, where m is the slope of the calibration curve at the lower concentrations of solutions on the filter. In those cases in which the element line was ratioed to an adjacent line as an internal standard, this line is listed in parentheses along with the element name (Table C.4) (Cremers and Radziemski, 2003). Note that some detection limits may be higher than expected in view of the emission line strength. This could be due to self-absorption or other effects related to high concentrations of the element on the filter.

Table C.3 Other detection limits

Material	Conditions
Naphthalene	20 ng on surface [Portnov *et al.*, 2003] via C$_2$, CN emission
Halon-14	490 ppm in nitrogen/Ar [Lancaster *et al.*, 1999] via F(I) emission at 685.6 nm
Halon-1301	750 ppm in nitrogen/Ar [Lancaster *et al.*, 1999] via F(I) emission at 685.6 nm
FM-200	170 ppm in nitrogen/Ar [Lancaster *et al.*, 1999] via F(I) emission at 685.6 nm
HFC-134a	530 ppm in nitrogen/Ar [Lancaster *et al.*, 1999] via F(I) emission at 685.6 nm

Table C.4 Detection limits obtained from AAS solutions deposited on a filter [Ratio lines: 393.4 and 396.9 nm Ca(II) and 247.8 nm C(I)]

Element (ratio line)	λ (nm)	μg/cm^2	Element (ratio line)	λ (nm)	μg/cm^2
Aluminum	308.2	8	Bismuth (393.4)	289.7	47
	309.2	34		293.8	62
	394.4	16		302.4	33
	396.1	21		306.7	15
Barium (393.4)	413.0	165		472.2	644
	455.4	84	Boron	249.6^a	412
	493.4	86	Cadmium	441.5	2313
	553.5	45		508.5	228
	614.1	59	Chromium (393.4)	357.8	77
	649.6	226		359.3	124
	705.9	110		529.8	40
	728.0	207		534.5	298
Beryllium (393.4)	234.8	657		540.9	23
	265.0^a	212	Cobalt (393.4)	340.5	164
	313.0^a	100		345.3	53
	332.1	73		350.2	125

Table C.4 (Continued)

Element (ratio line)	λ (nm)	$\mu g/cm^2$	Element (ratio line)	λ (nm)	$\mu g/cm^2$
	399.5	242	Scandium (393.4)	335.3	126
	412.1	71		337.2	122
Copper (393.4)	324.7	48		467.0	81
	327.3	419		474.3	82
	353.0	1181		507.0	101
	515.3	301		523.9	157
Gallium (393.4)	294.4[a]	107		535.6	102
	403.2	62		567.1	56
	417.2	45		621.0	114
Gold	267.5	384	Silicon (393.4)	251.6	172
Indium (393.4)	303.9	245		288.1	50
	325.6	43		568.8	14
	410.1	38		624.3	55
	451.1	39	Silver (393.4)	328	78
Iron (396.9)	275.0	279		338.3	95
	302.0	121		520.9	71
	344.0	195		546.5	32
	373.4	258	Strontium (393.4)	346.4	44
	430.7	335		407.7	59
	438.3	50		421.5	87
	440.4	162		460.7	86
	526.9[a]	222		707.0	14
	532.8[a]	419	Thorium	411.6	54
Lanthanum (393.4)	333.7	80		438.1	184
	375.9	112		439.1	96
	398.8	40	Titanium (393.4)	308.8	117
Lead	280.1	116		323.4	51
	283.3	223		334.9	98
	287.3	83		336.1	321
	357.2	42		365.3	87
	363.9	45		368.5	90
	368.3	51		375.9	61
	373.9	33		439.5	64
Lithium (393.4)	460.2[a]	45		499.1	130
	497.1[a]	96	Vanadium (393.4)	289.3	132
	670.7[a]	374		292.4	80
	812.6[a]	114		309.3	56
Magnesium (393.4)	279.5	64		318.3[a]	52
	285.2	86		327.6	144
	383.2	142		370.3	316
	517.3	78		411.1	47
	518.3	85		437.9	18
Manganese (247.8)	294.9	177		446.0	40
	356.9	420		459.4	56
	482.3	126		488.1	101
Nickel (393.4)	310.1	1005		572.7	52
	341.4	222		624.3	50
	344.6	353	Yttrium (393.4)	430.9	35
	361.9	43		442.2	76
Rubidium	247.2	65		452.7	65
	780.0	9		464.3	89

	490.0	38		334.5^a	112
	508.7	49		468.0	204
	520.0	68		472.2	149
	546.6	29		481.0	85
	552.7	93	Zirconium (393.4)	327.3	200
YO	597.2	33		339.1	228
YO	613.2	24		349.6	93
YO	616.5	59		357.2	135
Zinc (393.4)	213.8	340		407.2	193
	330.2^a	181			

^{a} Unresolved lines.

REFERENCES

Aguilera, J.A., C. Aragón and J. Campos (1992). Determination of carbon content in steel using laser-induced breakdown spectroscopy. Appl. Spectrosc. 46: 1382–1387.

Aguilera, J.A., C. Aragón and F. Penalba (1998). Plasma shielding effect in laser ablation of metallic samples and its influence on LIBS analysis. Appl. Surf. Sci. 127–129: 309–314.

Aragón, C., J.A. Aguilera and F. Penalba (1999). Improvements in quantitative analysis of steel composition by laser-induced breakdown spectroscopy at atmospheric pressure. Appl. Spectrosc. 53: 1259–1267.

Arca, G., A. Ciucci, V. Palleschi, S. Rastelli and E. Tognoni (1997). Trace element analysis in water by the laser-induced breakdown spectroscopy technique. Appl. Spectrosc. 51: 1102–1105.

Archontaki, H.A. and S.R. Crouch (1988). Evaluation of an isolated droplet sample introduction system for laser-induced breakdown spectroscopy. Appl. Spectrosc. 42: 741–746.

Arnold, S.D. and D.A. Cremers (1995). Rapid determination of metal particles on air sampling filters using laser-induced breakdown spectroscopy. Am. Ind. Hyg. Assoc J. 56: 1180–1186.

Arp, Z.A., D.A. Cremers, R.C. Wiens, D.M. Wayne, B. Sallé and S. Maurice (2004). Analysis of water ice and water/ice soil mixtures using laser-induced breakdown spectroscopy: application to Mars polar exploration. Appl. Spectrosc. 58: 897–909.

Asimellis, G., S. Hamilton, A. Giannoudakos and M. Kompitsas (2005). Controlled inert gas environment for enhanced chlorine and fluorine detection in the visible and near-infrared by laser-induced breakdown spectroscopy. Spectrochim. Acta Part B 60: 1132–1139.

Assion, A., M. Wollenhaupt, L. Haag, F. Mayorov, C. Sarpe-Tudoran, M. Winter, U. Kutschera and T. Baumert (2003). Femtosecond laser-induced-breakdown spectrometry for Ca^{2+} analysis of biological samples with high spatial resolution. Appl. Phys. B 77: 391–397.

Bassiotis, I., A. Diamantopoulou, A. Giannoudakos, F. Roubani-Kalantzopoulou and M. Kompitsas (2001). Effects of experimental parameters in quantitative analysis of steel alloy by laser-induced breakdown spectroscopy. Spectrochim. Acta Part B 56: 671–683.

Bauer, H.E., F. Leis and K. Niemax (1998). Laser induced breakdown spectrometry with an echelle spectrometer and intensified charge coupled device detection. Spectrochim. Acta Part B 53: 1815–1825.

Beddows, D.C.S., O. Samek, M. Liska and H.H. Telle (2002). Single-pulse laser-induced breakdown spectroscopy of samples submerged in water using a single fibre light delivery system. Spectrochim. Acta Part B 57: 1461–1471.

Berman, L.M. and P.J. Wolf (1998). Laser-induced breakdown spectroscopy of liquids: Aqueous solutions of nickel and chlorinated hydrocarbons. Appl. Spectrosc. 52: 438–443.

Buckley, S.G., H.A. Johnsen, K.R. Hencken and D.W. Hahn (2000). Implementation of laser-induced breakdown spectroscopy as a continuous emissions monitor for toxic metals. Waste Manage. 20: 455–462.

Bundschuh, T., J.I. Yun and R. Knopp (2001). Determination of size, concentration and elemental composition of colloids with laser-induced breakdown detection/spectroscopy (LIBD/S). Fresenius J. Anal. Chem. 371: 1063–1069.

Cabalín, L.M., D. Romero, J.M. Baena and J.J. Laserna (1999). Effect of surface topography in the characterization of stainless steel using laser-induced breakdown spectrometry. Surf. Interface Anal. 27: 805–810.

Caceres, J.O., J.T. Lopez, H.H. Telle and A.G. Urena (2001). Quantitative analysis of trace metal ions in ice using laser-induced breakdown spectroscopy. Spectrochim. Acta Part B 56: 831–838.

Capitelli, F., F. Colao, M.R. Provenzano, R. Fantoni, G. Brunetti and N. Senesi (2002). Determination of heavy metals in soils by laser induced breakdown spectroscopy. Geoderma 106: 45–62.

Carranza, J.E., B.T. Fisher, G.D. Yoder and D.W. Hahn (2001). On- line analysis of ambient air aerosols using laser-induced breakdown spectroscopy. Spectrochim. Acta Part B 56: 851–864.

Chadwick, B.L. and D. Body (2002). Development and commercial evaluation of laser-induced breakdown spectroscopy chemical analysis technology in the coal power generation industry. Appl. Spectrosc. 56: 70–74.

Charfi, B. and M.A. Harith (2002). Panoramic laser-induced breakdown spectrometry of water. Spectrochim. Acta Part B 57: 1141–1153.

Cho, H.-H., Y.-J. Kim, Y.-S. Jo, K. Kitagawa, N. Arai and Y.-I. Lee (2001). Application of laser-induced breakdown spectroscopy for direct determination of trace elements in starch-based flours. J. Anal. At. Spectrom. 16: 622–627.

Cremers, D.A. and L.J. Radziemski (1983). Detection of fluorine and chlorine in air by laser-induced breakdown spectroscopy. Anal. Chem. 55: 1252–1256.

Cremers, D.A. and L.J. Radziemski (1985). Direct detection of beryllium on filters using the laser spark. Appl. Spectrosc. 39: 57–63.

Cremers, D.A. and M.J. Ferris (1996). Unpublished results.

Cremers, D.A. and L.J. Radziemski (2003). Unpublished results.

Cremers, D.A., L.J. Radziemski and T.R. Loree (1984). Spectrochemical analysis of liquids using the laser spark. Appl. Spectrosc. 38: 721–729.

Cremers, D.A., F.L. Archuleta and R.J. Martinez (1985). Evaluation of the continuous optical discharge for spectrochemical analysis. Spectrochim. Acta Part B 40: 665–679.

Cremers, D.A., M.H. Ebinger, D.D. Breshears, P.J. Unkefer, S.A. Kammerdiener, M.J. Ferris, K.M. Catlett and J.R. Brown (2001). Measuring total soil carbon with laser-induced breakdown spectroscopy (LIBS). J. Environ. Qual. 30: 2002–2206.

De Giacomo, A., M. Dell'aglio and O. De Pascale (2004). Single pulse-laser induced breakdown spectroscopy in aqueous solution. Appl. Phys. A 79: 1035–1038.

Dudragne, L., Ph. Adam and J. Amouroux (1998). Time-resolved laser-induced breakdown spectroscopy: application for qualitative and quantitative detection of fluorine, chlorine, sulfur, and carbon in air. Appl. Spectrosc. 52: 1321–1327.

Eppler, A.S., D.A. Cremers, D.D. Hickmott and A.C. Koskelo (1996). Matrix effects in the detection of Pb and Ba in soils using laser-induced breakdown spectroscopy. Appl. Spectrosc. 50: 1175–1181.

Essien, M., L.J. Radziemski and J. Sneddon (1988). Detection of cadmium, lead, zinc in aerosols by laser-induced breakdown spectrometry. J. Anal. At. Spectrom. 3: 985–988.

Fichet, P., P. Mauchien and C. Moulin (1999). Determination of impurities in uranium and plutonium dioxides by laser-induced breakdown spectroscopy. Appl. Spectrosc. 53: 1111–1117.

Fisher, B.T., H.A. Johnsen, S.G. Buckley and D.W. Hahn (2001). Temporal gating for the optimization of laser-induced breakdown spectroscopy detection and analysis of toxic metals. Appl. Spectrosc. 55: 1312–1319.

Franzke, D., H. Klos and A. Wokaun (1992). Element identification on the surface of inorganic solids by excimer laser-induced emission spectroscopy. Appl. Spectrosc. 46: 587–592.

Freedman, A., F.J. Iannarilli and J.C. Wormhoudt (2005). Aluminum alloy analysis using microchip-laser induced breakdown spectroscopy. Spectrochim. Acta Part B 60: 1076–1082.

Gautier, C., P. Fichet, D. Menuta, J.-L. Lacour, D. L'Hermite and J. Dubessy (2004). Study of the double-pulse setup with an orthogonal beam geometry for laser-induced breakdown spectroscopy. Spectrochim. Acta Part B 59: 975–986.

Gonzalez, A., M. Ortiz and J. Campos (1995). Determination of sulfur content in steel by laser-produced plasma atomic emission spectroscopy. Appl. Spectrosc. 49: 1632–1635.

Grant, K., G.L. Paul and J.A. O'Neill (1991). Quantitative elemental analysis of iron ore by laser-induced breakdown spectroscopy. Appl. Spectrosc. 45: 701–705.

Hahn, D.W. and M.M. Lunden (2000). Detection and analysis of aerosol particles by laser-induced breakdown spectroscopy. Aerosol Sci. Technol. 33: 30–48.

Haisch, C., R. Niessner, O.I. Matveev, U. Panne and N. Omenetto (1996). Element-specific determination of chlorine in gases by laser-induced-breakdown-spectroscopy (LIBS). Fresenius J. Anal. Chem. 356: 21–26.

Hemmerlin, M., R. Meilland, H. Falk, P. Wintzens and L. Pauleri (2001). Application of vacuum ultraviolet laser-induced breakdown spectrometry for steel analysis–comparison with spark-optical emissions spectrometry figures of merit. Spectrochim. Acta Part B 56: 661–669.

Huang, J.-S., C.-B. Ke, L.S. Huang and K.C. Lin (2002). The correlation between ion production and emission intensity in the laser-induced breakdown spectroscopy of liquid droplets. Spectrochim. Acta Part B 57: 35–48.

Huang, J.-S., C.-B. Ke and K.-C. Lin (2004). Matrix effect on emission/current correlated analysis in laser-induced breakdown spectroscopy of liquid droplets. Spectrochim. Acta Part B 59: 321–326.

Hybl, J.D., G.A. Lithgow and S.G. Buckley (2003). Laser-induced breakdown spectroscopy detection and classification of biological aerosols. Appl. Spectrosc. 57: 1207–1215.

Idris, N., H. Kurniawan, T.J. Lie, M. Parded, H. Suyanto, R. Hedwig, T. Kobayashi, K. Kagawa and T. Maruyama (2004). Characteristics of hydrogen emission in laser plasma induced by focusing fundamental Q-sw YAG laser on solid samples. Japan. J. Appl. Phys. 43: 4221–4228

Ishizuka, T. (1973). Laser emission spectrography of rare earth elements. Anal. Chem. 45: 538–541.

Ismail, M.A., H. Imam, A. Elhassan, W.T. Youniss and M.A. Harith (2004). LIBS limit of detection and plasma parameters of some elements in two different metallic matrices. J. Anal. At. Spectrom. 19: 489–494.

Janzen, C, R. Fleige, R. Noll, H. Schwenke, W. Lahmann, J. Knoth, P. Beaven, E. Jantzen, A. Oest and P. Koke (2005). Analysis of small droplets with a new detector for liquid chromatography based on laser-induced breakdown spectroscopy. Spectrochim. Acta Part B 60: 993–1001.

Khater, M.A., P. van Kampen, J.T. Costello, J.-P. Mosnier and E.T. Kennedy (2000). Time-integrated laser-induced plasma spectroscopy in the vacuum ultraviolet for the quantitative elemental characterization of steel alloys. J. Phys. D: Appl. Phys. 33: 2252–2262.

Khater, M.A., J.T. Costello and E.T. Kennedy (2002). Optimization of the emission characteristics of laser-produced steel plasmas in the vacuum ultraviolet: significant improvements in carbon detection limits. Appl. Spectrosc. 56: 970–983.

Knight, A.K., N.L. Scherbarth, D.A. Cremers and M.J. Ferris (2000). Characterization of laser-induced breakdown spectroscopy (LIBS) for application to space exploration. Appl. Spectrosc. 54: 331–340.

Knopp, R., F.J. Scherbaum and J.I. Kim (1996). Laser induced breakdown spectrometry (LIBS) as an analytical tool for the detection of metal ions in aqueous solution. Fresenius J. Anal. Chem. 355: 16–20.

Kurniawan, H., S. Nakajima, J.E. Batubara, M. Marpaung, M. Okamoto and K. Kagawa (1995). Laser-induced wave plasma in glass and its application to elemental analysis. Appl. Spectrosc. 49: 1067–1072.

Lancaster, E.D., K.L. McNesby, R.G. Daniel and A.W. Miziolek (1999). Spectroscopic analysis of fire suppressants and refrigerants by laser-induced breakdown spectroscopy. Appl. Opt. 38: 1476–1480.

Lazic, V., R. Barbini, F. Colao, R. Fantoni and A. Palucci (2001). Spectrochim. Acta Part B 56: 807–820.

Lazzari, C., M. De Rosa, S. Rastelli, A. Ciucci, V. Palleschi and A. Salvetti (1994). Detection of mercury in air by time-resolved laser-induced breakdown spectroscopy technique. Laser Part. Beams 12: 525–530.

Lo, K.M. and N.H. Cheung (2002). ArF laser-induced plasma spectroscopy for part-per-billion analysis of metal ions in aqueous solutions. Appl. Spectrosc. 56: 682–688.

López-Moreno, C., S. Palanco and J.J. Laserna (2004). Remote laser-induced plasma spectrometry for elemental analysis of samples of environmental interest. J. Anal. At. Spectrom. 19: 1479–1484.

López-Moreno, C., K. Amponsah-Manager, B.W. Smith, I.B. Gornushkin, N. Omenetto, S. Palanco, J.J. Laserna and J.D. Winefordner (2005). Quantitative analysis of low-alloy steel by microchip laser induced breakdown spectroscopy. J. Anal. At. Spectrom. 20: 552–556.

Lucena, P., L.M. Cabalìn, E. Pardo, F. Martìn, L.J. Alemany and J.J. Laserna (1998). Laser induced breakdown spectrometry of vanadium in titania supported silica catalysts. Talanta 47: 143–151.

Martin, M. and M.-D. Cheng (2000). Detection of chromium aerosol using time-resolved laser-induced plasma spectroscopy. Appl. Spectrosc. 54: 1279–1285.

Multari, R.A, L.E. Foster, D.A. Cremers and M.J. Ferris (1996). Effect of sampling geometry on elemental emissions in laser-induced breakdown spectroscopy. Appl. Spectrosc. 50: 1483–1499.

Neuhauser, R.E., U. Panne, R. Niessner, G.A. Petrucci, P. Cavalli and N. Omenetto (1997). On-line and in-situ detection of lead aerosols by plasma-spectroscopy and laser-excited atomic fluorescence spectroscopy. Anal. Chim. Acta 346: 37–48.

Neuhauser, R.E., U. Panne and R. Niessner (1999). Laser-induced plasma spectroscopy (LIPS): a versatile tool for monitoring heavy metal aerosols. Anal. Chim. Acta 392: 47–54.

Noll, R., H. Bette, A. Brysch, M. Kraushaar, I. Monch, L. Peter and V. Sturm (2001). Laser-induced breakdown spectrometry – applications for production control and quality assurance in the steel industry. Spectrochim. Acta Part B 56: 637–649.

Pakhomov, A.V., W. Nichols and J. Borysow (1996). Laser-induced breakdown spectroscopy for detection of lead in concrete. Appl. Spectrosc. 50: 880–884.

Paksy, L., B. Német, A. Lengyel, L. Kozma and J. Czekkel (1996). Production control of metal alloys by laser spectroscopy of the molten metals. Part 1. Preliminary investigations. Spectrochim. Acta Part B 51: 279–290.

Palanco, S., S. Conesa and J.J. Laserna (2004). Analytical control of liquid steel in an induction melting furnace using a remote laser induced plasma spectrometer. J. Anal. At. Spectrom. 19: 462–467.

Panne, U., R.E. Neuhauser, M. Theisen, H. Fink and R. Niessner (2001). Analysis of heavy metal aerosols on filters by laser-induced plasma spectroscopy. Spectrochim. Acta Part B 56: 839–850.

Pardede, M., H. Kurniawan, M.O. Tjia, K. Ikezawa, T. Maruyama and K. Kagawa (2001). Spectrochemical analysis of metal elements electrodeposited from water samples by laser-induced shock wave plasma spectroscopy. Appl. Spectrosc. 55: 1229–1236.

Pichahchy, A.E., D.A. Cremers and M.J. Ferris (1997). Detection of metals underwater using laser-induced breakdown spectroscopy. Spectrochim. Acta Part B 52: 25–39.

Portnov, A., S. Rosenwaks and I. Bar (2003). Emission following laser-induced breakdown spectroscopy of organic compounds in ambient air. Appl. Opt. 42: 2835–2842.

Radivojevic, I., C. Haisch, R. Niessner, S. Florek, H. Becker-Ross and U. Panne (2004a). Microanalysis by laser-induced plasma spectroscopy in the vacuum ultraviolet. Anal. Chem. 76: 1648–1658.

Radivojevic, I., R. Niessner, C. Haisch, S. Florek, H. Becker-Ross and U. Panne (2004b). Detection of bromine in thermoplasts from consumer electronics by laser-induced plasma spectroscopy. Spectrochim. Acta Part B 59: 335–343.

Radziemski, L.J., T.R. Loree, D.A. Cremers and N.M. Hoffman (1983). Time-resolved laser-induced breakdown spectrometry of aerosols. Anal. Chem. 55: 1246–1252.

Radziemski, L.J., D.A. Cremers, K. Benelli, C. Khoo and R.D. Harris (2004). Use of the vacuum ultraviolet spectral region for LIBS-based Martian geology and exploration. Spectrochim. Acta Part B 60: 237–248.

Rai, A.K., H. Zhang, F.Y. Yueh, J.P. Singh and A. Weisburg (2001). Parametric study of a fiber-optic laser-induced breakdown spectroscopy probe for analysis of aluminum alloys. Spectrochim. Acta Part B 56: 2371–2383.

Rieger, G.W., M. Taschuk, Y.Y. Tsui and R. Fedosejevs (2002). Laser-induced breakdown spectroscopy for microanalysis using submillijoule UV laser pulses. Appl. Spectrosc. 56: 689–698.

Rodolfa, K.T. and D.A. Cremers (2004). Capabilities of surface composition analysis using a long laser-induced breakdown spectroscopy spark. Appl. Spectrosc. 58: 367–375.

Rohwetter, Ph., J. Yu, G. Méjean, K. Stelmaszczyk, E. Salmon, J. Kasparian, J.-P. Wolf and L. Wöste (2004). Remote LIBS with ultrashort pulses: characteristics in the picosecond and femtosecond regime. J. Anal. At. Spectrom., 19: 437–444.

Sabsabi, M. and P. Cielo (1995). Quantitative analysis of aluminum alloys by laser-induced breakdown spectroscopy and plasma characterization. Appl. Spectrosc. 49: 499–507.

Sallé, B., J.-L. Lacour, E. Vors, P. Fichet, S. Maurice, D.A. Cremers and R.C. Wiens (2004). Laser-induced breakdown spectroscopy for Mars surface analysis: capabilities at stand-off distances and detection of chlorine and sulfur elements. Spectrochim. Acta Part B 59: 1413–1422.

Sallé, B., D.A. Cremers, S. Maurice, R.C. Wiens and P. Fichet (2005). Evaluation of a compact spectrograph for in-situ and stand-off laser-induced breakdown spectroscopy analyses of geological samples on Mars missions. Spectrochim. Acta Part B 60: 805–815.

Samek, O., D.C.S. Beddows, J. Kaiser, S.V. Kukhlevsky, M. Liska, H.H. Telle and J. Young (2000). Application of laser-induced breakdown spectroscopy to in situ analysis of liquid samples. Opt. Eng. 39: 2248–2262.

Schmidt, N.E. and S.R. Goode (2002). Analysis of aqueous solutions by laser-induced breakdown spectroscopy of ion exchange membranes. Appl. Spectrosc. 56: 370–374.

Stepputat, M. and R. Noll (2003). On-line detection of heavy metals and brominated flame retardants in technical polymers with laser-induced breakdown spectrometry. Appl. Opt. 42: 6210–6220.

St-Onge, L., M. Sabsabi and P. Cielo (1997). Quantitative analysis of additives in solid zinc alloys by laser-induced plasma spectrometry. J. Anal. At. Spectrom. 12: 997–1004.

Sturm, V., L. Peter and R. Noll (2000). Steel analysis with laser-induced breakdown spectrometry in the vacuum ultraviolet. Appl. Spectrosc. 54: 1275–1278.

Sturm, V., J. Vrenegor, R. Noll and M. Hemmerlin (2004). Bulk analysis of steel samples with surface scale layers by enhanced laser ablation and LIBS analysis of C, P, S, Al, Cr, Cu, Mn and Mo. J. Anal. At. Spectrom. 19: 451–456.

Sun, Q., M. Tran, B.W. Smith and J.D. Winefordner (1999). Direct determination of P, Al, Ca, Cu, Mn, Zn, Mg and Fe in plant materials by laser-induced plasma spectroscopy. Can. J. Anal. Sci. Spectrosc. 44: 164–170.

Theriault, G.A., S. Bodensteiner and S.H. Lieberman (1998). A real-time fiber-optic probe for the in-situ delineation of metals in soils. Field Anal. Chem. Technol. 2: 117–125.

Tran, M., Q. Sun, B.W. Smith and J.D. Winefordner (2001). Determination of F, Cl, and Br in solid organic compounds by laser-induced plasma spectroscopy. Appl. Spectrosc. 55: 739–744.

Uhl, A., K. Loebe and L. Kreuchwig (2001). Fast analysis of wood preservers using laser induced breakdown spectroscopy. Spectrochim. Acta Part B 56: 795–806.

Van der Wal, R.L., T.M. Ticich, J.R. West and P.A. Householder (1999). Trace metal detection by laser-induced breakdown spectroscopy. Appl. Spectrosc. 53: 1226–1236.

Wachter, J.R. and D.A. Cremers (1987). Determination of uranium in solution using laser-induced breakdown spectroscopy. Appl. Spectrosc. 41: 1042–1048.

Wallis, F.J., B.L. Chadwick and R.J.S. Morrison (2000). Analysis of lignite using laser-induced breakdown spectroscopy. Appl. Spectrosc. 54: 1231–1235.

Whitehouse, A.I., J. Young, I.M. Botheroyd, S. Lawson, C.P. Evans and J. Wright (2001). Remote material analysis of nuclear power station steam generator tubes by laser-induced breakdown spectroscopy. Spectrochim. Acta Part B 56: 821–830.

Williamson, C.K., R.G. Daniel, K.L. NcNesby and A.W. Miziolek (1998). Laser-induced breakdown spectroscopy for real-time detection of halon alternative agents. Anal. Chem. 70: 1186–1191.

Wisbrun, R., I. Schechter, R. Niessner and K.L. Kompa (1994). Detector for trace elemental analysis of solid environmental samples by laser plasma spectroscopy. Anal. Chem. 66: 2964–2975.

Yamamoto, K.Y., D.A. Cremers, L.E. Foster and M.J. Ferris (1996). Detection of metals in the environment using a portable laser-induced breakdown spectroscopy instrument. Appl. Spectrosc. 50: 222–233.

Yamamoto, K.Y., D.A. Cremers, L.E. Foster, M.P. Davies and R.D. Harris (2005). Laser-induced breakdown spectroscopy analysis of solids using a long pulse (150 ns) Q-switched Nd:YAG laser. Appl. Spectrosc. 59: 1082–1097.

Yaroshchyk, P., R.J.S. Morrison and B.L. Chadwick (2004). Dual beam spectrometer using laser-induced breakdown spectroscopy. Rev. Sci. Instrum. 75: 5050–5052.

Yueh, F.-Y., R.C. Sharma, J.P. Singh, H. Zhang and W.A. Spencer (2002). Evaluation of the potential of laser-induced breakdown spectroscopy for detection of trace element in liquid. J. Air Waste Manage. Assoc. 52: 1307–1315.

Yun, J.I., T. Bundschuh, V. Neck and J.I. Kim (2001). Selective determination of europium (III) oxide and hydroxide colloids in aqueous solution by laser-induced breakdown spectroscopy. Appl. Spectrosc. 55: 273–278.

Zhang, H., F.Y. Yueh and J.P. Singh (1999). Laser-induced breakdown spectroscopy as a multi-metal continuous-emission monitor. Appl. Opt. 38: 1459–1466.

D Major LIBS References

Books and book chapters on LIBS, laser-induced plasmas, and plasma physics and spectroscopy

Adrain, R.S. (1982). Some industrial uses of laser induced plasmas. Ch. 7 in *Industrial Applications of Lasers*, ed. H. Koebner, Wiley, New York: 135–176.

Cremers, D.A. and L.J. Radziemski (1987). Laser plasmas for chemical analysis. Ch. 5 in *Laser Spectroscopy and its Application*, eds L.J. Radziemski, R.W. Solarz and J.A. Paisner, Marcel Dekker, New York: 351–415.

Cremers, D.A. and A.E. Pichahchy (1998). Laser-induced breakdown spectroscopy. In *Encyclopedia of Environmental Analysis and Remediation*, ed. R.A. Myers, John Wiley & Sons, Ltd, New York.

Cremers, D.A. and A.K. Knight (2000). Laser-induced breakdown spectroscopy. In *Encyclopedia of Analytical Chemistry*, ed. R.A. Meyers, John Wiley & Sons, Ltd, Chichester: 9595–9613.

Griem, H.R. (1964). *Plasma Spectroscopy*, McGraw-Hill, New York.

Griem, H.R. (1974). *Spectral Line Broadening by Plasmas*, Academic Press, New York.

Griem, H.R. (1997). *Principles of Plasma Spectroscopy*, Cambridge University Press, New York.

Kim, Y.W. (1989). Fundamentals of analysis of solids by laser-produced plasmas. Ch. 8 in *Laser-induced Plasmas and Applications*, eds L.J. Radziemski and D.A. Cremers, Marcel Dekker, New York.

Lee, Y.-I., K. Song and J. Sneddon (1997). Laser induced plasmas for analytical atomic spectroscopy. Ch. 5 in *Lasers in Analytical Atomic Spectroscopy*, eds J. Sneddon, T.L. Thiem and Y.-I. Lee, VCH, New York: 197–235.

Lochte-Holtgreven, W. (1968). *Plasma Diagnostics*, Wiley, New York.

Miziolek, A., V. Palleschi and I. Schechter (Eds) (2006). *Laser Induced Breakdown Spectroscopy*, Cambridge University Press, Cambridge.

Moenke-Blankenburg, L. (1989). *Laser Micro Analysis*, John Wiley & Sons, Ltd, New York.

Raizer, Y.P. (1977). *Laser-induced Discharge Phenomena*, Consultants Bureau, New York.

Radziemski, L.J. and D.A. Cremers (Eds) (1989). *Laser-induced Plasmas and Applications*, Marcel Dekker, New York.

Radziemski, L.J. and D.A. Cremers (1989). Spectrochemical analysis using laser plasma excitation. Ch. 7 in *Laser-induced Plasmas and Applications*, eds L.J. Radziemski and D.A. Cremers, Marcel Dekker, New York.

Root, R.G. (1989). Modeling of post-breakdown phenomena. Ch. 2 in *Laser-induced Plasmas and Applications*, eds L.J. Radziemski and D.A. Cremers, Marcel Dekker, New York.

Singh, J.P. and S.N. Thakur (Eds) (2006). *Laser-induced Breakdown Spectroscopy*, Elsevier Science BV, Amsterdam.

Weyl, G.M. (1989). Physics of laser-induced breakdown. Ch. 1 in *Laser-induced Plasmas and Applications*, eds L.J. Radziemski and D.A. Cremers, Marcel Dekker, New York.
Zel'dovich, Ya.B. and Yu.P. Raizer (2002). *Physics of Shock Waves and High-temperature Hydrodynamic Phenomena*, Dover Publications, Mineola, NY.

Conferences

LIBS 2000 (Pisa, Italy)
Corsi, M., V. Palleschi and E. Tognoni (Eds) (2001). Special issue, 1st international conference on laser induced plasma spectroscopy. Spectrochim. Acta Part B 50: 565–1034.
LIBS 2002 (Orlando, FL, USA)
Hahn, D.W., A.W. Miziolek and V. Palleschi (Eds) (2003). Special issue on LIBS 2002. Appl. Optics 42: 5933–6225.
LIBS 2004 (Malaga, Spain)
Laserna, J.J. (2005). Third international conference on laser induced plasma spectroscopy and applications. Spectrochim. Acta Part B 60: 877–878.
EMSLIBS 2001 (Cairo, Egypt)
Harith, M.A., V. Palleschi and L.J. Radziemski (Eds) (2002). Special issue on 1st Euro-Mediterranean symposium and laser-induced breakdown spectrometry. Spectrochim. Acta Part B 57: 1107–1249.
EMSLIBS 2003 (Crete, Greece)
Anglos, D. and M.A. Harith (2004). Special issue on 2nd Euro-Mediterranean symposium and laser-induced breakdown spectrometry. J. Anal. At. Spectrom. 19: 419–504.
EMSLIBS 2005 (Aachen, Germany)

Articles (in order of year published, most recent last)

Loree, T.R and L.J. Radziemski (1981). Laser-induced breakdown spectroscopy: time-integrated applications. Plasma Chem. Plasma Process. 1: 271–280.
Radziemski, L.J. and T.R. Loree (1981). Laser-induced breakdown spectroscopy: time-resolved spectrochemical applications. Plasma Chem. Plasma Process. 1: 281–293.
Radziemski, L.J. (1994). Review of selected analytical applications of laser plasmas and laser ablation, 1987–1994. Microchem. J. 50: 218–234.
Rusak, D.A., B.C. Castle, B.W. Smith and J.D. Winefordner (1997). Fundamentals and applications of laser-induced breakdown spectroscopy. Crit. Rev. Anal. Chem. 27: 257–290.
Song, K., Y.-I. Lee and J. Sneddon (1997). Applications of laser-induced breakdown spectrometry (LIBS). Appl. Spectrosc. Rev. 32: 183–235.
Rusak, D.A., B.C. Castle, B.W. Smith and J.D. Winefordner (1998). Recent trends and the future of laser-induced breakdown spectroscopy. Trends Anal. Chem. 17: 453–461.
Hahn, D.W. and M.M. Lunden (2000). Detection and analysis of aerosol particles by laser-induced breakdown spectroscopy. Aerosol Sci. Technol. 33: 30–48.
Knight, A.K., N.L. Scherbarth, D.A. Cremers and M.J. Ferris (2000). Characterization of laser-induced breakdown spectroscopy (LIBS) for application to space exploration. Appl. Spectrosc. 54: 331–340.
Radziemski, L.J. (2002). From LASER to LIBS, the path of technology development, Spectrochim. Acta Part B 57: 1109–1114.
Tognoni, E., V. Palleschi, M. Corsi and G. Christoforetti (2002). Quantitative micro-analysis by laser-induced breakdown spectroscopy: a review of the experimental approaches. Spectrochim. Acta Part B 57: 1115–1130.
Vadillo, J.M. and J.J. Laserna (2004). Laser-induced plasma spectrometry: truly a surface analytical tool. Spectrochim. Acta Part B 59: 147–161.

Winefordner, J.D., I.B. Gornishkin, T. Correll, E. Gibb, B.W. Smith and N. Omenetto (2004). Comparing several atomic spectrometric methods to the super stars: special emphasis on laser induced breakdown spectrometry, LIBS, a future super star. J. Anal. At. Spectrom. 19: 1061–1083.

Lee, W.-B., J. Wu, Y.-I. Lee and J. Sneddon (2004). Recent applications of laser-induced breakdown spectrometry: a review of material approaches. Appl. Spectrosc. Rev. 39: 27–97.

Articles (in alphabetical order for last name of first author)

Hahn, D.W. and M.M. Lunden (2000). Detection and analysis of aerosol particles by laser-induced breakdown spectroscopy. Aerosol Sci. Technol. 33: 30–48.

Knight, A.K., N.L. Scherbarth, D.A. Cremers and M.J. Ferris (2000). Characterization of laser-induced breakdown spectroscopy (LIBS) for application to space exploration. Appl. Spectrosc. 54: 331–340.

Lee, W.-B., J. Wu, Y.-I. Lee and J. Sneddon (2004). Recent applications of laser-induced breakdown spectrometry: a review of material approaches. Appl. Spectrosc. Rev. 39: 27–97.

Loree, T.R and L.J. Radziemski (1981). Laser-induced breakdown spectroscopy: time-integrated applications. Plasma Chem. Plasma Proc. 1: 271–280.

Radziemski, L.J. and T.R. Loree (1981). Laser-induced breakdown spectroscopy: time-resolved spectrochemical applications. Plasma Chem. Plasma Proc. 1: 281–293.

Radziemski, L.J. (1994). Review of selected analytical applications of laser plasmas and laser ablation, 1987–1994. Microchem. J. 50: 218–234.

Radziemski, L.J. (2002). From LASER to LIBS, the path of technology development. Spectrochim. Acta Part B 57: 1109–1114.

Rusak, D.A., B.C. Castle, B.W. Smith and J.D. Winefordner (1997). Fundamentals and applications of laser-induced breakdown spectroscopy. Crit. Rev. Anal. Chem. 27(4): 257–290.

Rusak, D.A., B.C. Castle, B.W. Smith and J.D. Winefordner (1998). Recent trends and the future of laser-induced breakdown spectroscopy. Trends Anal. Chem. 17: 453–461.

Song, K., Y.-I. Lee and J. Sneddon (1997). Applications of laser-induced breakdown spectrometry (LIBS). Appl. Spectrosc. Rev. 32: 183–235.

Tognoni, E., V. Palleschi, M. Corsi and G. Christoforetti (2002). Quantitative micro-analysis by laser-induced breakdown spectroscopy: a review of the experimental approaches. Spectrochim. Acta Part B 57: 1115–1130.

Vadillo, J.M. and J.J. Laserna (2004). Laser-induced plasma spectrometry: truly a surface analytical tool. Spectrochim. Acta B 59: 147–161.

Winefordner, J.D., I.B. Gornishkin, T. Correll, E. Gibb, B.W. Smith and N. Omenetto (2004). Comparing several atomic spectrometric methods to the super stars: special emphasis on laser induced breakdown spectrometry, LIBS, a future super star. J. Anal. At. Spectrom. 19: 1061–1083.

Index

Note: Page numbers in *italics* indicate figures and those in **bold** indicate tables.

Handbook of Laser-Induced Breakdown Spectroscopy D. Cremers and L. Radziemski
© 2006 John Wiley & Sons, Ltd